The Telemachon

G.A.Howkins

G.A.Howkins asserts the moral right to
be identified as the author of this work.

Imprint : independently published.
An imprint of 'Psychezoion'.
This edition April 2018.

A catalogue record for this book is
available from the British Library.

ISBN 9781980439851

This novel is entirely a work of fiction.
The names, characters and incidents
portrayed in it are the work of the author's
imagination.

Thanks to the E.S.A./Hubble Telescope for
allowing use of the glorious Carina Nebula
image 'Mystic Mountain'. Original image by
ESA/Hubble (M.Kornmesser),
warping and recolouring by G.A.H.

To Denise, my dedication.

MAPS
OF THE
JOURNEY

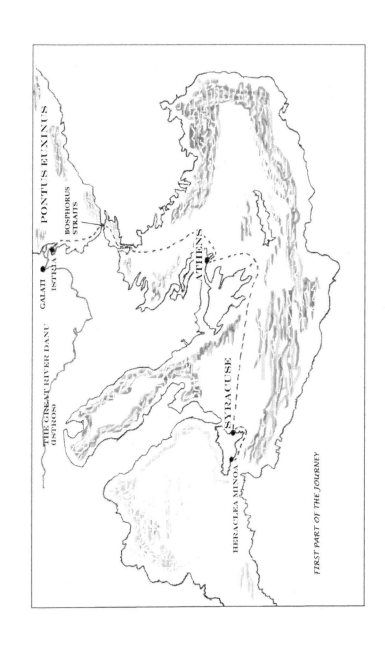

THE GREAT RIVER DANU (ISTROS)

GALATI

ISTRIA

PONTUS EUXINUS

BOSPHORUS STRAITS

ATHENS

SYRACUSE

HERACLEA MINOA

FIRST PART OF THE JOURNEY

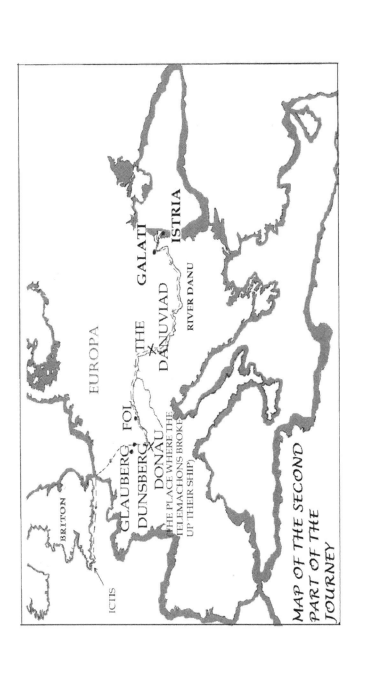

MAP OF THE SECOND
PART OF THE
JOURNEY

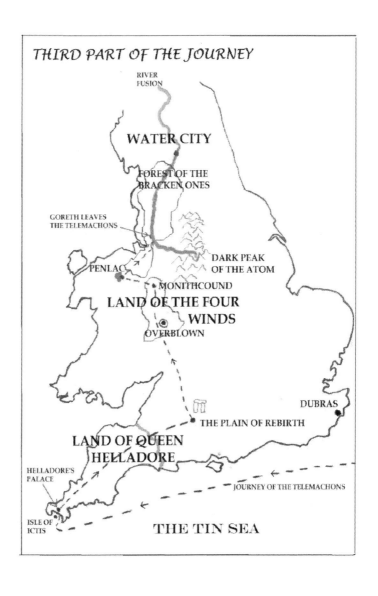

1
Something on the ship

These mortals yearn for our power. If I stretched my flaming red wings and summoned the Meltemi I would fly faster than this little boat. But I cannot use them. Not yet. My strength grows, the nearer I get.

Chanting, always chanting in my head. I hear their thoughts; their desires. A constant need for this or that; the bare heads always wanting a red hat for their hatred and so I brush them with my red wings and they gain strength as do I. These voices swarm around me on the ship and are carried to me from my homeland. Faint they are and tainted by the salty wind. But soon I will feel the clear fresh water against my briny lips and the divinity will clamour in my veins. The time will come, for it must come, it shall come and for us it will come. Me and my people.

For this time now, I must lie patient in the hold of a ship with these others. The blood courses through my veins and even yet I feel it changing. Heat in the blood grows more familiar and I become languid. But inside the charm works and the sea quarks jump and crash against each other in the myriad ticketing fleas, some splinter and fuse into gluons, others spiral and elasticate an expanding pool of plasma; a fountain falling aurora borealis swathing the skies to teeming colourful life just as in the starry explosion that made us all.

My blood will transmute into ichor. Nails grow longer. My skin begins to fall away, piece by piece, discovering the amber glow beneath. Thankfully the process is slow: I am able to muffle the spaces in my mortal skin with my garments; the dead skin I hide and shuffle off into the sea.

I know what I will become.

Thousands of years ago I came this way once before, encouraging my people to travel by the Great River. Telemachus approaches now. We pursued the water to its source and went further. On the banks either side of the River some of our people settled and worked the land. We found the cave dwellers. They were few in number and were allowed to mingle with us. War would have been pointless and taken our energy away from recreating the forested land. So we accepted integration: we learned their knowledge of the earth; they learned our value for cooperation.

Telemachus is a danger to us. He and his, have different gods. If they ever take hold, my existence would be threatened. I would become a mighty torrent like the Great River but all my surge and power turned against me with my people's tidal change in belief. Generation would reverse itself, strength build exponentially and like a river flowing backwards in terror from the sea, I would be rolled upstream and squeezed through the original pinpoint source.

I would be somewhere else, something else
There! Another scrap of skin sloughs to the floor.

2
Istria   334 B.C.

The water slapping in waves against the wooden hull. Gluck, gluck. An almond shaped eye, painted in white and blue, delineated by a clear black line, like kohl around the rim, pushed forward on the prow of the merchant ship and sighted its progress.

Ahead was Istria: a Greek colony city which was the last marker for civilisation before the mouth of the Istros, the Great River that surged from the known Greek world deep into the unknown barbarian world and perhaps to another inhabited place beyond that.

He could, Telemachus supposed, after leaving the harbour, simply bypass the river and continue to Tyros or Berezan, in fact any of the other Greek cities founded around the shores of the Pontus Euxinus. That way he might avoid the terrors and adventures to come; move on from those cities to found a new colony on the available land situated close to this hospitable sea. It would be far easier. He had the trading vessel he was standing on, the war trireme accompanying it and the warriors it held, captained by his trusted friend, Eucleides. He had too the former slaves who had joined him in Syracuse at the start of the journey: Pelisteus, Belisama, Tyracides and Melissa. He had been proved wrong in his belief that they would end their particular journey in Athens. They had shown greater resolve and remained with him. Not that the voyage so far had been that challenging. The winds and currents helped rather than hindered them and the boats made good time all the way from Athens through the Propontis past Byzantium, between the Dark Rocks and into the Pontus Euxinus.

Telemachus intended to make one night's stay at Istria and after provisioning the ships, to round the headland and enter the Istros' mouth. The flat marshy delta to be encountered would not look dangerous but nevertheless carried an inherent risk peculiar to that kind of maritime terrain. The channel of water selected to get to the main river would run shallow at certain points where the silted mud had accumulated. He would not want to look foolish in front of the others by stranding their only means of transport.

Their captain, Thocero, would take the initial blame if that happened as his boat would be leading the way but ultimate responsibility would rest with him.

Briefly, his mind flitted ahead along that huge river breaking from its source somewhere in the deepest western corner that could only be described as unexplored Europa. He wondered at the numberless and nameless people who had travelled the Istros all those aeons ago and who were now the Scythians and Celts and the many other unfamiliar tribes that existed along its banks and off into the hinterland surrounding it. They came in a search for space, food and survival. What had their descendants made of it? Did they live in temporary nomadic villages or had they built cities with walls? Possibly neither, maybe they lived in trees or caves and tunnelled into the rock like the Petrans or perhaps they lived over the water as did the Venetii.

The only evidence he had come across concerning these people was either anecdotal from Greek traders bringing the tin, fur and amber produced in those places or what was held in the book of maps locked in the desk of the captain's cabin. As to the former, those Greek merchants were the last link in a long supply chain extending back into the Celtic lands. Their knowledge was consequently mercantile and not substantially concerned with Europan customs and habitations. The maps, however, were a different matter altogether. They were physical, could be held in the hands and judged for their true worth. Yet that worth could be just as ephemeral as oral stories recounting the Celts' dubious cults and the human sacrifices they made to their gods. Those maps – Hecataeus' maps – given to him in good faith by his mother who had obtained them at Delphi where they had been left as a votive offering, purportedly by the mapmaker himself, could be a hoax.

If so they were a beautiful deception.

In Athens he had taken the atlas to the chief librarian. The man had scrutinised the papyri, page by page and then had given his opinion that they were genuine; some of the maps might have even been drawn by the great cartographer himself rather than his assistants. Telemachus, astonished, had questioned that and in response the librarian had produced an authentic handwritten document by Hecataeus kept in the archives. When compared to the text on some of the maps in Telemachus' possession they were indeed similar. What cast doubt on the maps was that although

Hecataeus had been a wide traveller in his life-time, no one had assumed that his journeys were as extensive as evidenced by the maps in the book. If they were to be believed, then it appeared that the Miletan had travelled through central Europa along the River Istros right to its very source.

The librarian had turned the pages back to the first map which showed the Istros' conjunction with the Pontus Euxinus and tracing with his finger the river line into the Scythian interior, he had left Telemachus with a challenge.

"My lord, there is only one method by which you can begin to prove these maps and their creator to be genuine." Telemachus continued to regard him, waiting for the answer. "Find this second marked city along the Istros in its location as shown here and you will indeed have a valuable document in your hands." The librarian's finger rested under the name 'Galati'. Anticipating Telemachus' response, he ended – "Nothing is known about this place and I only use the term 'city' because its existence on the map implies that a sizeable number of the local population live there."

A slim figure slid to the prow beside him. Telemachus brought his thoughts back from the library in Athens to the view in front and the woman beside him.

"We should be in Istria by the afternoon, Belisama."

Her broad-brimmed hat jiggled in response. As a red-haired woman, her skin was particularly sensitive to the sun's rays and she took special care to protect it whenever she could.

Of the former slaves taken on board at Syracuse, she was the least forthcoming so when she spoke after a few moments' silence, her simple statement startled him.

"My homeland lies in that direction, far into Europa at the other end of the Great River."

Telemachus wanted to know her commitment to the journey they were making. "Do you want to go back?"

She replied, without any feeling in her voice," I must. It is unavoidable."

"You say that as if you have no choice in the matter. At any point you can leave this ship whenever you want to. Naturally, I would prefer you to stay: your knowledge of the local people and language will be greatly needed on this expedition. But I am not forcing anyone to follow me who is not willing."

"Like I said to you – I must," repeated Belisama. There was a touch of anger about her manner which raised questions in his mind. Seeming to realise that, she suddenly changed her attitude. "Telemachus, I want you to promise me something, if you think you can agree to my request."

"What is it?"

"I want you to tell me that you will not kill or enslave any of my people."

Telemachus thought before he answered her. There was no point in making an empty promise.

Belisama, we go to found a city. Where that new home will be I have no idea at the moment. Sometimes new settlers are welcomed into a land, sometimes not. Even though we are prepared to put much effort and toil into farming and making fruitful the land that was empty and barren before, still we will be called thieves and intruders by those who are jealous and insecure. If we are attacked, we must defend ourselves. But you know my views about slavery. I will not enslave anyone and that is a promise I can keep."

"Ah, but can you make a better one and free those who are captive?" This interjection came in jovial tones from a white-bearded, thin man standing next to Melissa further down the deck, who had obviously been listening in to the conversation.

He was the most recent passenger taken aboard the ship in Athens and a temporary one. His plan was to purchase a vineyard outside Istria and to retire there after a lifetime apparently spent as a trader in goods between Athens and Istria. Telemachus had learned not to accept the first thing said to him by people about their past lives. He had been taught that recently by an uncle with three names who had done his utmost to kill him.

"If I set out to free every slave in the world, these two ships I command would not move one daktylos[1] away from the Istrian harbour."

"You would certainly upset the many slave traders in that port," agreed the other. "On the other hand, if your wish is to set up a city where slavery is prohibited, that is a different matter. A few would see it as an aim deserving the highest praise; most would consider a city where every man is free, plainly impracticable."

---

[1] 'finger-span'

"And women," added Telemachus.

"Women?" The man, whose name was Histarchus, sounded sceptical. "That is new."

"So new it is revolutionary," broke in Melissa beside him, not disguising her enthusiasm.

"And possibly one step genuinely beyond the practicable," said Histarchus, ignoring the comment from beside him. "Still," he continued in mild tones, "who can question the motives of a brave and adventurous leader about to enter the territory held by the barbarous Scythians? Certainly not me. My lord Telemachus would be doing the civilised Greek world a great favour by travelling the River Istros and bringing back information about what lies along it." Privately, Histarchus believed that Telemachus could be making a reckless mistake in using a river route to search unknown land rather than going by the more familiar coastal trade routes around the continent. Notwithstanding that, he was intrigued by the endeavour. "Perhaps, in my own small way I might be allowed to assist?"

"I would be glad to discuss it between us at another time," replied Telemachus. He was distracted by a boat approaching from Istria; certainly, a Port Authority customs vessel, coming to check their cargo and guide them to a specified mooring site.

3
Embarkation

Telemachus and Eucleides attracted some attention when they put their boats to the moorings at Istros under the direction of the customs vessel. The focus was not unexpected. What port is not entertained when a fully manned war trireme, gloriously painted in blue, white and gold swings expertly into its waters and comes to rest? Its mariners were fine, healthy looking men and the dock side crowd wondered from which Greek city they had set out. The only clue as to its identity was in the name painted on the side - 'The Telemachon' - and few standing there realised it derived from the name of the man watching on the other boat that accompanied it. In Sicily, before they had left, a name had been chosen by vote from several put forward. The crew had opted for the one invented by Eucleides who had explained that it was based on the name of Telemachus and it would also be the word for the journey they were taking and the search that was at its core: a city free from tyranny, serving its people's happiness.

The passengers in Thocero's merchant trader also garnered curiosity, particularly the women. Slave dealers at the jetty glanced surreptitiously and after making a quick assessment for cash value, checked to see if there were any tell-tale signs for slavery on them.

A calculation for tax purposes had already been made by the customs officers and Thocero was required to pay a tithe for the goods he was carrying, either in kind or cash. The trireme, after a thorough search, was charged at a flat-rate cash payment as only provisions for the men had been discovered. Telemachus, Thocero and Eucleides all knew that there was a secret hoard of gold kept on the trireme; in the wooden base that the statue to Poseidon stood on, to be precise. That money was a lifeline for what would be a long expedition and they would not see it reduced by large margin simply for entering a port. It might not be taxed at all and if discovered the whole amount would probably be taken as a fine: the risk attached to it just had to be taken.

Telemachus assumed that a warship's arrival into the harbour would attract special interest from the ruler of Istros, whoever he might be and contact with a custom's boat would not suffice. So it proved. Not long after they had moored the two ships up, there came a squad of ten armed cavalry men and an officer. They were palace guards and issued Telemachus with strict instructions on how his men were to behave while in the city. Anyone found to be carrying a weapon would be arrested. Passengers and crew could enter the city but in groups of no more than ten; they would first have to report to the barracks near the harbour's main gateway to the inner city and from there would be accompanied around Istros by guards. Only two groups at any one time would be allowed to wander the streets. It was made obvious that the king of Istros might want to talk with Telemachus but at a time he would choose and they were to inform the guards when their intended date for departure drew near.

"Well, this king lacks nothing where security is concerned!" exclaimed Eucleides as the Istrian guards clattered away over the stones, leaving himself, Thocero and Telemachus on the dock.

"It would be a natural dupe who allows a fully manned trireme from Zeus knows where to sail up to his city gates without taking the necessary precautions," observed Thocero who was a man not averse to risk himself but balanced it out on a basis of cool calculation.

"Even so," suggested Telemachus, "such caution shows there must be good reasons for it, unless he is a natural tyrant controlling every contact his people make with others."

"A tyrant such as that would have sent his own trireme out to either engage us boldly or turn us away," added Eucleides.

"Perhaps, even at this distance, he has already heard about King Alexander of Macedonia overrunning Greece and is worried about where his ambition will lead him next," offered Thocero.

"The ruler here is quite likely to be in the pay of Alexander, who after all, is a richer man now he has plundered Thebes and his Illyrian and Thracian territories are not poor in silver mines." Telemachus paused. "We heard it in Athens anyway. The young king is not interested in taking a city he has already vanquished, such as Athens or easy pickings like Istria. He wants fame and glory by uniting the Greeks behind him against a far bigger and constant foe. The Persian Empire entices him like a fat treasure chest with a rotten old lock. One blow of his Macedonian phalanx will open it."

"So the problems that trouble this king must be local ones then?"

"I am sure we will soon find out, Eucleides." Telemachus was wanting to get on. "But now we need to organise a rota for our men and women to visit the city."

4
Rescue

"Have you asked the waggon master to stop at the harbour so that we can see the trireme from Athens?" Xura was persistent, always persistent.

Chalestrus looked at his nine-year-old sister and curbed his irritation. Why their father was continuing to send them to the summer palace outside Istria he did not know. It was a routine for the hot summer months that should have ended for him at least two years ago, when he turned twelve years of age. Like his friends from the aristoi amongst the clans, he should have been sent to train in the city gymnasia so that he could become a renowned warrior. Did his father not want a strong son to defend their family's interest, the kingdom?

"You know that father has instructed him to do that already, Xura."

"Yes," added the woman who was their attendant, "and please remember, My Lady, that the king has expressly forbidden you to leave the carriage. You must stay inside." This was a pointed reminder for Chalestrus rather than Xura but by proxy communication she avoided the direct conflict and insults that would follow. Now it was Xura's turn to be irritated and she shook her veiled head and sighed loudly.

"We're here and there it is!" shouted Chalestrus, poking his head through the window in the covered waggon. The vehicle came to a rumbling halt near a collection of street vendors and at a safe distance from the trireme.

"What a magnificent sight she is!" exclaimed Chalestrus again.

The brightly painted warship loomed over the fishing boats that were moored either side. Above them, wind and sun-beaten crewmen worked the deck or lounged nonchalantly against the starboard bow, observing the jetty life.

Telemachus had already gone into the city with the first groups given permission to do so.

The jetty was packed with stalls selling goods that had just come off the merchant boats in the harbour. All sorts of goods were being sold including Cretan pottery, cloth dyed brilliantly, olives, cheeses and other foodstuffs, spices imported through the Ionian cities and exotic birds in wicker cages. This last stall was very close to the place at which they had rested. The waggon master thought it might be a treat for young eyes.

Just as he drew up near the trader however, a sudden commotion broke out. A sailor, noticeably drunk, staggered and fell into the stall. One of the cages, the largest and holding a Rose-ringed parakeet, bounced to the ground and sprung open.

The bird popped its head through the open door, flashing its red circled neck common to the male of the species. For a second or two it seemed to be dizzy, then squawking loudly, "Let me out! Let me out!" it squeezed its body out of the cage, spread its wings and flew.

Unfortunately, it must have been still disorientated by the fall because it flew straight into the waggon occupied by the royal children.

Xura shrieked with fright as the confined space was suddenly filled with flapping wings, pin-sharp claws and a jabbing beak.

She hurtled out from the carriage, followed quickly by her attendant. After a brief period though, Chalestrus exited the waggon, a superior smile on his face, his arm wrapped around the body of the beast, his hand firmly but without cruelty, grasping its neck.

The incident did not go unnoticed.

A small wizened man, lazing on some stone steps under the shade of a carob tree, stood up quickly after seeing the children. He studied them hard and then hurried away.

"Let me out!" came the familiar cry. Caught and trapped, the parrot tried to twist his head around to see who had him. Its marble eye rested on Chalestrus.

"If you don't keep quiet, you will be first onto the altar pyre as a gift to Poseidon at the next Istrian festival," said Chalestrus with good humour.

The parrot became sheepish, which was quite a difficult feat for a parrot.

"Oh!" said Xura, delighted, "Can we keep him?"

"Of course, now that he has behaved himself." Chalestrus was utterly pleased and put on years as he used the opportunity to exercise authority and munificence all at once. He ordered one of the two guards riding his horse alongside them to pay the vendor the money for the bird and have it sent to the summer palace. Passing it over, he then ushered the others back into the carriage, clambering in next to them. The waggon driver called out, reins were shuddered. Horses moved off.

At the other end of the city, a little later, Telemachus came away from the bath-house, newly refreshed. It had been very pleasant. He had stood under the carved gorgon face gushing water from its pouted mouth, scraped his skin and rubbed it with sweet smelling oil and finally rested on the steps by the large circular pool, eating fresh orange and talking with the Istrians. He was pleased to hear the Greek tongue spoken widely in this unfamiliar place and from what he learned it was a language commonly used along the Istros. Telemachus was doubtful about this. None of the people he had spoken to had gone further inland than the next settlement, a small Scythian village. It was necessary to come away from the baths after a short while, he could not stay there with his men long; the others had to be relieved from the Telemachon so that they could enjoy a respite too.

The four Istrian guards who were detailed to watch over him had not been exceptionally restrictive in limiting his wanderings through the city, although he could guess that he had not come across the route to the palace yet.

Stepping out onto the street, he looked ahead and what he saw startled him. The street rose in a gentle slope along its length and at the top of the rise a covered waggon appeared. At the same time as it came into view, two other events happened in quick succession. Someone had thrown himself from the terrace of a house along the road onto the driver and the impact knocked the man off the waggon. Passing a side street, the guards accompanying the vehicle were immediately set upon by numerous armed men, running out with long spears raised. The guards either plummeted to the ground, thrown by their rearing horses or were run through with the spears.

Telemachus glimpsed frightened children's faces at the waggon windows.

He turned to the nine men and four Istrian guards behind him, grinning. "I don't think they were expecting us." He sent some of his men and the Istrian guards to deal with the attackers while he himself and the rest waited for the oncoming carriage.

As it wheeled furiously towards them they started to run either side of the road, increasing their pace while it drew level. Telemachus was the first to haul himself up onto the waggon, closely followed by the others. He used the window to lever himself up to the carriage top and to the front of its roof, below which sat the driver. One of his men had also made it to that point and they held on to the roof and to each other to stabilise themselves. They looked down grimly upon the man who was whipping the horses with his reins.

Telemachus made a threat to throw the man off the waggon, breaking his neck, if he did not stop. The driver, realising that four opponents had clambered on, assumed that the situation was hopeless. He began to rein in the horses. The prospect of being caught and tortured in an underground dungeon was not an appealing one and as soon as the waggon had stopped, he leaped off it, attempting to escape by an alley. Telemachus' crewmen ran after him and he was soon brought back.

The children and their servant were brought from the carriage. The girl, wide-eyed and pretty under the veil was visibly upset but not tearful.

The boy, from a noble family by the look of the design on his chiton, the chain and seal that hung from his neck and above all the thin gold circlet around the head, had removed the fearful expression from his face. Telemachus was amused and not altogether surprised when the boy boastfully announced that he was the Prince of Istria. Such boasts would lead to more trouble and an early death. The boy could at least begin with expressing some gratitude and finding out who his rescuers were. That way he might make sure that he was not simply exchanging one group of captors for another.

The prince did finally thank them and indeed made a request that Telemachus should return with them to the Istrian palace, where the King, his father, would no doubt show his thanks for their rescue.

Telemachus politely declined the offer and suggested that if there was any reward to be given, then removing the guard over his ship and freedom to come and go as they pleased would be welcome to his own people. Learning his name, the prince left with his entourage.

5
King Istar and the Gift

The short stooping figure in front of him negotiated the twisting tunnel and rough ground quite nimbly. Squirming flames from wall torches lit their way. At first they had descended from the palace above, now it was fairly level but before them Telemachus could see the bottom of what seemed to be a spiral staircase built of brick.

The king, without a word, took a first step and began to climb, expecting his companion to follow him. The stairs were steep, around and around they went. Telemachus could hear the small gasps coming from the other, who nevertheless maintained a strong steady pace.

When he had first seen the king on arriving in the palace at his invitation – an invitation that could not be refused – Telemachus had been quite shocked. After seeing the healthy vitality and handsome appearance of his children, he had expected their father to be a much younger man. Nothing could be further removed from his expectations than the figure presented by King Istar who appeared as old as the Great River itself, his white beard stuck away from his chin in braided points like an aureole around the lower half of a star. As his son, he wore a thin gold band on his head but decorating his neck was the barbarians' prized piece of jewellery, a torc in solid gold. This was a further surprise. Telemachus had not expected the king of a Greek city to be displaying any barbarian tokens on his person. There were similar features in his face to those in his children and he walked with a slight limp, possibly from a past war wound, he thought. His manner was polite and not arrogant, it hinted at good diplomatic skills which had protected his city from war for a long period.

Eventually they reached the top. Pushing at a wooden door, Istar led them both into a very large room which allowed daylight in from above.

The king stood aside and watched his guest's reaction carefully.

If he had been alone, his jaw would have dropped but he was not alone and he could feel the king's gaze on him.

The room was filled with treasure of all varieties: open chests of silver and gold coins, jewel encrusted gold hilted swords and wonderfully designed shields hanging on the walls; small chryselephantine statues of the gods; another open chest laden with cut jewels sparkling yellow, blue, green, red and sharp diamond.

Telemachus was speechless. Istar was showing him not only his kingdom's treasures but a trust that he was not sure he deserved.

As if reading his thoughts, the other spoke for the first time since they had left the palace rooms.

'You are amongst the very few who have seen this but all of my people know about it. Much of this treasure stays here temporarily, riches come in and go out again to the temple treasuries or to pay for what the people need to be happy. But the most valuable stays here."

The king walked to a peg like any other on the wall, from which hung a sword in its scabbard. Compared to its bejewelled fellows, it looked far less impressive.

He took it off the peg by the belt and handed it to Telemachus with care. "Sometimes, in our avarice, what is truly worthy escapes us."

Telemachus held the scabbard and studied it. The weapon, even under scrutiny, was without distinguishing marks – the hilt was admittedly silver and the leather sheath finely illustrated with sea beasts but Telemachus was looking for a sign, something unique, giving the reason for it to be here at all.

Pulling the sword slowly from its scabbard, he found it. In gold letters two words were inlaid under the hilt. On one side was the word '*Ekdikairsair*' (Revenge) and turning it over Telemachus read '*Patroklus*'. His heart missed a beat. "This cannot be," he whispered.

"Draw the sword fully," urged the king, as if eager to know something. He plucked a cuirass, solid forged bronze, from its hung position on the wall and flung it down at Telemachus' feet. "Strike!" he commanded. The younger man stared dubiously at the fine armour and then back at Istar. The king nodded.

Taking the sword out, he swung it with his good right arm and all his might. The blade hit the cuirass with a terrific ringing clang and cut it cleanly in half.

The devastating sight and sound sent a thrill through them both. Istar gave words to his marvelling. "The sword of Achilles!"

Telemachus did not question it for one moment. In handling and using the weapon he had felt that additional strength had come to him from somewhere.

"Troy is just a boat-ride away from us," continued the king. "That sword was taken from Achilles' grave and eventually given to the kings of Istria. Throughout the millennia, despite the political squabbles and rivalries for power that sword has always remained in this city. Its protection."

Telemachus slid the weapon back into its scabbard and hung it in its buckler back onto the wall peg.

"Now," said the king, moving off to an arched opening giving way to an adjoining room, "I want to show you something else."

The smaller space was occupied by curious things, all arranged and stacked neatly. There were instruments for measuring and viewing and boiling, scrolls and papyri some open at diagrams mapping the stars or revealing the inner universe of the human body and then there were the glass bowls.

It was the material that constituted these vessels which first caught his attention. They were an opaque white colour and then objects in the bowls could be dimly seen, held in some colourless preservative solution. Telemachus was used to the kind of glass which was deeply coloured and shiny, not this glass, which you could almost see through.

"Ah, the finest artificial crystal produced from the workshops in Rhodes," commented Istar helpfully, "almost as good as amber. The Rhodians are looking for a method in mixing the sand and soda by which they can produce pure transparency. But as with amber, my friend, what you see trapped inside provides far more interest."

Telemachus took a step forward to see what was in the bowls. What he did see sent a shudder through his body but whether it was a shudder of revulsion or fascinated delight, he could not tell.

Staring up at him was a small face, a miniature face, but the body to which it belonged was something he had only seen before in mosaics, on painted amphorae and standing as statues in a temple precinct or on a stone relief.

The hairy face with its glassy, visionless eyes was joined to a man's torso that led seamlessly into the body of a horse.

Telemachus jerked his head back, an instinctive repulse. "Beautiful myth given monstrous life!" he gasped.

"No, in fact it wasn't. The being was taken from a pregnant mare grazing the slopes under Mount Olympus. It was still-born."

"It seems more adult than child," queried Telemachus.

"The king glanced at the bowl. "Who are we to say what a centaur should look like at birth? Look in the others and you'll find creatures more curious and perplexing."

Telemachus did so and it was just as he had said. The bowls were small or large, depending on the size of their contents.

One diminutive bowl contained what appeared to be a bird, only this bird had a head shaped like a crocodile, red eyes, wispy gossamer strands instead of feathers and a strange leathery parabola etched with silver markings around his back which, Telemachus presumed, served it for wings. He could not work out how it might function. In the next pot was a fish without fins but with limbs and green fur that looked like seaweed and which entirely covered it. Another contained a very large butterfly but one like no other: the wings on this extended in a series of spines either side of the body and so close together as to be almost touching. Between the gaps was a fine meshy hair and a pattern in green and gold was stamped upon them like the sun shining through leaves. The insect's skeleton, if insect it was, resembled a human figure, as a mandrake root sometimes imitates the form of a man.

"The philosopher who caught that," said the king, staring at the same creature, "told me that when it flew, it made the sound of a siren song in the air. He was so entranced listening to the sound that he almost failed to capture it."

"And now it lies here," murmured Telemachus, ". . . . dead. What will we do when they have all gone? Will the gods create new creatures for us or will they curse us for our destruction and leave us to play grim games in barren lands?"

"Death is not inextricably linked to decay and forgetting. The beings here are embalmed for posterity. That fish for instance, with its limbs, proves does it not that the theory devised by Thales of Miletus was right – all things were created from water? Someday perhaps, the gods will allow us the power to make these preserved beasts live again or give life to new ones."

"For what purpose. On a whim? Because we can? If we are to discover the best in Nature for our own well-being we must work with her and not against her. Diminishing her diversity and creativity is poisonous to our own survival."

"I agree," said the king, "but to ensure our own survival we must gain knowledge through exploration and study and as you will probably find in your planned journey along the River Istros, that hungry search will always have fatal consequences."

He went to a cabinet standing in a darkened corner and took out another glass vessel, a conical flask with a cork stopper. The glass was similar to the others – clouded with whiteness and opacity but inside could be discerned a blue jellied emollient, an ambrosus which glowed strangely in the darkness. The light emitted was so strong that the flask might be used as a lamp in a very dark tunnel.

Istar tilted the bottle slowly from left to right, then back again. The substance flowed but thickly, heavily.

"I have lived a long life, Telemachus – on the whole a good one, with many things around to keep me in comfort and to employ my interest until the day I die. I would, however, regard these as all worthless and my life's purpose but to seek a sudden end if I had lost the two children you rescued today."

Telemachus began to remonstrate; it would have been a simple duty for any man to do what he did but the king stopped him with his free hand upraised.

"No, I wish to show my gratitude. Please do not refuse my gift."

"It would be ill-mannered if I did."

The king placed the flask on a table beside him.

"Inside this glass is an Ambrosus, a salve with extraordinary power. It has been brought here from the sanctuary at Mount Olympus and the priests there tell that Hermes the Trickster came down from the mountain himself to leave the transmutative in the shrine as a gift."

"Transmutative?"

"This substance is only to be used in times of dire necessity; once it is used up there is no more to be had as my philosophers know only too well, having tried in the time elapsing between two Olympiads to discover its formula and constituent parts. Having said that, there is enough substance in the bottle for several applications.

When you do apply it, you must smear it over your face completely, eyes closed; a totally enclosing mask which seals your face."

"What then?"

"It dries on your face very quickly and the effects are felt running throughout the body. Once dried, you open your eyes and find that you have become whatever you wanted to become as long as you started with the thought about something solid and living."

Telemachus had heard many claims from wizards and shamans, cult priests and others in his time but this was preposterous. However, the position of himself and his people in Istros could not be endangered.

"How long does the transformation last?"

"Until you can reach the nearest flowing water to bathe the face of the thing you have turned into." The king understood Telemachus' doubt. "I can only tell you what I know about the Ambrosus and I know because I have used it myself." Istar' expression showed that he expected queries and an argument from the other but Telemachus remained patient.

"I mentioned a gift to you earlier: well, what I would like to give you is actually a choice of two gifts – either the Ambrosus or the Sword of Achilles. Which do you choose?"

"My lord, this is just too much – your generosity is very great," came Telemachus' immediate response. And indeed, as far as the sword was concerned, it was a magnificent offer.

The king's face, more priest than king and more wizard than priest was towards him and bore a charming smile. He was waiting on his decision.

It suddenly felt like some kind of test. Surely, thought Telemachus, he must choose the sword. One blow from its cutting blade would be a hundred times more powerful than a thousand concocted ointments credited with magical attributes. And this sword was much more than a plain blade. It was a whisper, no, a roar from a time when the Greeks were united together with one common aim. Grasping upon that hilt, your hand closed over the same place where once had been the hand of the most famous hero at the walls of Troy – a warrior who had gone against his own king and another to achieve victory and immortality: a courageous individual who by his deeds overcame despots. Whoever held the sword would have a truly powerful symbol for his people. It would give them great strength; it would be adored.

Telemachus paused.

"I choose the Ambrosus."

The king cocked his head on one side as if to criticise his decision, "Are you certain?"

Oh, he was certain. There was no doubting now. Telemachus wanted his people, those who sailed in the Telemachon and Thocero's boat to believe in him, not some relic from the past, no matter how worthy it was. This sword, if accepted, would become his prop, a forever reminder of someone else's triumph and glory. If taken away it could have a devastating impact on morale and self-belief and the blame for its loss would be thrown upon him. Then say he did choose it. It would be difficult to estimate how the Istrians would react.

King Istar satisfied his caution. "You have chosen wisely. My people would not have been happy with the sword's loss although I would not have informed them until you were far away from here. In my own mind you have asked for the most necessary item for your journey's success."

He took from his gown a silver coin and threw it to Telemachus who deftly caught it as it spun through the air. "Tell me," said the king, "what do you see on its face?"

Telemachus inspected the metal. "I see two faces," he said slowly. "They are side by side but the one on the left is inverted."

"Exactly," spoke Istar. "My people think that the image represents me and my son, the one in his right position in authority over them, the other yet to come and to be turned into his rightful position. I, on the other hand, know what that image truly means as I designed it myself."

"Something to do with the Ambrosus?" interjected Telemachus.

"Completely so," stated the king. "In some of the Istrian coins, the inverted face has been stamped on the left, in others on the right. What it refers to is the transmutative effects belonging to the Ambrosus. Once used and transformed, the user might become something that accords with his own identity more closely than when he was a man. He may wish to remain in that shape. This is the inference from the coin with the inverted face turned to its proper view. But the drachma showing the reversed face on the right gives a warning about a much more dangerous potential contained by the Ambrosus. Despite the person choosing what he or she is to become, sometimes the form chosen is totally alien to the user's soul. In that event they may have little control over what they do when in that new body."

"It seems to me that a man or woman should be happy with the body they already inhabit."

"You are right," agreed the king, "and in fact the most successful users of this metaphysical gift are those who have the greatest personal integrity. They can cross over into any outward shape with their soul intact and the ability to exercise their own will is undiminished."

"Be that as it may, this ointment could be riskier than the danger it is supposedly helping to avoid in the first place."

"Perhaps. Use its transformative power only in times of great necessity," urged the king, handing over the Ambrosus.

Telemachus took it, almost reluctantly.

"There is something else I wish to warn you about," continued Istar, "and it is about the first part of your journey along the Great River."

"We would welcome any advice about that."

"When you leave the mouth of the Istros, all civilised protection will end, barring the will of the Gods: once you trust yourself to the Great River it will conduct you to the barbarian heartlands where savage rites take place, human sacrifice and to believers in the Wolf. After the mouth, the river courses through lands that on your right belong to the Scythians and your left, the Thracians. If you survive their attentions you will arrive at Galati, a city ruled by the Getae tribe, the wolf adorers. On the death of their chieftains they strangle those closest to them and hurl their bodies into the same tomb to serve their needs in the after-life. This is all I know – not my bravest warriors dare take that journey down the Great River towards them. You are either the bravest man I have ever met or Zeus' greatest entertainer."

"I have met Thracians and Scythians. The Thracians were hard drinkers certainly but tough fighters and completely loyal if you gained their trust; the Scythians were skilled, accurate bowmen. They seemed decent enough."

"Yes, civilised when they have to be, when living amongst us but when back in their own communities they return to barbarism."

"How do you know they do not take civilised manners with them to influence others?"

Amusement gleamed in the king's eye. "My young friend, like others of your age you overestimate the good in others. Surely you would recognise that the strongest personal motivation – especially for you and your peers – is ambition, to win a place in the polis for yourself by gaining influence with others?" After assent from Telemachus, Istar continued. "The only way for those returning to achieve the respect they must have is to prove that their traditions and beliefs have not been overcome by the Greek. In essence when back in their homeland, they will themselves become more barbarian than the barbarian." He stopped to allow the thought to sink in, then switched the conversation. "Anyway, what were the circumstances in which you met these Scythians and Thracians?"

"They were in my father's employ and his opponents' too."

"Really?" said Istar, greatly interested and about to broach the subject of his deepest curiosity. "And who is your father?"

"Timoleon."

The answer seemed to shake the king. Was it trepidation that Telemachus detected come and go in his demeanour? Whatever it was, he felt a new respect and attentiveness in him from Istar.

"The Corinthian general?"

"Yes."

His fame travels even to these shores. He has completed a wondrous service to Greater Greece in beating back the Carthaginians."

"Have you heard any recent news about him?" asked Telemachus eagerly.

"Only that the Syracusans hold him in great esteem and he continues to work and restore good order where anarchy and chaos ruled before. That is a man whose personal integrity would not be distorted by the Ambrosus."

Relieved to hear that all was well with him, Telemachus returned to matters more pressing.

"You asked to be informed when we were to depart. It will be tomorrow at sunrise."

Now Istar felt relief and he smothered the gladness in his tone of voice. "We will pray to the Gods that they may help you. I can provide a guide into the main channel for the Istros. Have you any other aids?"

"Thank-you but it will not be necessary. We have maps and a Celt to guide us."

"A Celt?"

"A woman. Her name is Belisama. I believe she was born at the source of the Great River, although she is quite reticent about her origins. It was a long time ago, much has happened to her since then."

"Remember what I said about returning exiles. Can you trust her? You will be journeying from the mouth of the Great River to its dark soul. Perhaps she may not be able to evade that confluence when her path crosses with its beginning. Malice could seize her and betray you."

"We trust her."

"Well, your father accomplished a marvellous task in defeating the tyrants and bringing democracy to Sicily but what you intend to do is much greater. No Greek has crossed the unknown European continent by the River Istros and returned to further our knowledge about it."

"Hecataeus did."

"Hecataeus did travel our shores but he wrote down what our traders told him about Scythia and Thrace. One man, Herodotus of Halicarnassus ventured into the hinterland but did not get far. He was honest enough to admit it. But I have read his 'Histories' myself – indeed a copy of it is kept here and I find what he says about the Scythians accurately concurs with our own merchant's experiences. Anyway, Telemachus, don't let an old man's chatter keep you from your destiny or deprive the Telemachons of your guidance."

He offered his wrist and Telemachus grasped it, feeling the other's bony hand wrap around his own. "I wish you and your people success and happiness for the future."

Telemachus looked into the old king's face and knew that his words were genuine.

6
Galati: A Strange Wonder

The city of Galati was a secretive city. So secretive that after dusk, conversations had to be carried out in whispers. This was by long-standing order of the Wolf Masters. They were six in all: six Pelts or office holders committed to efficiently managing the intricate administrative structure that kept the population under control and tightly focused on their own tiny roles in the functioning state as the Pelts were on their individual government departments.

Three men and three women comprised the Wolf Masters. They were bed partners. This was allowed because all secrets by their very nature have to be shared and whereas one is a danger to the state, two is a safety valve.

Unusually, one of the Pelts was a black woman whose mother had been a Libyan slave. Her father, a Wolf Master in the previous generation, had held a remit which included the buying and selling of slaves through Galati's river harbour. Her father's influence was a powerful one indeed to ensure her position in the governing pack; this despite the intervening years that had elapsed since he had relinquished his own post and also the obstacle that was Galati's enforced xenophobia.

Not only was Rhodessa not descended from the Getae tribe, she was neither Thracian nor Scythian. Galati had a strict rule for foreigners: they were not to step through the gateway into the city. In fact, a particular place had been built for foreign visitors – who were mainly Greek merchants – a little further down the river to which they were ordered every night so that their ideas and customs did not pollute the general populace. This place was a building that served its guests' needs and was mockingly referred to by the Galateans as 'The Palace of Fools'.

Anyone seeing Rhodessa would naturally realise that it was not only her father's authority that had made her a Wolf Master. It was also her natural beauty. This had won her partner's support before he too had become a Pelt. Although it had been arduous, her partner, Bhusa, managed to win his family's confirmation for her position. That was how it was. When the change occurred from one Pelt pack to another, it happened after a complex procedure whereby the Wolf Masters were nominated, partnered and confirmed through interrelated agreement by the most powerful six families in the state. No other citizen in Galati took part: the consideration to give them political power was treated as dangerous in itself, Galatean citizens and Getae tribe members belonged to the state.

Any opponents to the system and indeed it was surprising how many were denounced in this matter, were dealt with swiftly. After denunciation, they disappeared.

But their disappearance was not final. Pack after Wolf Master pack had gradually evolved a system which would distract and give relief to people's frustrations with the harsh conditions imposed on them. Slaves could be owned so that the citizens might not dwell on their own political captivity. A limit was placed on the number of slaves that could live in the city and also the time they could be there. When the allotted time had passed, the slaves were executed, replaced with others and the cycle was repeated. This had not happened to Rhodessa's mother; that woman gave thanks to the Wolf God every night for the time she had fallen onto her master's lap.

Possessing slaves could not suffice as the only agency for the people's willingness to conform. Entertainment had to be provided and as Suhdo, the Wolf Master for ceremonies, had put it, entertainment was the forest in which the people's political thoughts got lost.

Naturally, ceremonies were given high status in Galatean society. The blood-thirstier they were, the better; it was after all, demanded by the Wolf God. Why he demanded them was not made quite clear but the people never questioned it. Whenever an extreme action was commanded by the authorities, they only had to mention the Wolf God's name, Lupa, for the people to be acquiescent. This had taken much education and 'entertainment' throughout a generation to achieve. It helped that all contact with the outside world was limited and the Galatean's thrill for spilt blood was provoked to a crescendo in the festivals dedicated to Lupa. It was here that the disappeared political dissidents briefly resurfaced along with the common criminals, only to be torn apart by starved beasts taken from the surrounding forests or exotic landscapes further afield. The Galatean's natural human sensitivity was being perverted in both subtle and obvious ways.

The subtle method was to convince the population that their city was a fine place to be and a pleasure to live in. Admittedly, there was very little similarity between the homes rented by the ordinary inhabitants, which were small and those owned by the Wolf Masters and their senior servants of the state, who lived in variously sized palaces, but the streets were clean and all facilities maintained with due diligence. Astonishingly, there had been a small protest by some people when the last green space in Galati had been closed down to make way for a market. The rebellion was efficiently quashed and Lupa's maw had been stuffed to satiety at the next religious festival.

That was several years ago and everything since then had settled into the natural state controlled by the Pelts. Until now.

The Wolf Masters had reconvened their fourth meeting with the same topic for debate and still there appeared to be no solution to the problem.

Galati contained a large population that required a good constant food supply. Some of this came from the Great River itself, other food was grown on the land which had been converted from forest outside the city's gate.

Because foreign contact was limited, very little was actually imported from the Illyrians further down the river or the Istrians at the Pontus Euxinus. A significant portion however, came by hunting in the forest. The forest was endless and bountiful. From it was brought the wild boar, the pheasants and partridges, the stag and deer, the badger and bear which nourished the people. The hunting parties were large and very successful. Yet recently all that had changed. The hunters had come back with empty bags. They had told of successful catches and carcasses stored close to campfires which had been dragged away by morning. All without a sound; just an overpowering smell like hot, wet, animal hide. There were no tracks, only a trail left by the dead catch as if being dragged to some distance. When the trail marks were followed, they suddenly vanished. What the hunters could not understand was how one creature could have dragged up so many bodies, if one being it was.

Not only had the catch gone. So too had hunters. And it had been five days since the last hunting party had left the city. It was feared that they had been taken.

Military detachments had been sent into the forest over the past few days but as yet to no avail.

A noisy argument was going on between the Pelt Masters in the Hall of Decisions.

"Burn the forest!" The inane suggestion preceded by the speaker, Bhusa, thumping the table at which they sat, shut everyone's mouth. But not for long.

"Oh yes," started up Cordyr, her manner seething with sarcasm, "Let's all play at fire and burn Galati to the ground!"

"No, I mean we should burn a controlled area. First trap the creature, whatever it is, then surround it and kill it."

"Whatever it is – exactly. We do not know what 'it' is and so how can we set a successful snare? We are ignorant as to whether it crawls along the ground, rises from the forest lake, burrows up from the earth or arrives from the clouds."

Judging from the lack of ground tracks I would suggest the latter – flight is how it travels and we already know that meat will pull it from the sky. We need to burn a small clearing, far enough away from Galati and the surrounding farmland to make it feel secure. Place the meat there. Set the trap." Bhusa always spoke like this: clipped and direct, complete self-assurance. It was why he had risen so quickly to become a major presence within the Hall of Decisions.

"We have tried everything else. Why not this?" said Suhdo, resignedly.

"What if game is not its only meat?" suggested Cordyr. "We have, most evidently, lost hunters. Who is to say that it is not acquiring a taste for two-footed animals? Another point is can there be more of them out there?

Perhaps this creature is the scout for its fellows from the Shadowsick Forest." What Cordyr had named was a far region in the vast woodland which no Galatean had travelled to and entered. Everything was possible in the Shadowsick Forest, including it being a habitat for previously unknown flesh- eating creatures.

"So you are suggesting that first it takes our hunting catch away from us and having discovered how easy it is, the beast or beasts will come to Galati and take us?"

"Unfortunately, that is my conclusion, yes."

A shout pierced the air and a man ran into the hall, having pulled himself from the guards at the door. He was carrying a sack and flung himself down on the floor before the startled Wolf Masters.

"Forgive me!" he gasped. A guard was already raising his javelin to stab him in the back.

"Hold!" Bhusa ordered, raising his arm. The guard stopped and took a step back obediently.

"Forgive me …" repeated the man, who looked like a Galatean soldier but whose uniform was in tatters, "… for this intrusion my masters but I had to see you urgently and the guards would have made me wait."

"What is it?" said Cordyr, ignoring all decorum.

"I am the only surviving member from the military detachment and last hunting party sent through Galati's gates."

The six Pelts were taken aback. Altogether that was nineteen men lost to the city. Whatever malevolent force was exercising its powers beyond the walls, its strength seemed to be growing.

"My men came across the hunting party and this is all we found. Have I permission?" The soldier appeared to be requesting their assent to reveal what was in the sack. Bhusa did not suspect trickery so he gave it.

The distraught man upended the bag. From it tumbled two white skulls, picked clean and fleshless. They fell onto the ground but a third object came out after them. It failed to hit the floor but instead, as if blown by the faintest air current, it rose up glistening, slowly wafted to the ceiling above on a perfectly vertical route.

Each Wolf Master's head rose with it. They had never seen a feather like it before. Bhusa had imagined the male peacock's feather to be the strangest and most wonderful in existence. What his eyes took in, far surpassed anything else in it virtuosity alone.

There was a design like a curling lightning bolt from the plumed tip to the shaft bottom and it ran without interruption in its pattern from side to side and down along the vain to the quill. The colour lying peripheral to the bolt was the deepest blue flecked with gold but the pigment which made the flash was truly indescribable. None there had seen the colour before: it changed from one moment to the next and appeared to float and shimmer above the surface on which it rested, yet its volatility did not affect the sharp silhouette that was etched across the plume. As it rose in the air a harmonious hum could be heard emanating from its centre.

One or two servants in the hall clapped hands to their ears, afraid that their minds might be turned if they allowed themselves to listen.

"What….?" The perplexity in his face finished the sentence for him.

"It is a small feather from the creature's wing," spoke the disturbed soldier.

"Small!" came a sibilant hiss from Bhusa. What he was seeing was at least as long as a tall man's leg.

Losing interest in its ascent, the feather was now slowly revolving and curling over like smoke from a dying fire, beginning to drift earthwards.

Entranced, Bhusa stepped forward and reached out to grasp it.

"Don't touch it!" yelled Rhodessa.

Her partner, wrenched from the spell, hurriedly backed off and the feather came to a gentle rest at his feet.

"Sometimes what is most pleasurable to one sense is the most toxic to another as with certain flowers, the leaves or thorns dealing death to those who touch." Rhodessa kept a garden, one of several in her palace that contained such plants. Despite living on the same estate, Bhusa knew nothing about its existence.

"She is right, Master. I covered my hand before placing it in the sack. I would not touch anything from that creature's body after having seen it."

"You saw it!" broke out Manwyr, Cordyr's partner, the Wolf Master responsible for buying and selling in the city and even now could not help wondering how much wealth could be earned if the creature was caught alive or dead and sold to the foreigners in the Palace of Transients.

"Yes, I did, only just for a few moments as it rose away from the place where the hunters and my squad were caught but what I saw was enough to warn me away from anything connected to the beast. I knew I had to bring back some proof concerning my companions' fate and what attacked them so there it is." The man pointed at the feather and skulls. The Wolf Masters contemplated him.

"Tell us what it looked like," commanded Manwyr.

The soldier hesitated as if reluctant. Then, water gushing from a broken dam, his words came rushing out. In a simultaneous act, he was both expressing what he had witnessed and purging his terror.

"My squad had found the hunting party alive and well in a clearing although the squad after several days tracking had not been able to see, never mind capture, any animal in that forested region. They spoke about hearing that sound which you have heard here, produced by the moving feather, although we of course had no clue as to its origin. It was evening and being thirsty, I left the others to collect water from the nearby river. Leaning from the river edge to scoop water up with my hog-skin I was suddenly alerted by the black water below turning bright white, a reflected image that mirrored what was behind me. I turned and saw in the dark sky, above the place which held my companions, what appeared like a lightning bolt travelling earthwards. But whereas those earthly strikes disappear in a flash, this bolt remained transfixed like ice in air. It made exactly the same marking in the sky as the sign on that feather. At the end was an iridescent halo of light, again above the grove I had just left."

"You had a choice," probed Rhodessa gently. "You could have fled or you might have returned to report on what you saw. Which did you do?"

"I crept back," asserted the man. He was beginning to relax and vaguely began to wonder about the reward for his evidence to the Pelts.

"Good man," said Suhdo tonelessly.

"Were there no screams or cries from your friends?" asked Zalso, another Wolf Master and Suhdo's partner.

"Nothing. Apart from that hum in the air, my companions were soundless. When I made my way back, using the trees to disguise my approach, I could see the source for the light and understood everything. In the clearing sat the creature, the bolt streaming from its tail. The beast seemed to be roosting and was positioned over the ground where once my companions had existed. That arced light was cast by the flames that sprung from its body, yet these prongs did not emit heat. Smoke poured skyward, which now covered the body that was like a bird but not a bird and now uncovered or wrapped around the long cylindrical neck extending to half the tree lengths around. The flame did not burn and the smoke did not choke. The neck was scaled like a snake's and the head too was serpentine; a forked tongue slithered out of the mouth intermittently. It did not see me but did detect the last remaining body, either unconscious or dead beside a bush. The body was a hunter's and noticed by the creature whose neck quickly bent and gathered the man up in his jaws, lifting and stuffing him under its great body, deep into the plumage. Having done that, the creature's head raised to the sky, wings outstretched. Flames leaped more wildly from its hulk and the creature stood on two feet. A trilling came from his mouth; the surrounding light was blue, the feathered barbs radiated fluctuations in colour at the core of the flames and the smoke…. it …was horrific….it….it… was beautiful!" The man stopped, exhausted.

Even the Wolf Masters were shocked. They were experts in deception however: their shock registered with onlookers as considered thoughtfulness.

"But what is it?" murmured Bhusa, finally.

His question could have been one asked of himself but the soldier realised it was for him to answer. He stared at the feather fallen on the floor and something stirred from a childhood memory. "You know, my grandfather used to tell me many stories about the forest and the world beyond, the infinite enigmas and beasts that wondered there. This creature, if it wasn't for the fact that it consumed human beings and its size was huge, would be such a one as he told me about: the Psychezoion.

The Psychezoion. The pet of Zalmoxis.

With one name, the soldier had verbalised his own death warrant.

Cordyr acted with quick efficiency. "Guards, can you escort this man to a guest-room on the lower floor?" The palace soldiers realised fully what this meant: excluding family members and government personnel, the only 'guests' in the xenophobic palaces belonging to their masters were political ones kept in cells below ground. They moved with too much alacrity. Cordyr frowned. "Be gentle with him, he has survived what no Galatean has done so up to this point. Make sure he has plenty of delicious food to suit his choice." She really did mean this. He had provided them with useful information entirely at his own risk. The least the Wolf Masters could do was to give him a tasty meal before they murdered him. Besides, she did not want any tantrums on the man's part before he left the hall. That would not be a good precursor to the decisions they had to take.

"You can go." This last command was given to the various attendants and remaining soldiers, who withdrew silently.

A brooding fell upon the august company after the others had left. Bhusa's gaze flitted from the objects left on the floor to the painted panels around the vast hall. The light that clarified the images there descended from the opaque glass-covered atrium in the octagonal building's roof above and from quivering torches placed in the spaces between the panels. There were ventilation spaces but no windows; they would have allowed too much daylight and observation of the secrets processed in that room.

Those painted images narrated Galati's founding by the god Lupa. Behind him Bhusa felt the Wolf God's presence again – a statue group more than double his own height which showed Lupa, wolf's head on man's body, about to spring upon a Galatean enemy, a goat-footed satyr, creature of the forest. Bhusa knew that these images and more were repeated throughout the city. The people had come to believe in them and the customs and rituals that perpetrated their belief. It gave them an identity as a people; kept them under control.

Only, it was a complete lie: a constructed myth.

Secular power and authority resided in the hands of those who understood this. Religion was the subterfuge.

As he sat around the semi-circular table with the others, himself and Rhodessa at its centre, Bhusa was impelled to speak first. His father it was and others, who had promoted the new religion which had replaced belief in the old god, Zalmoxis. Zalmoxis, the god who had been a man, a Getae that had travelled abroad, met Pythagoras and returned from Samos completely smitten by the Eleusian mysteries. A man who taught that this life was not to be so valued since people would cross over into immortality by going into a cave. He had proved this to the Getae himself by digging a chamber underground and living there for three years. When he came from below with the knowledge he had gained, people treated him as if he had risen from the dead. He had become a god.

Bhusa's father had thought about becoming a god. The pharaohs did it. Why not him?

Powerful theatre was required to make a god. It might have been enough for Zalmoxis to emerge spluttering into the light after three years' commune with the concealed universe below. But it was not enough for Zalmoxis. When he came up from his underground chamber and out through the mouth of the cave, something else came with him. Witnesses swore that they had seen a beast, half-snake, half-bird, fly up from behind, all aflame and ascend into the sky. It was a soul beast, the Psychezoion. Later, the Galateans said it was a ***daimon***, perhaps Zalmoxis' own. He kept it as a pet for all that time below and conversed with it, scrivening secrets for recreation and immortality.

In the end Bhusa's father had decided against transcending his own mortality. The trouble with being a god in your own city is that the people can see you. Divinity moults on regular contact, especially in a small place. He would be blamed for any unstoppable natural disaster – a crop failure, a plague – best to spread the responsibility amongst a caucus, concentrate on producing a legacy that would ensure wealth and power for his family. Besides, a threatened god can always project himself into the sky at any time. Bhusa's father had the wish but not the means.

So Zalmoxis had returned, if not him, at least the Psychezoion; then the god would come after his pet.

"This is a challenge to us," stated Bhusa, firmly.

"In more ways than you think," replied Suhdo.

"Meaning?"

"Meaning that we should not take any action which smacks of panic to the people; it is a sure method for undermining our own authority."

"I take it that you are referring to the witness?"

"Indeed yes. I know in more normal circumstances secrets are to be kept but this is extraordinary. It will be out in the public street before you can take any action to stop it. After executing the witness what happens next? Do we go on to kill the guards that heard everything spoken here and who took him down to the cells, the attendants who served our food? No, I suggest that we reward the survivor with gold, warn him that he is not to talk about his experience until we make an announcement to the city. His family and friends know us well enough to respect our wishes – we will say the same to the guards and attendants. It will give us the time we need to prepare our response. I move that this decision be taken now."

The last sentence was the protocol for a vote. Five hands were raised around the table. These included Cordyr's own, since she had reconsidered her initial action after Suhdo's warning and Bhusa sealed the decision with his agreement.

"Now," continued Suhdo, "the real problem is the Psychezoion and we must ask ourselves the reason for its return."

"Could it be to take revenge for the priests of Zalmoxis?" suggested Cordyr.

In the previous generation all the priests administering Zalmoxis' cult had been gathered up and executed. They themselves had been, in fact, the real motive for the alternative religion. Bhusa's father and his co-conspirators had faced too much interference and opposition from them when trying to administer secular government. A new divinity and religious conversion was the excuse required to eradicate their power. Of course the Zalmoxis priesthood had refused to convert, opting for suicide.

"If that is the motive, what indeed will be a satisfactory revenge?" wondered Bhusa aloud, "Galati's obliteration?"

"The Psychezoion might have come for us, its leading opponents," said Zalso cheerily. The others stared at him.

"Zalso, this creature is just that - something not human, without rational power and certainly lacks the ability to distinguish one human from another as regards who was responsible for opposing its master and who was not," countered Bhusa.

"I am not so sure. The Psychezoion was a god's pet, cared for by a divinity over three long years. Zalmoxis may even have created the beast himself. We must be cautious when estimating the creature's capabilities."

"That is heretical. Zalmoxis is dead; Lupa our protector," warned Cordyr.

Zalso laughed contemptuously. "If we cannot talk freely amongst ourselves, we should throw the city gates open to the Psychezoion now. Please, Cordyr, let us forget our own propaganda and plan sensibly when faced with destruction."

For the second time Cordyr fell silent, beginning to feel the others' accumulated impatience.

"We now understand what is responsible for our hunters' deaths but we lack the knowledge for stopping it," Bhusa said. He picked up and shook the hand-bell placed nearby. A door opened and closed, then an attendant appeared at his elbow. Bhusa handed her a towel from the table.

"Take this and wrap the feather in it that you see on the floor. Avoid touching the thing. Carry the feather to Doctor Eudeos and ask him to analyse the constituent parts. Perhaps we may learn something. Describe to the philosopher everything you have seen here concerning the feather and ask him to be careful in the handling of it. He must report to me at the first change of the palace guard tomorrow." When she had left, Bhusa turned back to the others. "Sometimes a body's essence can provide the means for its own annihilation."

"That might be possible but could take too much time. We cannot do nothing while Zalmoxis' pet ravages our hunting parties and farmland. It may even decide to come straight to the city to nourish itself on the people. We cannot allow that to happen – the fight has got to be taken to the Psychezoion, if only to assess its power."

Zalso, responsible for the city's fortifications, always preferred offence to defence and the others were used to his aggressive manner which always bubbled under the surface, ready to break.

"You intend to lose more Galateans and so hastily?" His partner, Suhdo, had felt herself forced into the marriage between them. She locked the bedroom door every night, threatening him with death if he ever touched her. He could have whoever he wanted and all the power granted by the Wolf Pack but her own body was sacrosanct. Zalso conjured up anger for appearance's sake but really could not care less: he preferred men anyway.

"No, my dear wolverine, I do not."

"Mercenaries then?" asked Bhusa with a puzzled frown because it had been a generation since the Galateans had last used foreign mercenaries.

"I suppose so."

"Where from? At such short notice?" asked Manwyr, incredulous.

"At this moment," continued Zalso steadily, "I have in chains nearly a hundred Hellenes and Syracusans on a war trireme at the river port. They call themselves Telemachons, derived from the name of their ship and their leader, Telemachus, who is held captive with others on the accompanying vessel. The boats arrived a few hours ago on their way up river and were quickly boarded. Gold was found hidden on board the merchant trader."

"Gold?" said Bhusa with interest. "That is usually being carried from the north, mined in the Pretannic Isles, to the south or from the Land of the Gauls eastwards along the Istros; I have never heard about it being transported westwards along our river from the Euxinus Pontus."

"More importantly, when have you ever known a Greek trireme to be sailing up the Istros through Celtic country?" Manwyr, as usual, was irritated by Bhusa's notorious cupidity for sparkling unnecessaries. He kept his own palace like a scholar's paradise, packed with scrolls ancient and modern – happily Cordyr shared his enthusiasm.

"Never," admitted Bhusa. "What are their plans for themselves and the gold they were carrying?"

"Failed ones already, if they can be stopped as easily as this," came Zalzo's dismissive comment. "We can guess what they are trying to do. What all Greeks do as soon as land runs short or internecine squabbling starts up. Pack their weapons and sail out to eventually take someone else's land and women. This time the Greeks, these Telemachons, have taken on a challenge that they have hugely underestimated. What madness overcomes them? How can they expect to survive this journey into the Celtic fist of Europa? But their concerns should not be ours and we must use them for the solution to our own predicament. They could not have arrived at a better time for us."

"You are about to suggest that we send these Telemachons to fight with the Psychezoion," anticipated Bhusa.

"Any disagreement with that?"

"Absolutely none on my part. I cannot speak for the others," said Bhusa, looking around.

"What is to stop these Telemachons from agreeing to the task and then simply leaving?" asked Rhodessa.

"Their oaths sworn to their gods?" Zalso was smiling and he only smiled when planning malice.

"You don't mean that."

"No I don't. We have their gold without which they could not bribe their way past many Celtic tribes along the river and we will take hostages."

"Hostages?"

"Yes, there are crew and four ex-slaves on the merchant boat, one a Celt who would be a useful interpreter further on into the west. We will keep them all and also a handful of the Telemachons to encourage their friends to return after they have completed their task. That is, if they are able to return."

"And just suppose that they accomplish it to our satisfaction, what should be done with them then?"

"Do you know," said Zalso unexpectedly, "I actually think we should let them go free." There was obvious disbelief on his listeners' faces. "Does anyone question my integrity?" The sudden outburst from the military man caught them all by surprise and unnerved one or two. Yet they should have been well used to his volatile temper by now. Bhusa made another mental note to guard himself against the volatility and to bring the date even closer when he would have Zalso removed from the Pelt circle. The Galatean commander of fortifications tried to resume a calm manner. "There would be little reason to kill them when there are tribes all along the river waiting to do that already if they knew of their coming. They would pose no danger to us on their release. In fact if they killed the creature that is threatening us we should really give them most of their gold back – excepting a small portion which we can divide and enjoy amongst ourselves." Zalso eyed Bhusa when he said this; the latter, along with the other Wolf Masters recognised a weak attempt at ingratiation when he saw one. Again, this was unlike Zalso.

"What if they refuse to hunt the Psychezoion?" queried Bhusa.

"Oh, in that event I rescind all those generous impulses expressed just now and will use the Telemachons as bait for Zalmoxis' revenger."

"A small rippled relief flowed around the table. This was more like the Zalso they had come to love and distrust. Rhodessa felt a slight thrill at the edginess he inspired. Such a shame his inclinations lay elsewhere.

"Besides, I have met with their leader, Telemachus. He is a young man burning for glory and the chance to become a champion, a true leader for his people. He will not pass up this chance to make his name eternal on the lips of the human race. Even the Gauls would be impressed by something like this – a man vanquishing a god's curse: a rampant soul-beast quieted."

"Are we to meet this young hero?" asked Rhodessa interested.

"He is outside the Hall now," replied Zalso.

"Bring him in," urged Bhusa. "Let us hear how a hero speaks."

7

The Cave of Zalmoxis

The underground chamber was deep. Very deep. And very old. Telemachus had never been inside the home of a god before. He had been inside several temples in Sicily and in one or two even into the *naos* where the god was said to live; his or her presence indicated by the eternal sacred flame fed there or an ancient wooden idol that had inhabited the sanctuary long before the temple was built on it. Magnificent as these buildings were and the images they contained, after the first excitement Telemachus' rational mind had come into play and he questioned the divinity's real existence.

Here it was different. Occasionally in the temples when he had reached the inner naos he had begun to feel something else. In this space now, that same reaction was beginning to form, only intensified. In both places, the naos and this cave, the feeling provoked was based on the same factor: simplicity.

Telemachus stretched his torch out as he walked around. Its light fell on the solitary bed cut from the rock wall, the heavy wooden table. The niche for the bed reminded him of a burial, isn't this what some people did with their dead? There were shelves gouged into the chamber sides and he wondered what might have been kept there, food probably, scrolls perhaps. This was existence stripped to the essentials but richer in a way and a preparation for what was to come.

He remembered the challenge the Wolf Masters had set him days ago in their Hall of Decisions. There was no mistaking the implied threat if he had refused. To get immediate release for his people he had to please them. In truth though, he was intrigued by their predicament: its connection with the man-god Zalmoxis and the havoc wreaked by the Psychezoion.

He had therefore accepted the challenge but not without a condition. He wanted to get inside the underground chamber that Zalmoxis had created for himself. Telemachus had made this request quite expecting the Pelt Council to turn to him and say that its location had been lost years ago or more likely, owing to their new found devotion to Lupa that the cave had been filled in. But no, the original location was known, in the forest land outside Galati and it had lain undisturbed since Zalmoxis had left.

After ensuring that the Telemachons were released, Telemachus had left for the site with a few of his comrades and some Galateans provided by the Wolf Masters. They also gave him a waggon filled with ropes and tools.

When he had arrived at the cave, Telemachus found the place in a rocky outcrop shielded by trees. This rock contained a wide entrance leading underground but it was obstructed by a large boulder, above a man's height. After toiling for hours, using the ropes and tools given to them, the stone was successfully rolled aside and the dark, musty entrance exposed.

The others were about to go down with him but he stopped them.

"Let me go down first, Eucleides and I will call up for you and the others if there is any danger. His trireme commander, although doubtful, made no objection.

So he had descended, just as Zalmoxis had done all that time ago. Telemachus wondered if he too would return to the surface with something discovered in the subterranean world. Had Zalmoxis found the Psychezoion in here or had the creature come to him from somewhere else? This was the necessity for his search, to see if there remained any clues to its existence and even better, its destruction. It was the important condition he had laid down in accepting the task from the Wolf Masters.

He anticipated their reluctance when making the suggestion to reopen Zalmoxis' underground sanctuary and got it. The stone blocking the chamber's entrance had been there for many, many generations. Ever since Zalmoxis had risen from the dead with his Psychezoion and exited his temporary home. Zalmoxis commanded the sealing up. Before that the stone had closed the cave mouth for the three years he had been below, mysticising his human form into a god's.

Telemachus understood their fears. They did not want to restore any belief in Zalmoxis. This might be hard to accomplish, particularly when the Galateans came to learn about a Beast in the Forest. Mixed with this was the superstitious expectation that if one occult creature had emerged from such a place then there may be more down there or worse. They made all this known to him but the Greek argued effectively that by descending into Zalmoxis' world he might find the solution to their curse.

His demand prevailed and here he was. Telemachus continued his exploration. On any flat walls that were available, text was written in faded yellow paint. Sometimes there were mathematical ratios and numbers as if whoever had written them was working on a particular concept in his mind. He could not decipher these in the short time available but easily recognised the textual poetry and the moral urgings that interweaved with them. They were lines crafted into the grave hexameters reserved for pronouncements from the Delphic oracle or Homeric hymns sung at Delos. They were, Telemachus knew, straight from the mind belonging to the first Greek calling himself a philosopher: Pythagoras. The man from Samos believed in reincarnation. Telemachus briefly played with the idea that he might have reincarnated himself as the Psychezoion but dismissed it.

Turning back to the chamber itself, Telemachus gingerly walked around the edge. He only had the one torch; it was dark and the ground underneath jagged and uneven.

Above ground, the others heard a sudden cry spring from the entrance.

"Eucleides, Thocero, down here! Bring the others!"

The two men whose names had been called glanced at each other and then, buckling on their swords and grabbing the ropes, led the Telemachons rapidly into Zalmoxis' cave.

"Where are you, Telemachus?" shouted Eucleides as the gloom descended upon him. But when he rounded a corner, his commander could be seen in the glow of the torch he held.

"Here," spoke Telemachus, waving the firebrand. "Step lightly or you will fall."

The men made their way to him and Telemachus used his light to show them what lay beyond. Behind him, the chamber wall abruptly ended in a large space. Within that space were four tunnels radiating away. Each shaft could be walked easily by a tall man; in fact their ground was flatter and more even than that belonging to the chamber.

The blackness within them seemed equally impenetrable but after moving his light to illuminate the four passages, Telemachus drew his torch back to the one he had selected and held it steady. Although his hold was firm the ribbons of flame bent from side to side, uncontrollably.

Eyes alive with excitement, he spoke to them, "We must choose one of these to walk and with her breath the Earth goddess Ge has shown us the way."

They moved into the tunnel warily, igniting several more torches in case one was blown out by the gentle breeze they could feel coming at them.

Not long after starting down the passage, Telemachus, leading, abruptly halted. "Hush!" he hissed. They stilled themselves and listened. Beneath the quiet and slight movement in the air arose a sound with which Telemachus was familiar. The sound was distant but unmistakable. He had heard it described in the Hall of Decisions and after finding Doctor Eudeos had witnessed the noise himself when the philosopher, his hand covered, waved the feather in the air to show him.

He gestured for the others to move on and they worked themselves along the walls with even greater caution. Some way further up, the main tunnel gave way to a large tunnel joining it. The men moved in and looked around. The roof space was huge and there were stalactite points hanging from the ceiling. One dropped liquid slowly from its tip to the ground. It was the largest and curiously was shaped more like a spear point than a stalactite since the base fixing it to the rock above narrowed, leaving two triangular corners clearly defined rather than a widened circular join.

A glimmer came up from the floor and Tyracides the Messanan whispered, "What's this?" Before his friend Pelisteus or Telemachus could stop him, he had grasped the Psychezoion's feather in his hand.

A tearing sound erupted in the air and a blue-white lightning bolt milked the darkness, spilling over his fist. He screamed and let the feather fall. His face was twisted in pain. The others could see his open hand as he stared at it – a jagged red weal now marking the palm.

"Are you alright Tyracides? Can you move your hand?" Telemachus spoke. The other gasped a comment in reply, opening and closing his fingers to test it. "Well, the Psychezoion must know we are here now and I think we have just been given a demonstration concerning how dangerous this cursed creature is going to be to kill or capture."

"Surely captivity is out of the question – we'll be lucky to kill it and keep all our men alive," warned Eucleides.

"Maybe," replied Telemachus. He paced around the antechamber, still talking. "We must not forget that this is the god's creature. If we destroy it will we invite divine wrath down upon our heads?"

"There are many gods," answered Eucleides, almost amused. "If you are frightened by the one, get yourself another. No man achieves anything worthy by giving into sacred fear. And when death faces you, so be it; it is a worthy pretence not to fear even that."

"I am not like you, Eucleides, although I hope I have the same courage. I would persuade divine enemies to become my allies." He stopped his pacing and stood near the large strangely shaped stalactite. The point released another drop of fluid, splashing down with a slight echo onto the dark floor.

Telemachus raised his head to the ceiling above and cried out with self-assuredness, "Zalmoxis!"

The name bounced and reverberated around the enclosed space. The Telemachons felt a thrill running up their spines and fear in their limbs. Telemachus was calling up a god. Was this wise?

No answer. Just the steady drip from stalactite tip to ground.

"Zalmoxis!" Louder still.

In the black depth something changed. When the next drop fell from the limestone and hit the ground, there was a chime like the single clap of a bell.

Telemachus peered and his third utterance, in contrast, was almost a whisper, a confirmation, "Ah, Zalmoxis!" Behind him, fearful faces watched in amazement as the stalactite rocked itself loose from the roof and fell toward the ground with a crumbling thud, its tooth crushing into the ground.

After the thud came a rumble, the Earth beneath their feet shook. Slowly, the transfixed rock shard became molten, malleable; another shape evolved. The body was animal but the head was human. It pulsed with a dark, constant rotational change mutating through diverse suggestive forms, all redolent of the world beneath, never clearly animal nor human: a shining membraneously winged and two-footed bat, a silk-furred large-handed mole, a stick-framed wide-elbowed cockroach; all towering over the Telemachons, menacing them. Yet, the human head which surmounted the changing body, thin, without any hair on scalp or chin, was almost benign as it regarded them through wide blue cat eyes set in ashen skin.

There was a sound that evoked the wind through tree tops when it spoke.

"What do you want from me?"

Telemachus paused and then answered him indirectly. "We want to bring peace to Galati."

Inexplicably, a tear slid from the god's eye down his cheek.

"They have abandoned me. I can do nothing."

"But you can recall your daimon, your pet. It seeks vengeance and is taking innocent lives!"

"My command over the Psychezoion ended on the day it rose from the dead with me. Now, while it roams above, I inhabit the layers beneath, unable to rise again and living with the buried offerings made aeons ago by my true believers. My memory is being destroyed by its rage."

Telemachus saw a chance. "Then help us to stop it. You must."

"Must!" rumbled Zalmoxis, clearly angered. "Why must I help a people who have denied me and substituted a man-made wolf god for true belief? Ask Lupa for respite!"

"The Galateans are without fault," insisted Telemachus. "It is the Wolf Masters you should blame for leading them astray. Punish them."

"As I have said already, I am powerless beyond the ground beneath. But you have been selected as their champion. Behave as one, use your resourcefulness and what has been given to help."

"Given?"

"By King Istar. The Ambrosus."

"But what living thing is fiercer than the Psychezoion – what do I change myself into to overcome it?"

"It is not that you should change yourself."

Telemachus thought for a moment. "You mean that the beast itself has to be transformed?"

"The Psychezoion, as powerful as it must appear to you, has a weakness that can be exploited. It never wished to be free from me because a part of it is me. My substance made the creature. It flew from this chamber thinking it wanted freedom and indeed every day it spent apart from me, my pet increased in size and strength. Occasionally, when I was walking the surface it would return to me for companionship but one day it simply vanished never to be seen by me again. Yet I hear from you and the bats that twitter in these tunnels that my pet has come home again, only to destroy. Let me tell you that destruction is not its true nature. It yearns to be what once it was: diminished in size and power and in the warmth, underground. To defeat the Psychezoion take some Ambrosus and dip a spearhead into the ointment. Then throw your spear with the greatest accuracy and find its heart."

On the last word the pulsations running through Zalmoxis became wilder and then reaching a crescendo finally exploded into fractal fragments, leaving the solid stalactite behind.

It took some moments before they recovered themselves.

"Well, now we know," said Eucleides with finality.

"And we must put that knowledge to good use before the creature takes more victims," said Telemachus as he moved off to follow the source of the breeze down the tunnel.

They went with him and it wasn't long before they could see a light in the distance and eventually stood at the exit in blazing daylight.

The natural light after the darkness was welcome but what it helped them to see was a grisly sight indeed.

Below them was the rocky floor of what looked like an abandoned quarry. The tunnel had come out into the middle of a steep cliff which fell away sharply. There was a small plateau before the tunnel's exit and a path winding down precariously to the quarry.

At ground level, sun reflecting from a feathery sheen, lay the Psychezoion, resting in the nest it had built. The eyes were closed, the long neck outstretched. Meshed in with the tree branches and brushwood making up its bed were Galatean skulls and skeletons, picked clean and white. The creature was enormous but a man could still reach the heart with his javelin.

Telemachus took a spear and a quiver holding six arrows from two men. He lay them on the ground and took out from the pouch at his waist the flask that Istar had given him.

"Is that the Ambrosus?" asked the man whose quiver had been taken. "What is that – a magic or a toxin?"

"Both, we hope, as far as that creature down there is concerned." Their commander dipped the spear point and arrowheads into the jar, making sure that each was thoroughly coated with the yellowish jelly. "There is no use in us all descending and risking ourselves so Eucleides, Zipleus, Thocero,

Taranus and Agenor – you come with me. The rest stay here, unless I call for reinforcements."

Tyracides stepped forward. "Let me go, Telemachus, I want to make amends for what happened earlier."

The Corinthian studied him doubtfully but relented. "We all learn by our mistakes, Tyracides. If you can promise me that you will control your irrational impulses then yes, you may go with us." The Syracusan with a glad expression tugged on the helmet thrown to him by one of the others. Pelisteus patted his arm.

"Did Zalmoxis not say it should be a spear point that reaches his heart? Asked a Telemachon anxiously.

"Who can doubt the iron messenger as long as the message gets through?" Telemachus answered him.

He got up from the ground and keeping the javelin himself he passed the quiver over to Agenor, who for years had been a trusted accurate archer within his military command back in Sicily.

"We must make our way down without any sound that might alert the beast. Follow me. The rest of you stay back within the shadow of the tunnel.

Slowly they descended, sticking closely to the rock face and away from the edge. The humming sound they had heard in the tunnel became louder, the closer they approached. A slight wind was blowing through the quarry and the creature's feathers fluttered and sang in the current.

Telemachus was hoping to take the bird snake quickly before it properly awoke. Its nest, he noted, was placed near to water falling down the rock into a cold pool.

The men manoeuvred themselves into positions assigned by Telemachus. They kept themselves hidden as much as possible behind the large boulders that lay around the quarry. There was no avoiding the fact that they had to wake the creature so that its massive body was lifted off the nest and the chest could be exposed. Telemachus and Agenor were near one folded wing while Eucleides and the others were at the beast's head.

The Psychezoion rested, eyes closed, forked tongue flickering in and out of its mouth. The scaly head, flat on the ground was just an arm's length away from his sword. Eucleides knew he was there to disturb the creature, to raise it from the ground. Why do that when the head could so easily be lopped from the body and the beast destroyed? What was so essential about the heart being pierced with the Ambrosus when they could avoid further trouble by him taking action now? Eucleides decided on that instant and raising his sword brought it down expertly to cut the neck.

The head was sliced from the body and Eucleides stepped back, unable to believe his luck. He looked towards Telemachus, joyful. But his commander's changing expression, to one of horror, gave him warning. He turned back and found that the neck was not still and not bleeding. Instead it had begun to squirm and a tremor shot through the plumed body. He and the others retreated.

The beast lifted itself from the ground and even while it moved, the neck grew back another head. This though was different to the reptilian one that had been there before. What now swung on the end was the hairless head of Zalmoxis, angered and searching. He immediately found Telemachus with javelin raised.

Overcoming his shock, Telemachus took a few steps forward and threw the spear with all his force.

Too late. With agile speed, the Psychezoion turned and the spear shaft grazed its feathers. There was a thunderous flash as the weapon disintegrated in mid-air.

Men were now scattering in all directions, running for cover but Agenor had fitted an arrow to his bow and was taking aim. Before he released it, the Psychezoion reared upwards, wings flapping. A wing tip knocked Agenor from his feet, spilling the arrows out of their quiver. The sudden force had left him levelled and choking.

"If it flies we are doomed!" yelled Thocero to the others by the boulder to which he had run.

The Psychezoion continued to work its wings but seemingly for a purpose other than flight. The body colour was changing like an iron bar heated and under terrific temperature, from sore red to furious white. The gold flecked blue of the feathers did not lighten, however. They grew darker while the unknowable colour that made the wriggling design in the feather's centre whitened. A lightning bolt streamed from its tail upwards into the empty blue sky.

Something seemed to snap. There was a violent hiss and feathers from the Psychezoion's body were catapulted outwards to spray the surrounding area.

Feathers became orange darts and hit both Zipleus and Taranus still running a retreat. Their bodies were lit up and for a moment showed a prism of colours, like a rainbow within their outlines. Just for seconds, then the colour faded and nothing but ash piles were left behind in the places where they had been moving.

All the time a trilling sound could be heard which seemed to change with the beast's movements.

Telemachus became desperate. He realised that any moment now, the beast would fly. The arrows Agenor had dropped were too close to the creature for him to retrieve. *Not as he was.*

It was an impulse fed by urgency. Pulling out the flask from his pouch and releasing the stopper, Telemachus shook two globules of Ambrosus into his hand. He wiped the ointment around his face and rubbed it in.

The jelly tingled his skin. He thought hard. The terrifying Psychezoion with a human head waving on the end of a tubular neck, lashed and flapped before him. He thought about flight. The prickling was an electric wash that charged his whole body. A cloudless blue sky became black and then blue again. His arms moved spasmodically and the cool air rushed through his feathers. A buoyancy raised him up, just in time as a feathered dart from the monster, now red now burning orange, sped underneath and buried itself in the place where he had been.

Eucleides gasped, without comprehending what he was witnessing. He had been watching out for Telemachus and had seen his actions with the Ambrosus.

After applying it, the man seemed to shrink in stature, but not by much. His figure moulded as if being worked by two huge invisible clay worker's hands and his shape changed into that of a bird: the beak popping out of his face, his arms revolving into long pinioned wings and his two legs extending, covered in snowy white fur and pointed into claws bigger than the head. White head, golden eye; white feet, black talons. Along the Istros, Eucleides had learned, these birds were known as 'River Ghosts': their spectral mix of white and brown plumage – white plumage on the main body and a brown mask across the face – made for an unsettling sight when they flew and hunted, especially near dusk. The Osprey's feet are designed to pluck fish from water but this Osprey, much larger than normal, had a greater challenge to match.

Having risen and soared into the sky, it dived. Skimming the stony floor with its feet, an arrow from Agenor's quiver was quickly grasped and pointed forward.

Eucleides recognised his friend's tactic and called out to the others. "Agenor! Thocero! We must bring the creature around towards us!" Without question, his companions obeyed the command. They rushed out along with Eucleides and taunted the Psychezoion with their swords and spears.

The monster observed them almost with amusement as they waved their weapons uselessly. He was just about to return his attention to Telemachus when Eucleides managed to stab him in the side with his javelin. It was only a pin-prick but amusement became annoyance on the face like Zalmoxis' and the creature spun back to the men.

Meanwhile with every effort so that his avian muscles strained to their utmost, Telemachus had reached the zenith of his climb upward. From this height, the Psychezoion looked small in the quarried world down there and the men were mere flies picking at its flanks.

He faltered, bent his head and beak forward; fell.

The rush was exhilarating and his speed increased as he described the perfect downward diagonal of an isosceles through the smashed air. His human mind wanted to laugh out in its excitement but the predatory bird intelligence stamped out the distraction, giving his wings a slight adjustment to hone his trajectory. The round gold eye was ready for the kill but not with beak or claw.

The Psychezoion's neck shifted once more. It heard a whistling noise pass by under his wing; a bit of brown grit shot into his flesh.

Telemachus rammed the arrow deep into the monster's chest. He half-expected to die on the creature's feathers just as he had seen others fall victim to them. The fatal, conducted bolt did not occur but he had enough to contend with in simply bouncing from the brute's plumage and falling away. He flapped his wings which saved him from crashing to the floor but in the event almost collided with the quarry wall. Again several wing shakes turned him away but not before he suddenly found himself flying through the water gushing from the quarry top. The water pressure forced him down, losing height.

Thocero and the others saw the osprey emerging through the veil of water, flop to the ground and rolling helplessly along. As the bird rolled it seemed to expand like dough; feathers retracted, wings turned back to arms and as the rolling body became inert, Telemachus' transformation to his original form was complete.

The Psychezoion with the arrow shaft buried deep towards its heart, also appeared to be struggling. The neck reached upward and Zalmoxis' head was mouthing words to the sky but nothing came out. Its wings stretched outward in an attempt to fly but suddenly there was a collapse. The monster imploded and shrank in size. Zalmoxis' head vanished, to be replaced by the familiar snakehead and now the Psychezoion was no larger and no more terrible than a farmyard chicken. From a figure of dread, it had once again become a pet and flapping away up the quarry face it found the tunnel mouth and fled back to Zalmoxis' underground chamber.

The others hurried to see if Telemachus was seriously injured but apart from minor bruises their commander seemed relatively unharmed.

"Do we follow it?" wondered Tyracides, peering up at the quarry face.

"Only to escape from here," answered Telemachus. "When we leave Zalmoxis' sanctuary, we will not roll the stone back to seal the chamber. Let the Wolf Masters do that again – if they are brave enough to take the consequences."

"Will the Wolf Masters accept that we have overcome the Psychezoion if we don't have any proof?" said Agenor.

"Somehow, I think that the ashes of our friends, Zipleus and Taranus, will not be enough," added Thocero bitterly.

"How can we trust them? They are already holding our crews captive. What is to stop them from slaughtering us all as soon as we return?"

"I fear that is exactly what they will do," replied Telemachus. "They are barbarians without any civilised values, having made a religion out of their savagery. We must do what they least expect – return by night to the harbour, release our comrades and flee."

"What about our gold?" asked Thocero.

"That must be the price we pay for our lives."

"But this is hardly heroic, Telemachus, particularly for yourself. I have just seen you defeat the beast that has terrorised their people. They will hardly believe that you have accomplished the challenge, even if their hunters now fail to be eaten, when they wake to find you have fled the city."

Eucleides intervened. "Thocero, we cannot fight off a city with a trireme and a trading boat. This is the time for wisdom and circumspection. Even if it was possible and say somehow we were able to bring down the Pelt with a hundred warriors, would you want to live in such a city, where the inhabitants allowed themselves to be ruled by wolves?"

"I suppose not," grumbled Thocero. "It just seems that we are not building on our victory here today. Our names will not be made famous for what we did and our reputations will be scarred by the way we plan to leave Galati. This makes our journey along the Great River more difficult. Every Celtic warrior between here and the source will treat us as running hares to send their dogs after."

This was in fact a very good point. One which persuaded Telemachus to refresh his thought.

8
Wolf Masters

Suhdo placed a finger on her lips. The action was not necessary. It was meant as a warning for Rhodessa standing right next to her but the latter did not need to be reminded of the danger they were in. They were both standing at a wall in which a hole had been drilled through to the next room. The hole was large enough for any sound to be conducted through and although Suhdo disliked the cramped space, the hole and the secret space that she had built into her bedroom behind a wooden panel years ago, served its purpose well. Her bedroom lay beside the reception hall for important guests to the palace. The listening space was created by a competent craftsman, now dead, who installed it when her partner, Zalso, had been away for a week on what he liked to refer to as his hunting trips. Since then she had gained much useful information via this secret spy hole and she knew that this occasion might be the most rewarding yet.

Telemachus was in the hall with Zalso. She had already been made aware that this would happen a day earlier. Telemachus had sent one of his men to tell her. What he had to say, this man called Eucleides, might have guaranteed his execution on the spot but Telemachus had judged the situation well. He could feel the tension between the Wolf Masters that time he had spoken with them and accepted the task for destroying the Psychezoion. He must have even sensed the differences between herself and Zalso; that was probably not difficult as she never bothered to hide them. The risk was of course reduced by the message which Eucleides carried in his hand from Rhodessa and Bhusa. That certainly made her sit up and plan for her immediate future. It was time for herself and Zalso to part company; frankly it was a relief.

In the hall, Telemachus was assessing the effect of his words on Zalso. He had just told him that he was willing to commit the Telemachons to his service.

Zalso leaned forward from his throne and looked at the young man intently, "And why would you want to do that, son of Timoleon? Don't get me wrong, I do value your proposal but really, you cannot wonder that I question your motives. You have come to my palace after a few days in the palace, saying you have conquered the monster that has terrorised us, although not even a tail feather is brought to prove that claim and then offer me your hundred warriors. I thought you were wanting to make your name along the Istros and to establish a home for your people at the other end of the world?"

"Please do not mistake me in turn, my lord. I am determined to find that home for the Telemachons. It will happen. To make it possible though, I need my gold returned to the ship and if it is possible a further addition would be received with thanks."

"Why do you think I might need the Telemachons?"

"These are dangerous times and it is at such that men like mine, mercenaries fighting for their living, can be employed to bring greater stability to a city like Galati. You set the task, we complete it just as we did with the Psychezoion and then after payment we will be on our way."

"The Psychezoion?" said Zalso, puzzled because he thought he had just dismissed that topic.

"Ah, yes. You need proof. There are two of my men outside the door, can you send for them?" Telemachus noted the narrowing of Zalso's eyes. "Don't worry, my lord, they are unarmed."

The Wolf Master hesitated and then sent a slave to the door. Eucleides and Thocero entered carrying something on two poles which they shouldered in and laid on the floor. At a signal from Telemachus, they quickly pulled the covering cloth away to reveal a small cage. Behind the bars, trilling with the sudden light and staring at Zalso was the Psychezoion

"What – is this Zalmoxis' beast?" cried the Wolf Master. "How can this be possible? I thought the creature was much larger. Can this be its young?"

Telemachus explained what had happened but changed the circumstances so that he did not have to mention the Ambrosus. With the astonishing creature before him, its projectile feathers protected by the closely knit bars of the cage, Zalso was prepared to believe that an ordinary javelin had not killed it but somehow had shrunk it in size.

"Apart from our military service, this is another gift we bring you," said Telemachus.

Zalso viewed it, shocked but fascinated. Ideas were already forming in his mind. With this beast he could reinstate the Old Religion, be the saviour of his people, disband the Wolf Circle. All the power accumulated by the Pelts could be removed from their control and be placed under his own. He licked his lips thinking about it.

"How soon would your men be ready to fight?"

"We have some weapons but we will need more."

"You can take some back to your ship from my armoury. You can also have your part of the gold that was originally taken. By sunset today, be prepared to move on my enemies. I will send you a message with an army officer."

Behind the wall the two women were removing themselves from the cramped space, quietly but swiftly.

Telemachus inwardly rejoiced but did not betray his emotion when Zalso spoke treachery. He knew that somehow those words would be conveyed to Suhdo and the other Wolf Masters, perhaps by paid informers or listening holes. That was the ultimate irony in these most secretive palaces: information slid through them as easily as rain down new guttering.

For his part, Zalso maintained the pretence that he knew nothing about Suhdo's listening chamber. Just as he pretended ignorance concerning her poison garden. Or her numerous liaisons with young men in the city. These little ignorances were required deceit for the successful manipulator. There was only so much that fear could win and the terror he instilled in others achieved quite a lot. Though too much exerted pressure could snap the catapult and enable people to transcend their psychological bonds. This had obviously applied to the systematic belief that had been imposed for years on Lupa. In that instance it was not the people who had reacted but something else. The time had come for a change and he would be the nemesis for that transition.

A hard rapping sound knocked on Suhdo's door. It was the sound made by a sword pommel. Rhodessa looked at her companion with a frightened expression.

"Hide!" hissed Suhdo as she approached it warily under the growing foreboding that they had left it too late to leave the room. She tried to find some weapon with which to defend herself. Seizing a pair of scissors from her dressing table, she dropped them into a pocket in her gown.

Suhdo opened the door with a panache that she hoped would not reveal the inner turmoil.

" 'Scuse me, your majesty," came the rough voice from the Sergeant-at-arms standing before her, sword out. His scarred face was grinning from ear to ear. He loved it when roles were so quickly reversed and power collapsed from the mighty, especially women. "But my lord Zalso suggests that it is best if you keep to your quarters for now, until he is able to speak with you."

Suhdo could have shown anger but that would have just been wasteful and silly. She chose instead to phrase a question into a demand to retain an authority that no longer existed.

"When will that be?"

The veteran showed disappointment. He had expected fear.

"When he is ready, my Lady." The last two words were pronounced with heavy sarcasm and he found himself staring at the panelled oak door which had just been slammed, missing his face. For a moment he thought about going in there and giving her a good slap. But then he checked himself – roles could be reversed yet again, leaving him vulnerable. No, he would have to wait until she had fallen all the way from her plinth right to the dungeon below. Then the fun could really begin. Zalso certainly wouldn't mind. Women meant nothing to him.

On the other side of the door, Suhdo waited for the explosion of fury. She was pleased to have seen that there was only one guard and if he had come in she would have used the scissors straight away, when he least expected it – first into the eyeball and then into the neck. She had dispatched a young deer like that once, when her brother had scoffed at her presence on a hunting trip in front of their father. He never treated her with contempt again after that.

The expected intrusion did not occur and once she was sure, Suhdo retrieved Rhodessa from her hiding place.

"What do we do now?" she asked, having heard the exchange.

Suhdo took her by the arm and steered her to a large wall hanging. Behind that was what appeared to be plaster but was actually fabric. Suhdo tore at it quickly with her scissors and revealed a door. She turned to Rhodessa and said fiercely, "Zalso thinks he knows everything about this palace but it was originally mine and my family's. This is a hidden passageway, one amongst several – we can use it and the adjoining rooms and passages to get to the stables. There are loyal servants there who will help us to escape. But we must hurry before Zalso discovers our absence."

In the reception hall, Zalso watched Telemachus and his men leave. He could have had them killed, he thought idly but that would have been a distraction from his real purpose. Better to use their military experience rather than to waste attention on them when he had much bigger game to chase. He had told Telemachus to be ready the next day. Well, they would be required sooner than that. He would ensure too, that the Telemachons would form the vanguard in the fight against his enemies. That way, he could counter two problems with one solution. Hopefully, the Telemachons and their leader would perish.

There was a hiss in front of him. The Psychezoion's head stretched out on its long neck between the cage rungs, swinging to and fro. Zalso tossed it a grape which was snatched from the air and swallowed greedily. The guards' eyes tried to avoid it.

Zalso sent for his second-in-command. He was glad to see that after the first surprising glimpse of the Psychezoion, the man's attention was locked solidly onto himself alone. Very wise. The general waited for his orders.

"Xoras, prepare your men," said Zalso. "We go to war."

9
The Revelation

Back at the river port Telemachus made his own preparations and they had nothing to do with battle. Zalso's men still guarded them – six on the 'Telemachon' itself and three on Thocero's merchant boat. Yet more were at the port gates. All these soldiers had been given new instructions by Zalso to let their former prisoners work freely and without interference. Telemachus used that to his people's advantage over the next few hours. He had reduced the terrible creature which had been slaughtering the Galateans in the forest and this city's response to that was to devise a plan to massacre each other in a debilitating civil war. Their fate was in their own hands, not his. He had done all he could do for them and he was not about to spill the blood of his own people by taking sides in their conflict.

And so at the right time, efficiently organised, hands were laid on Zalso's guards in both boats and they found themselves over the side and spluttering in the water with the Telemachons laughing above them.

Zalso's commander had been seized and remained on board the Telemachon with the threat to the harbour guards that if they attempted to follow, he would be killed. This confused them enough so that there was no pursuit. A short distance away from Galati, the commander too was thrown overboard and the Telemachons watched as he dragged himself up onto the river bank, mouthing curses at them that could not be heard because the tireless, sweating effort exerted by the Telemachons over their oars ensured an ever quickening pace in the water and a widening distance between themselves and Galati.

Telemachus then, was not a witness to the long war that consumed the city, only being ended when the people themselves requested help from outside. King Istar sent his Istrian army which defeated Zalso and treating all the warring leaders with no special favour, put the remaining Wolf Masters to the sword; they having been condemned in court as war criminals. The Psychezoion had been deliberately freed by someone in the palace and had vanished.

The two boats had been travelling up the river all morning. Telemachus was in Thocero's craft, leading the way. They were setting the pace, otherwise the trireme with its scores of oarsmen might have left them far behind. He was standing at the stern, checking back over their course to make sure that no one was following them, when he heard a quiet voice.

'My lord Telemachus ....'

Behind him had appeared three figures. Two of his men from the trireme, who had been amongst several transferred to row the trader and a third. The third man was standing between the other two, his arms restrained by them. It was the merchant from Istros, Histarchus. He seemed to be remarkably calm despite his predicament. Unusually for the warm weather, he was wrapped in a thick woollen cloak.

" .... I think you need to see this." Continued one of those holding him.

Histarchus was staring with those large globular eyes of his, completely unperturbed. When the cloak was pulled away from his body, he made no move to prevent it.

They all looked in wonder at what was revealed, even the sailors who had seen it already, below deck.

Beneath the cloak Histarchus wore nothing: his arms, torso and lower half were bare. But it was not human skin that now lay exposed. It was the scaled skin of a fish. There were dark brown spots on a lighter ochre background and his sides were infused with a luminous bluish tinge. Even his face seemed to carry a roll of skin around the wide mouth.

"He looks like an Istran salmon!" cried out another member of the boat crew, astonished. And it was indeed true – he resembled nothing more nor less than those murky giants gliding along the deep river bed whose length can equal a small man's height.

Even his voice when he spoke, seemed to have changed and come bubbling up from under green, river weeded stones.

"It must surprise you, Telemachus to have found such a guest aboard your craft: an uninvited guest. Yet the unwelcome ones here are you and your Telemachons. You are the transgressors into my land. This river and the fertile lands from which it takes its water and gives it back is my territory, to be used by the people I have nurtured. I brought them here; they followed my silvery track into the mountains and settled along it. I am the water that gives them life. You will raid and pillage, taking from my people what is rightfully theirs."

"As to pillaging," replied Telemachus, "your people-the Keltoi- are not slow in practising that on others and will soon, no doubt, come into Greece to satisfy their longing for what we have and a desire for telling great deeds in battle. We, on the other hand, are only honest travellers and simply want a safe passage into Europa to its other side. You know my name. Will you give me yours?

"I am called Danu," came the answer. "Listen to my warning. Do not squander the creatures in the Great River or bring death to the people along its banks."

"If you are the god of this river, I would rather travel along it, myself and my people, with your goodwill and without hindrance. If we are left to pass in peace by the Keltoi dwellers on this watery inroad, then there should be no excuse for violence on our part. We have no control over events however, if people attack us we must defend ourselves. Yet there is something we can promise. That is, while we navigate the Great River we shall not feed from the fowl that paddles on its surface or forage through its reedy beds, neither shall we pluck out the quick-scaled creatures that swim its depths – not without your permission.

"Sometimes," replied Danu slowly, "the most successful approach to your destination is achieved by divergence and the allure of what is most difficult."

Telemachus was hoping for a friendly acceptance but instead he was left with an aphoristic riddle.

Danu remained still as a pike behind a rock in one moment and then shot out across the deck in the next. Running on his bare, wet-glistening feet, he jumped high into the air and over the handrail, making a perfect dive into the green river water. Before he hit the surface the crew could see his two separate legs fuse into one strong fish tail. There was a splash, a brief jagged shape gliding under the water and he was gone.

"Passenger overboard!" came Thocero's humorous tones from the stern, where he had followed the proceedings closely.

"Will he be watching us, sire?" asked a man, referring to their vanished god.

"Oh, I am certain he will," replied Telemachus. "If nothing else, I have no doubt about that. We must live with the promise we made to him."

10

A Strategy

Over the next three days the two boats made good headway along the Istros, with no interruption. There were sightings of the local people here and there but they were very occasional; caught in the middle of some task either chopping wood, hunting hogs or the particular preoccupation for women – washing clothes at the river's edge, they paused and stared, fascinated or, as in every instance with the washer women, lifted their dresses up to free their legs and flee.

There were settlements that had to be circumvented and consulting the maps drawn by Hecataeus, the voyagers were able to name them as they glided by. After leaving Galati, they found Braila which was a much smaller settlement near the tributary river Lalomita, then Bucharest, a little larger and between the tributaries Olt and Vedea, a fortified place that was larger still, Craiova. Its size probably owed to its comfortable position. Frontally protected by the Istros and a different river on each side, the Craiovans had only their backs to defend.

But it was their own defence that the Telemachons had to consider. When they rested they slept outside their boats after first constructing a rudimentary palisade on the river bank around the moored ships. It was best to travel at night. In this manner they could slip silently by the smaller communities without raising the alarm. Of course, the trireme had to be disguised so that it no longer resembled the Greek warship it was and this could be done with relative simplicity by using cloth to cover its silhouette and caulking the painted eyes at the prow with river mud. This worked surprisingly well. The men though, asserted that it was not just by human means that they were enabled to travel invisibly past the Celtic communities. Many had witnessed the River God Danu and his return to the water. None dared to fish from the river after that, keeping strictly to Telemachus' promise that only game from the forest would provide them with the nourishment they needed. It was this contract with the god, they claimed which ensured their safety.

Telemachus, the maker of that contract, agreed with them and ordered further offerings to be burnt to propitiate the river. His faith was not shaken when again they sailed by a tribal home – the largest so far, Craiova – and at the last moment a hail of arrows was sent thudding into the wooden hull of the trireme.

He ordered a war footing immediately on deck and sent a signal blast ahead on the aulos to Thocero to speed up. As they gained pace and waited in readiness for another attack, eerily it never came.

The Telemachons' leader knew that this incident was just a warning. It was as if the barbarians were saying to them, 'We can take you any time. This is our land – foreign to you, home to us. We know its traps.'

Votive offerings to Danu were not enough. The gods expected requests for help and sometimes they gave it. Continuous pleadings for more only earned their contempt. They expected mortals to use the intelligence and initiative with which they had been endowed and to become independent; just as the gods themselves had separated from the Titans at the beginning of creation.

Telemachus decided to consult his people. Tracing the river line through the maps in the periplus devised by Hecataeus, there were three major tribal centres to be passed. Belgrada first and after that Buda and Pest with the mighty Istros coursing its way between them. He could see that before the first of these there would be the opportunity to shelter the boats at the base of a mountain range. It was here where his consultation could be made.

What was clear was that there had to be a different strategy for making their way through barbarian territory. The river was not an open sea. Any traveller on it could be easily watched from the forest or the mountains above. Telemachus was surprised that there had not been a full-scale attack already. He had ideas for improving their safety but was open to suggestions.

The people on the ships with him might offer a better way. As the journey had progressed from its very beginning in Heraclea Minoa, Telemachus sensed a change in attitude. He was treated as undisputed leader of the expedition, supported loyally as he was by both Eucleides and Thocero. But from simply being two ships manned by crews seeking adventure and booty, the expedition had changed into something else. It had become what he originally had wanted it to be: the search for a destination. The change had come in Athens. There some men in his crew had returned with boys, girls and women from the slave market, asking for them to be included on the voyage. Those with the boys and girls he marked out as lost causes and made sure that they remained on the Piraeus jetty when the boats left. Love between adult men he could accept but pederasts were something else. It evoked the Persian yearning for eunuchs and young brides or Boeotian practises and neither were manly or civilised. If the Athenians had implemented laws to prevent pederasty amongst their teachers and stop the stalkers in the gymnasia, the least he could do was to exclude them from the tiny community aboard his ships. The women, though, he accepted. There were only a few and they took the places of the pederasts and several male crew who left in disgust, complaining about the diminishment in strength at the oars. Telemachus realised that this could become a sore point with the remaining crew and so he had the women trained by those who had bought them. After a time, they too could take the oars for short periods, tend to the sails and cook the food that was needed to keep everyone in good humour.

In accepting the women aboard, Telemachus was also thinking to the future. Seeing women amongst them, the communities they came across would not fear for their own women. Aboard these ships Telemachus had his own living population. The Telemachons were not just a band of marauding male warriors; they constituted a floating polis. Telemachus had noticed the changing relationships amongst the four manumitted slaves from Minoa. Only the love affair between Tyracides and Melissa had lasted, that between the potter and the Keltoi had not. Their separation had been amicable and it had caused no problems. Belisama had chosen Agenor as her next lover and made the trireme her new base. Telemachus hoped that she would not make a habit of transferring her affections. That would cause ructions. He had assumed a fierce independence was uppermost in her nature, now he had changed his view and was beginning to think a selfish gratification for her basic desires was her prime motivation. Either that or she felt chronically vulnerable without a man's protection.

The place they drew the boats up to, was a sandy cove. It gave way to grass and a bushy area of flat land which suddenly became a steep mountain slope.

It was dusk. Telemachus got the men to chop and clear some bushes, using the wood to build a fire so that they could cook a stew with some salted goat meat and vegetables from the hold in Thocero's boat. The mooring spot was well disguised by the hills on a bend of the river which helped to make the firelight undetectable. Even so, a patrol was sent out to ensure that there were no spies about or ambush planned.

Once wine and water had been mixed in the krater and given out, proper discussion began.

"We must think about how we are to proceed from here," said Telemachus. "So far, our journey up the Great River since Galati has been relatively comfortable. You are all experienced enough in venturing through new territory and so you know as well as I do that this tranquillity cannot last." There was a low sound from those surrounding him, indicating agreement. "We have to, then, prepare for the worst and anticipate it. If a village along this river finally takes it into their heads to make an attack upon us, what will happen?"

"We either die or kill those who mean us harm." The response came from Melissa and the gathered crowd were somewhat surprised that it was a female voice and not a masculine tone that had answered.

"Yes, but if we succeed in preventing their assault what comes next? We may have defeated one community along the river that means us harm but then what about all the other ones which hear about it? The next settlement will have the excuse to act against us and so will the next one and the next after that. All the River People strung along its course will rise up and destroy us. The different tribes will combine against us because they are the Keltoi and we, the Greeks, are their common enemy. But our destruction will be certain long before that. We are only two boats and ninety people in strength."

"It will be inevitable, the longer we stay on this deliberate track," spoke up Eucleides. "What if we left the river altogether and changed direction?"

"Divergence…." added Tyracides, thoughtfully, "…. that was what Danu spoke about before he plunged back into his domain. The River God's suggestion may be the best."

"We may know little of the Istros," came a warning from Croebos, a Rhodian who had won a laurel for wrestling in the one hundred and seventeenth Olympiad[2], "but we understand even less about the forest that surrounds it."

"With this," urged Eucleides, pulling out the cord around his neck on which hung a small grey stone, shaped like an arrowhead," my Anatolian course pointer – and our Hecataean maps, we will find our way through." The turning lodestone came to rest after moving side to side, the sharp end indicating north. Eucleides, his strong figu e, standing, lit by the wavering flames that crackled and spat over the charring, held the metal up for the gathered faces to see.

"Yes, Eucleides with such fools and your courage and the determination from all who sit around this fire tonight – we could find our way through and out of the dense forest," agreed Telemachus. "But the problems encountered there could be far greater than the ones we are attempting to deal with on this river. At least here we have some awareness concerning the potential enemy and where he might be found. Amongst the branches and leaves or ponds and stream-sodden ground we could be taken unsuspecting at any time. The effort in cutting our path through the thickest undergrowth will tire us and those who watch will simply wait for our exhaustion to overcome us and make their task far easier. No, if we are to go through the trees we must at least give ourselves a chance by allowing the autumn winds to strip the branches bare. For now, we must choose differently. The Great River remains the quickest means for this stage of the journey."

He was expecting the question. As his gaze wandered over the many fine faces turned towards him, hopeful faces belonging to good strong people, he considered who they were; what drove them on. Croebos of Rhodes, who had spoken earlier, a man that had joined him in Sicily trying to escape the grieving for a family slaughtered by Phoenician pirates landing on his island. Sostis from Naxos, a prince of his tribe with several brothers whose inheritance would have been Naxos itself but he chose instead to join Telemachus and his expedition at Athens. Then there was another champion from the Games, Pelos, a sure-footed sprinter gaining his victory at Isthmea and having fought beside Telemachus since they were boys together in Corinth. Many there were who had likewise come from that home city such as Agenor on the far side of the fire - a clever commander, or Polydeuctes,

---

[2] 330 B.C.

Kleptomenes, Aristopolis, Talos, Stellarstasis, Podiason: all courageous men on land and tough oarsmen on water. There were more he could name; he knew them all by their decent actions and was convinced, now that he had sent those others away at Athens that the best and the good had been retained. The best of them all was Eucleides, the Macedonian. His loyal support was as constant as the moon. Pelisteus and Tyracides had helped him greatly in Minoa and with the women, Melissa and Belisama, had become firm believers in the expedition. The other women who had joined in Athens, becoming freed from their slave status once they stepped aboard, they too had gladly taken on new responsibilities and duties that were integral to a cooperative endeavour. Eris, Hebe, Selene, Adrasteia, Chara, Chryseis and Andromeda: the names were Greek but most had been sold into slavery from Africa or the Levant and one or two came from Athenian households rich in daughters but poor in the capability for mustering a dowry. Anyway, his musing was broken. The question came.

"Where and when will that journey end, Telemachus?"

Eucleides had spoken. He was probably wanting to clarify what they had all needed to know. Being honest with himself, Telemachus knew that he was wrong not to tell them in Athens. He had wanted them first, to accomplish a small part of the journey together. Everyone here wanted something different to what they already knew – the constant warring between cities, destroyed homes and lives lost, lost opportunities for themselves and the children they hoped to have, a debilitating sense that the best society could offer had already been promised to others. The women felt this and so did the men, although the latter tried to disguise it. Trained all their lives to compete well and to enjoy it, that is what they attempted to do. But away from the public sporting and artistic events where the best could be easily judged and rewarded, the men understood that real success and prosperity in the polis depended on not what you knew but who you knew and which phratry you belonged to. Their only option for creating genuine success for themselves was to fight as mercenaries and steal what they wanted. The Telemachons thirsted for change to their lives and Telemachus wanted to provide it.

"It is in the hands of the gods as to when our travelling will cease but I can say that where we are going, no Greek has been."

Heads were still, expectant.

"The Tin Isles."

There was a murmurous sea surf, sudden chatter. It was both relief and excitement. The Pretannic Isles – a land at the world's edge and a myth even to the myth-making Greeks: a green land, fertile but barbaric and inaccessible. Above all, the source for tin – that prized ore which when mixed with copper produced an even more valuable metal and had ushered in a new age for the Hellenes: bronze. The forged tin ingots were carried into Europa by Celtic traders along the rivers to Massalia from thence to the Mediterranean and Aegean Seas. Not only tin came from there but gold too and other goods.

After the excitement caused by finally knowing their destination and the vocal reaction, there was quiet.

It was a long way.

And there were many obstacles.

Eucleides for a brief moment reminisced. When the Telemachons had passed through the Bosphorus, they learned that the young Macedonian King, Alexander, had crossed over with his army just a month before. After paying his respects at the tomb of Achilles, he had moved on, intending to conquer the Persian empire. If not for his trouble with Alexander's father, Philip, he himself would have been with that army moving east. Instead he was going west to a strange, almost terrifying place. There were no regrets for him. He had seen what life was like at a despot's court and was under no illusion. His men might love him now but Alexander would tire of fighting and become as drunken and corrupted as his father, only putting about a dream of further conquests to keep the young lions in his army happy and to maintain his authority. His own interest was best served by being at Telemachus' side. He was an explorer, a discoverer, a maker. No doubt there was the conqueror in him too, wasn't everyone moulded to be that through military training? There was nothing wrong with taking from others if you were in need or they had hurt you but sometimes it was better to offer something in return so they would continue to give. That was life. Only the very simple and very, very greedy believed otherwise. Those mad ones continued to take until they destroyed themselves. And others.

Belisama, amongst the Telemachons, listened intently. She would not be going to the Tin Isles; her departure would happen before that. Right from the beginning her plan was to get home. Even her relationship with Pelisteus had been predicated, in hindsight, towards that end. What else but instinct could have impelled her to form the connection with a pottery slave when she was married to the pottery owner's nephew? As it was, Pelisteus had plucked her from a civil war in Minoa and settled her on board the Telemachon, a ship bound for her homeland. She had naturally made it known that she was a Keltoi and could speak the language about which they knew nothing. This served to increase her value with the expedition members and moderated Pelisteus' reaction when she had to tell him about Agenor. The very fact that it was Agenor also helped as he was an important man amongst the Telemachons, one who had played a vital part in Telemachus' battle with Porcys, back in Heraclea Minoa. She felt more secure with him. Perhaps he might want to go with her back to her tribe when they reached the source for the Istros. They would accept him. Despite what the Greeks thought they were not savages. She had lied to the others when answering their queries about her origins. Her undisclosed trauma about the past and consequent memory loss was a necessary subterfuge. She had been made a slave by Keltoi tribal war and had been passed on by Greek traders, that was true but there would be no advantage in revealing her people's beliefs and practices to the Hellenes.

Other Keltoi slaves had adapted to the Hellenic culture quite happily, even the men. They were too easily impressed by the grand stairways to the temples, the colour and statuary, vivid festivals, incessant talk in the agora and city streets, luxurious goods and abundant food in the stoa markets. How the Greeks loved to talk! It was the reason why the language had been so easy to learn. You could not get away from it. She, on the other hand, yearned for quiet. That quietness which existed in the mountains and forests of her land. The only disturbance there was the bubbling track made by a falling mountain stream or a heron's flapping wings and the soft splash as it landed at the forest edge's lake. A grove might be marked out as a special place for a god or tree spirit but not by enormous, heaven-bearing marble statues – a simple wooden image would suffice. Her people had created stone monuments and temples to the stars and gods in the past; you had to travel many miles to worship or bury your dead there. Belisama had not reached the age or indeed suffered the death in her immediate family which required her to undertake that journey. For a long time, life had been simple and happy. It was only with the arrival in their valley of another tribe that it had all ended. Fortunately, her own village had been quick with its defences. The new arrivals had attempted to barter for land. They had been pushed from their own settlement further north by marauders who had made a habit of raiding them. Protection for her own village should have come from the city on the hill away along the Great River – Bittupen, the hill of the world. A quarrel between the prince there and her own tribal chief had led to that help being withheld. Belisama wondered if her village had survived. Her knowledge about it was ended on the day she was trussed up like corn in the crop field and taken to be sold into slavery.

"In anticipating your response, I did not expect silence," laughed Telemachus, "and for so long too!"

"The Pretannic Isles are, without doubt, going to be a challenge," said Agenor, with emphatic understatement. "Now you have made the objective for our expedition clear, we can only return to the original point – how do we avoid the conflict with the Celtic settlements along the Istros? If we are not to go around them by redirecting our route through the forest, then what is the answer?"

"You have already given it," replied Telemachus. "Avoid conflict. That is what we must try to do." He held up Hecataeus' periplus for all to see and stretched out one of the maps. It was more for effect. People standing behind the fire could just about see Telemachus' finger resting on a line illustrating the River Istros. Even so, it seemed to them that the point indicated was not that far along the line wriggling back towards the sea.

"We are here and according to Hecataeus we have already passed four Celtic cities and six tributaries to the River since Istria. Those cities are: Galati, Braila, Bucharest and Craiova. If we continue at this pace, we will come across even larger communities – the first one being Belgrade, then further on, Buda and Pest guarding the river and facing each other across the water. If we provoke their enmity it will be the end for the Telemachon, for Thocero's boat 'The Apollon' and for you and me." He stared meaningfully at those around him. "We must make peace with these places and convince them to allow us through. There is a suggestion that I am going to make and that I hope you will accept."

"Tell us, Telemachus!" urged Eucleides.

"I will then. We Greeks are perhaps not the best people to show others how to live peacefully. Yes, we united and punctured the ambitions of that menace, the Persian Empire but since then all our time has been wasted in internecine strife with the Persians backing one side or the other to their own advantage. The new weapon of choice was cash and it served effectively to bring Greek cities to their knees."

"Oh, no," groaned Eucleides, rolling his eyes up and throwing his arms out like a satirical actor in mock despair, "spare us the history lesson!" The onlookers laughed. "I really did mean…. tell us!"

"I mean to assert that throughout those warring years there was one thing and one only which could make the warriors from every city throw down their weapons and join together with all others from all parts of the Greek world in peaceful festivity." He waited.

"The Olympiad!" rang out Melissa's voice, startlingly clear.

It was an invigorating reminder of the best in their homeland and the Telemachons echoed Melissa's response by shouting its name again, "The Olympiad!" and cheering.

Telemachus smiled and waited for the noise to die down. "Just that – the competition to end all bitterness and promote the best in our society. We have in the games, the means for our survival and the opportunity to connect with the several communities that live on this Great River all at once, for the better."

"Danu would be pleased," commented Thocero, recalling the figure he had seen diving overboard.

"But what about the practicalities, Telemachus?" asked Agenor. "How, when, where and most importantly, who are we to organise these games with?"

"The most prominent cities on the map for this next neck of the river is Belgrade, followed by Buda and Pest beyond that. We could site the games off the river bank between those places – find a nice plateau. It is going to be essential that our negotiations with the king or High Chief of Belgrade succeed. He is the key to the communities in that land."

"But what if the King of Belgrade is at war with those other two cities?" spoke up Croebos.

"Every war needs a truce," suggested Telemachus.

"Then again," added Eucleides, "what are we to negotiate with? It seems to me that to gain what you want in such a procedure; you must have something to offer the other side. We have very little, in fact probably nothing that would appeal to them, especially military strength. When two ships go against a city, the city will win every time." A brief moment after he had spoken, Eucleides worried that he might have caused offence to his listeners and said, rather too hurriedly, "Even though the crew are the finest fighters in Greece and 'The Telemachon' the swiftest trireme on the Aegean or any other waters."

The people looked back to Telemachus for his response, following the discussion avidly.

"We actually have much to offer, Eucleides. First, our reputation as Greeks. Who amongst the Celts would not desire to pit themselves against the Hellenes in competition and human prowess?" There was an approving affirmation from the onlookers. "Prizes are secondary to the endeavour and performance during the Games but I grant you that they need to be worthy. Our champions at Olympia and the other Games are given laurels, oil and when they return home, dinners for the rest of their lives at public expense together with estates in recognising the honour they have brought to their cities. In these negotiations, I have said that it is crucial we win over Belgrade to our side and of course that means gaining the support of its king. To him I can promise a wondrous gift: the Ambrosus."

A concerned buzz arose from the crowd. The story about how this magical ointment had been used by Telemachus for capturing the Psychezoion had been told, retold and added to in the nights since departing Galati. It had begun to add to his presence and some Telemachons, not the warriors naturally, had developed an awe for him. It was a gift from the gods that might totally eclipse his own human ingenuity. As such, Telemachus would be relieved to see it gone.

"Apart from that there is something else we can give to the Celts – an idea. But in this I am totally dependent on you playing a part when we find ourselves in their company."

The Telemachons listened.

"We must convince them that this expedition is not one to establish a homeland for us but is solely about trade. We travel through their communities to the Tin Isles – some call that country Albion – for the purpose of trade, establishing contacts and a trading route. On our return we will bring gold, tin, leather, amber and fur. We will have built another boat to accommodate all the goods we intend to trade with them and others. We will tell them that this is just the first of many such expeditions and that in future we will bring them luxuries from the Aegean that they have never seen before. By instilling this idea in them – that we can be important for their future – we ensure our safety and free passage along the Istros, that they call the Danu. Actually, we must get used to calling it by that name."

"Yes, but why then, if we concentrate on this stratagem, do we need the Games?" asked Melissa.

"Goodwill and influence," replied Telemachus. "If we concentrate only on the trading ploy, we must use that idea and negotiate with every individual community inhabiting the river, over and over. By establishing an Olympic event we can bring those community representatives to us and negotiate all at once. We could promise a cash toll to pass through. That will be our partial influence, the rest will be achieved by our finest athletes at the Games themselves.

The plan appealed greatly to everyone present and there was no better suggestion. Telemachus put the matter to a vote and it was carried unanimously.

Agenor asked that they end the night with a sacrifice to the god Danu, requesting his support for their encounter with his people and this was done.

At dawn the following day, the Telemachons sailed for Belgrade.

11
Faramund

The smell of roasting hog clung to his nostrils. He was hungry. Faramund ignored the clamour for attention from his stomach and re-immersed himself in the latest problem he had invented for himself: how do you shift a great weight with least effort? He supposed it depended on how you defined 'great' and 'least'. To overcome a challenge, first break it down into small steps and test each solution that you construct. Sitting there, he felt a large hand squeeze his shoulder.

"What are you up to now, Faramund, not playing with another of your wooden toys again?"

Said by anyone else it would have been an insult but from the large warrior that strode to his side and remained standing, he accepted the greeting for what it was. Berengar was a boyhood friend from years back which actually were not that far behind them. He certainly looked like a defender of his tribe and heroic marauder, with the great bronze sword at his side, the otterskin breeches and red-dyed woollen shirt. An impressive appearance was further enhanced by the gold torc around his neck while ritual serpentine tattoos winding around both arms were proudly revealed by his pulled-up sleeves. The relaxed manner was not entirely ingenuous though. Berengar was tainted with frustration. Like Faramund he had just passed his second decade and still he had not killed a man in battle. Worse still, he had not even marched to battle. To raid, to fight; this was what made a Celt's blood run in his veins, this was what being a man meant and how could you sing songs of the heroes at the fires and feast with the other men if you had not yet done this one brave thing: taken an enemy's life and sent him to the land below so you could step into his place as an adult man in the upper world? You could only achieve importance in the tribe by standing with your tribal brothers before the enemy, having stripped the clothes from your body and about to give yourself over to the protection offered by the battle god Rudianos. He might have got that experience a year ago against the Macedonian King Alexander, who had driven the defeated Triballi army to Peuke Island where the great Danu River meets the sea. He had been in the wrong place at the wrong time, although some cowards might suggest the reverse was true. His village had yet again been moving west to more fertile ground and when the horseman from King Syrmus had arrived from across the Haemus Mountains to request help, it was already too late.

"Better to play with toys than kill children with swords, Berengar." Now it was the other who could have felt insulted but again friendship intervened and instead he looked with admiration at the contraption held in Faramund's hands.

"I know that what you hold there is not a toy and you know that the sword which hangs from my side will not behead children .... Only our enemies. No matter, why are you sitting here, hungry, when you could be at the feast?"

"Oh, I'll be there soon – I was just putting the finishing touches to this. It will take a little more work yet."

Berengar ignored the excuse and took up the device held out to him by his friend. Faramund's reluctance to attend the feast plainly owed to the fact that the young hunters and warriors, those wanting to be combatants at least, would eat first. Others – the women, children and slight young men like Faramund would be served afterwards. If he showed his face early, it would only excite abusive comment.

Looking at what Faramund had made or rather what he had paid to have made because he could not believe that his friend had actually built this mechanism of wood, iron, spindle and handle all by himself, Berengar tried to work out its purpose.

Faramund seeing his perplexity, gave him a clue. "It is meant to prove my theory that you might be able to move a great weight with minimal effort."

"I see," said Berengar, dubiously. He had observed huge rocks being levered by great oak poles managed by a dozen strong men. Some of those thick poles had snapped like twigs. He could only wonder how something as small as this could lift a large weight. But he also knew that Faramund possessed wisdom far beyond his years. He could name the stars and their position in the sky throughout the year; he could predict the weather; eat mushrooms from the forest without falling ill; track any animal through that same forest avoiding the attack of others and come back with it for his supper. Most of all, he could invent things or create uses for simple everyday items that had not been thought about before. This cleverness was combined with a stupid tendency to voice his own opinion whatever the topic. He seemed to forget that he needed physical strength to defend himself when he upset the wrong people and in Faramund's case that was usually anyone physically stronger than him and again with regard to Faramund that was practically every male in the village over the age of fourteen. At such times Berengar provided the protection he needed but they both knew this could not go on forever. Berengar's tone was almost a plea as he said to his friend, "Faramund, why don't you become a priest?" At least this would guarantee him some status within the tribe and a purpose for his thinking. He could devote his mind to the gods and they would look after him.

Faramund sighed. How many times now had this same conversation been repeated with Berengar?

"I think the gods would withhold their communication if I was responsible for the divination. Besides, Thoros would not allow it." Thoros was the chief druid over all the others living in the villages along this part of the Great River. A relatively young choice for the position, in his thirtieth year, he was guardedly jealous about it and had been brought up in this same community before it had moved westwards. Thoros was not about to encourage any potential competition from his own community to take even the initiatory druidic rites that would begin to impose on his influence.

As to Faramund's first statement, Berengar had begun to think that his friend might even doubt the existence of the gods. If that was true, he was a dead man.

Berengar gave the wood and iron mechanism back to Faramund and offered him his hand. "Come on Faramund, it's time to eat." If not priest or warrior, perhaps his friend would be happy simply tilling the soil, something not as important but still valuable. Somehow, though, Berengar realised that such a life was not in his friend's destiny.

Grasping Berengar's arm, Faramund pulled himself up and then carefully placed his invention inside the doorway to his round-roofed dwelling next to the fire he had built to give himself light while he worked.

They joined the other villagers eating, drinking, talking and listening to the bards telling tales about the gods and heroes. Bronze cauldrons filled with beer or mead swung from poles waist-high, while pigs in plenty turned on spits over the various fires, glistening fat dripping from their bodies and hissing into the flames. Berengar steered his companion over to the feasting table where yet more meat and cooked root vegetables were piled high. He separated and taking an empty plate began to choose his food.

Faramund did the same and cutting a hunk of pork laid it on his plate. He began to ladle out vegetables for himself. Not far away were three young men with the ritual tattoos denoting their major hunting successes on their bare arms. They had drunk much mead and laughed uproariously together over something said. Noticing Faramund the tallest one and loudest, placed a finger to his lips, grinning. The others hushed, anticipating fun.

He leaned over, drunkenly. "Thanks, Faramund, so kind to think about the appetite belonging to a real man, for a change." Winking broadly, the lout began to pull the plate towards him. It didn't get far. A heavy iron war dagger plunged into the meat, smashing the crockery plate beneath.

"I believe you have made a mistake," came Berengar's grim warning, his bared teeth seething below the heavy moustache. He lifted the meat into a fresh bowl and with the dagger still sticking from it pushed the whole dish towards the other. "And because I believe you to be an honourable man, I think you will make amends by spooning out fresh vegetables for my friend."

The lout looked at Berengar and recognised him, then at the knife. The invitation was unmistakeable. He was intoxicated and could be brave but not that intoxicated that he was not brave enough to look foolish. Without looking up, he filled the bowl with steaming new vegetables and then together with his companions moved off.

"You know, Faramund," said Berengar thoughtfully, "if only some Celts' courage reached the same level as their arrogance we would have beaten that Greek king Alexander back to his Macedonian fort."

Before Faramund could reply, a shout broke out at the other end of the feasting area. Pipes were blown to attract attention and several men, one horse-mounted, made their way to a central place amongst the feasters. The village elder accompanied them.

Even as he rode through the crowd, many grasped where he had come from and who had sent him. The inference was not given by the large fox furred cloak draped around his bare torso and the leather trousers covering his legs, but by the spear he carried. More a weapon made for ceremony rather than war, the shaft was topped by an oversized but perfectly shaped amber spearhead. The amber was an unusual red in colour. It was the insignia of the King in Belgrade.

The herald pulled his horse to a stop and waited for the people to gather. He then breathed in deeply from the diaphragm as he was trained to do so that his voice would be projected as far as possible.

"People of the Dardani tribe, I come to you from Garudian, king and lord of this valley and much else besides. He sends you a message, through me, that Greeks have come to his city."

There was consternation. Faramund, listening with Berengar commented to him, "I thought Alexander had led his army east, to conquer the Medes?"

The herald held his hand up and the noise abated.

"These Greeks come in peace and in two boats. They simply want to travel up the Danu with our goodwill."

"Goodwill!" shouted a burly, bearded man, "Not so long ago they drove brave Celts to the Danu Isle and slaughtered all but a few. I say kill them!"

There was a danger that other voices would quickly join with his and the messenger spoke to forestall them.

"The Greeks we warred with were Macedonians – these are not from Macedonia but far away across the Aegean from Athens and Sicily."

"Athens!" snorted another. "About as Greek as you can get and they're all as bad as each other!"

"Do you want to protect your honour as Celts and prove that we are better than any Greeks?"

The question momentarily surprised his listeners. Of course, that is what they wanted to do and it sharpened their attention to what he said next.

"What if you were given the opportunity to show your strength and qualities as warriors – beat them in something that the world over they have boasted their superiority and in which they believe themselves to be invincible?"

His listeners were caught.

"I mean, my brothers - an Olympiad." The herald paused for just a few moments to allow them to consider. They had heard about this Greek habit for taking part in festivals to display athletic and aesthetic prowess. Boxing, running, throwing and poetry. It was strange. Even stranger, they stopped wars for it and all the Greek tribes, even those fighting each other, competed.

"We don't stop wars to play games!" yelled a contemptuous young man, the one who had attempted to take Faramund's meal from him. "That is a Greek custom. Leave the Greeks to play with themselves!" There was laughter. "When we fight a war we don't stop until the red blood pours from them, or us!"

But a dissenting opinion made itself heard from another part of the crowd.

"That's true brother, but I, for one, would like to know how to better a Greek in any situation, particularly where it is to be a competition in strength."

This last came from a man naked to the waist and as hard as a mountain with muscles that bulged like its peaks. Toruc, a village champion in the tree throwing contest that was held between the valley settlements at the beginning of the New Year. What he said, particularly in matters like this, was always treated with respect.

The herald took his cue gratefully.

"Whoever competes in this Games and becomes a champion will be rewarded for the rest of his life by King Garudian. His name will live forever through the singers of songs as they travel from place to place. It will not be easy. Hard training will be required to achieve victory. Let us show those Greeks that true excellence in speed and strength lies here in the land of Danu!" There was a cheer from some in the crowd which the messenger was relieved to hear. "I will have notices put up with the permission of your headman. They will name and describe the events to take place. People will go amongst you to make a list of those who are wanting to gain fame for themselves and their families through these Games. Not everyone on the list will be able to go – only the best. First you must hold events in the village to see who shows the excellence that can represent us. We will call those Games by our own name – the Danuviad – and it will be held at the end of a full moon cycle on the flatland between Belgrade and the oppidas, Buda and Pest." Having done his duty, the herald dismounted and led his horse away in the direction of the Headman's dwelling.

People returned to their feasting with more to talk about. Keen excitement was evident but opinion sharply divided. Some were wanting to test themselves at the forthcoming Danuviad, others were fixedly opposed to it. Berengar immediately wanted to put himself forward. As he said to Faramund, this was a fight without blood and just as much honour could be reaped from it. Over the next few days the excitement did not fade but actually increased as the Headman began to organise the qualifying athletic events. Soon, many of those who had been opposed to the Games, changed their minds once they saw the preparations. Different spaces in the village were dedicated to different events and these ranged widely in their organisation from running with sword and shield in hand, running without, jumping over a cart – the length jumped being measured, what the Greeks called the Pankration but the Celts recognised as a fight to the death, sword combat, weight-lifting, throwing the spear to the greatest distance, boxing and the chariot race. There were other competitions too. They were all individual events.

The full moon's cycle was almost complete and the strongest athletes had been chosen. Some were to be entered for single events only, while others got more. One man of the six to go had successfully qualified for three events and that was Berengar. They all knew that there would be a further test to come in the Danuviad itself because they were to contest against other Celtic villages before finally competing with the Greeks themselves who would have the advantage of extra time for training and assessing the competition they were to face.

One evening Berengar was sitting inside his round-roofed house inspecting several spears laid on the ground at his feet. He was deciding which one to take with him and use at the Games. In two days he would be leaving. It was quiet except for the crackling flames on the hearth set in the centre, its smoke rising towards the central hole in the roof. Berengar's wife, two years younger and seven months pregnant with his child, had gone to visit her parents on the other side of the village.

A familiar call was made from outside, he answered and Faramund came through the doorway. Berengar realised straight away that his friend was going to ask him for something. Faramund detested asking anyone for anything that he could do for himself and not being a deceptive person, it usually showed on his face as to what he was thinking following a problem that had arisen.

This time there was no problem and Berengar offered a filled mead cup to his friend to ease the asking. Faramund took it gratefully and almost drained the beaker with his first draught. This is going to cost me a lot, thought Berengar, amused.

"Berengar, you know we have been friends for sixteen summers now, since we were first able to walk."

"Faramund," said his friend, impatient as ever, "I have known you long enough to understand when you jump and dodge in your conversation, rather than getting to the point."

Faramund blushed and gave an embarrassed cough. It is no wonder that he has never been accepted by the other young men in the village, thought Berengar. The other tried again but persisted in his digression.

"Well, listen, Berengar, you above all must understand how difficult it has been for me to gain any standing in our village." The warrior Celt nodded, sympathetically. "I have never had the physical stamina that you and others can show. For someone like me there must be an opportunity to make my name widely known and suddenly, to acquire reputation and status. I have thought about it for a long time, puzzling about how I can achieve this. Then the god, Danu, answered my prayers, making a barren hope into an abundant destiny. He brought the Greeks into our land and the Danuviad with them. After the messenger from King Garudian had come and gone from our settlement, I suddenly realised what should be done. But to do what must be done will take your help as well."

"Go on," said Berengar with some foreboding.

In his nervousness, Faramund began to rush his words. "You have been chosen to take part in three events at the Danuviad. I want you .... I.... I.... would like ... " with heavy emphasis on the last word, " you, to give up one of your places to me."

Berengar sat back shocked, not sure if he had heard correctly. This was something unexpected. A terrible birth of protest and argument arose in his mind. What possible madness possessed Faramund to ask him for this? Those arguments began to fall from the tip of his tongue.

"But Faramund – you know I will not immediately compete in the events at the Danuviad. There has to be success in the qualifying events against other settlements at the place where it is to be held. You would never get through that!"

"I am not asking you to step aside then," said Faramund, calmer now that he had voiced the unvoicable.

Berengar's mood, however, was the mirrored opposite to Faramund's equanimity. He was beginning to seethe. "You are wanting me, after all the hard training I have had to do and the sweated effort to succeed here amongst my family, friends and the Elders - you are saying that I should give that up in front of my tribe? Then, when I have done it, to betray them all and give my place to you?"

"Yes, I am Berengar. Yet it does not have to be done as blatantly as that. You still have the other two events. You can plead an injury for your third event and then request that I compete in your place. The Games officials may reject me but your nomination will be treated seriously, particularly if you became champion in the other two sports."

Despite his attempted persuasion, Faramund could see that his friend was becoming more, not less, infuriated. He raised his hands as if in surrender and gave in to the other's anger.

"Look Berengar, it was just a thought. I can see that I am asking too much. Forget it."

There was a cessation. The phrase 'too much' twisted up like a poisonous snake that has been apparently knocked unconscious but without warning rises up against the one who hunts it, its head back, ready to strike. For Berengar, the sound of these words keyed directly into his memory. A memory recall in which he lay close to death. A chance encounter with another hunting party from the Scordisci tribe had ended in a bloody skirmish that day. He had been brought out from the forest badly injured, his wound already infected since it had taken from one night to the next to return from that part of the woodland where they had been hunting. Over the next few days, despite leeches applied to his wound and prayers said by Thorus, the Chief Druid himself, nothing seemed to be effective. Then Faramund had come quietly by. Berengar, in his delirium, could not even recognise his friend but he was told by his wife that Faramund had applied a poultice. What was in it nobody knew. He came every day to change the dressing and the warrior's strength returned. On the fourth day he was able to recognise Faramund and thank him. It was then that Berengar offered his friend anything he had for saving his life, nothing would be 'too much'. Faramund had replied that what he had done was what any true friend would do for another. He did not expect a reward because he knew that Berengar would do the same for him one day if the need arose.

So this was it. He must risk his own reputation; he was obligated. Berengar did not try to dissuade Faramund from the course he had chosen. The expression on the other man's face during the discussion had been fixed and purposeful. Yet, Berengar understood his friend's necessity. To survive as a man in the tribe you had to be ruthless with your enemies when at war and loyal to your friends and comrades. Perhaps with men like Faramund, those who were not natural fighters and could be taken as such, ruthlessness was to be used against your friends as well to get what was needed.

Berengar told Faramund that he would give up the event to him at the appropriate time. The latter thanked him profusely but there was sadness in the air. Both saw that a bridge had been crossed which could not be re-crossed together. It was difficult to imagine that their friendship would last beyond the Danuviad.

12
The Danuviad

Telemachus regarded the list in his hands with amazement. On it were twenty different events and beside each one was a name:

Sprint.	Pelos
Pankration.	Croebos
Boxing.	Polydeuctes
Long-cart Jump.	Sostis
Javelin.	Agenor
Discus.	Demaraton
Axe-throw.	Pelisteus
Sprint with armour.	Lysimachus
Wrestling.	Eucleides
Chariot Race.	Belisama
Sword Duel	Artorius
Tree-lift.	Stellarstasis
River Swim.	Bauxus
Boat Race.	Akeron
Rock-haul.	Phildoktopes
Archery.	Eris
Tower Climb.	Herophon
River Swim (underwater).	Tyracides
Chasm Leap (through fire).	Thocero
Sling-shot.	Antipater

His finger moved to a name on the list.

"Eris? A woman? What does my best archer, Agenor, say about that?"

"He couldn't say anything. She beat him in the trials. He was not happy about it but fortunately his consolation was qualification for the javelin." Eucleides knew there was more to come. Telemachus' finger moved again on the list.

"Belisama for the chariot? Another woman?"

"Like Eris, she beat the men fairly. There will be no opposition from them over her selection. The competitions were held in the open for all to see – they witnessed the skill and fearlessness with which she handled the chariot. Apparently, her father was a charioteer without sons. There was nobody else but her to train and that was what he did until the day she was taken."

"I thought that she could not remember anything from her childhood?"

"Her memory quickly improved when she was persuading me to let her take the trial," smiled Eucleides. "We have had a female champion in our own Olympiad's history: the Spartan princess, Cynisca. So there is a precedent for this."

"I don't think you will find, no matter how hard you search your own memory, a female Celt racing her chariot in any Greek games. That is the important point - not only is she a woman, she is a Celt. Don't you think that will anger the people along the Danu? They could see her as a traitor; it might stir up the Celts to attack us and destroy what we are setting out to achieve."

"It might do," admitted Eucleides. "But I prefer to think of her as the making of these games."

"Why? Explain yourself."

"This Danuviad is not an Olympiad," began the veteran with an obvious tautology. "There are differences."

"Several events would never be seen at Olympia, Nemea or the other important festivals. Certain it is, that you would not see women taking part with men."

"More important than that, Telemachus?"

He thought for a moment. "Greeks compete with each other."

"Exactly!" enthused Eucleides. "This Danuviad will be the first games in which Greeks will compete with Celts and not with each other. We will present Belisama as symbolic for this competition in a grand speech before the chariot race. She represents division becoming unity, in herself and the excellence for which she is striving. In her victory she will not only be winning for us but showing the best in every Celt and giving them the triumph as well. The success of this festival and what you want it to achieve for our journey, Telemachus, will depend on her success.

"Let us hope she wins the chariot race then," came the other's laconic comment. But before Eucleides could make a testy reply, Telemachus became more positive. "No, no, Eucleides, it is a good idea and one that I accept. I will have to speak to King Garudian first though, to gain his support. There must be a decision to place the chariot race as the last event and for it to be given greater significance through that speech you mentioned and some spectacular rite that will precede the race. We must encourage the Celts to feel glad whether they win or lose. Another matter strikes me now – can we ensure that no fatality occurs during the festival? That too could spark an angry reaction in the watching crowd if a Celt dies."

"That could be possible in the Pankration, boxing, chasm leap and particularly in the sword duel. I'll make certain that additional training and safeguards are given. The judges too will stop the event if things become volatile."

"Unfortunately, it could be impossible to stop a rolling chariot," murmured Telemachus.

"There will always be a risk when one mortal pits himself or herself against another. We cannot guard against everything."

Telemachus agreed and they both moved on to continue supervising the flat plain that the king in Belgrad had designated for their use. He had also sent men and materials from his city to help in the site's construction. As they walked along the river edge, the two Greeks had a clear view over the work that was taking place. It was impressive to see what had been accomplished in just the few days since they had moored up to the land. The area had been mapped out and sub-divided into those places where the different sports were to be enacted and buildings were being erected to accommodate athletes and important visitors to the games. The majority of visitors, whose numbers could not even be guessed, would have to raise their own shelters with animal hides and wooden poles. Telemachus had ordered a curving channel to be cut from the river to purify the site as it ran through, carrying the sewage waste back to the main trunk well away from the area and where it would be swept downriver by powerful currents.

"We don't want Tyracides and Bauxus to experience an unpleasant after-taste on completing their swim, do we?" he had said to Eucleides.

Back home the Greeks were used to competing or attending games which had been sited in places with spectacular panoramas over other mountains or the sea. This was to honour the gods for whom they were being performed and also to please themselves and encourage the athletes. To achieve such splendour usually meant that rock had to be cut from other rock and magnificent marble imported from over long distances.

Here, that was not practical. Wood was the chief building material, although beauty could be had in the surrounding forest, the distant mountains and of course, the Danu itself. Earthworks were raised which took shape as tiered seats of beaten mud, veneered with wood and having a clear aspect over the track and field events below. Time was short and speed essential. But what was aesthetically possible was done. The gods, Danu for the Celts and Poseidon and Zeus for the Greeks, could not be disgraced. With that in mind, Telemachus had the statue of Poseidon removed from its base, which of course, contained the secret gold hoard and repositioned on land in a temporary sanctuary. Likewise, the Celts created their own shrine with a carved wooden image of Danu placed at its centre. Telemachus had decided that now their journey was through land rather than over the sea, they would transfer their worship to Zeus, who could offer greater protection. Consequently, he had a wooden carving made to replace the stone Poseidon. The sea god would be propitiated at these games with sacrifices and the athletes' sweat. The king of the gods would receive his due praises at the Danuviad and be persuaded to travel with them on 'The Telemachon.'

*   *   *   *

A roar like a dozen ships being wheeled on the dolkios[3] banged against his eardrums. The Celt before him had just thrown his javelin and a mighty throw it was. It had landed just before the chain stretched across the beaten ground which marked out a distance of half a stadia[4] away. Further than the chain, about a tenth of the length again, stood a man shape made from wicker. It marked the javelin field's termination as it was assumed no spear would reach it. The Celt turned and gave Agenor a satisfied look as he made way. He was from the Oppida at Heuhenberg and the men from that hill fortress had given a good account of themselves at the Games in competition with the other Celts from Belgrad, Bud and Pes. But not so well against the Telemachons. Agenor was as surprised as his fellow Greeks at the rivalry evident between the different Celtic settlements. So much so that the

---

[3] A paved road for ships to be wheeled across the Corinthian Isthmus.

[4] About 304 feet or 91 metres.

Greek competitors had been applauded by certain sections in the crowd, once the onlookers' own representatives had taken themselves out of their event. Now it was his time and his would be the last throw.

He tilted his head skywards and uttered a prayer to Zeus. He could not fail the other Telemachons. Gripping the bronze-tipped shaft in his right hand, he began the run up to his mark. Quickly his legs pumped - as fast as a flapping bird's wings across the ground – all the while his eyes fastened on the target. In what seemed to be a single movement and dynamic recoil, his body stopped, hopped and the right arm thrust the javelin forward into the air. The spear tore upwards, seemingly ever upwards and attaining its zenith…. curved down. Before landing, it smashed like a meteor through the wicker man's head.

Agenor was the last javelin thrower. The feat was unbeatable. Again a rushing sound came from the crowd and the accolade washed over him like falling surf. His heart buoyed up on the cheer. He saw the other Telemachons amongst the spectators wildly applauding him, Telemachus at their head, a wide grin on his face with his two hands clasped in the air indicating jubilation. Agenor fell to his knees and thanked the God of gods.

Telemachus regretted the fact that he was not to take part as a competitor himself. It was a decision made at the end of a conversation with Eucleides and Thocero. They felt that the opportunity for revealing courage and gaining honour should be shared with others. After all, if it was not for them, there would be no expedition and who finds true worth and trust in following a self-serving glory seeker who cares nothing for the lives of others? Telemachus could only heartily agree with this, particularly as his fame had already been assured in the stories circulating about his encounter with the Psychezoion. Yet Telemachus felt impelled to lead at every turn and chafed inwardly when he thought a Telemachon had not achieved their best in the competition. Fortunately, this happened only once or twice during the whole Danuviad but in the main he was deeply grateful for the commitment and talent shown by the Telemachons in their events. It was inspirational. How could his search not succeed with people like these? The Celts, too, displayed the qualities only found in champions. In one instance surprisingly so but it had nothing to do with physical strength and the Celts had to be encouraged to acknowledge him.

It was soon after Agenor's event. Telemachus had seen his strongman, Stellarstasis, lift a tree trunk above his head, hold it steady and then throw it to the ground. The wood made a deep thud and raised dust as it bounced on the beaten earth. Up to yet there had been no major distinction between the competitors before going on to the heavier and thicker trunks. Stellarstasis received polite applause. But what happened next was without precedent in any competition and nonplussed the crowd.

There was to be one final competitor: a Celt from the village of Slat called Berengar who was to try the weight before the trunk was to be swapped for a bigger one. The man came out into the arena to that part dedicated to the athletic trials but there was something wrong. His arm was in a sling. The audience fell into a concerned silence. Surely, he was not going to try to lift the tree with one arm? Berengar called out. He had a loud vibrant voice; more use to him than that injured arm.

"People of the Danu I beg your forgiveness! As you can see I am unable to take part in this event but I hope my success in two previous challenges has pleased you!" Indeed it had. Berengar had made himself a champion for the Celts in those two events, already making himself a renowned Danuvian and the crowd listened with respect.

"The judges in this great festival have allowed me to nominate my own replacement and I have chosen the man that would best serve you." Now the people were expectant. From the wooden tiring house where the athletes prepared themselves, a door opened and shut. As one, heads swivelled to the sound.

Faramund walked before them into the stadium: scrawny, long-limbed and petal-delicate. He was not even dressed like the others. Whereas they merely had a cloth wrapped around their loins, he was fully clothed in leather trousers and woollen shirt.

The crowd laughed. A sound which was irresistibly converted to jeers.

Berengar raised his arm. Some in the audience thought it was meant for them. The jeering, although slightly diminished, nevertheless continued. In fact, Berengar's signal had not been to stop the noise but to summon a covered cart which was driven out towards him and the wooden trunk he was standing at.

The new intrusion mollified the people's vocal scorn and the jeers died away as they saw it brought to a halt and the covering pulled away by the two men sitting in it. What was revealed to the watching crowd was a gleaming copper barrel half the size of a man if stood on one end. After the men had cut the ropes holding it and by the way they both had to exert their full force simply to roll it from the back of the cart to land on the ground, even though it was on its side and by the noise it made – a cloud splitting boom as it made contact – the audience realised instantly that it was solid metal. The next thought that struck everyone in almost the same moment was that *no man could lift that weight*.

Berengar bellowed again.

"My friend, Faramund, invites all his fellow competitors to lift the weight!"

The crowd teetered on jeers again in its response but that was superceded by their attention moving to the other weight-lifters standing by. Those looked at each other doubtfully and then with outright trepidation at the barrel. Some individual voices in the crowd began to be heard – "It's madness!" "Only an immortal could lift that!" However, in the moments that followed there was a subtle shift - mild urgings at first to the competitors and then the Telemachons in unison began to call out to Stellarstasis. "Go on Stellarstasis! Have a go!" "Show them what we're worth! Eventually, they began a repeated crying of the first part of his name – "Stellar! Stellar! Stellar!" followed by a chanted command, "Lift! Lift! Lift!" Like gathering clatter produced by dead leaves in the autumn wind, the Celts began to yell out their own competitors' names in rhythmic persuasion so that once more the stadium was alive with noise.

A Celtic athlete pushed his way forward to the weight and looked down at it. There was a handle at either end; they had not been bolted on but seemed to be a seamless part of the barrel itself. Pondering, he decided to lift it up to a vertical position by one handle just to test its weight. After grasping one handle with both hands, he breathed in and pulled with all his strength. Nothing happened. He let go, puffing and panting. After recovering himself and angry now, he tried again. Accompanied by grunts and groans which to the spectators seemed to emanate from the barrel itself, the drum was shifted upwards by just a hand length and then dropped.

Every one of the weight-lifters made their attempt, without success and the worst returned miserably to the tiring house. Stellarstasis made the best effort. He had almost managed to raise the barrel upright but was forced to release the handle when it had reached a forty-five degrees' angle. He, with some other fellow competitors, was willing to stay to see what Faramund would do, not finding it credible that the weaker man would beat him.

Faramund, for the second time, found himself under scrutiny. He went to the cart and returned with a bulky sack. Laughter occurred again in the audience when they saw him struggling with whatever heavy objects were contained within it. "Do you want some help with that?" came a shouted question and there was another eruption.

The young man took no notice and extracted from the bag various metallic parts which he began to piece together. Once finished he pushed the mechanism forward so that two thick metal bars from it went under the middle part of the barrel. It was only now that the spectators understood there was a gap between the drum's body and the floor. The bars under the barrel joined with the base of a metal pole, rectangular in shape, looking like a chariot axle, that extended to the same height as Faramund's head. There was a handle coming from back of the pole at about the same level as the Celt's knees. He looped link chains over the barrel to the top of the pole.

Berengar shouted out an announcement to the puzzled spectators with as much bravado and drama as he could.

"Celts and Telemachons! Faramund will do what no other man has done here today! He will lift the copper barrel off the ground!"

Faramund slowly turned the handle and bit by bit the shiny copper mound and all its massive weight rose upward from the earth. There were gasps from the crowd.

The Telemachons, those who had spent life-times travelling through Greek harbours where cranes lifting loads from boat to jetty were a frequent sight were less impressed but admired the ingenuity even so. The cranes they had seen were worked by several men at a time not just one and a feeble looking one at that. The Celts too had the image of huge stones being lifted when they saw the copper barrel rising – magnificent megalithic stones in their circular temples to the sun and stars. They thought particularly of that Plain of the Temples in the distant country Albion which these Greeks called the Pretannic Isles and which some amongst their own tribe had visited on a sacred journey.

When the copper drum had risen to waist height, Faramund stopped turning the handle and stood back. Shyly, he turned to the tiered seats. The people took in this strange looking slight man and his formidable bulk-shifting machine, they hesitated and then responded with loud applause. But even as the clapping faded away, critical comments were yelled out, "It wasn't him that lifted it!" "He's no champion!" and more amidst boos and hisses. The dissatisfaction was voluble and growing.

Telemachus decided to do something before it got out of control. He raised a placatory hand to that section in the tiered seats reserved for King Garudian and other Celtic leaders over the Danubian domains, making his way down and out onto the field, all the while keeping his hand high. Distracted by a new figure marching into view, those that had made their anger known, desisted. What Telemachus said next though, might have caused a riot.

"Celts! You should be ashamed of yourselves!" His strong, clear voice would have echoed around Greek Stadia, which were often cut from stone; here his words were soaked up by the mud banks and the people themselves. Telemachus had gambled correctly: the sight and sound presented by an isolated man admonishing them, they who sat in their hundreds, was enough to subdue them.

"This," continued Telemachus placing his hand that he had held high down onto Faramund's shoulder, "is a young Celt of genius! He has done as his friend said that he would do and with the tool that he has created, lifted what no other man today could hold up. All the competitors here should be proud for their supreme effort and training, diligently carried out during the past weeks. But I ask you, regard that machine. Did that take a few weeks to make? I suggest that it took a lot longer than that – much of this man's life… years spent in accumulating knowledge and thinking creatively has passed into it. "Nevertheless…." Here, Telemachus stopped and beckoned Stellarstasis towards him, "I agree with all of you that this competition was primarily about human strength. Therefore, I suggest that these two men are both crowned as champions: Faramund for his strength of mind and Stellarstasis for his strength of body. Celtic genius and Greek brawn! Imagine what might be achieved in this world with that combination. Let us celebrate the Celt and the Greek!" With that Telemachus raised the hands of Faramund and Stellarstasis into the air and joined them.

A roared approval greeted his action and this time when it fell away there was no criticism, only a tangible excitement amongst the spectators for more events.

By the time Tyracides was preparing to compete against the other finalist in the underwater river swim, six events had already gone and the Celts had been victorious in four. To qualify for this one there had already been several races and the competitors had been whittled down to two for the championship. Victory in this aquatic event rested not only on who could gain the bank on the far river side first but who came up to the surface least times to take in air. Thus the one who was swifter through the water and remained longer under the surface, without having to breathe air, was rewarded with the victor's trophy.

The Celt he was matched against, looked more Greek than Celt, with his black ringleted hair, shoulder-length and shining under the sun. The barbaric blue tattoos stamping his arms and legs promoted his difference. Something else notable was his failure to offer libation to the River God, as Tyracides had done, before they entered the water.

"Do you not need to ask the Water God's permission before travelling through his domain?" asked Tyracides.

"When I swim, I feel that Danu and I are as one. His strength is my permission," Bauxus, the Celt, had answered.

Both were tensed and naked, ready for the race into the water. The bronze Carnyxes blared and they ran: their unearthly tones accompanied the whole event.

Plunged into the river, Tyracides sensed its cold rills rolling along his stretched limbs and ribs as he made his way across the flowing current. He saved his breath, spending it on powerful spatial strokes across as much distance as was possible. Beneath the surface the water was murk brown with mud in patches but would suddenly give way to light from above. At last after eight strokes, he had to swim up for air and breaking the water's limit he gulped a lungful before heading down again. Before his descent, he had checked for the distance remaining and for Bauxus. The Celt was nowhere to be seen. What happened next was the subject of a discussion he had with Telemachus after the race and which the Corinthian made him swear on his oath not to reveal to anyone else.

"But you must have seen Bris underwater while you raced against him, Tyracides?"

"No, sire, not seen but I was aware that he swam by my side. My attention was fixed on getting through the water."

"What happened the second time that you went down – is this what you want to tell me about?"

"Yes, Telemachus – when I submerged again I found the water even cloudier and as I had not seen Bauxus above, I tried to detect him below. The mud in the river was behaving like cumulus clouds in a windy sky; sometimes they covered up all light to see by and at others passed and made way for the sunbeams to pierce the green weeded depths. There was definitely another body alongside me, which I thought strange because if it was the Celt, should he not have gained the advantage in keeping underwater and by now be leading me?

Anyway, I peered to my right and there indeed was Bauxus, swimming. Having seen me regard him, a curious thing happened. Effortlessly and despite all the power I was using with my muscles strained to the utmost, he began to move ahead. Then as he did that, a horror began to happen to him. The very mud in the water appeared to spiral and wrap itself around his body. Like one of my wet clay pots on the wheel, his figure revolved and stretched as if the material it was made from could be shaped into anything it desired. And it did. The being I saw in that river was no longer human. It was more like an eel, or dolphin with a faint connection to human traits. It was growing larger and reminded me of the size of the river itself. Then, wilfully, the creature stopped all movement forward and turned its head around at me. Telemachus, I was with you on Thocero's boat after we left Galati – I could not forget what we all saw then. What I witnessed today in the river's underworld was that same face with the goggle eyes and the wide split mouth – the face of Danu."

Before he had come to this country, Telemachus would have sought to rationalise Tyracides' experience, told him that such things could not exist. His own people had built wonderful houses for their gods and their enormous images were placed inside. It was to encourage respect for them in those sacred places. And fear. Yet in the cities, there were some who were beginning to lose that fear and deny any divine existence. They spoke about war, disease and men's hatred for each other as the cause for worshipping the gods. Without such calamities and the evil in human nature to create harm there would be no need for religion and society would be free to make a real advance. Telemachus himself had begun to believe this. That was before he had gone through the Bosphorus with the Telemachons, crossed the Formidable Sea and tracing the setting sun, come here, to another country. Here, the monsters lived; there were no kind gods and divinities ate mortal flesh. At the present, Danu seemed to be benign. He was just biding his time.

Telemachus wondered why Danu had not drowned Tyracides.

"What did the creature do then?"

"He did nothing…. But I did. I am ashamed to say I panicked. I kicked upwards and came to the surface but even as the water dripped down my face, I grew angry. Was this fair, that the Celts should send a god against me? I could not allow myself to be beaten and so I immediately returned to the depths.

The monster was there, gliding along without any urgent pace, seeming to show utter contempt for me. I thought, I'll show you! And grabbed hold of its leg. Danu was completely unperturbed and continued to meander on his way. He actually turned a circle – I had the distinct impression that I was being played with. I knew this could not go on since my lungs were ready to burst. But just before I decided to release my hold, the creature made a sudden, powerful move with his legs. My grip was broken and I was flicked off as easily as a child might be unexpectedly thrown by a horse. The seismic turbulence in the water threw me to the surface again and I came up coughing and choking. Wiping my eyes and recovering myself, I saw Bris touching the white marker on the opposite bank before returning.

I swam on, touched the mark on the riverside and returned but by then, of course, the gap was too wide between us and Bauxus won the race."

"Are you telling me, that the person who was swimming across the Danu against you, was the river God himself!" exclaimed Telemachus.

"I can only tell you what I saw," said Tyracides. "I saw the beast but I did not see Bauxus and when I did see Bauxus the beast had dissolved away. When I confronted him in the tiring house, he appeared to be genuinely puzzled but then laughed and said that such an excuse for losing the race could be used successfully with Greeks but ask his people amongst the spectators if they had seen a god-in-the-water!"

"Could there have been something in the river with both of you?" enquired Telemachus.

Tyracides shrugged his shoulders. "Perhaps." But Telemachus, watching him knew that he would not change his mind.

"It is important that we do not look like fools and poor losers, no matter what you experienced," said Telemachus putting his hand on his shoulder. It was then that he made him swear not to tell anyone else.

Returning to the spectators' seats, Telemachus viewed the progress of the remaining events closely. The Telemachons were competing exceptionally well. Although there were injuries, none were fatal. Three events were particularly prone to this risk: the chasm leap, the duel and the chariot race. The chasm leap was an artificial one, although the organisers had debated whether or not to use an actual chasm along the river. There were difficulties in arranging for such a location to be spectated without breaking the rhythm of the other events' performances in the Danuviad. It was decided to construct a wooden runway, about half a man's height off the ground with a very wide break in it towards the end. As a further trial where one runway ended, a wall of fire was to be built up before it, fed by bracken and maintained by slaves. Any competitor would have to leap through the flames and land on the remaining part of the runway over the substantial gap. The distance from the beginning of the second runway to the landing spot would be measured as the jump length for each competitor. The fire wall was there to make the jump more difficult to assess for the athlete and there was the real possibility that some contenders might fail to bridge the gap properly and break bones in falling; even their necks.

The leap turned out to be one of the more spectacular events – a frisson came from the vision of each athlete bursting through the fiery wall. It was not without risk when doing that either. Thocero's long hair caught fire as he leaped the ignited air and had to dunk his head in a water bucket, put there for that purpose. Thocero's jump was the longest though, by far.

Getae tribesmen won the next two events- the long-cart jump and the axe-throw but Eucleides gained the victor's crown in the wrestling, despite being matched with a man from Bud who was just as experienced a veteran and more powerfully built. Eucleides would have preferred a younger, less experienced opponent but he used the other man's heavy weight to his own advantage and eventually weakened him through exhaustion, toppling him onto his back.

Belisama watched the Danuviad's progress engrossed. She had never witnessed anything so exciting, except in war- but that was a bad excitement, bad thrill. Here, it was appreciating people at their best with all the war skills employed in peaceful competition. Snippets from these games would last long in her memory: Polydeuctes with his flashing fists, dancing around and pummelling his opponent's body; Lysimachus in the armour sprint – the fierce menace, gleam and ferment from metal men on the run – Lysimachus himself using a fallen man as stepping stone to his victory; Eris hitting the heart on the wicker man while simultaneously knocking her opponent's arrow from it; Artorius and his Celtic match fighting each other to an exhausting standstill, swords at each other's throats after a wonderful display – the crowd calling for both men to be rewarded with a champion's crown.

These and many more were her thoughts in the build-up to the chariot race. She was looking forward to it with an increasing thrill but not without some trepidation. Her training in the previous weeks had restored to her the skills she once had over horses and chariot. It rekindled a fond remembrance too, of her father's teaching. The day when she had mastered the turn at a gallop with the horses and her father's shouted comment – "We'll soon make a man of you!" followed by a loud guffaw. Her mother, naturally, disapproved, fearing for her safety. But even she was impressed by her daughter doing what a man was able to do and doing it much better.

The harness had been fitted and Belisama stepped into the chariot with her spearman. Well, that is what he would have been if they were riding to battle but in this instance he had no spear, just his own weight to counterbalance hers in the speeding chariot, especially useful in taking corners to prevent the vehicle overturning.

Melissa waved at her from the crowd. She and Belisama had maintained a strong friendship despite her separation from Tyracides. It was surprising how her former lover had adjusted to the new circumstances and how little jealousy he had shown when she had chosen Agenor. In fact, she had to admit to herself that he had shown none, which was unusual for many men. If anything, it was Agenor who was slightly jealous and that was something she just could not understand.

She had been told that Telemachus was to make another speech to the crowd with the Celtic leaders stood beside him and that was to be followed by one from King Garudian. She listened but with only half an ear as all the time she was checking her competitors, the course and her impatience to start. There were some pleasant references to her Celtic origin and praise for her courage. The audience, which had been curious when she took the chariot, were enamoured by the speeches, applauding them warmly.

Belisama was already aware that the crowd, Celts and Telemachons alike, had already decided that her chances for victory in the race were zero and considered she would be lucky to survive it intact. There were some seasoned charioteers out there on the track to compete with her: men who had used their vehicles in battle at the centre of chaos and whose superb control had brought them safely back out again. She tried to ignore her own feeling that the opportunity for winning was frail.

A libation to the gods Danu and Zeus was made in the Greek way, the carnyxes blown and all chariots lurched forward. There were six chariots in total. Apart from her own, there was one provided each by Bud, Pes and Belgrad, one from the fortress at Heuhenberg and another from the settlement at Slat, driven by a Celt who had been champion in two events already, Berengar. Slat's village Headman and the Chief Druid, Thorus, had not been happy about Berengar's actions at the tree-lifting contest despite the public acknowledgement given to Faramund, although Thorus' antipathy was because of that very fact. The Slat charioteer had been forced to withdraw in Berengar's favour. It was no use for Berengar to protest his poor skills for driving the chariot. A refusal, they were adamant, would mean his banishment from the tribe or worse - that his honourable offer to become a human sacrifice for the war god, Rudianos, in the next tribal conflict would be accepted. Losing the race, would result in the same decision.

Lined up and readying for the signal, horses snorting and champing on their bits, Belisama was conscious that the other contestants had concentrated their attention on the trumpeters. Only one took a moment to shout a mocking comment in her direction – the tall warrior Coccidus from Heuhenberg.

Silence marked the crowd's readiness; King Garudian gave the signal and the bronze horns were lifted. Whips cracked and the horses surged forward. A cacophonous support spouted from the audience for the individual competitors. The track in front was oval shaped and by one end, at a safe distance, stood a rank of drummers. When the chariots had completed a circuit they all beat their skins once, two circuits – twice, and so on.

On the first turn, the charioteer from Belgrad took it too wide, the vehicle swung out at the sharpest point and almost overturned. The horses, being dragged off the track, were in no position to recover themselves and had to be retired. Belisama had carefully aligned her chariot at the centre, with Coccidus on her left and Berengar to his left, while the charioteers from Bud and Pes were to her right. The problem with taking a central position was the risk for being crushed by those on your left and right.

That was beginning to happen now after they had completed more than one lap. As the vehicles rushed on into the straight, the wheels attached to Coccidus' chariot and the Bud's chariot began to bang into her own. The man from Bud tried to steer his vehicle away, with some success, but Coccidus was more reckless and seemed to be driving purposefully to collide with her wheels. Both Belisama and Coccidus knew that if the wheels interlocked for the turn they would both be out of the race.

Belisama made a decision and shouted it into the ear of her Spearman. He, taking a spare whip, immediately ran up the chariot pole – a practised battle technique – and from the top of it slashed at the nearside pony's neck, the side that was pulling Coccidus' chariot. The animal, feeling the sudden pain, veered away, pushing its mate and forcing Coccidus to slow the rolling vehicle while he regained control.

An advantage was granted to Belisama and her chariot pulled away, readying for the bend. Likewise, Berengar and the others kept steady control as they swept around it, closely pursued by Coccidus. The drummers in unison raised their fists and beat their sticks down four times.

Coccidus changed his tactic and cut to the inside track, bringing him alongside Berengar. The two were neck and neck with Belisama in front. There were four laps to go.

But on another turn, unexpectedly, the chariot from Pes began to pull away and overtake Belisama. The cheering from the crowd redoubled. Irrational again, Coccidus, having edged forward swerved drastically in front of Berengar and Belisama. They had to draw back. The man from Pes, having seen what Coccidus had done to Belisama, tried the same trick and brought his chariot into contact with the Heuhenberg warrior's. What occurred then was really not what the Persian had wanted. The contact was a hard collision and made the chariot bounce. Coccidus staggered back, lost his footing and fell out at the back before his Spearman could grab hold of him.

He fell onto the ground and it was only his helmet that prevented him from being knocked unconscious. Coccidus climbed to his feet, dizzy, clutching his broken arm and looking for the quickest way off the track. Owing to his actions, he was half-way across it. His Spearman had halted the chariot further up and was now turning it back to retrieve his master.

The other contestants drove on, disregarding, around the course. Berengar took the lead. From their vantage point, the watching spectators could see immediately what would happen if Coccidus did not get away from the track quickly. His chariot had returned and the Spearman was pulling him onto the standing board. Then the reins were flicked and the ponies began to move off. But the wrong decision had been made. Rather than moving across to the innermost lane and the safe space inside the oval stadium beyond that, the driver decided to head towards the outer lane and the spectators. The mistake was lethal.

Coming around again, the other chariots saw the obstruction. The Pesan drove to the left to avoid it and in losing the lead was forced against Belisama's chariot which swung against Berengar's.

This time the impact was so great that the chariot was lifted up onto one side and both Berengar and his companion were toppled out onto the ground. The Spearman landed first and then Berengar, directly on top of him. A wail rose up from the crowd where his wife was standing with their new-born babe in her arms.

Having seen what happened when Coccidus had failed to leave the course early enough, the guards on the periphery did not leave it to the contestants to help themselves as they did before but rushed over and dragged the chariot and men away.

Now it was just a contest Belisama, the Pesan and the man from Bud. A luxury of space had been granted by the previous mishaps and all three chariots spread out across it, not wanting any further devastating contact. Belisama took the inside track, the other two the outer. It was not just a matter needing human skill but the quality in the horses. Belisama had chosen hers carefully, gambling that her horses bred for their stamina and agility near the Rhodanus River would overcome all the others, including those Carpathian Mountain horses that frothed under the whips and were straining tight to pull some of the other chariots.

The Budan was ahead, but it was deceptive as he was on the outside; Belisama passed him on the turn and then began to make clear headway before he could recover his distance on the straight track. The noise from the crowd expanded as people changed their allegiances from their own lost contestants to her and she raced towards the guard with his javelin levelled to mark the winning line. He lifted the lance and she rushed past: a champion of the Danuvian chariot race. A massive tumult resonated from the crowd and the carnyxes blared the end of the event. With her victory, the Telemachons had won one more event than the Celts but from the response made by the spectators it was certain that the Telemachons had gained the goodwill for which Telemachus had been hoping. The injuries sustained by the charioteers were not fatal: the worst were those suffered by the fallen Spearman who had not only hit the ground and broken his leg but had cushioned Berengar's heavy fall, paying the cost of a cracked rib for his courtesy. Berengar did all he could to aid his companion but there were other concerns on his mind during the aftermath.

It was those concerns that brought both himself and Faramund to Telemachus' tent, where it had been pitched on the riverbank close to the moored trireme.

They stood before Telemachus and Thocero, waiting for his response to their request.

"So you want to join our expedition?" Telemachus had condensed Faramund's long preamble, a wayward list of motives for joining him, spoken by a man who was shy in getting to the point and perhaps many other things.

"If you will have us, sire," came Berengar's low voice.

This utterly surprised Telemachus. He could understand why Faramund, a man whose wit had been clearly proven in the stadium, could speak Greek but not this tree-lifter.

"Where did you learn to speak my language?"

"My friend taught me," said Berengar, gesturing towards Faramund.

"He has instructed you well by the clarity of your speech."

Telemachus considered them. Faramund's cleverness reminded him of his friend Gnosemus, another thinker, whom he had lost in Heraclea Minoa back in Sicily. Unlike the more dignified Gnosemus though, this man seemed somehow to have a separate vivacity and bubbly excitement about him that was curiously overlain by his shyness with others. Berengar was a bluff, big character, tough and expressing his own opinion even to ill-manneredness. But honest. He would surely tell him the real reason why he, a champion of two events at the Danuviad, would want to leave his people. A matter he shared with Faramund who had glossed over it during his appeal.

The question was asked by Telemachus and Berengar answered it plainly, while Faramund looked uncomfortable. Berengar told him about the expected punishment for giving way to his friend in the weight-lifting competition and the unachieved victory in the chariot race. He also added that he would like to bring his wife and baby son with him.

"Have you thought carefully about that Berengar?" said Telemachus. "By the glimpse that I had of your son earlier, he must yet be new-born. It will be a hard journey for battled men – how can you hope a baby will survive it?"

"He is my son," replied Berengar, "and not only that, he also has my protection. His mother is a hardy woman and will fight like a wolverine to nurture him. I love my tribe but I know how it treats the sons of those who have broken trust with it. I must leave and my family must go with me. If we do not go with you then we must find another way."

Telemachus wanted to take them with him. "There is another problem. We, the Telemachons, are guests in your country. How can we insult the hospitality given to us by accepting you on our expedition? Your Headman will complain to King Garudian and everything we have set out to do to gain the friendship of your people by these games will be undone."

Thocero intervened. "Telemachus, I would be happy to make way on my boat for these people. They have talents which will be invaluable to us on our search – strength, invention and speakers in both the Greek and Celtic languages. As for this Headman, he will still be in the vicinity somewhere. Let's find him and offer a gift for these people's freedom. I can't see that he will refuse – he'll get gold and will maintain his credibility by telling the village that Berengar and his family have indeed been exiled."

This gave Telemachus something to think about. Thocero was not a man for spending his gold freely. He hoped it had nothing to do with Berengar's wife who had rushed to her husband's side when he had fallen from the chariot. Her pretty looks had stimulated much sympathy from the male spectators in the crowd. That would be stupid and Thocero was not a stupid man.

"Alright Thocero, your plan has much to commend it and if you are willing to offer gold for our guests so am I."

The relief on the faces he saw before him was obvious.

After they left, Telemachus turned to Thocero.

"So why did you really want them on board, captain?"

"I was impressed by them….by their natural abilities. They seemed to be honest people."

"You say that and yet Berengar lied to his people by pretending to represent them at a Danuviad event which he had no intention to complete."

"He did that for friendship."

"Yes, and it might be that at a time when we most need him, he will disappoint us too – for friendship."

"It is Faramund that interests me most," returned Thocero, side-stepping an argument.

"Faramund"

"Yes. We have had to give away the Ambrosus, a god-given gift. It might be that Zeus, since we have been making sacrifices to him, has given us Faramund. Human wit to replace magical enchantment. We have seen one machine created by Faramund. I believe there will be others to come. We might find ourselves truly grateful for his inventions.

"You mean, like Daedalus, he might create wings for us so we can fly to the Tin Isles?"

"We can only ask," smiled Thocero.

13
A Pass of Fools

The Danuviad having ended and goodwill achieved beyond expectations, the Telemachons packed their necessities back into the ships and set off once more. Peaceable terms had been made and Faramund, Berengar and his family went with them.

'The Telemachon' and Thocero's boat 'The Singer' made an unrushed passage along the Danu towards Bud and Pes. Telemachus had asked the captain why he had called his boat by that name. Thocero had replied that once, a long time ago, his mother had taken him to an oracle to find out his destiny. The oracle had told his mother that her son would become a renowned teller of mighty tales one day but only after he had sung the water to fire. "They always pronounce in riddles," affirmed Thocero, "and this has puzzled me whenever I think about it. The only way I could make sense of the prediction is by naming my boat as I have done." Telemachus thought his friend knew very clearly what the oracle had meant but said nothing.

The Telemachons were accompanied on their way to the settlements by other boats carrying the princes of Bud and Pes. A warm welcome was given when they all moored on either riverside midst the two towns.

Both the trireme and the trader were well stocked with food provisions so it was not thought necessary to stay long for that purpose. Information about what could be found upriver was essential however and apart from the Hecataeus maps giving geographical outlines and hints for urban centres to come, the Telemachons required factual verbal accounts. Like the food and other physical commodities, this could be found in the markets too, from the same people – the traders. They were used to continually travelling up and down the river, taking news along with cash from the local inhabitants. By this means, it was discovered that there were two peoples living beyond Bud and Pes on the river - the next major settlements the boats were to come across. The People On The Plain would be friendly and give them no trouble. The People Beyond the Mountain Pass were a different matter. Because they existed between the mountains around a tributary which fed the Danu, they very rarely came down to the Danu and probably would not interfere with their journey anyway.

"That may well be," said Belisama to the leather merchant with whom she was dealing and whose responses she was interpreting for Agenor and the others beside her, "but why are they different?"

The young red-haired Celt put down the leather hide he had just shown her onto a large pile. "The People Beyond The Pass have strange attitudes and stranger customs. Yet they believe that everyone else should hold to these beliefs. Anyone who do not conform to their principles, they treat with hostility and contempt. They believe those people are cursed by their god, Danu and so can be treated with less care than they would use with their own herd animals." The young man lifted his hand in the air to show them. "Do you see that?" There was a gap where his index and second fingers should have been. Despite not understanding the language, the Telemachons guessed his question and nodded.

"That is what they did to me so that I could never again pull another bow-string. I had hunted for food in the valley and was roasting a wild boar. To them, eating pig's meat was a sacrilege: you should only take food from what Danu provides – the fish in the river. So they chopped my fingers off before I was allowed to go." Disgust spread over his listeners' faces as they heard Belisama's translation. "Yes and there is something else you should know."

"Go on," said Belisama in his own tongue.

The Celt watched them closely, curious about their reaction to his next statement. "They are ruled by children."

"What!" exclaimed Agenor when he had heard, aghast. "What, by Hades, does he mean?"

"Half their ruling council seats are taken by children and the Bouleuterion leader is a boy with the power to make the final decision. The people in the village believe that the next generation is the most important, consequently the adults have no self-respect. Everything should give way to the young – Danu has ordained it. The adults sacrifice themselves to their children. Literally so. Every year at the winter solstice the boy leader chooses an adult, either male or female, to be burnt alive so that the new year can begin and the new generation be born."

"What is certain in such a society," said Agenor grimly, after he had heard Belisama, "is that the children are pampered."

"Are those people demented!" broke in Tyracides. "Have they lost all their rational senses?"

"In one sense you might say that," mused Melissa, "but in another who can deny that the principle is a good one – society does depend on our young. Yet they and my fellow women have been subjected to utter savagery and torture whenever wars take place. Women and even children are raped when men plunder and lose their own humanity. Thus in another sense you might say that children are taking their revenge in that place for the horrors that exist outside it."

Agenor disdained a direct response to her but made his own point. "Who are the adults that have produced such a system – because it is they that are the ones who will benefit in some way. These child councillors will be bizarre levers for pressing their own demands."

"What do these people call themselves?" asked Tyracides.

Belisama put the question to the Celtic trader who replied with one word. They all laughed. The word in Celt sounded so similar to a Greek word.

"Did he actually say what we thought he said?"

Belisama repeated the word to the others clearly so that there could be no mistake.

"Fools," she said.

Faramund added an explanation. "The village they come from is called 'Foll'- hence their own name for themselves as its inhabitants."

"Well," said Agenor. "As long as these uncivilised Fools stay away from us, I couldn't care what they call themselves or how they treat each other. Let's get back to the boats and make ready to go."

With that, they all took their leave from the stallholder.

Telemachus got to learn about what they had found out and brought it into his planning for the next stage of the journey. From his maps he understood that the Danu went on much further into the land mass and he could also tell by the papyri that using the rivers noted there to cross Europa would only take them so far. At some point they would have to tramp their own Dolkios and carry the boats or boat in pieces perhaps from one river to the next. It would mean that or abandoning the boats altogether. Telemachus was loath to do this. Waterways were the quickest and most effective means for transport. There was the sea to come, that lay as a barrier between Gaul and the Pretannic Isles. He supposed that he could always hire boats out to convey his people but those boats would not have the same sea-going genius built into them as was obvious in 'The Telemachon'. He had got to love the ship and the freedom it gave.

That liberty, however, came at a cost. A sombre mood descended upon him as he watched the still land move past under the steady beat of oars hitting water, worked by his men. They had been travelling for many days now and had passed the People of the Plain who recognised them as the Danuviad champions and gladly had cheered them on. The forest was insurmountably thick. Trees, rank upon rank, were massed on the hills. Some sloped to the river in clustered groups, like a defeated army running to the water with a desperate urge to throw themselves in to escape whatever was behind. What lived in that forest? What could live there? They had come to a place without light. He could feel it. A suffocating cloth that had suddenly been dropped, blasting his vision but offering no warmth in recompense – just those massed piny needles that formed a dense thicket defence to deflect the honest gaze from what ate away at the wooden core. The sun was shining in a cloudless sky but it could not pierce those tree-tops, could not stir those roots. This was not Greece. Suddenly a breathing sadness filled his throat. What would he not give to see his father's face again or hear his voice? Staring at his hand, he thought not for the first time about the last touch it had been given by his wife Clytemnestra. That touch should have been a firm grasp. He could have saved her but she had let go. She had plunged to her death.

From the corner of his eye, he saw something move. Looking up he found that a long-legged pelican was lifting itself from the river bank; flapping upward, it heaved and wheeled away above the distant scintillating water; baggy throat under the beak filled with fish for hungry young. Telemachus had never seen one outside Greece.

This was not Greece. Blue sea, crystal at its edges, was replaced with brown river water here; bleached rock, scented herbs and the constant, hot, life-endowing sun with rain, mud and encroaching cold as the winter drew on; colourful, smooth-stoned temples sprang joyous festivals with rough, hewn wood or stone monuments and capitulation to fickle gods.

The movement under his feet was reassurance. So was that stork flying over the tree-tops. He shook himself inwardly: this was not how he should lead the Telemachons. Fear and doubt were mere self-indulgence. Come, come, he admonished himself. They had travelled further along the Great River than any Greeks before them. They could not turn back now, even if they had wanted to. The only answer for them was to get away from this river and break through that forest cover. At some point they would have to strike northwards.

According to his maps, the Great River ended at a place called Donau, a small settlement. It was here that the Danu was born from two other rivers. One, called 'The Brig', tracked north but to where was not known as that area was the subject of the final and least helpful chart in the whole periplus. The river Brig was a small one and somewhere along it, Telemachus expected that they would have to leave the waterway and rely on other means for transport.

Already the skies were beginning to darken as the boats progressed up the river. Another sign that they should abandon this waterway was the narrowing of the banks - still wide but a younger course nevertheless, compared to the massively mature torrent that poured into the Pontus Euxinus at the other end.

Telemachus ordered the boats to be moored. He avoided travelling at night whenever he could. The trireme drifted in to a bank on a river bend and the anchor was thrown before it could go any further to get stuck on the mud. As he scrutinised the forest edge with apprehension, Telemachus caught sight of something floating in the water. It seemed to be river weed but there was too much purpose in its movement. He bent forward to get a closer look. The flotsam was slowly, definitely making its way to the river's edge. It seemed to take some time. Telemachus thought about calling someone to his side but just at that moment the mass suddenly rose from the water as if shooting up from the mud itself. The shape was small, much smaller than a man; it was the brown river weed come to life. Two arms appeared from either side of the heap and cleared vegetal strands away from what was clearly now a pale face in the dusky light – a child's face that spluttered and giggled and then laughed out loud. The sound was quasi-human. It tailed off into a haunting shriek and then the thing ran and its dark form merged with the spiky tree shadows and the dusk. A shudder had passed through him at this vision. His horror intensified in the realisation that he had seen this face before, only it was older. It had been on board his ship: it was Danu.

"Telemachus!" Berengar called as he walked up to him in some haste. The other turned. "Have you noticed anything about this place?"

Initially Telemachus thought he was referring to the apparition at the river bank and was about to confirm it when Berengar continued, heedless. "It is very like that site the stallholder was telling us about, the one to which he was taken by the People Of The Pass. Look over there." His pointing finger indicated a tributary river flowing into the main channel. Beside it and receding into the distance were a collection of hills.

"Yes, you are right. It is very like that. We'll double the guard tonight."

"I'll take a duty tonight, sire, if you wish."

"Thanks, Berengar. That would be welcome."

The Celt marched off. Despite his outwardly tough manner, Telemachus had come to understand that he was a forgiving man. His friend Faramund had placed him in a difficult situation at the Danuviad and yet the friendship seemed to have been maintained on this journey. From his encounters with Faramund, Telemachus knew that the latter felt tremendously obliged and would not let him down: they were both honest people.

For several days they had been confined to the boats now and it was time to stretch their legs on land. But he had seen the phantom and Berengar had reminded him where they might be. If not for that, his inclination would have been to allow everyone to encamp by the river overnight. As it was, he would have to compromise and at least prepare for a meal to be enjoyed by the water and then return to the boats for a closely guarded sleep.

When Melissa heard that they were to go ashore she was glad. She did not like the cramped conditions below deck, the claustrophobia made worse by her memories of being transported as a slave to become some man's plaything. Of course, now, travelling with Tyracides made it far more comfortable. She felt happy thinking about him. He loved her, truly, and she loved him, truly. Tyracides was the kind of man, who, once he had committed his love, did not take it away. She repaid that trust with her own and they believed firmly that not even death could break their compact together. But that still did not remove her dislike for travelling by boat.

The experience was made easier again by pleasant company. Of the women who joined the Telemachons in Athens – Eris, Hebe, Chara, Selene, Adrasteia, Chryseis and Andromeda – all were aboard this vessel, Thocero's trader. The men joked about Thocero and his floating harem. This, she thought, could not be further from the truth. He treats us with the greatest respect. I wonder where his affections are kept, if he does not seem to be interested in any of the women aboard – in the young men comprising his crew? The cabin boy? Thinking about that: actually the cabin boy, Leonis, bears a marked resemblance to Thocero in the thin nose and broad eyebrows. Perhaps he is related, maybe even his son. When the old crew departed in Athens to be replaced by some of Telemachus' men, this youth stayed. No-one interferes with the boy; he seems to have Thocero's special protection. If he is his son or a nephew, why not just say it? Thocero has a great regard for us and the new crew have that in greater part for him. He carries authority with an easy confidence, like Eucleides or Telemachus himself. He can laugh with the men, turn them merry in a moment, but knows where to draw the line.

We women are convivial together. There is a close experiential bond between us: slavery. That encompasses being taken without warning from your homeland – having to travel and mine happiness from the vast, potentially endless seam of misery. That is what kept me and Belisama together in those first days in Syracuse. But now, I don't know. We have drifted apart. She in one boat, I in another. The other women do not like her. They say that she is more man than woman, despite her beauty. Who knows what Belisama has suffered in the past? She did not disclose it to me. I wonder why she is still with us. I thought that she was simply using Pelisteus, the expedition, anything, to return to her homeland. Well, this is her homeland. She could have had the pick of the Celts at the Danuviad when she won the chariot race and rejoined her people with great honour. But she didn't.

Here comes Tyracides with his wonderful protective warmth, ready to help me into the boat that will be lowered now over the side to take us to shore. The others have mixed feelings about this land, understandably. On the whole, I like it – the trees and mountains are pretty, the climate is cool but there are plentiful furs to keep us warm. As everywhere, the people are mixed, some good, some bad. The men divide into two: those who strut their arrogance – the leerers and lechers and belchers, who treat women as if they are nothing – determined to live down to the backward, savage characterisation for the Greek; then there are those who treat us with courtesy and politeness but in their eyes lies still the condescension we are used to on Greek streets and have come to escape. Berengar and Faramund, though, were different.

"What are your thoughts, my heart?" called out Tyracides as he came up to her.

"I am thinking about the greenness of those trees," she replied. "How solid and fertile everything is. In Greece, the trees were sometimes sparse and the land not always good fertile earth but harsh, ungiving rock."

"True, the land here yields much but back in Greece we made even the rock give us fine buildings and paved streets. That forest you are praising might appear to be attractive on its exterior but once you step inside your appreciation would soon change to fear and an urgent need to find your way back out again. Unfortunately, I think that one day we will have to do just that – go into it and out again to find our own land."

"Tyracides, don't think about the forest. Let's think instead about the child we will have once our journey is done."

The man grasped her by the hands. "Nothing better than to plan for that!" he exclaimed, "But we shall do, once you have travelled just a few paces over water and are safely placed near a warm fire on the river bank, enjoying a hot goat-meat stew!" He pulled her playfully to the ship's side and helped her over it into the small rowing-boat to join several others.

The rowing-boat went back and forth several times, as did the other one from the trireme before all the Telemachons had got to the riverside and were fully engaged in building fires and preparing food. The freedom to roam the river was exhilarating and noisy cheer went up like smoke around the camp fires. In the forest of ash and oak, the breeze sent a whisper through the leaves and fringed by trees, the shadowing mountains stared down.

Melissa was with a group of the women – Eris, Hebe, Chryseis, Selene and Adrasteia – who were busily skinning the rabbits caught by Berengar, Talos and other young men from the forest's periphery. They were working near some bushes which themselves were not far from the trees. While their knives cut and sliced, the chatter was equally sharp. But it came to one of those moments which strikes even the liveliest conversations: a pause and momentary silence. And in that silence, a twig snapped.

Melissa froze. "What was that?" she whispered. The others stopped what they were doing. The sound had originated not from the bushes but the trees. They listened.

Faintly, they heard another noise. Remote as it was, no woman there could mistake it. It was the cry coming from a child in distress. A continual, insistent weeping.

The women had moved downstream from the others so that they could wash the blood from the skins and meat, allowing the deitrus to be carried off by the current, away from the encampment.

"We must get the others, said Eris.

"No, wait, it's going," came Selene's worried tone and indeed the sound was becoming more indistinct. The women moved spontaneously together. They were drawn as if on a single spider thread towards the treeline. Melissa was the first to get there and through the close-knit branches she thought she saw a small boy, perhaps six or seven years old, fair haired, sitting with his back to a tree, weeping.

"Hello!" she called to him and ducked under some thickly leaved branches to get closer. "Don't be afraid!" Yet when she raised herself up, the boy had moved away and she just glimpsed momentarily his fur trousers and fair hair. He was not too far away and was walking without hurry, as if in a sulk. The temptation to follow was strong.

"Melissa!" The others had stopped at the forest boundary, reluctant to go further. It had been Selena who had called. Their anxiety grew. Melissa crushed herself through more tugging tree limbs, protecting her face with her arms. She felt the pressure of clawing bark ease and stood up straight, letting her arms drop. The glade before her was a large space and at the other end was the child facing her. But something was not right.

Melissa called back to her friends, "It's …." but before her words could be finished, they were stopped by a hard hand over her mouth.

The five women at the edge heard the throttled choke and shouted out her name frantically. Selena and Eris went into the undergrowth.

Their yells were heard by Tyracides first, who came running and soon after the rest of the Telemachons left their fires to see what was going on.

When the women shouted out to Tyracides what had happened, he did not break his run but with sword drawn smashed through the vegetation. Many others followed him, Telemachus amongst them.

They rushed into the glade where Melissa had been but of her and the strange child there was no sign, except one. Faramund's keen eyesight detected it. While hunting around the opposite side to which they had entered the space, he plucked something from an outstretched twig and called Tyracides over to him. As Faramund held it up, Tyracides found himself looking at a long golden hair that could only have come from Melissa's head and which sparkled even in this dim light. Tyracides turned to Telemachus.

"I must go after her. Every moment counts."

Telemachus did not waste time by arguing with him. He wanted to send out a large search party but the risk was too great. "Go then, certainly, but take others with you," He looked over the Telemachons gathered to the front. "Who will help to find Melissa?" A chorus answered back with arms raised. "No, you cannot all go. There may be an army in there waiting to massacre us. It could be those demented People Of The Mountain Pass we have been told about."

"The mountain children?" scoffed a voice from the back.

"I do not think the stallholder was telling us the whole truth, either that or something was lost in the translation. We cannot afford to fight the unknown and lose the expedition but Melissa must be helped." He searched the raised hands and willing faces, then gave out the names. "Tyracides, of course, Herophon, Faramund as tracker, no Berengar - you have a wife and child here, Pelos, Sostis, and Artorius. Eris?" She was standing with hand up.

"Remember my skill at the Danuviad," she said, firmly.

"Alright. You better use that knife to cut the hem from your dress, otherwise you will slow everyone down. Now, get your weapons and pray that Hermes will lend your ankles wings. I can only give you until tomorrow and the morning after that we will have to leave whether you are here or not. The people he had named hastily went back for their weapons and then together, disappeared into the forest.

"What now?" said Eucleides after they had gone.

"We wait."

"Do you really mean to leave them if they do not return?"

"I am responsible for a hundred people, Eucleides – men, women and now a child, who look to me for guidance through the clear and unclear dangers ahead. Every daylight hour we spend motionless on this river attracts the wrong attention, most probably from those barbarians who have taken Melissa."

"I will sacrifice to Zeus for their return."

"It may be that their safety will receive a greater guarantee if you offer to Danu as well," said Telemachus with perception. "We must make friends with strange gods to restore our loved ones."

*   *   *   *

Firebrands plucked from the river camp fires lit the way as Tyracides and the others pushed themselves through the undergrowth. Night was falling when Melissa had been taken and the darkness became complete with the passing time, a clouded sky and the dense foliage. They had travelled as fast as possible, cutting and slashing, yet trying to mute the sounds they made in their pursuit. Faramund, beyond the glade's long grass had been able to discover tracks on the muddy ground and knowing they would have to stop for rest when the torches burnt out, the pace had been increased.

At the first bird's song the next day, the rescue party was up and resuming their search. The worry was that the quarry might have been lost altogether but the Telemachons came to a huge beech tree around which more than a dozen bodies had lain down and the marks on the trail after that suggested they were not far off.

Faramund realised that they were all heading on a direct route to the mountains above the trees. Further on, following a stream sloping upwards, the terrain became a little more arduous although there was compensation in that the trees themselves began to thin out.

Finally, they reached the forest perimeter, were through it and climbing yet another slope, Tyracides in front. He was the first to see over its peak.

"Down!" he hissed.

The others reacted instantly, falling flat onto their stomachs. Tyracides flapped his hand, crouched for precaution and his companions paddled towards him on all fours. They gathered near the rise and peeked over.

Before them was a relatively level plain, scrub and grass covered, which rolled out at some distance to end at a pass between two mountains. In the middle of the plain was a rocky river bed but the water in it was more like a wide stream than a river. There were indications that it could swell and become a torrent at certain times in the year. Next to the water were the abductors and Melissa. They were all standing while several mountain ponies they had been riding were allowed to drink. Melissa had her hands tied in front of her. The Fols, because it was unarguably who they were, were at such a distance that there was no need for whispers.

Tyracides flung himself onto his back on the slope and groaned, "Zeus! Zeus! If ever I see that stallholder again, I will strangle him!"

"Why?" said Herophon, puzzled, "What has he got to do with this?"

Eris had already noticed. "Just take a closer look at them, Herophon."

He did so. There seemed to be a curious anomaly in height between those standing near the mountain ponies. "What - are those the children that the Fols worship?"

"They are all Fols, Herophon, but some are not children," said Eris.

"Dwarfs!" rasped Tyracides.

"Why would the stallholder lie to us?" queried Herophon.

"It might not be that his words were mis-spoken," ventured Eris, "rather that they were misheard and falsely translated."

"But Belisama is a Celt – how could she misunderstand?" said Pelos.

"There are many tribes living along the Danu and near its source," explained Faramund. "I believe she is actually from the Helvetii – they live to the west of the Danu's source and there are certainly differences in the way they speak so she might have made a mistake in her translation. It cannot be helped but now we know better. So what are we going to do?"

"They are probably on their way back to the mountain village and if we are to believe at least some of what the stallholder told us then it is the dwarves who run that place. It is curious as to how such a community was formed – why are there such a number of them in the village and how is it they command authority?" mused Faramund.

"We leave our weak babies in the mountains to live or die by the will of the gods. Could that be the answer here? That many communities have left their babies out over the years to be taken in by one village? said Eris.

"But how is it that the different babies have the same condition?"

"Have we got time for this!" said Tyracides testily "At this moment they are getting back onto their horses and riding off. We must stop them before they get to their settlement – this place they call Fol."

The rest saw the sense in this and as soon as they were able, without giving themselves away, they clambered over the rise and continued the pursuit.

It was rocky ground with the shallow stream winding this way and that until they came to a pass where the mountain divided into two and presented itself as two monumental walls like dense iron, projecting to the sky. Standing at the bottom and staring up, you could not see where they finished. It would have been the best possible position to set guards and they could not but wonder why there were none to be found.

"What does this mean?" asked Sostis.

"That Fol itself is some way from here or that the settlement itself is so effectively defended by other means, it has not been deemed necessary to employ a guard duty in this spot." Tyracides peered through the gap and traced the path-line, dappled with overarching tree branches, ascending an incline. Beside it the water was tumbling in the opposite direction. Surely, this would be far too tricky for the horses to attempt?

"How can we be certain they came this way?"

"There has only been this one track," said Faramund. "They will have dismounted and led the ponies. Perhaps there is an easier path which will separate from this one. Wherever they are," he finally warned, "they must be much closer now so we should stop talking altogether."

"Why don't Ii sprint on ahead and see if I can find them?" asked Pelos. The others, in admiration of his stamina, agreed this was the best thing to do. Pelos put the bag down that he had been carrying, unbuckled his sword but kept the dagger at his waist. Lighter now, he set off and the others were amazed to see him moving with speed and agility up the slope.

"He's a mountain hare!" blurted out Faramund, before stopping himself in embarrassment, having ignored his own caution.

They continued at a slower pace after him. Trees began to appear again beside the water and then Faramund was found to be right in the idea that had occurred to him earlier. For there before them the path divided into two and at the junction stood Pelos, gesturing.

When they came to him, he told them that the ponies had been led off along the lateral track which seemed to curve around the mountain, while Melissa and the majority of her abductors had gone by the track that led upwards.

The track, as they climbed it beside the now gushing water, turned out to be much more than that. It became a widened route, artificially cut into a series of long steps. Three times they came to a level plateau with the water falling in a roar from above them to a large pool beside the flattened ground on which they stood. Or rather sat, because at the third resting place what appeared to be stone benches had been carved from the rock for that purpose. Resting after their exertions, Faramund began to voice the astonishment they all felt.

"These plateaus have been cut from the rock!"

It was true. The benches were surrounded by flat land on which had been laid polished stone tiles. Yet again the water adjoined this terrace but did not remain still. Perpetually swirling and bubbling, it was stirred by a waterfall crashing into it from above - a foggy liquid haze was sent up at the back where the water wall made contact and pulled from the front edge where it was collapsing into the pool below. The din was terrific and the companions had to shout to be heard by each other without fearing that their voices might be detected by those they pursued.

Not resting long, they began to climb the stairway to the next level, unaware that eyes were following them from behind.

The fourth causeway was the steepest, longest and by far the most difficult. Tyracides understood why a sentry detachment had not been necessary at the mountain pass below. These steep, elevated steps were a splendid defence in themselves, guaranteed to slow an invading force and which could be made totally inaccessible with certain additions.

Then an iron handrail suddenly appeared either side of the steps to support those who were ascending and the water's force inexplicably diminished. Gradually at first, then it became a narrow water spout. The answer lay in the rock face behind it. The rocks gave way to mammoth stone blocks that had been cut so precisely, they interlocked without any material being wanted to fill gaps between.

"It's a dam!" yelled Faramund.

Incredibly, that was exactly what it was and Faramund had thrown up all caution because the Fols they chased were nowhere to be seen: the steps rising way above them and then disappearing into an arched entrance positioned in the dam wall were empty. The stone bastion stretched across a widening gap and if they bent their heads right back, they could just see the top edge of the dam, over which a water spillage was happening, forming an ooze that trickled down.

Faramund was in awe at the ingenuity that had created this. He had come across other bulwarks to store water for use by the tribes but nothing like this monster.

Tyracides was first through the arch and up the stairs, sword and shield to hand. There was no light; the stairs spiralled up and they held tightly onto the handrail for guidance as well as safety. At last they reached the upper steps and a doorway blazing with light.

If they were to be jumped upon, it would happen just as they exited through that arch. Tyracides paused and whispered to Pelos behind him, who passed the message on. They readied themselves with sword and shield, then at a signal all rushed up and through the doorway.

They could so easily have been taken but it was the only option that was to be had. Tyracides, first out and blinking in the sun after utter darkness, could not believe his luck. No blade had come slashing down onto his neck when he came up from the stairs. No thundering rush of metal and flesh had greeted him or any of those that followed.

Instead there was emptiness and silence. The Telemachons found themselves on a long walkway above the dam with none but themselves around. Eris, with bow and arrow raised, was the last to come up.

They took their time to check that there were no signs for an immediate attack upon them in the close vicinity or at a further distance before lowering the shields.

What lay before them was a vast reservoir filled to its maximum. The huge expanse was edged on both sides with roads that led to grey rectilinear shapes in the background. It was unclear because the distance was so great. The river that fed the reservoir seemed to come from the centre point in the artificial construct and could be just discerned as it etched the snow-capped peak that cut the skyline behind the built edifice.

"Oi!" gasped Sostis. "I have seen acropolises on several hill tops in Hellas, all magnificently built but I have never seen until now such a fortress cut from the mountain rock – it is immense! Is this Olympus and is that the abode of the gods?"

"Is that what you think – it's a fortress?" commented Faramund. "Look more closely. There are individual buildings on terraces, even greenery between them, implying gardens or crop allotments."

On closer inspection it was found to be true. There was a defensive wall, certainly, but that was a boundary marking the bottom of the incline which carried all the terraces and buildings. Faramund wondered why more of the flat land between the dam and this city had not been utilised for homes. In fact, some had been and an earthwork rampart had been dug up around them but serious attention had been given to designing the second bulwark, made with the same accurately cut monolithic blocks as formed the dam.

"What are those holes in the mountain?" Faramund again, drawing their attention by directions to indents on both upper and lower levels in what they all realised now, must be Fol – no simple village as the Celtic stallholder had implied but a curious and wonderful city engineered with great skill and cunning into the side of a mountain.

The 'holes', all eventually agreed, were arched entrances into the mountain itself. They were fascinated by the thought of what may be inside but Tyracides soon punctured the marvel by bringing their minds back to the real purpose for which they had come.

"That must be Melissa down there!" He was pointing off to the side, where a reservoir road dipped around to meet the river and stayed alongside it to enter the city via the gap of Fol's first wall and then the more palatial entrance that marked the second bulwark. A small group were arriving at and moving through the earthwork gap, after being stopped by the patrol on duty. There was some discussion and then they were allowed to go on, unhindered.

"What are we going to do?" asked Eris.

"There is only one thing we can do," answered Tyracides. "And that is to go in."

The others regarded him in astonishment.

"We would be walking into a trap of our own making," Faramund asserted simply.

"How else are we going to get to her? Anyway, there is little point in us all risking ourselves. I can go in myself."

"No," said Herophon. "You need our support. We must somehow trick ourselves through that gateway."

"Why not take the honest way," came a cultured voice behind them, "and come at our invitation?"

The Telemachons spun around.

From where they had just come – the stairway onto the parapet, was gathered a number of armed men. At the other end of the walkway where additional tower-capped stairs adjoined, more men were coming towards them. They had been so silent.

Silent and almost nonchalant as they came up to them. Dressed in chain mail and with swords still in the scabbards, it was as if they had come out for a pleasant stroll in the sun, along the dam.

Tyracides' gaze travelled back to the original speaker; more guards were behind him. The Telemachons were outnumbered three to one. But what was noticeable was that some of these guards, including the speaker himself, were only waist-high.

Smooth-chinned, black hair cropped and shaved above his ears, the small man regarded him with amusement. "I know exactly what you are thinking but please avoid making a fatal mistake: some of us are closer to removing your manhood than others. He pointedly nodded towards Tyracides' genitalia and tapped his sword. "Besides, even if you escaped from us up here, I cannot guarantee the safety of your woman down there."

Tyracides re-sheathed his sword. His companions, realising their predicament, did the same.

"Very wise," said the dwarf, with approval. "My name is Folson and I have come to escort you into our fair city. First you will unbuckle your swords and give all your weapons over to us, then we can enter Fol."

They did as commanded and were taken back down the stairway. On their descent, despite being weaponless, Tyracides wondered if they should make an attempt to overpower their captors – in the darkness and confusion they might have a chance – but the warning about Melissa was one he could not ignore.

It took them some time to cover the ground between the dam and the city. Folson and his guards were horse-mounted while they themselves had been placed on a large cart. "They haven't tied us," observed Eris. "It's not out of kindness," muttered Herophon. The cart rattled on at some speed which slowed when they had to negotiate several bridges. These bridges spanned wide water channels that had been cut from the reservoir.

"Where do these conduits go?" said Artorius.

"Most probably to irrigate the crops or orchards on the other side of the mountain," suggested Faramund. There was no further talk after that as Fol loomed nearer.

Their reticence was due in part to anxiety but as the cart rolled on they could not but be absorbed by what they found around them.

The gate by which they entered the citadel was composed of a colossal bronze statue, a gigantic man with legs astride and palms upwards supporting the stone top of the bulwark on his shoulders. His head was stretched forward and on it he wore an enormous gold hat, cone shaped, stamped with circles and other signs. Traffic into the city passed between his legs.

They were into the flat region between the first and second gate they had observed from the dam. People walked in the streets and only the children gave the cart a second glance as it drove past. Tyracides did not speculate on that. Without their helmets and dressed as now, they could be taken for Celts themselves. They had bought the leather, wool and fur garments on the Danu: items practical for the cold weather which was getting colder the further west they journeyed into the mountainous terrain.

The people, though, in their appearance were unique. A mixture of dwarfish and ordinary sized residents in Fol were to be expected after the encounter at the dam but here it was much more than that. Eris as a slave, had seen various races from across the known world walk the streets in Athens and so had the other Telemachons as they passed through. Yet this was a settlement right in the centre of the Celtic territory and nowhere else on the Danu could match it. Every skin colour was contained here, from the blackest Nubians with short, curled ebony hair and dark eyes; to the palest skinned Hyperborean, blonde hair over the ears, piercing blue eyes above beards trimmed and plaited; to the olive skinned Mediterranean folk, probably Greek. As to be expected, there were many red and dark-haired Celts mingling with the rest. All these people were different, yet their costume was similar - woollen shirts, occasionally linen, leather jerkins or cloaks made from various materials, a short tunic with the legs covered in linen or alternatively fur or leather trousers. The colours used to dye the clothes were startlingly diverse and jewellery in the form of torcs, nose-rings, earrings and finger rings abounded.

Most remarkable were the women. Bare-armed and without head-covering, they carried themselves confidently through the streets and were treated with respect by the men. Eris, looking around her, felt that she was missing something. Then it came to her. Everyone here is happy, she thought; there are no covered women hurrying through the streets to avoid being propositioned by a man, no men being berated by their masters, no beggars with arms outstretched and pleading for money. None of that. Just a genuine togetherness and acceptance that was totally opposite to every city she had known. Why then, had they taken Melissa? Don't accept the first presentation of anything she reminded herself.

Tyracides, for his part, was sitting in the cart wracking his brains as to how they could rescue Melissa. Of course, the problem had become much worse – they all needed to find a way out of Fol now. The deadline for their return set by Telemachus seemed hardly possible in the present circumstances. Tomorrow the Telemachons would sail without them and they would be left stranded in this city of Fools.

14
Costus the Cobbler

The Grand Vizier of Fol, inside his palace scoured into the mountain, looked down at his courtiers from the burnished throne he sat upon. The throne was built low to the ground so that the Vizier did not have to jump to position his dwarfish stature on its seat. Correspondingly, the throne surmounted a stepped dais which raised him above the heads of those who came to lobby him for special favours such as a small change in the law that would benefit the manufacture and sale of goods they produced, a position in the administration or indeed just a plain lump sum cash payment provided by Fol's taxpayers. If the Grand Vizier thought about it deeply, he would have realised that the outward signs of power such as this elevated throne or the tall golden conical hat he wore on his head, that had its precious metal stamped with calendrical and constellatory symbols and was wound around a simple withy framework and which at important times in the year was detached from his head to play a significant part in the strange incantatory rites that went on for days- all these were illusory: real power did not reside with him. How could it when he did not want to use it to benefit others? But he did not think that deeply. He was after all, just Costus the cobbler and in the last three years, he had commissioned some wonderful shoes for himself, made to his own specific design. They were dyed green leather, golden buckled and platform-heeled. Certainly difficult to walk in but who cared about that when he made such an imposing figure by wearing them? Another advantage was that if they were propped on the footstool and stared at very hard, his courtiers' faces were blotted out.

What the Grand Vizier, formerly Costus the cobbler but really deep inside always Costus the cobbler did understand, was his own boredom. With great surprise he had discovered that luxury bored him. He was reminded of that when his eyes lifted from his shoe tips to the vast surrounding cavern chamber. On the upper levels, above this grand audience chamber, he could see the entrances and doors to scores of rooms and some tunnels leading to who knows where into the mountain. So many rooms. How many could one man and his immediate family actually inhabit during a year? Some he had never visited and certainly not those tunnels. He shuddered. His people had come from those tunnels and others in the mountain, a thousand years ago. They had picked a way out. Stone-cutting and metal forging magic had created this wondrous city, this silver nail thumped into the mountain sole. After all that time, his people had got used to the natural light and he, for one, was not about to venture a regress back down a tunnel to claustrophobia.

Best to leave well alone. As with the luxury. In fact, he could not but choose to leave it alone since he did not own it. His pale green eyes roamed the upper echelons. All these rooms and he did not own one of them. At least he owned his cobbler's shop and the rooms above it. Costus felt not like a Grand Vizier but like one of the ordinary citizens of Fol. They did not have property rights over their own homes but rented them and their lives could be disrupted at any moment on the whim of the landlord, particularly if they complained. Why were they so happy? Was it the generous holidays given to them, the frequent street theatre and musical events, the mushrooms brought from the neighbouring mountains?

Anyway, he only had a few more weeks to serve. A smile played around his craggy features. To serve. How ironic. When the summons had first come to him as he knocked a nail into the last shoe for that day, he had almost fallen off his chair. It should not have been such a shock. Everyone knew that a Grand Vizier was to be elected by lot from the general population every four years. Fol had once been a proper kingdom governed by hereditary monarchs but after a disastrous succession of them ending with one had fattened and gorged himself on different meats and taken to roasting and eating his own subjects, it was decided to change the constitution.

Initially Costus had, after getting over the shock, been tremendously excited by his lottery win. He had imagined the changes he might make to benefit his neighbours and the city - better cobblers' shops (his own in particular and one or two belonging to his friends), finer quality shoes for the citizens, that sort of thing. When he thought any longer than a few minutes about what he might do for Fol, he ran out of ideas. This was just as well because when actually taking on the powers and responsibilities held by the Grand Vizier, he learned that there were none. The genius he would have exercised to improve the lives of Fol's inhabitants was severely curtailed. It was ferociously limited by those who actually did govern Fol – the ones who traded in goods and services and most of all, money. They had their representation in the exclusive circle of senior advisors which perpetually attended the Grand Vizier and no action could be taken without their personal signatures attached to it. Given the limb of power but not the muscle wherewith to use it, Costus became frustrated. That did not last long so he became bored. In this boredom there were episodes when thinking about his little shoe shop lifted his mood a little. It was perhaps the destabilising effect following from his sudden promotion to Grand Vizier that made him question even these cheerier periods. He remembered the occasional visits paid to the shoe shop by his Uncle Votless and over the nice, crusty bacon sandwich and beer one night, he had asked the question, 'Why are we so happy?' Uncle Votless had grinned and given him a broad wink. 'It must be in the bread …. or the beer!' he had answered. The old Fol had been right on his first assumption. It was in the bread. Unbeknown to both him and most of Fol's citizens, the food manufacturers added a secret ingredient derived from a mountain plant – on that stimulated a sense of well-being amongst those who ate the dough.

He felt a tickling sensation on his nose-tip. Bollarchus, yammering away at yet another request from the dough manufacturers for money from the treasury, his plaited beard bobbing up and down over his furred and richly embroidered gown, stopped. The Grand Vizier had slowly raised an index finger from his hand resting on the throne arm and the rest of his body remained rigid. Bollarchus, playing the game that the Vizier's every wish was his command, when in fact the reverse was true and every one of the Vizier's wishes was his to command, made a strenuous effort and reformed his features to show concern. The expression was replicated by the twenty or so courtiers crowding in their finery behind him. Bollarchus watched as the dwarf's eyes almost crossed in their attempt to assess the foreign body that had landed on his nose.

"Your highness, a big fat fly has just landed on your proboscis.

In response, very, very slowly, as slow as a wounded snail, the dwarf turned his hand palm up, the index finger still raised. A middle finger flicked up.

Bollarchus stared at the two-finger salute which openly displayed Costus' annoyance with him. There's no need for that, he thought.

Costus reassigned his attention to the fly and uncrossed his eyes. There was a momentary pause and much faster than a corn scythe, his right arm swung in the air, its large hairy fist clamping tight.

"Got you!" yelled the Grand Vizier, delighted. He could move fast when he wanted to. A sea-over-shingle-rush of applause sounded from the watching courtiers.

Costus smiled. Big as the fly was, it rattled around inside the dwarf's fist as if trapped in a jar. He hopped off the throne and walked over to two columns behind it.

Inwardly groaning, Bollarchus, along with the other court attendants, was well aware what would happen next.

The Grand Vizier looked up to the shimmering gossamer that was a lethal trap filling the upper space between the columns, its edge just above his head.

"Come here, my pretty! See what I've got for you," he cooed.

The silvery strands quivered and vibrated to the harpist's plucking fingers. Only, it was not a harpist's fingers plucking. These fingers were not smooth, they were hairy; they were not fingers but legs, huge legs. And the legs belonged to a spider the size of a dinner plate.

It had dashed forward from a darkened corner and waited in expectation. You could almost hear it panting.

"I Know you much prefer mice but here's a starter before your main course," chortled the Vizier and he threw his captured fly into the web. It struck against a strand and before it could make any attempt to escape, the spider had jumped and injected a powerful anaesthetic into its body. The fly wriggled, then was still. All became a monumental blur as the spider wrapped, rolled and bowled the juicy flesh into a little glinting bundle.

Costus backed off, all the while watching, entranced. He might not be partial to going down tunnels but he enjoyed seeing his pet, trap live things and killing them.

"Sire! Sire!" Bollarchus almost lost control over himself, trying to recover the Vizier's senses back to practical matters.

"Yes, yes!" came Costus' sharp tone, wanting to hurry court matters up himself now and get them over with. "Yes, my most trusted advisor, you can have the funding requested for your bakers – just get your gold from my treasury, I'll sign the order, but what about the cobblers eh?"

"Cobblers?" uttered Bollarchus, mystified.

"Yes, cobblers. You are always petitioning for the bankers, bakers, farmers, alchemists, dam makers – and let me remind you that dam was built three generations ago, how come we are still paying their grandsons – but what about the cobblers? If it wasn't for those fine men and dwarves this city would not exist. They produce the quality footwear that is required to get all those others you claim for, to their places of work. On the backs of their labour, this city, Fol, has grown to its fullest height." Costus made a dramatic gesture and pushed out his chest, drawing himself tall on his platformed shoes.

"Please, please, sire!" said Bollarchus, attempting to soothe him. "If you want to petition for the cobblers, I will do it on your behalf and produce the document of enactment for you to sign. You can be certain they will get what they need."

"Thank-you!" the Grand Vizier replied, adding great emphasis to the second word. He thought gravely for a moment and then finished, "And whatever you ask for them, you can have!"

Bollarchus almost laughed out loud at the simplicity of it. This job was like squeezing the juice from large, ripe lemons: only, there weren't any annoying pips to deal with. He decided to change the topic in case the Grand Vizier immediately attempted to retract what he had just offered.

"Now, your highness, do you remember those Greeks we brought into Fol?"

"Bollarchus, do you think I have the memory span of a deflowered earthworm? Of course I do." Costus was only pretending annoyance. Really this incident with the Greeks was a spot of interest on the page of his otherwise dreary, powerless and luxuriant life.

Avoiding the Vizier's question because he knew the answer to that one, Bollarchus pressed on. "What shall we do with them?"

"Do? Why, let them go, naturally."

"Go?" The senior advisor sounded confused.

Costus sighed. "Bollarchus, maybe we can actually avoid these monosyllabic, minimalist sentences and actually get on with the business?"

For a moment, the advisor wondered if the Grand Vizier had been visiting the library to catch up on his education. He was about to dismiss it as a habit completely out of character but then made a mental note to check with the scroll warden.

"But sire, we arrested them. Don't we want to keep the woman they were trying to rescue – not only her but the other one that came with the rescuers? You know that we need more women to increase the birth rate in Fol. Just lately there have been too many women dying in giving child-birth."

"I understand that. However, I think if we release them into the city and persuade them to stay for a few days, they will want to remain here." Costus' expression became a little vacant, "Everyone in Fol is so ridiculously happy," he scratched his head. "It must be in the bread or beer or something."

Bollarchus kept his face as blank as a pan of milk. "You might have a point there."

"What, about the bread and beer?"

"No, no – I mean it is quite right that our citizens are happy." A sudden worrying thought came upon him. The silence was uncanny. He turned around and there were the courtiers he had forgotten about, ranked face upon face, avidly listening to every word spoken, the musician's instruments hanging listless from their hands.

Bollarchus affected a jolly laugh. "Aren't we all happy?" he asked them. Twenty or thirty heads nodded in unison. "Right then, let's get this party back on to its feet. Play on!" The last was a command to the musicians who quickly returned to playing their instruments while the courtiers went back to dancing or replenishing drinks.

With the comfort that noise restored, Bollarchus resumed his discussion. "That happiness is infectious," he continued, thinking about the bread, "and I am sure that with a few healthy meals of good Fol food inside them, they will forget about leaving."

"Quite so," enthused the Grand Vizier, glad to see that his advisor had accepted a two-way traffic in advice for once. "But I don't want them released until they have feasted with me in my own chamber. I want to enjoy their company and learn something about the shoe-making practices where they come from."

"That can be arranged," replied Bollarchus. He had no real qualms about it. The Vizier had been prevented from learning secrets during his tenure and would not endanger the city by chit-chat with the Greeks. Bollarchus promised himself there would be dough-based food in plenty served up to his highness' guests.

Tyracides, Melissa and the others received the news of the intended release with mixed feelings in their prison and not a little suspicion.

"I think this meal with their Grand Vizier is just deceit. After it, no doubt, something ghastly will happen to us," said Melissa, despondent.

"Remember what happened to Odysseus' men when they ate the food provided by Circe!" commented Pelos to the others. Faramund did not remember as he had not heard the story so they told him.

"Is it likely," the young Celt responded, "that they would let us dine with their ruler and feed us their magic at his table, when they could have done the very same to us in the prison here?" They all concurred that it was strange but nevertheless determined to be careful about the food and drink they were offered.

Tyracides was more concerned with the impossibility of getting back to the Telemachons at the appointed time. Telemachus would be leaving the river bank where they were supposed to re-embark even while they were presently talking. Sostis, the youngest, was close to despair, "What are we to do?" he cried. Tyracides comforted him.

"We know that he will follow the Danu as far as he can. That gives us a definite route and somehow we will join with him again."

Conversation was interrupted by the guards who took them out to another place where they bathed themselves and were given rich, clean clothing and then accompanied to the Vizier's private chamber.

The guards stood back and Tyracides knocked on the large wooden door. A loud clicking of platformed shoes could be heard against the stone floor, approaching. The door swung and there before him or rather below him was Costus.

"Greetings, my friends!" beamed the little man and waved them in." Do come to my table – I have been looking forward to this gathering. We can learn so much from each other!"

Amused by the informality and the cheerful appearance made by their host, the Telemachons entered.

It was a sumptuous room, if 'room' it could be called. It was more like a spacious hall and in the corner was another door, presumably leading to the bedroom. Around the walls were hung colourful tapestries showing heroes battling with fabulous creatures and from the ceiling looped chandeliers pinioned with lit candles.

"What are those?" asked the instinctively curious Faramund, pointing up.

"The candles?"

"No, the shields around the candles."

"Oh, they are made from glass – it helps to protect the flame."

"I have seen that substance before, transported from the Ionian cities but nothing so clear, so transparent!" said Melissa.

There was more to marvel at. The long table in the centre was packed with vegetables and fruit of every description accompanied by various cooked and steaming meats. The fruit was colourful and luscious, all different sizes and shapes.

"How do you grow such fruit!" exclaimed Eris and before she could help herself, "The climate here is so cold!"

Costus smiled, glad to reveal the ingenuity that was Fol. "We grow it under the glass you have just remarked upon – on the other side of the mountain. The vegetables are cultivated there too, all irrigated by water from the dam you passed. Now," he continued, "let us sit down, enjoy what is on the table and you can tell me all about where you have come from and why."

They sat down, Tyracides casting meaningful glances at the others while his host and the servants were not looking. If Costus had been more observant as the time passed, he might have noticed that the Telemachons ate only what he ate and that in small quantities. Later on in the conversation, Faramund suddenly said, "This bread tastes very strange – sweet and spicy."

"Really?" answered Costus, "I have eaten so much of it in my life that, I must confess, the taste was hardly noticeable any more. I have left off eating it recently – to lose this." He patted his stomach.

"Yes but it is very nice," mumbled Faramund as, lifting a goblet containing the last dregs of wine to his mouth, he spat the morsel into it. Despite what he had just said, he was not about to take any risk. They, for their part, took his previous comment as a warning and avoided the bread all night. At an opportune moment, Faramund emptied his goblet's contents under the table, where it was wolfed up by one of the two hunting dogs the Vizier kept.

During the meal, Costus apologised profusely for Melissa's abduction – since no harm had come to her, the others and Melissa herself, accepted his apology with good grace.

"But why was it done?" Melissa asked.

The dwarf, in an endearing way, was slightly embarrassed. He chose honesty rather than duplicity and told them about Fol's declining population.

"There must be an easier way rather than filching people from the countryside," said Tyracides. "I am sure that with all you have to offer here," he gestured to the table and the room, "there would be hundreds of people wanting to come and stay."

"You would think so wouldn't you?" rejoined Costus. "But the fact is that we do not want a sudden influx of newcomers into Fol. What we have got here has taken generations to achieve. The mountain and forest is difficult land to work and disease strikes the city occasionally. Summers are hot, winters are very cold. It is not like the lands from which you originate which is either warm or very hot. The advantages we do have here are fresh, clear water and once the trees have been uprooted, fertile soil. From what you have told me, your own cities are beautiful and the sun god smiles constantly – why would you leave such a country and travel the unknown world to these Tin Isles as you call them and what we refer to as Albion?"

"I for one," answered Pelos, "am sick of war and where we come from is continually riven with conflict. In my short life I have been forced to work as a mercenary – that seems to be the only business which provides a man with the things he needs. I am looking for peace. That is what Albion means to me."

"Sad, that a man has to move from a beautiful country to find it. But isn't war a condition of humanity? What makes you think that this Albion will be any different?"

"With Telemachus we will make it different," said Tyracides. "He has told us what he knows about the country from the maps he has and the people who have informed him. He says that the climate is not so cold as it is here in the winter because the mountains are smaller, although it is not as hot as in Hellas. He has promised we can build a city where everyone will be free, equal and happy. Tyranny of any kind will be rejected."

"I would like to meet this Telemachus of yours. Do you think he would have room on his expedition for a poor cobbler?"

"Which poor cobbler?" asked the perplexed Tyracides.

Costus told them about Fol's political constitution. He had only been half-serious in his request but he began to think. Meanwhile he went on to elaborate on the nature of Fol.

"You know, it is a good system because in electing a ruler from amongst the citizens every four years, one man – or dwarf," he emphasised with a smile, "cannot monopolise the government and become a dictator. Every man or dwarf has a flaw. A person susceptible to human weakness cannot be entrusted with total power over others. What is Telemachus' weakness?"

"If I knew, would I tell you?" said Tyracides with good humour. His mood shifted suddenly. "I understand his strength too well and when he says he will do something it would only be an embrace from the King of the Dead that will stop him. So I realise, Costus, that in sitting here around your table as guests, we have lost our places on the expedition unless we do something about it."

Tyracides then told the Vizier about their missed appointment with the Telemachons. The conversation carried on without Costus making a direct response but then after they had been entertained by Eris revealing her archer skills by shooting her arrows the length of the hall to find an exact target, Costus returned to it.

The Telemachons got to learn that lately he had become unhappy with his city and his own place in it. He had been Fol's ruler for the past four years and yet was unable to carry out any major change to improve the lives of the poorer citizens or indeed reduce Fol's isolation.

"But when you see the citizens, you don't think the city is isolated," remarked Pelos. Costus told them that the people were the result of slaves being brought in generations ago to replenish the population. This had worked only for a time and Fol was once more facing a cyclical depletion.

"When we were driven through the streets in the cart, there were many people around," said Faramund.

"Yes, but how many young people did you see?"

That made them think and they realised that what he said was right. Younger faces and children had not been prominent in the crowds. Of course, with the dwarves it was sometimes difficult to guess at age – some could have been either thirty years in age or a hundred.

"To get yourselves back to your people will mean a tough journey through the forests and mountains between here and wherever you are able to get to in order to find them. There are many dangers ahead: Men with Flaming Crowns, the Water

Daemons and many other beasts unknown, exist in that furious interior. Some even say that the original Mother and Father of the god Danu live in a certain region and that they guard a pit into which are thrown the spirits of all the men, women and creatures who have died in and on the Great River. This pit is the entrance to the Laboratory of Remaking where beasts come to life again as humans and men and women, if they have lived good lives, are renewed as beasts. The evil doers are annihilated, their names destroyed and any memory of them wiped out."

"Superstition," said Faramund.

"You could be right," agreed Costus. "Still, the least you must have to find your way through such regions are reliable guides. I may be able to help you with that."

It was then that they heard his offer to lead them through the forest. He would choose from amongst some close acquaintances of his, not cobblers, but people who had intimate knowledge of the woodlands.

"Why would you do this?" asked Melissa.

"Although I don't look it, I am actually one of the younger citizens of Fol," said Costus. "There is no real happiness in this place; indeed, there is something almost sinister here which I want to escape – my position as Grand Vizier has allowed me to discover the obstacles to a better life in this city and they are insurmountable. Best to move on." The last was said with relief and briskness. He looked at them for a response.

"So, you feel powerless to improve life here?" asked Tyracides.

"I feel like someone who has lived all his life in a house surrounded by a wonderful landscape, living in peace with his neighbours and then one day he decides to climb the mountain next to his home. It is a singular peak with a magnificently open view all around." Costus stopped and his piercing gaze rested on the listening Telemachons. "I have got to the top of that mountain and what I see everywhere is devastation: the final corruption."

"If you were to climb to the top of the mountain you know to exist," said Tyracides carefully, "surely what you would find is that wondrous dam on one side and the finely laid crop terraces it irrigates on the other? That does not imply disorder or ruination to me."

"What you see is not what you get," said Costus, flatly. "Just as it might appear to anyone on first sight that the constitution which guides Fol is democratic when in fact, it is not. After all, we dwarves came out of the mountain to make this Fol but now we are a minority within our own city walls. To pluck a dwarf like me, just an ordinary cobbler without wealth or connections and make him the Grand Vizier for four years – that would be a true democratic expression would it not?"

"Some would say so, but I assume you are going to tell us otherwise."

"I am!" said Costus, bringing his fist down onto the table and making them all jump. "What you see in me is a mere emblem for the state. I should be answering the needs of all Fol's citizens, instead I am used to fool the Fols – my overriding function is not a democratic one but to serve the interests of the select few in this place, those who punch the gaps that made the toothless grin in this 'happy' city's face."

"When we establish a better city," spoke up Pelos, "what we require is optimism – you must have that to draw up a humane constitution."

"Oh, I do have that in surplus," refuted Costus, "but to be optimistic without realising how greed can destroy the best in society is to be an ineffectual dreamer whose ideas will be manipulated into disrepute by those wanting exorbitant profit. You need me for the new constitution you will eventually establish – I have experience." He uttered the last few words in a tone that was grandiose but after a few seconds added, in a humbler manner, "Anyway, I can mend your shoes." The people around the table laughed.

Tyracides was beginning to think of how his fellow citizens and colleagues might react to the Grand Vizier's words if they had heard them. He was reassured to find, on surveying the room they sat in, none of the servants were present. Costus must have chosen his time.

The rest of the evening, with the servants still absent and no other intruding, was taken up by planning what they should do next. Costus made them aware that to leave the city was not going to be a simple matter. They decided to leave a day for preparation before slipping away.

15

Encounter in
the Black Forest

Eucleides and Thocero were anxious about what had become of the search party and Melissa. That was on everyone's mind as the anchors were reluctantly lifted and the boats sailed on up the river. The other matter concerning how long their river journey would last was also uppermost in their thoughts as they moved on to Ingol. Their boats were swift under the oar, Ingol quickly passed and Donau was reached in less than two days. It was at this settlement, the birthplace of the River Danu, mothered and fathered by the tributaries Breg and Brigach that Telemachus told them to break up the ships.

There was strong resistance to this at first. The oarsmen of the Telemachon had grown understandably attached to the ship that had carried them so far, receiving and giving loyalty in turn. Thocero too was reluctant at the idea that his own vessel, which had been a livelihood for many years, was now to be destroyed. Yet as a trader, he understood that it was necessary to use all the resources at your disposal to meet changing needs and circumstances. If his boat had to be dissembled for its timber to be sold on and reap their people benefits, then so it had to be. "We might be able to sell the whole boat," Telemachus had told him, which would have avoided the destruction. There was no such choice open for the Telemachon. Telemachus was adamant about that. The last thing he wanted to hear about was a marine fleet, built with the same design as their trireme, manned by Celts and invading the Greek coasts. To please his men though and the others who sailed with him, he had more than a hundred pendant charms made from the ship's boards. They were given the same likeness as the statue of Zeus that had stood above the Telemachon's deck and with those pendants hung around their necks, it could be said that the Telemachon would always be with them. Everyone was happy about this and the trireme was taken apart. There were good proceeds from its wood, while 'The Singer' was sold in its entirety to a Celtic merchant who employed it to transfer amber from the north.

They had set up an encampment near to Donau and Telemachus was thoroughly busy bartering with the local chieftain and his tribe to provide themselves as comfortably as possible for the long march north. The chief was a shifty, sly-looking man who tried to exhort as much as he could for the reasonable but standard provisions required by the Telemachons. In these matters Berengar, the Danuviad champion, proved to be a clever interpreter and forceful negotiator, seeming to decipher the man's thoughts as accurately as his words. Telemachus was grateful and a friendship sprung up between them when he recognised that the Celt possessed a trustworthy and principled character.

The Donau chieftain, on consideration, was not to be trusted and even when the goods had been bought from him, it was essential to check their quality and that they had been delivered properly at all. There would be no serious problem – Donau village was not large and its chief could ill-afford to provoke confrontation with a hundred experienced Greek warriors. Still, sometimes the stock quantities fell short or the horses to be bought were weak so the slyness had to be challenged firmly.

Striding through the camp to check yet another delivery, Telemachus was reminded of times past with his army. Then as now, he was used to the busy activity caused by a military force readying for action. Back then, the action was invariably a battle and the excitement would begin to rise in the veins: beat in the heart. You tried to take your mind off it by focusing efficiently on the simple tasks allotted to you – this applied as much to the most senior commander as to the ordinary soldier. Today, they were getting ready for another stage of the journey, one that would have to be forced through impenetrable forest untouched by human foot and over morose mountains, jealously guarding their easier accesses. No, truly, it felt more than ever like the arrangement necessary for war rather than for just travelling.

The subject of the missing Telemachons was deliberately raised by the others on a routine basis. No-one wanted them to be abandoned. There were long discussions speculating on what had happened to them and where they might head if they had got back to the river only to discover the Telemachons had left. Berengar was concerned about his old friend Faramund; he seemed to have forgiven the latter's manipulation at the Danuviad and in his newly established friendship with Telemachus raised the matter several times. Eucleides brought it up too. His worry was the effect such a neglect would have on the morale of the others. How could the Telemachons have trust or owe loyalty to leaders who deserted their own and left them to an unknown fate? Finally, Telemachus had had enough and like a scolding parent bringing his sullen children together he reprimanded them, stating clearly what he believed would happen.

"I do not think that they are dead. Somehow, using their intuition and talents, they will have escaped their captors and fled north. That is their direction of travel. They know where we ourselves are going – Melissa and Tyracides have seen our maps. They will follow the North Star and I am certain that we will all meet again at Ictis. That is where the tin comes from to make the bronze that is transported down the River Danu and the Rhodanos." Ictis was a small island before Albion which was a major trading point between the Celts of Pretannia and those of Gaul. For a millennium, tin had been bartered by the Pretannic peoples and exchanged for goods brought from Gaul.

Berengar, listening, thought about his wife, Ula. She was brave but could she cope with the challenges ahead? Even more worrying was the risk to their son, now that the boats had been destroyed and their way was to be made by foot or pony. He had been pleasantly surprised though when he had found Ula in their makeshift tent, constructing an apparatus from leather, linen cloth, wool, fur and a wooden framework.

"What is that?" he asked.

She turned amused eyes towards him. "Well, unless we are going to leave our son behind, I thought I would make a carrier for him."

"Really? Is it strong enough?" He checked it over. The main part was a kind of wickerwork basket with holes to allow free movement for the arms and legs. Through these holes extended water-proof hide, with the fur turned inwards to enclose the limbs. The interior of the main basket was thickly lined with wool and fur for warmth. Two broad leather straps cut through either side for the arms of the person carrying it.

Berengar whistled. "Love of my life, your wit surpasses my estimation. This will keep Herne safe and warm while we travel."

He patted the head of his son, its curly hair as soft as a moth's wing. The child, crawling over the furs on the tent floor, looked up and cooed in response. Attempting to stand, he fell back again after a few balanced moments. Berengar made no move towards him: the boy had to learn and besides the furs would prevent his head hitting the hard ground.

"I hope you have made some good warm clothing for yourself and the child. It is winter and the conditions can only get worse as we travel north on higher ground."

She picked one of the furs up from the ground.

"Not only for us, Berengar, but for you too. You need something more than just the love of your wife and son to keep you warm, great though that is."

He looked at the thick, cushioning garment she had given him. It was a finely made cloak with a metal clasp sewn in at the neck. The fur was both inside and out. He would be kept reasonably warm in the coldest conditions. Again, Berengar appreciated his wife's adaptability. Perhaps he was worrying too much for her on the journey ahead. He brought her to him and kissed her on the mouth. She pushed him away, playfully. "Not in front of Herne, Berengar. Our child is going to grow up a handsome man with fine manners."

"That is a certainty with you as his mother," agreed her husband.

Her light-heartedness disappeared as she began to ask about the next stage of the journey.

"Berengar, you know that the Donau villagers have been warning us about what lies ahead?"

"I can just imagine their pleasure in describing the difficulties," said her husband fiercely. "Pay no attention to them, they are not a nice people. I'd have thought they would want us away from their village rather than frighten us and be encouraging us to stay here."

"They say that the trees are so densely grown in some parts of the forest that the sun is blotted out and all is dark. They call it the Black Forest. Only rivers pass through it, feeding lakes and swamps. Things come from the water or ride over the mountains at night."

"Such stories are told by our own tribe," soothed Berengar. "They are spoken to warn children from places that are a danger to them or frighten strangers we did not like." The only fault that

Berengar could find in Ula was her easy belief in superstition. He trusted in the gods but unearthly creatures swarming in every river or under trees in forested shade were mere phantoms in the human mind not the gods'. He became stubborn in trying to rid her of such beliefs. "Did any villagers tell you that they themselves had been attacked by these creatures – had their children taken by them?"

"No, but -"

"That's right, they wouldn't! Otherwise the scars produced from such an encounter would have to be shown or vanished children explained to the neighbours! But to see these phantoms come and go without trace is far easier to describe and exaggerate especially with no proof required. They did just witness them after all. I can guess up to a dozen villagers told you and the others that they had detected these creatures in the forest."

Ula nodded her head and then, just as quickly, resisted. "There are beings in existence which are familiar to the gods but not to us. Did not Telemachus defeat the Soul Beast – the Psychezoion – or was that just a tale told to frighten children?"

Berengar could not deny it. He could have gone further and said to her that the beast he had seen was not all that large, though strange. He did not want, however, to continue the argument. Besides, there was just too much to do.

That same day, Telemachus led his Telemachons into the forest.

To the east and further north, a smaller group of people were also making their way overland with some rapidity. Speed was imperative. Tyracides and the others had escaped from Fol and were journeying deeper into the mountains. Melissa was fearful that they would be chased and caught but after two days in the mountains, it appeared that the city had not sent a search party after them. Melissa puzzled over this and Costus tried to enlighten her. "They know about the tribes and other things that lie in wait for us. Their assumption is that we will die from cold and exhaustion on some mountain pass, if we are lucky." He grinned and patted her leg. "Let's prove them wrong." Tyracides was none too pleased with the familiarity shown by Costus to his wife but then passed it off as a matter of geographical standing because the dwarf could not reach her arm.

Whenever an essential campfire was built every night, a check was first carried out on the surrounding area before it got dark.

Usually this meant sending out three of their number who would seek for the highest vantage point to reconnoitre. Sostis volunteered himself enthusiastically for this task, being the youngest and curious. He continued to practise his athletic strength and agility by climbing the tallest trees or scrambling quickly up lower mountain slopes over the treeline. Faramund would go with him, in case any tracks, human or animal, were discovered and it was also not missed that Eris would be keen to go.

They travelled for many days, northwards, aiming towards the coastline which marked Gaul's boundary and the beginning of the sea that would take them across to Ictis and Albion. Just as Telemachus had hoped, Tyracides and his companions bore in mind all of the discussions they had engaged in with Telemachus over the periplus devised by Hecataeus. They did not fool themselves that the land could be crossed with impunity and expected any sea view would cost them much more than only a month's travelling. Meanwhile, the nights grew colder. A warm room under a sheltering roof was an increasingly attractive idea with every day that passed but any settlement they came across was given a very wide berth.

Together, at night around the warm fire, they rested weary limbs. The last pitchers of wine from Fol were taken out and made to last, while for entertainment they told each other stories and conversation bounced between the philosophical and the intimate. The best in human nature – a capacity for cooperation and friendship – can be nurtured under hardship and so it was with these eight people. Tyracides and Melissa had their friendship and more. All but Melissa and of course Costus, had exhibited their prowess at the Danuviad. For the umpteenth time, Tyracides was pressed to tell how he had swum against a River God. The other athletes showed appreciation, then made sure to acclaim their own victories. Faramund, reticent as ever to boast about his gifts, was persuaded by the others to explain the mechanism with which he had won the weight-lifting competition.

"Could you invent something for me?" asked Eris tentatively. A surprising attraction had grown between her and the young Celt. At least, the others had found it somewhat strange. The Greek men had assumed she would look to one of them for love. They, like her, were athletic, disciplined and worshipped the same gods. Yet this was not what happened. Instead, her attention was caught by the Celt, whose body was puny in comparison. The same could not be said about his mind and the others had to admit that this strength in Faramund was what must have aroused her desire for him. He was always ready with an answer, despite his shyness.

"I think I could, yes."

"What would it be?" Her expression showed a wrapt attention.

"You are an incredible archer," as ever, Faramund was too quick with his praise for something he seriously liked. The flames from the fire lit humoured faces, even Sostis found his liberal praise a little naïve. Faramund paused and blushed, recognising what the others thought. It was just for a moment. "I think, however, that I could invent something which might make you yet more powerful."

"What would that be?"

"A weapon to defend your beauty."

"My bow is at hand."

"I could make you a better one."

Eris was intrigued and so were the others.

"It could allow you to shoot more arrows at a faster rate and be smaller than the one you carry now, although slightly heavier. The major differences would be that you'd have to use the bow horizontally and instead of releasing the drawstring with your finger and thumb, you would press a lever."

Eris was at first interested in this new weapon but on reflection, she decided against it. Her bow was light and easy to carry. When she used it, the bow felt like an extension of her arm and besides, there were many memories that it provoked: her life and independence had started with the archery training given by her Scythian father. The bow was symbolic of their people; it had made them powerful, able to defend and extend their land. A skilled Scythian archer, shooting arrows from a galloping horse was a deadly opponent. She did not express these thoughts to Faramund as she did not want to upset him. He was always excited about anything new that came into his mind. The others showed a certain fascination for this new bow and the discussion about how it could be made went on for some time.

In spite of the diligent precautions taken to ensure their safety at night, the group was so constantly alert that it made getting to sleep at night very difficult, particularly for Eris and Melissa. The sounds that came from the forest darkness surrounding them did not help. Noises like those made by owls and wolves disturbed but were expected, it was those others, that could have been the gruntings made by bears or wild boars or sounds that seemed to bubble up from swampy mud and hiss from swiftly moving tree branches even though there was no wind. They were alarming because they were not expected. Sometimes quasi-human moans erupted from the secret recesses and these, if anyone would but admit it, completely unnerved them.

One day, they had been following a forest river for some hours and before the daylight had completely failed them, a halt was agreed. A makeshift shelter was erected under bushes and blankets put down. Then they decided to go fishing for their meal.

Scanning the flat river mud, Faramund called the others over to him. He pointed to something on the mud. It was a trail of tracks that suddenly ended. Clambering down from the river bank, they got a closer look. Faramund warned them not to move onto the mud.

"It can be like quicksand and you will be sucked into it so beware!"

They were able to get a better view without risking themselves and discovered that the tracks were similar to those made by human feet. Comparable and yet where the toes should have been there was a webbed shape. Pelos wondered whether it was a wading bird rather than a human.

"But look at the size of it and the shape around heel and instep!" remonstrated Herophon.

If the tracks had been made by a wading bird, it would certainly have provided an obvious explanation for their abrupt conclusion. The bird would have lifted itself and flown away.

"There are large birds on this river," continued Pelos. "We have seen how impressive they are with our own eyes."

"If indeed the creature had not been a bird, where had he gone?"

"Might he have jumped into the river?" asked Sostis.

That was possible. But Sostis was peering closely at the marks and he was nearer to them than the others.

"Just a moment – they have not been made by one creature but a number."

What do you mean?" called Melissa.

"Here, there is a cluster of them. It's as if many had been standing here stationary."

"Did they all simply alight, stand still and then lift off again?"

"That is one possibility," agreed Sostis to Melissa's question.

"They must have been birds," stated Pelos firmly.

"No birds such as we have seen," said Faramund.

"Let's get on with catching our dinner," warned Tyracides.

The others saw to this but no amount of searching could snare the fish that were required for the night's cooking, not from that place, anyway. It seemed that the water had been emptied of life. They decided to move downstream and almost immediately, Herophon caught a wriggling piece of silver meat on the end of his spear point. He pulled at the cord attached to the shaft and lifted the fish from the water. Soon the others had also reaped a nourishing harvest from the water and there was food in plenty to fill their stomachs before they went to sleep.

That night the guard was doubled and regularly changed. The next morning brought an exceptional fog. It seeped in, making milky shapes which seemed to swallow everything but the few paces before them as they moved. Again, they followed the river-line rather than needlessly striking into the trees.

The sun could not be felt above them, yet its light silvery disc was ever present, floating high up. Bit by bit as the day progressed, it burnt through and the fog dissipated. Pockets on the river, little muddy bays, still stubbornly held on to the damp white swirls and it was one such which they came to, on rounding a bend where they came face to face with the Diluvia Men.

Seeing them, the Telemachons immediately reached for their weapons. At first, Tyracides couldn't work out whether they were stuck fast and in need of help or deliberately hiding to ambush anyone they came across. He thought it might be these who had left the footprints in the mud they had seen the day before. Fog blowing over the figures only obscured them further. At last, Tyracides could see that these beings did not seem to be alive. They were not struggling, despite the fact that the river mud was clamped around their legs just above the knee. Their bodies were rock still and not a limb movement or an eye blink was detectable.

Tyracides overcame his uncertainty and slowly moved forward. The others, peering around in case it was all a clever trap, moved reluctantly forward with him. They got to the edge of the rocky ground before it sloped downward to the flat muddy expanse which contained the upright bodies.

Confident that he was just beyond arm's reach of the first, Tyracides held his ground and tried to understand what was out there.

Eight men appeared to be static in the mud going back to the river. In fact, three were actually in the river itself and whereas mud surrounded the lower legs of their fellows, only water partially covered their own limbs. Tyracides thought that they might be statues, perhaps left as votive offerings to the River God by the people in these parts. If that was what they were, then surely they could have been better carved. He thought that the river deity might find these roughly hewn, man-shapes displeasing.

Closer now, he was regarding the shiny, wet mud from which they appeared to be made and that lay as skin, if they had been living things. Tyracides learned that his impression there was no movement was wrong. For in this mud which caked them moved small animals that could only have come from the river bed. Simple worms and eels, tiny frogs and fishes, all moved together in the ooze, creating a vibrant layer of life. This was why the monuments gave the impression they were roughly cut.

He also saw that each effigy was positioned in a different manner and were not merely standing. The one nearest to him happened to be one of the three in the river itself. No other effigy had been placed between it and the river bank Tyracides stood on. The face of this creature could be made out and it was an expression of utter pain, although the cause for this was not quite clear. He did have his arms behind his back as if his hands had been tied but they too were in the water. He was sitting with his knees up and the river water was up to his waist.

Now, Tyracides understood that each individual figure had the marks of capture on him and was straining to free himself or was suffering in some horrible way. He looked to find if there was a woman amongst them and there were two.

It was an eerie tableau but then some madness must have gripped Sostis and the stupid boy threw his spear at one of the stooping Diluvium Men. Tyracides called out and tried to stop him when he saw his weapon being lifted but it was too late.

The spear flew towards the sitting figure Tyracides had observed but instead of sticking into it or bouncing off, the shaft and point was swallowed up by the primeval embryonic mulch that moved on the surface. It was as if the iron-tipped weapon had never existed but an instant later there was a consequence. The recumbent figure stirred and slowly stood up. The Telemachons drew back, terrified. Those other figures around and in the river were all moving now. They were not mortal and much taller than men.

Once stood to its fullest height, the being before Tyracides shook itself like a dog. The mud came off in large chunks and splatters. Tyracides saw that his hands were shackled at the wrists but as the mud flowed from his body, the chains just dropped into the river as they had nothing solid to fix to. What was underneath that loam was certainly not solid. It flowed and waved and rushed around inside the silhouette of a human body like the river water in its channel. Eyes in the face were caverns under rock ledges and the open mouth was a jutting chasm with interior stalactites and stalagmites for teeth.

The giant began to wade towards Tyracides and after shaking the mud away in a similar fashion the others behind him came too. Brown river weed rippled up its torso like chain mail. Rather than do nothing or flee, Tyracides called out to the approaching daemon with all the fierceness he could muster – "What do you want with us?"

Breaking its stride to stoop so that its head was on the same level as Tyracides', the creature opened a mouth that projected no sound. Instead the speech struck Tyracides as a clearly formed thought. To Tyracides it came as Greek but to Faramund it came in his own Celtic tongue.

The projected thought was implacable, terror-ridden and came with sounds familiar in a watery cascade:

"Your humanity!"

Faramund, seeing Tyracides struck motionless with fear, took the initiative and shouted to the others, "Run!" He went to Tyracides and pulled him away by the arm. Stumbling at first, Tyracides regained his self-control and began to move. Yet the one notion filling his mind at that moment was – 'How do you fight water?'

Desperate, Tyracides tried to find a means for escape as he ran with the others. There were only the trees, sturdily rooted in the ground. "Get to the trees!" he bellowed at the others. "Tie yourselves to a branch with your sword belts. A premonition of what was going to happen was upon him. The others rushed to the nearest ones and did as he asked. They scrambled up into the boughs. Melissa was tied to a thick branch by Tyracides and

Herophon with Faramund helped to secure Eris as neither possessed a sword belt. Costus was thrown into the lower branches of an oak by Artorius and finally several in the group had to make do with clinging to boughs after climbing rapidly.

The water divinities – for this is what they were, sons and daughters of the River God Danu – moved slower than expected away from the river in their pursuit. Slow they might have been but terrible in their accumulated force. As they approached the Telemachons, their great arms swinging to the ground, they got closer together. Then their arms swung up and they combined, arms interlinked, as if ready to dance a rite on the threshing floor. They began to revolve and astonishingly the gods did dance. Their human disguise dissolved into one massive shape stretching up and the Telemachons' faces registered hopeless disbelief as they saw before them a mountainous wall of water looming. It was a tidal wave but this one composed from the river water which reached its zenith and then in one crashing swoop surged over them.

A weight Tyracides had never known before, dropped onto him. He held his breath as the watery force buffeted his body against the tree but the branch he clung to broke off. His body was spun away in a watery torrent.

Herophon and Artorius were knocked from their positions too and were dragged off. The others managed to hold on. Costus, at the junction between branch and trunk on the oak tree Artorius had helped him up, was saved by the water forcing him against the bark and holding him there. Of course, there was only a certain time they could all hold their breath underwater. Costus felt his lungs almost burst before the waters receded. It was only for minutes that the wave, coming and going as it did, covered them.

The water had travelled in a curve back to the river and that is where Tyracides and Artorius found themselves bobbing to the surface and being carried by the current. After the first gasps of air they were able to swim to the river's edge and pull themselves onto the bank.

The others, sodden, descended from their safe havens. Recovering from the shock, they made a brief search for Herophon who was the only one missing but he could not be found. The immediate area had been devastated by the flood but it was confined to a relatively small space and actually looked like a wide running track filled with broken trees and flattened bushes.

It swept from the river in a wide arc to rejoin again further up. The urgent necessity after the search was to dry off and get warm. Fortunately, the horses that had bolted at the first appearance of the water daemons, were found, not far away, in the forest. The Telemachons dried themselves off with woollen blankets and set about building a comfortable fire which did something to alleviate their spirits, although not much.

"Do you think Herophon is dead?" asked Sostis, whose bluntness was a particular trait that the others had tried to modify without success.

"Taken by the water daemons more like as we've not found any sign of him," asserted Artorius.

"It's strange how those sprites came to be there and tied up like that," observed Eris.

"As to that who's to know?" continued Artorius, "but I do know why they awakened and attacked us – because of that young fool over there," he said roughly, indicating Sostis. "If he had kept his spear close then we would never have suffered a threat to our lives and furthermore lost a good man, a champion from our company."

"I think I can tell you why they were tied up," Faramund said, as much to prevent a bitter argument as to answer Eris. Everyone's face turned to him. "It was a story told amongst my people and it concerns the rivers in this region. Those beings who chased us are the Children of Danu. They had been caught and punished by the all-powerful god because of his dispute with them."

"What dispute was that?"

"It was an argument over power and survival. Apparently Danu accused his children of neglecting their duties. The tributaries that fed his river were drying up or in some instances were leaking poisons into his body. They should have prevented this from happening. The Sons and Daughters blamed the mortals living around the rivers. It was they who greedily consumed water from the tributaries without any thought or care for the gods and the waste flowed from their settlements to pollute the water courses. But Danu refused to believe that mortals could hold such sway over the gods and considered instead that it was the weakness in his immortal children: their choice for inaction rather than divine action that was at fault. He chained them up near one of the tributary rivers, with the single provision that no mortal would be allowed to punish or insult them further and if that happened they would be released from their incarceration."

"Now the spear thrown by Sostis has set them free," intervened Tyracides, "and at liberty to do what?"

"It is hardly likely that they will take revenge upon their father. If their progenitor dies, so will they. Much more possible that the subject for their grievance will be us, the mortals who intoxicate them with our avarice."

"Us in particular?"

"If we offer them sacrifice, they may turn their attention elsewhere."

"Have we not already made a sacrifice to them in the person of Herophon?" said Costus angrily.

Faramund calmed him. "We are not sure that he is dead. We may find him yet but sometimes it is said that the Children of Danu take people away, only for them to return later as their emissaries. These gods, if they intend to do their worst to us, may not come in the form of water next time but may shape-shift to the forest swamp or mountain height. It would be no harm and perhaps mean great security for us to offer something up to them.

Pelos, listening to Faramund, wondered what kind of man he was. His assumption in the past was that the Celt could be compared to the questioning philosophers back in Greece. Faramund's present words contradicted that idea. The philosophers he had heard about and occasionally met when they taught in the city gymnasia or agora avoided any discussion about the gods and people often thought they were either sceptical or heretical in their beliefs. The Celts were different though. It was rumoured that some tribes still practised human sacrifice to their gods. When they rubbished human life like that before their divinity how must the people themselves live happily? Yet none of those back home had seen the gods, despite what they claimed. Here, in this foreign, green and perturbous land, he and the others had met with them. From his own experience, they were worth placating.

"Alright," acknowledged Artorius, "let us do that. We have enough problems from the inhabitants in these lands, we don't want to contend with their gods as well."

"I thought we just had," muttered Sostis. Then he quickly deflected any potential animosity by changing the topic. "This river we are following – what are we going to do when it gives out, as it must do, the closer we get to its source?"

"We have a little way to go yet," said Tyracides, "and it has been useful in leading us directly north from the dam at Fol. When it comes to an end, then we will strike out in a north-westerly direction through more mountains to the coastline at the sea between Gaul and Pretannia. Once there, we will hire a boat to take us to Ictis. That is where Telemachus and our friends will be headed."

What will we use to pay the hire with? We have no money."

"There is a faint possibility that we may reach the coast at the same time as Telemachus. In which case all our problems are solved. But that is hardly likely. We might barter fur hides and antlers we could pick up on the way. In the end, if we are desperate, I have my sword and you have your bow, Eris."

There was an ironic cheer from the rest.

Eris cuddled up to Faramund for extra warmth. They had both grown more familiar with each other since Fol.

Tyracides, noticing, said, "I shouldn't make yourself comfortable there, if I were you."

"Why ever not?" she replied.

"Because it is your turn to take guard duty and just so that you are sharp for that, you can serve it with Artorius."

Eris got up and marched off.

Tyracides smiled at her disappearing back. Despite everything that had happened, he retained his sense of humour.

16
Tomb

For days the Telemachons had been making a way through the forest. It was just as they had been told. Sometimes the canopy overhead was so thick that no sunlight would reach them for a whole morning. The people they did see – the occasional hunter or two – fled on seeing their numbers as they moved through the trees. Berengar had informed Telemachus that this part of the forest belonged to the Sequani tribe but that people from other tribes sometimes trespassed there to take game. If this was so, then news of their presence might soon spread to the Sequani and their strength would cause concern and more likely than not, conflict.

Telemachus had this to deal with and the other problem – the lack of money. His men were mercenaries after all and were in the habit of being paid for marching. He understood their loyalty and that it could last for a long period without payment because they did believe in this expedition to set up a new homeland but his authority rested on him being able to provide them with something that was more than just a hope. No provision would lead to their trust being undermined, just as it should be.

So he found it of more than just a little interest, when Berengar told him that in the direction they were heading they would very likely come across the Tomb of the High King at an oppidum called Glauberg.

"High King?"

"The hero of the Sequani, their ancestor. They worship him at a shrine built nearby.

"Many pilgrims visit from the Sequani territory surrounding it and make offerings in the shrine," added Costus.

"Is the tomb closed or can people go inside?"

"Important people, tribal leaders and the people they choose can pay their respects inside the monument. It is heavily guarded."

"I hear," said Costus, sensing the Corinthian's interest, "that the tomb is filled with gold and other precious gifts. Some valuable items are also kept at the shrine."

"Gold is what we could always do with," said Eucleides.

Berengar was dubious about what he was hearing. His own people had intermittently warred with the Sequani but nevertheless he did not wish to desecrate their sacred places.

"You mean to rob them? My friends, that could be a very rash action. Glauberg is not far from the Gated Walls at Dunsberg and that is a Celtic city where many thousands live. If we raid the tomb and try to escape, there will be an army to hunt us down. Do you want to take that risk?"

The others pondered for a few moments and then Telemachus spoke again. "We have food and our own full strength at this time but that is all. Other than that we are desperate for additional resources. Much money has gone: spent on supplies. We must get the cash from somewhere to pay for our crossing over the sea to reach Albion and beyond. This opportunity has been placed before us by our own gods and my feeling is that we must take it. It might be the last piece of luck we get before we reach the coast. As for the consequences, well, having spent some time amongst the Celts, Berengar, I can say that your people are no different to ours in the quarrels they make – tribe will fight tribe and take slaves just as in Hellas, city will vie with city. We are travelling beyond the goodwill we created with the Danuviad. These people did not take part and do not know us. They are likely to be hostile in any event. But I do not want to offend the hero or ancestor in these lands so what is the answer to our problem?" Berengar looked uncomfortable. He did not have a solution.

Telemachus wanted the Celt's friendship to remain firm but he owed a duty to every Telemachon.

"Look, Berengar, I hear that your wife is a very devoted woman. Will you do me this favour? Go back to her and make a sacrifice to your gods. Pray for divine inspiration and seek for a message from them. Ask for their help in this matter and then return here to tell us what they say."

Berengar realised that he was being offered a choice to either leave the Telemachons forever or to return. He went back to Ula and told her what had been discussed.

Not much later he came back to the tent where the others were still gathered. The fact that he had come at all, gladdened Telemachus and his companions. But Berengar had returned on a condition.

"Then what did your gods say, my friend?" asked Telemachus.

"They said that you must pass by the tomb and go on your way." The Corinthian frowned. "But," added the Celt, "if any member of the Sequani raises his hand against you in an aggressive act, then you may take the gold from the tomb but nothing from the shrine."

"Ah," said Telemachus, pleased with the outcome.

"Apparently, the gold in the tomb was stolen in raids on the Aedui and Helvetii tribes many, many years ago."

"Please don't say that the gods want it returned to those tribes," said Telemachus with a smile, clapping Berengar on the arm.

"No, you can use it to your own satisfaction. The gold will eventually find its own way home."

Eucleides was already trying to think of a way he could provoke the Celts in Glauberg.

"If the Celts do attack us and we take their treasure, there is no point in taking it all. We have a long way to go before we reach the sea and we cannot be burdened with carrying a great quantity of heavy metal, no matter how precious it is," said Telemachus.

"Assuming there is that much to be had," commented Eucleides. "But you know, Telemachus, a small pot filled with coins carried by each of a hundred men soon adds up."

"We'll decide when we see it," declared Telemachus. Something in him hoped there would not be too much treasure. He did not want his warriors driven greedy by it when there were far more important matters to hand. "How is your baby son, Berengar?"

The tough features on the Celt's face softened and he answered, "Healthy and stronger every day, Telemachus. He seems to enjoy travelling and seeing the world from his mother's back."

"Good, there will be more journeying for him to do and the least he'll gain from it is a pair of sturdy legs."

Telemachus, once the others had left him, thought about Berengar's boy. He recalled the child he never had, whisked away by his wife as it lay inside her womb, when down a Sicilian cliff she fell to her determined death. Was that a son or his daughter? He would never know. He thought less often about it now. He was too busy trying to reach Albion with his people. There was little time to spend on anything else other than that sole aim. He would settle to his future, once he had found a new homeland in the Pretannic Isles.

Yet any man needs beauty and some comfort in his life so Telemachus had found his attention drawn to a young woman who had joined them in Athens. Her name was Hebe. She had taken the oars at a vacant seat on the trireme and proved her worth through hard effort. During the Telemachon's voyage she had fallen in love with Zipleus, another crewman but he, tragically, had been lost to the Psychezoion, near Galati. She was miserable for days after that. What revived her spirit was the spectacle at the Danuviad and more importantly, a friendship that had sprung up between herself and Ula, Berengar's wife. Telemachus presumed that she had discovered a new motive for her life in being able to help with the Berengar family's son. She felt a poignancy when she carried out the common tasks needed for the growing child. Thwarted dreams for what she might have lived with Zipleus. In that both Telemachus and she shared the same tragic theme, a loss of someone each had once loved.

That could have been the reason for why they had begun to find warmth in each other's company. Not that they ever spoke about their previous lovers but for the one time. Thereafter, it was never raised again. From the crew she had already heard stories about Clytemnestra and the events in Minoa. Telemachus had appreciated at first-hand Zipleus' bravery before he was extinguished by the Psychezoion's fiery breath. New love does not require an old bow; the arrow must sing when it is released.

So they had spoken and begun to feel a closeness. Telemachus was still wary. He did not want to lose anyone else. Already, Clytemnestra and his parents were far from him. He would never see his father or his mother again – of that he was sure. He had changed. He hoped that his hot-headed, jealous youth was behind him. The soreness over Clytemnestra's betrayal, first with Eupolemus and then in taking her own life away from him, had healed. He was much more judicious in how others might perceive his actions. Asceticism, however, was never going to be an impetus for his own daemon: he had begun to desire another human being.

It was a strange land he had come to. So cold at times. Snow, he had seen for the first time, when they had left that stopping point on the Danu where Tyracides had gone with the others to search for Melissa. After sailing away, the snow had come down like blown froth from the beer these Celts brewed. Big flakes had fallen thickly, some straight down from the skies, others slower and slanted, yet more flakes were whipped in by the wind, on a diagonal curving rush. He tried to see how they were constructed and caught them in his palm but fixed in the warm flesh each became an instance of tearing feathery crystal before dissolution restored a simple water bead.

Catching at civilisation in this place was like trapping those snowflakes. Some settlements displayed civilised manners but move on to the next and the fragile courtesy was replaced by utter barbarity. At the Danuviad, where the spectators had come from far and wide, he had learned much about these savage places: young men and women garrotted and sacrificed to swamp gods, numerous beheadings with the grisly skulled products placed in monumental stone niches. He had fought with their superstition, defeated a god's pet – the Psychezoion – but to overcome the Celtic deities themselves might be an impossible task. But then, he was not here to do that: he was simply travelling through to set up a civilised city somewhere at the end of this journey. The problem was that often your experiences change what you finally create. His ideas about the gods, when he was in Minoa with Gnosemus or Syracuse with his father, were sceptical ones. He had heard the philosophers' talk. That was then, a time before he had come into conflict with the gods and had never seen them except as stone effigies in and around the temples. Now, because of his encounter with these religious monsters that ruled the Celts, he was being forced more strongly towards his own gods. Beyond the polite rituals carried out for his people, he must resist that. There would be no religious strife in the city he would make. Religion was almost always manipulated by priests as a source for empowerment. Rulers used religion to make divinities of themselves. Indeed, he had heard that the young Macedonian ruler, Alexander was busy conquering in the east and recreating himself as a god-king. These godly men's liberties thrust shackles on others.

In a way he was sorry that they would not be raiding the shrine at Glauberg. It could have served as a sign to the Celts that the Telemachons were not afraid of whoever came after them. Such an action, on the other hand, could unite all the tribes in the region. Berengar recognised the possibility, which is probably why he had forbidden it through his wife's omen.

The Celt was able to show them an easier route to the tomb via the River Nikros[5]. They used it as a guide northward. Hecataeus' maps were no longer relevant because the Telemachons had gone much deeper into Celtic territory than his periplus had charted. Berengar said that the river would join with another, much longer one, called the Renos[6] and it was there it would have to be left in order for them to get to the Tomb. The monument was built on a flat hill surrounded by springs and was well fortified. By horse, it would be at least two days' travel.

"How do you know all this?"

"I have visited the Tomb."

"Then you have seen the interior?"

"Yes."

Telemachus thought carefully. The whole plan was becoming more difficult. If it were to be done, then he would divide the Telemachons up at where the two rivers met. Fifty of his best men would go with him and the rest should continue to travel north. Berengar would be going with him. He told the Celt about his plan.

"We will use all the horses we bought at Donau; we will become a cavalry regiment."

"And what about those who are left?" said Berengar, thinking about his wife and son.

"They will go by the River Nikros and then the Renos northwards. The money remaining will be used to hire boats at the next settlement we come across. Your advice was to leave for the monument at the place where the two rivers merge. Well, I think that we could accomplish much distance and a faster pace by using the horses at a canter on the flat river plain along the Nikros. We will rejoin the others after we have visited the Tomb."

"That Tomb may be ours but not in the way you would like, Telemachus," came Berengar's laconic comment.

"Come, come, my friend, this is not like you. You are usually far more optimistic about a challenge that arises."

"I have come into contact with the Sequani tribe. They are a tenacious people and do not take an insult lightly."

---

[5] The modern River Neckar.

[6] Gaulish name for the River Rhine.

"I do not doubt that but remember, according to the response granted by your prayers, it is they who must deliver the offence. Without that, we cannot move against them."

Telemachus smiled at the big man. He found protocol to the gods a tedious routine but a favour for a friend was another matter.

For his part, Berengar was at first unsure whether Telemachus was mocking him or reiterating a promise made. Yet on his experience of the commander's genuine qualities, he decided the last applied.

The next settlement they did come across on the Nikros was not so large that it could pose a real threat to the Telemachons and not so small that it could not provide the boats that were needed for transport. Berengar conducted negotiations and the matter was soon settled. They did not make an overnight stop. This was a relief to some villagers but a disappointment to others. Many young men were particularly taken by the attractive looks of the Greek women. Eight river craft were hired and Telemachus, with his fifty men, sat astride their horses on the riverside dock to see them off. The mounted company impressed the fishermen and traders and comments were passed. Eucleides and Thocero sat on Telemachus' left, Berengar was to his right.

The villagers assumed that Berengar led the company. He, after all, was the Celt. But as they viewed the men on their horses and saw quite clearly that Telemachus was dressed in a finely worked cuirass with its Greek design in the winged viper head emblazoning the chest, partially hidden under his plush red cloak, they began to perceive the truth. Berengar was a strong, presentable man but Ula's home-spun cloak could not begin to compare in value to the metal on the man's chest who sat next to him.

"What are they thinking, I wonder?" asked Thocero, noticing their stares.

"So long as they keep to themselves and do not attempt to interfere with us, it does not really matter," said Telemachus. "We will be gone quickly and we have not seen anyone ride from the village to inform others. There must have been questions about our intentions, Berengar. How did you answer them?"

"I told them the only thing they would believe if you were a Celt in this village suddenly descended upon by a large body of armed men."

"Which is?"

"That I had been sent by a chieftain from the north to recruit mercenaries for his army. You, being those mercenaries."

It was a good explanation, Telemachus judged and said so. "This place is far too small for them to risk losing people in a battle, whereas the gold we gave them for transport has secured a momentary trust."

"What could be troublesome is that we are splitting our forces," said Eucleides. "The majority of our men are going with us to the Tomb while the remainder are travelling with the women on these river boats."

"Don't worry," replied Telemachus. "Enough men are in those boats to afford the women protection. There is not sufficient crew in each boat to overpower them. I have told the captains we will be meeting with them further up the river after it joins with the Renos."

Thoughts to safety had not only disturbed Eucleides. It was also in Hebe's mind as she helped Ula on board their selected fishing vessel, a larger boat than usual but not meant for carrying passengers.

They stood on board, waiting for the last Greeks to embark and watching Telemachus with his mounted cavalry. Ula stared anxiously towards Berengar, pleased at least that he was in the front rank with Telemachus and could be easily seen. She raised their son and waved at him. He lifted his arm in response.

"He will be good? Yes?" she said in her imperfect Greek to Hebe, anxiety creasing her face.

Hebe put a comforting arm around her shoulders. "You mean safe? Yes, he will be safe, Ula. Don't worry."

As for herself, her eyes searched for Telemachus, her heart beating faster, not wanting him to leave. He was watching her and the last Telemachons moving up the gangplanks onto the decks; his men and their mounts chafing at the bit around him. His arm went up and it was meant both as a farewell to her and a signal to his companions. The horses were urged into a walk, next a fast trot and the company moved off.

When he had gone, Hebe felt his absence. He had a reserve in him which Hebe, knowing his history, thought she could understand. Once betrayed, it was difficult to put your trust in someone else. She should certainly know it. Having your own father sell you into slavery saw to that. He was a man who cared for nobody but himself yet the paradox was that he had surrounded himself with people throughout his life. Currently, he was on his fourth wife and fifth child, the previous three wives having died in childbirth or after enduring some peculiar disease. One went under suspicious circumstances soon after he had served her an anniversary meal to celebrate the day he had bought her from the slave market. He had blamed the oysters. It was curious how the gods allowed the worst to survive the best. What did they get from seeing these cold creatures – passionate only in their own selfishness – devastate the lives for those around them? Perhaps it was entertainment, laughing at the gross behaviour and cruelty on show such as performed in some depraved satire. Another thought, might it be a means for control, to keep humanity in the mud and remind mortals that they could never be better than the animals with which they shared this world and in many cases a lot worse?

Over there, riding away, was a man she could begin to trust. He was so different to her father and truly, all the men she had ever met. Not that she had picked lovers like olives from a tree. There had only been one to whom she had lent her heart. To remember him walking into that crowded slave market, coming right up to her, her heart hammering under ribs, thinking to herself that this was it, this was the point at which her life would get better, him buying her and them both walking out from the agora together. But a shocking thing occurred. He just looked at her, said not a word, showed not a single expression on his face – just stepped away and turned his back. All human love, by rights, should have died within her that day. Later, in going over it, she realised the nuances recognisable too, in her father. She must have been blinded to them at the time. It must be why her father had allowed him access to her; one serpent recognising another. A single moment in that slave auction stuck to her, a conscious memory on her part, an unconscious movement on his. She remembered how, when his eyes were on her face, his hand had gone to that part of his chiton at the waist under which, she knew, his money-belt lay.

She was a possession to be bought and sold. In that market a man had decided the expense was too great, just as her father deciding about her upkeep had consequently handed her over to the slave traders.

Intuitively, she regarded the men on the boat with her, searching for danger. She was relieved that the young man everyone had first perceived as Thocero's son was with them. It turned out that he was in fact Thocero's very much younger brother. Leonis was an open, approachable person with good humour written all over his face. He was diligent in his work, whether that was repairing boats, obtaining food or erecting a shelter. He was impeccably courteous to the women. The two other Telemachons with him were similar in their manners and could be trusted but of course in situations like this it was the unknown Celtic men on board – those controlling the boat – who had to be watched with care. Long-haired and moustached, blue spiralling tattoos around their arms and legs with one actually peering through a wavering flame mask, they spoke little, only communicating in guttural growls to guide the vessel. From what she could work out, the tattooed face who growled the most seemed to be the pilot. There were five of them. Hebe had small hope that the atmosphere would improve.

"Do you trust them?" she asked Leonis when they were a few hours into the journey. She felt free to speak because none of the Celts on board, apart from Ula, seemed to understand Greek.

"As much as I trust an untrained horse. But don't worry Hebe, we will be there to catch you if the horses buck – won't we my friends?" He prompted the other Telemachons on the boat who were within hearing distance and they all shouted back a cheer. The Celts muttered to each other in the background.

"How long will it take us to get to the River Renos?"

"If the wind continues to blow the sail in the right direction as it is doing now, we will make good time and perhaps be there in two days. That is what was promised when we hired the boat, anyhow."

"Do you think the crew will cheat us?"

"No," he indicated the other boats following behind them on the river, all within sight. "If they did that it would have to be an organised assault, ten individual sorties on ten different vessels. They do not want to lose the men or the transports that provide the village with food during the winter. We have yet to pay them half the hire money at the destination."

"Maybe that is when we should be most aware," said Hebe.

"Yes, I think we will be," assured Leonis.

Her misgivings continued however and were only intensified when she helped Ula to wash the baby and themselves in the river. The boats had moored after a day's travelling and having continued throughout the night. They were accompanied at a discrete distance by Leonis and two other Greeks. While she was in the river and Ula was at its edge with her baby boy, she thought she saw something move behind the bushes to her right. It was too tall to be an animal. Leonis could be heard talking with the others well away out of sight. She did not say anything to Ula, not wanting to frighten her. When she got back, the captain gave he a lascivious grin. More than ever, she hoped to get off the boat soon.

At the necessary time, after they had gone from the Nikros to the Renos, the Telemachons disembarked quickly, collecting themselves into an informal battle line. The village chief, who had travelled with them, took a final payment and then ordered the boats home. They were rowed down the river because the wind had dropped and not one Telemachon felt sorry for their leaving.

17
Moment of Truth

It was during the journey through what they thought was an easier part of the forest, although the ground was boggier, that they came across it. Little warning came except the distinct lack of birdsong from the trees. The quietness, a complete silence but for their own voices, was unusual. It made them subdue their own human chatter.

Melissa was in front of Tyracides. She suddenly caught her foot on a route and fell headlong through a bush, crying out.

Tyracides went through the canopy and reached down to help her up. A strange sound, half-way between a rattle and a gurgle, broke his attention. Something large was very near. He slowly turned his head upwards as the others behind him also broke through the greenery.

Ahead was something that was not quite a tree and then not quite a man-made tower. It lifted like a huge beech with branches spread but was a translucent white colour because the skin or fabric was not bark but bone. The shape was bulbous: each bump in the structure was a skull, hollowed eye pits rolling their darkness. At the base lay a rectangular entrance without a door. That strange sound that Tyracides had heard came from the living creature that was stretched before the wide entrance as if to guard it. It was a huge serpent but no such beast as this had ever been witnessed by Celt or Greek.

The yellow and black reptilian scales twisted around the neck to end in an avian head, wavering on its own fleshy pole. The eyes over the cruel beak glittering, darted this way and that. That sound, louder now, was coming from its open mouth which showed a forked tongue tipping in and out at a rapid rate.

A pervasive putrefying stench coloured the air, despite there being no fleshy remnants on the bones in the tower.

Pelos, Sostis and Faramund rushed to engage the beast, while Costus deliberately made a fuss over Melissa and Eris placed an arrow in her bow.

The creature also benefited from two huge humanoid arms either side of its neck that presently rested on the ground and made it look like a sphinx in shape. With these two scaly arms, it hauled its body forward and lunged the head towards Sostis.

Anticipating that the tongue would strike, Eris had released her first arrow and a juddering shriek emanated from the creature as its eye was pierced by the shaft.

Blood pouring from the wound, the monstrous worm reached out a hand in its pain and snatched Sostis up. The companions could see their friend's arms and legs protruding, writhing between the monstrous fingers. The worm squeezed him like clay and the grisly movement stopped. Eris shot another iron-tipped barb at the uninjured eye but the shaft flew harmlessly next to the creature's head. Seeing from where it had come, another hand reached out and caught hold of Eris as she was fixing a third missile to her bow-string. Faramund went forward and furiously hacked at the arm that was holding her. Tyracides ran forward with Pelos and attacked the other side.

Held high in the air and much closer, Eris used her advantage by firing straight at the other eye. The arrow was accurate and dug deep. Another wail rose up. The worm dropped both Sostis and Eris, seeking to tear both shafts from its eyes. Tyracides took his chance. He ran with all speed along the neck to a place where it was narrowest. His sword swooped once, twice and three times. The neck slumped and the head rolled off along the ground.

Faramund went immediately to Eris who had been flung into a bush. She was badly scratched and bruised but otherwise no bones had been broken.

Sostis, however, had given up his spirit and the body was buried where it lay, with the honour he deserved. They mourned the loss of such a brave companion.

After the silence, Eris was the first to speak. "Where are we?" she asked, looking up in wonder at the skeletal mouth to the tower of skulls. Not even Faramund knew. There had been no such place described in the lore of his land. He could only guess and make it a sensible one.

"It resembles some kind of tomb or monument."

"One that was guarded," said Pelos, "as they often are…. If there is something valuable inside."

"I have something here which might prove that to be true," said Tyracides. He was coming away from where the monster had fallen, his arms and hands covered in its gore. Hanging from his hand as he raised it to show them was a golden chain and at the end of it was attached a large bronze key. "Whatever this opens lies inside that tower."

Tyracides, Pelos and Faramund too, wanted the women to remain outside the structure while they explored within. Costus offered to wait outside and guard them. Melissa and Eris rejected this idea though, insistent that they should all go together into the tree tower. Costus thought that this would be better as there would be greater safety in numbers. He would remain outside to ensure that no dangerous miscreants would be following them through the doorway.

"You have just contradicted yourself," said Faramund, amused. "How can there be safety in numbers when there is only one of you beside the entrance? Anyway, I always thought that dwarves were most at home in a dark and spiralled world."

"I did not explore the shady interiors to my palace at Fol and I don't intend to start now," said Costus sniffily.

"Your claustrophobia will have to be overcome, Costus." Said Tyracides with finality. "Thanks for your willingness to keep our backs safe but it would be impossible to leave you here on your own. Your own eyes have seen the strangely formed beasts that roam this forest. We should go in together." Seeing that he was not going to get what he wanted, the dwarf rallied himself.

"Of course! What was I thinking about?" He drew his sword and made a few feints at an invisible enemy. "I will lead from the front," – here he stuck his chest out – "No more giant worms will attack us! Not if they don't want me to detach their heads from their loathsome bodies!"

"Like you did with the last one, Costus?" queried Pelos. The others laughed.

"Come then, my brave warrior, formerly a Grand Vizier and cobbler, let us go in to meet our destiny," said Tyracides. "Don't you go first though. I will just be happy if you place yourself behind me and guard my back!"

The surprise was that thinking it was a tower, they expected to go up after stepping over the lintel but what they found instead was a stairway which descended and broadened into the gloom. Raising his head, Faramund could see in the distance an aperture open to the sky. Round and round and up the inner well of the tower were climbing rows of skulls with faces showing inwards as those outside the structure faced outwards. With his practical mind, he wondered where the rain went when it fell into the tower and instinctively inspected the ground around his feet. The floor he stood on was dry enough and the answer lay in two channels cut either side of the stairway, running in parallel descent. Dry as yet, they were quite capable in feeding any drainage water to whatever was below.

And from below, they could hear the unmistakeable sounds made by a river in full flow, the reverberations multiplied by the rock and evident space surrounding it. They met each other's astonished gaze with incomprehension.

"Do we really want to go on?" Costus asked.

"Why not?" answered Pelos.

Costus kept his patience and temper. "Friends, you may have already noticed my aversion to such places but my feeling is no idle or simple repulsion – it is justly earned. My people have spent their lives underground, hacking out precious minerals from the rock and working it into objects for functional use or ornament. No-one knows more than they the dangers that can suddenly rise from subterranean passageways or fall with a wallop onto your heads."

"We at least owe it to ourselves to find the lock which this fits," said Tyracides, showing the key that now hung around his own neck, although on a greatly shortened chain. "We exchanged the life of its keeper for one of our own. Sostis would have wanted us to go on."

"Go on into what!" snapped Costus. "At any point we could reach a dead end. That river you hear below could lead us on a steady course but then drop into a black hole. The light we see at the moment is given by those oil lamps in their alcoves along the stairway but they could soon end and let me tell you, adventurous Telemachons, no night-time above the surface contains the utter blackness that can, in a blink of an eye, blot out your vision below."

"He has a point," said Pelos, dubiously. "Who built the tower in the first instance – this stairway, these lights on the wall which need to be replenished? Whoever it was I don't trust them, for the simple reason that any builders who use skulls for stones are not to be trusted."

"I agree with Pelos on that," said Eris, "and don't you think that there is something utterly banal in that key you are waving around Tyracides?" She liked him but she wanted him to use reason.

"What do you mean?"

"I suggest that if the worm was meant to guard something truly valuable, whoever its masters were, they would not be so stupid as to hang the key to that treasure around their guard dog's neck."

"It is not a key; it is bait," came Costus' assertive support.

At that moment a whirring noise could be heard from behind them. They turned to see what they thought was an open entrance to the tower being closed off by a heavy iron door that had slipped smoothly from above the rectangular space into thick metal runnels framing it. They rushed to the entrance but it was too late.

"Now we can start to worry," said Costus.

Pelos hammered at the skulls with his sword pommel but when it smashed through bone there was an uncomfortable clang of metal hitting metal.

"Iron walls!" he said in despair.

The others ran around the bulged circumference, testing the space, but found it hopeless.

"That has given us a partial solution to our dilemma," said Costus ruefully. "There is only one way out now – and that is in."

Tyracides took the key from around his neck as if to fling it down but then thought again and tucked the object into an inner pocket, ashamed that he had led his companions into what was turning out to be a trap. "Keep your swords ready and let's proceed with caution!" he told the others.

They descended the stairs for a short flight only to come to what seemed like the round floor of the tower. The stairway, however, continued through a large hole in the floor but the steps became metal rungs positioned in the rock. Light came from below.

Tyracides regarded the others' nervousness and prevented any inactivity by thrusting his body into the emptiness. "We have to go on!" he urged. They could do nothing but follow.

Once through, they found that the rungs took them down into a large concave space that became a tunnel, unusually lit by the daylight falling at intervals from shafts to the surface. It gave them some comfort.

"We can use this to get back up!" said Eris, standing under one. They crowded around her to inspect. It would not be easy.

"That is a very long way to go and there don't seem to be many places to put your hands or feet," said Pelos.

"It will take much effort, that is certain," said Faramund, "but certainly we have a definite exit route here and if it's not to be attempted now, we can always return should there be problems ahead."

"But you don't mean to go on!" exploded Costus. "This is the means for rescue and we have the strength to achieve it. If we continue, what will we do for food and sustenance?"

"Have you not noticed the bat droppings around us?" replied Faramund mildly. "We can still hear that water flowing nearby so we are not liable to thirst and there may be fish."

An argument began concerning what they should do next and came to an end with a reluctant compromise: everyone should explore a little further for an hour. If there was any obstruction or real danger encountered, they would return and attempt to climb up to the surface.

In a short time after they had moved on, the source for the running water they had heard was discovered. It was indeed an underground river which seemed to pop from nowhere to accompany the path they walked on. The current flowed quite strongly and when they bent down to taste the water, it was clean and sweet.

"What was that?" said Pelos, suddenly backing away from the edge. A shadow moved under the surface and was gone.

"Fish!" yelled Costus with delight, "See!" He pointed and indeed there was a small ball of silver fish bouncing from one edge to another.

"What I saw was larger than that," observed Pelos.

"Where you have small fish, you will find a bigger one snapping at their tails."

"This was no fish!" Pelos insisted.

The others ignored him to concentrate on the good news.

"Does this mean, Costus, you might consider exploring further?" said Tyracides, chancing his luck.

Costus paused. The tunnel underground had been a surprise to him. He had not expected so much natural light to be getting in. Surprisingly, he rather liked the subterranean level. It must be his ancestry at work. "We might go on a little further but only as long as the light remains in the tunnel."

"Good man!" Tyracides slapped him on the back.

"And what about those who so obviously maintain this place?" asked Pelos.

"We might be able to escape from here before meeting them. We need to keep our wits quick," said Tyracides.

"Whatever this place is, it is obviously important to those who use and keep it," said Melissa. "This tunnel must lead to some place or some thing which would be worth discovering."

"Isn't it more important that we get out of here and continue with our attempt to meet up with Telemachus in the north? This is just a distraction from what we should be doing."

"Not necessarily, Eris," came a mild interjection from Faramund, who was holding up a cord at the end of which swung a small metal ingot, one end piece shaped like an arrowhead. The others watched it swing. They were familiar with this sight; it had helped them on their journey many times before.

"Your lodestone," said Eris. She and the others noted how its whirling pendulous movement eventually came to rest, the sharp end pointing the way up the tunnel.

"Northwards – the direction in which we are going anyway. Who knows? It might be an easier path to follow down here underground rather than up there through the forest and its inhabitants."

His voice carried conviction but Pelos remained doubtful. "If we go, our pace needs to increase and we cannot proceed without some natural light. The last air shaft must be our exit to the surface." They all agreed that this was the best option and resumed their course along the tunnel.

It was a long hard slog. Very soon the torches disappeared from their alcoves and the declining but uncluttered path became a series of ascending and descending craggy promontories. The river itself could be touched in some places but fell steeply away at others. Costus was almost lost to it when they all had to jump a break that had opened up in the path. What was a gap that could easily be bridged by their longer legs nearly became his burial pit as he lost balance landing on the other side and would have fallen into the river below if Tyracides, going before, had not turned and quickly grabbed him. They pushed on. Hours turned to what seemed like days and the river, fortunately, did provide them with the necessary food and drink to carry on.

The surroundings changed. From what had been a partially artificial passage at the start, the rocks bearing the gouges made by many hammers and chisels, became a wide, natural passageway with confusing exit tunnels to the sides. Faramund was firm in his leadership, not pausing for argument while Tyracides' stern support ensured there was none. Tacitly, everyone accepted that they had gone too far to make a return; that line had been breached many distances ago.

Yet the air shafts persisted. Even in the spaces with the highest roofs there was still the comforting round crow above, with the light, a fallen marble column, beaming down.

Finally, the river itself disappeared over an edge into an iron grey mouth that slitted like a sneer from the rough ground ahead. The water dropped in a boil and a roar, refusing to provision them any longer and their spirits dropped with it.

But they continued forward without talk, knowing full well if they were to indulge in it the only result would be arguments and recrimination together with a whole lot of wasted time.

So they didn't stop. They forced themselves on despite weariness and aching limbs. Shortly after the vanishing trick played by the river, they were rewarded. Or thought they had been.

The tunnel came to an end in another wide space and this one in its far reaches revealed a stairway such as the one they had come in by. Light flooded the steps from above but beyond these was a darkened recess and from it there ran two armoured men with swords raised. By the look on their faces, they were not about to be satisfied in merely taking the Telemachons as their prisoners. There was hardly any time to retaliate, yet Eris managed to fit an arrow to the bow that always went with her and loose it at the first man. It pierced his throat and he lurched to the ground. The second man had reached Tyracides and was bringing an arm back to scythe his sword through the other's head. Tyracides saw a gap in the defence where the shield had not been kept tightly close and took his chance. He kicked viciously at the man's groin who squealed and folded up into a sitting position. Tyracides drew his own sword and without pause, stabbed him between the collar bones. He stepped away as the blood spouted and the man gasped his ghost.

The speedy onslaught left them all shocked and panting. Melissa was about to speak but Tyracides warned her with a finger raised to his lips and with the same finger pointed to the concealed area from which the two armed men had just sprung. Had he heard something? Another gesture from Tyracides and they all moved cautiously as one towards it, their weapons in hand.

When they came around the stairway foot, they found themselves looking at a door that was ajar and now they were certain that there was someone else behind it. From the gap into the immediate gloom came a strange luminous green light. A voice spoke.

"Hello! Is there anyone there? Apart from my guards of course and hopefully they are as dead as fallen leaves in autumn."

The speech was Celtic. Faramund had to translate but what struck everyone was the sound. The voice was projected as if through water, bubbles seemed to erupt, yet everyone understood it to be a young voice.

Faramund took over. "Why don't you come out to us?"

The young voice was irritated. "Did you not hear me say the word 'guards'? That is exactly what they are or were and I am their prisoner. So excuse me if you can work that one out by taking a small imaginative jump in your imagination and coming to the conclusion that I am manacled and unable to do that – which I am."

Faramund told the others.

"Does he think we are fools?" said Tyracides. "Even if he is a prisoner who is to say he is not being forced to entice us in by other guards?"

Melissa was fascinated by the voice. "Have you ever heard such a sound?"

Faramund put Tyracides' doubts to the prisoner who was beyond the doorway.

Another rising petulance of bubbles was the answer. "If you don't believe me, fair enough but just push that door wide so you can see in, won't you?"

Faramund moved towards the doorway. "What are you doing?" hissed Tyracides.

"No, it's alright I think but just make yourselves ready in case I am wrong."

He got to the wooden door, its grille in the centre and cautiously used his foot to move the obstruction on its hinges. Taking a quick step back, he enabled everyone to see what was inside.

The door swung slowly back all the way. As it moved, the greenish light grew brighter and there sitting on the floor was a large shape manacled at the wrists to the wall. The room was bare and there could be no hiding place for anyone else.

They were amazed.

"Have you ever seen anything like that?" said Eris.

What looked like a man was propped there, face towards them – a man because he had two arms two legs and a head. But beyond that the details diverted. The most obvious difference was in the skin. The green luminosity they had seen in the doorway was in fact coming from his body. It glowed a constant green light, powerful enough to clarify most of the room confining his large figure. A second surprise came in his face. Faramund had expected a young face for that voice he had heard but not a bit of it. This visage was old, the skin wrinkled and long whiskers drooped around a lipless downturned mouth and fell from the chin. Such a contrast between the elderly face and its young speaker he found very strange and not without a certain charm. That face though was definitely not human. He had seen heads like that when carefully peering into brown river water; they swam by completely engrossed in their own watery world, those goggle eyes fixed elsewhere on small prey in the weeds leading their long bodies on, sliding by under his gaze. This being belonged to the water. You could tell that by his webbed hands and webbed feet; the roughened scaly skin. He had hair: long thick strands around his head but no hair that Faramund had ever seen before; this grew like soft green ferns at the bottom of some strange pool.

Faramund's momentary assessment was broken by a gasp from Tyracides behind him.

"Danu! He is like Danu!"

And who should know better than Tyracides – the man who had swum against the river god in the Danuviad?

Although not understanding Greek, the creature's head lifted at mention of the god's name. "How is it that he uses our god's name with such surprise?" he asked Faramund, guessing that it was he who had spoken to him earlier. Faramund explained it to him while the others continued to gaze at the chained creature dressed in a simple robe.

When Faramund finished, Tyracides said simply, as if having a one-sided conversation with himself, "Only, Danu's skin did not glisten like that under the water."

The shape at the end of the chains urged the young Celt to translate everything and he did, also asking the creature, "What are we to call you?"

"Call me Goreth, the name I was given by my parents and tell your friend here that this luminescence from my skin is something natural to our people and can be turned on and off at will."

Faramund spoke to Tyracides and he replied, "Really?" but there was a nuance to his tone that Goreth did not like because in the next few moments the green light faded from his skin, allowing utter darkness to seep in. There was utter consternation from the others.

"Tell him to lighten up!" yelled Costus in his own Celtic tongue and almost immediately afterwards the room was illuminated by the now comforting presence of Goreth's body.

"We can't stop here much longer – surely there will be others to come after the guards we encountered," said Pelos. "Goreth needs to be released and quickly."

They checked his manacles which could only be released by unlocking a padlock. Pelos went out to the guards to search for the key but none could be found. He took the boots from one guard and brought them back into the cell to give to Goreth who duly tugged them on.

"They'll be no good unless we can get him loose from those chains," commented Costus.

"Wait!" said Melissa abruptly as she watched Tyracides investigating the chains again. "Tyracides, what about that key you found around the serpent's neck?"

Tyracides took it from his garment and fitted it into the chunky metal, muttering, "Why, by Zeus would they ….?" Before he had finished the sentence, there was a soft click from the lock and the hinge flew back, opening the manacles. Goreth pulled his hands away, rubbing his sore wrists.

"How long have you been here?" asked Faramund, helping him to his feet.

"Less than two hours. I passed by you under the river on my way here."

Realisation came to Faramund. He called out to Pelos. "You were right a while ago, Pelos. That was not a fish you saw in the river – it was Goreth."

Goreth noted the communication and guessed at its meaning. "My passing did not go unnoticed then, despite my swimming without these human rags." He held up his arms from which the robe draped as if that was even more distasteful than all the chains which had bound him. "You are lucky to have one who is so observant amongst you," he said, nodding towards Pelos.

"Yes we are but Goreth, how is it that you were imprisoned here? What did you do to deserve this?"

"Can you not see the answer in my face?" replied the creature. "You humans cannot tolerate beings who are different. Those who do not share your features or beliefs, you hunt from their homes and existence. The seas and rivers run dry of life and all land is emptied before your ravening desire for conquest and assimilation. Even while you do that you turn on each other and concoct destruction from bitter hatred.

My people are far older than yours, we arrived with the rising sun in a time before your time and a time of plenty. We kept to the rivers because that was where our arterial life lay: where we lived serene. But then you mortals came and our peace soon came to an end.

At first we were treated with wonder. Our likenesses were carved on your monuments. But that did not last. Hateful individuals amongst your kind provoked a fury against us and the sacred fires of our settlements were extinguished. Perhaps there may be one or two of us left, still wandering the forests in Europa. As indeed I have done since the burning of my own village two full moons ago. Yet it was rumoured that one settlement other than our own still survived and it could be found far to the north over the sea that borders this country you call Gaul. In another far country it lies, the land I think you call the Pretannic Isles."

Faramund translated his words to the others. They were all for taking him with them.

"He needs to cover his head," urged Tyracides, "otherwise he will find himself the first target in any conflict."

Faramund pulled his hood up. "Have your people got a name for themselves?"

"The Orsook," replied Goreth, "but amongst you men we were given another name, a name we did not feel insulted by – the Fish People."

"Goreth," said Faramund, "we are travelling north ourselves, hoping to reach the Pretannic Isles. Would you like to travel with us?"

"Yes, but I fear that to get free from this underground prison will not be as simple as you think."

"Do you know anything about it that you can share with us?"

"Those two out there," said Goreth, referring to the fallen guards, "wanted to take me up the stairway after they had brought me from the river. They hauled me along with them but we only got as far as the open doorway in the building up there. We were suddenly greeted with the sight of people battling each other – a full-scale conflict in progress. They dragged me back down, chained me and were about to return to the surface when you arrived."

Costus interrupted and translated his words this time. He was getting impatient to do something. "We cannot wait around for the final victors up there to come down and slaughter us all!" he added. It carried the conviction of common sense and everyone wanted to get to the fray, if it was still going on, to find an opportunity for escape. They were about to leave when Goreth put a hand on Faramund's arm and stopped him.

"Has he still got the key that freed me?" he asked, pointing at Tyracides."

"Yes, he placed it back around his neck – why?"

"When we came back down from above those guards were saying something about the Shrine of the Lock. I couldn't hear everything as they had left the cell and were deliberately lowering their voices. I have a feeling that this shrine they mentioned lies above our heads and that key might be even more useful than it has been already. Your friend would be wise to keep it safe and close."

"I am sure he will," said Faramund and spoke briefly to Tyracides. The other touched the metal at his neck as if to reassure himself that it was still there. Then he made his way out from the room to the steps. At the bottom of the staircase, he warned his companions.

"Whatever happens we must try to stay together and present a united front – protect each other!"

They climbed the steps quickly, eager to be out into the sunlight and fresh air, their former tiredness forgotten.

A dead body lay in the doorway of the building which enclosed the stairs. From the exterior came shouts, curses and the killing violence of swords in collision.

They peered from their safe haven into a melee of bodies squirming for advantage. By the number fallen already, the fight seemed to be in its closing stages. There were many soldiers on horses and it was apparent that they were overcoming those fighting from the ground. One cavalryman in particular caught Tyracides' eye. He had just killed a warrior who had attempted to run him through with a javelin and now was looking this way and that for another challenge or to go to a comrade wanting help.

There was something familiar in the way the man held himself on the horse, in that brilliant armour with the winged viper's head boldly struck at its front.

He grinned in utter relief and shouted his excitement to the others. "It's Telemachus!"

They were joyful at the news but remained careful in making an exit from their place of safety. Telemachus was less wary when he saw them. Leaping from his horse, he ran over to Tyracides and embraced him, then Melissa. Already the situation was coming under his men's control as they went about collecting the injured Sequani, tying their wrists and forcing them into a nearby building.

"We must move quickly," Telemachus shouted to them, "before reinforcements are sent from Dunsberg." During the battle, he had seen two Celts being sent away by a commander and they had rushed off.

The Telemachons gathered together and began to inspect the site. The few ordinary citizens, old men, women and children had already fled and Glauberg appeared to be deserted.

"Who is the little man?" asked Telemachus, amused, as he noticed Costus moving with them.

"That little man has a large talent," said Tyracides firmly. "Already, he has been a shoe cobbler and a powerful ruler in the space of one life."

"A powerful ruler only if he did not cobble his subjects and rule his shoes," remarked Telemachus. "And who is the man in the shroud?"

He had stopped before an imposing building which stood out only if for its remarkable size. Yet his gaze was fixed upon Goreth with suspicion and not without reason for Goreth was almost fully covered.

Tyracides thought he might as well get this over with and avoid wasting time in a spoken preamble. He looked towards Faramund, who nodded and said, "Goreth, throw your hood back."

The Orsook did so without hesitation.

There was an astonished gasp from the watching crowd as his head and face came into view.

Telemachus did not know which was more wonderful, the stone monument he was standing beside or the creature that had just revealed itself.

"We found him locked beneath the ground in that building from which we have just come," said Tyracides simply.

Under the sunlight Goreth's skin shone but did not exude that eerie luminous colour it had done in the tunnel. Standing there, surrounded, Goreth looked vulnerable – like a fish out of water.

Berengar stepped forward, "When I was last here, that building did not exist."

"Underneath it is a tunnel that leads all the way back to a city called Fol. We should know, we spent two days tramping its route," said Tyracides.

Telemachus was tempted to ask what was Fol and why was Goreth imprisoned but there were more urgent matters.

"We will talk about this later. For now, we must enter the tomb. We have had their god Danu's permission to enter because of their offence to us."

"I am not certain," said Berengar, "that a serious offence was given when they simply refused our request to pay respect to the warriors buried within."

"Well, I was offended," said Telemachus lightly, "and it was they who lost their temper when I showed it. Be that as it may, we will not damage anything within the monument and only take what is necessary as a fine for their insult."

Berengar was not seriously annoyed and did not force the point. They proceeded to the door of the tomb.

Telemachus was impressed by the two tall statues that stood on either side, guarding the portal. Wood. It was one of the major differences between these people and his own: their love for wood. Back in his own land stone was the basic building block for houses, places of worship and sites for administration. Stone endured. It fixed. Mighty forces had to be applied before it could be torn apart. That's why his people's monuments were written in stone; they could remind the future that it existed only because of the creativity and life that had gone before. Wood, over the years, rotted. It was temporary. But then, it seemed to him from what he had heard and seen in Europa that many of these Celtic communities were not permanent: shifting from one place to another, attacking and being attacked, their state was fluid. With them, defence was no defence – wooden ramparts, stilts on water. They needed to stay in one abode, think and build better, engineer their own safety. Find stone, you Celts and construct. Even when the lower part of the city had been invaded, Hellas could occupy its acropolis high up in the safe mountainous height of stone overlooking the invaders. For months on end, yes, beat them back too. The Celts liked their mountains but they did not use them properly. Some oppida existed on mountain tops and hills, it was true, like this Glauberg and Dunsberg not far away, but too few. More frequently Celts left elevated places to gods. He remembered sailing along the Danu and up the Nikros. Those curious stone megaliths occasionally circling the hill-tops. That was their one use for stone – to honour the gods – and these stone circled spaces were ruled by their Druidic priests.

Some of those men had more authority than the kings and chiefs who ruled over the tribes. He also knew that there was a sacred place in Pretannia in which huge monuments were situated. It was a flat plain filled with circular stone temples and where famed warrior lords were buried. People from all over Europa endured much hardship to travel there, give respect and make offerings. Feasts were given at the summer and winter solstices. The gods had marked the plain out as their own through markings in the ground, strange coloured rocks, air congealing to flames above the earth. The Celts moved their feet on that ground, half in dread, only food and intoxicating mead could help them to enjoy the presence of their gods and the sacrifices that were necessary.

So these thoughts flitted through Telemachus on seeing the grim figures set out as a warning either side of the door. Carved in oak, they were silhouetted sharply against the green grassy dome that was the tomb's roof. They presented as warriors guarding the entrance. One swung an axe from a standing position, the other, crouched, was shown plunging his long sword into someone, anyone, who dared to pass through the doorway.

"Berengar," said Telemachus, noticing that the doors were sealed and no lock was evident but comforted that they were made from wood and not iron. "Take some men and find something around here that will help to break those doors open." I'm testing his loyalty again, thought Telemachus but it had to be done to ensure that he wanted to be one of them, a Telemachon.

A little while later the Celt was back again with the others, hauling a cart. From the front of the vehicle poked a heavy column of iron that had been extracted from some building nearby. It was chained in to an immoveable position in the cart and everything behind had been reinforced so if pushed from the front, it would not break out of the vehicle. Telemachus realised immediately that Berengar intended to use it as a crude battering ram.

More soldiers were called up and they got their shoulders behind the cart. The wheels began to roll, the soldiers ran and at a shout from Berengar they released it and let it roll. The cart smashed into the doors. There cracked out a wrenched splitting sound and the wood cracked across but held. The men had to heave the cart twice more at the entrance before the ram burst the doors open.

Telemachus did not go straight in. He stood musing at the strange runic signs around the frame. He called out to Faramund who had to push his way past those gathered around him.

"Faramund, can you make out what these say?"

The young man carefully checked the symbols stalking across the door beam.

"It says 'Tomb of Orsek, High King over all the tribes of Danu.'"

"Is that all?" asked Telemachus, "Without threat or curse for those braking the seal?"

"None," replied Faramund.

Telemachus was dubious. "Nevertheless, we may meet with a spring-trap or a planned collapse once we enter."

"I don't think so, sire," said Berengar. "The tomb was opened on the summer solstice, once in the year. Select visitors were allowed in to view the body and then after they had left, the entrance was resealed.

"Who was Orsek?"

"Our great ancestor, the first king, lord over all that generation who first travelled the Danu and the other rivers in Gaul, settling on their banks."

"Was he a great leader?"

"The greatest in his time."

Telemachus pushed open the doors and the dim chamber lit up. It was a very large chamber and with Telemachus entered Eucleides, Berengar, Faramund, Tyracides, Costus and Goreth. Others were kept back outside the barrow.

A gold emblazoned chariot and a cart stuffed with goods for the after-life stood apart on one side of the room while next to the long, far wall, lay the body for whom this tomb had been built, suspended on a wheeled bronze couch, covered in silver leaf as reflective as water. The couch was an extraordinary length and the reason for that lay inside for not only was the man contained there a tall one but he was wearing a conical pointed hat fashioned in silver; figured representations of the sun and moon and starry constellations whirled around it. "It is as though he was buried yesterday," whispered Telemachus.

Tyracides called Costus over to look inside. "That is the kind of hat you were wearing when I first saw you at the court in Fol. What does it mean?"

"It signifies," said Costus, thankful that the couch was open-sided so that he could study the spectacle without help, "that this man was not only a highly regarded warrior and King but he was also an emissary to and from the gods – a worker of magic, the Druid for his people. He was given infinite trust by them." Costus stepped back and added, "In my case, the druidic crown was only a token, not the substance. It was the people who surrounded me that exercised substantial power – I was just part of their deception."

The receptacle's back wall was set with illustrated plaques showing a people in movement being led by a single figure away from a scene of battle and burning towers. There was something unfamiliar about the one leading and those who followed. It could be just the crudity or lack of skill on the metalsmith's part, thought Telemachus. He reached out to the long robe that covered every inch of skin, to the man's arm. With a shock he touched softness. There was still flesh on these bones. That is impossible.

By his arm rested a long, bronze sword with an amber hilt. Around his head he wore a helmet, almost Greek in style but for the fact that this hid the whole face and had simple features – eyes and an open mouth – engraved on the metal. It was in effect, a bronze mask.

Telemachus reached out again, with both hands this time. Berengar, aware of what he was about to do, remonstrated. "Sire, this hero's body has rested undisturbed for a thousand years. Is it wise?"

His chief continued without hesitation, ignoring religious custom. He did though take the utmost care in freeing the warrior's head from his helmet. The others craned in. As the metal lifted up, the soft ferny hair fell down and the face surfaced, bridging a thousand years. The gasp from the onlookers was audible, followed by a passive, stunned shock.

It was not the skull of a mortal man that had breached time and come to them, it was the full and fleshy face, supernaturally preserved, of the Orsook, of the Fish People.

Goreth, overcome, fell down on one knee before the figure and chanted words, whether it was in joyous thanks or a plea for forgiveness, no one knew. Faramund and Berengar found it as incomprehensible as did the others standing there.

The action made by Goreth restored awareness.

"Perhaps we should burn the body," said Telemachus.

"Burn it?!" shouted Faramund and Berengar together, incredulous.

"Don't you see what this means to the Celts? For countless generations they have been worshipping what they thought was a warrior king of their own people when all the time it was actually a hero from the beings who existed here a long time before they came. In their rage they will tear the body to pieces – at least we can give the king a proper burial, one carried out with respect and honour. The Celts will ensure that nothing remains of Orsek – if that was his name – they will not allow his body or this tomb to continue. The monument represents an affront to their identity and culture as this land's inheritors."

"But Telemachus," said Faramund, "aren't you missing something? Those illustrations on the couch – don't they tell the same narrative that belongs to the Celts' history: a people burnt out from one land only to move on to another and presumably take that by force from those who once lived there? Another point, by burning the king's body are you simply not just initiating the same cultural destruction?"

"What do you suggest then, Faramund?"

"I think we should put the helmet back and then let the tribe that arrives here decide for itself what they are to do. They may decide to take a look under the helmet as we have done but then go on as before in their old ways. If a crime is to be committed, let them be the ones to call it down upon themselves."

"We have come into this tomb so its sacred nature will have been desecrated for them. They will not restrain their own curiosity and if the tribes around here have hunted Goreth's people to extinction, they will certainly not stop at eradicating their last footprint from this land. But I will make myself agreeable to your suggestion, Faramund."

Meanwhile Goreth, hearing his name spoken, asked Berengar to translate. They conversed in low tones and it was then that Goreth asked for something he wanted to say to be translated into Greek. When he heard the translation, he stood up to the others and reiterated in perfect but bubbly Greek: "I fear that our history in this country will be obliterated but while I remain alive the true history of my people will be told elsewhere, in another homeland."

Berengar patted him on the back and said in Celtic, "We will tell that history as it should be told – truthfully – and together we will make a better history and a better future, my friend."

They continued to search around the tomb for other things of interest and found in a cauldron, under the lid, gleaming gold coins piled high. Telemachus decided to take a major portion but left the remainder. In another area they discovered, on a table, a bronze chest with a lock. On the lid was another runic inscription which Faramund read out: "Strong enough to kill the serpent that guarded me: strong enough to use what is inside."

The lock could possibly be opened with a key. Everyone looked towards Tyracides. He paused, unsure that what might be kept in that chest would be pleasant.

The key was in his hand and then pushed into the lock. It fitted. He turned the key and there was an audible click. The chest lid slowly lifted.

Tyracides was ready for anything, whether that was an inanimate stationary object or some missile aimed to project as soon as the container was opened. What he got was an alloyed fear in one way and a riddle for his mind in another. Why had something so small been held in such a large chest? The small pouch, tied at the neck with a leather cord was positioned centrally, beckoning him. On the inner part of the chest lid, another runic message. Faramund translated without being asked. "Cast into the river for new life."

Taking the small bag out, which slipped easily into his hand, Tyracides untied the cord and poured some of its contents into his palm. He stared at the hard white spheres that rolled onto his skin.

"Perhaps they are seeds," mused Telemachus next to him. He was glad to a certain extent. Tyracides would begin to build a reputation amongst the men, once they learned about him killing the serpent which had guarded the tunnel. If what had been contained in the chest was a grand warrior's weapon like that which lay beside the king, then he would have had to allow Tyracides to keep it. Telemachus needed champions around him, yes, but not rivals. Seeds were much less dangerous. "Take them. We may find them useful, although how anything could grow after being entombed here for a thousand years is doubtful."

Tyracides shut the chest, turned the key and placed the pouch in his clothing where once the key had been. Costus, nearest to the king's body and staring at it, suddenly cried out, "Telemachus, look!" Everyone turned and found something remarkable. As if the opening and closing of the chest had caused it, a change was occurring in the face on the corpse. Formerly, the skin that was slightly green in colour and was so fresh that it would not be surprising to feel a warmth there, was starting to pale. The almost kindly fixed expression that also conveyed a firm authority, loosened. That vegetal hair, glossy black streaked with grey, became molten and then aqueous, dripping into the coffin. The face dissolved too, dissoluting to a watery puddle as with the rest of the body and all that was left became a rich soaking gown, shoes, a helmet, a sword. The legend dominant over that tomb for a millennia, had left.

Faramund, lost in his own thoughts, did not seem to have noticed the hero's going. "Why strong?" he said, to no one in particular.

"What?" asked Tyracides.

"Why," repeated Faramund, "did that inscription imply that you had to be strong to use these seeds? What are they for?"

"We will find out in good time," answered Telemachus. "But if we don't move quickly there will be no need to discover the reason, as we'll be dead, executed for trespassing in this tomb. We have enough gold to help our expedition for the moment so let's get on." Actually, the commander had been disappointed by the gold found in the tomb, rather than having every soldier lending a hand to transport it, three or four would suffice. He began to consider the shrine but there was no time.

The urgency for them to part company with Glauberg was compounded by the news from a look-out that he could see a large force approaching in the distance, from the north.

18

Formus

The mass of horses galloping along the beaten mud road from Dunsberg to Glauberg made a slow thunderous sound which was echoed and then swallowed by the forest. This was an easy ride downhill. In front was Glauberg, its wood and stone buildings on a gentle incline sloping up towards the main feature, the green, domed tomb of Orsek. They would have to slow the horses, not only to suit the topography but also the events that had arisen there.

Two men rode at the head. One was heavier in his saddle, his was a stockier figure and the hands that held the reins were like bear paws. His face down to the nose was protected by his helmet's metal face-plate and the cheeks down to the chin by bronze flaps which rattled as he rode. His mouth remained unprotected, apart from the drooping moustache on his upper lip which swung to below the squared chin. He sat astride a black stallion, a proper horse not a mountain pony, one that had been bred to the highest quality by those in Dunsberg who had made their wealth on horse-trading and he, Corix, King of the Sequani and seated at Dunsberg, deserved the best mount in the Oppida. He cast an irritable glance at the man's horse that rode alongside him. It was pure white, another stallion, which predictably was trying to get ahead of his own. Where his Chief Druid, Formus, had got it from he did not know but it was typical that when his king had been sold the best animal in Dunsberg's stables, he had gone elsewhere and returned with one that was better. Corix had never asked him where he had got it, had not commented on it at all and likewise Formus never informed him. Their relationship was based on what they could keep from each other. It was an uneasy alliance but it was one that had to be maintained. There were only two significant clans amongst the Sequani, one ruled the druidic priesthood and therefore was able to place Formus in his position, the other held monarchical right over the land which he as the eldest son to this other clan's leader had ruled for three years. It was a tense contest constantly fought.

Corix understood where real power and influence over his people resided. In this person sat on his white horse not quite next to him, its head a full neck-length in front of his own black stallion's. It made him fume inwardly. He might have his people as the soldiers, the strength to defend their land and to conquer and extend to other territories but it was a strength lent and not given. Real strength – the hearts and minds of the Sequani tribe – was made over by them to the gods and the priests. How he wished for such power and influence.

Yet, Corix had been taught his history well. Generations ago there had once been an attempt by a Sequani monarch to wear both the secular crown and the druidic Golden Hat but the coup had failed and the tribe came to the brink of annihilation through civil war. Fortunately, the gods knocked some heads together and an agreement was made. The two incumbents removed themselves from their positions and were replaced by others. War, the most dreadful kind, had been averted.

Events happen and their history told but human beings have a mania for ignoring their application to the present. It seemed to Corix that there were two kinds of people: those who were self-aware and learned by the mistakes made by them and others and then there were the blindly ignorant, only pushing selfish wants and who would justify the killing of a newly born innocent baby to satisfy their own egoistic desires. Of the latter, such a one was Formus. It might have been the situation in the historical record that a Sequani king had tried to monopolise all power for himself but there was nothing to suggest that a similar revolt could not be staged again, only with the players and roles changed. Formus was manipulative and ambitious enough to attempt sole leadership over the tribe. His malice had become clear in the manner he had pursued the Orsook.

It had taken years to extinguish those people, if they could be called people. He had voiced his support for the campaign to purge their sacred land of them. They were an offence to the gods – actually claiming that their culture had existed in this country long before the Celts had arrived when everyone knew their origins were in the lakes and mountains of the hoar-frost islands far to the north. Oh, they might have presented themselves at *about the same time* as the Sequani who had been brought here by the god Danu but their outrageous lie deserved a righteous punishment. So he had led the attack on their settlement and killed many in the fight. Those that survived he had handed over to Formus, thinking that the latter might carry out the usual practice, sell them into slavery and use the proceeds for building the shrines and temples. Later, he came to learn that this was not what had happened. The druid had made it his own vicious pleasure to torture the victims, forcing them to renounce the gods they worshipped, idols created in their own false image. Only a few renounced but met their end anyway. Corix got to know the limit to Formus' cruelty from this episode: there was none. He was a man without any merciful inclination whatsoever. Yet this in no way made Corix afraid. His opposition was guided to become less blunt, more tactical.

The latest dissension between the two involved the very destination for which they were riding.

Glauberg was a holy place to the Sequani. For as long as he could remember, the clans had sent family members to the High King's tomb and to the shrine so that they might take part in the ritual observances and respects, particularly at the summer and winter solstices. The festivals could become uproarious: much mead and wine was drunk; boasting tales told about brave deeds in battle and the hunt came from the warriors; epic myths sung or chanted by the bards. That was in the more peaceful times – when war with other tribes was happening, the captured prisoners were garrotted or beheaded, shedding an altogether grimmer light on the festival.

The climactic moment for these ceremonies was always the opening of the tomb when Formus, as the high priest organising them, would enter the monument while drums were beaten and the spiky headed carnyxes blared the echoing call. His reappearance would be announced by him brandishing Orsek's great sword and in the war years he continued on to swing it down and lop the heads from the prisoners' helpless bodies.

Very few people were ever allowed to go inside the tomb. Formus, one or two attendant priests and a few wealthy aristocrats who had given significant gifts to the shrine. He himself had been granted entry once, at the finale to his coronation. His disappointment had been immense when he found himself inside the tomb. Somehow it lacked the grandeur that should belong to a hero's resting place, particularly this warrior.

He had been so dismayed by the experience, wondering in part about the burial he would get if this was how a renowned warrior and first king's grave was marked that he had made an unforgiveable mistake. A few months later, he had mentioned it to Formus. To his surprise the Chief Druid agreed and after a time came back to him suggesting a solution. He thought that the answer was to move Orsek's body north to Pretannia. The destination would be the Great Plain of the Stone Giants – that boundary land between this world and the next which all Celts across Europa would like to visit once in their lives. No greater honour could be given to the First King. Formus had already sought and gained the support he required from the other druids, both here and in Pretannia.

This was not good. Not for Corix in any way and not for the tribe. How could their festivals take place without the physical presence made substance by Orsek's body? The rituals would be powerless. Without the hero, too, the grip over the land would be weakened – his remains there gave a glorious record, a reminder of what had been accomplished in the past and could be achieved in the future. He gave them strength. In essence he was the Sequani tribe. These were the arguments Corix used to dissuade Formus from what he proposed. One, the king was sincere about. It did worry him that the religious festivals would be missing an earthly link. In wanting a bigger tomb for the High King, he was hoping that those hearts and minds belonging to Formus and his druids could be gradually weaned away to look more favourably on secular kingship itself. There was no denying the power contained by Danu and the other gods but their interests would best be looked after by Corix, rather than the priests.

Formus dismissed his reasoning. He said that by conveying Orsek to the Sacred Boundary, the standing of the Sequani tribe amongst all Celts would be greatly enhanced. Spiritually their hold over the country would be strengthened by their champion claiming a grave memorial overseen by the Stone Giants.

Formus was holding back. He did this at times but it was even more certain at this moment. Corix was well aware that Formus wanted to improve his standing amongst all the druids in Europa. These people travelled to each other's festivals as guests and ambassadors. Within their tribes they had the authority to start a war with another one or indeed end it by means of oracular prophecy. So Corix found it no surprise that he would use Orsek's remains for his own gain. Formus' interests were aimed above the Sequani but not towards the sky gods as they should have been. It was the personal influence with Celts everywhere that he wanted to extend.

Therefore, that was no puzzle. The difficulty in this suggestion was the ease with which he was prepared to see the High King removed from his own land. Formus had built up a reputation over the years in his position as the protector of the High King's body and its tomb. He was the only one allowed to touch the body – no one had done so apart from each appointed Chief Druid for a thousand years. By removing the hero's body to another place far away, it was as if he was saying that this land and that particular history of the Sequani was not important. When Corix had questioned what would happen to the tomb, Formus replied that two other kings from the more recent past, one being Corix's great-grandfather, could be installed there.

Corix racked his brains, trying to remember the tomb's interior as it had appeared all those years ago at his own coronation. Of course his attention had first been focused upon the king's head – he was utterly disappointed not to see the face as the rumour had it that the body was so magnificently preserved and the corpse itself was completely covered in that rich purple dyed material – a cloth he had never seen before; it shone so in the flame light. His attention had slipped to those figures on the couch's interior. They were suggestions for human bodies really, not substantial in detail. The artist had not been terrifically skilled in his representation: heads slightly out of shape, eyes overly large. People were fleeing from enflamed battlements and a toppling city in one plaque, travelling in boats on a river and curiously swimming alongside them in one more, building a city anew in the last.

Corix forced himself to think about Formus. What was he trying to do? Usually if you moved something about such as treasure and that was what Orsek represented to the Sequani – a tribal treasure with incredible value – you were trying to hide it. How did this link in with Formus' other obsessions: his antipathy to the Orsook for instance? The Orsook. Figures on a couch interior. A High King's helmeted face. A merging together of ideas so sudden, so precise, the utter realisation made him gasp.

"My King," shouted Formus, turning his head back over his left shoulder, "are you alright?" The voice carried above his mount's galloping.

"Yes! Yes!" replied Corix with added testiness.

"Would you like us to slow the pace?" The comment just bordered on a sneer.

"No, not until we get to those trees."

But even when they had got to the woodland, Corix did not want to reduce speed. It was imperative that they get to the tomb and for him to enter it, despite expected protestations, at the same time as Formus.

When they got to Glauberg, their quarry was gone and they found the sacred site, as expected, victim to a raid by a large force which had completely overcome the small duty guard positioned there.

"Thanks to Danu that the shrine remains safe!" called Corix, leaping from his horse, "But see! The tomb!"

A door littered the ground in broken pieces and the battering ram which had authored its destruction, lay redundant beside a shattered entrance.

"Lord Corix!" yelled Formus, pulling his horse up and dismounting hurriedly. "You don't mean to enter the tomb?"

"Of course not!" said Corix, standing aside from the doorway in a quick movement, his hand held out to usher the druid in. "There are probably still raiders inside waiting for us. Would you like to go inside and deal with them?"

The king could rely on the cowardice that played an essential element in Formus' character. The High Priest hesitated.

"No? Well then," continued Corix, "allow me to forage them out." With that he drew his sword and went in.

His practised military awareness had served to inform him that no raider was to be expected, either in the tomb or anywhere else in Glauberg. They had all left earlier but would not be so far away.

Formus made himself follow the king into the tomb. He had taken a small dagger from his belt.

Inside, a cauldron lay on its side, some gold coins sparkled within. "They must have panicked and left quickly when they knew we were coming or otherwise they would surely have taken it all from the pot," said Corix. He moved out to the High King's corpse. His eagerness was obvious but Formus did not comment. They simply stared in dismay at what was there. The drenched remains of the King's body presented a poor spectacle.

"What have they done?" muttered Formus. His shock was pretence. He was actually pleased about what had been done. Now the proof that Orsek was not the first High King of the Sequani, the first Celt to settle in those lands but instead a river creature close to Danu's heart, leading his people to claim this country for their own – that evidence had been destroyed totally.

It was the only benefit from this ransack, thought Formus. The consequence it brought was that he could no longer carry out his plan to make Orsek a holy relic to be buried on the Great Plain. The idea had been a long time in the making, certainly longer than Corix believed. Now his ability to deliver that relic had been severely limited and his reputation amongst the Chief Druids in Pretannia would suffer. Yet another danger to contemplate was that someone, or some few, in the band of tomb robbers had seen Orsek's face. If the High King's true identity became known, it wouldn't be long before the Sequani would surmise correctly the reason why he as chief Druid had pursued the Orsook with so much determination. It must not happen.

"They have made the greatest insult against our people and have shamed us," continued Formus, answering his own question. Corix watched him calmly, suspecting where this was going to lead. "If we stand by and do nothing, soon we would have all the other tribes riding down on top of us to take our land away." The king could not argue. He knew the tribes living around the Danube, the Nikros and up in the mountains. Any evident weakness would attract them like flies around a rotting carcass.

"So, we go after them?" said Corix.

"And destroy them," affirmed Formus.

One of their own men appeared at the tomb entrance and addressed Corix. "Sire, we have captured one of the robbers. They left him, thinking he was dead but he had been knocked unconscious."

They went outside and found a Telemachon with his head hanging low, dripping blood and groaning as he was held by two Sequani.

"We need to find out who these desecrators are," said Corix. One guard pulled the prisoner's head up by his hair. Under the flowing blood, eyes closed, Demaraton's face could just be seen. The head was dropped again.

"I already know something about them," replied Formus.

"Really? How did you come by that information?" Corix was impressed.

"A friend of mine, Thorus, the chief amongst the druids on that part of the River Danu along which these people sailed in their trireme."

"Trireme? Greeks!" Came the unbelieving cry from Corix.

"They call themselves Telemachons, after their leader and their ship."

"How did they manage to pass through the tribes down there without being taken?" Corix had heard that Greek traders ventured along the Danu and even as far as the Nikros but this was the first time in his thirty-four years as a Celt that he had heard about a Greek war trireme sailing upon the sacred Celtic rivers.

"It seems they gained goodwill by setting up contests which involved themselves and all the tribes in the region. They named the event the Danuviad."

"Fools! Fools!" exclaimed Corix. "They offer their guest-friendship without limit and the Greeks have tricked them into granting safe passage. Then that travel without hindrance ends up here – some of our best men killed and our High King's corpse obliterated. Did your friend not suspect this: could he not have warned us sooner?

"They lost track of them at Donau. Their claim was that they were heading north and attempting to set up a trade route, promising to return with tin and other goods to benefit the settlements they had sailed through."

"Their intentions are certainly not that now. No Celtic oppida would allow them back after this. When did you learn about them, anyway? Corix's tone was harsh.

"A few days ago from a messenger. But there was no way I could suspect that this was on their minds. Isn't it the height of stupidity to be in the middle of your enemy's country and with a much weaker force to rob and injure him? What can they expect from that but to be surrounded and annihilated themselves?"

"The need for gold must have been desperate," said Corix.

"This claimed intent for trade was a ruse. That is plainly not their motive."

The hanging prisoner groaned.

"Take him to the chief's house and secure him – I will be along soon," Formus ordered the guards and then, after they had gone, to Corix, "Whatever that man knows, we soon will. One of my slaves is from the east and understands Greek to be able to translate."

"I would have thought a scream is understandable in any language," commented Corix drily. "Do we really need to waste time here – wouldn't it improve our chances for catching them, if we started the pursuit immediately?"

"My friend, Thorus, believes that they are making for Pretannia. What I suggest, my lord, is that I hand-pick some brave warriors from Dunsberg and with them go after and punish these tomb scavengers. It may mean that I go to Pretannia itself. If so, all well and good because then I can visit my sacred brothers at the Plain of the Stone Giants and set up a memorial to our High King Orsek."

Corix studied the High Druid, wondering, as ever, what he really desired. The small thin frame, the fine, immaculate black hair and beard decorated with cords, blue ritual tattoos wriggling down his bare arms: all denoted a tidy vanity to disguise his unruly ambition. Ceremonial washing kept him cleaner than the poorer Celts but he was tough, not soft. All that religious washing, thought the king, could not remove the blood of the Orsook from his hands. This priest was a natural killer. He was also the same age as Corix and had travelled more widely than him, making powerful allies amongst his holy brethren. The time might come when the High Druid could consider that the Sequani might be better off without their king. Altogether, mused Corix, Formus was a dangerous rival and his absence was only to be welcomed.

"Of course, you might come too," offered the High Priest. Then before Corix could answer, "But that would leave the kingdom without its king and protector. It is perhaps best that you stay here."

The king was provoked by a condescension in what he said but kept silent. Formus took this as agreement. He brought out the small dagger which always went with him as a useful tool for sacrificing animals in religious devotion. His sharper stare scrutinised the iron blade: its cutting ability was quickly assessed and found satisfactory. Opening his hand, he showed Corix the handle – gold wire was moulded over it to look like thin rope wound laterally around the stem, the pommel was a red haematite stone while the bronze cross-bar tips ended in two fierce dragon heads back-to-back, their ruby jewelled eyes shining.

"I love this," said Formus. For a moment, the king wondered if the spoken words were for him or the druid was having a conversation with himself.

"It is a fine-looking blade," Corix nodded.

Formus raised his head and the eyes in his face seemed to stare through him. They were blank.

"No, you mistake me," he said and then expression returned to his voice and face while his hand closed around the handle.

"It is not the dagger's artwork that pleases so much as the function. That is what excites me. I press this tip against certain parts on a prisoner's body and then into them and that man or woman will jabber away their innermost lives and associations. Sometimes all I have to do is bring the knife to within a hair breadth of that spot and the same result is achieved." Formus frowned. "But if that happens, it is far less stimulating." He shrugged his shoulders. "When they have blurted all their secrets, I stick them anyway."

Corix had stared into the eyes of seemingly demented opponents in the battle terror all around. They had seemed to be inspired by blood-lust and no doubt his appearance to them was exactly the same. But it was no passion for killing that motivated either him or those others: it was fear and self-preservation. To hear these words from a man who would always be an onlooker at those battles, who got his pleasure using a knife in the peace of a half-darkened room, made his gorge rise. He sinned the weapon he carried, blasphemed against the gods of war.

The druid stood up putting his blade away, for the moment. Corix raised himself too. He was thankful that the priest was smaller. Sometimes he sensed that the other was made uncomfortable by their physical disparity. He tried to encourage that feeling by putting his hand on the priest's arm as if to restrain him. Formus looked up, querying.

"Keep me informed," said the king and squeezed his arm a little harder than was necessary.

"Naturally, my lord," replied Formus, although both knew that it would be something that Corix would get to hear about but never everything. As if he thought he had not done quite enough for the king, Formus said, "I will gag his mouth so that the screams cause less disturbance." He left.

Corix would comply with the High Druid's wishes. The Greeks – these Telemachons – could not go unpunished; that was certain. Yet he would choose the men to go with Formus and they would certainly not be his best warriors. It appeared that the tomb raiders had no more than a hundred men in their fighting force.

Well, he would only grant an equal number to Formus. He could get additional reserves from his fellow druids in Pretannia if he wanted them. Corix was not prepared to send a substantial part of his army off to leave the homeland weakly defended.

That might have been in the king's mind but when they returned to Dunsberg and told the people what had been done at the High King's Tomb, they were met with a furious response. Formus could have had many more volunteers for his punishment squad than Corix had been prepared to give him. It took all of the king's persuasion in reminding his people that there were other dangers from the Aedui tribe and the Helveti to deal with, before the situation was calmed. So, in fact, Corix did have to give some of his best warriors to Formus in order to keep the numbers of those leaving small. There was a reciprocal benefit. Those particular soldiers wanting to go were religious fanatics and in any serious matter for placing their loyalty, they would have opted for the druid rather than the king. Best then, that they did go.

19
Destruction of a People

Formus came away from his dead prisoner, having learned everything he needed to know. All about Telemachus and where he had come from. All about the journey along the Danu after the killing of the Psychezoion, the Games at the Danuviad where the Telemachons proved themselves champions; how the woman, Melissa, was abducted before they had got to Donau and subsequently the Telemachons divided. He was told in painful shrieks about the attack on the Tomb of the High King at Glauberg and how the Telemachons had come together again. It was at this point that the man's panted narrative became much more interesting. He explained that the search party had not only brought back Melissa but also two other people. One was a dwarf and the other by his description was an Orsook.

This news had come unpleasantly to the High Druid. He thought that every one of those miserable creatures had been eradicated by the Sequani soldiers under his direction. Why had this particular Orsook joined the Telemachons to travel north? Was it simply because he had nowhere else to go or did it mean more than that? It could be that there were more of his kind living in the Misty Isle. Yet none of the Pretannic druids that he had met could tell him there was an Orsook settlement on the isle. But it was a big country. The priests knew more about the land and people over the sea in Gaul than they did about what lived in the mountains further north in their own home. There was little real interest about the creatures he described and their curious webbed hands and feet. One or two put forward the view that this probably resulted from an insular community not welcoming fresh blood into the settlement: it was well known that deformities could occur in such circumstances. Formus had argued with little result and then decided to keep quiet. There was poor reward in stirring up antipathy towards himself when he had worked so long and hard to develop these alliances in the first place. They would only change their minds if they saw the evidence for themselves.

The Orsook, called Goreth by the prisoner, could provide that opportunity in himself or with the discovery of the Orsook village he was clearly intending to join.

If the Pretannic Celts were not to be engaged over the presence of these creatures in their lands, the Sequani Gauls surely would be.

During the next few days, Formus moved from one Sequani village to another with his soldiers, gathering support. By the time he was ready to pursue the Telemachons, his volunteer army had swollen from one hundred warriors to five times that number. He was careful though, to keep about him the original recruits from Dunsberg – they became his personally favoured bodyguard whom he could rely on as he knew each one by name and they saw him as a communer with the gods.

The High Druid relied on this loyalty and in particular on two close advisors: one a former slave taken as a child in a tribal conflict with the Helveti tribe and who had worked himself up to a trusted position in Corix's army. His name was Artemius and it was only in the last few days that the king realised where the captain's own trust was actually placed. But again the king was wrong. Artemius, after long lessons learned in his slave childhood put trust only in himself and – because they were so fickle while he possessed a surprising sense of humour – in the gods. His attitude to the druid was a feigned respect and no one around who thought they knew him, doubted that it was genuine. Artemius understood opportunity when it was offered and did his best to deceive and please. With Formus he had developed something like an easy friendship and could say things that Formus would tolerate from only one other. That was the Lady Andraste, noble of the Sequani tribe, whose residence was situated in Dunsberg but who, since the death of her second husband and the marriage of her third and youngest child, travelled tirelessly from one place to the next, overseeing her land and ensuring that it was farmed properly.

She was a formidable woman, strong in bone and mind. Despite her forty-one years she was still attractive with a piercing green gaze and a thick plait of hair coiled into a single cone on top of her head. How she had come to meet the High Druid and where, was a complete mystery, almost as mysterious as the fact that they had soon become lovers. His innate cruelty was matched by her fiery temper and so either by deed or wish, he chose not to reveal that side to her. Instead, at those times he could not supress his urges to hurt, he used other means for gratification.

These three then, were talking together in a house given over to them in the last village. They had succeeded in recruiting yet more warriors to the army they now controlled. Artemius thought it time to discuss the situation more openly.

"Why are we using all this time to recruit, Formus, when by now we could have easily overtaken the Telemachons? It doesn't seem like a proper chase to me."

The druid from his sitting position around the fire looked up to the smoke disappearing through the central hole at the apex of the curved roof. His head moved quickly, beard cords swinging. Artemius was reminded of a bird, a hawk on a tree branch, ever watchful, ready to fly.

"What if I told you, Artemius, that my intention is to destroy the Telemachons and their new friend, the Orsook, but not necessarily on this side of the Tin Sea?"

Artemius saw Lady Andraste through the flames opposite. A half-smile was on her lips, her head turned towards the druid. She knew.

"My answer would be that I believe once we are on the Tin Isle, it won't be just the Telemachons we will be chasing."

"Correct," said Formus, lowering his head now to meet the other's gaze. "Do you realise how big that island over the water is? How much land lies there for the taking?"

"It might be large," replied the warrior, "but ours is far greater and there is more to the east."

"Larger perhaps," agreed the druid, "and full of forests."

"Exactly – wood we can use to burn and produce heat for warmth or cooking and to build boats."

"We do that and we clear land but it is not enough. You have lived here all your life – surely you have wondered why it is that the tribes here are in constant conflict? It comes down to the land, land that is not cleared fast enough to produce the food for our growing population. Pretani is different. There are forests, yes, but more space is available for growing crops. I have seen it with my own eyes. And the inhabitants are fewer and cast out wider around the island. If land or food was in short supply, how could the Plain of Stone Giants exist?"

This was true. Artemius like other Celts in Gaul had heard about the great feasting and revelries that occurred there twice in the great annual journey of the sun. For those willing to make their own trek from Gaul, the food was free.

He began to consider his own attitude in all of this. What Formus seemed to be implying was a move northwards, a change of home. He was not averse to that. Still young in years, Artemius lacked a wife and family. He had thought about leaving before but he had not imagined going north.

"If we want land, Formus, why not go east and south? Take it from the Greeks?"

"I am not afraid of battle but those lands are even further away and the Greek cities can raise large armies. We cannot settle and work new land with dead men."

"The Greeks are led by a Macedonian king called Alexander," added Andraste. "He has forced a settlement with Celts to the north of his country – they are too afraid to attack him."

"We have to be realistic about what can be achieved," continued Formus. "I have a large force behind me now but it is not enough take on an army of thousands."

"So this business with the Telemachons and Orsook provides an excuse to gain admittance to the Tin Isle with a large military force?"

"Oh, I am completely serious about punishing the Telemachons for what they did to the High Tomb and for pursuing the Orsook," said Formus with a touch of anger.

"The point is," came Andraste's soothing tones, "We have friends in Briton who would welcome us, especially when they know that we are chasing Greek thieves who have plundered the monument to our High King."

"Greece is not our natural homeland. Briton is the land our ancestors travelled to over a natural causeway that bridged the Tin Sea."

"And I always believed that Gaul was our homeland," said Artemius, not restraining the irony in his voice.

The druid retrieved his cup of broth from close to the fire and took a sip. "Artemius, we are a people who have always moved from one place to another over the generations. From river port to mountain fort to flat farmland. The motives for that have usually been hunger or a battle lost and consequent threat of enslavement. Up to yet in our own lifetimes we have probably been reasonably lucky. We have not lost a major battle and we have not needed to uproot ourselves. I say 'we' but I am well aware that you yourself have not been so fortunate."

"That is right for myself Formus but how can you say that your people have lived their history in continual flux? What about Orsek, the High King, does his tomb not show that he has been here for a thousand years? What is that if it is not stability, history, a solid homeland?"

Formus, for a moment, considered telling Artemius the truth. Although it would have won the argument, Formus himself would have sacrificed his position. It was impossible. Not possible for several reasons, not least being the motivation for his pogrom against the Orsook.

As if reading his thoughts, Artemius raised another matter. "Where do the Orsook come into this – why is it that we have enslaved them and sent them away? From what I heard they were a peaceful people who were not interested in disturbing others."

Inwardly Formus laughed at the man's naivety concerning the fate of the Orsook. But then his ignorance like so many others was what resulted from the druid's own ingenuity. The Orsook village had been as far away from Dunsberg as you could get without leaving Sequani territory altogether. The soldiers he had used had come from nearby Celtic settlements, he did not use his own fanatical supporters in Dunsberg – although they would have exulted in such a deed – because they were too near the court and the public centre of the country. The king had to be involved of course and just as speedily removed from the conflict area once it had ended. The defences raised by the Orsook had been pitiful. They were probably relying on the nearby river if attacked but Formus had made sure that exit was obstructed.

Afterwards, he had marvelled at how easy the eradication had gone. He was expecting some difficulty in trying to engage the Celtic villages with his plan. It was wonderful how enthusiastic they had been. Rich payment and the promise that they could keep anything looted from the Orsooks did not a little to inflame their willingness. The king's presence after the battle was a bracket, a brief secession in the violence for the Orsook prisoners. With him gone, the overseeing Celts abandoned themselves to an orgiastic slaughter culminating in the prisoners being piled high and incinerated.

So Artemius would have known nothing about this. Unfortunately, Corix got to know. One of those very same Celts, thinking he could make more gold from the situation and suspecting that the king was being kept deliberately uninformed, had travelled the long distance to the court and told him. After that it was shame that kept the king's mouth shut. As for the villager – he returned home and on the very night he returned his house was burnt down with him, his wife and three children inside it. Both villages got the message. Shame and fear were tools even more powerful than the divination equipment kept in the High Druid's bag of tricks. Right now Formus had to keep this very effective warrior on his side so he told him something he could believe.

"The Orsook were not so peaceful as you have been told, Artemius. I am somewhat reluctant to tell you this because you were born from the Helvetii yourself but the fact is that your tribe were preparing to encroach on our territory and to move the boundary of theirs forward. The Orsook were living near to that line and about to join the Helvetii against us. That is why we had to act." The druid paused to let this sink in. There it was again, he thought, that useful little tool of shame. More than ruminating on whether the information was true or not, Artemius would be more concerned with the presumed guilt of his own original tribe, the Helvetii. It was time to direct his attention away from the Fish People.

"Now look, Artemius, what I want you to think about is this: even in your short life how many times have we, the Sequani, had to deal with incidents on our borders? Too many. If it is not the Helvetii then it is the Aedui or the Senones tribes. We are constantly attempting to protect ourselves. Do you agree with that?"

"Yes."

"Then what is your solution because if you do not have one, I do. It is to set up a colony elsewhere. The Greeks do it, so do the Etrurians, then why can't we? I have already spoken with the king. He favours the idea and all of those who will be journeying with us are wanting to set up a new colony as well." Actually this was not quite true. Corix would be told at the time of departure. Formus anticipated no objection from that quarter. The king would be glad to see his High Druid depart, even if it meant losing several hundred fierce warriors. Then he might be able to absolve the destruction of a completely innocent people from his conscience.

"Will you be coming with us, Artemius?" asked the Lady Andraste.

"I will be glad to do that. I have always wanted to see the Stone Giants of the Great Plain."

"Your first sight will probably be of Dubras when we cross the Tin Sea," said Formus, getting to his feet, "that is the first port of call for those wishing to cross into the country."

Artemius got up with him and now the certainty of what he was going to do came as a relief. For too long he had struggled with his differing tribal origin while living amongst the Sequani. The rise to his present position in the army had only come with the unfailing number of Helvetii writhing at his sword's tip: the doubters were satisfied for the time being but no matter how many men he killed, the doubt continued to survive. Only by placing a sea between himself and the tribe that had given him birth would he gain true acceptance from the people he had adopted.

20
Wrath and Reconciliation

Condensed in water: an evolute in water. Then the flood snaps at bearing the bundled, brittle life. Muscular spasm and pain press out the essential wail – a siren for birth. My essence is water. Liquid fire that rolls a current through the arteries and pumps a heart. Look at my hands. Look at my hands! The skin wrinkled, pale, pores clammed tight in their deprivation. Water, water, cooling sweet water. I must hurry.

This covering is a rigid pupaed wrap. Still, though, it can serve. I made it, perfected it, accompanying each one of my people into existence through the fleshy tunnels. What webbed hands, what webbed feet – a powerful spine as well for manoeuvrability along liquid alleys and roads and blue salty plateaus.

Out from the water and sometimes in, I took this skin on. My people liked it when they saw me so I kept it and inhabited the design. But not all the time.

Not everyone liked the skin. Those others, the mortals, attacked my people because of their differences. They called them 'The Fish People' because their pores clamped tight without water and yes, they were jealous when they learned that the Orsook could breathe under the rivers, lakes and seas and not die.

But the mortals made us die. All along the bank of my river, the Danu and within the hinterland of the continent they call Europa, by the waterways and marshes – we died. Even the Orsook began to curse their skin when they found that they could not run from water and survive. I sent some northwards, traversing the riverlines to the lakes over the Tin Sea. Now with the Orsook ground to ashes in the earth and the body of their first High King returned to water, I must follow.

He was right in the first instance of recognition, Tyracides. Danu is who I am, not Goreth. So I must continue the deception. Pretend ignorance where there is none. Feign weakness to excite mortal sympathy or bullishness and keep them unaware. They must not know that my tongue can speak a thousand and I understand their every word. I take very public lessons from Tyracides. They are surprised how fast I acquire their Greek language; it must be that you were struck by Zeus' lightning bolt for by your accent you could not be distinguished from any Hellene, they joke.

So therefore, I must get to the Orsook survivors in the Tin Isle. Since leaving the High Tomb at Glauberg, we have made good progress but no one doubts that we are being pursued. Seeing Orsek's face in the tomb was a shock. My one and only earthly son.

Goreth could not help his reaction there and it had been remarked upon by the others. Better controlled was his apparent disinterest in the hard, white bubbles spilled out onto Tyracides' hand. If anything, the sight for him had been more startling than seeing his son's dead face. He understood what those solid round globules were and their significance.

They were taking a rest now before entering the port of Kaled. Telemachus had suggested that it would not be clever to spend more time than necessary there with a gathering army behind them and therefore, at last, they had rested by this river which led to the port and the sea.

He felt its silvery ripples in in the mid-day sun pulling at him. His body thirsted for water.

From where she sat with Telemachus on the river bank, Hebe was disturbed by a sudden rushing draught close to her. It was Goreth running at full speed, his gown stripped from his body, at first in his hand and then flung to the ground, leaving him perfectly naked.

The Telemachons lying at their ease, laughed at the display. "Go for it, Goreth!" called Talos. With an inner reprimand, Hebe enjoyed the briefly glimpsed strength and litheness in the running figure. Really, there was not that much difference – apart from the hair texture, the healthy green hue to his skin and the facial details – to other handsome young men. Indeed, he could be regarded as more appealing, particularly in the way he dived, a superb arched curve into the water which hardly broke the surface. He stayed under for considerably longer than a human.

"Should he be down that long?" shouted Chryseis to the others, forgetting or just possibly seeking reassurance.

"He can stay down as long as he wants, he's Orsook!" yelled back Aristopolis.

"Let him stay down there forever and good riddance!" growled Berengar. His wife, playing with their son nearby, hushed him.

At last Goreth came to the surface without a splutter and waved to the crowd at the riverside. There were cheers, jeers and handclapping. Telemachus said to Hebe with a smile, "I'm glad that wave is not a farewell – we would be missing much if we lost the last man of the Orsook race." But when she replied, "I think so too," a shadow passed over his heart.

Later that day, they cooked river fish at several fires and ate with relish the evening meal. Goreth had caught many of them. He was sitting with Telemachus, Hebe, Eucleides, Faramund, Berengar, Ula and the child and several others. Ula was spooning soft fish meat into her boy's mouth. She cast an admiring glance at the river carp, its long length turning on a griddle over the flames.

"How did you capture such a beast, Goreth? Surely there might have been enough power in that tail to avoid your grasp?"

"It wasn't difficult," said the Orsook, his voice coming from below bubbles. "Once I had wrapped my arms around it and stopped the gills from working."

"an embrace that suffocates," murmured Eucleides, "and brings food to our stomachs. A very useful, affectionate gesture, that. Affectionate to us, I mean – not for the fish."

"If he hugs and kills his own kind, what does it mean for us?"

That voice came from Berengar and suddenly the light-heartedness was gone. The others looked at Berengar with incomprehension. How could he say such a thing? After what had happened to Goreth's people?

The Orsook's eyes were on Berengar's face and there was a long pause.

"'My kind', as you say, died at the hands of your people. Isn't that so, Faramund?"

Faramund was taken off-guard by the question but assumed he was really being asked to say something temperate and rational in the matter. "Yes, well, as I understand it, there were one or two Celt villages near the Orsook settlement in the east and they – er – felt threatened by them so there was a battle."

Goreth felt the anger of Danu rising within him and Danu tried to calm his own mood by using Goreth's mortal rationality. But it was little use. Goreth opened his mouth but Danu spoke from it.

"Two villages. One settlement. It was not an honourable battle - it was a bloody massacre. My people were wiped out by a deliberate and planned genocide."

Berengar leaped to his feet in fury. "One of those villagers was my own cousin – trying to defend himself and his family from an invasion by the Helvetii treacherously supported by that Orsook settlement!"

"If your cousin died," said Goreth deliberately, " it was only justice at work."

With a raging howl, Berengar threw all of his tremendous height and muscle at the more diminutive Orsook.

And then a remarkable thing happened,

Remarkable in two different ways: first in what Berengar experienced and second in what the onlookers witnessed.

Berengar himself expected to land on and grapple with Goreth's body. Instead he felt nothing and seemed to pass through the creature but by exerting his will he just found his feet before he fell. Standing up, he could sense a burning tingle wherever his bare skin met the air and Goreth was nowhere to be seen, except perhaps in the luminescent green ribbons of light that folded and wrapped around his own body which reminded him about what Faramund had said about the shining that had come from the Orsook's body in the underground cell beneath Glauberg. The midday sun still beamed down but his companions, the cooking fires and horses had gone. He was somewhere else. Then, in an instant, he was falling from a cliff. He had jumped backwards and was facing up. There was Goreth reaching down with his hand as if trying to save him – the expression on his face so curious. Down Berengar went and plunged with terrific force into the water below. He was pressured into the depths and lost all ability to control his actions: jerk-spun this way and stretched taut, that. Constantly, there was that huge water-milled force – roar, crack and guttural wrench – another's definition for his puny frame. Soaked, he was, sodden, powerless.

The Telemachons watching, saw Berengar fly through the air at Goreth but just as quick, Goreth put his hand out to take hold of the Celt's wrist. At the moment he touched it, motion became inaction. Berengar's movement was frosted in mid-air. He hung like a child's kite on Goreth's webbed hand but did not crash to the ground. Telemachus tried to turn his head to Eucleides and

Faramund to Eris but they could not. Nothing was able to move. The air was solid.

So it went on like this for no one knows how long; time, at this point had ceased, could not be counted.

But life is more powerful than time ant time is not a dead matter which meant that Berengar moved again. In very slow motion, he was lowered to the ground. His legs hit the earth and the limbs on his body reacted as if he was flailing in the very deepest water. It was shocking to see how he choked, as if his lungs had reached breaking point and the air that surrounded them was not air but water. Berengar's legs buckled beneath him and he fell back slowly, almost with sluggishness, but definitely drowning.

Then Goreth pulled him up as if out of water and with that tug, time shifted again. Normal motion resumed – although Berengar's response was far from normality.

He came up and when Goreth released him, fell onto all fours coughing, sputtering. Faramund and Ula, the toddler in her arms and crying to see his father in such a state, rushed up to him.

"He will be alright," said Goreth calmly, "just give him air and space to breathe."

Eventually the hacking coughs did subside and Berengar was able to recover himself.

The others were perplexed. They could not understand what had just passed and regarded Goreth with fearfulness. It was left to Telemachus to put it into words.

"Goreth, what was that?"

"What do you mean?" said the Orsook, his large eyes calm and fixed upon the other.

"How did you do that to Berengar in mid-air? What divine power do you possess or were able to call upon?"

Goreth made it all seem very plain. "it is true that I have more strength than you assumed. I simply used that strength in my one arm to stop him jumping on top of me and lowered him to the ground. The sudden halt in his impetus took all the wind from his lungs and he reacted by choking."

Nobody believed him. But everyone there, even Faramund and Ula, could see that in the argument between them, Berengar had been wrong to provoke trouble.

"I have never seen in my life such strength in one arm and would have much preferred to have seen it used against our enemies." Telemachus paused and then with abruptness gave voice to what was really on his mind. "The concern is this, Goreth – how can we trust you not to turn against us? We do not know where you have come from or who you actually are. We do not even know why you travel with us, only perhaps that you need company."

"I know who he is," said Tyracides firmly. "I swam against him at the Danuviad." It was what they had all known all along. They just wanted the confirmation.

"Are you …?" began Telemachus but did not finish with Goreth's real name because of superstition, something remarkable for him to feel. Then, "But if that is true, why would you want to help those who have destroyed your own people. Unbelievably, there was an exasperated retort from Berengar. Telemachus, at this moment, ignored him.

"The tribes living on the lower reaches of the Danu are different to those inhabiting this region, young lord. They had great respect for me and occasionally, I would help them. Is it not fit and pleasurable to strive in healthy competition, especially to win honour? So that is what I did in the river, my river."

"But the question remains, why are you with us – what is the real purpose? I understand your wanting to leave a country where none of the Orsook remain alive but where is the lure for going to Pretannia?"

Goreth's face became pensive. "Now, Telemachus, why should I trust you and your Telemachons after what has just happened? Hatred breeds hatred and like a swarm of locusts, it will settle. The deadly cloud will fall on any nourishing peace settlement and ravage it to bloody remnants. When such fury is released, who speaks up for the innocents – those who are forced to take sides by threats against themselves and their families?" Goreth looked towards the man he had just humiliated. "Berengar." The Celt, sullen, turned and responded to the call of his name. "Come here."

It did not sound like a command and that was just as well, otherwise the hefty Celt would not have made a move. But the way this was spoken was different. No parent speaking to a troubled child could have used a gentler manner and yet this was an adult to an adult; there was no condescension in the tone. Berengar went nearer by a few paces to the Orsook immortal and stopped, waiting.

"I wish I could pull that hatred from your heart but it is not for me to do that – you must willingly push it from you. In the noisy locust predation, truth is first consumed. Do you want to speak up for the innocents, Berengar – to show genuine courage against swarming hatred?"

"Innocents like my cousin? Of course, I do."

"Perhaps I was wrong, Berengar, in what I said earlier. Maybe your kinsman was forced to do what he did and the Orsook were forcibly recruited by the Helvetii. If I am wrong, I apologise – please forgive me. But what will it take for you to be released from that anger aimed at the Orsook and myself? I recall a small child many years ago, playing with his friends on the banks of the Danu. He was a red-haired boy full of adventure and spirit but as you might expect, not much caution and self-awareness. He dared his friends to a challenge and swung from one tree branch to the next as they reached out over the water. The others followed. The challenger stretched his hand out for another branch, his whole weight swinging and it was then that his luck ran out. Do you remember what happened then, Berengar?"

Amazed that his deeply buried memories could be unearthed so easily by another, the Celt answered, wondering where this was going next. "Yes, Ii could not possibly forget. The branch was rotten and it broke away, dropping into the river and taking me with it. I went under, hit my head on a rock and passed out."

Faramund broke in. "The current swept him away – we could all see his head just showing at the surface and thought he was lost. Then his moving head came to a sharp stop as if he had met with an immoveable blockage underwater. Almost at once he was being propelled in the opposite direction by something that was beneath him. But we could see he was still unconscious so I told the others to form a line, linking each other out to the river's edge and myself and another went in up to our thighs."

"I regained consciousness," continued Berengar, "I woke to find myself sitting astride the back of a dolphin. My first action was to fling myself off it and start swimming."

"Berengar was close by when he did that, so thankfully we were able to grab hold oⱼ him. I was nearest and pulled him in. But, my friend, I have to correct you on one idea that you always had about that incident," Faramund said, staring apprehensively at Berengar.

"Why? What do you mean?"

"The others behind me could not see what I saw clearly, even when it did turn so rapidly and head for the deeps. What you thought you sensed with your confused and stunned mind, Berengar, was no dolphin." Faramund turned and looked deliberately at Goreth, willing to accept a new realisation about their past. "It was a man shape."

"But you always agreed with me in front of our families that it had been a dolphin," said Berengar.

"I did not have the courage to disagree with you and be derided by the warriors. They would have laughed at me, humiliated me – I was never brave enough to withstand that."

"So it was not a dolphin that saved my life at that time but a 'man shape'. Who was the figure in the water which was not quite a dolphin and yet not quite a man?" The Sequani Celt had already understood the answer to his own question and simply wanted affirmation as he turned to face the source for it.

"I rescued you," said Goreth. "I could have ignored your plight. You were from the race of men, what concern were you to me? At least that is what I should have thought, wasn't it Berengar? With your hatred I might have turned away then, especially as I knew how the Orsook would be persecuted by your generation and your tribe. Why did I help you?"

"I don't know," said Berengar.

"You were a child and you had fallen into my watery domain, helpless. That river teems with life and those that die do so to feed others so that they may live. But Man and the Orsook and the Gods are not animals; they should not kill because they can and when the passion drives them. Surely their intelligence should make them better than that? The instinct must be to preserve and protect life, not waste or perish it when life is at its most vulnerable. This is what civilises us and without that instinct, without that action to help each other, then human society, the Orsook and the Gods all die together. You have lost your cousin, Berengar, I have lost a whole people, at least in this known part of Europa."

"You are the God Danu – how is it that something should remain unknown to you?"

Goreth sighed. "I am no god, Berengar, I am what you believe me to be. Everything immortal in me is engaged in a very human desire: to find what has been lost and return to a normal, happy society again."

"Well, perhaps we might both find that, by going to the north," observed Berengar. "meanwhile, I owe my life to you. Let us start afresh."

Goreth extended his arm, "I am willing. Take my hand and seal a new friendship." Berengar eyed the hand that had so recently brought a shocking unreality to his senses. Goreth's eyebrows lifted and he winked. There was a firm smile which showed genuinely in his eyes. They shook hands.

21
Across the Tin Sea

The Telemachons had stayed in Kaled's port for two days before they hired boats to cross the Tin Sea. They were desperate to get away as fast as possible of course but the bartering over hire agreements and loading procedure, held them up. At any moment they were expecting the Celtic army from Dunsberg to descend upon them. Faramund and Berengar were able to learn from the locals in the port that an army was on its way, led by a druid called Formus, his military commander being a young man from the Helvetii tribe by the name of Artemius.

Telemachus wondered about the speed of their pursuit. He was well aware that travelling at a mere horse trot would have brought them into contact by now. He discussed it with Eucleides who suggested that their slow pace was deliberate.

"But why?"

"We are not their true prey."

"We robbed their High Tomb. The High King's body – the one they regarded as the first ruler - was liquidised in front of us. We are going to be held to account for his destruction. Surely they must want us caught and punished?"

"No doubt. Yet how do you explain them holding back? It cannot be fright that delays them. Their force is much superior."

"You have already considered it. Eucleides."

"Yes."

"And?"

"They must want to follow us into Pretannia. We are their excuse to do that with the large army they have."

"But won't the Celts in Pretannia be suspicious themselves and stop them at the coast?"

"As Faramund told us – they are led by a druid, an important one. Apparently he has friends in the Misty Isle, particularly at the Plain of Stone Giants. You know how these druids work with one another across Europa and with what importance they regard Pretannia, their Sacred Isle."

"If so, why would he desecrate it with conquest?"

"He may or may not intend to do that. The important thing is to remove ourselves as a priority from his plans."

"I assume he will think that we are headed to Dubras[7] on the first stage of our journey that being the nearest point to Gaul for crossing into the country," said Telemachus. "Therefore we must change direction half-way across the Tin Sea, go further west along the coast and then northwards on a central axis through the mainland."

"It is not in the contractual agreement for the boats and the pilots we have hired," murmured Eucleides, drily.

"The pilots are not to be informed about the change in plan. We will persuade them to change direction and land on an uninhabited coastline. Once we have beached the boats, we will burn them."

"Is that necessary?"

"I would rather," said Telemachus with great firmness, "destroy the boats than kill the pilots. If the vessels are left and the pilots steer them back to the home port, there is no quicker way for Formus to learn exactly where we went. The information will be sold as soon as those boat captains step onto dry land. The Telemachons' lives are at risk and there can be no time for pleasantries."

"No compensation for them then?"

"We will pay them the hire money and a little more. They will probably be glad to have escaped with their lives. Once we journey on the mainland, we will avoid the Plain of Stone Giants and the faster we can get away from the southern land in Pretannia, the better for us."

"And as well, the sooner we can leave this port the better it will be for our chance to escape," advised Eucleides. "I am surprised the people here have been so amiable when they might have already heard about our actions at Glauberg."

"Their existence is based upon mercantile trade and its free passage through their port. It is a habit kept for even us – Greeks who have upset a neighbouring Celtic tribe, yet as we have seen, the Gauls war with each other as much as the Hellenes with their fellow Greeks at home."

"Nevertheless," said Eucleides, "the nearer Formus gets with his army, the more willing they will be to throw us into irons."

---

[7] Celtic name for Dover.

So the urgency was clear and that very day the Telemachons boarded the boats seeing the water was calm and the skies clear, then sailed for Pretannia. While still within sight of the port, a crewman called from the masthead on Telemachus' boat that he could see a great host arriving at the metropolis they had left, shining with weapons of war. They made sure all sails were fully employed on the boats to make certain they were out of view themselves and then on the display of a signal flag from Telemachus' ship, the Gaulish captains were encouraged to change course and aim for another entry point into the country. There was no blood shed and the transition to the new course went smoothly. The boats were all now heading for Ictis along the Pretannic coastline running westwards.

22
Albion

It was the white cliffs at Dubras that had given this land its name – 'Albion' – 'white lands'; they loomed like mountains of ice above the cool blue sea. The Celtic inhabitants used that term for the country, once having passed this way over those white cliffs, maybe in that distant time when Albion had been connected to Europa and all the Celts had to do to get here was to walk, before the sea washed over their footprints. At one time it must have been the biggest causeway in the known world, offering hope and new life for those fleeing from tribal conflict and certain death.

Telemachus mused on this as he sailed by the chalk escarpment thrusting up from the depths. Little did he know that the sun would turn on its annual course around the Earth fifteen times more before another Greek would come that way again with an intention, like Telemachus, that was not devoted to trade. He would be returning from a journey to explore these islands and as far as Thule before writing about what he had found so that his fellow Greeks could understand what lay on the other side of the world. His name was Pytheas and it was by the terms that he used – Pretannia, the Pretannic Isles, Pretanike, the land of the Albiones, Albion, the country of the 'Pretannoi' or tattooed ones, that the alien became familiar to the civilised world. Much later, Pretannia became Britannia and then Britain.

Whatever name by which it existed, Telemachus was fully aware that he knew very little about this long country. Some things he could pick up from Faramund and Berengar. There was also information given grudgingly by people in Kaled port. Numerous tribes ruled over the land and they did not always live peacefully with each other. It seemed that the Plain of Stone Giants where the Celts buried their revered ones and worshipped the Sun God was also used, such as with Delos and the Hellenic Games, as a place for settling differences and bringing about peace between people if it could be achieved.

Where the Telemachons intended to land ashore, on the mainland of Albion over a narrow seaway between it and Ictis, a passage would have to be made through the territory belonging to the Belgae tribe. Further north would be the Atrebates, Catuvellauni, Coritani and further north still, the Brigantes. Beyond that would be a place too cold and too wet for comfortable living, certainly for Greeks. Where they might settle in this land was a topic beginning to be much discussed by the Telemachons. When it would come to the time for a decision, such a matter would have to be agreed by a vote and consultation with the gods. Telemachus thought he should not impose a home on them but if the land under consideration was not fertile enough or could not be easily defended, then he might be able to persuade them away from it.

Certainly there would be bare opportunity to place themselves in the southern part of the country: it was crowded and if the Telemachons excited hostility too many tribes could descend upon them in a concerted attack. In fact, that was probably what Formus would try to arrange when he got to this side of the Tin Sea with his army. Unless the Telemachons could get through these southern territories with the greatest speed, they would be trapped.

No, it would be north for them and meanwhile, they would try to bypass the numerous hill forts he had heard about and the Plain of Stone Giants which would be many days' travel from here. Higher ground might be best, somewhere with fresh rainwater as a plentiful resource, higher ground but level and without stones so crops can be easily grown.

He had decided against burning the boats. Eucleides was right. It would be a waste. The Kaled pilots and crew had been put ashore midway between Ictis and Dubras. Their disembarkation point had been chosen with care. It was after they had passed another port and Telemachus calculated that it would take them half a day to get there from where they were landed and another day to get back to Gaul. While they were doing that Formus would have arrived near Dubras with his army – he would never be allowed into the city with a force that size – only to discover, eventually, that the Telemachons were not in the vicinity.

He and the Telemachons would be already on their way through the kingdom of the Belgae, only, as Eucleides and he had just recently become acquainted with the fact, the territory ruled by the Belgae did not belong to a king. When the pilot in their boat had been asked about the country and who governed it before he was put ashore, the man rudely sniggered. Pinned to the mast with Berengar's hand around his throat, the pilot recovered his manners, squealing out that it was a woman who ruled the Belgae and she had done so for some time. His skinny neck pressed again, the man had given the name of the queen as Helladore. "She cannot be very terrible if you sneer at her," said Berengar.

"No-one laughs at her court," he had said. "In her nature she is more man than woman and in her cruelty less man than monster. I am ashamed to admit it but even at this distance from her throne, the laughter that came from my mouth was produced by fear rather than mockery."

23
Queen Helladore

Bordoric's sweating, frenzied face was a breath away from that belonging to his friend Ortix. Anyone seeing the contorted detail in their expressions would assume the hatred for each other as given. None would have guessed at the former friendship. Except the watching crowd. They recalled that friendship as they watched the soon-to-be fatal combat and recognised that it was not hatred that dug into the flesh of these faces: it was the desperate desire to live.

Grunts and groans lifted from their struggling bodies to the bloodied setting sun above as they pushed and heaved and cut and slashed at each other. There was some blood but there might have been more if the two men had not been so skilful with shield or sword parry or had not been protected by the chain ring vests or the iron crown helmets. To Bordoric, it felt as though they had been fighting for hours but in reality it was one sixty-fourth marker on a time candle.[8] He sensed rather than saw the sun sinking behind Ortix's head, since one eye was closed by a bruise that had resulted from a swinging blow delivered by his friend's shield. At the instant the sun was sucked into the underworld so would both their spirits go with it. This was the rule for mortal combat in the land of the Belgae. Their fighting space was a grove cut from broadleaf forest, one large enough to contain the duellists, the spectators and of course, Queen Helladore herself.

Against exhaustion, the pace in the fight quickened. The men were in a race with the setting sun. Placed in a semi-circle before the crowd, were the archers. When the red disc in the sky fell and blotched out, the bows would be raised, arrows released. Both men would be squirming in the mud. Only one event would prevent that: a combatant's death before sunset.

The sporax glistened, a milky shimmer that stretched between two trees behind the fighting men. Its wispy filaments covered a

---

[8] 15 minutes – the candle was divided into 16 hourly segments, 5.00a.m. to 9.00p.m. for summer.

wide space and the men were trying to drive each other towards it.

Queen Helladore yawned as she watched them. Sat on her sedan throne, that had been brought to its position by four muscular slaves, her long black hair swept behind her ears, the fierce blue eyes under their broadly etched dark brows observant of everything despite her present boredom – she was a striking figure. She wore a dress that on the surface was made from animal hair, perhaps mink or rabbit and underneath was linen. Unusually – unusual that is for any other woman living in Belgae because she had made it a Law of State – her dress was cut off above the knee and her finely shaped legs were exhibited for all to see. At her waist she wore a jewelled dagger and over her shoulders down to the thighs, a long cloak wrapped her in warmth. The cloak itself was noteworthy in that it was made from blue and green peacock feathers and wool; the eyes in the feathered vanes stared with suspicion at everyone around her.

The queen glanced at the sun's lowering position and at last some interest was revived. She focused on Bordoric in particular. Irritating, self-obsessed, usurping Bordoric who thought he could deceive her in his role as her fourth husband and consort. It did not take him long in the marriage to begin conspiring with others to place himself on the throne and get rid of the detested title 'consort'. Naturally, he had not realised when he became her husband that even that title would not have been his for very long since her own real interest lay in the wealth and estates his family had given to him. He was stupid, Helladore decided. Stupid not to have learned from the deaths of her previous husbands. Brainless to think he could outwit her. The punishment for treachery was death but it could be avoided if Bordoric agreed to trial by combat. He had done and it was then left to the Queen to choose his opponent. She had wanted some amusement and therefore selected his closest friend who ironically had not been party to the conspiracy. No matter – Helladore was notorious for punishing those who displeased her by pitting them against their nearest and dearest. In the past she had forced mothers to kill daughters, fathers-sons, sons their fathers, wives-husbands and in one particularly juicy incident, a grandfather his grandson. That had been unique. The old man was close to death and yet had been forced to kill his young, healthy grandson – the last in his family line. You'd have thought he would kill himself, rather than go ahead with it but no, he did as he was told. The potential for evil in human beings never failed to surprise Queen Helladore.

A thudding sound from the combat area reawakened her attention again. Bordoric had somehow managed to overcome his friend and was dragging him to the Sporax. This would be interesting. She had only witnessed once before what happened when a person came into physical contact with the finely webbed Sporax strands and she would like to see it repeated. However, this desire was watered a little by the fact that Bordoric was getting the upper hand in the combat. Above all, she wanted her husband dead – killed in a suitably gory manner and converted to ex-husband material.

It was gladdening to see the metal coppery sun fusing with the horizon and being poured like molten metal in a smithy into the mould of the ground. Only moments were left. The surrounding atmosphere was cooling tangibly; light dimmed in rapid sequential shades. At the captain's command, archers' bows were readied. They were so near that total darkness would not be enough to prevent the targets being hit. The many archers would ensure that the combatants' bodies would bristle with hedgehog spines.

Bordoric's opponent, Ortix, had been pulled right up to the apparently fragile strands interlacing the trees. Seeing them closer now, terror gripped Ortix and with a despairing effort he was able to twist around and yank up one of Bordoric's legs. The other man, unbalanced, fell. And because he too was close to the taut web between the trees, his body crashed into it. There was a murmur from the watching crowd, a knowledgeable sound marking sympathy but also guilty shuddering thrill.

Bordoric struggled to free himself but he was stuck fast. Every tug from his arms sent a semaphoric tremor through the strands. The archer captain's eyes were fixed on Helladore's face, waiting for her signal. The sun was down.

Ortix had retreated along the ground and with relief was taking in Bordoric's predicament. He looked around for his fallen sword, found it and grasped the hilt.

Helladore said clearly, "Just Ortix, leave Bordoric for the moment." The captain understood and delivered a command to his men. Ortix had just drawn his sword back, ready to plunge it into Bordoric's stomach but before he could act, a dozen arrows were fired and thumped into his back. He lurched forward with a groan.

A shivering scream emitted by Bordoric brought the attention of the audience around to him. The eyes bulging in his face were horribly focused on a dark corner to the web which was disguised by abundant tree foliage.

From the obscurity, a solid massy lump formed under the pale moonlight. It was held aloft on eight long and hairily delicate legs, though the delicacy was in proportion, since each were as thick as a man's thigh and the length of half a tree branch. The spider edged its way forward along two silk threads, roads leading down to the trapped prey. As it moved, it tapped the silk with two forelegs, sending deliberate vibrations down the lines, testing for the relative strength and dynamism of its victim. Bordoric, feeling the movement and seeing for himself the long-legged death that approached him, tried to wrestle more furiously with his sticky bonds. Having gauged the response in these flimsy movements, the beast was unimpressed. Four globular eyes around its head, the two in the centre being biggest, pinpointed Bordoric's location. Its poison sac churned and up an internal canal flowed the agent of paralysis. From the wide-plated fangs on either side the head, began to drop beaded venom, the colour of corruption.

Helladore's subjects, standing in the grove, moved back as one, utterly revolted. Her archers though, held to their places. A ghastly silence had overtaken all, which was suddenly broken by the creature on the web. Opening its jaws, it let out a long wailing howl. There was utter shock. The sound was an exact imitation of that which had just left Bordoric's lips. Completely confused, thinking there was another human victim trapped in the Sporax despite having seen minutes earlier that there had been none, Bordoric paused his movements. It was then that the giant spider leaped. Landing with its body over the man, the fangs sank into his torso. People in the grove heard bones crunching as one fang broke into his chest. Venom sprayed and his body was suffused: first rendering all actions static and then liquefying the internal organs for easier digestion by the beast at a later date.

Moving its abdomen over Bordoric, the spider squirted fine silk from the spinneret nozzle heads, deftly rolling the dead body around with its forelegs so that a fuzzy cocoon was shaped.

That Bordoric was dead could only be a certainty. The archer captain looked to his mistress for further command. Helladore raised her hand and let it fall in a slewing movement. The arrow punctures would have no fatal consequence but their impression would be symbolic. A necessary message concerning the relentless nature of the law in Helladore's land.

For a second time the arrows hissed in the air but this time the target they found was the silken cocoon. Not one arrow hit the spider but it instantly froze. The head turned and all its shining eyes faced the onlookers. Some people panicked and moved away quickly, remembering the leap it had made onto Bordoric. Helladore's archers continued to remain in position but were hastily refitting fresh arrows to their bows. The beast held itself fine-tuned for action and in the next moment scuttled back along the thread lines to its abode.

Queen Helladore leaned back against her sedan and gave another order, "Get him down and burn his body." The archers replaced their bows with burning brands from a nearby fire and held them against the strands connecting the cocoon to the web. Other men came out with their long spears raised to ensure that the giant spider would not attack again. Its food was being taken so it was very possible but many such events as this had previously taught the queen and her guard that the beast was quite timid when faced with a real threat. Only when a victim was safely trapped by silken manacles that held like iron would it venture to attack. After some time, the strands melted, showing that they were organic not metallic and letting the body drop to the ground.

As it was being cleared away, Helladore turned to the courtier closest to her, who was always at her side, the Lady Bellosa, her sister.

"Tell me, my Lady, have you seen to the guests tonight? Are they comfortable?"

"they are, your majesty. Their one discomfort is the guard I have placed at the chamber door but I have assured them that this is a custom applied to any strangers who come into the palace and they accepted that."

Helladore viewed her sister with approval. She kept her close because she was harmless, harmless that was, to Helladore herself. She could be relied upon to do the right thing and to do it efficiently. In looks, no two sisters could be so dissimilar. Bellosa's appearance was a mirrored distortion of the queen's own beauty and her ugliness to Helladore was a fact that was very satisfying. The rumour at court was that Bellosa had ben fathered upon the Queen Mother by a wandering bard who plied his poetics trade from one tribal capital to another. The man had been as physically attractive as a decomposed corpse but his voice and his song enamoured all who heard to the point of seduction. Which was exactly what happened with the Queen Mother. Helladore's mother had successfully organised a palace coup with another lover six months later and had removed her husband from his crown – in fact, literally when he was executed – before he had got to see the unedifying spectacle that Bellosa presented at her birth. She had been kept in her proper place ever since, particularly by Helladore. Beauty was what commanded men's attention and allegiance. They would forgive anything as long as their other needs were met. Helladore had chosen the right man to wed her sister. He was one completely devoted to acquiring material wealth and if that meant marriage to a woman whose appearance led to the conclusion that she had been fathered by a man with the looks of a decomposed corpse, then so be it. He knew where his duty and prospects lay. It lay with Queen Helladore and he serviced her whenever she required it. Unlike his wife, the figure he made was most marvellous, which was why he had been invited to marry into the royal family. One ugly royal was enough.

Helladore returned her thoughts to their present guests.

"Their king is called Telemachus, you said and the people with him are mostly Greeks. Tell me more."

"My Lady, Telemachus leads them but he rejects the term 'King'. The others look to him for guidance and they seem to be proud warriors. Yet some are not Greeks but Celts and there are women amongst them."

"Celtic women following a Greek warrior chief? They risk my scorn coming into this land. From where have they travelled?"

"Magna Grecaea and through the territory of the Scythians by sailing the World River, the Danu."

A tinge of wonder was upon Helladore's face and then quickly controlled. "To the furthest places we send our tin? But how is it that they have not been stopped and cut down by the Keltoi tribes in those places?"

"It seems that our gods are with them – they have made as many friends as enemies. The Celts that accompany them were formerly Greek slaves they have freed and some who have joined them from the Dardani tribe."

"I am more interested in their enemies," broke in Helladore.

"Formus," informed Bellosa emphatically.

"Formus? Well, well, he is certainly a fierce enemy to make. Even I would think very carefully before going against him with all the allies he could persuade on to a battlefield through the Druidic Order on this island. Telemachus and his people must have committed some dreadful act against the gods to excite his hostility."

"They raided the High Tomb at Glauberg."

"Did they really?" Now Helladore did not bother to hide the astonishment as her eyebrows arched.

"And destroyed the High King's body."

Helladore gasped, leaning back on her ornately carved throne. This news disturbed her. For a minute she did not seem to be able to respond. Feeling her sister's gaze, though, she gathered herself and decided upon what should be done.

"What possesses men to come into another country where they have been welcomed and destroy a revered, sacred body? There is no alternative. I cannot allow them to proceed any further into Albion. All of the Telemachons must be detained and executed."

"There are other things you should know," said Bellosa, understanding that her own survival at court was dependent on obedience and the ability to provide information that was complete to her sister.

"Yes?"

"They are pursued by Formus with an army of five hundred men. He has recently landed at Dubras. Then there is something very strange."

"In what way?"

"The Telemachons are accompanied by an Orsook. His name is Goreth and is amongst a small group of friends always at Telemachus' side."

Hearing this, Helladore partly realised why Formus had arrived with an army. His insane hatred for the Orsook knew no territorial bounds. He would certainly punish the Telemachons for their desecration at Glauberg but a much more important objective for him would be to kill this Orsook who had managed to avoid death in Europa.

"What are your thoughts, Bellosa?"

This surprised the queen's sister. Rarely did Helladore ask for advice from her. It was, of course, a gesture – a pretence that Bellosa was an equal in the courtly circle. This actual condescension constituted reward for good information. But Helladore did not want an opinion.

"The High Druid brings an army with him. Why does he need it? Surely, he could have utilised his allies to capture these Telemachons? We are no bound allies of his and yet knowing about their actions, we are ready to capture and execute this lost band of Greek and Celt adventurers. Formus stands to lose the friends he already has over here by his incursion. There might be some other reason that drives his actions. Stories are told that the Orsook in Europa are not the last of their people. Some might still exist on this island – to the northern country, the mountainous lands and lakes – in that region inhabited by the Brigantes. They say that the Brigantes protect them and treat the Orsook as semi-divine."

"The Brigantes themselves deny it!" scoffed the queen, forgetting herself for a moment. They aver that these stories are nonsense and no such creatures have ever lived in their land."

"We must ask ourselves, My Lady," continued Bellosa with a tone designed to calm," why it is that this Orsook, the last of his race in Europa, is willing to accompany these Telemachons. Go where? If the direction they travel is northerly, then that in itself might substantiate what I have just said."

Despite herself, Helladore became intrigued with the point that her sister raised. She had always been curious about the Orsook, those quixotic amalgams of human and fish. Their destruction by Formus was unnecessary and her agents had made it clear to her how he had tried to keep the deliberate genocide from his own people. The creatures posed no substantial threat to him – they were not warlike and it made her wonder about his motive for taking such action. She had met with the druid herself and within a short time had recognised a mutual affinity for malice. Yet even pleasure in cruelty must have a plan, an objective. So what was his?

Helladore's plan was simple. It was to focus cruelty on those people surrounding her and a few outside the immediate circle. In this way she created terror and terror was a superlative tool for maintaining her rule. She enjoyed exercising violence against the human beings who came into her personal orbit; a malicious gravity kept them in position. It exorcised the abuse she had suffered as a child. A counterpoint to her detestation for human beings was her love for animals, a whole variety of which she kept in her palace. Daylight hours in the palace gardens were filled with whistles, hoots, gibberings, roars and cackles. Believing she was a witch, her people assumed that these noises arose from yet more fellow humans magically transformed by the Queen's wicked powers. So, for the Orsook, unusually, Helladore took to sympathy.

If, as Bellosa had implied, Formus' intent was to chase this Goreth and the Telemachons all the way to the north then his ultimate objective must be to find and eradicate the Fish People that were rumoured to survive there. In that case, the Telemachons were not his real concern and in fact if she executed them, it would interfere with his means for discovering which northern land the Orsook inhabited. The Queen debated this theory with her sister.

"You could give the Orsook free passage to the north and execute the others," said Bellosa helpfully.

"The problem is that without the Telemachons beside him, he is likely to die alone, not getting to the place where Formus wants him to be."

"My Lady, the Orsook are not easy to capture – they are as slippery as fish!"

This attempt at humour met with a scowl from the Queen. "Be serious, Bellosa. You know how easily his kind were caught in Europa. He is in my palace at this very moment. All I have to do is to arrest him and wait until Formus gets here."

"I just meant to emphasise that Goreth himself has escaped the mass murder perpetrated on his fellow beings," added Bellosa weakly.

"He has been fortunate," said Helladore. "I think it might be better if I allowed the Telemachons to continue on their way although the desecration at the High Tomb in Glauberg cannot go unpunished."

"What will you do?" asked Bellosa.

"I will speak to them tomorrow and then decide."

"And what about Formus, if you do let them go?"

"If I allow them to live, I will explain it to the High Druid in terms he will understand."

Formus would be rational thought Queen Helladore. From past meetings between them the druid had counted on her as a supporter, if not a firm ally. He would not lose such a friendship over this matter. Already the Queen had made her mind up to ushering the Telemachons through her land. Only if this

Telemachus and his people were arrogant, rejecting the punishment or recompense she required for their sacrilegious pillage, would they find that their first journey into Albion would be the last one they would ever take.

24
Telemachus Enchanted

Queen Helladore looked and listened. Telemachus was speaking in front of her. She was absorbed by his words but it was not necessarily the words that fascinated. The Greek was youthful and confident before her. The leather jerkin he wore, stretched over his wide chest and shoulders then ending just above the muscled biceps, covered nothing but strength. Bare-headed, his long hair, dark as crow wings, flowed over the shoulder pads upon which his armour would have rested but Telemachus had come in peace, not war and his cuirass rested elsewhere. His words were expressed to annul distrust.

"We, the Telemachons, ask only for a safe escort through your domain. We mean no harm and are seeking only to find some place in Albion which is free from constant warfare and that will accept us."

Helladore felt her heart beat faster than usual. What was wrong with her? She had experienced dozens of men in her life before this – why should he be any different? He inescapably was. Just hearing the voice held a clue. The tone was firm, unyielding; sculpted mouth giving expression to sounds that were precise yet did lull and soothe in their impact. She grasped at the words that resolved from the sounds. This was due in some part to Telemachus having only just begun to master the Celtic language. But if what he was saying had been said instead by a Celt, she would still not have understood the communication – her whole psychology found it confusing.

"Freedom is our aim. The freedom to live and cooperate together as equals for a better society and to build the greatest city the world has ever known."

Bellosa had noticed her Queen's absorption. She knew at once what it meant. It was the same pattern repeating itself in her behaviour. The method she practised to gain a gratifying conclusion to her lust. That it was lust, Bellosa could not doubt. How could it be dignified with the name 'love' if the man to whom she was attracted unfailingly ended up dead? The Queen was like a poisonous horse-fly skimming over the courtly herd until she found a stallion in robust health then would drop down, fasten herself to him and drink up blood in a toxic exchange until death sealed the wound. Not a full day elapsing since her last husband had gone and already she had found herself another stallion. Bellosa was grateful. This meant Helladore would be distracted from her own husband and Bellosa loved her husband very much indeed.

"We have come from the other end of the earth for just this and nothing else. Those places the Telemachons have left are back in the past. We will never return. The future holds our only promise."

She had felt that love sometime after the wedding day. It was not a marriage she had been looking forward to – a partnership brokered by her sister for her own purposes. Besides, she believed all the talk at court about her new husband. After all, what else had she to go on? She expected as a consequence to be spending her time with an intensely selfish and arrogant oaf who would hardly speak to her. In fact, the experience was very different. It would be too bold to think that he cared deeply for her – he just managed to consummate the marriage and only occasionally slept with her at all. But he was not what the court and presumably the Queen, thought of him. After a long time she got to realise this only because he allowed her to know and that was only because he came to realise how much Bellosa hated her own sister. Dorstoric, her husband, was playing a crucial game within the influential land aristocracy overseen by Helladore. The Queen had changed the Belgae tribe she ruled in this part of Albion. It was an accepted fact that most Celtic tribes reserved their aggression and enmity for those other tribes that attacked them. Behind the borders in Queen Helladore's country, however, the viciousness worked within and nobody was deemed to be worth anything without showing an obvious callousness to others. Dorstoric had grown a public perception about himself which had matched what was expected and given him success. He was clever. But at what cost to himself? It must be an exhausting effort to continue the deception with the Queen in those waking moments after all passion was spent. Bellosa accepted that her husband held no steady eroticism for herself but she believed he regarded her with some affection and trust. She yearned for the day when somehow his affection might become an enduring love.

"So we place ourselves before you, Queen Helladore and warriors of the Belgae tribe, to ask that we may at this time begin to create a strong bond of friendship between your tribe and our people. To allow us to travel through your country and then, wherever we settle, our people will flourish at the will of the gods and we will repay your friendship with the fine things we can create and in times ahead, the protection we can offer with our growing population."

A watching warrior sniggered. Telemachus understood. He was standing with just four Telemachons – Eucleides, Berengar, Eris and Faramund – while the rest had been enclosed in a compound from which the only immediate chance for release would be thoughtful diplomacy. That amused soldier revealed the irony in this Greek interloper with his tiny force promising protection to a country that owned a powerful army and dense population.

Overhead sloped the high roof covering this large chamber in the palace. It was made from rushes and no doubt would rot in just a few years. Very different from the marbled halls and tiled roofs he had left in Greece. Everything below the roof was made from wood and straw and mud. It was the same with the other buildings he had seen. Stone was only used for containing the worship rituals to their gods – in those curious circular sanctuaries that seemed to have their perimeters made from massive lintelled doorways. He had glimpsed them on the hill-tops while sailing along the coast. And it was to another hill they had been brought – this palace fort belonging to the Queen.

He had admired the huge earth embankments, the winding path to the main gate, overlooked at every point by the defenders. This hill-fort would be no easy conquest for an opposing army. Looking again at the vaulted timbered roof, Telemachus changed his mind about its temporality. It was a sturdy trap for everything inside the building. The only visual relief was the hole at its apex which allowed acrid smoke from the fire on the central hearth in the hall to drift through it. Light through the window spaces in the oval construction fell onto the rows of blue tattooed warriors collected on benches – without their weapons but a continuous intimidation.

His eyes drifted back to the beautiful woman on the throne, coppered hair against a face as pale as abalone shell. Pale, yet not suggesting frailty or weakness in her beauty. It was strange how she leant forward, her arm wrapped around the bronze sceptre that was more like a staff in its length. In her demeanour she was an old crone leaning on it for support but her beauty and the way that her gaze seemed to pierce him added up to a powerful and intriguing presence.

Helladore, as if a disorientation had passed, seemed to awaken herself and settled back onto her throne. The soldier's snigger was a reminder that she needed to exercise command over both herself and others.

"Prince," she said, "for I assume that is what you are, you demand much trust for very little evidence that your intentions are indeed friendly and benign towards us. Suppose we allow you through our country and you do prosper in the years ahead. Your great city is built and it becomes rich. What can make us believe that you will not return with a mighty army to our country one day, having remembered its own riches and attempt to rob and destroy us?"

Her warriors drummed their heels on the wooden floor to signify support for what she had just said. Bellosa remembered not to underestimate her sister. She may have appeared to be hypnotised by Telemachus' imperfect Celtic speech but in fact she had heard and weighed every word.

Telemachus could translate better than he could speak the language. He could have had Berengar or Faramund speak for him, but if this was the island to which he had led his people, he would have to lead by example.

"My Lady, what have you seen with your own eyes that makes you believe this? Yes, there are brave warriors amongst us but there are women and children too. We are a people seeking refuge, we would not harm anyone."

"Is that how the Sequani tribe experienced you – as people who passed harmlessly by? They must have confused you with some other raiders then, other raiders who stole votive gifts from the sacred monument at Glauberg and ruthlessly destroyed the body of their revered ancestor, the High King."

A growl erupted from the warriors seated below her, behind Telemachus' back. The son of Timoleon had to exert control before things got out of hand.

"It is true we were responsible for the trespass at the sacred site but it was not as you heard it." Helladore was about to speak but Telemachus pressed on. "We were at the tomb not to steal from it but to rescue a friend of our company who had been taken and imprisoned there."

A slight crease furrowed Berengar's brow as he stood with Telemachus while the faces of the others remained neutral.

"Then surely he must have committed some wrong to deserve it and you increased that wrongdoing by being there yourselves."

"He committed a wrong only if you believe that a person with different features to the rest of us causes offence and should be imprisoned."

"If I believed that, my sister would have been jailed years ago," replied Helladore. Her soldiers laughed. Bellosa blushed. "But who is this person that was taken prisoner at Glauberg – why is he not here to explain himself?"

"I am here!" came a loud, bubbling voice projected from the rear of the hall. A tall figure strode in, followed by two of Helladore's guards, scuttling like puppies. When the central firelight struck his face and powerful frame there was an instant reaction from the seated soldiers: a murmuration rippled up, registering the surprise that all felt on seeing a living Orsook – perhaps the last one existing anywhere in the world.

"My L-L-Lady," spoke up Faramund nervously before Goreth had got to a convenient space close to the Queen, "You have heard how the druid Formus hates the Orsook. This is the reason for his chasing us to Albion. He wants to capture Goreth." Faramund gestured towards his friend.

Helladore glanced at Faramund but deciding he did not deserve her lengthy attention, had transferred it to Goreth, steadily noting every facet of the creature's wondrous appearance.

She addressed Goreth directly at last but in such a way that those listening almost believed that she was talking to herself. "You know – I have often wondered why Formus was so fixed on removing the Orsook from his land. Now, one of that race he hates so much stands before me and I still cannot understand it. Formus is in Albion with his own army. I do not find it credible that he is here simply because of one creature." She spoke to Goreth directly. "It cannot be what you are but what you have done. Why do you think he is following you?"

"Sometimes men become famous for an idea and it becomes large in the popular imagination, even if that idea is conceived in evil. That obsession grants them status and wealth. Soon, they cannot give up the concept that has made them famous in society, even if they wanted to."

"There are such men …. And women," replied Helladore, "but I doubt that Formus is one of them as you describe it. He is completely at one with his own fixed conception and nothing will tear him away from it. However, what he is doing now could have been done in the past so where is the additional motivation for his actions? Why have you, Goreth, together with the Telemachons, upset him so much – please try to tell me the truth, Goreth. We like to hear the truth, don't we, my warriors? This last assertion was directed to the sitting soldiers. They picked up on it – a few echoed the word from their mistress' lips, "Truth," and then the remainder joined in and all bellowed out, "Truth!"

Goreth replied evenly, unintimidated. "It is true, Queen Helladore, that I had been captured in Glauberg and held there underground until the Telemachons rescued me. I could have freed myself from their shackles if I had so wished. But it was in the Telemachons' destiny to meet me at that place, that time and I am nothing if I do not fulfil human destiny. You ask me for the truth, Queen and as I would never wish you to bed down with a lie, I will reply with simplicity and honesty." Listening to his words, Bellosa's pulse beat harder at a pertinent reference and her thoughts flitted protectively to her husband. "We -   the Telemachons – were in a desperate situation once I had been rescued. We had killed the guards at Glauberg because they attacked us. There in the tomb were the gifts scattered all around. To get to this land, we would have to hire transport and provide for our needs so we took the gold."

An angry exclamation rose up from the seated warriors.

"But we only took what was needed!" rang out a different voice – Telemachus' voice – above their heads. The hostile buzz paused and the Corinthian pressed his advantage. "Yes, we were wrong to take anything at all but you are soldiers like myself and as such we obey and honour the gods, we know our duty yet we must also admit that part of that duty is to use our wits when providing for ourselves and our comrades." There were several acknowledgements from Helladore's men. "Most coins and treasure we found there was left behind and afterwards we prayed to the gods that we might make some recompense to the First King of the Celts in that land and restore to him the honour paid by his people. At no time did we enter the shrine in Glauberg and attempt to take any of the far more valuable gifts that had been left there since the monuments were created in ancient times."

"Well, thanks for that!" jeered someone from the back benches.

"I do not mean to show disrespect," said Telemachus quickly," and yet I cannot but be plainly aware that we have caused offence. If we can make reparations to you at least in part for what was done at Glauberg, then we would be glad to do that. Perhaps your Queen can judge what might be appropriate." Could it be that Telemachus had noticed how Helladore had earlier devoured him with her eyes? Faramund thought that the commander was playing a very risky game with the queen. He had heard something about the way she behaved and hoped Telemachus was not going to lose everything in one hasty move.

"It is the Sequani tribe you have wronged," replied Helladore. "Yet still, they are our allies and are Celts. They trade with us and some of their people make a sacred visit each year to the Plain of Stone Giants for the Great Festival." She was wondering what might satisfy her warriors' desire to punish these people. The wish to please people crossed her mind rarely but it was her own want for Telemachus that nurtured an uncharacteristic generosity.

She paused as if thinking, though she had already decided upon what might be done. "So because they are our allies, we must respect their grievance and punish you."

Helladore noted the look of concern on the Telemachons' faces at this news.

"Do not worry, Telemachons, I will grant all you have asked for – safe passage through my territory to the north."

"Then where is the penalty and how is it to be paid?" queried Goreth.

"You have all requested this from me but it will not be something enjoyed by all."

There was realisation by the Telemachons and consternation. They all looked worriedly towards Goreth. All, except Telemachus.

The queen spoke again. "One of your men will remain here with me as a hostage and that man will be Telemachus."

The captives stared at each other, completely dumbfounded. Eucleides offered himself up immediately as a hostage instead but was brushed aside by Helladore. Only their commander himself registered less surprise. At last, Berengar tried to rescue the situation. "My lady, this man is a hero to his people. He has led them skilfully and well. Without him they would be like a sailing ship lost in sea, fog and lacking sail, oar and anchor. We implore you to leave him with us. When Formus gets here with his army, he will demand Telemachus' death."

"Do not worry about Formus in that regard. Even with an army of five hundred men, he is no match against our force consisting of thousands. He is aware that coming into Albion as he does, the very worst action he can take is to break his friendship with us and become our enemy. Look to yourselves Telemachons because I can offer you no protection beyond my borders. Formus pursues you and you must take to speed and the northern lands to evade him. Either you can stay here with your leader and I must give you all to Formus or your leader stays here with me in safety and you have a chance to escape. What does your commander, Telemachus, say about that?"

Chief amongst the Telemachons, Telemachus thought about the woman he loved, Hebe. For indeed he had found love again, with her. Now it was to be ripped, once more, from his grasp. Helladore was a beautiful woman, assuredly but he had knowledge about the atrocities she had committed, terrible acts that could not be disguised with a lovely face and were certainly enforced by an evil mind. His first duty however, was to the people who had given him their trust. He was under no illusion as to what the queen's hostage taking could mean for him personally but an opportunity for escape had been made.

"Telemachons, we have no choice. Formus is approaching with his army and will be at this country's borders anytime from now. You must put distance between yourselves and him. For our mistaken action at Glauberg, it is just that I remain here. It may be that in the future Queen Helladore will be merciful and release me. Today we must make amends." Telemachus was confident about a return to his people, less sure that it would be motivated by the Belgae Queen's goodness.

Hebe certainly did not accept that. Later in the morning she requested and was granted a meeting with Helladore. Throwing herself at the monarch's feet, she begged that if Telemachus was to stay she would be allowed to stay with him. Of course the plea was rejected and the monarch, with a plastered smile across her face suggested circumstances might change in the future and lead to Telemachus' release.

With that faint hope Hebe was led back to the compound by palace guards and then a whole cavalry regiment escorted the Telemachons to the northern boundary and oversaw their exit from Helladore's land.

25
Helda and the Witch

Helladore glanced down at her sandalled feet as she trod the well-worn path, her familiar route, into the enclosing forest. Such dainty human feet. She revelled in her own beauty and she certainly did not want to ruin that loveliness by catching her foot on some fallen obstacle and twisting it or have some furry tusked, wild beast running low to the ground, crashing out from the bushes and snapping it up as a delicacy. The path might be often used by herself but it was always susceptible to change and encroachment, particularly in *this* forest.

By constantly ducking under low hanging branches and circumventing wide prickly bushes she kept her progress steady. Bees kept up a buzzing drone as they flew from one open-mouthed flower to the next, pollen bags stuck to their legs. She admired them their focus and loved them for their plump juicy bodies.

Warm. Spring was in full growth and she slipped the heavy woollen shawl from her shoulders. She should be happy but she was not. Already a month had gone by since the Telemachons had left, closely followed by Formus leading his Sequani army. She had expected an angry response and even threats from the druid when he found out what she had done. There was little, barring an unexpected politeness and diplomatic acceptance. He had not done so much as made a demand for Telemachus or asked for permission to ride through her domain. Instead, he had travelled along the border to pursue his quarry north.

A conflict successfully avoided and her guest restrained at his leisure in her palace. She should be happy. She was not.

By this time, the Greek lord should have easily succumbed to her seduction. Yet no matter what she did or how, Telemachus was like long grass before a wild storm, bowing down and allowing it to brush over rather than standing tall and inviting her passion to wrap around him. If it had been anyone else, particularly a Greek like himself, she might have thought that he preferred the company of men but his chosen companion was a woman. That same woman who had wept at Helladore's knees for his return. Seeing her human frailty, the Queen had dismissed the idea that such a creature could hold any power over her lover.

In that she had been wrong. Telemachus' stubbornness was rooted in the attachment he felt for Hebe and no matter what wiles Helladore had practised upon him, he refused to give way.

So she had come here, to the primeval dense complexity that had nurtured her. Tremorous lines that gave her strength.

Unknown to the Queen, someone was observing her with small curious eyes. Above the path was a small hill and on its brow a little girl, no older than six years, had rolled onto her stomach and had sighted the monarch as she made her way along the track. The little girl's name was Helda and she had been sent by her mother to fetch some ripening pears from a wild pear tree which grew in the forest not far from the village where they lived. It was alright, that particular tree grew on the periphery with other fruit trees in a safe area *but do not go beyond that grove* warned the mother and *be back soon*.

The girl had just collected the pears for her wicker basket and had finished munching on one. They were lovely ripe and the juice dribbled down her chin. While she was wiping her face with the hem of the green woollen dress she wore, the noise made by undergrowth being pushed aside had come from below. She rolled over to see what was causing it.

Helda had never seen a queen before but instantly she recognised that this must be that wicked Queen Helladore who ruled over the country. Stories about her abounded in the village and were eagerly listened to because although the village was the nearest one to the hill fort where she lived, it might as well be the other side of Albion. Helda's settlement was only a very small one and as long as it sent the quota of crops and animals demanded and to be enjoyed by those in the Oppida, no one came to disturb them. Her father and mother both scolded her when she had used the word 'wicked' to describe the queen. And because she wasn't a naughty girl, Helda had done as she was told and had not repeated it. That was the Queen Helladore down there too. She was certain and nothing would change her mind about it. You could tell by the hair as red as fire and the pale face like the moon's face against a dark night sky. The small gold coronet on her head gave it away and…. and…. what was that long metal stick in her hand? Helda searched for the name in her mind. The older boys and girls had called it something. Stipter? Scipter? No …. Sceptre!

That was it. Sceptre. Her friends told her it meant that someone was a king or queen but Helladore's was different. Some people suggested it had the power of the gods within, like a druid's staff.

Realising all this should have made the little girl turn and run as far away as possible but she couldn't.

Helda thought she was not being naughty. She was only curious.

And the little girl left her basket heaped with pears. Excited and trembling, she moved further and further away from the fruit grove and away from the village and came closer and closer to the murderous Queen.

The path went this way and that, up and down and down even deeper. In her other hand she was carrying a large vase, evidently empty. At one place the Queen suddenly stopped. Helda, who had been flitting from tree to tree behind her, brought herself up just as quickly behind one which just covered her slight frame. She squeezed her breath in and shut her eyes tight, hoping that she might disappear. As luck would have it, two squirrels dashed up the tree she was hiding behind, rattling the foliage. Helladore's piercing gaze found them when she looked behind her with suspicion. Seemingly satisfied, she resumed her march into the forest.

It was not much longer after that worrying moment for Helda, that the Queen seemed to have reached her destination. The track had come out from the main part of the trees and more or less ended at a dell, two sides of this hollow being rock that climbed upward.

Somewhere in the background Helda could hear a watery force flowing. Her impulse at this juncture was to find a covering that was nearer to the Queen. Helladore's back was turned and she was at an appropriate distance. Ahead, closer to the dell was a soft-leaved bush that would give her the covert position she required. Helda darted out from the trees along the ground, into the bush. She peeked between the leaves and found that she had a clear view of the Queen.

Although Helda could feel the roaring water in her ears, she could still not detect where it was coming from. The wicked, pretty Queen was standing by the rock hollow. Normally in places such as that you would expect the water to come tumbling over the top into the deep pool below. There was no waterfall and where the pool should have been was a mere dry dip in the ground which Queen Helladore now moved into, after placing her vase on the bank. The child followed her movements closely. Saw that she had flung her shawl onto the dry pool's edge and was now – horrors! – taking her gown off. Helda covered her face with her hands in embarrassment.

She knew after a while that she could not remain blind forever, if just for her own safety. She squinted through her widened fingers and found that the Queen was standing naked next to the upclimbing rock with her sceptre thing stretched out towards it. Swiftly she hit the rock with it three times and the metal produced a ringing sound that jumped all around the natural hollow.

The watery roar in her ears suddenly increased and then above the Queen water gushed out in a stream from half-way up the wall-face. Calmly, the Queen remained still as the flush of water hit her head. It seemed to Helda that she must have done this many times before because she was not in the least bit frightened. The water slapped on her head and drenched her body. Although powerful, it was evidently not strong enough to knock her off her feet.

Helda's hands had dropped to her sides now but as she continued to watch, one hand found its way back to her face, her mouth in fact, in an involuntary attempt to stifle a scream.

Queen Helladore had bowed her head and stretched out her arms as if submitting herself to the watery onslaught. As the water rushed over her body, running over it to fill the stone basin in which she stood, a startling change was happening. The water became a colour that was like blood but not so opaque that Helladore's figure could not be seen under the cascade. What had pulled Helda's fist to her mouth was the sight of Helladore's body visibly undergoing a change before her: growing larger, blacker, hairier, sprouting other limbs in addition to her own arms and legs which were extending and becoming pointed.

The whole lower half of her body was filling out into a bulbuous shape, four legs either side and now the creature was turning and Helda could detect two shorter limbs either side of the head which were the fangs. Hair sprouted from its body like black wires. The beast was now about three times the size of Helladore's original human body and the gushing water that had now lost its redness looked like a mere trickle bouncing off the hard shelly surface.

A jerk and the massive figure twisted around on its six legs. Helda, panic rising, tried to keep as still as possible. The legs reached out again and the spider lifted itself away from the water and moved onto dry land. For a few moments there was stillness as if it was listening for something. A huge vibration rattled its body. It was shaking itself and the water splattered from it like thrown darts. Droplets showered the bush where Helda was hiding. The girl wished with all her heart that she had listened to her parents' advice and had not followed Helladore into the forest. She could run and try to get back to the village but the girl was afraid that nothing would escape detection from those six black observant eyes that crowned the head of the giant insect. She was sure that the moment she burst from the bush those fangs set near the eyes would quickly snap her body in half. Therefore, the right thing to do was to stay hidden and bide her time, watching for the right opportunity.

Helda prayed to the gods that the spider would simply go, move away as far as possible from the bush she hid within. But it didn't. Instead, it turned around slightly and then lowered its abdomen to the grassy patch upon which it stood. From the lowest part where small bumps extruded, came a thin stream of silk. Now Helda could see that the beast was directing her silk around and then into the vase she had left earlier. All it needed was a touch from the spray and the vase was half-filled with shining gossamer. Helda noted the curious patterning on the large two-handled pot – a continual circular chain comprising green serpents on a yellow background biting each other's tail. The silky jet ceased as suddenly as it had started and then the monstrous creature moved towards the bush which covered Helda.

With great courage, Helda held her ground and refused to give into terror and run. She made herself as small as possible while the great head tore at the top leaves above her. It did not last long. There was a gulping sound and the creature moved off. Peering out again, Helda saw that the spider had returned to its original position near the vase. It seemed to be hunched over it; the vase the size of a bucket against its vast bulk and buttressed by the cloudy silk that had been laid around it.

Those bronze jaws were just above the open rim of the vase and then something glinted from the spider's mouth. It oozed out slowly, a liquid amber colour and dropped with a plopping sound into the pot below. A thin gelatinous strand remained attached to the creature's jaws for brief moments and then was blown away in the breeze.

Satisfied, the insect raised itself up and moved back to the pool. Under the waterfall once more, it held still and everything that Hilda had seen happen before occurred now in reverse so that the beast figure reshaped and shrank back into the beautiful figure of Helladore as the water ran red and then translucent. With the Queen's back turned and the water's noise distracting her attention, Helda finally broke out from her hiding place and made it back into the trees.

Queen Helladore felt herself restored. Or was it changed? She thought about it sometimes. Neither shape – woman or spider – was more or less comfortable to her. It was just that she had spent the last thirty annual cycles investing the body of the woman rather than the spider. What had happened before that? She did not know. Her intuition was that this had been going on for a very long time back through many changes on the land and back to her original birth but whether this was as a human or an insect or some other animal she did not understand. What she did have in her mind and body was the ability to live a long, enduring life and she had survived longer than anything around her. Survival is success, there was no moral counterpoint to that and therefore gratification of her bodily needs, its pleasures, would continue that urge for survival. All she had to do was to preserve the strength from that instinct within her and defend herself against any predatory assaults.

She brushed the hair away from her face and stepped out of the waterfall. Her sceptre was standing vertical on the bank where she had stuck it into the soft mud. She waded over, reclaimed it and then returning to the rock face struck the wall three times. With the last metal chime fading into the stone, the water spout thinned and then stopped altogether. At her feet, the water drained away.

Once out of the pool, the Queen dried herself off with the shawl she had discarded earlier and after dressing herself, wrapped it around her damp hair. In the warm summer sun and light breeze she would soon be totally dry.

She took up the sceptre and cleaned the end in the little dribble of water that remained in the pool. Going to the vase, she used the sceptre to stir the liquid held there. After stirring the contents thoroughly Helladore cleaned the sceptre again and picked up the vase by its handle.

A fragrance had issued from the vase while she had mixed the concoction within. It reminded her of how much she loved the broad leaves on the Approdisiae Bush. She turned her head towards it. Then stood stock still.

Something was not usual.

She went to the large plant and carefully moved aside the stems. Walking to a part further away she again delved down. There at the bottom was a broken and flattened area: signs that something or more likely, someone, had been squatting there for a definite time. Helladore's extraordinary hearing sensed a cracking twig, a movement not so far away. The Queen spun around and sprinted towards the source back into the forest line, along the track.

All she wanted was a sight and as she came in amongst the trees that is what she got. Ahead, running between the trunks with the sunlight striking her intermittently was a girl who could have been no older than six years of age. Her long blonde hair bounced off her shoulders as she ran, the terrified face, crooking back, briefly glanced at Helladore. The Queen stopped. That was enough. There could not be that many six-year-old girls with fair hair living in the village settlement nearby.

A plan had already formed in the Queen's mind. She would send her guards into the village to take the girl into the Royal Household as a personal servant. The parents would not argue – terror and gold would keep their mouths shut. She doubted that the girl would tell her parents of today's events. She should not have been so deep into the forest on her own and that guilt would prevent her speaking. If she did, then it was just too bad for the parents.

Helladore went back to retrieve the vase and rod. At a quick pace she returned by the forest track to her palace.

26
Spider Spittle

The chamber in the private wing of the palace was richly decorated as befitted a queen. The beamed, vaulted ceiling rose up over the room space into a shape which was hexagonal but suggestive of a dome. Heavy, wooden furniture crafted with great skill predominated on the floor space: the bed at one end, a couch, low table, chairs, wardrobe, desk, set of drawers. Luxury congealed on these and around the room so that a court sycophant might admire the gold leaf thickly layered over the carved animal legs with wooden hooves supporting the couch, the jewel encrusted marquetry spanning the table's surface, the rich tapestry detailing legends important to the Belgae people hanging on the walls and on every functional base upon which a person could sit or lie were soft, comfortable fabrics made from bear, wolf, otter or rabbit skins. A genuine warrior however, would not care for such frippery.

A sweet, pungent scent, like mint, intoxicated the air. Telemachus wondered where it came from at first, then decided that it must be a perfume worn by the Queen herself. Her skin must have been oiled with it, it shone so healthily. She was reclining opposite him on the couch, the table between them. Her shoulders, arms and legs were bare, her red hair unclasped, spreading thickly and glorious over the furred rabbit cushions that propped her up.

She was relaxed and Telemachus had seen her like this three times before. On each occasion she followed the same obvious pattern of seduction and each episode finished with a petulant bout as he rejected her advances, firmly and in his own mind, kindly. It was beginning to wear him down. He realised that it was only her interest in him that ensured he was still alive. That favour though, would not continue much longer if it met with constant rejection, particularly with a woman such as Helladore. Over the past month Telemachus had sought for weaknesses to be found in the place he was kept or the method by which he was guarded. There were none. No doubt the guards' lives depended on keeping him close. The only time his shackles came off was before he entered his windowless room or went into the secure bathhouse. He had requested exercise and was granted it. Every day a sword was pushed into his hand and he would find himself duelling with a soldier from the hill-fort. The Celts wanted to know if there were any Greek tricks with the sword that they should learn.

"Are you well, My lord?" Helladore looked at him with a smile on her lips as she said it.

Telemachus returned her smile. "I am very well in body, My Lady but as for my mind that is a different matter. You have treated me generously and I am grateful but you must understand that my place is not here but with my people."

"Oh, but I do understand that Telemachus," replied the Queen with some reproach. "If it is one thing I have come to appreciate this past month it is that your heart does belong …. To those people you lead."

"Then why am I still kept here? Is it a ransom you want and has a message been sent?"

"One step at a time, my prince. You have been here a month, surely you have the patience to wait a little longer?"

"It has been a month in agony, not knowing anything about what has happened to them."

"Then let me relieve your worry. I have some news. Would you like to hear it?"

"Of course," said Telemachus, trying to control his eagerness. Even a lie from the Queen might be something to work on.

Helladore said, "First, let us have some wine." She turned and called out, "Helda, serve us from the vase."

Telemachus was startled by the girl, who had maintained a silent presence behind the Queen's throne until this moment. The child was very young and had bright long hair that reached to her waist. Without a sound and eyes averted, she crossed to an open-necked pot beside the Queen from which a long spoon protruded. The jug was a curious one – a circling chain of green serpents bit into each other's tail against a yellow background. It signified the eternal round of life on earth fed by the sun's unlimited energy. The girl was spooning out some of the liquid contents into two shallow drinking bowls. That sweet pungent odour again, but now Telemachus realised that it was rising from the silvery spangled liquid moving in the bowls and not from the Queen herself.

Helladore took a bowl for herself from the young girl and one for Telemachus. She offered him the cup. Noting his hesitation, she said, "Really, Telemachus, if I had wanted to poison you, it would have happened a long time before this. Look, I will taste it myself to show that it is harmless." She swallowed from her own drinking cup and then passed it over to him, taking the other one back for herself.

The scent rolled up again into his nose. This liquid did not have a vinous movement but was sluggish like overflowing lava. The pungent aroma was becoming very pleasant.

"I have never seen or smelt wine such as this," said Telemachus.

"Taste it!" laughed the Queen. "This is the finest wine that you will ever drink in this world. Tell me what you think. I will guarantee that you will want more and perhaps I may give you a barrel or two to take to your friends."

Telemachus took a first sip.

"Hold it in your mouth, before you swallow," warned the Queen.

He did so and it was a curious sensation. Initially what he felt in his mouth was more like food and dry at that, rather than drink. It was sweet: a golden honeycomb but flaked and drier. All at once the substance melted and he was able to swallow it easily.

"That is astonishing!" enthused Telemachus.

Helladore enjoyed the delight on his face. "It is a whole new way of drinking that this wine encourages. You imbibe it slowly, sensually – it encourages ease and profound reflection." There was no importance attached to the words she spoke to him now because what this potion caused after its primary sensual contact was a forgetting. The drinker's original willpower would be sapped and bent towards the object he looked upon, anything else became a tiresome distraction. What Helladore needed to ensure was that Telemachus would drink the bowl empty and that his attention would remain on her while he finished it. The potion's effects would last far beyond the drinking, for two, maybe three cycles of the moon at least. Enough time to make him her own and if he ever attempted to escape, well, there were other spells she could concoct to punish him for that.

"What do you call this?" wondered Telemachus aloud.

"Our herbalists call it by one name but the people call it by another – 'Spider Spittle'."

"Why do they call it that?"

"Observe it in the bowl – does that silvery sheen not remind you of dew and gossamer webs on the morning's grassy forest floor?"

Telemachus stared and could do nothing but agree.

The content in the bowl was like striated, whorled silver – fluffed cotton heads immersed in metal. He dipped his finger and lifting it out found a long silken line attached to it from inside the cup. It did not release from his finger until he had scraped it off on the bowl's edge. For a moment he thought about not drinking it at all but only for a moment. What he really wanted to do was to drink this delicious wine until it had all gone. It was not an insatiable thirst that gripped him but something else. He continued to sip from the silver while talking with Helladore.

He began to understand that where the Queen sat was a beauty which captivated everything around it. Her voice grew more melodic. The skin of her face, neck and arms was as pale and smooth as the curved aperture of a sea conch. That hair was deeply, richly red, so profuse so soft he longed to plunge his hands into it. His eyes greedily slid over her pert breasts and long shapely legs. There was nothing more that he wanted than what he saw before him.

"Now, Telemachus, let me tell you the news."

"What news?" He scratched around inside his head to recover his mind. "Oh yes …. Of course." Then almost without interest, "Please tell me, if you think it important."

Helladore registered his listless response and like an attendant doctor monitored the symptoms. She was satisfied and the beast within her got ready to pounce.

"Your people, the Telemachons, have widened the distance between themselves and Formus and his army. It did not help the High Druid that he had to trace a route around my country while the Telemachons travelled directly northwards. Formus has underestimated the tribal territories he had to pass and is delayed by negotiation. What did he expect in leading five hundred Gauls through Albion?"

Colours – bright, cogent – poured into Telemachus' eyes from where Helladore sat. His heart bounced from note to musical note emitted by that sweet spoken voice and leaped into the poorly lipped entrance to her instrumental throat. His wine cup lay empty, exhausted in its magical function which now effected an arterial course through Telemachus' spirit.

It was as if he had been pierced by an anaesthetising fang. His mind quivered and lay still, only waiting for something to exert control over it. Helladore leaned forward on her elbows, watching him. To Telemachus, her movement was acutely entomological, as was the way she looked at him.

This is the moment she thought. Reaching out her arm, she patted the space beside her on the couch. "Come to me," she cooed. Telemachus moved to that vacuum beside the Queen, drawn and rolled on an invisible thread, at once euphoric and will-less.

27
Division and Death

The information that Helladore had given Telemachus concerning his people had not been entirely accurate. It was true that Formus was struggling to rediscover their tracks but what the Queen was ignorant about was that three amongst the Telemachons - Eucleides, Thocero and Agenor - had refused to leave Telemachus as a hostage when the Queen's guards had left them at the border.

A discussion had followed in which Tyracides tried to persuade them not to go back.

"We all respect your loyalty to Telemachus but he himself would not wish you to risk your lives in such a manner. You saw how the Queen looked at him. She wishes to keep him as a hostage and it seems to me that his life is not in danger. He is in the safest place presently, while it is we who need to escape Formus by travelling north to secure our own lives. We require your help to achieve that."

Tyracides had gained much respect from the Telemachons. He had shown irrational behaviour in the past such as his ill-judged snatch at the Psychezoion's feather in the Cave of Zalmoxis but Tyracides himself had put this down to a lack in military training and had worked hard to master his impulses in emergencies and to develop a more reflective approach to difficulties that arose. In all ways his manner of life could be regarded as commendable and so his advice was taken seriously. Only Eucleides and of course, Telemachus, could carry greater authority and strangely because he was so set apart from all – Goreth as well.

"The time for that to happen – to find a home for ourselves – is not to be easily measured," said Eucleides. "I, for one, don't trust this Queen of the Belgae. Remember the stories we were told about her, to keep us frightened when we were imprisoned at her capital? Those husbands she got rid of? It won't be long before Telemachus outlasts his novelty and will follow them in the same way. No, we must attempt to get him back. You are right though, Tyracides, to strike northwards as fast as possible with the majority of our people. I and my two companions here," continued

Eucleides, placing his hands on the shoulders of both Agenor and Thocero, "will attempt to do something to retrieve our lost friend. So we part company with you now and will return with him if we make a good sacrifice to Hercules for his help in this labour."

Tyracides saw that there was little use in trying to dissuade them further.

Someone else stepped forward and joined the small group. It was Goreth. "I think I might be able to help. You have come too far with Telemachus to relinquish him to such a creature as Helladore." Eucleides and the other two were pleased to accept. The decision was made and the Telemachons separated: the many to travel beyond Queen Helladore's northern border and the tiny few to return back to her palace.

If those three returning Telemachons, together with Goreth, had seen the change wrought on Telemachus they might have been much more concerned about the possibility for rescuing him. Helda could see it and she was only a six-year-old child. She was aware what the Greek had been given to drink. After all, she had been at the scene of its manufacture. Despite herself, she found a certain fascination in analysing the effects on Telemachus, for whom she felt very sorry. Helda perceived the Greek lord's enthralment, the growing ignorance for everything around Helladore and the total focus on the Queen herself. Was this what love did to you? She wondered but then she got cross with herself because she knew how the substance was created which Telemachus had swallowed and she knew what the Queen was.

Helladore fully realised the girl had observed everything that had taken place at the waterfall, her sanctuary. When first brought to her, the child had confessed all. There were then two options for the Queen – either to kill the child or to keep her. Her instinct was to kill but it rather amused Helladore to see the girl shake whenever she came near her. Gradually, as the Queen kept her close from day to day, this stopped. Helladore did warn Helda never to speak about the incident to others but when they were alone together the Queen would talk about it and in such clever, manipulative, light-hearted terms that the girl began to doubt what she had witnessed.

"How can you believe that monster was me! The bush obscured your view. I do keep such a creature, my dear, here in the palace grounds and someday I'll show it to you. For now, you must stay with me and be my servant. If you serve me well, I will let you go back to your parents."

As a silk-rolled empty carcass husk after being fed upon by the only husband I allowed to live, since he is of my kind and helps to execute human husbands at the Sporax, thought the Queen.

These reassurances from Helladore helped to strengthen the only hope to which Helda could cling. She tried so hard to believe the Queen that she began to think she might have fallen asleep under the shrub and dreamed the whole episode. In fact, this was the manner in which she presented it to Helladore's sister, Bellosa, who did not hesitate to befriend the Queen's youngest retainer and most recent whim.

"It was strange that this vase present in your dream then made itself apparent in the Queen's hand when you followed her from the forest and it ended up as a container for the wine which she served to Telemachus, wasn't it, little girl?" Bellosa's method for befriending small children was clumsy in the extreme. She lacked any maternal affection and inside the palace walls children were neither seen nor heard – not as a result of any code of conduct but for the simple reason that they were not there. Nevertheless, she could tell from the blank expression overwhelming the child's face, that Helda had had been completely confused by the question. Bellosa bared her teeth in what she considered to be her most encouraging smile and changed the query. "When you followed her to the waterfall, was the vase in the Queen's hand then?"

The child's eyebrows knotted, her forehead rumpled and she tried very hard to remember. "I – think – so," she said at last.

Bellosa sighed. She wished another adult was here. This was like looking for a lost diamond in a swamp.

"And as you told me, the substance that the Queen called wine came from this vase and was served by you to Telemachus and made him 'funny'?"

"It wasn't my fault!" gasped the little girl.

"There, there, of course not, my dear," replied Bellosa in a soothing tone which to Helda seemed more like a hiss. "If it was anyone's fault it is to be blamed on that nasty spidery beast which produced it in the first place."

"But you said that was a dream and so did the Queen!" whispered Helda, more confused than ever.

"And so it was," said Bellosa with firmness. The wine was probably in the jug all the time and my sister had probably taken it to the waterfall to refresh herself with it. Neither the beast nor the Queen made the concoction – you just imagined it while you were asleep and sheltering under the bush. Now, what's this, little girl?" Bellosa had scooped up a biscuit from the plate beside her and waved it in front of Helda's face. The girl's eyes appraised the sweetbread with its embedded jellied fruit and she cried excitedly, "It's a cookie!"

"Just so!" Bellosa was pleased with the response, this talking with children was not so difficult after all. She felt genuinely warmed. "This is for you but save a bit to show the cook in the kitchen and tell him that I said you could have another one just like it." The child was just about to rush off when Bellosa stopped her with a stern warning, "Helda! Be sure not to tell Queen Helladore that we have spoken of this!"

"I won't ma'am, replied the girl using the courtesy she had been taught and then ran out.

As soon as she had gone, Dorstoric stepped from behind the open door that had hidden him.

"Did you hear everything she said, husband?"

Bellosa's question was needless – the utter shock on his face was answer enough.

"Can we believe her?" he managed to say.

"We are all aware that strange things exist in the forest and stranger things still within Albion's further reaches. Why is it that Helladore visits the forest so frequently? Well, I think I can tell you. First, you must understand this. Helladore was never my sister."

"Yes, the whole court knows that. She was adopted by your father."

"After my mother died," explained Bellosa, "the king, my father …." At this point she stopped. Dorstoric sensed a cumulous anger in her which surprised him. Her father had died some years ago after being thrown from his horse in the forest. He had assumed that the reason she never mentioned him was because of her sadness over his death. He realised suddenly that this conjecture was very far from the truth. Her vitriol loomed large in the room." My father went into the forest and came back out with this woman. I was fourteen at the time, my father's only daughter. Can you imagine what I felt when he adopted her as his second daughter. Only after that time she was no more treated as a daughter as I his heir. She was his concubine, his mistress, his whore! He changed the laws of the land so that she could inherit the kingdom that was rightfully mine. I was his natural child and older but that no longer mattered. She gained everything by the changed statute but it did not stop there. Her new allies at court spread the rumour that I had been bred by some wandering troubadour. My whole life has been fashioned by that creature!"

"Including your marriage," said Dorstoric sorrowfully.

"Oh no! I have never regretted that!" Bellosa laid her hand on his arm. "It is the one action in which she has failed, thinking that my unhappiness could only be increased in marrying me to you and using you as she does. Your company is the one beautiful blessing that has kept me alive these past few years. I could not bear it if you left me." A tear rolled down her cheek and it saddened Dorstoric, increasing his guilt. This marriage had been forced upon him by circumstances: a choice between imposed love or death. While the death had been avoided, there was certainly no love and though Bellosa lived in hope, he felt imprisoned with a woman he did not love at one end of his cage and a demon lover at the other.

Dorstoric quickly changed the topic. "Do you believe what the child said about Helladore is actually true and not a dream?"

"Oh yes, I do believe it," replied Bellosa bitterly. "How could someone who treats other human beings so cruelly be human herself? This transfiguration in the forest was truly witnessed by the girl and is a genuine explanation for what Helladore is. Everything make sense knowing it."

"Well, many bestial acts are committed against their fellow beings by people who may have the monstrous in their natures but are not actually monsters. I must see it with my own eyes before I believe."

"But I have seen it with my own eyes," admitted Bellosa.

"What! When?"

"Just before my father died. Like Helda I had followed Helladore into the forest and everything happened in just the same way that the girl had described it, only Helladore had no desire then to concoct an aphrodisiac and bring it back to the palace in a vase."

"Aphrodisiac?"

"Yes, that is surely what she created to affect Telemachus, as it has done."

"Did you inform your father, the king, about what you had seen?"

"It took me some time to face him with it because of the hold my so-called sister had gained over him but it was not until I tried to explain what I had witnessed that I fully realised her power. His reaction was unexpected – not even anger with me for having said something against her. It was though he was bound by the most powerful spell and could not speak anything remotely critical against her."

"Made powerless by a spell – or an aphrodisiac?"

"Since the child has informed us about her experience I have begun to think so. What puzzles me is that despite Helladore's nature – her inhuman essence and inclination to kill for pleasure – she has allowed Helda to live. I mean why would she do that when the girl could report to anyone what happened at her sanctuary in the forest?"

"Indifference?" muttered her husband. "It might be that she does not care whether people hear it or not. All sorts of stories are told about her already. One more does not matter and can be easily dismissed with ridicule, particularly if a child is the source for it. Look at what happened when you tried to tell your father. He did not do anything and ended up dying soon after he had heard anyway. That was surely not a coincidence."

Bellosa took a step away from Dorstoric, as if estimating him and with something close to a stricken expression on her face, uttered what was a plea, "But what do we do, Dorstoric?"

The aristocrat in him muffled an immediately generous response phrased in terms of action. "We wait."

"Wait? For what?"

Dorstoric was thinking rapidly about the situation, *his* situation. Sympathy for Bellosa did not affect that in any way, shape or form. In fact, it momentarily crossed his mind that it might be to his advantage to go to Helladore and give Bellosa up. He considered the outcome. He had himself just suggested that the Queen was indifferent. It was hard to calculate what her reaction could be. She might perversely decide to cut him free since he now understood what she was, if the little girl was to be believed. If that resulted, he would not reckon worthwhile odds on his own survival. Bellosa was her adopted sister and like her attitude to certain clan leaders within the kingdom, even Helladore would avoid having to kill when other solutions were to hand.

Before he could answer, Bellosa spoke again. "How long are we going to live like this, Dorstoric? That woman is a danger to you and to me. You may not last long in her favour and despite my royal status there will come a time when she feels her power is so inviolable that she can act with impunity against me. We cannot afford to wait."

"So ….," began Dorstoric, going over to a gilt and cushion covered couch in the sumptuous apartment and languidly stretching his limbs out along it, "your thoughts as to what should be done are?"

Bellosa regarded him with doubt for the first time in the conversation and wondered if she might trust him completely. "You do know that your time with my adopted sister is limited Dorstoric – understanding what she is, her history with former suitors and now this new fondness for the Greek prince, Telemachus?"

"How could I be so unaware, my dear? Perhaps you are right: I am being cautious at a time which requires risk and some innovation."

"That is exactly what we must do. We must take the initiative that is offered through this new companion she has chosen. He is an unknown to the court so any sudden calamitous act could be credibly blamed upon him – right up to the Queen's own death."

It was not such a shocking suggestion, particularly after Bellosa had disclosed her adopted sister's origin – this weird organism from the forest depths, neither entirely human nor completely beast.

"You plan to murder her and inculpate him?"

"Wouldn't that be the most effective way to rid this country of the monster?"

"Not necessarily."

"Why not?"

"There will," said Dorstoric, using the slow habitual drawl that was his manner when considering anything of importance, "….be consequences."

"Of course there will," snapped Bellosa. "We just have to make certain to take control quickly and forestall them."

"Surely it would be better to make it plainly obvious to people what Helladore is: to expose the monster in her before we kill her?"

Bellosa frowned. "That would be difficult."

"But very, very, necessary."

Bellosa was beginning to comprehend what he was getting at. "I think you might be referring to some public and spectacular display of her monstrosity."

"Continue," said her husband in encouraging tones.

"One in which she has no restraint over her own metamorphosis. Are you thinking about the water in her own sanctuary?"

"Yes, I am."

"But there will be immense problems with that. I cannot remember its whereabouts since it was so long ago. We will need to steal her sceptre before travelling into the forest, then discover the place and make the water cascade. Only a small amount of the water can be brought back with us. Will the magical effect remain once it is taken away from its source? Again, will the quantity we bring back have enough power to effect any change at all?"

"We don't know until we try," said Dorstoric, with the same assurance in his voice as before. "Helda will show us the way."

"You want me to persuade her?"

"Yes."

They discussed the details of what should be done. The relationship between these two was a strange one. Neither quite trusted the other and yet there was enough motivation for both to go ahead with the planned assassination. If anything, it was more urgent for Dorstoric to take part than Bellosa. He agreed with his wife's implication that the presence of Telemachus would mean the extinction of his own, even if he informed on his wife. Bellosa had less to worry about than he if she did nothing so it was incumbent on him to keep her enthused over his strategy. His recent thoughts intending betrayal quickly disappeared. His wife's corroboration for Helda's experience had convinced him.

During the interchange Dorstoric wanted to uncover the ideas Bellosa might have concerning their own future after the Queen was gone. To some extent he was testing the influence he had over his wife. He expected her to suggest that she would reign as queen and all-powerful monarch herself, while he would be her consort only. He prepared to argue it out with her. Surprisingly, her view was that they should both rule as peers. This was a satisfactory confirmation for his own sway over her and bode well for him in getting to accept any future mistresses he might have. Bellosa had put up with his nightly visits to Helladore, after all.

Bellosa dreamt on. This was the opportunity to show Dorstoric what he meant to her. It would be his salvation. His gratitude to her would become the true love for which she had constantly craved. After Helladore had been removed, they would live together in their marriage as properly committed partners for all to see. No more separations at night when he went to visit that spidery whore.

And so, mutually blind to the other's nature, they took the essential steps towards the Queen's murder. In this strategy the little girl was to take a crucial part. It was easy to gain her help once they had promised that she would be returned to her parents. It was Helda who stole the Queen's sceptre – a particularly tricky operation since Helladore seldom let the rod out of her sight. However, one day the Queen left it safely locked away – as she thought – while on a two-day visit to another part of the country. Helladore did not like risking it on long journeys. Helda knew where the key was kept to unlock the secret compartment in the desk that held the sceptre. She brought the staff back to the other two and then they all set out for the secret place in the forest. The nightmarish vision of Helladore still fresh in her mind, the little girl found the path easily enough and striking the rock at precisely the same spot, water soon cascaded down. Collecting some in two pots they carried with them, the company returned to the palace fort, the guards saluting Bellosa at the great gates. The sceptre was restored to its safe place and the water stored away from prying eyes. A day later, Helladore returned.

The public spectacle which Bellosa and Dorstoric had referred to in their plans was indeed about to happen. A feast to Belinus, God of earth, was to be organised very soon when the crops were in the ground at that part of the year called Beltine. Everyone living in the land ruled by Helladore would present themselves and it would be the perfect opportunity to expose her.

People living in her territory were divided into twelve clans, each led by a tribal chieftain and a druid who also served as an important advisor amongst the clan leader's military force. Prime in importance amongst all these chiefs and one who balanced on a cliff edge in coming close to being executed by Helladore as a potential rival was a forty-year-old human ox with drooping moustache named Calevenorix. Immensely tall, with stubbornness to match, Helladore kept his loyalty – just – through occasional gifts of slaves and exotic goods imported from abroad. She never made these so frequent as to appear weak and he did not insult her authority by asking for more. If his brains had equalled his brawn he would have gained greater influence over the other clans but although he was respected for his strength and courage by the others and also, sometimes, his opinion, Helladore was not seriously concerned about him.

The festivities were held on the flat death land below her palace fort. They took place annually and much mead was consumed together with imported wine contained in amphorae; songs were sung in praise of the heroes; religious rites and sacrifices administered by the druids.

The Queen herself was a central onlooker at the main ceremony which began the proceedings. She sat at a long table in front of the stone altar where the High Druid stood. Either side would be her immediate court circle including her current lover, as in this instance Telemachus and then the clan leaders sat on the remaining seats. The animal to be sacrificed would be held on the altar or before it, depending on its size. For an event such as this only a four-footed beast would be acceptable to the sun god. Calevenorix had been given the honour to kill it. A young bullock was to be offered. The kill would need to be clean. Sometimes these particular beasts could cause problems if death was not swift. Calevenorix felt the great weighty axe in his hand and regarded the fine edge. To the north of him up to the foot of the hill topped by Helladore's citadel, were buried the dead. To the left, to the right and behind him, outside of this ceremonial circle were the barrows, the burial mounds that housed the dead, his people's ancestors. The Children of Llyr, those beings who controlled the underworld, had to be placated. Otherwise they might rise up, their terrible forms sifting through the soil, bringing the dead with them. Corn had to grow to feed the living people. Therefore, he who provided the nourishing life force to soil and plant, Belinus, must be encouraged. And that divine motivation could only be achieved with a clean, violent death.

A druid raised a war trumpet, the carnyx, to his lips and blew. A low bass note thrilled through the ears of the attendant crowd. Calevenorix crouched into his battle stance beside the ox and suddenly lunged into a sprint in a wide arc around and behind the animal, all the time elevating his axe. It was the momentum he needed to deliver the force. Coming to an abrupt halt on the other side of the bull's neck, his body arched back and then forward, arms stretched taut, scything down the great cutting iron wedge to slice through the beast's neck.

Its head fell onto the stone altar while the remainder keeled over. Blood was everywhere. An air-splitting cheer went up and the crowd began to chant the spell of blood and earth and renewal, an appeal to Belinus. Dusk dropped and the huge fire behind the High Priest's back was cracking and spitting.

Bellosa was sitting next to Helladore and on her left sat Dorstoric. She could see that Telemachus was very different to the man who had first appeared on Albion's shores, a moon cycle ago. He was nothing now but the Queen's fawning pet. Reduced from a great hero, the Prince of the Telemachons, to a slave and the Celts treated him with disdain. Those great exploits they had been told about by his warriors who had been held captive here in the land of the Belgae, all added up to nothing under the sorcery exercised over him by Queen Helladore. That it was magical enchantment from deep under this world was stark. You only had to look at him.

After the sacrifice came the meat and the drink. Honey-dew mead and beer served by the female slaves from the flagons poured into horn or pottery cups. On Helladore's table only gold or silver touched the drinkers' lips. Bellosa and Dorstorix bided their time. They were used to these Beltine festivals hosted by the Queen and as the drink flowed freely, Helladore drinking almost as much as the men, they prepared for the event which had come to be almost as important as the sacrifice to Belinus. At last a drunken voice called out from a clan leader at the table.

"Will you do the honour of dancing for us, my Queen?"

Helladore looked up and smiled. She signalled to a slave with her eyes and he brought her leather wrist bands with the small bronze bells attached to them. She made another gesture and a group of young warriors seemed to appear from nowhere amongst the crowd and took their position in a line on each side of the altar. They carried their shields but these were long ceremonial accoutrements made from bronze and instead of swords the soldiers carried wooden sticks with which to beat them and produce ringing percussive notes for the dance that was to take place. Also joining the warriors were skilled *crwth* players, three in all, carrying their wooden sound boards strung with boar gut by their side. These instruments could produce a resonant jangly whirr of melodic notes to accompany the lyrics chanted or sung by the bards to bring back the dead Celtic heroes and their exploits to the listening audience. It was with such an instrument as this that Bellosa's mother was won over from her husband the king for a night, through honied words and a deft picking of strings with a quickly moving bone shard. Other musicians joined as well – two carrying wooden rattlers and ski-stretched drums, another two with metal cymbals, more bells and wooden flutes.

They reached their positions and the music started up. Helladore took her blouse off and underneath to the waist she was completely naked except for the blue woad paint that had been drawn over her breasts, stomach and back in whirled lines and circles and where, here and there, an oak leaf pattern could be discerned. The lines were so numerous around her fulsome breasts and the aureoles that they appeared densely blue. The nipples stood pointedly, proudly in the measure of her excitement. As she stood up and tied the tinkling bells to her wrists, her flounced skirt hung loosely over her swelling hips down to her small ankles. Applause: polite, forced, expected, accompanied her first movements out to the dance space but before the half-hearted clapping died away, it was overtaken by the sinister beat from the warriors' shields. She seemed to follow the sinuous pattern on her torso, revolving several times, her skirt stretching out like a dark moth, newly metamorphosed and preparing for its first flight. Raised arms in the air and shaking bells on her wrists, Helladore swayed out to the altar which had only just seen a ritual sacrifice. The oxen's body had been pulled away but the head remained and its blood continued to drip down the stone.

Everyone recognised the dance she was about to perform. It was the one most fitting for the feast of Beltine: the Dance of Fertility.

The crwth had started up, their plucked melody making some attempt to ameliorate that tangible aggression from the shields. Helladore had finished her evolutions and now stood still, apart from her sandalled feet which under her lifted skirt were seen to be stamping out in time to the unified drum-and-shield beat. Her movements – to the side, to the side and to the front – were repetitious, almost hypnotic and what was uncanny was the way that the top half of her body remained so still, her face and chest forward to the watching audience. It was almost as if she herself was poised on a mound, the mound was her skirt which was adorned with long silvery coils and tassels. Near the bottom, they shook and tremored as the small animals of her feet tried to beat a way out of the trap. With the music growing in volume, the flutes added another pitch and yet pursued the ostinato. Then speed and volume came to a shocking stop. But the feet continued to struggle. The trumpeters lifted their instruments vertically above the crowd and from the bronze dragon- headed mouths issued a deep phobostic wail. At that instant Helladore thrust her torso out to the audience, breasts hanging loose, her arms elbow-crooked outwards like pneumatic spider legs and face twistedly wrapping a protruded tongue, fanging the air. The feet paused.

At the table, Bellosa and Dorstorix allowed the music and movements to restart before slipping away but only to where their own slaves had been ordered to wait.

The carnyxes had finished and the other instruments resumed the same diatonic phrase as before. Flutes with crwth fashioned a softer sound, while the rhythm on the shields was slower, quieter.

And now Helladore, in her dance, performed actions that were familiar to the many women in the audience. She wove a skein into cloth. She was the loom and in the next moment her body was the bobbin, turned and mingled through a thread framework, leaving behind her spooled creation. It seemed to those watching and listening that Helladore was beginning to emulate the crop cycle and hunting practices that brought them food and life. Her dance and the musical notes underscoring it quickened its pace once more.

In all this, Helladore had been totally absorbed by her own performance, her gesture and rhythm tuned only to expressing a symbolic narrative.

But something jarred her peripheral vision. She seemed to come to herself and wondered why Bellosa and Dorstorix were suddenly before her with water pots in their hands.

Before anyone could stop them, they had flung the water over her. She was gasping and drenched. The first thought that occurred to Helladore was that this was some kind of joke. This water that dropped over her head and scoured her breasts soon told her something very different. Its touch brought an immediate and horrified realisation.

Uproar resulted from the assault. Hands were laid on Bellosa and Dorstoric despite their relationship to the Queen but Bellosa managed to scream out, "My people! It's not us you should fear – look at her!"

Some amongst the crowd reacted naturally to the command and turned their attention back onto the Queen.

Helladore could not stop what was happening to her. The water, having changed colour the moment it touched her skin, dripped bloodily onto the ground. She was increasing size visibly, her arms and legs extended into haired piston segments while the main part of her figure swelled into two further sections. From head to toe her human skin flayed off. Ripped, in diaphanous pieces, it blew away on the breeze.

People at the altar were retreating from the being that had risen up over them. The lords at the table hastily left to fetch their weapons. In the face of this unexpected menace arms that had restrained Bellosa and Dorstorix dropped their hold.

Telemachus, who had observed the dance closely and sat fixed in his seat when his lover had broken into bits, reforming into this horrible monstrosity, did an extraordinary thing. He rose up from the table and without a weapon started to walk towards the creature as if going to meet a friend. He was oblivious. Warning shouts from those who had just been dining with him were ignored. Anyone could see by the empty expression on his face that his reasoning powers had fled. Was it fear or the magnetic pull of the witch's sorcery? No one there that day could doubt that it was the latter. Fear would have made him run – either away from her or towards the beast with a sword in his hand. This insensate walk to his doom was the simple logic of his condition for the last month while in her company: humanless, a victim.

He came close to the mouth and fangs. Stopped. It was as if he was offering himself up. The crowd behind him was much depleted. Some had left to escape to the palace fort for safety but those that remained were the younger and older Celt warriors, ready to fight. Amongst those, four figures gathered and in his right mind Telemachus would have recognised them instantly.

Telemachus was reflected in the black spider's eyes and its pedipalp extended, brushing the prince. In some strange way it was almost repulsively affectionate, as if protective towards the man. Yet a moment later that changed as the head snapped forward and the fangs, dripping toxin, prepared to shoot down and bury itself into Telemachus.

In quick succession two arrows whistled to the beast and pierced the same eye. The giant arachnid jerked back. Behind Telemachus, Agenor lowered his bow and sprinted for him, quickly followed by Eucleides, Goreth and Thocero. They yelled out, "Get back Prince! Before it tries to strike again!"

The call from familiar voices stirred Telemachus. His face restored to itself a living expression. His comrades reached him and dragged him away just before the beast struck with its fang in a second attempt to destroy him. This time the fang found substance but it was only the soft earth where Telemachus had been standing.

And now the giant arachnid found itself faced with a line of warriors, shields up, spears and swords being thrust at its legs and sides. The black discus eyes peered from one point to another, estimating the nearest prey and the head jerked. A warrior screamed as a fang crunched through his stomach and he was lifted high into the air. His limbs squirmed for an instant but he was dead before he got to the creature's mouth. Briefly there erupted a gurgled sluicing while the juices were sucked from inside his body and then the empty carcass was blown away.

Goreth, Eucleides and Thocero had returned to the fight, leaving Agenor to tend to Telemachus. They flung themselves at the creature's legs, Goreth and Eucleides on one, Thocero another. Using the thick wiry hairs on the legs, they climbed upwards. The beast that had been Helladore had already fastened on another brave young Celt and was busy removing his internal organs after liquefying them with her toxin.

Using her distraction, the three climbed faster but the additional weight on her legs reminded the beast that there was another danger far more urgent to deal with. Its limbs vibrated and with a shout, Thocero dropped to the ground. He was unhurt since he had failed to get very far. The other two, at the top section of the leg, hung on grimly and with a hiatus in the juddering they managed to haul themselves onto the smooth carapace, thicker than armour plating, just behind the insect's head.

Below, men chopped successfully at its feet and whole sections came away under the sharp blades. Panic seemed to grip the monster. Its abdomen, comprising the bulbous lower section of the body, squirmed from side to side. Silk shot from its spinneret enveloping two men and they choked, drowning, in sticky gue. Thocero was caught by some of it but not badly so.

Goreth and Eucleides had worked themselves to a position just behind the eyes and where, beneath the shell, lay the brain. It was difficult to keep their grip and remain there but somehow they did. Helping each other to their feet they took their weapons – Goreth, a sharp three-pronged iron trident and Eucleides his bronze spear – then with all the force and steadiness they could muster, smashed the points through the eyes in the direction of the brain.

A sound like a high-pitched scream sundered the air: all movement ceased. Then the spider's abdomen sank to the floor. Its eight legs shrivelled up, withered into themselves. All the commotion suddenly stopped but there were still moans from the men who had been knocked aside by the spider's massive form.

28
At the Village Boundary

Once the power Helladore had wielded over her land had gone, the peace and good relations between the clans became precarious. Being the previous ruler's daughter, Bellosa took her place on the throne at the Belgae palace fort and Dorstorix was made her co-ruler. The change was accompanied by much gift-giving and as a reward for their part in destroying Helladore, Telemachus and his friends were freed and given five fine horses, sturdy travellers, to help them on their way. The Telemachons were desperate to leave as soon as possible and not only because they wanted to rejoin Tyracides.

"I have seen the contemptuous glances that the clan chief they call Calevenorix has cast at the new royal couple," said Telemachus to the others. "This land will not remain at peace for very long and so we must get far from here before we are involved in the anarchy brought by civil war." The others required little encouragement and so they left on the same day that Helladore had been exposed and killed.

They travelled north, following the stars and Thocero's lodestone which he was never without. Telemachus imagined Formus and his army would be in front of them and Tyracides in advance of that. He hoped the Telemachons had not been captured. It was a tough journey at the pace they forced upon themselves. Sometimes Goreth left his horse tied to the others and swam the rivers along the route. He had an uncanny knack for choosing only those waterways going in a northerly direction. They worried that they would lose him: fast as he was he did not swim through water at the rate of a horse canter. There were suspicions that he was enjoying the fluid sensations and sights of his natural environment. When the friends stopped to rest for the evening he would always turn up later, refreshed as if from a short walk.

For several days they journeyed like this through the land of the Belgae and then the country inhabited by the Atrebates. The villages they came to were small. All they had to do to be guaranteed a warm welcome in the Belgae villages was to announce the news that the Queen was dead. Other than describing their part in Helladore's death, the company limited their comments on what might happen next by explaining who ruled now and maintaining optimism for the country's future.

It was Telemachus who did the talking. His Celtic language skills had improved with an enforced stay at the Queen's court. Now that he had been restored to himself, regaining his independence and self-awareness, Telemachus was staggered by the occult force Helladore had exercised over him. The past month was hazy in his memory, the only clear centrifugal point being Helladore herself and the pleasure she took and gave to him. He was able to communicate with others at court but from behind an intangible wall. Always it was better to turn back from it and to converse with the beautifully real and solid presence that the Queen offered. Of course Telemachus had fathomed that the cause for his disorientation and the attack on his self-will had begun that evening when she had given him the delectable wine to drink. It was no wine but some concoction that contained a magic more powerful than any earthly intoxicant, a magical power that had coursed through his mind and body leaving perhaps a permanent scar or strange abilities behind. He was not sure which. If it was a scar, then that was the memory that he had lost all freedom, independence, to another. If abilities, it was the proficiency he had developed with the language these people spoke. But there was something else, a thing deeper than mere chatter. It lay in this new land to which he had come and that he had discovered when accompanying Helladore on her trips from the palace into the forest and hills surrounding it. Naturally, he realised now why she had to make those journeys, her monstrous nature being inhuman and wild, she must have found it difficult to be restrained by human dwellings. She had given him that wine more than once and he had accompanied her out from the fort more than once. Unstable memory ruined his recall about these visits to the wild but it was the emotional and physical senses that were strengthened by them and which seemed to be getting ever sharper. He tried to explain it to Eucleides when they all rested as overnight guests at a Belgae village. They both talked together at the edge of it.

"Do you miss Macedonia, Eucleides?"

"Yes, like an orphan misses his mother and father. Macedon made me what I am. I came down from my mountain village to make a living by the sword. The pure air up near the clouds amongst the oaks and pine gave my lungs life; coming down from there to the blue Aegean Sea, Poseidon granted me the expanse my heart craved. You Hellenes and us Macedons, what would we be without crossing the blue waters?"

"No regrets then, my old friend? If you had stayed at Pella, you might at this moment have been conquering the Persian cities with King Alexander. They say that he is a man and warrior like no other. Irresistible as the tide."

"I would not have survived his father's rule," said the other seriously. "That man was a tyrant such as the ones we removed from Sicily, only a better tactician in war and with a far more effective fighting force behind him. As for his son, well, let us not forget what he has done to Thebes. Razing the houses of his fellow Greeks to the ground does not suggest a man who is interested in liberty for his compatriots whatever he might say about those Greek cities in the east needing to be freed from their Persian overlords."

"Have we met with better rulers along the Danu or in Gaul or here in Albion?"

Eucleides broke into a chuckle, his grey hairy face cracking. "Probably not. Two-footed or four, we are all beasts by nature and beasts we shall remain."

"It is law that gives men civilisation."

"As long as that law sits on the shoulders of justice."

"Justice is as hard to come by here as anywhere else," said Telemachus. "It is a strange country that we explore."

"Further than strange, peculiar I would say. Look at these houses they live in. How can a man live in a roundhouse? Give me a house solid and square with more than one floor and one room to roam around in. Those straw roofs cover the whole building and make it look as if they are buried in the ground."

"Keep your voice down, Eucleides, we don't want to upset our hosts."

"Well, really, Telemachus, would you want to live like that – where everyone sleeps together and then where is the Andron, the place where men, both young and old, can drink wine together and sing the tales of their forefathers?"

"While travelling we have seen them do that elsewhere in open ritual spaces or the houses of their chiefs. Perhaps sharing everything together, including the space they live in, explains the Celts' attitude to their women."

"In what way?"

"That their women are given freedoms never allowed for in the east and in Hellas. Surely you must have noticed that, Eucleides?" The veteran did not answer. When he found himself in their company for any extended period, he treated all women like his own mother, with respect. Beyond that he didn't give them a second thought. "Remember some of those Celtic settlements in Europa – there were armed women amongst the men and that was definitely the case when we first met with Helladore in her palace hall. She clearly had female warriors included in her military guard."

"I daresay she did," agreed Eucleides, "but the population here does not seem so great as in our own homeland and it might be that if you cannot get enough soldiers because of the lack, then conscripting Amazons might be your only answer."

Telemachus almost gave up. Getting Eucleides to think beyond the geographical limits of his own closely kept belief system was impossible. Far easier it was to persuade him to any risky venture for the thrill or to travel the world in pursuit of something that might not be attainable. "Is there anything you like about this land in which we are trying to settle? Because if not, my friend, we could always continue travelling for the rest of our lives."

Eucleides cocked his head at Telemachus, recognised that he was teasing him and thought seriously.

"I like the land – it is cooler than where we have come from but still warm. The earth is fertile and produces much fruit, some I have never tasted before and good sturdy wheat crops. The forests are abundant with wild boar and succulent red meat can be cooked from them. I especially like this drink they call beer that has been offered us," said Eucleides becoming animated. "It tastes like warm bread and sings in the head. The cheese is different to ours too – it crumbles and softens in the mouth and is rich and creamy."

Telemachus was about to make a jokey comment concerning Eucleides' stomach but he wanted to encourage the effusiveness in his friend, a rare characteristic in him.

"What about the people, Eucleides, the Britons?"

"Ah, them. Well, they are the same as us and yet not the same. Whereas we are all marble and hot sun in the sky, they are all earth and wood. They are close to the things of the earth and those that live underneath. I felt that about the Celts in Galati and I certainly recognise it in these Britons. That's all I can say." The last was added with a simple shrug of the shoulders.

They were standing in the dusk at the village boundary, faces towards the forest's edge. The birds had gone quiet and the tall trees began to block out the little light that attempted to distinguish their dense forms.

"I think you have hit upon something there that I began to understand ever since the sorceress Helladore gave me her wine to drink," said Telemachus.

"Why, you are not suffering some sort of relapse from its effects are you, my lord?" replied Eucleides, anxiously.

"Don't worry, Eucleides, I am not about to lose my reason again." His friend was relieved. "But I will tell you that somehow I have been made to be different when I am away from human habitation and in the forest and near the rivers. No doubt the same will occur to me when I am in the hills and on the mountain tops."

"That, I think, is another remarkable feature in these people. They are much closer to the wild gods than we are. Pan is their father, Demeter their mother, while for us Zeus is our king and progenitor on the land. Their barbarity keeps them close to the wild. We were once like them."

"Their gods are nothing like ours, not even Pan and Demeter. It is what communicates itself with me when I walk in the forest."

"Speak to Goreth," advised Eucleides, "he above all, should know what is happening to you."

"I will."

Eucleides turned from the forest back to the village. "Meanwhile, Telemachus, where do we go from here?"

Telemachus followed his gaze and then stared up at the sky, the black cloth mint spun, its filtered tiny suns beginning to fix in ice around the reeling depths.

"We carry on. Northwards. That will necessarily mean us following behind Formus and his Sequani Celts, avoiding detection, but follow we must since he is chasing Tyracides."

"Do you mind that the Telemachons are being led by Tyracides?" asked Eucleides on impulse.

Telemachus looked surprised. "Why should I mind? He is a good man. We need more like him. People like you and him, Eris and Melissa will help us to get where we need to go and help to defend ourselves from such foes as Helladore and Formus."

"Where we need to go," repeated Eucleides, musing.

"Yes. That is what I wanted to discuss with you. Despite my mind being befuddled and blunted in Helladore's company, I was able to pick up something about Formus' intentions. Much of it was the Queen's conjecture about his motives but it sounded plausible. She had sent out scouts to report on his movements and to spy on his dealings with the local people he had come across. They brought back the news that he was finding it increasingly difficult to negotiate passage for his force through the territories held by different chiefs. If it was not for the fact that he was well known amongst the priestly caste, his army would have been utterly destroyed by a collective action against him."

"It's a pity that hasn't already happened."

"He has gained some sympathy because he carries the remains of the High King Orsek from Glauberg with him."

"Protected by the shadow he hates most," muttered Eucleides.

"Exactly. But what he requires is the ability to travel freely without harassment or attack in the Northern Lands, where he is unknown and will almost certainly be met with hostility."

"Almost?"

"There is a means for him and his army to be guaranteed absolute safety as long as he does not abuse the privilege."

"By doing what?"

"He will travel to the Plain of Rebirth, the Ancestral Gods and there dedicate and bury the first king of the Sequani. After that he will request the Rite to Amity; it is a solid wax cylinder on which are inscribed the sacred runes that will give him free passage through any tribal territory or kingdom he wishes. His desire will not be refused – he is a High Druid and belongs to that highest order which grants the rite. No High Druid has been refused up to this time."

"So what do we do once he gets his hands on that? His pursuit will be unimpeded; before long Tyracides will be surrounded and the Telemachons slaughtered."

"If we keep running."

"We could turn and fight and taking in the odds – five hundred to one hundred – be slaughtered as warriors instead."

Telemachus brushed aside the irony. "I am glad you said 'we' Eucleides because indeed by the time Formus meets up with the Telemachons, we should have rejoined them. To gain the Rite to Amity, Formus will exercise the little courtesy he has and be delayed at the Plain. We must take the advantage, by-pass him and meet up with our people. It is then that we must take some action to either distract him or attack and reduce his forces."

"It will be no easy task but you are right. If our only thought is to flee we will at some time or other exhaust ourselves and be in a poor condition to fight."

"Formus is a Celt but a Celt from Gaul. He is familiar with the region below the Plain of Rebirth but not the country to the north. There is a daimon whispering at my ear that somehow, somewhere amongst the mysteries hidden by this land there will come the help that we desperately need. But it will only come if we provoke it."

Eucleides was not sure if it was Telemachus thinking these last thoughts or the dregs from Helladore's potion revealing their enduring effects. On the whole, though, he definitely recognised this decisive individual as his former friend and much preferred him to the bleary eyed idiot he had seen sitting at Queen Helladore's side.

At that instant a cry shot up from within the forest. It was hard to say what had made it. A bird call, high-pitched but having enough sinister clarity to suggest the shriek from a woman. On its fading exit, other, numerous calls started up: a clattering laughter. After a few minutes they, too, died away, sharpening the silence by their absence.

The old warrior shuddered. "I could roam at will and take pleasure in it when I walked the woodlands in Hellas but the ones here are different. They contain base gods and occult creatures. I would rather sleep one night with an ugly woman than spend the same time in these forests, subject to those daimonic forces."

Telemachus chuckled. "At least you would have an excuse when the woman wakes up and complains about you sleeping."

Eucleides clapped the younger man on the shoulder, forcefully. "My lord," he said jovially, "we cannot stand around here all night if we are to get back to Tyracides and the others."

They returned to their guest quarters, safe for now, from strange sounds in the night.

29

Of Stones and the Bridge of Fusion

Formus stood on the small hill overlooking the Plain of Rebirth. Behind him was a large wooden building that served as a meeting hall for the important visitors to this place and behind that were a number of dwellings, some small for families and others much larger, again to accommodate the pilgrims and the people who accompanied their dead to be buried at this sacred place. Some of his men had slept in the meeting hall overnight, others had barracked in various homes and guest houses around the settlement. He himself, the Lady Andraste and Artemius had been accommodated in the Chief Druid's roundhouse. Effectively that man, Runegar, was the ruler of the Plain. Any king or queen or warlord stepping onto this land would only do it at his welcome and all their personal authority was held in abeyance before his, while they were guests here.

The plain in front was neither plain nor perfectly flat. It consisted of numerous structures engineered and built from stone, wood and turf. Stone and wood created the circular temples, huge blocks and posts; the grass turf rolled over the barrows, beneath which were housed the ancestors. Along the horizon, Formus' eyes tracked the sacred causeway that led to the biggest monument, in it the most powerful rituals and greatest offerings to the sun and moon were made at the most necessary times in the year.

This hill he stood on was fashioned by men but that space below had been marked out by the gods. As such, only the Chief Druid could hold it for them. Agreement between all the kings and tribal leaders of the lands bordering this site meant that protection was given it from any incursion and to the people who travelled there to worship.

The brilliantly bright, chipped whitened stones on the central monument, the stone sentinels themselves, gleamed under the direct sunlight.

At his feet, Formus could see people busied around the site preparing it for the next sacrifice and those others moving along the sacred route. They were on foot and walking in unison with a slow ritual tread. As far up as he was, Formus could just detect the hymnal chant used by the travellers to announce themselves before meeting with the sacred space.

Formus was somewhat irritated. He had never believed that it was going to be an easy matter to transport an army comprising five hundred men across Albion without hindrance and he was right. First, Helladore had refused him permission to travel through her lands and then he had to barter passage for his army not once but several times through the territory belonging to the Atrebates. Unlike the united land of the Belgae, the country to the east was held by several warlords and hence costly to travel through. He could not continue to leak gold as he had done to get this far and yet he would almost give what was left to bring the Rite of Amity into his hands. A soft footfall sounded lightly behind him. He turned around, expecting it to be the Lady Andraste and was surprised by the sight of Runegar, without attendants.

The Chief Druid was not a tall man but his presence impressed a certain authority upon onlookers. It was the manner in which he carried himself – relaxed, assured. His sleeved, embroidered robe was clean and ended above the ground. An idiosyncrasy for a man in his position was the smooth chin and the long hair on his head bound in one thick plait behind his head under a golden hat filled with signs of the moon, sun and stars, such as those worn by his fellow druids and sacred individuals on the continent of Europa. Formus himself had the right to wear one but found it cumbersome, preferring instead to wear a simple gold circlet around his own head.

The golden hat nodded. "Hello Formus, I am glad to find you alone like this – it gives us an opportunity to speak in private and perhaps be a little more candid with each other."

Formus looked to the side and waved away two of his own guards, who, catching sight of him, had begun to approach.

"Just what I was thinking, Brother Runegar. So much more can be achieved by the willingness of two rather than the reluctance of many, don't you think?"

Runegar ignored the familiarity that Formus had used, the term 'brother' being more commonly spoken between druids visiting each other in the settlements rather than to a priest such as himself who had authority over other priests and dispensed the sacred duties on this most holy site.

"Yes, I do. Now, Formus, let us get down to the matter. You wish to bury Orsek, the king of your kings, ancestor of ancestors, in this sacred burial place. Am I right?"

"As we have already discussed, my friend."

"Further, you would like to be given the Rod of Amity?"

"Only by your good graces."

"The question is, what more do you want?"

Formus looked at the grey eyes focused seriously on his and recognised a better man in them. He had heard about Runegar's good works amongst his own people and indeed with those from other tribes: the rich cash gifts to the Plain of Rebirth, donations from powerful lords, taken by him and diverted to some extent in helping to rebuild villages and families injured by war; his constant diplomacy between chiefs and kings and queens to maintain peace. Formus was not unnerved by seeing a worthy man as others might be. Others might feel inferior to such people, regretting their own deficiencies. Formus felt the opposite. He was the superior being. He knew that all worthy men die before their time. This world he inhabited was divided into two. The predator and the victim. You were either one or the other: it was the one and only natural law. This man that stood before him was a gentle lamb – soft and innocent, only resolute in its own stupidity before the sweeping sacrificial fang. Could he himself ever be like that? No, he could not, which is why he sensed the power inside himself and inwardly laughed. Predators like himself though, had to exercise great cunning so as not to be found out. The victim had to be teased and drawn. Made to feel above all, safe.

"Let me be absolutely honest with you, Runegar." The other druid smiled, searched for a rock and sat down. Formus, not wanting to upset the balance of trust by standing in an imperious position above him, also sat. "You are right," he continued, "I do want more. Something for which all right-minded human beings are greedy and desperate so I don't feel selfish in asking for it."

"Asking for what?"

"Peace."

"Ah, peace, my brother. You have a strange manner in pursuing it."

"Some might see it like that."

"And how could others view it – five hundred men at your command? An army in a country that has always treated you with the greatest courtesy and friendship?"

"Others might see how we have conducted ourselves already and understood some purpose behind our travelling. I would not want to hide the fact that we have come to wreak justice on those committing sacrilege against our people."

"I have heard about that."

"They journey north and as soon as we bury Orsek here, or what remains of him and give him the security of rest and honours that we could not guarantee at Glauberg, then we go north too."

"To capture and kill them?"

Truly, I hoped you would think better of me than that. When these people are caught, I will take the perpetrators from amongst them and after a proper trial before the gods, they will be punished."

"Then, what is next?"

"Then we will work to achieving our peace."

"Meaning?"

"We want to settle ourselves in this land and take ourselves away from the wars on the continent."

"Ah, is your greed for peace or land? The one does not necessarily flow from the other."

"We will go north, Runegar, where I know land is more freely available than it is here. I do not wish to take anything by force, only use what is going to waste. It might appear that I do have military intentions but believe me when I say that the men who accompany me are not mere warriors but pioneers and settlers in their own right. Yes, there are five hundred of them but what fool would bring an army into Albion to attack and pillage the people here? If that happened, it would take only a few days to raise an army from the tribes around that could be counted in their thousands not hundreds. We would be wiped out."

Runegar had to acknowledge the truth in this but he was still unsure about the Sequani druid and his motives.

"Formus, I hold an entrusted responsibility over the most sacred place in Albion. My own reputation is joined with it. People travel to the Plain from all lands in this world. What if I judged that it is right to pass the Rod of Amity to you and you broke that trust? That the Rod has allowed you a welcome in the lands of the North and the next thing I hear is that your 'pioneers' have not settled peacefully but instead have enforced their presence and carried out a massacre on the local population?"

"I need those numbers I travel with to build a settlement, not to carry out mass killings. Just as I have described the circumstances here in the south so it applies to the North. If I provoked trouble, my small force would be surrounded and destroyed. The population may be sparser but they are fierce. It is the followers to the goddess Brigantia who rule there – no?"

"The Briganti are the most powerful but before their territory lies the region where the worshippers of the Horned One live. They are called the Cornovi. Both peoples rule the skies from their elevated forts. Other tribes could exist that not even I have knowledge about. They probably come from the great island to the west and the cold regions to the north-east through seas jagged with ice and even from the south, from Europa."

In talking about this, Runegar seemed to have begun to settle his own worries. "In fact, Formus, you are perfectly right in what you have said, only a fool would instigate trouble in those regions. What makes you think that a place might be available for your settlement in the North?"

Formus' mind veered to the Orsook, somewhere he could force a gap by which he could enter that territory but to Runegar he said, "Your wisdom is great and recognised throughout Albion, Runegar, but I have travelled a little around this island and sailed the coast along the northern lands, occasionally taking horse with others to explore inland. The earth is fertile, producing many rivers and forests. None would wish us harm if we were to clear enough forestland to provide food not only for ourselves but for others."

"One year to clear the land, two years to do that and grow your crops. All that before you reach your place to settle and to get to it will take many more months at least. Do you have the patience for it, Formus?"

I do if I get slaves to work under my men's direction, he thought. "It will be diligently done my lord priest and the reward will be all the greater. Meanwhile, we will fish and hunt and employ the wood we have chopped to give us dwellings, food, fuel and barter in exchange for clothes from the Brigantes or any others who live by. The Rod of Amity will serve its purpose – a means for initiating friendship between ourselves and other communities."

"I will give you the Great Seal to aid your travels," said Runegar, making his decision.

Formus was about to express his thanks but the other man stopped him. "It will benefit you. Any of the tribes which pay their respects to the gods on this Plain will offer the necessities you require. However, you must not accept that the Rod will make your journey a simple one, without obstacles."

"I could never believe that but is there anything in particular that prompts you to say this?"

"The Rod will be your goodwill wherever you travel through the world of human beings but it is not a magic amulet, it cannot protect you and your followers from the Celestial Bridge if your fate is ordered by the gods to cross it."

"Celestial Bridge?"

Runegar made a sign in the air, a sacred one, for protection. He peered down at the human beings below, toiling to create the precise elements to elicit favours from omnipotent forces.

"It exists between the lands held by the Briganti and the Cornovi. Where it can be located in this world, specifically, no one knows. The bridge arches over a river, silver and turbulent. It was spelled into this world and yet, not of this world, by the supernatural exercise of the two gods in those regions – Brigantia, Queen over the sky and everything that comes from it and occurs within it and the other is the Horned One, Lord-Chief over all life on the earth, below it and above the ground. These two each built one part leading from their own people's land over the river towards the other country. The work took on a moon's flowering and waning. At the end they met in the middle, but not quite the middle."

"That is vague."

"There was no centre; Brigantia and the Horned One refused to join. Instead they created an illusion for mortals so that standing on either side and looking through ordinary eyes, you would think that the bridge was a perfect, sturdy thing to cross. Indeed, you would wish to, since whatever side you crossed from, the land ahead would be more appealing, more pleasant and more serene than the land you had come from, such is the game the gods play."

"But surely that gap can be leaped and if not, ropes can be thrown across it or boats rowed across the water."

"The silver flashes in the river are not the sun's reflection: there is no water. It will not support boats yet resists the forms of men who try to wade it. And as I have said, ordinary mortals do not see the gap in the structure so they walk the bridge."

"What then – fall into the water and drown in the water that is not water?"

"They fall, yes, but it is a drowning unlike any other. Their descent is into the Black Hole contained by the river of stars. Their mouths are filled with the other world so that a hunger for it grows and keeps them there. Few return."

"Few?" said Formus sharply.

"Only one I know about. I will take you to that person if you like."

Formus thought that he could spend his time more usefully than visiting what was probably an old man who had lost his wits. However, he had to react to this offer in a manner that was not offensive. Runegar had just promised him the Rod of Amity and had not denied Orsek an honourable burial at this sacred site. He was entirely sceptical about the whole story Runegar had just relayed to him. Stationed guards on borderlands were the most effective means for detecting incursions. The protection could be bolstered by a psychological barrier from stories such as this – designed to deter the religious and the superstitious. Despite his status in the druidic order, Formus treated religion and superstition as weapons to use on others, not as mind-wash for himself.

"That would be very kind."

The old man turned out to be a young woman, who, despite her speech and appearance seeming remarkably sound, was subject to periodic fits when the god Belinus 'took her' as she expressed it. He had come across such occurrences previously and was inclined to believe that it was a peculiar disease like the plague, only this manifestation did not transfer from person to person. It was illuminating to see how others regarded it. In the two cases he had known, one was a handsome young man and the other was an ugly little girl. The girl was viewed as someone punished by the gods for some personal or family misdeed and thus was despised by her community. The young man on the other hand was set apart as having a prophetic gift, the idea catching hold after he started to detail the dreams that came to him when he had been in the 'other place'. One or two seemed to match events that eventually occurred in the village. The elders there had then put him through training for the druidic priesthood. This woman had the same cleverness about her, the ability to change a weakness into a strength, repudiating victimisation. Her prettiness was anything but a barrier to that as Formus could see in Runegar's bashful behaviour towards her.

It would be useless to argue with Runegar about the fact that the girl had not actually been to the bridge herself but only in her dreams. Yet her description of the approach to the place where it could be found was precise and contained intriguing features, including that a direct path to it took one through a ruined and empty building, whose purpose was not clear and which was set astride the head of a small valley. The bridge itself she referred to as the Bridge of Fusion and the river, as the River of Bubbled Particles. She claimed to have been given these names by a child who had guided her over the valley pass to the place of crossing. The child had disappeared after she had stepped onto the bridge itself.

She had walked across what appeared to be a solid structure, the flashing lights flowing beneath and either side of her until coming to the centre, the floor gave way and her body dropped into what was a black hole before she was submerged by the River of Bubbled Particles. Beyond that she could not say since the Goddess Brigantia and the Horned One had forbidden her.

Formus itched to put her to torture, just so that he could prove her lie but of course the authority did not rest with him, only with the fatuous and infatuated man by his side. Runegar there, standing like a soppy hound panting at its master's command.

The woman did produce something that genuinely took Formus' interest. Something substantial. In fact, Formus had to admit to himself, he thought it wonderful and he was not someone who easily gave into that kind of feeling.

She had taken them to a table inside her house and on it was a shaped pottery like an upturned bowl, a cover. She had lifted it up and underneath was what looked like a metallic lump that from its size could be easily fitted into the hand. Briefly, Formus speculated why it had not been placed in a casket if it was a keepsake but he soon found out the answer. She asked Formus to pick it up.

Puzzled, he reached out to grasp it and expected to lift it with ease. Instead he found it had been stuck to the table in some way and said so. With obvious delight in her eyes, the woman said that it was not stuck, just very heavy and a strong man could raise it. Astonished, Formus took hold of the misshapen ball in both his hands and with a huge effort lifted it a little way above the table. He could not hold it for long however and soon let it fall back onto the surface beneath. With a thud, the lump almost split the wood.

The traveller over the Bridge of Fusion claimed that in the 'other' place from which she had returned, stones like this were scattered everywhere.

Formus questioned how she could bring such a heavy object back to her home alone and the girl told him that when she came from the other place she had not been sent via the bridge but had awoken, as if from sleep and found herself and the stone in the woodland on the perimeter of her settlement. The strongest man in the village did not find it an easy task to carry the stone back to her house.

The Sequani did not believe for one moment the girl's story about the bridge, although others here in this village near the Plain of Rebirth obviously did do. He wondered as to where she could have found this metal, since metal doubtlessly it was. With such a material one could work marvellous things. It was much heavier and harder than iron. If it was possible, just a little of this metal combined with iron could create weapons that would break the bones of the gods themselves. Just as iron made better swords than bronze so this new metal could be alloyed with iron for greater cutting and chopping force. Who knows? There might be a means for creating weapons solely from the metal itself if the problem of weight could be overcome.

Excusing himself to Runegar, he took the woman aside and offered her gold for the metal. Much to his surprise she agreed to sell it. Then he reasoned that there was not much reward in a stone lying idle on a table. He hired a small cart to take it back to his quarters. He and Runegar rode separately from it back to the Plain. Once returned, he handed the stone over to his best smiths and commanded them to work on it, breaking it into smaller pieces.

Soon after he had gone back to his guestroom to prepare himself for Orsek's burial which was to occur the next day, he heard a tremendous roar like the voice of a storm in the mountains. He rushed out with his guards to discover the reason for it and was met with the dreadful sight of his injured and dead metalsmiths. They had dug a fire-pit in a field outside the meeting hall with Runegar's permission and were now lying strewn around it, blood pouring from their wounds and their skin burnt raw. Only three had escaped with their lives intact, one being the ironmaster Formus had originally entrusted with investigating the strange ore. He was able to tell Formus that they had decided to heat it to test for malleability. Only a little heat had been applied with fire and bellows and the metal had changed quickly to a bright green colour. In the usual way for working it, they had struck the heated metal with a hammer. On the first blow there was an enormous explosion and the consequence was dead and wounded metalsmiths lying around the field.

Formus had sent others to tend the wounded and arrange a burial for the dead men. He also sent out to try and find any remnants from the metal around the field that were not already lodged inside his men's bodies.

Some were brought to him and remarkably, not only were they lighter – taking into account that they were smaller extractions from the larger piece but the colour had changed to a blue chroma, very different to the dull grey property it had possessed previously.

He had to think fast. The substance, whatever it was, would confer great power on the one who could use it properly. This gift from the Bridge of Fusion might mean that it would no longer matter that his army comprised only five hundred men in a land where thousands could be mustered in a few days. Armies and fortifications would fall before him, surrendering themselves on the mere suggestion that such might would be used against them. Rarely had Formus been so excited.

The news of this explosion had to be controlled and disguised. That was the immediate problem for him. A fortunate delay was granted to Formus in that as soon as they had got back from the village, Runegar had ridden on down to the Plain to prepare for sacred ritual. He had not seen the arrival of the cart with the stone in it, neither had he witnessed the destruction, although down there on the flat land below, surely all must have heard the detonation. There was more luck in that few, except the ironsmiths, had actually observed what had gone on. Where they were located, away from the Meeting Hall, was shielded by a band of woodland, deliberately maintained there for people's needs. At this very moment, Runegar would most certainly be making his way back to either satisfy his curiosity or cure his terror of the sound that had swamped them.

Presently, any explanation might suffice in the short-term. None amongst Runegar's people had been maimed or killed so he must express sympathy for a guest. What to say about the cause for the explosion, though? The evening sky above was grey and across its surface moved sombre, threatening clouds. A sudden lightning bolt was not impossible, particularly if it was cast by their own god, Danu, angered by the delay in punishing those who had desecrated the High King Orsek's tomb. It would provide a reason also for interring the king's body quickly after a great sacrifice and moving on without further tardiness.

The second problem was extracting the whereabouts of this supernatural metal from the girl. He considered that this did not add up to such a great difficulty if her ease in relinquishing the original stone was anything to go by. The girl evidently preferred gold to torture and for her knowledge and silence he would be willing to pay a reasonable price. Not too much. He had a short temper.

Formus saw that a figure on a white horse was riding up the lower hillside towards him. Runegar, on his own. He was tempted but only a little. Everything in the Plain of Rebirth had to remain undisturbed and he must leave it as he found it or bring those giant standing stones falling down over his head. He had got everything he had wanted and possibly much more in coming here. The same would happen on his next visit.

30
The Land Torn
by Four Winds

'*Somewhere far north to the Belgae and north of the Plain of Rebirth was a land torn by four winds. The land itself was green and fertile so it endured the fierce breaths from these four gods and existed, producing food enough to survive upon for the people living there. Their houses were made from rocks and their clothes were the rough hair hides skinned from the wildest predators that roamed the swamps and forests in that region.*

These winds each blew at a certain time in the year and the quarters of the year were named after their specific turbulence.

So, first came The Rain Drencher, pouring water into the dry river beds and making the swamps boggy again with mud, watering the deep pools. Tired of shaking and preening themselves and hiding under dripping boughs, birds would fly away seeking drier lands. At the Rain Drencher the inhabitants would take to their boats and oars, throwing nets out and hauling in shiny piles of wriggling fish.

Second came Ice Choker which, although at times lesser in strength than Rain Drencher, turned the world white and cold with its breath. Icy snow clogged everything. Sometimes, for days on end it would be duplicitous and become a slight breeze, the breeze so gentle it brought cold serenity. All was almost still, the icicles sparkled in the snap-shot sun that was fleetingly covered and uncovered with pale flying clouds; snow lay piled in mounds and the children of the inhabitants took out the temporarily useless smaller fishing boats – the circular skin coracles – to take them sliding, shrieking, down the snowy hills. At times like this, to be living in the Land of the Four Winds, was almost to be happy. But soon the Ice Choker would reveal its tricks – gather itself once more to whip up in frenzied ice, smashing off the icicles to send them darting at the tree trunks or the people who could be caught outside the safety of their homes.

Next, blows in The Howler, less cold but still bitter, meaning that the snow brought by the Ice Choker would remain on the ground for a month or more, becoming hard, then slush. The Howler was one that boasted its own name. It spoke of desperation from the east where it had scoured the Steppes. Many voices crowded together in this wind that set the teeth a chatter, yearning for its freedom to roam and pour a cold gloaming on the land to rip it from the brightness that belonged by right to the day. In dullness, days followed from the blackened nights and if one star shone in the sky it was regarded with the same importance as the moon that somehow seemed to be sickened with its own shining. At such a time in the year the inhabitants were reduced to eating hibernating animals since the bigger animals had gone to search for brighter days beyond this region's boundaries. Sometimes and then more frequently as the year progressed, the people were able to supplement their diet with fish that could be caught once the rivers' ice sheets had been pulled from above their beds.

Finally in this Land of Four Winds there was one that moved with it a kind of relief. It was from the south and broke the freeze with heat. This was the best time. Perishing limbs revived after the long cold months, blood flowed quicker to the heart and people began to make songs again. They called this wind The Breath of Belinus, the Sun God. All the animals that had departed came back and flowers danced on the mountain slopes, jouncing with colour. But The Breath of Belinus, being a sun god's, was hot and got hotter when the earth warmed. It got so hot in fact, despite the accumulated moisture from the previous season in the year that much of the water was steamed from the earth and the soil began to bake and crack. Grass turned yellow. Leaves shrivelled. Forests began to burn. People who had gladly shed their clothes in the first warming month hurriedly pulled them back on and covered their faces against scalding. Some panted their last breaths to an escalating heat and indeed amongst some older inhabitants that was also the case. There was plenty to eat and the population tried to cool itself in lowering rivers.

Any stranger entering this Land of Four Winds might wonder to himself or herself why the inhabitants stayed. What possible reason would prevent them from looking for a country with a climate more temperate and milder in its force? Well, at moments in the year these people were happy. Their appreciation of these periods was greater for the hardship they suffered at other times. But that was not what prevented them from moving away. Of course not. The real reason why they could not escape their harsh environment was because they were a people cursed.

It was something that had happened to them over generations. The same question was asked through the years by children of their parents, parents their grandparents – why had they not moved before the time of the sickness? The answer never varied. In the past when people had first arrived in the country, the winds had not been so strong and the first settlers thought that their lives could be happy there. They had stayed and built their community. The climate had changed gradually but in one particular year the switch was more sudden and drastic than ever before. By that time it was too late; illness had possessed the inhabitants.

This illness took only one form in those living in the Land of the Four Winds. In one way it could be described as being very mild; after all, it was only that their skin was blemished by small green freckles, slightly fungal in character, usually appearing on the arms or thighs. There were no other symptoms. Yet it was what resulted when they came into contact with other people who were not from their own country that had the most devastating impact.

If a stranger happened to cross the boundary between their own country and the Land of the Four Winds or a resident of this land visited that, then contact between the two peoples instantly spread the disease. That infection became far worse if it was contracted by anyone whose family had not lived under the Four Winds for generations. It was not just spots on the arms and legs but the whole expanse of the body was covered so densely in the freckles that they merged and the skin took on an unbroken green hue so unstoppable it turned the eyeballs from white to that colour. This was just the beginning. People affected in this way began to lose their fingers, toes and ears. As the infection sank deeper it got to the point that whole hands were lost but by then most of the victims had died from a weakness which had overcome their internal organs as well. Because the body parts atrophied like this, the sickness was viewed as a leprosy by those living in other regions and its origin in the people of the Four Winds made those others call it the Wind Leprosy – their superstition had it that the sickness was somehow conveyed by the Four Winds acting in an unnatural way on the land and people of that country.

Humans being what they are, it was completely predictable that people from the Land of Four Winds were not allowed to pass freely into other countries; they were stoned away if they made an attempt to cross the borders. Huge fences and walls were constructed along the borders to keep the people with the green freckles penned in. Before this tragedy the people living under the Four Winds had called themselves Borrumani or those who live with Borrum, god of the winds. The others who had trapped them behind the walls, after the tragedy, referred to them cruelly by the name 'Wind Lepers'.

So it was impossible for the Borrumani to go anywhere. Surrounded by people who detested them, afflicted by a disease that was fatal to others and domiciled in a country that they were beginning to fear, the Borrumani might be excused for possibly taking desperate action. There were those amongst them, insane and immoral creatures, who suggested that they should take their dead and catapult the corpses into the settlements and cities of their persecutors. By this means they would die, leaving the Borrumanis strong in their immunity and free to go wherever they pleased. Needless to say, this suggestion was laughed out of hearing, for what normal human being could propose such a vile plan? It would lead to human extinction since Borrum himself would punish those responsible.

No, the Borrumani would have to look to themselves and discover new heroes to find the means for their release. It is at crucial tense times like these that those people with the strongest characters and intellect to do good for others do step forward, helped naturally by wise and perceptive leadership. So it happened with the Borrumani. Wise leadership was contained within the person of their king, Hors Noremac, someone who had governed his subjects for many years. He it was who brought an end to the ideas about throwing infected corpses at the problem of the Borrumanis' imprisonment. All the potential instigators for this farcical scheme were rounded up, imprisoned and executed.'

"Where was I?" The Borrumani aristocrat, fair beard rolling down splendidly over his beaded gown, opened his eyes as if just awakened from sleep and turned to his secretary, a young man whose quill suddenly stopped scratching at the parchment on the raised wooden stand facing him.

"Your Majesty, you were just about to explain that new heroes were to be found amongst your subjects." The young secretary hesitated and pulled at his drooping moustache. It was a frequent gesture that the king recognised as a nervous preliminary to a suggestion. "My lord, Highness and Majesty, can I suggest a change?"

"Go ahead," said King Hors, pleased with his diffidence.

"Can we remove the word 'executed' from that last sentence? It might give the wrong impression about your rule and excuse me, Your Majesty, your character, to those reading these memoirs in future. This is the first volume concerning the history of the ruling Noremac dynasty, led by yourself and your illustrious father – now sadly passed from us – Airbla Noremac and I think the prime necessity here is to leave a favourable and kindly impression in the minds of those readers from the future. Words have to be carefully chosen and I know your late father urged us all to think inside the piggery and to go beyond our natural capacities as human beings but really, I am only here to serve your interests and I hope to create in this new project written – with your help – by me, a far more effective and powerful ruler in yourself than that presented for your father. It is only the truth we are conveying, after all," said the secretary with a simple shrug of his shoulders.

The administrator was an exceptionally clever young man, clever right down to the contrived mannerisms in diffidence he performed regularly to flatter the king's vanity: the frequent head bowing, moustache tugs and feigned nervousness, the constant plumping up of cushions or clearing away of clutter before the king moved to any place or sat down. About the only thing he was not clever at was preserving his own dignity. If his presence at the king's side had not been so familiar, he might have been taken for an older slave from a former generation.

That the young man, Netmapliar, was very clever – if cleverness is to be measured in rewards and honours while ignoring the people you govern – there was very little doubt. Despite his youth, the king paid him well and had given him a position as a ruling aristocrat in the second law-making chamber of the government. There was no real function in this additional chamber as the laws were created in the first one. Yet it allowed the king to stuff it with his sycophants, exercise his personal patronage to maintain a deadening grip over the way the country was governed and at the same time was a means for convincing the population that the creation of law for their benefit was 'fair' and 'just' because everything that was devised in the Lower House of elected representatives was passed up to the second chamber for careful consideration concerning its impact on the people. If they decided any law would harm the people in its present form they would send it back for reconsideration and changes. That was what the people heard anyway.

In reality, if the king and the barons who supported him did not benefit from the new law that was the sole reason it returned to the first chamber. As the years went by under the dominion of King Hors Noremac this whole process became much easier, with less and less potential laws being returned to the first chamber since the king also had his supporters amongst representatives there, in fact the majority as newly elected members from the population going into that chamber would quickly realise that it was only by the king's wish that they could be elected to that second chamber with its additional rewards on offer.

Several years after the king's coronation it became apparent even to the ordinary population, weltering under the constant lies told them, that in fact very few new laws benefited either themselves directly or the society in which they lived. These 'reforms' were never to improve the people's lot, always to worsen it.

Netmapliar was deliberately oblivious to all this. He attended the council sessions in the second chamber for perhaps less than half a morning's session on each of two days a week. For that he was given two gold coins minted with the king's portrait, representing payment for two full-day sessions. It was what a ploughman earned in two months by his sweat in the fields. Duty and obligation were concepts to be strongly projected in the king's memoirs by Netmapliar's hand but they were meant strictly for the lower orders; the elite thrived on their rejection, Netmapliar had worked his way into those aristocratic circles where maximum plunder was taken with minimum effort.

"Truth, my dear scribbler," responded the king, "lies netted in the map of deceit and you are here to guide me to the exact coordinates where I can bury it." It was the measure of the king's confidence in his own power over Netmapliar that he felt he could be so candid.

"So can I …?" asked the secretary with his usual pretended hesitancy.

"Of course, you can."

The king enjoyed these sessions. They were a relaxing break from negotiations with the barons whose avarice in certain individuals sometimes knew no bounds. Whether it was licenses for importing new goods into the country or mining certain land areas, a reduction in taxes on the goods they sold or a new law providing them with the ability to steal some commoner's land and call it their own – the list was endless. Everything was granted as long as the crown made its own profit from the changes by which the supplicant benefited.

He enjoyed these sessions almost as much as those he spent with his own private herd of pigs. They were his pride and joy. An interest he had developed from his time as a young lad. He was a little disconcerted to find that recently, though, the pigs had got suddenly nervous when he neared them. They used to be so happy with his petting. He must look into that.

Hors was otherwise very happy. It should never have been like this. The population he ruled should have been as turbulent as the climate they lived under. At the very least, the country's trade with other dominions should have suffered because of the disease his people carried. There was some instability but in general, with lucrative trade incentives, traders found ingenious ways around the problem and goods flowed in and out. Trade embargos set down by other kings and rulers were ignored and the smugglers carried out their work smoothly enough. Some of the smugglers lived in those other countries which had professed horror at the sickness. When you dug down under the hysteria to the actual facts you got to realise that very few people living outside the Borrumani borders had been infected. This was because the disease was not passed by the breath, as his own Chief Physician had discovered, but by contact with the skin and only then in particular circumstances – excessive sweating or an unprotected cut for instance. It was enough to stop infection by covering the skin with cloth. Therefore, the trade smugglers had all agreed to work together with their bodies covered and faces masked. The only significant difference between them was that the Borrumani traders had green clothing, in a strange hubristic reference to their disease carrying status while the smugglers from the other nations wore black.

Hors Noremac, in those quieter moments when he was alone and thinking about the kingdom, continued to be amazed in the situation that had been achieved. Such a kingdom as his, one surrounded by hostile tribes and its inhabitants infected with a deadly disease, should have descended into anarchy years ago with no possibility whatsoever that he would retain the crown. But the opposite had occurred and unbelievably his hold on power had not only remained secure but had actually been reinvigorated. The only conclusion Hors could draw was that greater stability had been won through fear. The population feared chaos so they kept themselves law-abiding, no matter what laws came into play. They were also thankful to the king himself that despite the hostilities with their neighbouring countries they were still able to buy the food and goods they wanted. There was no curiosity about where it had come from just so long as it was there and available. Other countries were hostile but what was the point of invading a disease-ridden territory? They feared the sickness so they occupied themselves with fighting each other and for longer than two generations now – ever since the leprosy had been known – the Land of the Four Winds had been at peace.

Naturally, King Noremac owed some thanks to his father, Airbla, for keeping the kingdom together while working under the same difficulties. But the previous monarch relied too heavily on the barons to enforce security and had begun to attract animosity from his own subjects. Food and goods were restricted yet the king did not share in his subjects' suffering: his life-style seemed to become more lavish rather than less. Hors, who had reached his coming-of-age at the time, knew that either their subjects would revolt and remove them both or the barons would do it with a coup. He was impelled to take action himself at the earliest opportunity.

King Airbla had therefore been found stabbed to death in his bedroom one evening with the murderer, his mistress, lying next to him. She had poisoned herself, presumably through remorse or fear of capture and the unpleasant instruments that would be used on her body to extract a confession. She was a mistress shared between both of them, unbeknown to his father. He had enjoyed her that very night before passing her the goblet filled with toxic wine. By that time, his father was lying bloodily soaked and dead in an empty bed-chamber, having waited for his mistress to arrive.

Well, she did, but only when it was too late for both of them and when someone else had got there first.

Hors lazily eyed his secretary, his scribbler. The boy, with his scraping and bowing, appeared so harmless. You could never imagine that he would be so handy with a knife. From pen to knife; the thought tickled and made him smile. By the forceful blows that he had glimpsed briefly on the body, the boy might have done as much damage with only his quill.

"Something amuses you, sire? I do hope it is not my clumsy suggestion."

Netmapliar's question brought the king's attention back to his task in hand.

"No, no – it is a very good suggestion," he assured the other. "You know how I appreciate a stab or two at improving my legacy."

The secretary's eyes blinked once or twice but the same obsequious stare remained. "Thank-you sire, but can we move on to the new heroes for your reign?" The tone was almost reproving rather than one made as a request.

"Actually …." began the king but broke off as his daughter entered the room unannounced. She was a pretty girl with dark hair distinguished by a single strand of grey that ran through it. The distinction made her seem more advanced than her twenty-two years and a confident bearing added to the impression. She was one of those people who are always about to do something and to relax was a distraction. Byncor had come to see her father to get something done and nothing should distract her. Except, there was. Netmapliar watched her hungrily.

She halted and did her best to hide the loathing. That slimy, toadish secretary was the last person she expected to see, having planned so often to avoid him.

"Oh, I had not thought you were going to write your memoirs today, father – weren't you going to receive a petition in the Royal Meeting Hall? I went there but finding it empty, came here."

"Not *my* memoirs, Byncor," said King Noremac gently, "but the true history of this State and the Noremac dynasty. The two are eternally linked and one cannot survive without the other."

"Yes, My lord. Can I ask a favour? Can we speak alone?"

"If we must, daughter, but you know I have the greatest confidence in my secretary, yet if it is necessary…."

"Please," said Byncor, determined and averting her eyes from the sly young man. She had always been puzzled about why such a weak creature could hold a powerful influence at court."

The king sent Netmapliar out.

He gestured towards a chair opposite. "What is on your mind, Byncor?" Although, he thought he already knew.

"Father, why have you not met with the petitioners today?"

"All in good time, my dear. All in good time."

"Do you know what the petition is about?"

"Yes, as well as you do." She certainly did, he thought, as some of the petitioners were her friends. They were sons and daughters belonging to aristocratic families at court, those friends being as young and naïve as she was.

She did not seem to have heard his reply. "Father, the people are appealing to you to release the cure for our national disease."

"You assume a lot," said Noremac in a soothing voice. "That I have the cure at all, for one thing."

"They know you have the cure! It is held in the Chief Physician's private laboratory. Why won't you use it?" Her anger was undisguised.

"Alright, we have a potion that could be effective but it is not yet fully tested. There is no point in rushing it, one has to be thoughtful, methodical. To do anything else would be to invite disaster."

"My lord, it is rumoured that you have been thoughtful and methodical for the past two years without any real consequence. The people are suffering! How can you go mon as you are and not be aware?"

It was the king's turn to be irritated. "Which *people* are you talking about? The ones I see in my kingdom are, in the main, very happy with their lives in this country. Of course, there is the problem with the weather but whatever we do we cannot affect that as it is controlled by the great god Borrum. As to the disease itself …." here the king raised his arms as if in despair, "is it really so bad? A little freckling on the skin, that is the only visible sign for us. Other than that, we are perfectly healthy."

"What! Please tell me father that you did not really mean that! How can we be perfectly healthy when we are shunned by everyone living beyond our borders? Is it healthy for our minds, particularly for people of my generation, that we are forced to live in this land as if it were a prison, our freedom to travel abroad completely restricted?"

"Believe me, my child, the pleasure gained from foreign travel is vastly overrated. In some ways I wish that you and your friends who think like you could visit other places and see the reality that exists there. You would be sadly disappointed. There are poor people amongst us, that is true but at least I ensure that they do not starve, whereas in these other countries people do starve and some to death.

"There are beggars on the streets! The numbers are growing!" Byncor cried.

"Now that, said the king firmly, "is a choice they make for themselves. It is not a style of living most Borrumani would choose but they seem to prefer it. Presumably they can get by and even enjoy themselves on the generosity provided by others."

Actually his daughter had raised a good point, in a figurative sense as well as an argumentative one. Begging had become a greater problem recently and those who did it had become an unsightly nuisance for people living in the oppida throughout the country. So he had organised a law currently to be passed in the second chamber which would allow oppida chieftains to place spiked points in those areas where beggars usually sat or slept overnight. The point of them being there would soon be made, thought the king, pleased with his new idea and they would return to the outlying smaller settlements from which they came.

This last remark by the king had an uncontrollable effect on Byncor. An angry bubble burst inside her and the complaints she had stored up for a long time came welling out.

"How are we to go on like this! No-one knows any different, sees any difference or hears anything different! It is stultifying. The only news we get is from and about other oppida, never about what is happening abroad, well, anything other than wars and invasions anyway. People are getting poorer in this country and yet they still believe they are better off than people who live elsewhere. I just don't understand it. People seem to be happy here living in their own squalor."

"Restrain yourself, Byncor!" said the king angrily. "Do not insult the Borrumani, my people, like that. If they think themselves better off than those unlucky enough to live elsewhere it is because they have good evidence for it."

"They have good evidence for the stink in their noses as they walk the streets but they don't seem to deduce that the cause for it is the collapsing waste system in this oppidum."

Hors Noremac was furious. "Now you listen to me, my girl, you have lived a privileged existence because of what I have provided for you – it would be very foolish for you to throw all that away on these stupid observations concerning this great society of ours for which you have no right, by experience or genuine understanding, to criticise. "The king paused on a sudden realisation. "These ideas are not just your own – who has been putting you up to this?"

"Kralmrax says …." Byncor began.

"Kralmrax! Kralmrax!" The king's eyes bulged. "Not that old ghost!"

"Please, father," said the young woman, visibly upset, "don't talk about my great-grandfather, your own grandfather, in such a manner. He is no ghost and is very much alive."

"Alive, but no blood relation to me," said the king disdainfully. "He is your mother's grandfather and I suppose, along with those ideas, he has also told you about his younger years and the impact he made on your mother's country?"

"He worked for progress in his own society – yes, he has told me."

"Everything?" replied Hors, eyebrows raised. Then, before his daughter could reply went on. "Did he describe to you the years he spent effectively plotting against the king in that country to improve the conditions of the poor people there which in the end resulted in the king losing his head?"

"No, he didn't," said Byncor vaguely shocked.

"Or that the barons he plotted with then took over and chose one amongst themselves to be the next monarch, an utterly despicable tyrant who not only starved the poor but killed them?" The king paused. "Don't answer that one because I already know."

His daughter was deflated. Hors pretended to feel sorry for her. He put his arm around her shoulders and gave a momentary hug. "My dear girl, some day you may be a queen over this land but before then you must learn to break through your own naivety. There are only two premises for a stable monarchy: to rule is tough and more importantly …. to be tough. Keep the people like a wild bear on a chain – at a safe distance, otherwise they will tear you apart. You have kindly feelings so brush them aside. Keep yourself safe and strong. The people won't love you for it but they will do something even better. They will respect you."

Deep, deep within herself Byncor had already grown up and was no longer dependent on her father's influence. She recognised that his philosophy was made from mixing extraordinary selfishness and fear. There had to be a better rule for governing than that. There just had to be.

"Well, well," said Hors and thought how he might cheer her up. "Listen, why don't we go down to my Chief Physician's laboratory to talk with him about the possible cure he has devised for the national disease?" Her lifted expression indicated that she was eager to do that and she did not let it fall, despite his next comment. "Then perhaps you might realise how very difficult it is to bring it to full fruition."

They went by winding passages in the palace down to the Chief Physician's chamber because that effectively was what it was. The physician, Conversevitae by name, ate, drank and slept his potion-making which is why his bed had been placed there next to the bubbling cauldrons and storage jars filled to varying degrees with powders of every hue. Byncor was glad to see that it was not so close that it was dangerous if he was to fall asleep on it during the day.

In that he was near to finding a cure for the disease that had terrorised a nation, Conversevitae appeared to be an exceptionally gloomy man. He suited his surroundings; the dim room was lit by several fiery glows and a single circular window introduced light from high above. A little more animation gripped him when he talked about his experiments and showed them the rat to which he had administered a dose of his potion. The rat had died and it was not a death without visible complications. She found her father's face looking at her meaningfully.

"The dose was too strong or did not contain the right elemental combination."

Byncor questioned him about the ingredients but Conversevitae as usual with men of his profession was evasive and secretive. She expected that. But there was something else that he was hiding, she was sure. She wondered where the deception lay in this smocked and smoky figure, his half-covered arms busy probing into corners to find the elemental jars that contributed to the potion.

And then studying him closely, she suddenly realised what it was.

His bared arms revealed no sign of the sickness – no freckling, no greenish hue, the skin was healthy, a little too pale but that was accounted for by his existence down here away from direct sunlight. She came to the only logical conclusion that could be surmised from what she was seeing: Conversevitae had found the cure. What followed from that, naturally, was that everything she had just been told was a lie. She quickly pulled her eyes away and focused on something else, in case the sorcerer should notice her attention.

So if that was a lie, what else might they be scheming and why? What would be the motivation for not allowing the people an antidote to this cursed affliction? There could be the potential for creating great wealth and power by hoarding this discovery. Only a select few might be administered the medicine. Byncor glanced quickly at her father's arms and legs but it was impossible to know, they were covered in cloth.

The physician had brought out a small pot from a shelf and opening it he scattered the contents onto a rectangular marble tile placed on the desk before the shelves. Black powder spilled over its white surface. He cast a confiding glance towards Byncor. "This is my most significant element for the cure to our ailment. Watch."

The princess did not like the tone with which he said this but nevertheless kept her eyes down. Conversevitae took a candle and touched its flame to the powdery pile. At once the powder on the tile caught the flicker which spurted upward in a fiery blue jet emitting green clouds and then itself changed from blue to green and eventually subsided into a sizzling suppurated mess, black and boiling, on the pale stone. Conversevitae looked towards Byncor for a reaction.

She pretended to be impressed but really wasn't. This pyrotechnic display could be produced by any travelling pedlar before he set about selling his goods. And so it was proved with the physician.

"Did you see the green clouds rise from the combusting powder?" he said earnestly. Byncor nodded. "In the same way," he continued, "the green sickness is expelled from the body when the powder is ingested."

"You mean," replied the Princess, finding it difficult to keep the mockery from her voice, "people can take this powder, burst into fire and billow up into the sky as smoky green clouds?"

Conversevitae gave her a withering stare. "No, My Lady, I am attempting to combine it with other elements so that does not happen. That is the stage to which I have got."

All this was beginning to make Byncor revise the assumption that he had found any cure whatsoever. The man was a charlatan – how could he possess the skills and intelligence to restore health to a whole country? Yet, maybe this was another performance but now psychological in nature. He was acting the fool, the insubstantial conjuror, to undermine her belief in an effective cure.

"Have you observed enough to appreciate that there is much more work to do to find what your friends are wanting?" remarked the king. His emphasis was such that it easily conveyed the impression only her friends were interested in gaining a cure, no one else.

"Yes, I can understand that now," she replied.

"Let us go then and leave our good physician to complete it." He led the way back to the apartments above. Every twist, turn and deviation in the passage was memorised by the Princess. She would get hold of the antidote, even if she had to return with her friends and steal it from Conversevitae's laboratory.

31
Vision on the Causeway

The different. The exotic. The godhead.

Goreth had pulled himself from the river water, refreshed and wet. Now that his body was dry, he wrapped a loin cloth around himself and sat down again, listening to the bird calls, watching the river flow and the blue chipped ghostly flash as a kingfisher winged down it, skimming the surface and away again into the dusk.

All sound hissed through his ears – the birds, the coursing river, the wind through the tree branches – setting up a fine harmonious melody in his head. He felt at peace and his body had quenched its thirst for water. Strange, exotic, godhead: that it should be serene when lying upon the most eruptive and formative change. This is what it is to be immortal – neither quite man, nor beast, nor plant, nor rock; neither quite man nor woman. Supremely powerful yet powerless. Powerless before the overwhelming power exercised by change. He was subject to it. Yes, because he was a god he could transcend it but only while he was above the Earth. The longer he spent in that exosphere, the weaker became his thought. On the living ground, his existence achieved fullness and the vitality was in the transition. He had taken part in many changes over such long periods of time from the minuscule to the enormous, the sensual to the inanimate: a photon of blinking light between particles in atomic space, that heaving volcano rising from its seabed, here the sweet and fragrant note drifted from the evening trumpet Moon Flower, there a massive fallen temple column weighted in blame.

Transition was occurring again. He had once been a female god and the people along the Danu had worshipped him as such. Then he had become male, strength replacing fertility, but this time this age wanted both strength and fertility. He would be neither male nor female. He would be both.

Already Goreth could feel and see the small breasts protruding from his chest. They were only perceptible with his clothes off and suited his delicately boned face. All body hair, apart from that on his head, had gone from above his waist. Below he had retained it, along with the phallus between his legs. The features that made him Orsook also remained. It was not such a drastic metamorphosis then. He wondered what triggered any change. He had discussed it with the other gods. Much theorising had been done – amongst those who were interested anyway, whereas others continued their obsessions and games with mortal men and women, convinced their pleasures and immortality would be enhanced by frivolous stories and ridiculous pastimes. All the theorising came to this: it was a mystery, the Mystery of mysteries. Their existence, a something, had originated in something else and that something might have changed from nothing. The importance was in the change; on that they were all agreed. This evolution was crucial to their being so they did not fight it when atomic or cellular rearrangement occurred within themselves. Goreth understood everything had taken part in his own existence as he had contributed to that belonging to others.

In certain situations, when urgency was required, he was able to transition himself but only on a temporary basis. If it was an uncalled experience as now, the shape lasted much longer.

A bush swept aside and Telemachus strode up to him. "Goreth, I …." The hero's voice trailed off and utter shock stamped itself on his face as he stared at Goreth's chest. For a moment he thought his eyes were playing tricks in the gathering darkness.

The Orsook god remained impassive, taking no offence. Why should he? Mortals are easily marvelled. Being as he was, meant that his body combined the best representation for the human shape, both provider and conceptor.

There was not much use in trying to hide his own reaction so Telemachus asked directly, "Goreth, what is happening to you?"

In answering him Goreth stood up, allowing the loin cloth to fall away from himself. It was a remarkable sight. This hermaphroditic figure standing tall and green-skinned under tree shadow and by lapping river water. "Do you think I am beautiful?" he laughed. The bubbling voice remained unaltered and for that Telemachus was relieved. In his own mind he thought, 'Strange – yes, 'wonderful' – yes but 'beautiful'? No. He paused for a moment. It was not sensible to offend a god.

Goreth had not asked the question seriously. He pulled his loin cloth and robe back on, unhurried and without embarrassment while Telemachus watched. Telemachus wondered whether or not any of the others would have reacted in a different manner. Probably not initially but then they would just ignore it. Goreth, typically, would not hide the change. The others trusted but secretly feared him.

Telemachus had never seen such a human shape before. There were babies born in his own country that were imperfectly figured but as soon as they were checked by the civic officials they were either thrust down wells dead or left to the mountain gods for their fate to be decided.

Goreth looked up, amused, while he was dressing and observing Telemachus' fixed stare said, "You are right, the change is remarkable," as if the other's thought had been spoken.

This surprised Telemachus from his stupor and shaking himself he recalled why he had come looking for Goreth.

Since leaving the land of the Belgae, after destroying Helladore, they had travelled northwards and had passed the Plain of Rebirth. They had also overtaken Formus and his army, leaving him – for the moment – safely behind. Now they were trying to catch up with Tyracides and the other Telemachons. The impression they were under was that the gap between themselves and the larger Telemachon group had been closing. Thocero, behaving as a seasoned scout and using the same skills that enabled him to climb his own ship's mast had, squirrel-quick, skimmed up to a tree top to see what he could find.

He discovered the Telemachons at a greater distance than he could shout over or at which he could attract their attention in any way. The stragglers behind the group were briefly glimpsed but then rounded a hill and disappeared from view even as he watched. Thocero had descended with the good news that at least they were in the vicinity. It was the time before dusk and Telemachus had ordered a rest for the night. That was an hour ago.

Telemachus observed Goreth as he collected some dried, broken twigs and a small fallen branch together into a pile. He was putting together the essentials for a small fire and he expected the Orsook to strike together a couple of flint stones to ignite it or to fiercely rotate a stick from side to side in a bored hole in the dry branch and produce the flame through friction and scorching. He did neither of these things but instead bent down, with his back to Telemachus and seemed to breathe over the collected debris. Lifting his head back, several flames could be seen twisting amongst the broken wood. Satisfied that the fire was secure,

Goreth got up and went to a leather pouch he had left nearby. He came back with a small corked, clay-baked bottle and two cups made from hardened leather.

"Something extra to warm us for the night," he remarked and took the stopper from it. It made a sound like a hollow thump and Goreth poured the mead into the cups, giving one to his companion.

"It was a gift given to me in the last Atrebate village we came through," said Goreth, referring to the bottle in his hand.

"I have never seen you drink this honey brew or even wine before," said Telemachus.

"In a large gathering – no, you have not. It is always best to keep wits about under such circumstances. On a cold night like this, with a friend who can be trusted, a cup or two can add warmth to the body and ease the conversation."

Telemachus sensed that this Orsook or god or whatever he was, was about to tell him something. With regard to Goreth, any words from him that shed light on his inner thinking would be at least revelatory.

His own attitude to Goreth changed according to the situation. Sometimes he was able to regard him as a fellow human being, a man like himself, trying to find something that was unattainable. But Goreth's mercurial changes constantly interfered with that comfortable perception. Telemachus could see the Orsook in him – in his features, the assured strength and grace in his own natural environment, the river, or the stunned reaction when he saw the High King Orsek's body at the tomb in Glauberg. Yet what else could he truly be other than a god, the divinity that was worshipped throughout Europa by its name Danu? How else could the violent encounter with Berengar be explained or this, his present manifestation as both man and woman?

"You wonder about me," interrupted Goreth's watery tone.

"I certainly do wonder," said Telemachus. "And I sometimes ask myself why you wish to be with us. You do not need our protection; it is us who require yours."

"Even the gods are driven by circumstance," said Goreth, taking a sip from his cup. "It could be that we have been placed together for mutual guidance along our separate paths."

"Up to now the paths have not been separate. We are both travelling in the same direction. Northwards."

"As yet, Telemachus. The time will come when I have to go my way and you, yours."

"How long have you been travelling, Goreth?"

"All of my life and more."

"Why?"

"Like you, to find a better place for me and mine."

"I have never heard you speak about your family, lovers, children. Have you known any of these?" Telemachus continued to sip from his cup.

"I have had many lovers and many more children. The lovers are gone and the children are now ancestors. I give guidance to their descendants, those that have not been slaughtered. But now, Telemachus, let us not talk about the dead but the living. Let us salute those who rely on us to bring them through and to give them hope." He raised his cup and so did Telemachus. They both drank back the remainder in one draught.

Goreth placed his cup on the ground and said to his companion, "I want to show you something."

Telemachus glanced towards the leather pouch lying not far away and Goreth, noticing, said, "What will be revealed to you cannot be found in a bag." He smiled and then as quickly, almost stern. "You trust me, don't you?"

"Of course."

"Then come with me."

Goreth rose and led the way from the fire he had just built.

His curiosity roused, Telemachus stood up and followed. He did trust him and he wondered what was about to happen.

The god did not walk far, just a little further than the patch of ground where they had been sitting near the river. Goreth went behind a bush towards the marshy ground that began there and disappeared.

He had not vanished altogether; his movements could still be heard. Telemachus paused. The night had come on and visibility was limited. The bush itself could just be seen, a dark mass against the darkening sky. His trust faltered. What was there to observe in these conditions? He pushed himself on and called out at the same time, "Goreth! We have small light by which to see – how can I be shown anything?"

As he rounded the bush, Telemachus came upon an illuminated figure, its body streaming light outward like a firefly but many times magnified. Goreth's luminous face peered at him.

Telemachus was reminded of the cell beneath Glauberg and how it had been completely lit up by this extraordinary power of his to cast light into the darkness.

"I said I would guide you." Goreth stretched an arm out and turned to what was behind him. Light seemed to travel from his arm and bounced into the blackness beyond, scattering the shadows and redefining another shape on the ground. "This is what I have come to show you."

Before them lay a wide track-way constructed from wooden planks and reeds. It was a road by which two carts could easily pass each other and Telemachus had never seen anything so large as this, constructed as it was in wood. This appeared to be the route's beginning: there was a large frame like a doorway the traveller had to pass through, to get onto the main causeway. The frame was solid, huge, having been made form three oak trunks. At either side stood a massive stone, pointed at the top. There were no images. Nothing had been hewn to a particular sign or shape. It was all completely natural. Goreth walked through the frame, stepping onto the timbers. Telemachus followed.

And it seemed to him that as he did so, as he moved via the same frame, the picture changed. Previously the causeway had seemed to go on forever but at this moment, standing next to Goreth, he could see that the other's light extended only a short distance and at its end the blackness rose up like an impenetrable wall. So stark was it, that the causeway appeared to finish abruptly. Indeed, it was more like a bridge than a road, with one end fixed solidly into the night while the end which they stood upon began in the light.

"Is this a road that leads to a real point or is it an occult distraction designed to trap us? Look at the gap in the causeway ahead. Four planks together are missing. No cart could pass over it."

Goreth stepped along the track to the place Telemachus had mentioned. When he advanced, the dark wall broke down before him and more of the roadway was revealed. Telemachus felt comforted a little by that.

"You are right, Telemachus, in suspecting this causeway not to be what its present shape is. I can only tell you what I know and what I know is not everything. I had thought you would be tested on your journey through this country not only by the usual challenges – the arduous travelling, the curious creatures and hostile people, the problem in keeping your own comrades united – but also that a challenge would come from its daimonia."

"Daimonia?"

"It is not simple to explain. Perhaps the best way to put it is the spirit that lives in the place. But it is not a single spirit, it is many possibilities. It is the direction of fate within the many choices in this land."

"A single spirit but many possibilities – that seems like a contradiction to me. Anyway, unlike my comrades I have always believed that I am the arbiter of my own fate."

"Above the gods?" questioned Goreth, inquisitively.

"Even though I know I am speaking to one – yes, independent of the gods."

"Then that is a principle you might prove immediately."

"How?"

"This causeway is very ancient," said Goreth, as if changing the subject." It is a roadway that was built by human beings in the past. Many were made and are still being made to traverse soft, marshy areas close by rivers, ponds and lakes. The people that lived then were much more attuned to the waterways and creatures that lived in them than they are now. They had a particular respect for us, the Orsook, as we did for them."

"Did that mean they helped each other? Were these trackways designed by the Orsook and mortals together?"

"They were built in the main by the Pretani people who lived here. Some trackways crossed the marshes to the dwellings that were built on wooden posts out over the water. Or they crossed from one such water village to another. The Orsook had no need for these causeways. They lived near the water's edge or in it."

Telemachus had grasped the implication in what was being said to him. "But this one is different?"

"This one is very different," affirmed Goreth. "The Orsook were…" then Goreth stopped to correct himself, "*are* skilful craftsmen. It was accepted that they could combine a specific magic with what they produced, suited to the thing's purpose. There were certain causeways established in those times, few in number and only in very special sites, that were designed to help the traveller cross land. But not across land in this world."

Telemachus gazed at what was solidly under his feet. He viewed Goreth and his radiating light, the track that still appeared to be a bridge and the density of dark nothingness around them.

He could firmly believe that at this moment the causeway, himself and Goreth were the only three figures in existence.

"If you come to this same place tomorrow at sunrise, you would not find this road. That is the cleverness in the Orsook's craft. It only appears at night and only then at certain times in the year."

"Roads that appear at an intermittent rate in time – not very reliable and without a consistent purpose," said Telemachus; a facetious comment to goad Goreth.

"Oh, the purpose is clear and personally definite. It is to make the traveller think."

"About what? A walk-way such as this, which is sometimes there and sometimes not, that leads off into darkness and can be lit up by a light coming from no ordinary source: I suggest to you that this is the Road of Destiny. Am I right? Is it my destiny?"

"The person that crosses these timbers might find that it is his destiny or hers or everyone's. It depends on what is seen and whether your motive for travel is selfish or selfless."

"I need not take this route," Telemachus almost muttered to himself. "Have I not encountered enough obstacles on my journey already? The Telemachons need me to lead them and I cannot waste more time on this." Louder still to Goreth, he said, "Let us leave this causeway. I see no point in pursuing it when we must rest and make certain that we find Tyracides and the others tomorrow, before Formus catches them up with his army."

Goreth stared seriously at Telemachus and his eyes were steadying. "as you said, you are the decider for your own fate. All I can do is show you the causeway once when it appears. After that it is up to you. Let me explain this moment, though. If you decide to spend any time on this track it will have no meaning in the mortal world. A day passed on these boards will not amount to a single breath exhaled in Pretannia."

Telemachus thought about this and Goreth gave pause to let him reflect upon it. Telemachus, suddenly, was tired. He should not be feeling like this – he was yet a young man. But all at once, he was conscious about his own mortality and the restraints imposed on him by the needs of others. There was so much to do: would there be enough time to achieve it all?

Goreth laid a kind hand on his shoulder. "It is no easy matter to be a good leader for your people. Much courage is needed and selflessness above all. You must crush the common human weakness – the greed, the jealousy and insecurity, which beset so many others who pretend to care for the people they govern. In so many instances these are the ones who die screaming in their sweated nightmares if not actually out of their beds on an assassin's sword edge. But a good leader needs the conviction from his own moral obligation to do the right thing by his citizens. He must be supported by those who can see this in him and they themselves should be selfless in this duty. Telemachus, you must inspire your people towards a goal for a better society, not simply promise them that whatever they want will be given to them. Happiness does not come with repeated satisfaction. It comes with imagination."

"I hear you, Goreth," said Telemachus rousing himself. "But how will the causeway help me in all that?"

"Use your own judgement about where it will take you. Develop wisdom. No-one and nothing can simply give that gift. Work for it. That is how others will come to trust the words you speak."

Telemachus faced the distant gloom ahead.

Goreth noted his reluctance and reassured him. "This opportunity comes to very few. The wooden road you see was built by both Man and Orsook to provide a bridge into the other place. It is a sign of their cooperation, their quest to explore and learn from the unknown. Many magical incantations were sung in its making, prayers chanted to the gods, sacred objects buried carefully beneath the timbers. It was told that a human and an Orsook builder offered their lives in sacrifice so that their souls could make the causeway live."

"What will we find?" said Telemachus in an almost hushed tone.

In response, Goreth raised his arm and swung it as if he was a discus thrower at the Games. What left his hand was not a metal disc but a scouring fierce light that arched over the lit part of the causeway and entered the darkened side. There it could be seen as a balled luminescence which exploded into sparky fragments, uncovering in its sudden flash yet more trackway with trees either side.

"Light smashes into dark," said Goreth simply, "and another world is made clear."

"It is very much like this world."

"This world, this universe: another world, a multiverse of possibilities. Step into it and see what can be found."

Telemachus made up his mind. "Let us go then."

"I cannot go with you, Telemachus. You must travel alone."

Telemachus was deterred. "But how can I do that, Goreth, without your help? I will not be able to see where to place my feet in the darkness without your light."

Goreth held out his arm to the other. "Take hold of my hand, Telemachus."

Doubtfully, remembering what had happened to Berengar, Telemachus took it. When he clenched the other's hand, he sensed a pulse ripple through his body and saw that the glow which had formerly illuminated Goreth's frame now departed from him and flowed like a hissing breeze into his own. Goreth was only visible now because of the light Telemachus projected.

"You may walk as far along the causeway as you need," said Goreth. "When you decide to return, run. With just four running strides you will be back to this same part of the traverse. If you find yourself in extreme danger with no way to return, call out my name twice."

Telemachus turned to peer at the way ahead, as if checking for the risks there, "but Goreth…" he began and turned back again. Where the Orsook had been standing was an empty space.

After several moments Telemachus started to feel the solitude. He was also angry with himself. If this was meant to test his character, he must surely have failed already. What must Goreth have thought about this obvious reluctance to walk the causeway? It was cowardly, not worthy for a hero or a leader. Surely, Tyracides would have behaved more manfully.

He took a few steps forward and listened. Utter silence. The light from his own body reached only so far, left and right of the track loomed massy shapes. An idea occurred to him. He wondered if he possessed the same facility for a flashing enhancement as Goreth had. He marked a spot to the left and then threw his right arm outwards as if hurling an invisible missile towards it. A ball sprung from his hand; it burnt with light but not flame, hurtled across the sky and landed in the place he had aimed at, lighting up the whole area for brief seconds. In that short time, Telemachus could see clearly defined, the oak trees and bushes packed along an extended woodland.

Except for those vegetal shapes, he was truly alone. The soft slap made by his sandals against the wooden planking as he walked was the only sound that could be heard. He moved over it for some time and what was strange to Telemachus was that the path did not deviate at all. There was no turning left or right with it, no sudden rise over an intruding hill; it simply drove forward, cutting the landscape, always pointing north. Another curiosity was that nothing seemed to overarch it. Trees, for instance, no matter how close they grew to the wooden walkway, would never stretch their boughs over it. Indeed, the giant beech trees, six of them, that he came across soon after he had begun walking and that were rooted in a line like sentinels to guard one side, were so lacking in branches on the walkway side that they looked as if they had been deliberately shorn of them but there were no roughened stumps to give real evidence for it.

And then he suddenly came to a chasm. It was a shock because the causeway had been on what was flat land, nothing rising or falling at all. Undisturbed itself, the causeway rolled over the break so that ahead it gave the distinct impression of being a bridge stuck in mid-air. Mist billowed up from below so Telemachus assumed that water must be at the bottom. He could see that the causeway bridged the chasm and continued on the other side but there was nothing holding it up from below or above and strengthening points at either end were entirely missing. The causeway was an engineering impossibility. There were two rails that ran along each edge of the causeway but they were too far apart for a traveller to stretch his arms and grasp both so it would be necessary to cling to just one as you moved. Anyway, Telemachus fully expected the causeway to bend under his weight, throwing him off-balance into the depths. He was astonished when venturing along the first part on discovering that the bridge held absolutely firm and there was no slackness whatsoever. He could not quite believe it as he made his way slowly and with extreme caution over the chasm. In the middle he pulled up, took a metal coin from his pouch and dropped it into the abyss. He waited. There was no repercussion but after listening hard for some time Telemachus did hear something like a muffled squabbling roar which soon died away. He moved off, quickening his pace and gained the solid land on the other side.

After continuing to travel the causeway for only a short time there was a perceptible change. The sky lightened and dawn was happening with the promise of a new sunrise. Yet, Telemachus had not been walking the path for such a length in time since leaving Goreth. Dawn should have been hours ahead.

As night diminished so did Telemachus' luminous presence and he was now a white shadow walking the boards. The land and what it contained became much clearer around him. Features shifted. What had been dense woody growth now became an open river plain. To the left was the river, its coursing wide and strong. But the waters were not clear; they were black. Curious about this strange pigment, Telemachus craned his neck forward to scrutinise the surface closely. Something had attracted his attention and shocked, he found that the river's surface was layered with dead and dying fish. Intermingled with these wriggling fish were birds from the river: ducks, herons, swans; all completely smothered in a black oily liquid that had glued their feathers, thus completely limiting their means for escape. No matter how they struggled, fish, birds and the viscous liquid mangled together were borne by the unstoppable current and rushed on – a vast swimming surface of the dead and the dying.

Lined along the bank, Telemachus could see people staring into the waters with dismay on their faces. They might have been farmers: behind them were neatly tended fields that were once fertile but now the crops standing in them were wilted and unhealthy in their growth. Where the fields met the river bank, black runnels, the same oily fluid killing the life in the river, seeped down the steep mud into the water below.

These people, men, women and children were oblivious to him. He waved his arms, the white light palely glimmering from his palms but they ignored him as if he was not there.

He continued to walk on. He could do nothing else. His heart was heavy and an ominous foreboding began to grow.

Soon though, the scene changed. The river, as if by some god's exertion, cleared itself and the water became clean again. No rotting bodies sailed by. Rose and gold streaks tinged the scarce clouds before the sun itself came into blinding view between the hills that now dominated the landscape.

Then, without warning, Telemachus came across people he could not fail to recognise. There were the Telemachons making their way across the land. A great crowd, led by Tyracides. There was no mistake, he could see them perfectly well. They were intent on their journey and he could make out Pelisteus, Eris with her bow slung behind her, Pelos, the Keltoi Berengar with his wife and child, the inventor Faramund, Costus on a pony, Melissa and Belisama, Polydeuctes, Lysimachus, Artorius, Sostis, Akeron, Antipater, Kleptomenes and a host of others. He searched for Hebe, beginning to worry that something had happened to her. She was in a small group behind Tyracides and he was thankful. Around her were others. He discerned them one by one. Eucleides! Thocero …. Had they deserted him while he was on the causeway and caught up with the others? How could that be? Others came into view…. Goreth! Then the greatest fright of all. Striding ahead, just before the Orsook was an unmistakeable figure. Telemachus gasped and leant on the causeway's wooden rail. Had he become a ghost left to wander this sorcery conjured walk-way while another spirit had invaded his body? Because there with the other Telemachons, purpose creasing his expression, was himself.

Telemachus almost panicked. He could not understand what this vision meant and cast around for answers. Was he wrong to trust Goreth as he had done? This causeway could be some supernatural means for imprisoning him while the Orsook by using his unearthly powers had gained control over Telemachus' body to some purpose that suited his own. He could instantly test this supposition by calling out Goreth's name. If the Orsook did not appear, then he was indeed trapped.

But Telemachus did not lose control of himself. He had to think a little longer before taking action. Goreth might have given him the explanation for this when revealing the causeway. If he called out now and the Orsook appeared, there was the possibility that he may look very foolish. Not like a wise leader at all. This then was a challenge to him. Make the right decision. By calling out now and betraying weakness, he would indicate an unfit nature to govern others. Consider the next action carefully and learn something more. Something that might be invaluable to his future. What had Goreth said: 'A multiverse of possibilities'? It maybe that what the Telemachons and his physical twin were doing across the river was not taking place in the here and now. He was here on the causeway now, so rationally it could not be. If it was an image of the future, he could learn from it. Another multiverse possibility: it might be the present as it could happen. What part did this pathway play in all of that? Was it his self-contained and present existence, a link to the world he had just left? He thought about stepping off to try it and find what would occur. Be cautious though.

Taking his sword from its sheath, Telemachus slowly pushed it forward into the air over the handrail. Almost on the instant, a pattern and its symmetry shifted. The content of the vision he had from the causeway – the Telemachons making their way overland – remained the same but the frame for it, that being the sky above and the river below, changed altogether. The water suddenly became a passing torrent while clouds in the sky sped by at a rate which matched the rushing current. Something pressed on his sword blade and the metal exploded. But it was not a normal explosion. The iron came apart, breaking into miniature globed particles curving up, down and to the side, leaving faint silvery tracks behind them. Against the rushing river they moved slowly, before the travelling Telemachons they sped quicker and then finally slowed against the flying clouds and disappeared out of the frame. Telemachus dropped the useless sword hilt and it clattered onto the wooden pathway. He could still see the last balled iron fragments that were his sword blade flowing upwards, then into and beyond the sky.

When the last glinting metal had disappeared there was another change in motion. Sky and river slowed their exhausting pace and returned to what fitted with the whole picture as before.

In all that had taken place and while he had been preoccupied, Telemachus saw that Tyracides and the Telemachons were well ahead of him now and he hurried along the causeway to keep up.

He was so eager in fact that he broke into a run and was into his fourth stride when the whole world shifted again. Too late, Telemachus realised that when Goreth had told him that running to return to the start of the causeway would take little time and space at all, then running forward to its presumed end would presumably operate by the same principle.

Only, it did not happen quite like that. When he stopped himself everything grew dark and then just as quickly recovered itself back into light. The Telemachons had not gone but it was no longer a scene describing the exile of a people. What the Corinthian could see from the causeway now was the construction of a very large city. Telemachus sought for the people he had recognised before, including himself. He could just pick them out, one by one. They were engaged in the different activities contributing to the city's establishment, some in trade to make the money required to pay for building works, others in the building and engineering works, yet others in farming outside the city.

Telemachus noted with interest that Tyracides was amongst this latter group, planting seed on his land. If he allowed his eyes to rest on one part of the scene, Telemachus observed that the thing he was concentrating on would magnify and become much clearer. Disconcertingly at first, this was what he experienced when he located Tyracides. His attention was focused on this strange phenomenon but soon what Tyracides was doing became much more engrossing. The former iron worker had taken a small leather bag from the river bank – it had been left to soak in the river water and he had just pulled it up – then brought it over to a lightly dug shallow trench in his field where he began to sow small white spherical seeds from it. Telemachus recognised them. They were the seeds Tyracides had found in the runic chest in Orsek's tomb at Glauberg. The chest that Tyracides had opened with the key he had got from the monstrous worm guarding the long tunnel that led to it.

This was not good. Telemachus had never felt comfortable about that discovery. What was buried in that tomb as an offering along with the High King's body, should have remained there. Transplanting it from one part of the continent to another in such circumstances might have ill consequences.

He deliberately switched his attention back to the city and the magnified focus sprang back to its original size. He had found almost every Telemachon and himself involved in the city's founding but one was missing. Wherever he peered – city, farmland or river, he could not find Goreth.

Time seemed to shift again. It speeded up. The buildings in the city grew upward from their foundations before his very eyes. Massive defensive walls circled the city and the farmland outside them were packed with crops. Telemachus saw that the plant grown on Tyracides' land was far larger than that grown on the neighbouring estates. It seemed to be a type of blue flower, then wheat: the head plump and heavy. As time passed, this plant seemed to take over the farmland adjoining Tyracides' fields so that one crop dominated.

That was foolish. Why wasn't there diversification? Anyone could see that if disease attacked the crop, the city would be stricken with famine.

And as the scene shifted again so it turned out. Blight did ravage the crops. The plants wilted, their heads bowed and blackened. Eventually the oily rot seeped from them into the river and Telemachus stared at the same despoiled surface with its deathly jamboree that he had witnessed earlier on in his travel along the causeway.

The city was no longer at peace. As Telemachus watched, two enormous gates in the city opened. From the one came Tyracides leading the Telemachons on horses and all dressed for war. From the other came a large body of infantry marching out, but these were Celts – he could tell them from their blue tattooed forearms and faces and the rounded iron helmets. They were led by one man on a horse, similarly tattooed but with stranger shapes on his arms. His grey beard and hair were plaited into cords. The thin dagger-nosed face stared straight ahead. If only Telemachus had known it, this was Formus. He knew the name, not the face but there was no-one at that moment who could tell it to him. The sight of this man and the warriors crowding behind him made Telemachus uneasy. Then he looked for himself on the Telemachon side but could find no trace. He thought about the situation evolving before his eyes and then it came to him that the man on the horse leading the Celts must be Formus.

What had driven Tyracides to ally the Telemachons with the force that had pursued them through northern Europa and Pretannia? These were desperate circumstances: the crops had failed; the city must be reliant on what had been stored but that would not be enough. Telemachus watched the two armies as they moved across the land in the same direction, following the river. It appeared that their march took several days as the sky darkened and lightened, each change marked by the two armies encamping for the night.

Then the disciplined forces were converging on a settlement that was very different to the city left behind. This community lived at the river's edge – it was filled with round dwellings under stone, mud and thatched roofs. In size the occupied land had expanded to twice that of the city and yet there were no defensive walls or ditches. His sympathy for the people who lived there mounted as Telemachus observed the armies moving in on their prey. An abrupt momentum came over the inhabitants. They started to rush from their homes in what was pure disorganised panic. It was then that Telemachus realised that the residents there were not human beings. They were Orsook. Some threw themselves into the river which, unlike the water upstream was free from debris and corruption. However, the opportunity for escape from their impending doom narrowed as the armies struck those houses on the settlement periphery. Burning torches were thrown onto the roofs and the fire roared up, stretching its flames to claw at more and more buildings.

Telemachus wondered why they had been so little prepared for the onslaught – not even the necessary sentries to give warning. As the shocking events rolled out, he witnessed female Orsook being cut down, the babies ripped from their arms and hacked to death. He was ready to turn his face away but a particular figure met his attention. The shape was running directly towards him and Telemachus had the disorientating sensation that the person was engaged in the turmoil and yet somehow separate to it. The figure loomed disproportionately larger as he approached, still running. His whole body was aflame. Everything behind this running body, engulfed with fire, dwindled away into nothingness and silence. Sound came from the being who ran. He was roaring but it was the roar from a blazing wildfire fanned by a rushing wind. And the screams from the massacre revived within it. Through the flames swirling around the head and face, as the body in a mass of fire ran towards him, Telemachus knew who it was. He could not help himself and shouted out twice "Goreth! Goreth!"

Goreth, if it was he, since this was a giant two or three times the size of Telemachus, stared straight ahead without responding. Now, the other could see that in fact the flames which wrapped around Goreth did not seem to harm him. The fire burned without scorching or singeing his flesh.

Telemachus suddenly felt himself scooped up as if by a tornado and felt that he was being rushed back along the causeway to where he had started.

The flames did not burn him either. There was terrific movement all around but he felt suspended in the arms of Goreth as he was carried back. There was calm but not in his mind. He felt a warning from the vision at the causeway and a despondency came upon him. At the bottom of that menacing despondency lay Tyracides, charging down upon the innocent Orsook with their chief persecutor, Formus, by his side.

At last Telemachus was set down by the entrance to the roadway, before the towering doorway framed from wood. The being who had brought him disappeared. In front of him was the Goreth he knew, inspecting him kindly. Before Telemachus had time to speak, Goreth forestalled him, "I know what you saw. You must decide for yourself what it could mean for your present circumstances."

Telemachus had already decided what it could mean for the future. His trust in Tyracides would never be the same. There was an inescapable fact in the events he had seen from the causeway and that was that throughout the latter part of them, his own existence had been entirely removed. He had always regarded Tyracides as an open, honest man. The insight from the causeway built by Orsook and men changed all that.

32
Enemies both visible and invisible

The Land of the Four Winds was feeling the first effects of the Ice Choker when Tyracides and the Telemachons moved onto it. They arrived by night – a still, cold night, bright with stars hanging motionless over the rolling land as the Telemachons stepped beneath. The voyagers were thickly clothed and hooded against the crisp, clean, icy air. Berengar was accompanied by his wife, Ula and their young son who was asleep on his shoulders. They had been making their way through a field when it was he who first spotted the dark silhouettes intruding upon the starred horizon ahead. The Telemachons were all stretched out in a line, haphazardly and followed by another line, then another. It did not serve for the greatest protection. Berengar called over to Tyracides in a half-whisper. The night was quiet, barring the hooted sound from an owl. There had been no sound from the weary travellers, just the long grass brushing against their legs as they moved forward. Tyracides' attention was easily attracted by the whispered word "Settlement!" from his friend. Nevertheless, he cocked his hand against his ear to urge Berengar to speak again. The Keltoi made another attempt, louder this time. "Village ahead!"

Tyracides jerked his head up and waved to the others standing around. They understood quickly and began to reform into a column behind him. Berengar, passing the child to his wife, joined with Tyracides.

"What do you think we should do?"

Tyracides glanced back at his exhausted followers. "There is nothing we can do except to walk into the place, asking for them to offer us food and rest. It does not look like such a large settlement. The worst they can do is to refuse us. It would not be worth their while to use violence."

Costus had come closer, catching the last words. "Yes, you are probably right but just to be safe, should we not keep some of our people back in case there is a risk?"

"We don't know who might be there," added Eris, her bow in hand and already drawing an arrow from her quiver.

"Put that away, Eris," said Tyracides in an even tone. "we must at least appear to be peaceful while we are in their village." Eris reluctantly complied. "But I hear you, Costus. It is good advice." He then divided the Telemachons up, so that a score stayed behind in the field, hidden, to watch the proceedings while the rest, led by Tyracides, walked into the empty streets of the village.

Because empty they were. That was unusual in itself. Their approach must have been discerned in some way so the Telemachons braced themselves for anything that might happen.

And what did happen was: nothing.

They walked the deserted streets, their movements almost seeming to echo in the evening air. Tyracides knocked on one door once and then several times. There was no answer so Tyracides tried the door, fully expecting it to be locked. It opened easily enough. A light was brought and he entered with Costus and Eris. Inside the large single room there were signs of habitation: beds on the floor, the central hearth with a stock of wood next to it and elsewhere in the room food stores that included dried beans, meat and bread. There were even clothes and bedding piled in a chest.

Misgivings overcame Tyracides even as he searched and came away from the house, ordering the others to explore the remaining dwellings. He knew what they were to find even before they reported back to him. Every house in the village was empty.

"well, the best that can be made from this situation," commented Tyracides to the Telemachons gathered around him, "is that we can eat and rest under warm roofs tonight, or …."

"Or …." said Faramund, looking down the street, "…. we can all be dead by dawn."

The others followed his gaze. Coming towards them were the people they had left behind in the field, being driven along by what were obviously the village inhabitants.

"No violence against them, just mass slaughter experienced by us," observed Faramund, drily.

The captured Telemachons trudged on. First came Aristopolis, the Athenian who had been placed in command. Tyracides gave him a reproving stare. He protested, "They were on us before we knew it! No marsh newt could have been quieter!"

It was a strange gap that the captors maintained between themselves and the captured. Notable because it was so wide.

There was little point in resisting. The villagers had shields and spears whereas although the Telemachons carried some weaponry, they had thrown their shields away days earlier to travel faster and lighter.

A man from the villagers came forward. He was surprisingly young – somewhere in his twenties – to be the spokesperson for the village. He wore a woollen tunic cut off above the knees and below them his legs were covered in leather trousers. He wore no head garment, not even a helmet and a long thick moustache marked his upper lip, falling below his jaw.

Tyracides was taken with the green freckles that decorated his skin. This was a new technique in tattooing he had never seen before.

The man, for all his youthful appearance, spoke clearly and confidently in the Keltoi speech which Telemachus had come to learn. Yet this was different to that used at Helladore's court or in Gaul. The words were familiar but the meanings of some he had to guess at and others had connotations which were confusing.

"Friendly enemies or enemy friends?" initiated the villager.

If it had not sent the wrong message, Telemachus would have frowned. He scanned the formation around the young man. Women, strong and tall, were there, as fiercely armed with weaponry as the men.

"Not enemies. We are friends."

"How can you be friends? You are not one of us. You do not live in the village."

From this brief exchange, Tyracides realised that the word 'friends' did not carry its usual connotation with these people. It could mean a resident and neighbour in the settlement rather than anyone, stranger included, who would behave in a friendly manner. The worrying implication was that they would dogmatically regard anyone from outside the village as a threat. He wondered what their word for 'friend' was in this context, if they had one. Not knowing it himself, he chose a phrase from what had been offered.

"Friendly enemies."

The young clan leader seemed to be satisfied and relaxed a little. "Have you come from far away?"

"Very far," said Tyracides, stretching his arm and pointing back, "across the ocean."

A puzzled expression flittered on the young man's face. "Ocean? What is that?"

"It's a very big lake."

"Ah, we live in the Land of the Four Winds, we have rivers and lakes enough. I am told that further north there are more lakes and bigger, perhaps some are as big as your ocean."

"Perhaps they are," agreed Tyracides. "I have not seen them yet."

The man looked at him seriously. "The last friendly enemy to come to our village died."

Tyracides heard a murmuring from the Telemachons behind him. They had spent enough time in Keltoi lands now to understand some of the language themselves.

"How?"

"You certainly have come from far if you have not heard about those unkissed by the winds when they travel through our country. Did the people you passed through not talk about it?"

Tyracides remembered that the Keltoi they had dealt with only wanted to take their cash and wave them goodbye as fast as they could. It would not have benefited them to warn about ant dangers ahead that might delay their paying visitors and change them to a dangerous encumbrance.

"Would you be kind enough to end our ignorance?"

"You have more to fear from us, with or without our weapons, than we do from you. Do you see these marks on my skin?" The young chief touched his face and now that he was aware the Telemachons could understand some of what he said, he shaped his words to their ears as well as to their leader's. "They are the sign for a true Borrumani, a touch left by the Wind God himself. It gives us a deadly power over others. What I mean by that is if we simply touch the skin belonging to a person who was not born in the Land of the Four Winds, that person loses limbs endures a long, agonising, cruel sickness before succumbing to the Shadow who rules underground."

The Telemachons broke out into nervous chatter and instinctively drew themselves away from their captors as much as they were able to.

The young chief raised his arm and the voices stopped.

"Our very breath would infect you with disease." Before the Telemachons erupted into further talk, the man spoke again, "So you see, you are entirely in our power. But please do not worry. We do not want to harm you."

Tyracides was worried. He had just led the Telemachons into a death-trap. At the moment, he was entirely dependent on the man saying he wished them no harm for a way out. "What do you wish us to do?" Tyracides said simply.

"Why have you come here?"

Tyracides explained.

"So you are just passing through, if we let you," the chief said at last.

"Yes."

The young clan leader paused. Neither he nor any of his villagers would want to put nearly a hundred people to death. Neither would they hand them over to King Noremac, a ruler they despised as a despot interested only in his merchant courtiers and his own personal treasury. However, Chief Coryumberix, as he was known, had something to prove with his people and this would grant that opportunity.

"We are a people at peace. The only struggle we have is with the wind. You, we do not know. It might be that we let you go, to find out later that you have murdered people before you came here or have devastated some Windlander settlement after you leave because you fear the Borrumani curse. In that event, I should feel personally responsible." Coryumberix hesitated. "How would you persuade us not to execute you all by touching you or arresting your people and taking them away to suffer King Noremac's pleasure?" The chief then put it plainly, "What can you do for us to gain our trust?"

Tyracides was at a loss. He looked around at the Telemachons and his eyes settled on one man in particular. He prayed to Zeus that he was doing the right thing and said, "Tell them, Faramund."

Confused by the sudden switch in attention from everybody collected there to himself and an imposed responsibility, Faramund stuttered, "M-m-m-me?"

"Yes," came a stern reply from Tyracides in an attempt to steady him, "You."

Faramund had listened carefully to everything the clan leader had said. He calmed himself and thought. To everyone there, it seemed as if he had retreated into a world of his own and the blank gaze on his face confirmed it. But then, after a minute or two, he said, "What if I showed you how to convert your constant struggle with the wind to a real benefit for your life here?" Close by him, Berengar began to smile.

"How would you do that?" replied Coryumberix, noting Faramund's suggestion with immediate interest.

"That field we trekked through just now to get here. The wind must blow strongly there at times?"

"All the year around it blows on that hill, even in the Breath of Belinus when the sun scorches."

"I have seen that you grow wheat to make bread. How do you grind the corn?"

"We use ponies to turn the grindstones that are as big as a house!" said the young chief proudly but with some exaggeration.

"Well, we shall build you a windmill with grindstones that are turned by the wind and you can save your horses for ploughing. You will increase your production of flour and bread many times over."

Tyracides following the conversation avidly, was glad that Faramund had found a relief to their predicament but at this point interrupted, "Wait, wait, my young inventor, we cannot stay her for so long that …." He tailed off when he saw Coryumberix's angered expression. He chided himself. They could not afford to let the village chieftain know that another Celt, a High Druid no less, was in pursuit of them accompanied by an army. "And then again, if the young lord thinks that this machine might be useful for his people, I would not wish to prevent us gaining his trust in that way. We will stay as long as necessary."

"Good," affirmed Coryumberix. "I think this windmill sounds as if it could have great benefits for us. We are not without building skills ourselves so it may not be necessary for you to stay such a long time. As long as we understand completely how it works, we would much rather finish it ourselves."

The chief was very satisfied with his bargain. Tyracides less so. He worried about the delay and the risks they might all incur by their staying in the village. If the Windlander leprosy did not kill them, then Formus certainly would. Costus and others soothed his fears when he spoke to them later.

"Formus does not know by which route we entered the Borrumani country," said Costus.

"Yes, remember, we lost them days ago by walking up the stream and getting our legs wet up to the knees."

"For you it was the knees, for me it was the waist," grumbled Costus. "An hour of cold water around my nether regions. It was lucky I didn't catch a chill and pass away after I got out."

"Well, let's pass over your nether regions, Costus …." began Melissa.

"Plenty have," interrupted the dwarf with a grin.

"And consider that our situation is not as bad as you might think."

"I'm all for colourful optimism in the bleakest moments," said Agenor, "but I am at a loss to find it here. Death in battle fighting for your homeland and freedom is a thing that can almost be welcomed. Gasping my life away slowly, after losing my limbs and Zeus knows what else happening to my body's internal organs is definitely not."

"Exactly," said Melissa. "Do you think that such a reputation as this land has got, will entice Formus' army into it? They would probably rebel first."

"This disease was unknown to us before we got here, perhaps they don't know either," said Tyracides.

"Does that matter?" replied Melissa. "Like us, their first instinct when they come across it will be to flee. We were able to be captured because our small force could not overcome a whole village such as this one. Aa Borrumani settlement will not attempt to engage with Formus' army, once they have recognised its size. Much better and less wasteful for them is to simply inform the would-be invaders how the Wind leprosy would destroy them."

"You are right," admitted Tyracides. "Now, please tell me how we can avoid contracting the disease ourselves when we are expected to live amongst them, building this windmill."

"It's all about hygiene," said Faramund. The others looked at him, wanting to know more. "We cannot possibly stay amongst them. That would be fatal to us. I don't think the Borrumani in this village expect us to live very long. That was the implication in the chief's statement that they would finish the building work and his urge to pass over the plans quickly to them. We should meet with him and ask for an area to settle temporarily that is set apart from the village. I am thinking that the field through which we walked and where we are going to establish the windmill would be ideal – down at the bottom near the woodland and stream. Strict social rules shall have to be put in place so that even an accidental meeting between us and the Borrumani is made more or less impossible."

"Do you think he will agree to this – giving away land to strangers, no matter how temporary, will not be a popular action for his people."

"He will do it," said Faramund confidently, "if he wants his village's food production and storage multiplied for the future. His villagers could see the horror on our faces when we learned about the disease. They understand that we want to leave as soon as possible. It will not be such a difficult task for the chief to persuade them to accept this."

So it turned out. Tyracides and Faramund met with Coryumberix and for their accommodation a designated region of land was given over from the field on which they were to build the new mill. With the chief's permission, the Telemachons cut down trees, erecting wooden buildings to house themselves. At the same time, they began to build the stone foundations on the hill-top to initiate the project that would provide for the village's future.

This took several days; meanwhile Formus and his army were getting ever closer. When the last foundation stone had been laid down under direction by Faramund, Formus was astride his white stallion. Artemius was on one side, the Lady Andraste another and his men behind, watching another of his soldiers riding furiously towards him. He had been sent as a courier to the settlement along the river. It was in front and just visible between the trees. The man was riding as if he had seen Hades himself. What on earth possessed him?

"Control yourself, Corus," said Formus as the rider lurched to a stop before him. He was gasping breath as if he had been galloping up the slope and not his horse. "If the settlement wishes to fight us we are ready. Is that what they want?"

"My lord Formus – you – cannot – go down there!"

"What? Calm yourself man. Speak clearly and tell me everything."

"The village is infected by the plague!"

Concern registered itself upon the faces of the men mounted immediately behind Formus and slightly further back whispered comments were passed along the ranks gathered behind them. The words 'village' and 'plague' were repeated.

"Order!" roared out Formus and the whispering stopped. "Tell me more," he said to the messenger.

"They carry the disease with them but are immune to it themselves. If we, who are not born in this country contract the affliction then it affects us like leprosy only death comes far quicker."

"What are these people called and what is the name of the country?"

"They are the Borrumani and dedicate prayers to their chief god, Borrum. The country is called The Land of the Four Winds."

Formus had heard the name before at the court of Helladore. It had been described as a weather-beaten region at a great distance to the north and disease had been mentioned. When pressed further the courtier went on to say it was a grubby little backwater, worthless, an island within an island, disease-ridden, whose neighbours had turned their back on it. Formus had paid scant attention until now.

"Is it necessary to voice the obvious thought that we should not risk going through this country?" asked the Lady Andraste.

"Not really," agreed Formus. "But where are the Telemachons and their leader, Telemachus?"

"They are either dead, having become the plague's victims or are travelling around the country to return to the route northwards."

"What is that there?" said Formus, suddenly shifting his gaze to a point behind the messenger's head. At some distance away, on a hill, was a building made from wood and stone. The edifice had been newly created and it was far from complete. Whatever its purpose, the finished building would cover a substantial area on the hill-top. Formus moved his horse to the side for a better view and traced the line of the hill down to a stream and some woodland. There at the bottom, just shielded by some trees was a collection of huts, again newly built.

"Are they expanding their settlement?" wondered Formus aloud.

On the hill, behind the mill foundations, hid the Telemachus and Tyracides. It was fortunate that they had worked quickly – the building thus far was greater than head height. The Telemachons, after seeing Formus' army collecting on the hill-top opposite had positioned themselves behind the windmill and were as still and quiet as the stone itself.

Formus was unsure. "What do you think?" he said to Andraste and Artemius. They searched the area with their eyes but could not find any signs of the inhabitants.

"Doesn't seem to be anyone there. No danger to us. It looks as if the settlement is going to get bigger," said Artemius.

"There might be movement on that hill," added Andraste, "but just see what's coming up on this one."

The others swivelled their heads. Behind the messenger another lone rider was approaching. He wore a hooded cloak which covered his features and was galloping almost as quickly as the messenger had done, towards them. Unlike Corus, this mounted figure stopped at a greater distance away but not so far that they could not see his face if only he took down his hood.

The messenger rejoined the ranks and as they all watched the new visitor walked his horse up and down along an imaginary line so that he could be seen by Formus and the whole army. He had the use of only one arm as just one hand controlled his horse's reins, although expertly done. The other arm hung down, a long sleeve enveloping it.

"Why do you come here?" shouted out Formus.

The rider continued his movement. He pushed fear before him, in his silence and dark hooded anonymity. After a few moments, the black horse drew up with a tight draw on the reins. Then a clear voice came from the hood.

"I come here to save you from death or to inflict it – it is your choice."

"Unbelievable words from a lone man facing an army of five hundred!" yelled Formus, angered.

There was no immediate response in speech. Instead, the horseman raised what everyone had assumed was his useless arm and at the same time threw back his hood. The grisly vision caused some onlookers to gasp with horror and exclaim, "Plague!" The arm raised high ended in a stump; the face was weltered with scars. In their sight, it seemed to some in the front rank that bits of flesh fell from his face. The revulsion and fear was tangible.

"Do you believe this?" shouted the plague victim, waving his stump. His voice and manner strangely exulted, a crooked smile on his face as he began to drive his horse towards them. The man was like some punishing demon or someone about to go berserk. Now that he himself was dying, he would introduce his deadly friend to others. Life was valueless.

Formus called out to an archer, who fitted an arrow and raised his bow.

Then he warned the oncoming rider. "Come you may but any closer and you will soon be joining your ancestors underground!"

Maniacal laughter burst from the diseased apparition.

"Do you think I care anything for that? Regard what is behind me and find those that will bring an agonising death to you – merely by their touch, if not their ravenous swords!"

It was true. Behind the rider was a crowd of Borrumani, armed and moving into view from the cover of the trees.

"Kill me and my severed body parts will be thrown at your fleeing backs! Stay and die!"

It was useless to remain. Formus knew that he must command his army to leave in an orderly manner or see them run and break up before this threat. The villagers would then slaughter them. Hurriedly, the druid gave the command to retreat and his army moved off, mounted cavalry first and then infantry with a speedy march.

When the Borrumani villagers reached the plague victim, just a few figures in the rear of Formus' army could be seen, gradually disappearing over the hill crest. They were followed by the villagers' jeers.

Coryumberix was the first to reach the rider's side. He grinned and slapped him on the back. "That was well done, Torcus. Now you can wipe that bread dough from your face and we can return to the Hall to share a pot of mead in celebration!"

Torcus first took his cloak and brushed off the honey-coated dough lumps festooning his face, then finished up by emptying a bottle of water over his head. Shaking it and laughing, he raised his stump to the sky before his comrades and said, "I knew the battle-god would compensate me for losing this one day and today was that day!" The villagers cheered and applauded.

The noise was echoed by the Telemachons on the other hill who had emerged from behind the mill and were waving their appreciation for what had been done, smiles on their faces.

"It is a pity they cannot share the mead with us," observed Torcus, waving back and then beginning to fit the hook he usually used back onto his fistless arm.

"That would be more than their lives are worth," came the dry comment from Coryumberix.

After Formus and his army had been frightened away, the Telemachons were granted a respite from their constant worry about him. At least their concern was reduced on that aspect but the fear that they might be infected by the Windleper disease continued. Coryumberix did his best to alleviate this by strict regulation for his people about when and where they might go. The villagers were not altogether happy about these new laws but they understood the necessity for them and accepted on the basis that it was temporary. The Telemachons were grateful to the Borrumani in the village that they learned was called Monithcound. Their suspicions about Coryumberix had ended when they saw how he had protected them from Formus. This new friendship and security surmounted the physical barriers between the two peoples.

And so the work on the mill progressed. The building now looked very solid and grand on the hill and around its base were Telemachons polishing the millstones, stretching the linen to fix to the wooden sail frames and taking more wood inside to continue the interior construction.

Although sparse, the living accommodation the Telemachons had arranged for themselves was comfortable. A stretch of river nearby had been given to them for fishing, washing clothes and bathing. Additional food and drink was brought and left by the villagers at the boundary line to their estate.

*   *   *   *

One day, it was to the river that Chara decided to take some linen to be washed. She had offered to help Ula, Berengar's wife, with cleaning her infant son's clothes and also in her basket were some of her own.

Tyracides stepped into her path. At once she became defensive. Chara was an ex-slave like Tyracides. Whereas she had been brought up in a rich Athenian's household, he had worked at an iron foundry in Syracuse. There was nothing wrong with that; it was not his former trade that concerned her. What did disturb her was that some male slaves had a particular attitude to the women taken into household service. They viewed them all as having offered sexual services to their masters. Somehow this made them feel resentful and they focused their resentment on the women rather than the masters. Chara knew that the sexual recrimination was true for many slave-owning households. In those cases, the female slaves were invariably forced to participate. Melissa herself, the companion to Tyracides, had endured such an experience at the hands of Porcys, her Syracusan overlord. But not all slave women were subjected to it. Sometimes they were lucky, as Chara had been and the masters were either devoted to their wives or if not, they reserved gratuitous lust for the hetaerae who provided services away from home.

When Chara had first known Tyracides on joining the expedition in Athens, he had treated her with perfect manners. She had got to know about his part in Telemachus' battle with Porcys in Syracuse and had respected him for it. But then everything changed and Tyracides' attitude with it. Chara could not fail to notice his growing interest in her – that and his increasing dominance amongst the Telemachons now that Telemachus was absent from them. What had once been a desire to do the best for others in working with them had become an obstinate protective stance for his own view, his own way of doing things which for him was necessarily right. He had begun to monopolise the important decision-making and others in the group were beginning to feel ignored.

Some amongst the warriors actually preferred this new direction Tyracides was taking. They wanted a man who knew his own mind, who was firm and clear in his direction. They easily bartered their right to be consulted and imposed no limit on Tyracides' power. Others such as Pelos, Sostis, the Keltoi Berengar and those who were not warriors amongst the men such as Costus and Faramund seemed to be biding their time, waiting for Telemachus to return. Most women took the lead from Tyracides' lover, Melissa; they showed utter support. Chara would not be surprised if Melissa had also recognised Tyracides' attention to her. If so, Melissa had not registered it in any changed behaviour with Chara herself. Maybe it was true then, that no matter how talented, there were those women who allowed themselves to be dominated by men in authority, yielding their own independence.

"Where are you going Chara?" said Tyracides with an attempt at lightness which did not work.

" Herne's clothes need to be washed," she said simply, mentioning Berengar's infant boy.

"You know the rule that has been laid down. No-one, man or woman is to go to the river without being accompanied by another. It is too dangerous."

"I will not be gone long." She saw his eyes moving from her face down to her breasts and legs, then slowly up again. Not even bothering to hide it now. Chara said nothing. She did not want to respond to his intimidation.

Tyracides savoured the long blonde hair of the pretty woman before him, creamy, smooth skin at the neck, soft, pointed breasts pushing taut at the linen and he wanted her. Despite the cold air, he felt a warm flush between his thighs.

"I can go with you if you like. For protection."

"That's alright," said Chara and in her attempt to forestall an impasse she almost pushed past him to get by. Slightly nervous, she repeated herself, "I won't be long."

Tyracides let her go. Slightly angered, he called, "It's at your own risk.!"

She walked on without reply and he stared as she went. His gaze followed her intently, particular interest was reserved for the path she took around the river bend and through some trees.

Turning around he made as if to go back to the encampment. Then a thought stopped him. He twisted around again to the delicate figure that had begun to vanish amongst the bracken. Alone and unaccompanied. A decision was made with the force of one hammer beat against the white hot iron he used to draw from the fire-pit. He followed her.

Chara had not gone very far around the bend in the river. She heeded some if not everything of the warning that had come from the man. It had disturbed her and now she wanted to get this washing done as soon as possible.

The river current was fast at this corner and loud in her ears. She began to pull the first cloth garment from her wicker basket and doused it in the water, squeezing the linen together.

She heard a footfall behind her. Before she had time to turn, a cloth was wrapped around her head so that she was unable to see and she felt herself dragged backwards. After a few moments, a heavy body flung itself on top of her and her arms were pinned to the ground. Chara struggled but she was helpless under the oppressive muscular force that frenzied above her.

But then there came a sudden cessation.

The weighty body over her was arrested in its movement. There was not a sound, not so much as a gasp. It began to fall sideways and saved from her despair Chara desperately continued to push at it; at the same time, she tore her blindfold off and tried to get to her feet.

"Steady!" warned a voice. Shocked again, Chara rubbed her eyes and searched for the origin of this newcomer.

Tyracides stood a little way ahead. The short scabbard at his side which contained his dagger was empty and on the ground Chara found her assailant with Tyracides' knife protruding from the back of his head. She could not quite believe it. Not since the assault began, did she imagine it could be any other than Tyracides forcing himself onto her.

She looked down and what had been instant relief was now replaced with sheer anguish. Her assailant, his leather trousers around his knees, was a Borrumani. Tyracides had thrown his knife from a distance and now she knew why. Chara broke down and wept.

Tyracides attempted to comfort her, without approaching. "Chara! Chara! What has happened is done. I shall have to return to the others and tell them about this. There might be some help we can get you."

"Can't you see what he did?" she gasped. "He has touched me. I have his disease!"

"We will speak to Coryumberix. There might be something they can do, we don't know until we ask them. Stay here until I can get someone to return with the means for providing you shelter." Tyracides was certain that it would be impossible to have Chara living amongst them again, unless the gods intervened.

He left her weeping beside the cold river, face down, the corpse of her attacker sprawled alongside.

Back at the encampment Tyracides told the others about the events and organised clean clothing and material for a tent to be taken to Chara. The Telemachons were angry about this insult to her but once more they found themselves in a hopeless situation. All they could do was to ask Coryumberix for his advice and who was to say that he would believe their account for why one of his own people lay dead on the riverbank with a dagger through his brain?

Coryumberix, when they met him, was far more understanding than they had assumed. He saw the body and the state Chara was in. Much more practically he realised that there was no reason why the Telemachons would concoct such a charade if in fact they had cold-bloodedly murdered the villager. A better plan might have been to drop the body in the river and allow the current to wash it out to sea.

"Is there anything that can be done for the girl?" said Tyracides about Chara.

Coryumberix considered the problem. "The other Borrumani in the clans beyond Monithcound think we are isolated. To a certain extent that is true but not totally. I do have people who from time to time bring me good information about what is happening in other parts of the realm and particularly at the court of King Noremac," Coryumberix frowned and pursed his lips together on mentioning the King's name as if he was about to spit. "It has to be good because I pay well. Unfortunately, that can be a two-way traffic and I am surprised that with the strange new construction rising in our village that we have not had a visit from the king's agents already." The chief brought himself back to the main point. "Anyway, what I meant to say was that the King has a growing opposition amongst the younger generation, including, some say, his own daughter. My informant tells me that recently she has given it out amongst her young followers that Conversevitae has found a cure for our national disease but it is being deliberately withheld from the people."

"Conversevitae? Who is that?" asked Berengar, standing beside Tyracides. Tyracides frowned at the intrusion.

"He is the King's chief physician and necromancer," replied Torcus, raising his hook to scratch his nose. "He works all days long away from the light deep in his underground laboratory, producing new toxins to pollute the ground and weapons of war for the King from his malignant materials. By accident, he must have produced something beneficial for once – if this is true."

"Then why do they keep it to themselves? What do they gain from doing that?" came another interruption, this time from Costus.

"Who knows with this King …." said Coryumberix, "he keeps himself locked away in his palace and pits the aristocrats and merchant class against the poor, which is the rest of us. We have only maintained some prosperity because we live at the edges of his kingdom."

"But excuse me, sire," said Ula, close to her husband Berengar. "What you seem to be telling us is that Chara could possibly be saved from this dreadful disease if somehow she could have that necromancer's drug administered to her."

"It is a possibility. But we cannot be sure that it actually exists."

"The King's daughter seems to be certain. We must try to obtain the cure. Chara has been like a younger sister to me. She is a kind, decent woman and the last person deserving to be afflicted by such an evil blight. Will you not help her by sending some men to the king's court to find the princess and beg for the cure from her?"

"My dear lady," said Coryumberix gently, "I may be young and my heart goes out to you but my responsibility within this village is to protect everyone's interests not just those of your friend. In fact, I should say that as you and your friend have just arrived at Monithcound, consequently I have no responsibility at all. You should look to your own leader for that."

Ula turned to Tyracides, who remained silent and impassive. She broke out then with an exclamation, "Are we just going to leave her to die and do nothing? How long has Chara got before the infection takes her limbs and her life?"

"It is different for each man, woman or child. Usually the stronger symptoms begin to take hold after a week."

Ula hung her head, the sadness at her friend's situation welling up inside her.

"Stop your tears woman!" came a brusque voice. Torcus pushed himself forward. "My chief," he said to Coryumberix, "if you give me permission, I will go to seek the princess and attempt to bring back that cure."

"And what if you are caught?" said Coryumberix, his reluctance evident.

"I shall not be," replied Torcus with stubborn self-confidence.

"You are only a man, Torcus, made from flesh and blood like the rest of us. Like the rest of us, what you desire and what you achieve could go their divergent ways much the same as your head from its body under the axe wielded by the king's executioner."

"My lord, it is not only the girl, Chara, I am thinking about," although in fact it was, since Torcus had seen her sad, beautiful figure at the riverbank earlier when they had gone to collect the corpse of the cowardly thug who had attacked her. " It is the antidote to our scourge that I may be able to bring back. Out here, living at the edge of our country we are closer to other Keltoi than to our own people. Soon, with this new windmill we will produce more than enough grain for our own use, grain we can trade. This cure itself will be valuable to us if we find the means for producing it in great quantities. The other tribes can take the medicine and associate with us freely. Everything is possible. It may even remove the disease from our own bodies."

"A villager in the accompanying crowd called out - "The disease is our protection. Once that is lifted what is to prevent other countries from invading us and taking what they want anyway?" There was an assenting noise from others.

Torcus turned and spoke louder. "That is what King Noremac has always suggested and the kings before him too. They are wrong. If the other Keltoi had seriously wanted to do that, all they needed to do was to amass their forces and rain down fire and arrows upon our heads here in Monithcound without coming near. We know they have the potential to do that."

"Torcus, listen to me," said his chief. The other turned back. "There is some merit in what you say and if all these actions are accomplished as you hope they could be, then Monithcound will prosper for its people. But if you fail we will have the King's army down on our heads and all who live here will be enslaved. Therefore, I cannot give you permission to go. However, should you suddenly be found to have left the village, neither will I send someone to hunt you down and return you here. That is as much as I am able to do."

"Thank-you, my lord."

Coryumberix placed his hand briefly on Torcus' shoulder. "Go with our good wishes and may the god Borrum bring you back to us safely."

Although many people wanted to go with Torcus when they heard these words, they understood that it would be impossible for them. Coryumberix had sent out a clear command that no-one from the village was to go with him so he was to be truly alone. The chief relented and offered help in one respect. He gave a sealed message to Torcus, telling him to pass it onto a man he knew, living along the route to Overblown, the capital.

"Of all my agents," said Coryumberix, "this man will serve you best and is to be trusted." Seeing the quizzical expression on his warrior's face, Coryumberix enlightened him. "He is my cousin." Then explained why he would be necessary. "Amongst those who support the Princess Byncor, he has been granted her special favour and will lead you to her. After that, it is up to you to gain and keep her trust. We will all, here at Monithcound, sacrifice to Borrum for your safe return."

33

Escape from Overblown

It was on the third day of the waning moon that Torcus reached the capital. He had been brought safely over the route by Coryumberix's agent, a small man who lost his farm to flooding in one disastrous year and since had earned his living by spying and messenger services which made him much more money than his agricultural activities had done. In traversing it, Torcus was astonished at the size of his country. This was the first time he had gone beyond the next settlement from Monithcound and he had always believed the Land of the Four Winds to be small in size.

The chief's agent was careful to avoid having to go through any settlements and they usually saw them from a distance, on a hill, the agent peering for routes around them so that they would not be discovered. What troubled Torcus was that they came across more than one oppida that had been struck by a calamity of some kind. In one village there had been a flood of river water through the streets; in another a mud avalanche had cascaded over house roofs. Being a bitter survivor from a catastrophe similar to the one he saw in the first village the agent exclaimed, "Fools! Fools!" at the sight. Torcus remonstrated with him, pointing out the need for sympathy rather than insults. He answered, "Can you not see how the river has been allowed to silt up near the bend? Note where their houses are built. On that bend! They should have taken the mud away on a regular basis – that would save them having to wade to their houses!" Checking the corner that the agent was pointing at, Torcus had to admit that he was right. Two settlements further on, the other village overcome by disaster through dumped mud excited a similar irritable explosion from the little man – "Fools! Fools!"

"Now what have these people done wrong?" sighed Torcus.

"They have cut all the trees down on the mountain above them. Trees that fixed the earth to the ground. Without trees – no stability – rain loosens the soil – the people below end up in mud to their necks." Again, when Torcus looked, the agent was proven to be correct. Only, judging by the state some houses were in, the mud must have poured over the necks and heads of some, suffocating them. This impression the agent gave – constant irritation with the real predicaments he saw before him – did not endear the man to Torcus. He seemed to have an unhappy nature and unhappiness was not a soft bed for trust. Torcus reminded himself that that the agent was a cousin to his own village chief and was trusted by both him and the Princess Byncor. Somehow, it still didn't help.

Yet, if actions were anything to go by, the man fulfilled his promise and they met with the king's daughter as planned. She was surrounded by guards, both male and female, but they were not the king's own – these were younger in age, raw recruits one might have surmised, looking at them – they had been selected by the Princess herself and were utterly loyal. The King had allowed it because he knew the families they came from personally and could trust that those aristocratic families feared him enough to keep their offspring in check. The agent left immediately.

They had met in a forest outside Overblown and he found that the princess was as much interested in the Telemachons as he was in the cure. Sitting astride a grey mare, her legs in cotton trousers and with a long rabbit-fur coat over which she wore the large diamond and gold insignia for her royal house, Byncor carried beauty and authority in a scale properly balanced. Torcus was not tempted to be flippant and the four guards around her, although they were yet to mature, had a set look in their eyes that would make a hard fight if it came to it. And if it came to that, he would be able to handle them – just.

Torcus passed the sealed letter over to her from Coryumberix during the conversation and she was satisfied. Scrutinising the young men who guarded her she chose one and said, "Scotia, your appearance matches Torcus' quite closely. Swap your clothes with him and give over your horse. Stay in the oppida until I send for you." That was how Torcus was smuggled past the King's guards at the gate and into the palace.

The princess had decided that if she was ever to steal the cure for the disease that had been the scourge of her people for generations, this was the time. Borrum had brought about the opportunity for taking and using it. The Telemachons would form the core of an army-in-waiting and to it she could add her young supporters up and down the country. Coryumberix might also add his own village warriors. It would be a credible opposition to the King.

Byncor realised also that the cure without its inventor would be of minimal use. Conversevitae must come with them so that more antidote to the sickness could be made. The princess understood fully the consequences for herself if she was caught by the King. She had heard the story about her grandfather's death and its circumstances from a cousin. Not for one moment had she believed it then nor had she changed her mind since. She had been given the account when she was a child. It was not any inner precocious foresight allowing her to sense the truth, rather it was the childhood beatings she sustained at her father's hands and the intense, stubborn hatred she had for him. The beatings stopped as she grew older to be replaced by a feigned kindliness towards her, mainly for the benefit of observers. It was a mannered performance, acted perfectly. Relief from the beatings and physical pain was mitigated by a constant worry. What was this leading up to?

As a child she tried to work out what she had done wrong to deserve the punishment. Was it the way she held her fork when eating ... knocked a cup over clumsily, soaking her dress .... answered back? Because she made all these mistakes and more, which would inevitably end in the harsh treatment. In the childish, enclosed world that she inhabited with a population of only one, she must be at fault to bring these storms down on her head. She was just all wrong.

Then she grew up. Her mind reached out to the news and events around her; her ears became larger, particularly when she was hidden. She had always questioned why she was the only child and now she learned the answer. King Noremac had always wanted more children but he only desired more specifically to enable the birth of one: a son, a male heir. A son was required by the primogeniture that applied to the monarchy.

Her own mother, Byncor heard, had conceived a son soon after she brought the princess into the world. There had been a premature birth and the boy had died. After that the queen became infertile, so it was given. Yet the King had many mistresses and not one gave birth to a child, either male or female. If one did have a son, there was a certainty that she would have replaced Byncor's mother as queen.

So the Princess came to realise that the reason for her childhood punishments was simply that she had been born a girl. Her punishment as an adult was that she was consigned to a precarious existence fearing for her life. Any wise words coming from her father on how to govern well, she treated for what they were: a facile attempt to keep her gullible. Time was running out for her. The King's promises to change the law of primogeniture were meaningless. He was the kind of man who saw women as only good for having babies and gratifying male desires. Noremac intended a man to follow him on the throne. One man he favoured in particular: the cousin who had given the detailed circumstances surrounding her grandfather's death. In her own mind, Byncor had predicted a situation whereby her own death would be precipitated sooner or later and her cousin adopted as the King's son and inheritor. She would do everything to prevent that from happening.

* * * *

The light glowed against Conversevitae's pallid features as he worked in his underground chamber. But it came from no artificial source. The light was radiating from a large moth whose wings rapidly fluttered every now and again. Ordinarily this would have sent the moth airborne but with this creature there was no such event because its thorax was tied with tiny threads fixing it to a central wooden stick on the physician's desk. The moth was very large – about as big as Conversevitae's face – he could feel a breeze from the flapping wings when it brushed against his skin. Incredible patterns in pink, yellow and blue whorled and etched them. Down here in the dim chamber the creature had provided an aesthetic splash and had gloriously fascinated the wizard for the last few days. It belonged to a species that was becoming extinct in the land and generally speaking each glowing individual lived for only three days in the swampland over which it flew. This particular specimen was in its death throes, having reached the end of its allotted time span.

"There, there, my lovely," murmured Conversevitae, "calm down. I am only here to help."

The wizard moved a small dish near to the moth. It contained a bright red liquid. Moving an ocular crystal towards his eye, he peered through it to the magnified image presented by the insect's body. A needle was dipped into the liquid at his side and then having found the area he wanted, Conversevitae pierced the moth's skeleton with it.

The substance at the needle's point was his own blood which had been infused with vaccine for the virulent disease that had attacked his people for so long. It was not for his own benefit that he carried out the experiment. After all, he had taken the cure in a single dose months ago and it had achieved everything desired. The disease had been completely purged from his body.

No, he was undertaking this medical exploration to find its effects on insects and animals. The Borrumani disease being so toxic, it had crossed from human to animal and over the generations the Windlanders had seen a decrease in the animals that roamed the wild. It had even spread to the bees and where once many a woodland would have been drowsy with buzzing from its wildflowers, now anyone passing through would be cheered rarely by the same sound. Unaccountably, the domesticated animals like goats, cows, chickens, working farm dogs and others had not been affected by contact with their Borrumani owners. It was evident they had developed an immunity and Conversevitae had used blood from such sources initially to produce his antidote.

What he was expecting from injecting the moth was something he was not quite clear about. Usually the contaminated blood from a Windlander, without the cure, would lead to fatality either instantly or painfully over several days. It was the unexpected consequences from introducing the blood with an antidote that he wanted to observe.

Extracting the needle, Conversevitae waited. The wings continued to flap. Satisfied after a few moments more, the physician left the desk and moved back to another table on which lay a flat piece of parchment. Beside it was a quill in a bottle of black ink made from water and crushed pigment. He took the quill out and made some notes, writing in the Brittonic language that would be understood by some in the tribes living in and around the Land of Four Winds who had been educated to read.

He stopped suddenly when there came to his ears strangled cries from outside his chamber door where the guards were stationed. A few scuffling moments were followed by a precipitous sound, like that made by two heavy bodies dropping to the floor. Conversevitae frowned and rose to his feet.

On the other side of the door, Torcus and one of Byncor's guards dragged the sentries' unconscious bodies aside as the princess reached out to turn the great iron handle that would gain them entry to the laboratory.

"Wait!" cautioned Torcus. "He may be armed and ready to stab at us as we go in." The princess dropped her hand and stepped back. Holding his sword firm and ready, Torcus grasped the handle himself, turned it and gave a forceful kick to the door.

With amazing heaviness, the wood did not swing back at once but only creaked open slowly. Torcus looked in, was disconcerted at what he found and then rushed forward, only to turn and immediately push the door against the wall with his whole body. "Check behind it!" he ordered the others. They did but as Torcus could feel already, there was no one there. The chamber was not that big and there were some dark corners, yet it was empty. They were perplexed. Moments before, Conversevitae had occupied this room. Despite the door's oaken thickness, they had all heard him moving around.

"Spread out," came another command from Torcus. "Investigate every space and cupboard." A brief search followed. Apart from themselves, the room was empty.

"What's this?" said one of the men bending down to what looked like heaped clothes near the desk.

Stooped, he kicked it with his foot. The pile writhed and up from it sprang a cobra's head, its hood outstretched and forked tongue flickering out. The jaws were opening, ready to plunge and the guard, shrieking, lurched back. His legs automatically carried him, trying to compensate for the loss in balance but it ended with him slamming himself into a sitting position and into the wall several metres behind.

As he hit the stone, there was a curious sound made by it, something like the gasp made by a person being winded. The stones appeared to fold around him where he sat, leaving another layer behind. Those around the guard shimmered and blurred, vibrating in the air, then disappeared altogether to be replaced by the collapsed Conversevitae, slipping from the guard to the ground.

"What daemonic magic is this?" spluttered Torcus.

"Oh, don't underestimate our chief 'physician'," the princess said. "His powers to deceive are great and his occultic source for them yet greater."

Conversevitae came around from his dazed condition and was able to focus his eyes at last. They first rested on Byncor. "My Princess," he said and in all seriousness, "You just had to knock."

Despite herself, Byncor smiled. "And if we had done, Conversevitae, what other disguise would that additional time allow you to take on? A three-legged stool, a lump of mineral on your desk, a burning candle or an animal waiting to be experimented upon? Ah, I see you have a rather wonderful insect over there. Alive, I hope." She moved nearer to the moth which, with all the disturbance had become perfectly still. The princess touched its wing with her finger and instantly it began to flap again. The dish containing blood did not escape her attention either. "What's this for?" she said to the physician, tapping it.

"Another experiment in curiosity – nothing important really," came a mild reply.

Torcus intervened, "My Lady, we don't have much time."

Her pretty eyes continued to gaze at the wizard. And then as if stimulated by some invisible bolt her entire demeanour changed. The face that had been calm suddenly became a snarling mask. She whipped out a sharp-bladed knife from some hidden recess in her gown and held it to the physician's throat. At the same time, she grabbed hold of the long sleeve on his and pulled it up to expose his thin, wrinkly arm.

"Don't tell me that you have not concocted a cure for the disease, Conversevitae, the evidence is right here. How long were you and my pig of a father going to keep it to yourselves? One year – two – forever? Or maybe not. Riches could be made by keeping it to the selected few. Prosperity unending for the aristocrats belonging to your circle while the rest of the people are condemned to poverty, disease and a restriction on their freedom to travel and learn."

The physician's eyes grew round with fright. He had never seen the princess behave like this in all the time he had known her – not so much as guessed at the potential for fury clearly released before him. He was about to open his mouth and lie but the dagger point pressed harder into his neck and blood began to dribble from it.

"Please! Please!" he shouted. "You are right! Just take that infernal spike away from me!"

She did as he asked and Conversevitae bunched up the material from one sleeve and pressed it against his neck, staunching the blood.

Torcus grabbed an empty sack from a corner and threw it at the physician. "Here, fill that with the ingredients you need to reproduce the antidote and the antidote itself." Before Conversevitae could reply, Torcus said, "We don't want a long debate about it – there is no time. Just get on with it."

The physician scrambled to do as he was told. While he did that, the guards outside were moved into the room, their hands and feet tied, mouths gagged. Conversevitae was forced to give up the key to the chamber and after locking the door they moved down the passageway by the route they had come. Byncor released the moth that had been experimented upon in the laboratory. It fluttered along the corridor following the faint light, tracing its way to an open window. Even in his now imposed restraint, Conversevitae watched the renewed vigour that the moth had collected from somewhere with analytical interest.

There was less difficulty than might have been for the small entourage to move through the palace and out into the streets. After all, Princess Byncor was at the centre of it and she had chosen a time to go down to the laboratory which coincided with the king's visit to a nearby settlement on official business. Any sentries they came across moved aside at her approach. The guards they had left trussed in the chamber would soon be discovered so the temptation was to move rapidly, exciting suspicion. This they avoided with their almost leisurely progress.

At last they were out and still there had been no alarm given with running feet coming up behind them.

Soon after the streets, they were into the forest and on their way with the horses that had been taken from the royal stables. Three days more found them riding at a distance past the windmill that had been built by the Telemachons and into Coryumberix's village.

Conversevitae had not tried to escape while travelling with them. There was no reason, in fact, for him to fear rough treatment at their hands. He had always behaved respectfully with the princess and once he had learned about Chara's predicament he realised that if he could save her, his protection amongst these people would be assured.

At first Conversevitae had been very afraid. In the last few years he had lived the life of a hermit; stuck in the laboratory beneath the palace, living at King Noremac's whim. He had not found this hard. After all, he could leave the palace whenever he wanted to and all his food and clothing were provided for him with extra money besides. The happiness in his life was given by his absolute freedom to engage in engrossing experiments. Separate to the work on the antidote for the national disease and the monarch's occasional medical ailments, he was allowed to pursue any medical, botanical, mechanical or metaphysical line of enquiry he preferred, for which the necessary equipment with their ingredients were all paid. What discoveries and lines of enquiry he had made!

Latterly, though, disillusion had crept in. What was the purpose for creating these scientific possibilities – opportunities to advance human nature itself and provide a better environment for human beings to live in – when all the time the application for them was stamped upon? This was most pertinent to his antidote for the generational disease which had ravaged the country. Conversevitae was completely baffled by the king's reluctance to reproduce it for his people's good. He pretended to agree with the nonsensical reasons put forward by his majesty but rationally that was only in the interest of self-preservation.

So truly this was a unique position that Conversevitae found himself in – more so when he listened to the discussions about Monithcound village and the visit by the Telemachons, people who had travelled from the other end of the known world.

There was only one person who could mingle with these people and the villagers freely. Him. He did not bear the wind leprosy since it had been neutralised within his body, neither could he be re-infected by the villagers. That situation would last only up to the moment he vaccinated the Telemachons but it was a status and position to be prized. There was enough vaccine in his bag to cure Chara and several others. Possibility for a cure would exist if they reached her while she was alive and able to respond. It would take more time to produce enough cure for all of the Telemachons and those who lived in Monithcound.

It was astounding to everyone who had escaped the palace that they had not been pursued, particularly with the princess amongst them. Luck had been on their side. The men stationed at Conversevitae's door had just begun a twelve-hour guard and it was only at the end of it that they were found. They had been tied expertly by Torcus and the princess' men so that even their gags remained in place. The great oak door had to be battered down before they were released.

By then, the night had fallen and it was too late to send out a search party. King Hors Noremac was seething with anger when Netmapliar first brought him the news but then, after he had calmed down and with the secretary's sly observations he began to descry a certain advantage.

"Sire, it maybe that Borrum has answered our prayers over this incident."

"Why do you say that?" snapped his lord, "I have lost my chief physician, daughter and the antidote that could prove my power over a national malady all at once. Where, possibly, could there be any benefit in it?"

The secretary made his response with care. He did not want to turn Noremac's hostility onto himself. "Well, sire, it might make the problem faced by your successor a little simpler."

"Explain yourself, scribbler. My ears are pricked." The king admitted to himself that the thought had already occurred to him but he wanted his secretary to bring it up from the murky bottom. He was good at that.

"It is this, Your Highness. Either princess Byncor has been the instigator in all that has occurred, breaking your trust and thus revealing her treachery or she has been abducted. Either way, if she sadly loses her life and her dead body is returned to the palace, your subjects will understand. Then, naturally, a new successor to the throne has to be adopted. I believe you favour her cousin for the inheritance."

"Yes …. mmm, well put Netmapliar. No other could have explained the matter so succinctly."

"Thank-you, Sire."

"But there remains the difficulty that we have the antidote but its inventor is being taken to Borrum knows where – the purpose being what?"

"The people who took it will not be stopping along the way to tell others about it. The reaction could be uncontrollable. Therefore, they will keep its secret until their journey's end is reached. What that end is, I'm afraid I can only speculate. Perhaps the cure is meant for the Borrumani, perhaps for our enemies abroad. There would undoubtedly be a high price paid for it by any of the monarchs and rulers over the tribes in the countries surrounding our own. I think in the end we will have to expect that news about the medicine will get out. He cannot stop it."

The King's temper flared once more. "If whoever receives it is a Borrumani, he will have started the process for his own death sentence. Once my subjects get to hear there is a cure and someone else has it, support will haemorrhage from me. My physician's cure will convey power to whoever holds it. I have to prevent that."

"We will," nodded Netmapliar emphatically. "First, we must find out where they have gone."

"My daughter, said the King grimly, "seems to have connections greater than I suspected. There are places in the country – at the furthest reach from the capital – where my influence is not as strong as it should be. The odd village scattered here and there at the borders, especially near the Cornovii Mountains to the north, contain dissidents opposed to my rule. Their populations are so small I had never thought about bothering with them before this. The garrison cost would have been prohibitive. Yet I have some fortresses keeping check on the northern border. Not many as we trusted that our invisible ally, the Wind Plague, would keep the invaders at bay. Byncor is most likely to be staying with other young rebels in one of those smaller settlements."

"What is best to be done, My lord?"

"I will send messages out to the commanders in those oppida including the fortifications on every other border. They will be told to seek out the princess and to report back anything unusual happening in their region."

"Very well, Sire, I will arrange for the messengers to ride as soon as possible."

"Soon is too late. Now will be acceptable," came the stern reply. Netmapliar bowed low and hastily scurried off to do his master's bidding.

34
Cure

Torcus lifted the spoon to Chara's mouth and urged her to drink it. Her blonde hair was matted with sweat, face as pale as limestone. A fever had invaded her and she was delirious. "Is Herne alright?" referring to Berengar's infant boy. "Is he! Is he!" Then, "No, no, that's not the right way! Do it like this."

In an attempt to break through the delirium, the Keltoi spoke gently to her but in loud tones. "Chara, you must drink this. It is chicken broth. You need nourishment." She seemed to wake a little from her illusion and sipped at the spoon. He gave her three more mouthfuls and at the same time wiped her head with a cloth held in his other hand. There was something incongruous about this tall, wide-shouldered powerful man sat hunched and protective over the frail smaller figure laid out on the bed. Several people were in the hut with her: all Borrumani of course, it being too dangerous for anyone else.

Conversevitae was on the other side of the bed, having earlier administered the vaccine from a dish at his side. Torcus looked at him for an answer to the question that was so plain it did not need to be asked.

The physician sighed. "She is at a dangerous cusp. If we had been any later, she would certainly be dying by now. Do you see that black outline around her nose?" Torcus nodded, apprehensive for the explanation. "Well, that is showing that both muscle and bone are being attacked. It occurs a day or two before a limb falls off. I will give her another dose later tonight and then tomorrow morning. If the black mark fades, it is a sign that not only is the cure working and we have saved her life but also her rather fine nose. Now don't give her too much of that soup. We want the vaccine concentrated in her body for the longest possible time."

It was worrying and the big Keltoi remained devoted in his attentions to the 'Greek woman' as the other villagers referred to her. The next day, Torcus was relieved to find that the mark around her nose had begun to diminish and her delirium had gone.

"That is a powerful medicine you have created," he said to Conversevitae as they stood together away from the bed, near the round wall of the hut.

Coryumberix was standing with them. He too, was impressed.

"You work a deep magic to drive plague demons away," he said.

"Some belongs to me," responded the alchemist, "after years investigating natural wonder but the remainder belongs to the body on which I operate – in the spirit and soul which inhabits that frame."

"And through which anatomical part does the soul live in its concentrated form?"

Conversevitae regarded the young chief with renewed interest. Such a query was unusual, to say the least, from the lips of a mere warrior, even one as senior as this.

"No single part. The soul is evidenced by every cell, each region in the body that traps it, right down to the smallest twig in the forest of veins running through the flesh. But it doesn't stop there. It is in the air we breathe, the water we drink. It is in everything. My work is to take the soul apart in one particular place, observe how it functions, repair it if it is impaired and put it back together again."

Torcus grew impatient with the conversation. "You might have repaired Chara's soul but what about the rest of us? Where are we going to get the source for the antidote in the quantities that we require to immunise every Telemachon and Monithcound villager?"

"The alchemist turned around to face Chara as she lay sleeping peacefully. "You are looking at it," he said simply.

"What – do you mean to use her like a trough of cattle fodder?" came Torcus' brief, angry riposte.

"No, no, calm yourself Torcus. Chara will provide some blood but only a little when she has overcome the disease within herself. We shall then use that in combination with additives I have researched and afterwards give it to more people. Likewise, they will contribute their blood for the good of others and so on. The whole process builds like heavy rain on a dam until the water rises and overwhelms the disease in one sudden rush."

"May it be so easy," commented Coryumberix.

"Even if it is," said Torcus, the soldier in him returning, "all this will take time which we might not have. Hors Noremac will already have sent out either a message to the border forts or his own army from the palace to scour the country for his daughter. How do we reckon with that?"

"The most urgent task is to immunise the Telemachons against the Wind Leprosy. Then at least we will have them to aid us if the King's troops arrive."

"How long will that take?" Torcus asked Conversevitae.

"If there are nearly one hundred people to vaccinate I should assume at least a week, depending on how many people I can vaccinate with Chara's contribution to the cure."

"Well, we shall not take up your valuable time any further," said Coryumberix, slapping Conversevitae on the back. "Get to it physician and give us more fighting men!"

35

Ghost Warriors

When Telemachus came back from the Causeway, he was an angry man. Angry because he had found that Goreth had lied to him. In fact, time did not pass as he had suggested it did on that Ancient Occultic Road. Whereas Telemachus was given the impression that the hours, days or years spent there would be as short as wing flaps in this world, he found that substantial time had been taken from his life: nine days in truth.

Eucleides, Thocero and Agenor had been glad to see him back naturally and celebrated with him but they resented the enforced delay. The resentment felt by all four focused on the same target – Goreth. While Telemachus had been away walking the Ancient Magic, the others had felt themselves penned in by Goreth. Their vocal frustration had been met with just one response from him: "He has gone where few people go and where he alone must go. Rest and be calm. Telemachus will return." No other explanation was forthcoming and it angered them so there was some protest. But how can you argue with a god? So they waited and reminded Goreth that Formus was behind them – was he telling them to remain idle and be slaughtered? His answer was that Formus would never find them, not in this particular part of the forest. And indeed it happened just as he had told them. From the tree-tops they watched Formus and his army pass by. Formus did not even search the forest but then, why should he? His concern lay with the main body of the Telemachons. He would little realise that the Telemachons had lost their foremost leader.

Telemachus had kept his self-discipline, not giving in to his anger about Goreth while with the others but when an appropriate moment occurred during their journey after Tyracides once more, he broached the topic with Goreth. They were riding before the others at a discrete distance.

"Goreth, why did you lie to me?"

"About the Causeway, you mean?"

"Yes," said Telemachus sharply.

"Would you have walked over those boards if you had understood what you understand now?"

The immediate desire in him was to snap back a negative. However, he didn't. He thought. If he had rejected the Causeway, all those images that were surfacing up into his memory again, would not be there. Somehow, he felt, they ought to be there. An important responsibility was in them which he could not quite grasp yet. They were important for his future, the Telemachon's future. To waste that vision would be to condemn something, no, everything, to a tragic destruction. At last he said to Goreth, "We lost nine days." He sensed the plaintiveness in his own voice.

Goreth turned his head and looked at him with those eyes, large and round as worlds.

"The cost in time is nothing compared to what you might gain. Hermits have spent years in isolation, uttering incantations to their gods, swimming in the silence of their retreats, just to experience a few moments of what you were fortunate enough to be given."

"But what did it mean?"

"It may not make sense to you now. Yet everything changes and future events help to decode the past's mystery. Change, transition, are the only fixed certainties of the human and divine condition. We do not know why it happens or how. It simply impels us."

"Your transition," said Telemachus emphatically and Goreth recognised immediately to what he was referring, "– you have no idea why or for what purpose that has happened?"

"Happening," Goreth added. "It could still be happening. Or not. Like you, I have my own divine message to decipher. Unlike you, it is not something with which I am unfamiliar. I have lived through this before. I was at one time Danu, the River Goddess. Then I became a god: my form as fluid as water. For what reason? I do not know. The commands given by Zeus over our manifestations are unstoppable. We understand as much about them as you mortals do the actions that we, the lesser gods have on your own lives. I can only wonder why I have been compelled to take on the signs belonging to both male and female with the desires for both."

"Could you be returning to the female body you once were? Do you feel it?"

"It is possible," admitted Goreth. "However, there is a slight pain with the transition and once a change is fulfilled, it diminishes. My discomfort has already ended. Therefore, perhaps, my form is already attained."

Behind them, Eucleides kicked his horse's flanks and rode up.

"You two must be completely absorbed by whatever you are talking about." They looked at him, puzzled by his rudeness. He said, "Can you not see what is ahead?"

On the path directly in front, that sloped upward to the crown of the hill, sat a warrior in full military garb, his sword and shield up, a powerful black horse under him. Light reflected from the bronze conical helmet and on his round shield was painted a hawk - wings outstretched as in flight, talons thrust forward ready to snatch up the moving prey.

They halted their horses.

"Does he have friends about, I wonder?" said Eucleides.

"Friends ready to spring upon us," cautioned Agenor, who had just joined them with Thocero.

The rider was so still he might have been a wind-cut pinnacle to the hill.

"By that helmet, he is no Telemachon, which would have been so much easier for us. He could belong to Formus."

"Get off your horses," commanded Telemachus. "If his allies are hiding somewhere, we will only make clearer targets by remaining on them."

They did as he said and decided to creep around the hill from different directions to surround him, all the while listening for others.

It took them some time to move closer to the top using the trees and bushes to cover their approach but finally they made it.

"He's gone!" Thocero yelled.

He was indeed nowhere to be seen as the friends appeared from the undergrowth in a circle, marking the perimeter of the place which shortly before had been kept by the warrior and his horse.

"How could he have come through us!" exclaimed Thocero.

Telemachus moved to a stone pile put there by human hands to mark the highest point and scanned the environs. There was an uninterrupted perspective all around. "He's over here!" came from his lips, as a familiar figure came into view. The others ran to him.

Standing stock still as before, was the same man they had attempted to surround. This time though, he was not sitting in the saddle but holding his horse by its lead. His face, again, was towards them and he was nearer than when they had first seen him.

Agenor was suddenly afraid. "See his face and arms! His legs! The skin on them is like death!" It was strange but true. All three features on the man's body were bare, unusual in itself in that the snow and ice lay everywhere and one would expect the soldier to be better wrapped against the cold. He wasn't and his flesh, as Agenor suggested, was preternaturally white.

Then movement. The figure was signalling with his arm.

"Is he calling us?" said Thocero, not believing his eyes.

The man, if man it was, turned away and took his pony up the track.

"He's not going to get very far that way," murmured Telemachus, who, like the others saw that the narrow path first directed its course to the next hill but shortly came to an abrupt stop. The man seemed unconcerned and continued as if he was going to walk straight into the vegetation-covered rock in front.

He strode determinedly forward. The next minute an exclamation broke from some of his onlookers. He and his horse had disappeared.

"The man is a ghost!" said Eucleides.

"We should get away from here," urged Thocero. "This is a demon-ridden place!"

"No, that is not magical trickery," said Goreth, "but I am not certain what it is."

The problem for the travellers being that the path was the only obvious route by which they could exit the forest and pursue their journey to the north, they decided to follow it, with utmost caution.

When they had got down to the other hill, they found that what Goreth had spoken was true. There was no conjuring in the warrior's disappearance. What they found was a covered tunnel, long ivy hanging down to disguise it. Pushing the leafy stems aside, they went in.

It was a small tunnel and the roof was just above their heads. As the exit was not far away, it was also dimly lit by daylight. There was no recess for a hidden assassin.

The five crawled along the walls to the end. There seemed to be no-one near so they came out into the full light. What they had come into was a large quarry with a flat floor. It had certainly been worked for many years and what had been dug out was perhaps an explanation for the strange appearance made by the man they were pursuing. The cliff-like quarry walls rose up in a grainy elevation of chalk. Way over the white expanse, on the other side, steps were cut and zig-zagged to the higher ground. Climbing up them was the man they followed. Nobody else appeared to be around. Yet as they went forward into the vast open space a curious event was unfolding. Sometimes from a mountain peak you might observe a thick mist cast upward by wet trees in the early morning, spreading out along a valley. So, here, the same natural phenomenon was occurring, only the mist was rolling along the rim of the quarry and falling, swathe after swathe, into it.

"Come on!" cried Telemachus. "Let's get to those steps while we can still see them!"

The five moved over the intervening space but they had not covered half the distance before the fog completely enveloped them. It was a white blurring haze, mixed with the chalk dust in the air and the friends were hard put to it to keep each other within sight.

They continued to attempt to walk forward, until Agenor tripped over a rock underfoot and fell to the ground. The others were going to his aid, when Eucleides called out with an urgent whisper, "Stop! What's that?" The others paused, listening.

It was a low whistle. Not made by an animal but a human and it sounded like a signal.

"Get together!" whispered Telemachus. The Telemachons drew inwards for protection and waited, swords out.

As they waited, the fog slowly began to lift. It had been a temporary dense thicket allowing them to discern only four or five paces in any direction. Now it broke into patches and the mist was replaced by shapes far more tangible and sinister.

Arranged around them in a circle, cutting off any means for escape were men dressed for war, their skins were painted white with chalk just as the man they had been following. The mist, in its leaving, had deposited them there.

That warrior who before had been half-way up the quarry wall was down now amongst their observers. He had placed himself in front, closer to Telemachus. For an instant the two bands of warriors eyed each other, not a word spoken.

Finally, the man near to Telemachus said in the Keltoi language that he could understand, "Sheathe your swords. It is useless to fight us. We outnumber you eight to one."

Telemachus bristled. "your numbers are greater but each man of us will take two of yours down. If we sheathe our swords what is to stop you from slaughtering us?"

"That," said the painted one, "is what we would readily do if you were King Hors Noremac's men. But I see by your helmets and garb that you certainly do not belong to his army. Whose then?"

"These men and I fight for each other. More of us have gone north seeking a better life. Perhaps they have gone this way?"

The leading soldier exchanged glances with his soldiers.

"The Telemachons, you mean?"

"That's it!" said Agenor, excited. "How do you know?"

"Not far from here, there is a village called Monithcound. Your people arrived there, half-way through the filling of the last moon. They were invited to stay because they had offered to build a great wind-machine that would grind the village's wheat crops at a much faster rate than the people could hope to do themselves. The machine has been built now and Coryumberix, Monithcound's chief is much pleased with it.

Clear excitement was evident amongst Telemachus and the others on hearing how close they were to their compatriots.

"Can you lead us to them, to our friends?" asked Telemachus.

The pitying expression was well hidden under the chalk mask. "Nobody has told you about us, have they?"

"Told us what?"

"That we ….," the chief of this warrior band hesitated, stopped by a thought that had flashed upon his mind, "…. that we in this Land of Four Winds are living under the oppressive tyranny exercised by our so-called King, Hors Noremac and his courtiers. We are the young, drawn from settlements along the border whose chiefs are in thrall to Noremac and are kept as minions to the king by the gold he can pay them. There are many more of us. We come to this quarry to train for the rebellion against Noremac that is certain to happen and our true leader is Coryumberix, the man who has been elected leader by the people in Monithcound.

"Will you lead us to that place?" interrupted Eucleides, repeating Telemachus' request.

"We will," said the painted leader, "on certain conditions." Inwardly, he had made a decision. Telemachus and his companions should not be told about the inherited disease that every Borrumani carried and could pass on. If they were, there was the possibility for panic amongst them and they would immediately leave to find Monithcound for themselves. Meanwhile, it might happen that their capture by the King's men would be a real possibility. In that event torture would reveal the quarry's existence and more importantly, information about the whole movement that was about to rise against the monarch. So what he said now had to stop that, allay the suspicions of Telemachus and his men and guide his own men in how they were to proceed.

"We can abide by conditions as long as they are reasonable ones," said Telemachus.

"Know then, that my name is Kellis and we, here," he indicated the figures around him, "call ourselves the Ghost Warriors. The chalk with which we cover our bodies is sacred and is as much a protection for us as is our shields and swords. It is our real armour because people cannot see who we are and while we wear it our god Borrumani protects us, causing fear in the hearts of those who see us. While it is applied to our skin, we take part in a sacred ritual and the combat we engage in is the greatest rite, greater than any priest's prayer or sacrifice offered to the god."

Kellis' young warriors were listening more avidly to what he was saying than the Telemachons themselves. This was all news to them.

"The chalk must not be knocked from our flesh, no human breath allowed to breathe upon it because the chalk is the residue of the Wind God's breath itself. The only mortal exhalation that touches it, should be that passed out by a human soul on its journey to the underworld begun by a stabbing sword point. Therefore, the conditions that I lay upon you must be these: if I show you to Monithcound there must be no contact between yourselves and my Ghost Warriors when we travel and if we have to rest, it is to be in two separate groups with no communication between us."

Those led by Kellis could now understand his intention and the silent command to secrecy. For their part, Telemachus and the others understood too, the powerful motivation inspired by sacred rite in the worship of gods, their own or others.

"I accept your conditions," said Telemachus. "As do my men."

They set off at once but although the distance to Monithcound had been described as only short, in fact they had to sleep in the eerily quiet forest overnight before they reached the village the next morning. By then, of course, no matter the precautions, Telemachus and his companions – all excepting Goreth – had contracted the Wind Disease. They, being so weakened by it, had to be helped into Monithcound by the Ghost Warriors.

36

The Plant of Infinite Want

With Torcus' tender attention and the medicine from Conversevitae, Chara had made a full recovery. The big Keltoi suddenly became shyer when the woman he obviously doted on had recovered her full senses. Chara herself, not just grateful for the help he had given her, saw the man he was and relieved him of his shyness. They grew close and their gratitude to Conversevitae was made known to him. The physician was encouraged but circumstances came to a complete turnaround with what happened next. Using Chara's blood, he piped it into the arm of a volunteer warrior from Coryumberix's village. The consequence was a near catastrophic failure. The man almost died from a severe reaction to what was given him.

"I thought I asked you to give me *more* warriors, not to take them away from me!" said Coryumberix vehemently. "Tell me why I should let you live or what good you can do after this!" His reaction would possibly have been more impulsive if not for Princess Byncor's presence in the hut that served as both his home and the administrative centre for Monithcound.

"What we want," said the princess with more restraint, "is answers. Why has it not worked?"

"But it does work, My Lady. The Telemachon, Chara, has been cured. She is free from the disease and will not be infected by it again."

"My man isn't," said Coryumberix, tersely. "Used to be a fine fighter. Now look at him. His arm is useless and he pants like an old man if he has to exert himself. A cured Telemachon woman in exchange for a crippled Borrumani soldier was not what we were wanting."

"Sire, neither was I," came the hasty reply from the physician. "The antidote has proven itself successful in one situation and futile in another. I think that the cause for its ill effects lies in the blood. A severe allergic reaction might have set in. I surmise it would be better to use only the patient's blood with the antidote."

"What does that mean for developing a cure that can be used by everyone?" asked Princess Byncor.

"I had hoped to immunise the Telemachons and the Borrumani in this village quite quickly but now the procedure will be much slower."

He had no sooner finished speaking when there was a sudden commotion outside. They went out to discover its cause, guards crowding protectively beside the princess.

Into the village had come the Ghost Warriors, carrying Eucleides, Agenor and Thocero – faint with illness – between them. Telemachus was slumped over Goreth's back. Outside Monithcound's perimeter were crowded the Telemachons, Tyracides to the fore, staring in disbelief, not having dared to believe that they would return.

"Who are these, Kellis?" called out Coryumberix.

Before the Ghost Warrior could answer, Tyracides shouted from where he stood. "It is Telemachus, who led us from Sicily with others who are our friends. Telemachus, who overcame the Psychezoion, escaped from the mountain stronghold called Fol and vanquished the monstrous Queen Helladore." He purposely neglected the tomb-robbing at Glauberg.

The clan leader was impressed but his response conveyed the opposite. "And as we see, overborne by our land's disease unless we do something about it soon."

He called for the painted warriors to bring all four into his hut where they were settled on blankets and Conversevitae could investigate their condition before treating them.

"How was it that they became sick?" asked Coryumberix of Kellis. "Did you not keep strict separation in force?"

Kellis shrugged his shoulders. "My lord, I do not know. We were all travelling together. The painted brothers and I were in front. We had to lead. Despite a gap existing between us, the wind was against our faces, blowing back. Borrum blew our infection onto them – perhaps that was it."

"Did they understand the risk? Did you tell them?"

"No."

The clan leader sighed. "Well, let us hope you don't come to regret that decision. Who is that strange being who accompanied them and yet seems immune to our disease?"

"They call him Goreth and refer to him as an Orsook."

"Orsook," repeated Coryumberix, musing. "He reminds me of the gods that were once worshipped here before Borrum stroked our land and the forest became still. Our bards tell us that those gods went north. Where is Goreth now?"

"He went to the Telemachons."

"I will speak to him soon."

Coryumberix's wish was not quickly granted since he was occupied in the next few days preparing his village for a possible assault by soldiers from the closest border garrison, who were searching for the princess.

During these few days too, Conversevitae applied his physician's skills to Telemachus, Eucleides, Agenor and Thocero. Gradually, their condition improved with the different treatment that he had prepared. At the same time Conversevitae went into the Telemachon community, after assuring them that he was immune and began to treat people. The individuals he applied his antidote to first, were those connected to the ones in Coryumberix's hut: Hebe, Belisama, Leonis and Tyracides because of his position. They were willing to undergo treatment after seeing that Chara had been cured and was restored to full health. Then he went on to administer the potion to Berengar, Ula his wife and their infant son, Eris, Faramund, Adrasteia, Melissa and Pelisteus, Costus, Aristopolis, Polydeuctes, Kleptomenes and in fact all Telemachons by the end of the fourth day. After that, he tended to Coryumberix and the other Borrumani, including the Ghost Warriors.

None of this might have been accomplished so quickly – everyone had been inoculated by the week's end – without the help that was allowed him by Coryumberix. Hebe, because of her importance to Telemachus, was his first apprentice and then later Faramund became his second, owing to his knowledge concerning herbs and plants. These two were as busy as Conversevitae in putting together the ingredients for the antidote as much as much as they were in dispensing and applying it to others.

All three were nearly exhausted by their work in achieving what was required. Everyone had to be immunised by the time the king found them, which was inevitable.

As it was, on the third day into the treatment a small patrol from the king's garrison paid a visit to Monithcound.

There were only four soldiers in this patrol. Coryumberix had prepared his village thoroughly and his scouts had given enough warning so that the Telemachons were able to clear away all signs of their encampment and remove themselves from the immediate territory.

Explaining the windmill and how it came to be built was a trickier affair. Coryumberix might be the chief in the village but his authority was completely subordinated to a lowly squad officer if that squad was on the king's business. Fortunately, the officer who arrived was familiar to Coryumberix, in fact had been a boyhood friend.

"Marvellous," he said, after inspecting the windmill and observing how the huge millstones revolved to grind the corn while the sails that were connected to them turned outside. He came back out of the windmill with the young clan chief and others. The wooden blades spun and creaked, spinning with swift, solid power under the pressure from the wind. A wind, thought the captain, that could blow even stronger. "What happens if the sails are blown faster?" he said suddenly to Coryumberix. "Won't the limbs fall off or the whole structure fall apart?"

"Our engineer has designed the building well enough so that does not happen."

"Who is your engineer, Coryumberix? We have been boys and men together in these parts and I do not believe we have met anyone with the ingenuity from which this device has sprung."

"You are right, my friend," said Coryumberix, ushering Faramund forward. "This is the man who has invented the machine and my villagers built it to his instructions."

Faramund's slight, diffident figure next to the sturdy, brash appearance made by his creation was almost ridiculous. The captain found himself doubting what he was told. However, his questions to Faramund concerning the mill's construction elicited a technical explanation covering forces, pressures and interlocking joints which went completely over his head and convinced him that Faramund was indeed the wonder creator he was presented to be. Listening to him, the captain decided that his accent certainly did not belong to anywhere he was familiar with. About to raise the matter, Coryumberix anticipated him.

"Faramund is from Clundover, a settlement in the south. He is a distant relation to me and I sent for him."

Coryumberix was certain that the captain would not take it any further. There was a settlement of that name in the south and the chief was quite certain that the captain, giving his service to the king at the garrison and nowhere else would know nothing about it. He would accept this statement – had to – otherwise he might endanger his own relationship with the clan chief. Not for one moment would he believe that Faramund had come even further than that, seeing how freely Faramund passed amongst them all without fearing infection.

"Yes, a marvellous machine," said the captain, passing on. "A wonder. But Coryumberix, you needed to ask the King's permission for this."

"I wanted to find if out if the windmill worked, first."

"And now I presume, you wish me to ask for the licence on your behalf?"

Coryumberix nodded. "That would be appreciated."

"Good," said the captain, brisk. "I will be happy to communicate that and I am certain that by my description of your kinsman Faramund's invention, the king will be pleased to grant you the licence. More than that, I am sure that he will take an avid interest in it, perhaps to build similar machines across his kingdom."

"I would be honoured to oblige the king in whatever he wishes," replied Coryumberix, trying hard to keep the contempt from his voice.

"His one single wish at this moment is to see his daughter returned safely to the palace. Whoever has taken her will soon suffer for it. I want you to keep your ears to the ground, my friend and if there is any news to inform me as quickly as possible."

"Of course, I will do my best. Now before you go, can we go to my home which is the Meeting House for our village and drink a flagon or two of sweet mead? Does that sound agreeable?"

"Very!" grinned the captain, slapping Coryumberix on the back. They withdrew, accompanied by his squad and several others. After a couple of hours, their stomachs full and thirst slaked, the king's squad got onto their horses and started back for the garrison.

In exchange for the mead, Coryumberix had won a reprieve; although the garrison captain had promised to return with the King's answer for the licence request, it would not be for another week at least.

Conversevitae and Faramund had worked to improve the effectiveness of the antidote successfully so that once Telemachus had received it, along with Eucleides, Thocero and Agenor, their health underwent a remarkable transformation. On the second day they were up on their feet, completely cured but understandably, still in a weakened condition.

Before then, Coryumberix had met with Goreth and had arranged for them to be alone in conversation. He felt sure that the unearthly Orsook held many secrets. What they were exactly, he did not know, but privacy perhaps would help to uncover them.

Close contact with the creature was a shock. He realised immediately that the union of male and female was there in its starkness, yet distinct. Neither male nor female, yet both. The face strong in its bone structure but soft in complexion, the eyes large, round and clear. Hair on the head was less hair than wool, mole furred in texture and growing in plaits shaped like fronds from some unknown water weed. When speaking, the voice bubbled from a slow, hot volcanic source or a deep aquatic cave where hid a monstrous river life waiting to emerge. Coryumberix thought he understood people well. Anything different was feared and that fear led them to destroy. How then did this being avoid destruction? Just by his appearance, decided the young chief. For how could anyone break and smash what he saw now? There was a strange beauty attached to it, a beauty not from this world.

"You have seen me already," said Goreth. The words were sharp, if from the depths. Coryumberix was brought to attention.

"Yes, of course, you came in with Telemachus."

"No," said the Orsook, prompting him. "You have seen me not only with your eyes but in your mind, in the songs sung around the fires at night: those words made by the ancestors, recitations from ages past."

And it was true. The moment he had spoken, there arose in the chief's mind a bardic song, one of many that he had heard as boy and man at times that celebrated the turn of the year.

Now is the time, for the change to come.
Seething rivers flood, ice-cold waters heat.
Hear for the sound in the tumult that roars.
There, in flowing chance, transit liquid boils:
Without the heat to burn
But with the power to be born.

Yours is the time, for the change to come.
Blow the dead from the trees like the fresh wind's breath.
Fill the skeletal dumb world with flesh;
Songs that yearn to sing, leaping freedom's rush.
Without the heart to run,
The track lies empty and unknown.

See that the shape in the water calls.
Britons gather, watch, for your fellow Orsook.
They, are your family and lover past.
Smile in loving clasp. Forbid broken trust,
That trains the mind to doubt
And all humanity to the rout.

Came the Orsook, on a day like this,
Bleary shadow wet, running river borne.
Led them away, from the Four Winds disturbed,
Took them up north for the City of safety
And final rest from hate
To counter the human defeat.

Come then Borrum, blow away the sad,
Teary enmity, draining man and woman.
Lead us to fuse and to dance still the storm.
Hating ourselves must stop. A discovery of calm:
And mattered River Fusion
Flows under the Fish People's sun.

At some time in the past, creatures such as Goreth and the
people of his own tribe had existed together. They were at peace
and happy but something disturbed that harmony. It meant that the
Orsook had to leave. No-one knew where they had gone, although
legend had it that they had left for somewhere to the north, where
human beings were fewer in number.

"These songs tell you where my people have gone," said
Goreth.

"Not the ancient poems, no," Coryumberix corrected him. "In
several stories of our heroes there is a suggestion that the Orsook
went to the mountains and lakes of the north."

"We are forever in movement," sighed Goreth. "Ceaseless change, ceaseless instability; seized by the unlimited yearning for peace and security."

Goreth reached to a pocket within his shirt and brought something out, enclosed by his fist. Light from the central hearth glowed on his face and arms. He brought his hand closer to the fire where he sat and opened it. On his flat palm lay a round white seed. Coryumberix bent forward to get a better view.

"I don't expect you to know what this is so I shall tell you," said Goreth. The chief did not reply. "This seed was taken from the High Tomb of Orsek at Glauberg. It had been stored there, along with others, for nearly a thousand years."

"Where is Glauberg?" asked Coryumberix.

"It is a sacred site guarded by the Celtic tribespeople in those parts and can be found in Europa in an area north to where the Great River Danu flows from its source."

"I have never heard of it," admitted the chief.

"There is much that you will learn once Conversevitae's drug has cured your people."

"But what I do understand is that to take an offering from a sacred shrine will invite a god's retribution."

"Yes and we shall allow that divine justice to play out while not letting mortal hands interfere."

"But you said this was a Celtic tomb that was robbed. My priest might advise me otherwise."

"It was a tomb maintained by the Celts surely but the king lying buried there was not a Celt. Orsek led the first settlers into that land along the Danu, crossing a continent. He was not a Celt. He was an Orsook."

"The Orsook were the first people in Europa?" said Coryumberix, disbelief plain on his face.

"Yes, although you will never hear the truth either understood or admitted by a Celt."

The young chief was suddenly fierce - his hand went unthinking to the dagger at his belt. "Are you calling us liars?"

"Take care and calm yourself," said Goreth. "A good chief stays his hand, at least until the speaker who tells him what he has never heard before has finished."

Coryumberix, after a moment, brought his hand away.

"I have one seed here, given to me by Tyracides, the Telemachon who has already forgotten his generosity." Goreth moved his open palm nearer to the chief.

"Seeds are important but not ones that have been buried with the dead for a thousand years. They need soil to generate."

"Something far more important than soil has kept this seed its creative power for a millennium," asserted Goreth.

"What plant grows from it?" Coryumberix was intrigued.

"None that grow on this Earth as yet."

"So," said the chief, frowning, "– it was never used?"

"Never. Orsek had been given them a few days before he died. By whom or where he found them – nobody knows. He was old by then and close to his death. He might have given instructions for them to be sown and tended but he didn't. Instead, he commanded his servants to place them in his tomb. People at that time believed he wanted to take them to the after -life with him and grow their spectral flowers on the dark river's bank flowing across the Land of the Ancestors."

"The seed crops flowers?" said Coryumberix, eager to learn more.

"First the flowers come, then the grain. Both can be used. When eaten, the blue petals can produce a feeling in the consumer that mimics intense bliss and is accompanied by vivid dreams, haunting narratives that persuade the dreamer they can have everything they desire without the necessity to make any moral or rational choice."

"I have learned that nothing can be gained without fighting bravely for it," commented Coryumberix.

"If it is battle dreams you want, this flower gives them to you. But do you fight for good or evil? The blue flower's delusion is that neither is important as long as you fight and enjoy the battle thrill, gaining the reward for which you seek."

"Then I know many men in the tribes around and some women too who would give much for this flower. What is the grain that is harvested after the petal?"

"It is food. The grain can be used to make a flour for bread. Bread with a deliciousness never tasted before. Yet it is not the taste that is important. This grain kills all disease. Once it becomes a perpetual element in the diet eaten by a human being, the body is protected from disease until it is worn away by old age. An old age which is made greater by eating this plant. When the crop is growing in the fields its power is so great that any insect which settles on the plant to infest or eat it is immediately killed."

"Everything? What – whether it be a moth, gnat, flying ant, beetle, butterfly, bee, spider, damselfly, millipede, centipede, mayfly, ladybird, glow-worm, grasshopper, wasp, caterpillar, dragonfly, hornet?" He could not believe it would be everything.

"All," affirmed Goreth. "Devastated."

"But that is just wonderful!" exclaimed the chief.

The river god was not easily taken aback by human opinion. After all, he had heard so much of it during his long life and all the while it was getting louder. Yet he did not even bother to hide his reaction when hearing this one. His face showed consternation.

But Coryumberix allowed himself to be guided by excitement, oblivious to the immortal's perturbance. "It is the pests on the fields that limit our food supply. Without them we could feed our village ten times over and more!"

"I take your point," said Goreth with an ironic tone unrecognised by his listener. "Why, with such grain as this not only would your village be easily fed but those others that lie around you could be supplied at a handsome price. Your fame and wealth would multiply and now that you have found a cure for the Wind Leprosy, your influence could easily be extended over the borders from within this country. Soon you will have more power than King Hors Noremac himself!"

The young Celtic chieftain stopped his own rush of thought feeling the now explicit criticism and reacted. "Goreth, I do not want this seed for myself – only for my people!"

"Ah, your people," said the River God, as if that answered everything. He turned to the hearth where the logs burned and white ash could be seen – pale white and red – accumulated in piles around the burning remnants at the centre. Without any warning, he thrust his hand into the blaze, scraping up a big fistful of this white ash and deposited it between them. No pain could be detected in his face and the hand showed nothing of scorch marks.

"Why did you do that?" the chief gasped.

"Pass me your dagger," said Goreth. "No harm will come to you."

With more than a little reluctance, the knife was passed over. Goreth took it in the hand that had deposited the ash. He used his other hand to place and fix the seed into the hot ash. "Another property belonging to this seed," he continued, "is that it can be planted into virtually any ground – hot, dry, wet or cold – and will take root. In this instance it will need an additive to spur its growth. The Orsook stretched his arm out over the seeded ash and then pricked his arm with the dagger's point. Blood issued from the wound and a large bright drop plunged sizzling into the ash and onto the seed. A small gout of white steam issued upwards and as quickly vanished but the ash around the seed quivered.

"Orsek gave a name to this seed," said Goreth. "He called it the Plant of Infinite Want."

Before Coryumberix could murmur anything, a stem had thrust its way through the white soil and was growing upwards before them. It stopped at head height as they sat on their low stools.

"This floor is made from hard mud," explained Goreth. "But already it will have sent its roots down into it through the ash. As I said, it will grow in virtually any substance."

While he spoke, leaves had begun to bud on the main stem. They unfurled but not before the trunk had divided into other stemlets at the top, making it look like a tree. And now other protuberances broke out between the leaves, much fewer in number. They expanded and burst into bloom, dark blue, almost black in colour: sombre explosions, closer to bruises than flowers.

The plant was more a bush than a tree and its furious growth did not slow. The dreadful blossoms petalled to their peak and in twos and threes broke off and bombed the ground. Goreth suddenly felt a wave of heat from the vegetation. It ate into his body and he felt blithely weak. From certainty his mind moved to doubt. But then he bolstered himself. His purpose had to be complete.

One brief moment and it seemed that all was still. Only for a breath. It was in a gasping movement that the plant shuddered and ear upon ear of what looked like corn gathered upon it, replacing the spaces vacated by the dropped florets.

Still again.

Coryumberix looked over the bush to Goreth, "What next?" he said, shaken.

"Death," answered Goreth.

And as if obeying a command, the plant reversed its impetus to life. The ears reached their plumpest state with a golden-yellow and then dried and blackened without being picked. They fell on top of the flowers that had gone before and added to the dark deitrus surrounding the main stem. Before their eyes, the waste turned into a liquefied mulch which sank into the ground and the plant collapsed, its substance unfolding like a beached jellyfish.

"The Plant of Infinite Want," restated Goreth, sadly. And his own energy returned. "Great benefit or violent dearth. What is it *you* want, Coryumberix? Because in this weed you will get both or neither. It is your choice. Your name, O chief, may be raised to the stars or be trampled underfoot and spat upon. If I was in your position, I would find another way to achieve that and not use this seed."

"How can I?" said Coryumberix. "That seed you held in your hand has already been planted. Tell me more. Does it grow as speedily as that in the fields? What is this dearth you mention?"

"My blood intensified its life so no, it would normally take a season to be nurtured from the earth by a skilful farmer. Were you not listening? The violent dearth comes with its fatal capability to remove all flying, crawling life that settles on its body. The environment around this crop would become a deadly zone prohibiting every biological species. That is not the end. This dark matter you see that is rotting from it, gradually builds in the soil over the years and leeches into the rivers, poisoning more life."

"Then for Borruman's sake why have you shown me this?"

"It has the benefit I mentioned – purging disease from the human body and giving life at the expense of all other living creatures. It is so powerful, even eating its seed is enough to reverse any magical enchantment."

"but what is the use in having such a benefit, if the outcome has that awful impact on what we require to survive? Why didn't you destroy the seed in the tomb rather than bring it out to tempt the foolish?"

"I did not bring the seed out into the daylight – it was a human being called Tyracides who did that. In the end it was a human choice and you must make that decision with your own free will. If you like it is a test, a challenge to discover whether or not you are worthy of the world we have given you. We gods cannot interfere, only advise."

It seemed that good and evil were inextricably linked in the Plant of Infinite Want. Foolishly tempting as it was, Coryumberix still found himself wondering if the two effects could be somehow separated so that only the plant's generic balm for human health could be preserved while its malicious effect on the natural world obstructed. He thought that if the crop could be grown for just one year, its magical grain harvested once and the plant then burnt, that might be a means for overcoming the problem.

He asked Goreth who else knew about the plant.

"Only you and me – not even Tyracides, who carries the propagating seed with him. I will tell him in good time."

They were interrupted by a servant who had come with the message that their guests – Telemachus and the others – were making a good recovery.

After Coryumberix had sent her away, Goreth made to leave but the chief stopped him with a hand laid lightly on the other's arm. "Goreth, I wish to ask a favour from you."

"Please do – it will be a pleasure to grant it."

"When you tell Tyracides about what he is carrying, will you let me be present?"

With unblinking, round eyes, the Orsook immortal looked gravely at the chief. "If you are certain you want to be there, then I will make sure that happens. I will tell Tyracides very soon. It has been a secret for too long."

37
Haired Ones

The old grey-bearded lightning talker inspected the brass rod that had been put in his hands. Trusted by his tribe to interpret secret messages left by the Storm God in the blasted boles of oak trees or cypher made by men and women on wood and metal, the druid knew that he would have to check the signs carefully. The man who had given it to him waited, not much patience evident.

Turning the Rod of Amity, the Grand Seal, in his wrinkled grasp, he stopped; his eyes puckering to scrutinise. Along its length ran the words requiring safe passage for the bearer:

Ρ υ ν γ α ρ Σ τ ο υ ν Κ ε υ π η Ω ρ δ η ζ Σ ο υ

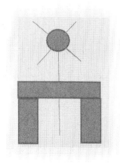

He interpreted it easily enough as, 'Runegar, Stone Keeper, orders so.' The symbol that followed the word 'Keeper' validated the whole object as a genuine instruction from the Druid of Druids. It showed the sun above the stone temple on the Plain of Rebirth. Four times in any one year this symbol was altered slightly and the lightning talker could tell from it that this man who stood dressed as a druid and a warrior before him, calling himself Formus, had been to the Plain of Rebirth and spoken to Runegar within the last three months.

The elderly priest passed the Rod on to his chief, a man equally as old and useless for battle but who had several fine sons to fight for him and hold the tribe together. "It is true," he said. "This man is who he says he is and has been granted the Rite of Amity by the Stone Keeper."

The elderly chief was relieved. He did not want war in his territory at this stage in his life, neither did he want to lose any or all of his sons who would inherit the land he had protected for so long. Behind Formus sat a strong, attractive woman, her thighs bare against the horse's flank. She might make a worthy wife for one of his sons but seeing her haughty stare; Formus' fierce expression; that other tough warrior – obviously a commander – on his own horse beside her and not least the hundreds of armed men on foot further behind those three; he decided not to pursue the matter.

For his part, Formus saw in front of him two scrawny looking old men. The one who held the Rite of Passage now, he assumed to be chief over the impoverished settlement that he could see near the lake. Some forty or fifty undernourished, hairy and lightly armed men were gathered behind. Three thin, ugly, big-eared men stood with the chief and carried enough mutual resemblance so that Formus could make a safe guess that they were his sons. Their wives would not gain much pleasure, he thought.

"Welcome, my lord Formus," said the chief, passing the Rod back via his druid. "I am pleased to carry out the Stone Keeper's command." He did not look pleased.

"You do not need to worry yourself," said Formus.

"I beg your pardon?"

"My army is large; your village small. I would not impose their empty stomachs on your hospitality. All I ask is that you provide us with some light provisions and your knowledge concerning the country we are to travel through."

The chief thought that in his request Formus was wanting what he said he would not want from them. A most contradictory man and not one to be argued with. At least, it seemed that he would not be stopping.

"You hold the Rod of Amity and my duty is to fulfil Runegar's sacred command. I will do it with pleasure. First I will order my men to fetch from the village everything we have."

This man is cleverer than he appears, decided Formus. He is making his settlement worthless to pillage.

"Thank-you. Your help is appreciated."

The old chief, with his sons and some but not all of his men, went back to the village to get the provisions.

It was then that Formus' army commander, Artemius, drew him aside.

"My lord, I do not like this. There is something not quite right."

"Why? What do you mean?"

Of late, the High Druid had begun to place an increasing trust in his lieutenant's intelligence. This had been inspired by the young man's ingenious suggestion for the metal found by the woman who had walked the Bridge of Fusion. They had offered her gold, not torture and she had taken them to a place where the metal, which they named Pyronite, was found strewn on a dry river bed. The Bridge of Fusion itself, was nowhere to be seen – removed by the goddess Brigantia and the Horned One so the girl claimed. Because the Pyronite ore was so heavy they could only gather small pieces. Even these were cumbersome on their journey. Artemius had been fascinated, as was he, by the metal and Formus allowed him to work with it, backed by a warning about what had happened to the metalsmiths who had applied flame to the substance on the Plain of Rebirth.

Artemius had worked wonders with the new metal. He had found that it could be easily chipped into small slivers. Then by shaping them he got arrowheads. Fixed to a shaft, wrapped in a burning rag and then fired after the rag had practically burned away, the arrow would explode on contact with its target. Small though the arrowheads were, the detonation could blow a man's chest apart or indeed any other part of the human body on which it landed. Human warriors were not the only obstacles that could be sabotaged with such a weapon. Formus dreamed for the day when they could be used in combination against a defensive wall or gate. For the moment they were stored safely in the baggage train ready to fill his archers' quivers.

Thus, he now took serious note when Artemius raised a concern.

"There cannot be more than ten houses in that village – not enough to accommodate up to forty men."

"Perhaps they pack them in."

"And their families?"

Formus appraised the size of the dwellings and saw that his lieutenant was right.

"Another thing," continued Artemius.

"Yes?"

"Have you seen how hairy those men are? Their long head hair and thick beards might be usual but hair sprouts from the back of their hands and if you observe carefully, their palms. They look like monkeys!"

Formus steered his attention to where Artemius had drawn it and again he had to admit that his lieutenant was right. Both he and his commander had seen such creatures at King Corix's palace in Dunsberg. The warriors they stared at did indeed resemble those animals.

"If they don't live there," said Artemius, "then where do they live and what is the purpose for those buildings?"

Just about to answer, Formus was halted, with his mouth open, by a weird gibbering cry that broke out and seemed to arise from somewhere in the forest behind the village. The High Druid was chilled. This sound was exactly like that sometimes produced by the monkeys at Dunsberg, just before they attacked each other.

The hairy ones left behind by their chief suddenly jerked their heads up as one and then turned, scampering off to the buildings behind them.

Formus and Artemius brought their horses back to the Lady Andraste, whose concerned expression matched their own foreboding.

"I think you should retire to a place of safety, My Lady," cautioned Artemius.

"Artemius," she replied, straightening herself in the saddle, "I may have the body of a woman but my inner strength is equal to any man's. Retire yourself, if you wish and I shall take your place." Formus smiled, not expecting anything different from her.

"Well said, Lady Andraste," responded Artemius. "However, I am sure you will not mind if I provide you with two companions to aid a warrior queen in case of battle. "With that, he called up two riders from their position on the left wing of the infantry and instructed them to keep her safe.

The warriors in Formus' army stared at the buildings and forest that lay in front. Whatever was going to approach would come from there. They kept their mouths closed and ears strained for any sound. After the previous unnerving shriek, all was unnaturally quiet.

"I was warned that extraordinary other-world creatures would appear to me the deeper into Briton I got and now that seems to be the truth," muttered Formus.

The soundlessness was broken by the wind or what they thought was the wind brushing thought the trees but when they looked they could find no movement. It was the same hiss that the breeze makes when scraping out leaves but this noise came from the breath forced through a thousand hairy mouths. Shapes could be seen jumping up and down at the tree line and then with a whoosh, a black cloud swirled up from the village buildings that undulated with the hiss and split apart into flapping dots, revolving like a tornado. Starlings. Hundreds in the sky, following now this bird, now that, then the next. A corner yanked upwards and evolved into a form that was more definite – a spear point; the feathery hundreds below spinning a thick shaft. From a vertical ground to sky position, it levelled to a horizontal, with the tip pointing directly at them.

"Shields up and over!" yelled Artemius.

And the weapon made from piercing beak, ripping claw and flying impact hit with full force. The cavalry fared worse than the foot-soldiers. Half were tipped from the saddle and left flailing on the ground while the birds attempted to peck frenziedly at their eyes. Fortunately, most were protected by their Grecian helmets. The horses, however, unable to defend their heads from the suffocating, pecking descent, panicked and ran off. The foot-soldiers had formed an impenetrable roof with their wooden shields and numbers of the starlings crashed against it with so much speed that they shattered their bones and bounced off, remaining dead or dying on the ground.

Whatever it was that drove these birds, it was not normal behaviour. The five riders at the front that were separate from the main army – Formus, Artemius, Lady Andraste and her two guards – had escaped the falling cloud and could see that the leaping shadows on the tree line had now begun to advance towards them.

Formus surmised that there was only one possibility to strengthen their position. His army was nearer to the village buildings than the opposing forces consisting of what could be observed as hairy crouching men. They were greater in number and his own warriors behind him required a defence provided by those buildings. They may or may not be empty. The druid decided to take that risk. He ordered his forces forward. At a run.

The hairy ones must have realised what they were doing but abruptly stopped advancing and held their position. This in itself was suspicious and Artemius, who was at the buildings first with his small cavalry detachment commanded his men to reign in.

"It could be that they have planned for us to do exactly this," said his captain as he pulled his horse up alongside Artemius.

"You may be right," admitted Artemius, "though I would have expected missiles to have rained down upon us from these hordes by now, if there was anyone here."

The captain and Artemius had stopped their horses on a roadway running directly through the village centre. The first house was only a few paces away.

As suddenly as they had attacked, the starlings – what was left of them – had lifted back into the sky. For a brief time they stayed there, circling and weaving. Then, as settling dust, they dropped onto the trees and their noisy twittering became silent in the gathering night.

Those men in the cavalry that had survived the fall from their mounts and were able to retrieve the horses did so. Gradually, the men regrouped and waited for Formus' instructions. He stared uncertainly at the village houses and then, reluctant, ordered the men into the settlement, slowly and on their guard.

The main expectation was that there would be a planned attack by reservists left behind. But the immediate onslaught did not take shape. What did take curious shape however, were the dusky silhouettes of the village houses; the silhouettes they perceived, was actually what they were.

The men were astonished at the houses that were mere facades, behind which lay sometimes rubble and sometimes nothing at all.

"What disaster struck here?" wondered Artemius aloud.

"Perhaps no great misfortune at all," replied Formus. "This concocted village that appears actual from a distance is to all purposes a mere shadow to fool the unwary traveller. Just as you might get at sea an innocuous merchant ship sailing close and at the last moment reveals itself to be a transport for brigands and pirates so the same with this artificial settlement."

"Ah, but if that is true," joined in the Lady Andraste, "Why would the pirates abandon their ship on the attack? Such a thing I have never heard of before."

"They haven't," came the short response from Formus, pointing at the tree-line where the hairy ones remained standing and watching."

"There were complete house here once," observed Andraste. "You can see the foundation marks on the ground. Whatever fate dealt them, I feel sure that they chose to build a new dwelling in the forest behind them. Maybe that is the reason they appear to be more like creatures from the forest rather than gainly men and women."

"It is a theory with which I could agree, My Lady but I would rather consider the more practical problem that we have which is to survive the night."

"Surely, sire," said Artemius, "the situation is not as bad as that? We greatly outnumber their fighting force after all and their leader is old and unadventurous. They might simply leave us to move on when daylight resumes."

"I would just ask you to think upon what has happened," said Formus. "Do you not think it at least unusual how those birds attacked us – driven by some supernatural impulse? As the Lady Andraste suggested, those tribesmen seem to be more attuned with the animal life in the forest than to ordinary men and women. Can they bring forces to bear that we know nothing about? Look at them. Do they seem to be watching us or are they waiting for something else?"

Artemius shifted his gaze uneasily. Formus had a point. The creatures had not withdrawn and in their brazen lack of fear almost taunted their opponents to come after them.

"We must either flee," continued the druid, "or attack them as soon as possible."

"I was never one for running away," said the young Helvetii, "moving backs present too broad and easy a target."

"Quite right," smiled Formus. "Now, we must somehow work out a means for getting at our Pyronite arrowheads without suffering attention from the birds or our hairy watchers. I am willing to bet that never have they met with such a powerful magical force as is possessed in that metal."

38

Confrontation

Goreth kept his promise to Coryumberix while in Monithcound and told Tyracides everything about the Plant of Infinite Want when the chief was present. Mindful that Telemachus might have changed his attitude towards Tyracides since he had walked the causeway built by Orsooks and humans, careful also to treat Telemachus with the respect his authority deserved, Goreth had included the Telemachon leader in his meeting.

When he had said everything that needed to be said there was, at first, a hiatus. It was as if each one was afraid to commit to an opinion and have it known to the others. Goreth broke the silence by repeating the warning he had made to Coryumberix. Yet, because he was a god and already knew what was in their hearts, he understood that it was futile. Not just one amongst them wanted the seed but all of them desired it.

"Orsek himself took this plant to his grave, understanding full well its malicious properties. Why do you all have to be convinced otherwise?"

"If he was so certain that it would have evil effects, why didn't he just destroy it?" asked Telemachus.

"He counted on the strength in his tomb's defences and perhaps assumed, wrongly, that the seeds would fail in their regenerative power as the years advanced."

"There must be some means for making good use of this plant so that people can benefit," said Coryumberix. "The answer might lie in the way we could grow it – perhaps under nets so that honey bees do not settle on it and die."

"The nets will have to be exceptionally fine to keep out the many more, smaller insects for which it would be fatal," said Goreth, with a grim expression on his face. He looked at the three men in turn. "I see by your expressions that you are all agreed on this. Very well." He moved to Tyracides and held out his hand. "Give me the plant." Tyracides took a step back from the Orsook, half in stubbornness, half in fear. "Tyracides, I told you to bring those seeds to this meeting and I know that you do have them. Give them to me or suffer the consequences."

The man gaped at the stern, ominous face of the god and realised that it would mean death to refuse. Beside him, on either side, Telemachus and Coryumberix made no movement. He took from his tunic the bag of seeds and dropped it into his hand.

Goreth opened the leather pouch, then produced two more bags the same size. He carefully distributed the seeds into the other two, leaving some behind in the original pouch. Pulling the leather cords tightly around the necks of each one, he called out to each man by name and gave him one bag.

All three were amazed. They had expected him to throw the seeds into the nearby fire which blazed on the hearth at the centre of Coryumberix's dwelling.

"But why do you do this?" Tyracides murmured.

"It is not for me to control your actions," said the god. "You are men. You will behave as you always have done in the past, here in the present and no doubt in the future. It is by your own free will that things around you are created or destroyed and if in the end you march towards total destruction who is to stop you? Certainly not those forces that exist alongside you. We will go on forever, whereas you can decide to live your mortality out of existence or gain wisdom and prove yourselves to be worth the creation." With that he turned and went.

They were left together, holding the seed for the potential saving or annihilation of the human race. Coryumberix pointed at some wooden stools near the fire and said, "Let us sit and talk agreeably."

The chairs were pulled up and they sat in a circle facing each other. For the first time Telemachus noted the steady, unblinking sea-blue eyes in Coryumberix's face. They made a sharp contrast to the red hair. In some men, he decided, this fixed expression could denote fanaticism, arrogance. The open-eyed gaze here, though, was one which suggested honesty as much as anyone could be honest in this harsh world. And something else. Curiosity. He had always found that an attractive trait in the people he met, whether man or woman. Curiosity about the world led to discovery and discovery to doubt. It is what a man or woman did with doubt that could make or break society. His assumption about the young chief was affirmed in what Coryumberix said next.

"Well, my comrades, while the King's physician has been immunising my people and you and yours, Telemachus; I have not been idle. For the first time in generations we are able to travel freely beyond the borders!"

"Yes, but you have to deal with those tribes that are unaware the infection has been eradicated," warned Tyracides.

"My messengers went days ago and have returned this morning," beamed the chief.

"What messengers?"

"Look," said Coryumberix. He pulled an iron poker from the fire and laid its red-hot tip on the ground between them. The dry debris instantly charred on contact. Drawing lines in the earth, Coryumberix began a running commentary. "This is where we are: Monithcound. To the north is the land ruled by the Cornovii tribe and I sent several emissaries to the first major settlement they came across there. Once they had overcome certain difficulties from the people with gifts of gold and a promise of trade in grain – that additional corn produced by your ingenious inventor Faramund from the windmill he gave to us, Telemachus – much information was learned. There are wondrous things in the north!" Coryumberix paused a moment. "Not all to the good admittedly but a lot was. Anyway, to the east ...." He drew a line, then ended it with a small cross, "I sent two more of my men."

"But that is within the Borrumani land," said Telemachus.

"Yes, I sent them for more practical purposes and to set to work on an urgent matter. A few days ago we were visited by a patrol from the King's garrison positioned here," Coryumberix, pointing to the small cross, drew another line from it southwards and finished by shaping a larger circle. "This is Overblown, the capital for the Land of the Four Winds and it is where King Hors Noremac is based – he rarely ventures from his palace. That was his custom anyway, up to now.

"And now he leaves his palace," suggested Telemachus.

"Yes."

"With an army."

"Unfortunately so."

"This is dangerous for you?"

"You have both seen that Princess Byncor, the King's daughter is here with us." Telemachus and Tyracides nodded.

"She is here without her father's permission. In fact, because she is here and because of what has gone on with the immunisation that Conversevitae has carried out, it is quite likely that after the King reaches the garrison, we will all be dead."

Tyracides and Telemachus looked at each other, not understanding.

"But how is it that your messengers were able to get back from the garrison without being arrested?" said Telemachus.

"And why does the King bring such a force against you?" added Tyracides.

"I still have some influence in the garrison through a boyhood friend and of course, gold. My messengers went on the pretext that they had gone to pay a deposit on a royal licence for our windmill. The commander was glad to accept the money and obviously did not consider it worth the effort to detain my men. They came back having learned that the king was on his way. Everyone believes that the monarch is distressed by his daughter's absence, naturally. We know the truth. For years our village has been seen as not worth attention, a rural backwater happy in its own isolation. Well, happy we were as long as we escaped the despot's regard. Isolated we were not. I have maintained contact with the princess, who, along with the majority of the youth in this country, are restless for change and an end to the corrupt government run by her father. We are ready to rise up at her command. The fact that she and Conversevitae are here, has been a closely guarded secret up to now. But that won't last for long. Princess Byncor has experienced the real cruelty that lies behind her father's sophisticated demeanour. He realises that she could lead a rebellion against him. That is why he wants her dead."

"All the same," said Tyracides, "it still puzzles me that the garrison commander did not take your messengers and torture them to get at the princess' whereabouts."

"He may have been told by Noremac not to take any action before his arrival. If his daughter dies in an isolated place away from the public gaze, he could construct a plausible cover for deliberated filicide."

Telemachus considered all that Coryumberix had said. He liked the man and he would offer help if he could but the probability that was becoming very clear was that this country would be levelled by civil war. He felt obliged to the Celtic chief for protecting the Telemachons from Formus and his revenge-thirsty warriors. But that protection had been paid for by the building of the mill. His own obligation was to find a home for the Telemachons and give them peace. That was a difficult task in itself. He felt the restless Tyracides beside him. It came into his mind that the potential for civil war and debilitating conflict stirred not only in the Land of the Four Winds.

"Coryumberix, I have met in you a man of honour. One who wishes the best for his people. I hope too, you can recognise that in me. The Telemachons and I have made a hard journey across known and unknown seas, lands and rivers to get here …."

"As have I," interrupted Tyracides, surly in not being recognised for his own leadership.

"Forgive me, Tyracides, I meant you also." But Telemachus knew he would not be forgiven and that the honest friendship which had existed between them since they had battled together in Heraclea Minoa was now becoming something else. He returned to what he was saying. "But 'here' is not where we should be. We wish to make our own freedom in our own place: a city we can call ours and build it so that the beauty in its architecture and the pleasantness of its people will be famed throughout the world. I do hope you will accept that. There is nothing that would get in the way of my helping you except for this."

Before Coryumberix had opened his mouth to reply, Tyracides made a surprising interjection. "I will help you, Coryumberix."

From the expression on the Celt's face, it was as unexpected to him as it was to Telemachus. In the tribe every person's public duty was to the chief – he had assumed it was the same for the Greeks and therefore Tyracides had just committed a transgression against his own leader. But he had to give courtesy where it was due. "Thank-you, Tyracides. We will be most glad to accept you into our ranks."

And then from a simple transgression that might have been forgiven, Tyracides went on to break the trust that is essential between friends and which was owed by a Greek citizen to the leader of his community. Not merely to break but to shatter it altogether.

"I think I speak for others amongst my companions when I say that it will not only be myself who would be happy to join with you in your fight against the tyrant in this country who calls himself King."

Telemachus was incensed. Everything he had begun to suspect about the man since the prophecy on the causeway was now laid bare. He grasped the certainty that the reason he himself was absent from that predicted future was because Tyracides had usurped his leadership over the Telemachons.

"Who gave you the right to speak for those others? Let them do what they think best for themselves! Have you truly abandoned everything we have worked towards on this expedition? It would be senseless for us to divide the Telemachons now and be distracted from settling in a place of our own choosing to live our lives freely."

"Telemachons!" said Tyracides with a sneer. He took the leather chain from around his neck, the one that clasped a fragment of the original ship that had brought them across Europa. After mockingly holding it out on his palm before Telemachus' eyes, he cast it contemptuously into the fire blazing on the hearth. It became in rapid moments a bright ember before disintegrating into white ash as the red flames rolled like storm-blown waves in cascades and deluged it. "Only a king or tyrant would stamp those that followed him with his own name! I thought you were the great democrat, Telemachus! Keen to give people liberty! Then why don't you give it now?"

"It was not me who created that name," Telemachus reminded him, "but the people of their own free will choosing it and voting upon it."

"You could have suggested something else."

"This is not about my name being used for the Telemachons," said Telemachus. "It is your jealousy and ambition that have provoked these words. I have heard from my friends how your arrogance grew while I was away and how you mistreated those around you. If anyone is the fledgling tyrant here, he stands before me!"

Neither of the two Greeks in the heated exchange between them had noticed Coryumberix stepping away for a few moments to the doorway. Their inattention was quickly jolted when the chief returned with two guards at his side.

They suddenly felt foolish but whether from the ill-discipline they had shown or the fact that they had been caught out by the young Celtic chief, it was difficult to tell.

Coryumberix's manner was stern. "Gentlemen, any bloodshed here in my house will have to be answered for. If you end up killing each other, I do not want your corpses leaving this house under the eyes of your people, who will naturally assume it was all arranged by me. You must settle your differences outside, in the open. Anyone who wishes to stay in our village and fight with us will be welcome and those who decide to leave will do so unhindered and with our good wishes. I will not take sides. The King's army is more than enough to occupy my thoughts."

The Histories written long afterwards record what happened next. Telemachus and Tyracides left the chief's house and went into the courtyard in front of it. They called out to the Telemachons they could see to go and fetch the others and before long every Telemachon had hurried to them, wondering what the urgency was.

All were gathered, none absented themselves.

There was Eucleides with Agenor next to him and beside him was Belisama, formerly Pelisteus' lover. Faramund was with his love, his bow-mistress Eris and behind them stood Berengar held close by his young son and alongside him was his wife, Ula. Next in a group together was Thocero with his younger brother, Leonis; Costus, once the Lord of Fol; Chara – now fully recovered – and close to her was Coryumberix's chief warrior, Torcus. Melissa stood, elegant as ever but troubled by this latest disruption of her husband; then Pelisteus, worried as a friend to both combatants; Hebe and beside her Goreth; Pelos, the swift-footed; Polydeuctes the boxer, whose punch could deliver an earthquake. So many came and so many more – Pelos, Aristopolis, Selene, Chryseis, Andromeda, Artorius and others – that it made Telemachus think even more when he saw them, how hopeless it would be if they allowed themselves to be divided, now or at any other time. He thought this but his anger at Tyracides grew sharper.

"You dog! You would want us to give up and perhaps even die here in this country – for what? To satisfy your own selfish needs rather than sacrifice them for the greater good of all of us?"

The people gathering there were astonished, struck by this uncharacteristic vehemence from Telemachus. For some moments they looked at Coryumberix, thinking that he was the target for their leader's attack but then, even more surprise, they realised that it was in fact Tyracides.

Tyracides was happy with the way events were developing. Telemachus did not look the assured commander. He was losing his inner control and an opportunity was waiting to be exploited.

"My friends," he said, "you might ask yourself what has stimulated Telemachus to such anger? Well, I will tell you. Free-will. That is the motive for his temper. The idea that you should all exercise your own choice in where you should go and with whom, rather than feel compelled to travel under his instruction is not one that he is willing to accept. Therefore he reacts to me as you can observe and betrays that very nature which was his all along. In Sicily he fought tyrants, out of Sicily he has become one!"

There were some jeers from the crowd against Tyracides at this: from Telemachus' many friends it was true but also from others who were not willing to allow Telemachus' heroic actions in the past to be wiped out by a few words from Tyracides.

"The only tyrant around here, Tyracides, is you!" yelled Thocero's young brother, Leonis. Again there were sounds from the crowd murmuring agreement.

"Listen comrades, Telemachus here wants us to leave Monithcound and travel on to the North. It is a year now since we left Heraclea Minoa and I think we have earned the right to ask when will this journey end? Can he promise us that the land where we settle will be any better than where we are now? For the last few weeks we have settled and built at Monithcound. I am sure you will not deny that Chief Coryumberix has dealt with us in an honourable and honest manner." There was assent from the Telemachons at this comment. "And now he needs our help, although because he is a dignified man he will not ask for it, hoping that it will be freely offered. At this moment the Borrumani king is riding up to his garrison nearby with an army. After he adds to his forces with the garrison troops, he intends to hurl himself upon the settlement here and destroy everything in sight. No man, woman or child will be left alive."

"Why .... would he do that?" called out Pelisteus from the onlookers. Someone answered him but it was neither Tyracides nor Telemachus nor even Coryumberix.

It was a woman's voice that replied. "I am the reason," and the Princess Byncor made her way through the standing bodies to a position near Coryumberix.

She was dressed in a fur-edged cloak and linen gown for warmth in the cold, Ice-Choker day and she moved with purpose. She spoke again but what many of the tribal Celts in that village had already guessed was confirmed. "I am the king's daughter,

Byncor and he comes for me." A worried chatter rose up which ended abruptly when the princess, raising her voice, spoke again. "The ties of family and blood mean nothing to him – he means to murder me."

The crowd, both Celt and Telemachon, was shocked.

Coryumberix spoke up to explain. "King Noremac treats his daughter cruelly and is as oppressive towards her as he is to us, his subjects. Many people in this kingdom agree with her, that the time has come to remove him from his throne."

"Let us, my people," called out Tyracides, "join with our friends and help to restore liberty to this land!"

While Tyracides had been talking earlier and the princess had been moving through the crowd, Telemachus began to feel something strange coursing through his body. At first it was rather like the tingling sensation to his skin that had happened when he had been infected by the Borrumani disease. But with that had come weakness and lapses into unconsciousness. This however seemed to be the very opposite; a curious strength began to flow in his limbs. It became a power he was not able to control.

What the Telemachons in the crowd witnessed next was again unlike the leader they had come to respect and admire. Telemachus took his sword from his scabbard and stepped before Tyracides, shouting, "These are not 'your' people to command as you wish. Show yourself to be a man rather than a coward and let the gods decide between us who should be best to guide the Telemachons to freedom."

To many standing there such as Eucleides and Agenor, this was a completely irrational, bizarre act. After all, Telemachus for the most part was enjoying the support of the Telemachons and might have won the situation around with words only. This was unlike the man they knew. Tyracides regarded it as a gift. If he killed Telemachus now, he would only be defending himself and he valued his own ironworker strength above Telemachus' lithe speed. He would have to react quickly though before the calls started for them both to stand down.

The sword was in Tyracides' hand before Telemachus' last words rang out. They began to circle each other and the crowd hurriedly cleared a space for them.

At the courtyard centre was a stone column, the height of two men and atop this was a carved figure in wood representing the god Borrum. He held an arrow on a rod in his hand and this easily turned to show the direction in which the wind blew.

Tyracides struck the first blow with a side-ways sweep but Telemachus dodged behind the stone column so that his sword struck the stone with a clang. Telemachus made a jabbing motion but his opponent jumped out of the way. Flurried, clashing blades struck in quick succession after Telemachus came away from the column and engaged with his enemy. During the rapid exchange, sharp iron sliced at Telemachus' forearm and he cried out. Only this was no human sound. The cry that burst from his lips was more like a deep reverberating roar. Nothing on two legs should have made it.

Despite his battle fury, Tyracides paused and stepped back with his guard up. Telemachus viewed his own seeping arm, the gore dripping to the ground. When his face turned back to Tyracides, something was not quite right. His face and head appeared to be changing shape: the neck lengthening, his skull bending, skin becoming furred – black – and silky.

Tyracides retreated one or two steps and now Telemachus, oblivious of what was happening to him, launched a ferocious assault. Despite his ironworker strength, it was all that Tyracides could do just to block the swinging cuts and thrusts with his own sword and by dodging behind the same column Telemachus had used. Those watchers at the crowd's front recognised that something was beginning to affect Telemachus other than the fight itself.

"What unearthly magic is this?" shouted out Torcus, backing away from Telemachus.

There was a stirring in Eucleides' memory. "It is Helladore's magic!" he shouted, looking on with frightened eyes." She has cursed Telemachus from the grave!"

At his friend's shout, Telemachus turned. Then his intent and will in the fight with Tyracides seemed to desert him. Just as Tyracides was about to take the advantage and deliver a mortal blow with his sword, Telemachus collapsed onto all-fours and the ironworker held back.

As he fell, his clothes split from him and the body that landed on the ground seemed to have jumped and landed as naturally as a cat on four paws. Only this animal was many times the size of a cat and to the horrified Greeks it was recognisable as similar to those leopards they sometimes created in their floor mosaics and temple paintings from the very real creatures that strode in their mountains. But this leopard's hide was black and if they had only known, was the same as those panthers that roamed in the deep Amazonian forest, another world away. An additional difference in feature too in the comparison between leopard and panther, was the eyes when the creature lifted its head to them. They were olive green in colour and no one could mistake them for belonging to anyone or anything else other than Telemachus. It was Telemachus' face trapped behind a witch's furred mask. The black leopard gave an almighty roar and sprang at Tyracides with catapultic power. The man was borne down, death was on his chest. Just as quickly as he had sprung though, the leopard leapt off and turning his back on the people, ran off into the waiting forest behind.

Tyracides recovered himself with remarkable speed and went to the garments that had been cast on the earth during Telemachus' magical shift from one shape to another. He stooped, scavenged and took up the bag of seed for the Plant of Infinite Want, tucking it away into his own clothes and pressing it close to the other one he held.

In the hours that followed, searches were carried out but no sign of the animal remained, barring a few paw prints in a mud patch. On returning, they counted someone else missing. Goreth. But he came and went as he pleased. It was hoped that he had gone after Telemachus and would bring him back.

39

Formus Defeats the Goranguns

Formus and Artemius had worked out a means for getting at the Pyronite arrowheads and the cart in which they were stored. It was only at a short distance but even then, the scouts that were sent out to retrieve it had come under fire from the archers in the woods. A man had died when an arrow had found its way under his shield to the artery in his neck. Having run the distance to the cart as planned, the men attached ropes and again evading the barrage of lethal metal – arrows stuck into their wooden shields like blades of grass in divots – they raced back with the rope ends. Twenty men got onto them and hauled with all their combined strength. On creaking wheels, the heavy vehicle rolled and came to them. There was a jubilant cheer as the men got to the covered cart and pulled from it the quivers with the Pyronite arrows.

"Take the archers to the right-hand side of those buildings and when I give the signal, ignite your arrows and fire upon the place where our hairy opponents are gathered in force," said Formus to Artemius.

"Is there a risk that we might set the whole forest on fire before we can get to their settlement and ransack it?" asked his military commander.

"The night is dark, which will give greater impact when those arrows make contact. Yes, a few trees will catch fire but snow is on the ground and the atmosphere too cold. The flames will soon extinguish themselves. The advantage is in the moment our archers get to work there will be little stamina for any fight in the enemy."

It turned out as the druid suggested. The arrows were lit and fired into that part where the hairy ones were conspicuously gathered. Most terrible were the screams and explosions as the heated arrowheads plunged into the men or trees they hid against. The forest was lit up as if it was day rather than night and those with Formus could see the numbers they were attacking. Not many – and amongst those, the few that still remained on their legs took to them, not having come against men before who, like these, could order lightning bolts down from the sky to strike at their enemies. They fled.

Formus ordered his whole army to chase after them with a shouted command to take no prisoners. It had been a long time since his men had experienced battle action and killing. He wanted to keep them sharp. Besides, the sight of slaughter thrilled him.

His men rode or ran into the forest, stabbing or chopping anyone they caught. When it seemed that no-one they opposed was left alive, Formus collected his troops together.

The bodies were inspected and amongst them were found the old chief, all of his sons and the soothsayer. Despite this and the broken bodies by the score lying all around, there were several men who insisted that a number of hairy ones had got away.

"Are you sure?" said Formus as he stood up from one man that had been killed by a simple sword slash. These beings they had just destroyed were indeed curious – not altogether beast but certainly not human men. Their foreheads jutted too far forward and the hair on their faces covered right to their upper cheeks. They were small in stature and the arms disproportionately long. Some differed from the others in that they carried less hair and appeared more human: such were the old chief, his priest and several others – all had been at that first meeting where Formus had initially dismissed their unusual features.

"Yes, sire. They followed the river and went in that direction." The man pointed to a waterway in the distance that was more a wide stream than what the speaker described and which disappeared into the thick forest.

The High Druid thought for a moment and then made his decision. "Artemius, prepare the men. We will go in after them. We will have to go through the forest anyway, so we might as well pursue the chance for spoils when it occurs. They will be making their way to the original settlement."

"What will we do with the dead, My lord?"

"Do?" said Formus, surprised. "How many of them are our men?"

"Just the two, sire, though they were brave fighters."

"Well, bury those men with the honours due to them but leave the rest to lie where they fell. Wolves and wild hogs will clean them up soon enough. More beasts thrive in these woodlands than those we left behind in Borrumania."

All that was done and soon the High Druid's army was on the march again, cleaving its way through the trees after the haired ones who had escaped.

They had not been an hour in the forest when they came to a settlement obviously abandoned in haste.

"It looks like those that escaped from us warned the women and children here, giving them time to flee before we came," said Artemius, reigning in his horse.

"An unusual place for habitation," commented Formus, taking in everything around. It was unusual. Formus had seen wicker huts like these before, but they had been on wooden platforms over lakes or marshland whereas these were built in the branches of large trees with corded rope ladders hanging down. Good protection from the beasts he had just mentioned and possibly others.

It was not only ladders that hung from the trees. There were too, ropes twisted and plaited from leather material that hung from the giant oaks and that were placed above the tree houses themselves. Formus wondered at their size. They must have done most of their growing in another, warmer age. Their trunks were ancient but massive in strength. In this Ice-Choker season that stretched its cold hand beyond the Land of the Four Winds, the leaves had been pinched from the boughs and the twiglets were completely bare.

"They used those ropes to swing from house to house," interrupted Artemius. "It must have been like a road in the sky."

"Useful military training could be practised up there as well," mused Formus. "Although, in the end, it did them little good." He turned to the practicalities. "Did the men find anything useful in the houses?"

"Yes – food, clothes, even some spare weapons. And we did find something else or rather," he corrected himself, "someone else."

"That's interesting. One person left abandoned in a deserted village. Bring him to me."

"It's a woman, sire."

"Young?" asked the druid, hopefully.

"Old."

"Ah, well, never mind. It is probably why she was left. Bring her to me now."

Artemius turned and called out above the heads of his soldiers who were working around them, busily engaged with setting up an encampment in the village.

His voice was heard and from the place where she had been stood, a figure came walking accompanied by two guards who hurried her on. They dodged the tied horses and the groups of soldiers, moving towards Formus. The High Priest viewed the short person with growing curiosity. She was bent over, limping and covered from head to toe in a hooded cloak. This person was not human. A perception that became full fact when she stood before him.

The cloak, big as it was, did not cover those lower arms that were so covered in hair. Neither did it shield the face from gaze. The face that was caught between weeping and snuffling. Those large eyes, flat nose and extended, whiskery mouth showing trepidation at her predicament. The creature wiped at her eyes with a cloak end, grasped in her long, bent fingers.

Artemius felt some sympathy. In her distress, this animal looked cute and vulnerable. It was good that she did not know Formus as he knew him. Otherwise, standing there at the mercy of the High Druid, her mere weeping would have become mortal terror.

"There, there," said Formus, seeking, with difficulty, to express a soothing calm. "My dear madam, do not fear us, we mean not to harm you. We only injure those who flagrantly ignore the rights contained within the Rod of Amity and attack us."

His words had the opposite effect to the one he had intended. There was more convulsive weeping. By and by, under the two men's long, patient stare, it stopped.

"That's better," said Formus. "There is no point in giving in to despair. You do not mean us harm so we will keep you safe. You don't mean us harm, do you?"

The creature's eyes opened wide at him, blinked. She shook her head vigorously.

"Of course not," he continued. "But naturally then, if you want to be our friend so we can keep you from injury by these nasty soldiers of mine who will instinctively take revenge for losing two dear comrades, you must answer our questions. You do understand, don't you?"

The primate face skewed towards the soldiers mostly engrossed in the dark evening setting up their camp under torch-light. It was not obvious that they were interested in dealing with her violently. Whereas, when she resumed her attention to the man who had just spoken, it suddenly came to her that he was very capable of such cruelty, despite his sympathetic pretence. She nodded her head, determined to survive.

"I am so pleased. It's nice to meet a …. a…. well, by the way, what do we call your people?"

"The Gorangu," she replied, speaking for the first time. Her voice was higher pitched than the human but considering her dilemma it was remarkably firm and clear. "I am called Dega."

"The Gorangu," repeated Formus, relishing the glottal sounds in the word. "Yes, so welcome to meet a Gorangun who does not want to waste my time. Now, my first question is – where have the people in this village gone?"

"North," came the simple answer.

"Where in the North?" Formus' tone was harder, implying that he would not accept simplicity again.

Dega made a sound which was the Gorangun equivalent to a human sigh and then explained. "The women and children have gone northwards to escape you. They were warned by the few men who returned from the battle. When they left, I could have gone with them but you see, my leg …." And here she tapped the limb she limped upon, "would have held them back so I told them to leave me." A warning stare from Formus reminded her to get to the point and she hurried on. "The place I think they might be making for is a land called Penlac. It is a lake or many lakes between mountains. I have not been there myself so I wouldn't know it to describe exactly what it looks like, neither have any of the Gorangu. While she was talking the Lady Andraste joined them, her maid carrying a torch to light her way. She gazed at the strange creature in the hooded cloak, unmixed wonder in her expression. Andraste had always been fascinated by the new, the different and Dega was certainly that.

"If it is unknown, then why use it as a destination. There is some other advantage it possesses that you need to tell me about isn't there?" Formus regretted the visit by Andraste. It meant that he could not dispatch the creature quickly as he meant to do, after extracting all the useful information from her.

"Yes. Penlac is a land filled with lakes containing sweet fresh water and plentiful fish. There is space enough for anyone to settle and high places in which you can live to protect yourself from sea marauders. Although that may not be necessary if you make peace with the people who rule there as they keep the land free from invaders."

"There is no guarantee that once your fellow Goranguns reach this country called Penlac, they will be welcomed by those who live there."

"We have far more in common with them than you might imagine," said Dega. She risked angering Formus because she could detect his great interest in her information and there was something else she was holding in reserve.

"What is that?"

"The people who rule there are not human."

"Not human?" interrupted Artemius.

"They are a powerful race who can breathe and live underwater as naturally as the fish in those sparkling lakes. They are the Orsook."

Formus held himself still, not wanting to betray his feelings but Artemius had no such misgiving and an exclamation came from him. "The Orsook!"

The old lady Gorangun looked from one to the other. "Yes, why – do you know these people?"

"We have heard about them," said Formus quickly before Artemius could speak again. "But anyway, will you be able to tell us how to get there – do you know anything of the land and terrain between here and there?"

"In my younger years I attended the chief of our tribe. We had many visitors come to us in our woodland, some were welcomed and passed on their way, others were not welcome and never left." Dega did not go further with the last statement. "Yet all gave their news about the pleasant and unpleasant incidents occurring beyond our own place and there were some that were making their way to Penlac. They gave us good details about how to get there."

"Then a safer journey can be had by you and by us as we make our way to this land," stated Formus.

It was a reassuring offer but Dega was not convinced. All her experience informed her that this was a man not to be trusted. However, she needed to increase her value and esteem with him.

She could do that now while she had his attention or later. Later might be too late.

"There is something else that you should know."

Formus raised his eyebrows and nodded at her to indicate that he was listening.

"The Rod of Amity you showed my chief – have you got it with you? Can I see it?"

Wondering what she was up to, Formus went to his horse nearby and came back with the Rod. He walked over to Dega and gave her the cylinder.

Her hairy hand clasped the ambassadorial token and brought it up close for inspection through her reddened eyes. She noted the words from Runegar etched and inlaid along the staff. Like her chief earlier that day she detected the deliberate flaw in the Rod of Amity. Where the symbol for the Plain of Rebirth was etched in the centre of the rod was a band of lighter coloured material, different to the extended cylinder either side. "My Lady," said Dega speaking to Andraste for the first time, startling her, "Could you ask your servant to bring her light closer that My lord might get a clearer view?"

Andraste ushered her maid forward with the burning torch and under its wavering radiance Dega held out the token for friendship to Formus. "Do you see that the central band of the Rod is a different colour?"

Formus held the end, briefly bent his head and then looking up said, "I do."

Dega tugged the instrument from him and swiftly smacked it against her leg. There was a hollow, wooden thump and the Rod broke into two, falling to the earth. This action was greeted with consternation by the onlookers but before they could react, the old Gorangun forestalled them. She spoke in a determined voice, "Like my leg, which I lost years ago, this Rod of Amity is false. Do you see what lies on the ground?"

The High Druid saw that the token was hollow and where it had split open, there was a parchment. Bending down, he pulled it out and retrieved it. He unrolled it slowly. There were just three words written on it with what must have been Runegar's, the Druid of Druids' seal beneath.

It was formed in the language made by the Brittonic druids to be understood by themselves and the chief of the tribes so he was unfamiliar with the script:

ΚΙΛΟΒΗΡΑ

Yet he was not that ignorant that he could not guess at its meaning. He turned the parchment towards Dega for an interpretation to confirm his suspicion.

"Although I only attended upon my chief," she said, "I got to learn what that means as there was only ever one message in a Rod of Amity that could be broken. It says: 'Kill the bearer.'"

Formus slowly lowered his arm. Everyone there understood the consequences of this announcement but he was affected in particular. It was obvious that Runegar had ordered the attack upon them. To Artemius and the other warriors this would mean that they were now to be treated as a hostile force within Briton. Formerly they could rely upon being treated as fellow Celts although this would not have lasted long since they had come here to take revenge and to sequester land for settlement. That ownership would have to be forced by arms rather than bargain. They were military men; it would not be hard to return to soldierly looting. For the High Druid, this matter was more serious. He had lost the support of the highest priest in the land and the sacred druidical matrix that bound it together. In the past he had been able to travel freely because of it; it had taken him to the seats of authority in this wilderness and in Europa. Now that was all gone and he would not be able to re-cross the Tin Sea even if he wanted to.

Characteristically, Formus did not spend much time in regret. Runegar's attempted assassination would not affect his own standing with his army, who looked upon him as their one and only leader, an authority second only in importance to loot.

He referred to the shrivelled old creature who had broken the Amity Rod. "It seems, Dega, that I am in your debt. You must accompany us and show the way to Penlac."

There was nothing to be gained in a refusal but the Gorangun voiced a concern. "My lord, I have no means to travel, my leg slows me down."

"She can travel by my side," spoke up Lady Andraste. "I will give her a horse and she can attend to me."

"There you are," said Formus to Dega, almost kindly, "It has all been sorted to everyone's satisfaction. You will leave with us in the morning."

They separated and the whole camp settled down for the night.

Andraste brought Dega into her own tent and after they had washed, the old Gorangun settled down by herself on the other side of the woven cloth that hung down and separated for privacy's sake one space from another. She lay down under the cover on her bedding with a candle beside her, after detaching her wooden leg.

Her new mistress also lay on bedding and before leaning over to the candle on a small adjacent table to extinguish it, she called out, "Sleep well, Dega."

Andraste's candle was blown and on the other side of the hanging cloth the candle remained burning and lit the Gorangun's face. But it wasn't the old creature's face. It had changed briefly in the bright illumination, as if made from the same soft wax powering the light source. The features flowed and the flesh reshaped under morphed pressure to become Goreth's face. He smiled and the high-pitched Gorangun voice was incongruous as it came from his lips. "You have been very kind to me, My Lady and I will sleep all the better for it." He paused and then raised himself up to blow at the candle. Before he blew, his features shifted again and wrinkled Dega's mouth pursed. Darkness blotted. Disguise upon disguise.

40

Conversevitae's Magic

King Noremac and his army had reached the garrison in the north. He had consulted with the commander there who, amongst other things discussed, had told him about the licence application for patent and trade by the villagers in Monithcound. Noremac was immediately suspicious.

"Who is the inventor for this 'windmill' – is he from the village?"

"His name is Faramund, Your Majesty. I believe he is a stranger in these parts, although so we were informed, a Celt and from Clundover in the south of your domains."

" 'We'? Commander, get me the officer from the garrison who actually spoke to these people." The captain was quickly fetched. The King questioned him closely and then sent him away.

Afterwards, Noremac coldly regarded the garrison commander, who lowered his eyes, feeling uncomfortable.

"Commander, did you not think that this 'windmill' that has been built in Monithcound was constructed in a remarkably short time? There are less than a hundred men in that settlement, yet this building seems to have been erected in not much longer than a week."

"My men inspected the settlement sire and found nothing amiss." He tried to say something that would please the king. "The application for the patent and trade licence is processing. Soon afterwards a deposit was placed for it by men from Monithcound."

"Is that so? How much?"

The commander told him and the monarch's eyes widened. "So much gold for so little a village? The clan leader there – this Coryumberix – he seems to be a young man with great initiative. In fact, just the kind of person my daughter would have chosen to have around her before she was taken from Overblown. I want you to leave an adequate force on guard here at the garrison, commander, but the rest of the squad must join with my army and then we will pay a visit to Monithcound. On the way there we will organise a sweep with detachments through any settlements we come across so as to check thoroughly for any signs that the kidnappers of my dear daughter might have left behind."

A day later, the tall oaken gates in the circuitous, timber-buttressed walls protecting the garrison swung back. Out from them came the King and his northern commander with the army marching slowly behind. It was rare for Noremac to be seen beyond his capital. With the Wind Disease having prevailed as it had done throughout his own lifetime, few people travelled out of the country and none at all settled permanently within it. The effect was stagnation – people put up with their hardship, not knowing anything different about how other Celts lived beyond their borders. Order was kept too by the King's military which made itself felt through frequent patrols which kept check on any signs for disturbance against the monarch's rule. Even the poverty he witnessed as Noremac rode through the various small settlements on his march to Monithcound could not shake his royal confidence in the way he ruled his subjects. For they were subjects, not people. He owned the land upon which they worked or begged and it followed naturally that he possessed their very body and spirit. This was not what his daughter believed, despite his attempts to train her and so she must be brought back to the palace, preferably in a state ready for her funeral.

It took a full day before Noremac was able to get his army to Monithcound.

While he was working his way towards the settlement, decisions had been quickly taken in the village itself. Telemachus' disappearance meant that Tyracides' leadership over the Telemachons was reinstated. This was not fully supported by those who had been close to the former: Eucleides, Agenor, Thocero, Berengar, Faramund, even Costus whose loyalty was mainly owed to himself. There were others too but for the time being they held their tongues, particularly as Tyracides changed his mind in deciding to fight with Coryumberix and chose instead to continue north in the same direction they assumed the panther beast – that animal which now caged Telemachus' soul – had taken. Such a turnaround did not surprise Eucleides who had always suspected that Tyracides' generous offer to Coryumberix was simply a means for goading Telemachus into a fight.

Coryumberix did not seem to be angered by Tyracides' capriciousness. He had spent some time in his hut along with

Tyracides and the Princess Byncor. When they emerged an hour later, there was an expression on his face suggesting hopefulness, when the news about the King leading his army towards their village might have had the opposite effect. Torcus, who had become closer to his chief in the last month, called out, almost jolly, "We have a strategy to defeat the King when he arrives, My lord?"

Coryumberix answered in the same manner. "Most certainly we do, my worthy warrior!"

"And will I be striding out to slay his soldiers with my double-headed axe?"

"No because when he arrives here, we will be gone."

"Gone? Where?"

"Where he least expects us to be. He might be standing amongst our empty homes in Monithcound but we will be stationed behind his gates in Overblown."

So that was the plan: a deft reversal of fortune if it could be accomplished as worked out by the three who had discussed it together in Coryumberix's hut. Speed was intrinsic to it. While Noremac made his way to Monithcound, Coryumberix would lead his warrior's south, the women and children moved out of harm's way. Princess Byncor was in no doubt that she could raise an army as they went from one inhabited place to another, although the process would not be without its difficulties. It would be a force filled with the disillusioned young in the country, those keen for change and to bring down the established, corrupt king.

"What will they be like against Noremac's older, experienced soldiers, though?" said Torcus dubiously.

"Some of them will already have been trained for war skills in their own settlements," answered Coryumberix. "Commitment, additional training and most of all, success, once we take the capital, will make an irresistible fighting force. And before you say it, Torcus, I know that overwhelming Overblown's defences will not be easy. Just remember will you, Noremac has reduced its capability by bringing the greater part of his army up here. A poor decision and one that will cost him his crown. Anyway, we cannot stand around wasting our time in idle chatter. Get the people ready to move out."

This was achieved in only a short space of time as the numbers living in Monithcound were smaller than the size of the army that was coming from the east. Another reason which helped them was the slowness with which the King proceeded. His contempt for the ordinary people, a rigid belief in their supposed inferiority to his natural rule, meant that he could not imagine a situation where there would be a mass uprising against him. There had been small insurrections during his reign but all completely suppressible. Taking such a large military force through the country as he was doing had not occurred to him because he sensed some enormous threat to his position. Rather, it was there to impress his subjects with the physical power he could exert against them if he so wished. He was not often away from his capital and so when he was seen by his subjects in the provinces he had to make sure they sat up and paid attention. In his own mind he was simply out hunting for his daughter and like any other recalcitrant child, when he found her she would have to be punished. Only, this punishment would be her last one. He realised Byncor had her supporters but always dismissed them as unimportant hangers-on. There was no thought in his mind whatsoever as he stopped the army every so often along the route, that his daughter would be starting out from Monithcound with Coryumberix and having the audacity to plan what she was in fact doing. He sent out search parties to nearby settlements and waited for their reports.

So slow, indeed, was the King's army on their march, that what might have been travelled in a day by one man on horseback at a fast pace, was only completed in a day and a half by the army with an overnight encampment.

They reached Monithcound in the late afternoon and once within sight of it, realised that something unexpected had happened.

A cavalry officer was designated to ride ahead into the village. What the King and his garrison commander had noted from an observable distance was that Monithcound lay empty and deserted. The cavalryman soon returned, his horse's hooves thudding past the austere shape that was the windmill, its sails turning creakily in the wind.

"There is no-one in the settlement, majesty," panted the officer. "But there are tracks through the snow as if a crowd of people has divided into two. Some tracks descend the hill from the village on its other side, disappearing northwards into the surrounding woods, while others exit to the west down that slope side and again into the tree cover."

What the listening King and his chief officers could not know was that Tyracides, to make up for his withdrawn offer to fight with Coryumberix had offered instead to conduct the women and children in Monithcound to a place of safety beyond the border. This suggestion had been gladly accepted by the Celtic chieftain. The King's physician, Conversevitae, had been asked if he wanted to stay behind to meet with Noremac or to travel west and then south with the princess. Neither proposition held any allure but Byncor made it very clear that it was his duty to remain with her.

"North, you say?" puzzled the King. "Surely that would take them into the lands held by tribes who are susceptible to our curse? They will be executed as soon as seen. It does not make any sense."

The cavalry officer said nothing. It was not his duty to theorise and if he did, his safety would only be compromised later.

"What do you think, Dacius?" said the King to the garrison commander. "You understand best this locality and the people who live within it."

"You are right, sire, when you say that in going to the north, beyond this country's protection, those from Monithcound who have chosen to do that will surely die. They have broken their bond with you, majesty, let them go to their doom. The others though, those that have gone westward, I think we need to be more concerned about."

"But doesn't that way lead to the Mountain Lands of the Ordovices? That group who go there will have the same problem as the other."

"My concern is that they are not necessarily wanting to get to the peaks where the Ordovices tribe has its eyries. Well before then, they will come across an ancient roadway which takes them south."

"South," repeated Noremac, now beginning to realise the significance of what his officer was hinting at.

"Although the track will not take them to the gates of Overblown, it passes by some settlements and ends not far from your city, majesty."

"But why would they want to go there?" muttered the King aloud to himself. He began to feel foolish and that was an unusual occurrence for him. "Monithcound must have less than a hundred warriors and some of them might have gone …." He stopped himself. "No, the case is that all the warriors are headed south."

"Coryumberix must be leading them, Your Majesty. He is young and ambitious. I am now certain that the Princess Byncor must be with him but what I am unsure about is whether or not Coryumberix is using her as a hostage."

The King had no such confusion in his mind about the situation. To some extent he would have to admit it. "Dacius, I think my daughter has betrayed me."

"But surely not, sire!" exclaimed the commander with some forced shock. "She must have been made to go, as a hostage."

"Not with what I understand of her behaviour for the past year or so. She has gathered around her a youthful coterie, a collection of moaners and complainers – who had got together a petition claiming that I had the cure for this country's disease, was withholding it and should immediately release the vaccine for the people's use."

Dacius was at a loss as to how he should reply. Kept mainly inside the garrison with his men and located in a peripheral northern post away from the daily news circulated at court, it was his lot to remain ignorant. As were most Windlanders in the northern domains. It suddenly occurred to Dacius that Coryumberix, the lowly chieftain of a small northern village, had known more than any of them.

"Up to now, I had not understood how serious she was about all this." What Noremac really meant was that he had dangerously underestimated his daughter's ability and commitment to put her revolutionary ideas into practise. Never had he considered the possibility that she might raise an effective fighting force against him. But this was the potential. Already she had Coryumberix and a hundred warriors on her side. How many more would she have by the time she got to the capital? When she had disappeared from the palace he had always known it was by her own decision. Conversevitae's absence alarmed him even more – yet he had considered it and came to the conclusion that in fact, this turn of events might be all for the best. He would go after them and hearing of his hunt for her, his daughter might decide to exile herself from the country. Then when he had got up there with his army, he would strengthen the border controls and make certain that if the vaccine had been put to any use, people further south in his kingdom would not get to know. Now, all of that strategy had been shattered with a clever move from his daughter. Her influence over his subjects would only increase when she moved through the land with the news that she had the means to rid it of the pestilence that had affected them for so many generations.

"We are more than a day behind them," volunteered the commander, "but it would be possible to cut them off before they reach Overblown. May I suggest, my lord, that we select a smaller group from our army consisting of the speediest riders and send them before us? A lightly loaded horse troop, fewer in number, would have more chance to narrow the gap between them and us. Once they have caught up and got in front, the necessity then is to obstruct any further progress by the princess' renegade band, delaying long enough for us to arrive behind them."

The King approved and any tardiness in his pursuit of Princess Byncor up until then was more than matched by the new urgency in his actions thereafter.

Even at the time that the King had made his decision to make haste in stopping her, the Princess herself had just finished addressing a meeting at the first settlement they had come to. It had proved to be an altogether different experience to the one she had expected. She thought it might be difficult to win people over, particularly because of all the years that her father and his father before him had imposed their authority in the way they had done. Hardship for the many was the norm so that less suffering was treated as if it were happiness. It was a surreal topsy-turvy world in which vices were admired and became the prerogatives of the rich while virtues were scorned and only deserved by the poor. Coryumberix spoke alongside her and they trusted him because by his voice and accent they recognised someone from their part of the kingdom. Yet, Byncor was able to offer them hope and a change to the rule that dominated their lives. They cheered her for this and they cheered her when she presented them with Conversevitae to explain that a cure for Wind Leprosy had been discovered. Within herself, Byncor noted the ragged clothes these people wore, the thinness of their bodies and wondered if they had the strength to fight with her for a new future. And then a curious, marvellous thing happened. Byncor had just finished her sentence with the words, "you must gather your strength and tear down this rotten, corrupt government," when out from the green forest came a mighty roar. It was a sound such as few had ever heard in that land: the deep-throated cry from the black throat of a panther.

Byncor had, of course, seen and heard it before. Along with Coryumberix, his people in Monithcound and the Telemachons, she had seen Telemachus transformed into the beast that had just roared from the forest depths. Fleetingly, she wondered why it was here, rather than tracking the Telemachons north. Byncor, though, showed more determination than her own father in pursuing an action and in this announcement from the forest she saw an opportunity which could be used for persuasion. It could go either way if the moment was not seized immediately. Superstition had to be harnessed to pull in the right direction.

"Do you hear that sound?" She asked the crowd. They were too much in awe of what they had heard to respond quickly and Byncor continued. "That sound is a message from our god Borrum, the bringer of winds." And indeed just at that moment a wind hit the tree boughs in a line, making the wooden limbs wave back and forth while the leaves rattled like quivering tongues punching plosives through a grey wintered mouth. "He is telling us," yelled Byncor above the rushing noise, "that my father, the King, is a traitor to this country and to you! You do not belong to any man who is willing to oppress you! You are the people of Borrum, the god of this land and he has sent me to release you from his curse, the Wind Leprosy. Take up arms against Noremac! Release yourselves! Let the strength from Borrum roll through your bodies and knock the despot from his throne!" As if in support, another growl was heard from the creature in the forest. A resounding echo went up from the throats of all who were gathered there.

Byncor and the others could not stay long in that village. Coryumberix believed that the King was already in pursuit. The best of the young people from that settlement went with them and they were soon on the move once more.

Over the next four days they stopped at as many such places. Each time the princess spoke to the people, their fighting ranks swelled in number. Byncor and Coryumberix grew in confidence and the initial aim to take the capital city became more than just a possibility.

This assurance was not dented by Coryumberix bringing her news about the military force that had been sighted, small but significant, after they had left the last village before Overblown. Coryumberix felt no shame in bearing the news to her as if a simple messenger boy. His attitude to the princess had changed somewhat, not that he had regarded her with any disrespect previously. On the contrary – he had noted with glad relief the meticulous organisation she had put into the promotion of a rebellion against her father. Right from the start the young chief had understood that an insurrection was what she had been planning for. The way she went about it gained not only his trust but that of others. Here, side by side with her, hearing how she spoke and persuaded the people who listened to her, not with any great oratory but with the simple needs and principles that the common citizens hungered to be expressed; this, he felt, warranted a greater respect for the princess. It did not mean he gave up his right to disagree with her. Given a complete freedom to exercise his own wish about how the country would best be governed, he would do away with the monarchy entirely. But this was not in the Celts' nature, not in this part of Briton anyway. Hierarchy was bred into the belief system that encompassed druidic magic and the monolithic stone circles separating the sacred sites on hill-top, plain and grove alike. All took their bearing and authority from the Plain of Rebirth. He would give it all up if he could. There are some battles not worth the fighting: too much could be lost.

The right to disagree with Byncor was one he exercised now as it was apparent that she wanted to try to outrun the detachment that was coming for them. Coryumberix protested and made it clear that he thought the idea was foolish: if they exposed their backs it would be an easy task for the opposition to slay them if they caught up. The other problem was that in being chased to Overblown's gates they would merely be trapped between the pursuing military and the King's men who guarded the walls. Again it would lead to their extermination. Princess Byncor bowed to his military sense and accepted the fact that they would have to deal with their pursuers first. Coryumberix regretted aloud the warriors he would lose in such a confrontation.

"There might be another way," suggested Conversevitae. He had been sitting with Faramund alongside him around the fire that had been built upon the largest space available in this last village before Overblown. The princess had begun to make this a habit wherever they stopped. She thought it drew her closer to the people and would give them the impression that she, unlike her father, would not be a distant, oppressive ruler.

"If it means that my warriors would not have to lose their lives while our enemies are forced to stop in their tracks and lose theirs, please do tell me," said Coryumberix, his scepticism evident to everyone.

"My Lord of Monithcound, you carry the answer with you."

"Really?"

"Yes, only you do not recognise its power, even though the Orsook, Goreth, as I have been told, has already given you some idea about its magic."

"The seeds from the Plant of Infinite Want? I am not a believer in magic, Conversevitae. I only believe in men's constant desire to commit evil. To destroy that, there are only other men's better characters and a willingness to fight. Magic is the stuff of air."

"You are wrong," replied Conversevitae, just as firmly. "The greatest evil can only be eradicated by the magical. Why do you think, for example, that Telemachus in his imposed state as a black panther, follows us?"

"The beast in the forest is not Telemachus. It is just a beast, frightening children in the stories they hear and following them in their sleep. We are not children."

"How can you say that?" called out Eucleides' voice from around the fire. "The struggle between Tyracides and Telemachus took place before your very eyes. You saw how Telemachus was transformed."

"I could not see properly because there were so many crowded around to watch the fight. Perhaps the animal had been attracted out of the forest by the noise. It then chased Telemachus into the trees or took him. I don't know, I couldn't see." His stubbornness was strange and shocking to those Telemachons gathered at the fire and who had witnessed the event.

"Princess," said Conversevitae, before any arguments could be started. "You've seen how I am defeating the Borrumani disease that has infected our land for generations?" Before Byncor could open her mouth to answer, the physician continued, "All I ask is for some seed to be given me by Coryumberix from the bag that he carries with him. Surely, to save our lives he would be willing to do that?"

The princess turned to Coryumberix, who already knew that the physician's appeal had worked. The young chief did not want to have her either ask or command him in front of the others so he pre-empted it. "My Lady, I will try anything to prevent my warriors losing their lives unnecessarily so let Conversevitae do what he must. I will give him the seed he wants but meanwhile my soldiers will be stationed to do battle with those hounding us."

The Princess addressed herself to Conversevitae. "Will you need anything else?"

The physician paused for a moment, a hand touching his brow, head bent. "I must choose some men and women from the village. They will be taught the magical rites to begin the spell. It will not take long."

"Very well," she responded. "I will ask the Headman here to assist you."

Hours after that conversation, the horse-troop sent out by the King days before had indeed succeeded in catching up with the small rebel army led by Byncor and Coryumberix. The mounted horse was led by a short, fat man called Mitshid who hid his corpulence under a thick, woollen shirt and deer-skin trousers. He was further wrapped by a bear-furred cloak. He jangled as he rode with the movement of the metallic necklaces circling his neck and the trinkets tied into his beard. His obesity was a direct gift from King Noremac. Normally such rotundity would not be tolerated in the King's army but he was a personal friend to the King and indulged by him. Just as he was a favourite to the King so the horse underneath him was a favourite of his own. He had a wide choice from his stable but this was the one he liked to whip hard. It had become favoured by Mitshid because it responded well to punishment. He had named the horse 'Farewell State'. Why that particular name, no-one knew. Over the years it had got thinner, parallel to its master becoming fatter. Once, it had been a powerful animal, allowing anyone to ride it. Now 'Farewell State' refused any rider other than Mitshid, the master who treated it most harshly.

Mitshid drew his horse guards up in a rank, fifteen cavaliers across and ten deep. The King had agreed to send a smaller force ahead but the size was relative to his own army, not to the numbers possessed by Princess Byncor and Coryumberix. Yes, the latter had approximately two hundred fighters with them but most of those were on foot and would find it very difficult to resist horse flesh and muscle galloping into them at speed and being hacked down by the sword-wielding riders on their backs.

As Byncor's and Coryumberix's men assessed their opponent's strength across the grassy fields it seemed to them that the terms for this battle were unequal. But there was something else to take into consideration.

Moving along two ploughed lines in front of Byncor's rebel army were men and women with bent backs.

"Are they sowing a crop?" exclaimed Mitshid to the mounted officer closest to him. He and the army behind watched the proceedings with growing bemusement.

"That is what they are doing, sir, see, they are dropping seeds into the earth. There is a druid with them and another, perhaps, standing by." The cavalry officer had noticed Conversevitae and Faramund ordering the event.

Mitshid peered forward in his saddle. Another exclamation came from him. "That is not a druid – it's the King's physician."

The seed had all been dropped and now there came a change in the event. A chanting was heard from the sowers, accompanied by drum rhythm and carnyxes were blown. The horns were blown in pulsed accord to enhance the drums.

"Shall we charge upon them, sir, at once?"

Mitshid was cautious and naturally superstitious. "It may be a religious rite. Even more important, it could be one devoted to Borrumani. We cannot give offence to the god – even if they are requesting his help against us."

"As you wish, My Lord but when do we charge?"

"We will wait until the rite has been completed."

The sowers had withdrawn from the ploughed earth and now were themselves taking part in the rite with movement as well as sound. Their bodies swayed together and turned, their feet stamped the ground. Conversevitae and Faramund were each walking along a ploughed, now freshly seeded strip. While they walked, they each held out a jar that contained liquid; this they dribbled along the seeded row. Then they stood back. The combined voices rose in pitch from speech to song, although it was not a pleasant one and constricted the flow of words that had been spoken previously to a repetition of just two – "Rise up!" The words became a musical wail: sombre sinister, deadly. Those men behind Coryumberix and Princess Byncor waited in their ranks, absolutely still. On Mitshid's side, some horses sensed something their riders could not detect: they shifted and reared slightly, having to be calmed. The birds in the nearby trees stopped their song.

"This is more than a prayer to the god for victory," said the cavalry officer Mitshid had spoken to. "It is a curse against us. Sire, we must attack now."

Mitshid was just about to reply when a shudder was felt by them all. It came from the ground. Along the ploughed lines where the Plant of Infinite Want had been sown the earth changed. It boiled up like slow lava from a fissure. But there was no steam. Thick yellow stems poked through the soil. Loud popping noises punctured the air. The amazed onlookers saw the stems widen and project branches. In minutes they grew three times the height of a single man and then just as suddenly, they stopped. They had grown so fast it was now impossible to see the opposing army. It was completely hidden as were Conversevitae, Faramund and the singers whose sound had been peremptorily blocked.

"We cannot see them and even better, they cannot see us!" shouted Mitshid. "Sound the charge before our men recover their wits enough to be afraid!"

The carnyxes were lifted by the trumpeters and from their dragon mouths the sounds for action blurted. At that, the cavalry urged their horses forward and all one hundred and fifty galloped across the flat land towards what looked like an oversized plantation of wheat.

The riders steered their horses between the stems as thick as tree trunks, intending to rush through as quickly as possible.

But as they reached the first row, the plants actually shook themselves. They had reached their full height and in one moment what had risen decided to fall. A whole vegetable mass collapsed on top of the horses in snaky coils, killing men and beasts together. A few unfortunates were left struggling for breath under the plants but soon dispatched, brought to a speedier end by Coryumberix's troops clambering about the piled yellow mass. There was only one exception to this – a cavalier who had managed just in time to evade being caught up with the tumble. He galloped away, succeeding in getting back to the King's main army a day later and reporting the disaster that had occurred.

If the King was shocked by what he heard, it was nothing to the impact upon Coryumberix. At least Noremac had some idea and had long suspected the power that his chief physician possessed. Coryumberix always scorned a belief in magic. This scorn had survived the incident with Goreth before the Orsook had divided up the seed. Somehow Coryumberix had managed to persuade himself that what he had been shown was a trick, one designed for the foolish onlooker. He could not will himself to believe the same after this. It was on a different scale altogether.

A complete military unit had been vanquished by magic. The Orsook's warning came back to him as if lit by a lightning flash. This plant, the very seed, was evil and no good could come from it. His attitude to the small bag containing his portion of the seed which he held in his pocket was entirely changed. He made the decision there and then to do away with it.

41

Tyracides reaches Penlac

When Tyracides had struck northwards through the land ruled by the Ordovices, he had taken with him those women and children that Coryumberix had entrusted to his care. The Telemachons followed him but only did so in the hope that they would come across Telemachus in his enchanted form as a black panther. How they would deal with it if in fact they did meet with him was not a clearly understood outcome – all they knew was that where Telemachus led, they would follow.

Out of earshot and well behind Tyracides; Eucleides, Thocero, Agenor, Pelisteus, Melissa and Hebe talked quietly as they walked through the forest. From ahead came the sound of swords slashing at the thick undergrowth and carried babies crying at the disturbance.

"Will we be getting any nearer to Telemachus in doing this?" asked Hebe, the anxiety accumulated by his disappearance beginning to tell on her.

"It is the only thing to do," said Eucleides. "We must keep ourselves together and wait for his return. I am sure that is what he would wish us to do. He will rejoin us."

"But how can you be so adamant, Eucleides?" spoke Melissa. "He lives on four feet now, not two. He might think like a beast not a man and perhaps does not wish to come back."

"The man has been enchanted by a witch, that is not to be argued with," added Thocero, "but it is a spell that can be reversed. The soul in the beast is still Telemachus. We must find a way to recover him."

"And how do we do it?" murmured Agenor. "The only people who could have possibly achieved that are gone. Our River God has decided to disappear when most needed and that old necromancer, Conversevitae, who I am certain is a necromancer has chosen to go south with his princess."

"As has Faramund," remarked Melissa sadly, who had grown to like the diffident inventor. "Together with Eris."

"More fool him," said Eucleides, sounding harsher than he meant.

"He thought that he had found Telemachus' tracks and they were leading south," said Agenor.

"Those paw prints in mud did not last long, certainly not long enough so that we could witness his proof," returned Eucleides. "I am not saying that he didn't find any. There are many creatures in this forest. He might have been mistaken. Personally, I believe that desire for revenge is stronger than you might imagine. Man or beast, Telemachus will want to finish what he started with Tyracides. That is why he will be keeping us close, right to the point he hunts his prey down. We are more likely to find the panther's fresh paw prints following behind us."

"It is not just the idea that Telemachus might have gone south which draws Faramund there," said Agenor. "His curiosity is not satisfied with only practical matters and engineering. He wishes to engineer the unseen. He is compelled to learn magic. Who better to learn from than Conversevitae?"

"If I know Eris," added Melissa, "she will put up with being away from us for only so long. Their place is with us and I believe we will see them again."

Eucleides tried to be more positive. "I hope so. I do miss his cleverness. I just think he was mistaken to leave."

"Do you think we will have any problems with Tyracides?" asked Melissa of no-one in particular. The others had begun to notice that the remarks she had made lately about her lover were becoming distant in tone, as if referring to a stranger.

"Only if we show outright opposition to him by continuing to talk about Telemachus," cautioned Pelisteus. His listeners sensed a double-edged warning in the assertion. They trusted Pelisteus, but he had been a closer friend and comrade to Tyracides than any of them, barring Melissa and nothing could be taken for granted.

"Where is Tyracides taking the women and children whom Coryumberix put in our charge?" Thocero did not restrain his irritation. "They only slow us down. Are we heading for any particular place where we can leave them or are they to stay with us permanently?"

At that moment, Tyracides himself made an appearance from around a bush, just in front of them. He had obviously heard the last question that was raised.

"I can tell you exactly where we are going, Thocero. There are mountains and lakes to the west of here. They cover a large peninsula and at its westernmost point there is a holy island positioned off the coast. It is ruled by druids. That strange place is not one we should visit as we would not be welcome there. But half-way along the coast in that direction and further inland there is a place where Coryumberix thinks that his women and children may be safely guarded. The people there live on the lake water and in it. The settlement is called Penlac.

"The inhabitants live in the lake-water?" queried Eucleides, mystified.

"Of course they would," said Tyracides, glad to surprise them. "They are Orsook."

The others stared at each other, wondering how this had come to be possible.

"But I thought Goreth was the only one of those creatures left alive," said Eucleides. "How did Coryumberix, who has been living in isolation with his own people, become aware of them?"

"Some seasons ago, the people in Monithcound rescued a Water-man, as they called him, from an Ordovicean hunting party north of the border. The Ordovicii took flight as soon as they recognised the green freckled skin on the Borrumani. The Orsook's injuries were tended by his rescuers and he seemed to be immune to the Wind disease. He was able to leave, fully recovered, sometime later. Before he went, he told Coryumberix that if his clan ever found themselves in danger, they should go to Penlac, a place in the western mountains which his own people ruled."

"So that is why we are going there," said Eucleides.

"Yes .... Coryumberix is sure that his clan's women and children will be carefully guarded by the Orsook until he returns to collect them. Once we have escorted them to Penlac, we will be free to continue to the North." Tyracides paused, as he prudently considered his next words. "Up ahead, the rest of us are gathered. You seem to be a little less willing to keep up with the rest. I understand your reluctance and what motivates it."

"You do?" said Agenor.

"I wanted to speak to you few here, before I spoke to everyone. Your hearts and minds are with Telemachus. I accept that now and have come to realise that I will never be able to replace him in leading you, us, to that proper destination on which we are all intent."

No-one spoke a word to interrupt. Tyracides could be arrogant at times, that was clear but he also had his good qualities. Stoicism in response to hardship was one of them and the ability to recognise, eventually, what was the right action to take for himself and others. The former virtue had made his years as a Sicilian slave if not tolerable, then adequate in preparation for rebellion. The latter had given him cause to regret what had passed in the last few days. Because the loyalty felt for Telemachus was so strong amongst his followers, Tyracides felt he would be foolish to ignore it. Even now that their commander had been magically enchanted to a roaring beast, seeming to be nowhere near, the Telemachons were still in effect led by him. Tyracides could not usurp that. The stubborn belief was too strong to turn – it had tidal significance and all he could do was use his wisdom and swim with it.

"Come, I want to show you something."

Tyracides led the way back and as they walked their breaths became heavier because the ground sloped upwards. Finally, they saw before them a tree line which was broken up with the sky showing between each trunk. It must be, they thought, the last of the forest.

And so it proved to be. Tyracides went between the trunks at the cusp of the hill they had just climbed, with Eucleides and the others following behind him.

They broke through and at once they saw that their position was on the peak looking across a river and its valley situated below them. In the distance were more hills that further away became jagged and mountainous. Interlacing the smaller slopes were lakes shining in the sun. The air became milder the further they travelled from the Borrumani lands. Winter was giving way to a welcome spring.

Collected at the highest space for a better view were the rest of the Telemachons with the women and children from Monithcound, the children held tight by their mothers. Tyracides strode up beside them and pointing for the benefit of Eucleides, Agenor and the rest, he said, "There, that lake in the middle, foremost at the foot of the grass and heather covered hill – that is Penlac."

Eucleides shielded his eyes and could faintly make out a large settlement. Some buildings were on the land, others on platforms above the water's edge. He thought what would Goreth have given to see this? Then he voiced aloud what he had been thinking since Penlac had been made known to him. "Do you know, I believe our River God is already making his way there, if he has not got there already."

Thocero agreed with him, "Where else would he go? It was his wish to meet those of his own kind in these isles and that settlement is where they were. A new home for him.

"Friends!" shouted Tyracides, moving to a high point over them all. "This is a good omen. We have found Penlac – its people will grant us the safety and respite that we need until we are ready to move on. We will go down to Penlac and meet with the Orsook who live there." A babel of Greek rose up from beneath him, intensified by the Celtic voices of the women, once they had the words translated to them. Everybody had got to understand that the Water People were no longer the stuff of legend – the Telemachons through their friendship with Goreth and the Celts because of their injured visitor to Monithcound. Tyracides raised his arm for quiet. "Women of Monithcound, Coryumberix has asked me to leave you and your children with the Orsook, where you will all be kept safely. We, the Telemachons, after resting, will travel on northwards. I want to tell you, Telemachons, that I know how it must have looked when Telemachus and I clashed weapons outside Coryumberix's hut. Well, he had been brought down by a magical curse. It affected his behaviour so that he attacked me. I had no such excuse in provoking it, only perhaps my own jealousy of his leadership. I can only offer my sorrow for what happened and say to you that I really do believe Telemachus will return to us. When that happens I will restore his trust in me. Meanwhile, I will make amends by leading you as best as I am able." This simple statement of his feelings went a long way to restoring sympathy and authority to Tyracides, despite his overbearing manner in the past.

Previously when Telemachus was absent from leading his people – as when he remained with Helladore – it should have been Eucleides as second-in-command amongst the warriors to take over the leadership. But he too had not been with the Telemachons and the only other Greek warrior of similar repute was Agenor. It was a strange thing but Agenor had made no move to oppose Tyracides when he took natural command. He possibly believed, as did more than just some others amongst the Telemachons, that Tyracides had led them fairly and well.

The journey from the hill on which they stood to the lake settlement inhabited by the Orsook took the best part of that day. When they arrived they were greeted at first with weapons, naturally. But when Tyracides had explained by an interpreter from Monithcound why they were there and was able to name both Coryumberix and the Orsook who had been helped by the people of the village, the atmosphere changed. The former guest at Monithcound presented himself and recognised many of the villagers travelling with the Telemachons. He turned out to be a son to the Water Sidhe in Penlac. The Water Sidhe was the person to whom the Orsook people there referred all the decisions to be made for the community's benefit. She was supported by a council and they all voted on each matter for consideration; the Water Sidhe had the final casting vote. The council could consider suggestions for action from community members but in practise it was the councillors who initiated laws and action in the settlement. To the Telemachons, it was a most undemocratic constitution, passing over the fact that during their journey they had also travelled politically from democratic consultation under Telemachus to the disguised autocracy exercised by Tyracides.

42
Telemachus Restored

Coryumberix bent low to blow on the small flame he had created, encouraging it to catch hold and ignite the other dry twigs he had piled together. It twisted, squirmed, wrapped itself around another few twigs poking up and then the bracken was firmly alight. The chieftain brought a branch and then another to feed it. Soon there was a sturdy fire blazing and all that could be heard in the forest glade he had come to, was the popping and crackling of fire, eating dry wood.

Once it was firm, Coryumberix stood up, pulling from his tunic the small bag containing the seed given by Goreth.

He had come away from the others to this solitary part of the forest so that he could not be prevented from destroying the seed. He had no doubt that that the others would argue with his decision. They had, after all, viewed its power in debilitating the King's squadron that had been sent to oppose them. There had probably been many brave men amongst that force thought Coryumberix. They should have been defeated by clean and principled fighting not by some demonic conjuring. The seed was bad just as Goreth had said and there should be no room for it on this earth.

Extending his arm to upturn the pouch and scatter it over the flames, Coryumberix suddenly felt himself thumped into the air. Arms flailing, he was knocked to the ground, metres away and left winded.

The black bulked figure was gathered as if to spring again. Its eyes were as hard as emeralds, lips grimaced back around the fanged incisors to shape a snarl. There was no human connection to it that would suffice, barring a rugged mauling and then extinction.

The Celtic chief remained absolutely still. He knew at once this animal had been Telemachus. It beggared his rationality but it was true. He wondered if anything of the man remained. His hand crept towards the great sword at his waist. The cat beast repeated its snarl; its emeralds following the slow movement. Coryumberix's inner query had been answered. Something.

He stopped his hand and let it loose by his side. The panther bent a head, opened its mouth and then dropped an object between its forepaws. It was the bag of seed that Coryumberix had been ready to destroy.

Snuffling over the pouch, the beast very delicately gripped the bottom in its teeth and upended the bag as Coryumberix would have done, only over earth not fire. Then shaking the leather pouch away so that it at last dropped into the flames, the beast stared contemplatively at the white pellets piled in a small mound before his snout. A long pink tongue jumped out from his mouth and scattered the pile. Then retracted into his mouth, taking a mouthful of the seeds from the Plant of Infinite Want with it. A gulp and the thick pink taper lashed out again and once more until every last seed had disappeared.

The big cat's head swayed and Coryumberix felt himself restored to a fine black focal point in a pool of green. Before he could think about doing anything else, however, the creature made a sound which was most unlike that usually produced by a panther: a whine. The beast collapsed onto its stomach. The whine became a sudden squeal and the skin of the beast rose up from its body as if pulled by some invisible hand. It ascended and folded like a dark cloak, finally squeezing into nothing. Coryumberix expected to see the animal's skeleton packed with muscle and flesh underneath but what was revealed was a pale body, a man's complete form with eyes closed: Telemachus.

Coryumberix rushed forward. No concern for the moment with the terrible occultic manifestation he had just witnessed and which would begin to hound his rationality from that time onwards.

"Telemachus! Telemachus! Can you hear me?"

Some sound came from the throat, a curious echo: resonance of the panther beast, prior to its existence being snatched away.

Telemachus opened his eyes. Confusion was apparent in them at first and then, "Coryumberix, is that really you or some demon sent to manipulate me?"

"Rest easy," replied the Celt, "What you see you can believe, although I would not have said that moments ago. Are you in pain?"

"Not greatly – some in my head but that seems to be subsiding."

"What do you remember?"

"Only my anger and the fight with Tyracides – afterwards, just the sound of my own breathing in the darkness."

"Strange that as an animal you followed us here, rather than track the man you were about to kill."

"What is the burning sensation in my throat?" said Telemachus, distractedly.

"It is the seed from the Plant of Infinite Want. I was about to destroy my allotment from Goreth before you attacked me as the panther and then ate it. Its power restored your humanity."

"The beast's conscious mind within me must have known that and perhaps there is the reason for it to be following you."

"If the seed was its objective then why not hunt Tyracides? He has two bags – his own and the one he picked up after the confrontation with you."

This left Telemachus thinking. With difficulty, he managed to get to his feet; the Celt lent a steadying hand. "Maybe, Coryumberix, it is my destiny."

The younger man looked at him and there was gentle mockery in his voice. "You don't seriously believe that do you? We must surely have greater control than that over our futures."

"As a beast I never knew and as a man, what I am learning all the time is that I know even less. We are two rational men, you and I, Coryumberix, but bad magic exorcised by malicious conductors has overtaken this world and is taking rationalism apart piece by piece. Those magicians are like Formus, Helladore and this King Noremac that you go to fight now. The battles with them are winnable – they can be defeated but there will always be others to fill their places and the war against them never ceases. Maybe I was never meant to contest Tyracides and he might be the best leader for the Telemachons rather than me. It is possible that my future lies here, joining with you and on my way to usurping Noremac. The vision I saw on the Bridge of Fusion certainly did not include me in the Telemachons' future.

"I wholeheartedly welcome you into the fight against Noremac, Telemachus," said the Celt, "but what is this 'vision' you speak about?"

"It happened before I was carried, ill as I was, by the Ghost Warriors to your village." Telemachus told him about Goreth guiding him to the Bridge of Fusion, what the Orsook had said about the causeway's origins and of the events he had seen from the Bridge.

At the end, Coryumberix was silent at first, then ventured, "As ever with these prophecies from the gods, the meaning is not conveyed simply. The immortals like to test us. While you strode the forest in your panther shape, we came up against a military detachment sent by Noremac ahead of his own army. Conversevitae and Faramund created a wonder with the Plant of Infinite Want – it grew visibly in front of our eyes: a year's growth squeezed into minutes. Then it fell back onto the King's horse troops, eradicating the whole force. You said that what you observed in the god's narrative felt as if it was taking place over many years. That might not be true, considering that we saw the Plant take such a short time to reach maturity.

"What about the buildings?" said Telemachus. "Their structures cannot rise in minutes."

"That, I cannot explain. Just remember what Goreth told you – the prophecy showed one of several possibilities. Some things in it might come true or all, or none. Only the future can reveal to you its importance."

"Well, there is one matter I am sure about because I feel complete relief from it."

"What's that?"

"The pain in my head and throat has gone. Eating that seed has broken the spell Helladore cast over me, forever."

Loud shouts broke the calm and came from the settlement behind them. Alarmed, Coryumberix kicked out the fire to score a safety of darkness. He quickly said to Telemachus, "It would be best if you stayed here – to recover your strength."

"No, I feel better now – I'll return with you." He was able to walk without help. The first person they saw, who narrowly missed running into them, was Faramund. The inventor stopped and despite the evident emergency taking place all around them, gasped, "Telemachus! Is that really you?"

Coryumberix had no time for protracted explanations and said, to forestall Telemachus, "Yes, Faramund, it is really him. Tell us quickly what is going on."

Faramund could not keep his eyes away from Telemachus although he spoke to Coryumberix. Likewise, there were others rushing around who pulled up sharply to stare and then continue on their way, still unbelieving and shaking their heads. "Sire, King Noremac's army has been seen at no great distance from here. We are moving out though it will be a hard task to reach Overblown before he finds and attacks us."

"Where is the princess?"

"She is with Torcus and her other army officers in the Headman's hut. A message has already been sent out for you but you could not be found."

"We'll go there – come with us Faramund."

"Sire, may I be excused? I am helping Conversevitae to pack his potions and equipment. They need to be made safe …. As does Conversevitae."

"From what I have experienced of that old wizard, I doubt very much that he needs anyone's help, excepting his own. But yes, the potions require proper packing so go and make certain that it is done." Faramund left but before he passed through the doorway he exchanged a hand clasp with Telemachus.

"I am so glad to see you again, Telemachus."

"As I am you," replied the other. "We will find our way back to our comrades soon." It was a statement but the tone was quizzical. Telemachus wondered if Faramund had decided that his future no longer lay with the Telemachons.

"Certainly, I am with you," answered Faramund with a firm nod. "But meanwhile I have much to learn."

"A clever young man," said Coryumberix ruminatively after Faramund had left. "I do hope that he does not become corrupted by Conversevitae's magic."

"I am sure he won't."

They decided to go and meet princess Byncor in the Headman's hut and by the time they had got there, the meeting with her army officers had broken up. Byncor's astonishment on finding Telemachus alive was clear but even clearer was the emergency created by the King's army and the need for themselves to reach the city of Overblown before he did.

43
Defeat and Death

In the race for Overblown's gates, it was Noremac who reached them first but he had not reckoned on his daughter's influence. As his army moved along the road up to the city's main gate, a soldier brought a message to the King who was riding behind the vanguard.

"Sire, the way is closed to us. They want to speak to you."

Noremac, without further enquiry, took his main retainers and rode his horse up to the front column which had halted before the entrance. Usually there would be market traders along the road here and a small crowd of travellers either buying from them or making their route into the city. Today, no stalls were evident and the only people on this road were his own army. There were other people however and they had collected in a mass at the top of the walls looking down at him. Some were dressed in military clothing, holding weapons, others were the ordinary citizens. The King probed the faces along the parapet until he came to one in particular; this man stood in a prominent position. Noremac instantly recognised him. He was a young noble of the court who had been seen in his daughter's company once too often.

"Arrevoes! Open the gates! Why have you shut them against your King?"

The response was sudden and all too clear. An arrow struck the ground just in front of Noremac's horse, causing it to rear up. With some difficulty, he managed to cling on and reassert his control over it. The man above leaned forward and shouted boldly, "You are no King of ours, Noremac! Your guards and supporters are all in the dungeons where they belong. If you are lucky, that is where you will find yourself, once the princess arrives and we have defeated those who are with you now!" When he had finished there came a flurry of arrows from the wall-top that narrowly missed the King as he had raised his shield this time but several retainers and front-rank soldiers were caught unaware and killed by them. The vanguard retreated to a safer distance, pushing the whole army back.

Noremac had truly underestimated the support for his daughter. To have overcome the men he had left behind, not so small in number and vigilant in their attention to duties, that support must have been great indeed.

He was trapped now in the worst possible position – between a fortified city from which an attack could be launched and an army fast approaching. Before any stratagem could be devised, it was already too late. Byncor and her force came into sight. The surprise was made all the greater by what the princess did next. She saw the situation her enemy was in – trapped as he was – and ordered an immediate charge. Her commanders did not question it. They realised that she had instantly recognised the advantage that could be gained – if only the city's military would give a reciprocal response. "If Overblown's been taken by my supporters and Arrevoes has taken charge, he will know what to do," she told her officers.

The attack was made and witnessing the instant engagement and fighting below him, Arrevoes did not disappoint his princess' expectations. The City's main gate opened and out stormed a host of armed men who pushed forward into the front of the King's army while Byncor's warriors terrorised them at the back.

Hemmed in from both ends, the king's infantry did what might have been expected. They broke ranks from the side and left and pulled away from the road. Pouring into the shelter offered by the trees, they ignored their officers' cries for discipline. One such officer shouting out was Soldidor, the captain who had been a childhood friend for Coryumberix.

Although it looked to Byncor and Averroes that they had their opponents defeated and on the run, the situation was much more volatile than that. In reality these soldiers were escaping and if allowed to continue running would very soon become a tactical guerrilla army fighting and harrying from the trees.

Coryumberix had already anticipated this action, sending archers into the trees each side of the road to await the coming men. When they did, the arrows fell in a sudden plummet from the sky taking Noremac's men in thigh and throat and face so that a good number were downed where they stood. Yet the soldiers from the king's army, panicked and undisciplined as they were at this time, were still too numerous for the archers. Soon the bowmen had been bloodily hacked to pieces by long iron swords and there came a moment, as in many battles, when a Tremorous shift in advantage occurs.

If the land each side of the road had not provided tree cover but instead had been rolling empty heathland or even spacious harvested fields emptied of their summer crops then all would have been well. The running soldiers could have been picked off by the archers at leisure, as if at a village target practice. But no. There was welcome safety in the girths of tree-trunks and thick leaf cover that both served to hamper visibility. So low is fortune at the height of the War God's fury.

Coward that he was, when the attack had come from the city Noremac had retreated from the front by riding along the road. His move had taken him into the main body of his men, a dozen ranks down. He felt safer and safer still as he watched the battle progress and saw that after the initial panic those of his men who had run to the trees and avoided being caught by the archers were now coming back and engaging with the confused fight taking place.

The sharp eyes in Telemachus' head had noted the king's manoeuvre. The sharper mind behind those sharp eyes calculated that at this shaky moment in the battle a decisive move could win all. He was with the Princess, Coryumberix and Torcus along with the rest of the cavalry who were gathered behind the infantry as it advanced onto Noremac's men. Some of the soldiers were also busily involved with protecting their flanks.

Telemachus leant from his black charger over to Coryumberix and told him what he was about to do. Coryumberix considered it and regarded the Greek sitting firmly in his saddle dressed in the bronze armour and red cloak that he had hastily fitted after Princess Byncor had come from the Headman's hut. "Telemachus – you have not recovered your strength fully. Let me do it. I shall lead them."

"There is no time to argue, Coryumberix – I am honour bound to repay the kindness you have given to my people."

"Well then, if that is what you are set upon. But I will be at your side." In truth, honour was at stake for both and Coryumberix could see that if Telemachus' proposed action was successful, he could not absent himself from it for the sake of his own standing with his army.

"Then, let us go," said Telemachus finally and with that they both drew aside. Coryumberix called to himself two cavalry officers and gave them their orders. When Telemachus and

Coryumberix moved again, they were at the head of a cavalry charge consisting of fifty horse. The tightly packed squadron galloped along the roadside and Noremac's men scattered to avoid being crushed to death by a tonnage of colliding horse muscle and hooves. The plan was simple. To attack where it hurt. And for the enemy that meant their king.

Men were trampled beneath the oncoming horses despite their attempts to avoid them. At the point where the distance to Noremac seemed narrowest from the roadside, Telemachus and Coryumberix swerved their horses into the massed column of soldiers with a spearhead formation of their own cavalry officers around them. They went in with their shields up to guard the reign hand and weapons swinging. By the very nature of the attack – unexpected as it was and a cavalry pressing on infantry – the enemy was forced to give way. An automatic response in those circumstances would be for the infantrymen to attack the horses with their short stabbing swords. But the difficulty was that in the crush instigated by the horsemen they found their arms pinned to the sides. All the nearest could do was gaze upward to the awful swinging double-headed axe gripped by Coryumberix and the blood-red sword in Telemachus' hand dipping in and away from their necks, taking their life-cord with it. For moments the dead and dying were held suspended by the living and then with another movement in the mass, dropped underfoot to create more problems for their comrades who were trying to maintain an upright position.

Meanwhile the king and his chief commander, Deophobos, had seen the infiltration which was beginning to advance to their own position, protected for the time being, at the centre.

Noremac looked for a way out. He was very much afraid and attempting not to show it. His reign had been a peaceful one – at least for himself and the elite he had gathered to him. The Wind Disease had guaranteed that major battles with rapacious invaders did not occur. The only purpose for which his army had been required was to put down domestic protest and revolts. These usually involved aggrieved petitioners and a supporting population from this or that settlement. His military had dealt with them harshly enough to set an example. Defenceless citizens were no match for his armed soldiers and the people died in their hundreds. Unfortunately, unarmed and militarily ignorant citizens were no great training for his army either, as the king was finding out. In this present conflict they might have defeated the archers but the direction of military advantage was beginning to turn yet again.

So the only way out was through his men to the other side of the road. Noremac turned to his commander and told him what he planned to do.

Deophobos was shocked. "Sire, we cannot leave the men – what kind of example would that set? They would think we are cowards if we run and do not attempt to withstand these attackers. Anyway," he continued, staring beyond the king to the route suggested, "I think that door has just been closed to us." Noremac turned around and saw that a fresh body of horsemen from the enemy had come up that side of the road now and were beginning an assault with the same tactic as Coryumberix and Telemachus were using. They had been sent out by Princess Byncor as soon as she saw what her commander, Coryumberix was trying to do.

It was speed that Coryumberix and Telemachus had relied upon to achieve their aim in getting to the king. They and those who rode with them had used it well. The Celtic chieftain and the Greek appeared to be irresistible as they pushed forward closer and closer to the inner ring of men that surrounded Deophobos and Noremac.

Now the king could see Coryumberix's sweating face, his arms and serpent-embossed breastplate covered in the spirted blood from the men he had already dispatched. His axe swung and crunched and lopped while beside him Telemachus urged his black warhorse on, over the fallen dead. The king's army was engaged at four points by its opponents and Arrevoes with his military that had issued from the capital's gate was slaughtering Noremac's troops at the front.

Ever nearer to him, so near that he could see their blazing eyes, Noremac understood fully what the outcome could be. Telemachus or Coryumberix, probably Coryumberix as he was the closer, would fight him and kill him. Noremac was under no illusion as to who was the better fighter and the most capable in such a situation. Tired as he must be, the younger man seemed to be driven on by a furious energy. The king saw that his head and body were well-protected by the bronze armour he wore. He used his shield well. But at the moment he was combatting the three infantrymen, Coryumberix's horse reared and its flailing hooves knocked down two of them. In that moment the king saw a flash of white skin and an exposed weakness. He bent down and took a long spear from a soldier standing nearby and rode his horse to within reaching distance. Taking the three-foot long spear in both hands, he chose his moment and poked its sharp iron point forward. Coryumberix had been dealing with the third combatant – his axe raised in one hand, he had allowed his shield to drop in the other. A fatal error: his neck was exposed. The spearpoint caught him under the chin and cut through the brain stem. His death came instantly. It was a sly intrusion into his bravery and the perpetrator did not even spend the time to pull the spear out but left it dangling and rode back. For seconds in a grisly scene the spear shaft hit the ground and held the riding corpse upright on his stallion's back like some dancing puppet to a war requiem but finally the body toppled from its place.

Even in the middle of battle, the Monithcound warriors registered their shock at his death. Some began an attempt to retrieve his body, Telemachus saw the danger in this distraction. He leaped his horse over one last obstruction and yelled to the others, "Revenge your chief! Follow me!"

Noremac had drawn his own sword but it was Deophobus' weapon that protected him from a swipe delivered by Telemachus to his face as he rode by. The commander prepared for another attack as Telemachus wheeled his horse around and came on again. Meanwhile the king's guards were being engaged by those who had followed Telemachus and a terrific noise was sent up from iron clashing against iron. Averroes' men also had broken through. The king, with his commander, was completely surrounded. As was their army. Back along the line both princess Byncor and Torcus were riding up. They came across the body of Coryumberix, set apart and ringed by shield bearers determined that their chief's body should not be desecrated further.

Telemachus was battling both the king and Deophobos. A cavalryman who had been knocked from his own horse but had managed to dispatch the soldier who had done it saw the unequal fight and grabbed a fallen spear from the ground. The weapon hurtled through the air and caught Deophobos in the thigh. A main artery was pierced by its point and blood sprayed up. With a groan, the commander slid from his horse. In the relief granted from this other combatant being disabled, Telemachus redoubled his attack upon the king. Older in years and by no means a strong warrior, Noremac was borne down by the blows and he too fell from his horse. Raising himself he tried to collect his sword and shield from where they lay on the ground but already Telemachus had dismounted and was levelling his own blade at the king's neck.

"Give the call, Noremac," said Telemachus. "Tell your men to lay down their arms or you die here and now." It was a hopeless situation. Already some men around him were submitting their swords. Their paymaster was threatened and all he could do was to express the last vestige of his authority.

"Will you behave honourably towards them?" asked Noremac. He wanted to maintain the fiction that he had been a benevolent ruler, if only for the historical record.

"More honourably than you behaved with them and the rest of your people," said Telemachus. "You will get a fair trial after the injustice you have forced on your citizens has been uncovered and assessed."

"You mean the injustice brought about by two generations living at peace?" scoffed the king.

"I mean the citizens that were murdered at your command, the cure for the national disease that was hidden from them and the poverty and debt that you forced upon the majority of your people to benefit the pampered few who surround you in your palace at Overblown."

"That is a long list," admitted the king. "Where do I start to refute it? Let me…." but before he could go on there was a sudden commotion. Some horseman thrust his way through to the monarch. A sword flashed under the sun and was savagely plunged into Noremac's neck. The king followed his commander and collapsed to the ground. None witnessing the strength in the arm that delivered the blow would say that the deposed monarch could or would survive such an assault. From the bloodied body on the ground, the men who were gathered there looked to the assassin. They found Torcus, his dripping sword held high and a ringing shout emerging from his lips. "Coryumberix is avenged! Justice for the people and justice for our chief! Let that be the new beginning for us, the Windlanders!" The words were taken up by those from Monithcound standing there and then everyone took up the cry, "Justice for Coryumberix! Justice for the people!" Eventually the shouts ended with the soldiers beating swords against shields in a tumultuous and noisy display.

Telemachus, after he had recovered from the surprise over the killing itself, understood why Torcus had done what he did. The king he despised had murdered the chief he admired. Coryumberix was a focal point for the people's rebellion against the king. Byncor too had led it but unlike Coryumberix she was a royal, an aristocrat in the capital. The chief, although young, had led Monithcound wisely and well. He was a man closer to the people and they felt his loss. Telemachus always sensed a certain shyness about Torcus, that kind of reserve which hid a magmatic passion. And so it had proven.

44
Penlac is Burnt

The two otters scrambled up to the two boys who held out their hands. With finger and thumb the boys carefully offered coarse barley bread crusts – wary in case they received a nip from sharp teeth for their generosity. But the animals were particular in taking their meal, balancing themselves on their hind-legs to reach up and take the food between their jaws. They then rolled onto their backs and holding the crust with their front paws began to nibble and swallow. It was clear they had done this many times before. The otters were not frightened of the boys nor the adults who sat close to them.

Berengar and Ula watched with delight to see how well their son Herne behaved towards the creature. He was not yet five summers old and was already using the respect that was necessary to please the River God. Normally these two animals would be amongst the skinned and cooking over their fires after a courtesy prayer to the god but these were kept as pets by Herne's Orsook friend, O-ta-ke-re. There were many habits and customs kept by the Orsook that marked them out as being different and keeping animals from the lakes and forests as pets was just one of them. They particularly liked otters for their cleverness and the birds from the forest for their song. But the birds were never caged. It was enough for an Orsook, child or adult, to go to a particular tree and whistle through the lips. If a bird was there it would alight, wings flapping, onto his or her shoulders.

"I am pleased that Herne has found such a good friend – someone he can learn from," said Berengar.

"Not so long ago these words would have choked in your throat before you could utter them. How you have changed," replied Ula, amused. Hastily, on seeing her husband's stern expression, she added, "For the better, I mean."

Berengar thought for a moment. "You are right, Ula, I used to detest the Orsook when I lived in Europa but that was before I came into Penlac and got to know them. Now I begin to understand their customs, the way they live their lives, the close

relationship they have with their natural Lakeland surroundings
….” He drifted off as if in a dreamy state, “the experience has
been truly wonderful …. And it has taught me ….” His voice had
been getting lower so that Ula began to lean nearer to catch his
words. He suddenly snapped out of his pretended trance and
clapped his hands around her shoulders, shouting loudly, “that
they’re just as bad as we are!” His wife shrieked, startling the
otters and the young lads. Berengar let out a huge guffaw to which
his wife immediately responded by punching him on the arm. It
was all good mature fun though; Berengar ended by hugging Ula,
adding a kiss on the cheek, while she mumbled, “You fool,
Berengar.”

Herne and his friend, O-ta-ke-re, returned to playing with their
pets after glancing in the adults’ direction to see that nothing was
amiss.

Still in his arms, Ula said after moments had passed, “No,
seriously Berengar, what do you think about the Orsook now?”

“They are a people at peace with themselves and respect the
place they inhabit. That is much better than what has been
achieved by the tribes living in Europa and indeed, here in Briton.
But even so, some are good, some bad. It is just that the way they
cooperate and help each other in their society determines that the
wiser individuals are more numerous than the bad. If I were to
judge them as a people I would determine my thinking on that,
rather than to assume they were morally better because we
persecuted them. Yes, we must make up for what we have done
through practical measures but it is for the children of the
persecuted and the persecutors to form a new relationship with
each other, not one based on a savagery committed in the past.”
He was looking at Herne and O-ta-ke-re as he said this.

“But it’s not just in the past, is it?” said Ula, quite bitterly.
“Our yearning for peace is to be destroyed again. Do we never
learn? What has been done in Europa will be repeated here in
Briton, if Formus gets his way. For human beings the self-
destructive cycle repeats itself. It is a wonder that the Orsook
accepted us here in their settlement, knowing us as they do.”

“They understand life as it is, not as it should be. So their plan
is to work with it, accept that Formus is on his way and prepare
for what may come. We might support that preparation.”

“More war?”

Berengar kissed her on her forehead and squeezed her protectively in his arms. "If it comes to that, yes. But you have your own warrior to protect you and little Herne."

"After all we have said, though, Berengar, about human beings repeating their mistakes. Is there no other way – a peaceful one, without lives being lost?"

"I am a warrior, Ula. It takes people far cleverer than me to avoid wars, or once started to bring them to an end. Perhaps Faramund might know." The last comment was added with a smile. "But then, he is not here with us and has gone south," – an ironic hesitation – "to attack a king."

The two boys continued to play. Their otters had run off and O-ta-ke-re was amusing his younger friend by dipping his head into the lake-water up to his neck, producing gurgle noises and bubbles as if drowning and adding to the show by flapping his arms. Of course, he could never drown and Herne laughed loudly. Soon they tired of that, drifting back to the adults.

O-ta-ke-re's thick bluish-green hair shone like sea-weed in the spring sun and he gave his head a dog-shake to dry it. They were both healthy and excited as children should look. Berengar observed his own son and decided that he must start him on his military training. It was almost never too early for that. In the Sequani village Berengar had come from, boys were trained to fight each other with sword sticks from the age of six onwards and they began to develop accuracy with the bow by hunting hares through the forest. He would be neglecting his duty, if he did not start this soon with his son.

A shadow passed over Herne's face. "Father, people in Penlac think that there are bad people about to come to us and they intend harm. They say that these people are from the same place as we come from, Europa, and they are led by a man called Formus. Is it true?"

"Herne," said Berengar gravely. "There are many bad things that can happen in this life but many good things too. You have, in your own short time in this world, travelled far and seen much. Don't waste your present time in fear for what may not happen."

"I've been told that the whole settlement – everybody in Penlac – is to move out," added O-ta-ke-re.

"And where," said Berengar, astonished, "did you learn that?"

"From my parents and they got it from the Water-Sidhe."

Berengar stood up. A kind of anger was upon him. "If there is a single fact recognised by everyone," he said, to no one in particular, "it is that a running hare will collect predators." He bent down, picked up his sheathed sword lying in the grass and rebuckled it around his waist. Turning to Ula he said, "I am going to Tyracides. Surely, we have enough people in this settlement, Telemachons and Orsook together, to stop Formus."

Ula knew better than to try and prevent him but O-ta-ke-re spoke up, "When the Water-Sidhe decides, we must do as she wishes."

With Berengar's gaze fiercely on him, the Orsook boy suddenly felt he had made a mistake and backed away as the Celt strode off.

Soon afterwards, Berengar found Tyracides in the dwelling that had been allocated him by the Orsook, a house on stilts above the lake. Inside the main room Tyracides was surrounded by his chief officers. They included those preferred by Telemachus – Eucleides, Agenor and Thocero – and those particularly favoured by himself – Pelisteus and Kleptomenes. Also, there was the Water-Sidhe's son, Su-Lance-du-Lac.

"Ah, welcome, Berengar," said Tyracides on first seeing him. "Perhaps you can help to convince my honoured friend here, Su-Lance-du-Lac, that to abandon Penlac would not be the best way to stop Formus coming after them – and us. It would, in fact, only serve to encourage him."

It was a relief for Berengar that Tyracides and the others held the same view as himself. Yet, by the stubborn look on the Orsook's face, it appeared that this stance was the losing one. He did not go to it at once – another opponent would probably cause the Water-Mother's son to leave so he tried to make the approach obliquely.

"Sire," he said, addressing Tyracides, "how much time do we actually have before Formus' arrival?"

"Two days, perhaps."

"That might seem a short time," mused Berengar, "but a lot could be prepared if we all worked together."

"You mean, if we all worked and stayed?" said Su-Lance-du-Lac. "That, I'm afraid, my friends, is not going to happen. We know how this man, Formus, hates us. If we lost a battle with him, there would be no mercy given: it would be the end of the Orsook, both here in Briton and in the known civilised world. I and my mother have heard what he did in the land of the Helveti from the mouths of those who experienced it directly and lived to tell.

"What?" exclaimed Berengar. "You have those European Orsook living with you here?" He was slightly stunned, remembering his dead cousin.

"Only two survived but yes, they are with us. Why? What do you want from them?"

"Nothing…. only, you must have learned from them that the only way to protect yourselves from a man like Formus is not to run but to stay and fight."

"You could not have heard me," persevered the Water-Sidhe's son, "I said that if we died, that would be the end of our race. We have a greater duty to keep than even upholding our honour. That duty is to our next generation: our unborn children and grandchildren. The Water-Mother has spoken and who better than her to decide?"

Berengar had no answer. If he had been an Orsook, he might have made the same choice. But then, he and Tyracides together with the others who had come to Penlac recently were in a parallel, if not matched situation in that they all faced Formus together.

It seemed that Su-Lance-du-Lac realised this too because he relented somewhat in what he said next. "Look, my friends, if you want to stay to repel Formus here, perhaps I can give you more than just comforting words. If I speak to the younger Orsook – those strong and fit enough for fighting alongside you – they might express a wish to stay. In which case, the Water-Sidhe and I would not object."

"Thanks for that, Su-Lance-du-Lac," spoke Tyracides quickly. But where will you and the rest of your people go?"

"Once more we will attempt to disappear into the river and woodland," answered the Orsook, "far away from warring Celts. I think you must understand if we do not say where we will be going."

"That would be best," affirmed Tyracides carefully.

The next day revealed a shock. While the Telemachons and the Celtic villagers from Monithcound slept, the Orsook had left. They took very few belongings with them. It was as if they had never existed. But for one thing.

Going down to the lake's edge, Tyracides, Eucleides and Berengar found a number of Orsook, some fifteen men and five women, sitting on the rocks there. When Tyracides asked where his people had gone, a young Orsook pointed wordlessly out to the massive shining surface glittering under the early morning sun.

"Into the water?"

He nodded.

Tyracides scanned the eerily placid water, gently rippled and reflective. There was no clue that all those men, women and children had gone into it: no anomalous silhouettes moving beneath its line, no bubble tracks. Their absence was absolute.

A questioning look appeared on Tyracides' face as he turned back to the Orsook, who had not yet spoken.

"Why are we still here?" suggested the Orsook in a clear enough voice, less bubblesome than his fellows. It was Tyracides' turn to nod. "We are to maintain Orsook honour and fight alongside you, if need be." He extended a hand in friendship and Tyracides took it. "My name is Ol-du-Brec. We may be few in number but our advantage is that we can use the waterways that go through your enemy's camp, without him knowing."

"While they had been talking at the lakeside, Agenor, Thocero and Pelisteus had joined them. More were coming from the houses on stilts.

Tyracides watched them and as if hit by a sudden realisation, murmured, "Not enough, not enough."

Pelisteus heard and asked, "What do you mean, my friend?"

Tyracides answered, "We have not yet sufficient combatants to face Formus and ensure us victory."

"But you said yesterday, sire, that the best way to stop Formus would be to oppose him and not give way," came Berengar's exasperated voice.

"Only if we could have added the Orsook warriors of Penlac to our force," said Tyracides. "Now it is plainly obvious that they have abandoned their settlement to accompany their women and children to another place." The Orsook looked angry at the remark but Tyracides forestalled him. "Forgive me, Ol-du-Brec, you and the others who stayed have made a brave decision but we have to deal with the reality of circumstances. One hundred Telemachon warriors and twenty Orsook – all as good as they are – together with Monithcoundian women and children, cannot hope to fight an army comprising five hundred trained military soldiers and avoid slaughter. We must think out a new tactic.

"You intend to retreat," said Eucleides, dismissively.

"Tyracides is right," came Agenor's interjection; support from an unexpected quarter. "What is there left to protect except ourselves? This village, Penlac, cannot afford us proper defence – it was the home of a people who could use the lake as their citadel and escape route, as they have done. We must go."

"Formus will arrive tomorrow and we must leave as soon as we can after we have taken a necessary measure."

"What would that be?" asked Berengar.

"There are food stores and clothing in Penlac. Even after we take what we require there will still be plenty left for Formus and his barbarians. We should deny them any material advantage and burn Penlac."

Ol-du-Brec and the other Orsook were clearly not happy about this but they did not argue. However, Pelisteus did speak up. "Won't the smoke from the burning buildings give them a clear signal as to where we are?"

"I think Formus will have more than enough information regarding that from the local inhabitants that he comes across. Formus is not a man for polite and patient questions."

Later, Ol-du-Brec and his companions watched the flames destroy their homes. These buildings had been built and rebuilt in wood and roof-thatch reed for the time it took to grow and die twenty generations from Orsook loins. Now the fire roared like a thousand beasts rampaging through the streets, reducing all that history to black char wrapped by dense, sooted clouds fuming into the sky. "Never, never, never," Ol-du-Brec promised himself as did the others silently around him, "will human beings learn about our Water City at the top of the world."

The smell of Penlac burning, guaranteed its secrecy.

45

The Gorangun Woman

Goreth's Dega nose twitched irritably. He-she could smell a scorching Orsook culture from miles away although that scent evaded human senses. On the other hand, what was not avoidable was the noise outside Lady Andraste's tent which was being caused by some event.

Dega roused herself properly as her mistress called to accompany her outside to see what was going on.

Andraste had already pulled on a yellow silk robe when Dega emerged from behind the screen which separated their sleeping space. "Come Dega, let's discover what all the commotion is about."

They got outside where small groups of soldiers and their camp-followers stared up into the early morning sky. Formus was outside his own tent and had been joined by Artemius. Both were looking up and at that point so did Andraste and Dega.

The blueness seemed to have been rent open by a dirty cloud, perhaps at four miles distance north from themselves. It was shaped into a funnel nearer the ground but its cause was difficult to say as it was particularly obscured by several low-lying hills.

Formus saw the women and called out. "Lady Andraste, please bring your Gorangun maid over here. She might confirm something for us."

The High Druid gave the Gorangun woman a hard stare when she stood before him. "Do you know, Dega, the Lady Andraste has praised you and remarked upon how attentive you are in your duties as a body servant." Andraste hadn't but Formus liked to play. "I take her word for it, of course. I only know that your attention to the duty I have set you as my guide to Penlac seems to be sadly lacking."

"I do my best, Lord," said the old lady, apparent fear in her lined face, "but it is difficult finding the straight track to a place of myth."

"As you seem to have proved. In your case the track that we follow has been exceptionally curved, almost to the point of being circular. And we all know that a perfect circle has no end point. Is that what you have been doing, Dega – leading us all on a circuitous route *without any point*?" While talking, Formus had lifted the sword from his scabbard and on his final three words had tapped the tip of it, once for each word, lightly on her chest just above the heart. More than lightly; the tip pricked and drew blood. The old woman began to breathe heavier, her fright increasing. Mercenaries outside their tents began to forget the burning embers in the sky and looked on with interest: they knew of what Formus was capable.

"My Lord!" gasped Dega, "What causes you to doubt me?"

"Look above your head," said Formus mildly. "We think that the smoky road you see there makes its way down to Penlac – that being the opposite direction to the one which you are leading us." Formus became more menacing. "Dega, what is the point of a guide who is unable to find a destination? In fact, what is the point of you?"

"How do we know that it is Penlac on fire and not some other settlement? I am not saying that it isn't and that I am absolutely correct in where I am leading you but it is best to make sure." Dega's confidence came from somewhere and was rewarded with the sword being lifted slowly away.

"We will find out what is burning over there. It is only a few miles away. If it is not the Orsook settlement then we keep on searching. If it is – all well and good, except perhaps, for you, Dega." He ordered two soldiers to go with the Gorangun. "These men will help you to keep on track. We wouldn't want our guide to get lost, would we?"

The men handled her roughly as they pulled her away. "Don't injure her!" Andraste snapped. "She is my maidservant and I will not have you harm her unless my lord's misgivings turn out to be true." They stood back then and allowed Dega to limp to the horse she was to ride.

The whole camp was roused and tents packed quickly for the march which would have an early pause just a few miles away.

Formus was convinced that the settlement on fire was Penlac and if it was, he would quickly do away with the old Gorangun woman despite any protestations from Andraste. He did not trust Dega and suspected that she had indeed wasted their time. Besides, he had threatened her in front of the men and it would not be wise to show them he was going soft.

*   *   *   *

Why is it that humans think they can treat the weak and the vulnerable as they do? In what dark space is humanity, in what part of their seed, their plant of human stock, lies this desire to pollute and obliterate? They view us, the Orsook, as the animal because our features resemble those of our underwater brothers and sisters. Calling themselves 'civilised', all their effort is turned to warfare and killing for killing's sake. It is a real pleasure for them and what is the only outcome? An end to their species. We kill only when we have to – to eat – and then we only take simple shellfish and the nutritious plants grown in healthy soil and riverbed. Humanity has taken the worst in animal nature and made it monstrous.

They think they are safe. Safe in the endless human feet pressing into this world's soil. Yet, just one disaster could wipe them out: a disease, a fiery rock from the sky and if any survived that cataclysm those last humans would finish by eating each other. The great world deity will laugh and breathe her relief. In less than no time at all any trace of the human occupation would vanish and we, the Orsook, will live happily again.

They think they are safe? The world and we, the Orsook, will bide our time. Those two who ride either side and keep me guarded – they have no realisation that theirs is a most dangerous situation. To them, I am just an old Gorangun woman with a false leg. Someone to be bullied, tortured and killed. Power lies in the unlikeliest places. That will be their potent realisation.

Formus has allowed us to lead the way. I am, after all, his guide. We are getting ever closer to Penlac. In just a little distance we will be through the trees, over the green hill and before Penlac, now reduced to blackened charcoal piles against the shimmering lake.

We have turned a corner on the path and are out of sight of the others. Now is the time. I bend low to my horse's ear and whisper.

It pauses. Understands. Then whinnying, raises itself on two back legs and paws the air. I fall to the ground and it races off.

A guard dismounts; strides to me. "Get up, old woman!" he snarls. He would prefer to kick me rather than help, but I hold out a hand. He reaches to haul me roughly to my feet. And grasps my hand.

A tremor passes through me. My face, in front of his, rolls like a breaking wave and my true image is restored. The guard sees it. In the last brief moment his existence is fear. It delights me.

*   *   *   *

"Where has the Gorangun woman gone?" said Artemius as he rode along with Formus and Andraste. They had come up to a turning in the track, rounding it. Although Dega and her guards had been riding along a little way ahead, they were nowhere to be seen.

"There's another turning further on, perhaps they are just beyond that," said Andraste.

Formus did not say a word in response but suddenly spurred his horse to go faster up the track. The others, after a moment, did the same. All three rounded the next corner almost simultaneously and then brought their mounts to an abrupt halt, horrified by what greeted them.

Two bodies were hanging from the trees. Thick, woody stems wound about their necks and tongues protruded from open mouths. This was not the only similarity. Each corpse – for it was evident that was what they were – had one arm outstretched as if pushing something away and the hand at the end of the arm was balled and blackened. Of Dega there was no sign.

"What sorcery is this?" exclaimed Artemius.

"The power that destroyed these men was not conjured by some old, crippled woman," decided Formus. "It came from whatever inhabited her shape. Guards!" Two men on horses hurried their beasts up to him. "Go with ten others and comb the area for the creature that has done this." He regarded the lowering sun. "Search until near dusk then ride on after us to Penlac. Whether you have found anything or not, we will have encamped there."

The cavaliers disappeared and Formus pushed his army on to reach the deserted, burnt Orsook settlement. All flames had died out by the time they came to the settlement's periphery. There was nothing left.

They soon discovered the cause for the fire.

"It appears the place has been deliberately set alight to spoil our foraging," said Artemius to Formus, both surveying the blackened remnants. All the stilted houses had collapsed into the waters beneath them. Those few structures that had been half-built with stone on land were now carbon filled husks still smoky topped and hot. "There is nothing to suggest a struggle with attackers. But there is one curious feature."

"Yes?" said Formus.

"From some of the houses and other buildings on the land, there are tracks made by many feet leading down to the water's edge. Yet none seem to return."

"Not so strange if you consider that the Orsook can live underwater. It would be their quickest, most natural method for escape. So they set fire to Penlac and went down to the lake."

"Perhaps not. Well, not the deliberate arson anyway. There are other tracks which show a smaller group was responsible for that. It seems that these did not escape by water."

"Where do they lead?"

Artemius gestured to the wooded area fringing the water and which expanded into a green density, north.

"They are using tree cover and go that way."

Formus stared first at the lake and then the forest. "Well, we have no boats nor the time to spare to build them. The people we follow are the Telemachons: it is they who desecrated our First King's tomb. Yet. I am inclined to believe that this division between lake and forest, Orsook and Telemachon, is just another trick, giving us the impression that they have gone their separate ways. Telemachus led his warriors here for a purpose and I mean to discover what it is."

Lady Andraste rode up as he finished speaking and almost to herself, spoke aloud, "This land is a green and fertile one with fresh water in plenty. Might it not be a reasonable place to take now that the Orsook have gone?"

"Study the view closely and add a touch of perception to this green and pleasant land, My Lady," said Formus with a touch of scorn.

Despite herself Andraste did just that. She saw the army behind them. The majority on foot, their officers mounted, they ranged in age from sixteen to sixty. Many were young men, some, like the veterans, were already battle-scarred. All had a common look in their eyes – a gaze made from fight fury and hunger but not a hunger for food. It was a gut pang for gold …. And something else. She saw the camp followers and their covered carts behind the main body of men; some even resembled men. Each day for them was a battle. She shuddered to think. What money the men had, a good portion was spent on them. It was desperation to dwell on what would happen to her and her female retinue without Formus' protection. It would be all the worse for their resentment of her power to command them. That command only lent by the High Druid's presence.

Her gaze averted from the army but it only fell on the burnt skeleton that had been Penlac. From the body of the hungry army behind her to the famished destruction before was the half-circuit for a vicious round that was a natural geometric progression. This settlement had not been burnt by their own hands but this army was the inevitable motive for it.

She felt gloomy.

Formus nodded with approval. "You almost grasp at this moment, Lady Andraste, what we truly want." She gave him a sharp look. He laughed. "My men are warriors not farmers. They must have men to plough the land for them and produce the food for their bellies, clothes for their backs. Oh, and when need be, rob those men's homes for money and women. For the present, that is what they must have."

"And what is it you must have, Formus?"

"Me? That is easy. I must have command over my men. More than that, I must possess a land filled with farmers – not the empty country you witness here with one burnt settlement and an uncleared forest. By the way, you must have spoken to your Gorangun woman – when she was around – about Penlac and its countryside. Did she give you the name of that forest?"

Andraste's attention turned to where the Telemachons had gone. "Yes, she referred to it as the Forest of the Bracken Ones." Before Formus could interrupt, she continued. "It is a great forest that extends all the way from here and swallows mountains and sea cliffs in its march up to a land of lakes much further north. In some part of that wooded area, Dega told me, there is rumoured to be chasms and entrances to the underworld that are all difficult to uncover and have been placed there by the gods since the creation of the world. In the past, some Goranguns and Celts have gone into that forest, trying to get to the other side. They have never come back. Another part of the forest is taken up with a river network on which, along its tributaries, can be found enormous dams made with tree branches, rotting leaves and mud. The Bracken People live there. Some say they walk on two legs and communicate with words, like real human beings."

"Perhaps those vanished Goranguns enjoyed the chambers and Bracken creatures so much they didn't want to go back," said Formus with a surprising attempt at humour. "If I had been such an adventurous Gorangun, I don't think I would have happily returned to my hairy village."

It was Artemius who returned to more serious matters. "Sire, am I to order our men to pursue the Telemachons into the forest?"

"We will wait for the dozen I sent to search for Dega first. Bivouac here and we will renew the pursuit tomorrow."

Dusk came and went without any return of the search party and the next morning it was feared that the men had got lost or worse. Formus ordered his men to pack up and strike out into the Forest of the Bracken Ones. The camp followers had to find another way.

46
A Return

It was at dusk, the night before, that the Telemachons were rejoined by someone they had feared was lost to them.

In a large clearing, Telemachons, Monithcoundian women and children and the twenty Orsook had set their small camp fires going to provide heat for food and light.

Eucleides was sitting along with Tyracides, Berengar, Agenor, Melissa, Belisama, Pelisteus, Hebe and several others, including two Orsook. Talking between torn mouthfuls of torn cooked pigeon, he was referring very deliberately to Telemachus. No matter how much it might annoy Tyracides, Eucleides intended to keep his memory alive and vital in the minds of the Telemachons, despite his absence. The Orsook remained quiet and just listened. It was noticeable that as a group they did not isolate themselves but were courteous and sociable. Tonight, they had scattered themselves around the different campfires.

"I have no doubt," said Eucleides, waving a pigeon bone in the air, "that Telemachus has somehow managed to rid himself of that witch Helladore's curse, become a man again and is on his way back to us as I speak."

"Will you accept me instead, for now?"

The bubbled question, that voice so easily recognisable, shook everyone to their roots. Berengar sprang to his feet with a broad smile and everyone began to rise.

Into the cast firelight walked Goreth.

If the surprise registered by the Telemachons was marked, far stranger was that displayed by the Orsook. One of them sitting at the campfire was Ol-du-Brec. As soon as he saw Goreth a look of wonder came over his face and he uttered a strange whistle: it was a call. On hearing it, all the other Orsook around the encampment stood up as if one person. For brief moments they were still, then they moved to Ol-du-Brec. He might have made the call but it was Goreth, standing illuminated and clearly defined against the fire, who drew them.

"Welcome indeed!" said Berengar. "Where have you been, Goreth? We thought you had returned to the water."

"Not so soon," answered Goreth, "there is much to be done before then. But as to where I have been Berengar, well that might be a help to all of us collected here."

"We are all glad to see you, Goreth," said Eucleides, throwing his pigeon bone into the fire and wiping his mouth. "What help can you offer us – is there any news about Telemachus?"

"Before he could reply, Ol-du-Brec broke in with an almost reproachful tone in his voice, "Yes, and where is the help for us, Danu?"

At the mention of the river god's name, a murmur rose from the Orsook standing there. A strange, trilling sound as if it had been produced by a flock of river-wading birds suddenly disturbed and taking to the skies. It was followed by an equally startled response amongst the Telemachons in the form of a quick burst of chatter. It died out as they sensed Goreth waiting for quiet. But it was Ol-du-Brec who spoke again.

"Will we have to suffer what our brothers and sisters have already endured in Europa? Where was your protection then? Already our people are on the move, having burnt their own homes to the ground. It is the same man, this Formus, who wreaks his hatred upon the Orsook. He will not be satisfied until we are all dead. So I ask you what can you do to prevent that, seeing how you could not prevent it in your own land?"

Goreth did not look angry at the challenge, he could not but accept it. "Ol-du-Brec, there is a force acting upon the river that even I cannot withstand. We have to allow the fate that rains down upon us from the skies and work with it, to our benefit. I have been into the camp of this druid, Formus; I know the man but he did not know me. I was disguised. For some time I was able to keep him from Penlac to give you the chance to escape but now he follows us. It is always assumed that between a pursuer and the pursued, the latter is in the weakest position. Not necessarily so. The hunted have their advantage and that lies in their ability to lead. The question we should be asking ourselves is: where do we take our enemy?"

"There is only one place, if we are to get anywhere and that is through the forest. It will make our pursuer's task more difficult," said Berengar.

"The Forest of the Bracken Ones contains its own risks," said Ol-du-Brec and he described the inhabitants of that vast tree covered region and the underground chambers that burrowed beneath. "Are you willing to take the women and children of Monithcound through that?" He had begun by speaking to Berengar but had now turned to Tyracides for a response.

Tyracides said, "First, what do you say yourself, Berengar?"

"My own wife and child travel with me. They will go where I lead and I will protect them," said the Celt. "The Monithcoundian women and their children are safe with us."

"I agree," said Tyracides, directing his response at Ol-du-Brec. "Whatever is in that forest is just as much a danger to Formus as to us. We have no choice but to go through it."

Ol-du-Brec did not mean to argue. He wanted to get his own companions to the Water City and what was being suggested would achieve that goal sooner rather than later. Besides that, he had been given an express instruction by Su-Lance-du-Lac to support the Telemachons in their journey to a new homeland in the north. One that would be as far away from the Orsook's ancient city as it was possible to be. He wondered how far along the route the Water-Mother and the others had got. They too would be making their way through the forest. But they would be using the River Fusion: along, perhaps, the longest river in the land with its powerful, fast-moving current. The Orsook would be quickly conveyed through that dark region and the Bracken creatures were not a problem. Once they had reached the forest's boundary, it was only a short distance from there to Water City. Considering it, Ol-du-Brec realised that it was the best access for the Telemachons into that area and raised the point.

"If we are to use the Forest of the Bracken Ones then it would be best to travel along the River Fusion. Only a short way. Many generations ago the trees either side of that water channel were cleared for a great distance and kept clear. It will help to speed our journey but to evade Formus we will have to break away and use other, smaller rivers to navigate our traverse."

"You and your people know this land better than any of us," said Eucleides. "We will follow your advice, naturally."

"Thanks, I hope to provide more help than a trail guide would for your journey to a new homeland." Goreth looked around at all the Orsook fixedly staring at him. "It seems that I must take the opportunity to renew my acquaintance with old friends. Will you excuse me?"

"Surely," replied Eucleides and watched as Goreth walked to another campfire where there were more Orsook than people sat around it. Like leaves lifting in a breeze, the Orsook who had stood, were compelled to the same place and began to sit down. The few Telemachons and Monithcoundians at that place moved elsewhere, unasked.

"Do you trust him?" said Tyracides to Eucleides when Goreth was safely out of earshot.

"He has been a friend to us up to now but how can anyone have complete faith in someone or something they do not understand? Goreth once shook Berengar's hand to end a fight, remember, and our Keltoi friend survived to recount the experience. He knows Goreth." Berengar, standing close by, heard the remark.

"Goreth is an ally to us but as to friendship – well, that can only be proven over time. His real concern is with his own people." Some of those listening – Agenor, Melissa, Hebe, Belisama and Pelisteus – were quite surprised by this judgement; they had assumed that both Berengar and Goreth had formed a close bond.

"Yet it appears that his own kind do not completely trust him. Ol-du-Brec is more than doubtful," observed Pelisteus.

"Maybe that is why Goreth is joining them now: to offer some reassurance," said Belisama.

"We could all do with that," Melissa responded.

"We can get it by putting a wide space between ourselves and Formus for the time being," said Tyracides firmly. "Agenor, in fifteen minutes time give instructions around the camp to retire for tonight and to be ready to move at sunrise tomorrow."

While Tyracides was giving that order, Goreth found himself opposite Ol-du-Brec, the sparks from the fire between them snapping and biting. All around the central light the eyes of the Orsook were upon him, glimmering, watching, waiting.

"How does one converse with a god?" said Ol-du-Brec.

"Without fear – but with honesty," replied Goreth. "As you, yourself have already done."

"It does not seem to get any clear answers."

"We are so used to giving them through oracles and you know how riddle-some they can be," observed Goreth, the corners of his mouth twitching. "When we step onto the earth we must use animal speech and be plain. So try me."

Ol-du-Brec drew back from the fire's heat and considered. "We may not talk as freely as we would wish, surrounded as we are by human beings and having to keep our voices low."

"Do not trouble yourselves with that. Regard that fair-bearded Celt sitting closest to us. In a moment, he will touch his ear."

The young man to whom he referred felt something buzzing and fluttering at the side of his head. He lifted a hand to his ear but whatever had been there was gone. His attention was taken by the Orsook at the nearest campfire. They were all looking at him but then went back to talking amongst themselves or at least two did, with the others listening. Normally, they spoke the Celtic language with that bubbling sound intermingling with it. Now, as hard as he listened he could hear nothing of the Celtic words since they were drowned out by the bubbling and yet another trilling sound capping it.

"I have sent something to dance in his head and it will jump from his to the others. He will be the only one to sense the spell which will continue to dance in all their heads with a lighter touch. You can say whatever you like. They will not understand."

Ol-du-Brec was certain about the truth of it, just as he and the others did not have any doubts about Goreth's identity. The news of his coming arrived at Penlac before the Telemachons. But Ol-du-Brec was not an Orsook who could be easily awed.

"I would have thought the Great River Danu provided a home for your being. It is the waterway that binds Europa together. Surely without you, its existence is threatened?"

"Not threatened as long as I exist," answered Goreth. "There are many great rivers in the world. You have one here; it runs through the Forest of the Bracken Ones."

"The Fusion," came a voice from around the fire.

"The River Fusion," affirmed Goreth. "It is the main artery leading to the heart of the north and will form an important part of our new homeland.

"The Telemachons also desire a new land for themselves. The north is going to be a crowded place." This new voice came from a female Orsook sitting at the fire. She was still young and had seen fifty summers come and go. The Orsook generally lived longer than their human counterparts and for them one hundred and thirty years was not an uncommon age to live to. Their bodies tended to deteriorate in the last five years and when death came their remains were burnt so the ashes could be offered at sea, or lake or rushing river. This Orsook woman had striking silver-grey hair that hung untied and low to her waist.

"What is your name?" asked Goreth.

"Chanson-du-Lac," she replied.

"You are the Water-Mother's daughter?"

"Yes," said the woman, unsurprised that Goreth knew.

"You have raised an important point, Chanson-du-Lac. We travel alongside the Telemachons. They are greedy for land. I have talked to their leader, Telemachus. He has told me how it is that his warriors found themselves on the Danu travelling through Celtic lands." Goreth paused, carefully surveying the upturned faces around the fire. "It was not necessity that drove them – they could have remained in a country called Magna Graeca where Telemachus' father had won mighty victories against their enemies. Instead they chose another course – one of plunder and fame. We look upon the Celts as our foe. This is only reasonable when the evidence for their persecution and destruction of our people in Europa is there for all to see. However, now we must recognise the common factor shared by all who oppose us. They are human beings. The friendship they pretend to have for us at this moment will not last. The Celts destroyed us in Europa and pursue us to extinction here in Briton. Already, you have been chased from your homes in Penlac. Alongside the Telemachons we march northwards – they stride into the unknown; you return to your city of origin here in Briton, the Water City. The Telemachons must never learn the whereabouts of that place."

"Do you believe that we would be stupid enough to tell them?" broke in Ol-du-Brec, irritation clear in his voice.

"What I am saying is that our attitude towards all human beings must change. Formerly the Orsook have been peaceful, attempting to live alongside the other creatures of this world in agreement and for the benefit of all. That worked well with our brother and sister species in the rivers and forests but has been disastrous in relation to the human race. We must change, otherwise we will not survive. Our settlements were invaded by the Sequani in Europa and your own friendly support for the Telemachons resulted in you, yourselves, putting Penlac to the fire. Henceforth, we must treat the Telemachons as our enemies."

"With your power, my lord," said Chanson-du-Lac, "why don't you sweep these Telemachons from the earth with the same force as the rivers break their banks under the tumultuous rain?"

"And as you did with the Sequani," added Ol-du-Brec sarcastically.

"There is a force greater than mine and it prevents me from intruding into the affairs of human beings in that way. Man and Woman are responsible for their own good, their own evil. I can only give choices. As to these Telemachons and Celts – I have already offered them a choice. It is up to them which one they make."

"What choice was that?" asked Ol-du-Brec, interested despite himself.

"I have given them seed for the Plant of Infinite Want. The crop from this plant may satiate their hunger and health for centuries into the future or in their hands it may work as viral human greed and annihilate their race. Considering the record left at this present time by human history, I advised them to destroy the seed."

"Better, perhaps, that they use it," said Chanson-du-Lac.

"The problem there," continued Goreth, "is that we all suffer in some way – the earth, rivers, lakes, animals and Orsook that drink natural water. Although humans will receive the greatest impact, we will not remain unaffected."

"Who carries the seed?" said Ol-du-Brec suddenly.

"There is no point in me telling you that." There was a sternness in Goreth's tone. "It would only end in theft or murder. You, Ol-du-Brec, with your followers must carry out that order laid upon you by the Water Sidhe and keep the Telemachons from discovering the Water City."

Ol-du-Brec was about to speak but then decided against it. The fact that he did not contradict Goreth's assertion about the Water Sidhe's order made clear that it was the truth.

Chanson-du-Lac observed Ol-du-Brec's rudeness with regret. He meant well and had served her mother loyally but was far too blunt. She would have to speak to him in private. Publicly, he commanded their small group but the Orsook who comprised it were thoroughly aware of who wielded the real authority amongst them. She was the only daughter to the Water Sidhe after all and despite her brother being older, as a woman the right to rule over Penlac would pass to herself. Penlac, of course, had been reduced to smoking black carbon but the Orsook who had lived in that place would still, in some future time, owe their duty to her. In that regard, she might welcome a new friend to her side who could bolster her standing. Chanson-du-Lac stood up and moved to a place near Goreth. The Orsook male who sat there, fiercer and older than the rest, respectfully moved aside.

"Have you come to make amends?" said Goreth with a smile.

"I have come to feel what it is like to sit next to a god."

"Is that what they say I am?" Goreth looked innocent.

"In our Hall For Reflection in Penlac, stood your likeness in wood."

"Which fed the flames," he reminded her.

"Burnt to the ground," Chanson affirmed, "and burned into our memory. It was old but not so old as is the original statue standing under the water jet of Founder's Fountain in Water City. That has been carved from marble. The statue was created by the Lord-of-Water, Orsek, while he ruled the Danu River in Europa. The same Orsek who was claimed as the Celt's first High King. What do they know about their own history?" she scoffed, "We understand it better than they do. When he became aware his life was coming to an end, he commanded his daughter, Sol-ay-sur-Pont, to leave the Danu River and to found a colony here in Briton. She was to take the statue with her."

"He did not have sons," Goreth added. "She was all the stronger for that and Water City is a tribute to its first Water Sidhe."

"And we have learned that to live peacefully with the Celts and other human beings is an impossibility. We will awaken ourselves: the placid lake's reflective surface will give way to a storm stirring fury. What was once peaceful becomes violent. We will defend the City-over-the-water to the last beat of our heart."

"You are not so different to human beings, then."

"If by using violence we can ensure peace for ourselves, no. But wouldn't any animal defend itself in such a way to secure its own survival? Orsook and human beings are species of animal; they cannot seem to rise above that, although the Orsook have tried."

"The Orsook might be closer still to human nature."

"In what way?"

"For instance, the Water Sidhe and her refugees from Penlac, including your own brother, will soon be knocking at the gates of the Water City. How do you think they will be greeted?"

"With concern and the greatest sympathy."

"Really? Has your life been lived with such insularity in Penlac that you know so little about the city that conceived your own settlement?"

Chanson-du-Lac hesitated, unsure. While they had been talking, the other Orsook had begun to chat amongst themselves. Ol-du-Brec, though, did not let his own attention waver from what they were saying. He made himself heard at this juncture. " The Water Sidhe was teaching Chanson-du-Lac to become the community's leader. Chanson had no time for anything else and it would have been too dangerous for her to leave Penlac."

"That is true," admitted Chanson, frowning, "but my brother, Su-Lance-du-Lac, did make more than one visit to the Water City."

"Any leader," remarked Goreth, "must be wise to the event taking place beyond the confines of his or her rule. That is worth some risk and your mother might have extended your education by sending you, rather than your brother. What did he tell you when he returned?"

"His task was to extend trading links between the City and our settlement. On his return, he was full of news about what he had achieved."

"You learned nothing about how the centre of the Orsook civilisation in this country is ruled?"

"Yes. He said the government was strong and the citizens were happy."

"Little enough. First, I may have been glib in describing the Orsook as taking on human characteristics. As you say, they will use violence to defend their homes and lives if they feel threatened, just as the human creatures do. But unlike human beings, individually, an Orsook will not kill another Orsook to exert his or her power over them for the sake of maintaining authority. Leadership is only granted by consent, not force. This is a principle acknowledged and kept to by every one of the water people.

"Yet, there is a yet," guessed Chanson-du-Lac.

"Yes – that is so," replied Goreth. "There has come to prominence amongst those assigned to govern in the city a certain Water Lord."

"A Lord?" interrupted the female Orsook, "I was never told this. It has been a custom, ever since the first Water Sidhe came to this land, that the right to rule would be passed only to a female Orsook chosen from amongst others by all Orsook citizens. That practice had been maintained in Penlac – are you telling me that it no longer applies to Water City?"

"Yes."

The Water Sidhe's daughter was visibly astonished as was Ol-du-Brec.

"But how did this come about?" said the latter.

"Fear bred instability. The Orsook in the city had learned of the fate met by their fellow beings in Europa. They wanted a change in approach to the human race that had persecuted them for so long."

"In Briton, we have not experienced such," said Ol-du-Brec.

"No," said Goreth, "but the High Druid Formus who chases after the Telemachons and is the reason why you are here – his real intention is not to capture the Telemachons but to hunt down and eradicate the Orsook."

At this moment, Chanson-du-Lac was more concerned with her mother. "You seemed to suggest earlier, Lord Danu, that the Water Sidhe and the others from Penlac would not be welcomed to the city. Has this Water Lord any bearing on that?"

"He cannot be seen to do anything less than to take them in, but your mother should be wary. She represents the old order and he the new. He has the support of the majority who live in the city and they trust him because he governs by consensus. There is unanimity there that should not be disturbed, particularly at this time when we face the greatest threat in our history. This is no time for division."

"My mother has just lost her home, as have those going with her. I don't think she will arrive in the Water-City only to immediately sow discord. What would be the point of that?"

"She has been used to the position of highest authority in Penlac – it may not be easy to feel herself treated otherwise by the Orsook in the Water City and their lord."

"I feel sure she will sacrifice her own ego a little to serve the greater interests of the Orsook people."

"Let us hope so."

"Goreth." The calling of the name the Telemachons knew him by was a surprise. There stood Agenor, who had come up softly. He too seemed rattled. On his approach he had heard the Orsook communicating with strange twittering sounds that he found indecipherable. When he stopped and found Goreth staring at him, there came an irritating feathery flap of wings near his head. He touched his ear and when Goreth spoke again he could make out every word as it was said, clearly, in Celtic speech.

"Agenor," said Goreth, mildly.

"Tyracides wishes you to know that we are all to start marching through the Forest of the Bracken Ones at sunrise tomorrow. He needs you to be ready."

"We will be."

47
The Calling

It was not unusual for Eris to be in Conversevitae's potion room. If Faramund was to be found anywhere in what was now Byncor's palace in Overblown, it would be here by the old necromancer's side, amongst the books, the bubbling liquids and the pungent burning odours of transformational magic. So Eris came here quite often to collect Faramund. Sometimes she left with him to return to their personal rooms on the ground level and at other times she did not. He would be too taken by a particular experiment or engrossed in discussion over a magical theory with his mentor to disrupt his learning and leave. She never complained; his excitement with the knowledge and practice he was gaining was obvious and besides, he reciprocated by not restricting her in any way. It was unusual however, for Eris to be in the wizard's chamber without Faramund being present.

She had come to find her husband at the set hour only to be told by Conversevitae that he was at the ironworkers' foundry in the city and would be gone for at least two hours. Eris had made to go but the wizard stopped her with a few words.

"Don't rush off just yet, my lady – not without some hot refreshment anyway. Would you like some mint juice?"

As it happened, Eris was feeling thirsty. It was a warm day she had spent in the courtyard practising her archery skills and the offer was welcome. She said so and Conversevitae set himself to preparing her drink.

"Faramund is easily the most talented apprentice I have ever had." He laughed raspingly. "In fact, he is the only apprentice I've had. But I would work with no other. I could see his enthusiasm and abilities straight away."

Eris looked around to find the latest work the two had been engaged in. Conversevitae noticed as he stirred and heated the mint juice.

"Ah, I see you are trying to detect our latest venture. Just view the table in the corner."

Eris diverted her gaze. A small brazier that could be easily held in the hand was piled with burning black charcoal under a covered glass flask containing green liquid. The liquid boiled slowly. A cork bung stoppered the flask but from it came a glass tube which fed into another glass jar and down this tube rolled a black distillate that was liquid and dripped slowly into the second container.

"We require a certain metal deposit from the iron foundry to continue that investigation and also a metal appliance that Faramund was keen to make himself.

"But what is it for?" said Eris.

"Perhaps a new metal will result that is stronger than the iron we have now, perhaps nothing at all. We must seek to find or find nothing at all."

Conversevitae brought the two-handed cup over to Eris. She leaned towards him from where she sat and grasped the other handle. He saw her soft white bosom beneath her linen jerkin and his loins stirred. Eris was an attractive young woman, shapely and strong. Unlike the other ladies of the court, she did not wear long gowns that covered her legs but took to short skirts which gave her more freedom in movement. Her legs were smooth and beautifully formed. These charms had not escaped Conversevitae in the past few months and he wondered how much of his own charm he could exercise over her.

"Do you know, my lady Eris, magic is a fascinating topic and it comes in an infinite variety of forms. Birth, growth and death each have their wondrous changes and it is for us to analyse and recreate them."

"Death is an end to magic, surely?"

"Some say it is the beginning."

"Then they are foolish and cannot think that life is worth the living," said Eris emphatically.

"Yes, that may be so. For the very poorest in our land there has to be hope for a better future even if that change in prospects occurs after their death. It is a question of belief. Those that believe the hardest will scrabble around for any justification to corroborate their view. They distort reality to match the philosophy that exists in their minds. I take a different approach – I change belief with my magic to match with the reality people find themselves in."

"Give me an example," said Eris.

"Well, do you see that needle on my bench?"

"Yes."

"If I poked it into the back of your hand you would feel pain. Your belief is, that it would cause pain."

"Of course."

"And the same would happen if I was to burn you with that flame under the flask."

Eris nodded, unsure where this was going.

"What if I told you," continued Conversevitae, "I could jab you with the needle or burn your flesh with that flame and you would feel nothing? Pain would be eradicated. As a warrior, you would no longer feel it."

"That would be a powerful magic indeed. Yet, I have heard that there are certain plants, if eaten, can achieve the same effect temporarily."

"This would last as long as you wish. There are no potions to be swallowed or solid matter eaten; it will result simply from your own belief. Do you want to see if it is possible?"

Eris knew that she should not, but she wanted to. He, after all, was only an old man and if it came to a trial of strength she thought she could better him.

"Let me assure you," said the old necromancer, seeing her hesitation, "that nothing will happen without your wanting it to and if you wish to stop the magic working, it will do so at once." *The gods of the forest will laugh over that lie and forgive me*, he thought. In most cases he had been successful in the past but there were some who were not susceptible to the influence.

Eris made her mind up. "Alright, Necromancer, cast the spell."

Conversevitae leaned towards her slightly. A slight sweet fragrance came from him, which surprised her but then she thought it might be due to the natural plants he worked with and concoctions he created in his laboratory.

The wizard touched the higher part of his cheek under the left eye and pressed on it to lower his lid a little and widen the eye.

"Eris, I want you to focus on the colour in my eye. Forget about any other distraction, just listen to my voice and follow instructions." Conversevitae had altered the tone in his speech. It was lower, almost melodic. She began to concentrate, hearing his voice describe what she saw. "Green, green, like the green in a vast field or a wide sea. Relax, imagine you are drifting on a small boat on that wide sea, only the waves lapping against the hull.

Green all around. Do you see how it swirls around my black pupil? Now, you too can feel your boat slowly turning around a black centre. A small whirlpool. It is not dangerous, only gentle." And she could sense herself moving, drifting. It was pleasant. She gave herself to the sound of his voice and the colour in his eye magnified so that she was entranced.

Conversevitae studied her expression. The full, red lips, perfectly soft and ripe, were slightly open, lax. The blue eyes blank. But he had to go carefully now, push her under to the most receptive level. "Eris, you feel at peace and very, very safe. You want to stay in that place that your boat has reached and feel the warmth on your face from the sun above. He slowly got up and collecting the needle from the bench together with a clean cloth, returned to his seat in front of her.

"That warmth is now spreading over your body. Can you feel it?"

"Yes," she murmured.

"Good. Your hand is very warm and tingles slightly. Whatever touches your hand, you will not be able to feel. Do you understand?"

Expressionless, blank, she answered, "Yes."

He took her hand and placed it on his leg, palm down. Like her lips, her hand was soft and well-shaped. She did not pull back. He felt the warmth from her touch through the cloth on his leg and it rose up his thigh.

"Did you feel anything?"

"No," came an answer in the same monotone.

He took the sharp needle and jabbed it quickly into the back of her hand.

There was no reaction. No sudden cry. He was satisfied. Almost.

"Or that?"

"No."

Blood welled from the spot where he had pricked her. Taking the cloth and pressing the place firmly, he dabbed until it was staunched.

"Answer me this, Eris, who is the man you have loved most in your life?"

"Faramund," she replied, without pause.

At the sound of his own name, the man hidden behind the column, near to the door, closed his eyes as if in relief and then opened them again. They were hard with anger. Faramund had returned from the iron foundry much earlier than expected to retrieve a tool from the laboratory. Approaching the closed door, he had heard the muffled sound of his wife's voice and was suddenly suspicious. The position of the door in the chamber was such that someone might enter without being detected. It was on an upper level, four steps above the main chamber floor and at an angle so that it was out of sight to anyone in the centre of the main room.

Faramund had crept in and was shocked to discover how close Conversevitae was to Eris. His first thought was to rush at the old man who was completely engrossed in what he was doing. Faramund was a rational man and that part of him wanted to be sure that there was no reasonable explanation for his mentor's strange behaviour. Every word spoken and action taken by the necromancer convinced him otherwise.

Conversevitae continued oblivious to the other man's presence. "Eris, I want you to hear my voice and know that it is Faramund's. It is his loving tone that you sense, strong and comforting. Do you hear me?"

"Yes, I do."

"And is it Faramund's voice that you hear?"

"My lover's, yes."

"You will feel something on your neck now. It is the hand of your lover caressing it." Conversevitae reached out his wrinkled hand to touch the bare smooth neck.

Faramund was ready to leap out and hurl the lecherous old goat to the ground. But that way would end in no positive outcome. Either Conversevitae could die, his head broken on the flagstones or, if not, the guards could be called from the end of the corridor and he would be taken straight to the cells. His work in this underground chamber had been rewarding in many ways. He was not about to give that up.

So, what he did do instead was to retreat quietly to the door and then made a play of shutting it loudly as if he had just entered.

Startled, Conversevitae kept his calm. To Eris, he said very quietly and in the same hypnotic tone he had used beforehand, "Forget everything I said after I asked you if you felt anything. Now, wake up."

She stirred back into a conscious state. The stinging sensation on her hand was there and she regarded it. "You were right, I couldn't feel a thing," she said, wondering.

"What couldn't you feel?" asked Faramund, walking down the steps.

"Forgive me, Faramund," said Conversevitae. "Your wife agreed to a small experiment in eye enchantment to prove if it worked."

"Oh, it works, Eris," said Faramund, not looking at his wife but fixing his stare on the old conjuror, "as I have seen several times before in this chamber." He was finding it difficult to control his anger. "Incidentally, Eris, I think your tunic is in some disarray over your left shoulder." He said this, all the while watching his mentor. Conversevitae did not blink. Eris smoothed the cloth, puzzled as to why Faramund should mention it.

"Have you brought the *aedile funicula* we needed from the foundry?" asked Conversevitae, hoping to move the topic on.

But Faramund was not to be distracted. "I have to go back for it," came his irritated response. "Don't worry about that – it will be done. I want to talk to you about something else, Conversevitae. Our time working together is nearly over. In fact, Eris and myself will be leaving Overblown in three days' time, after I have spoken to Queen Byncor."

"This is all quite sudden, Faramund," said the wizard. "What has prompted it?" Eris eyed her husband. Although it was actually no surprise to Conversevitae, the plan to leave was certainly new to her. Deep down, she welcomed it. Target practice in the palace courtyard was beginning to bore her.

"In fact," replied Faramund, "I have been thinking about this for some time. The working relationship we had was never the same as that between master and apprentice. There was no set date for its termination and it lasted for as long as I felt necessary to develop my skills and knowledge in the alchemical arts."

"Certainly, you have become more proficient in our short time together," admitted Conversevitae, "although it takes many years to master an acumen for releasing the generative forces trapped in this world." *Not so long as that*, thought Faramund. "I always assumed that you would learn what you could to improve your effectiveness in helping others and then return to the Telemachons. What will you tell the Queen?"

"Just that," said Faramund, curtly. "She will understand a wish to return to my people. Not only my desire, but also Eris'." He put a protective arm around his wife and thought, *I will not need Queen Byncor's assistance to do what I have to do.*

Conversevitae accepted what Faramund had told him. Realising the other man's suspicion he had no real fear that the other would start denouncing him before her. What use was that? It would be Faramund's word against his – with Eris unable to back her husband. The Queen would dismiss the charge as no real harm had been committed. He had made a special effort to regain the Queen's trust, since she had always seen him as her father's creature. Something like this if it was ever spoken to her, would finally lose that trust. Faramund and Eris leaving the capital would be best for all concerned.

Overblown had changed since Queen Byncor had become ruler. It was now a much happier place. Faramund saw that as he and Eris picked their way through the narrow, cobbled streets on their tall war-horses. Byncor had made over the beasts to them as soon as Faramund made it known to her that they were leaving. She was grateful for Faramund's support in opposing her father's rule – the spell-binding of Mitshid's forces through sowing the seed from the Plant of Infinite Want and most of all, the assistance he had given to conquering the Windlander disease. Faramund could see the benefit that Byncor's rule gave to the city in riding past the market-place. It had expanded greatly in size and was not the only one within the walls. All kinds of goods were sold ranging from exotic fruits and vegetables to luxury clothes and jewellery. Nothing had to be smuggled in as it had to be previously. The people walking, buying and selling in and around the stalls were as varied in their colour and size as the food that was displayed. Like the goods being sold, they came from every part of Briton and Europa. The noise and bustle cheered the spirits of those who remembered the suppressed and squalid lives that had been lived in the streets under Noremac's rule.

Despite his unhurried pace, Faramund was keen to leave the capital city's gates behind himself and Eris. He had taken an opportunity while Conversevitae was absent from the laboratory, to place his revenge for Eris' treatment where the former king's physician was sure to find it.

Back in the chamber, below ground, Conversevitae had the benefit of a servant to help him sort through any equipment and records that Faramund had left behind. The latter had not taken much with him – just an astrolabe to assess the night stars and a book containing analysis for his most important experiments. He had told Conversevitae to do with the rest as he liked.

The servant, a man, was almost as old as Conversevitae himself and had tended him for many years. "Sire," he remarked, "This cabinet on the bench is locked and there does not appear to be a key nearby. What do you want me to do?"

Conversevitae peered into the recess where the wooden receptacle was tucked. This was the space on the bench at which Faramund mainly worked and often he would extract items from that cabinet to be used in his experiments, experiments that had been highly interesting and beneficial to their work.

The 'lock' to which his manservant was referring consisted of a simple wooden bolt held by a metal padlock. With just a small forcing the bolt could be jemmied and split. Conversevitae handed the other a small, iron poker. "Don't mind the damage, just break it and we'll see what's inside."

The man took the tool from him, inserted the tip between bolt and door and wrenched. There was a cracking sound and with further leverage the bolt fell off and the door swung open.

Out of the cabinet fell the mummified shape of a bat. At least, that is what Conversevitae thought it was. Only, on closer inspection, he discovered that this bat was completely furless, the dried skin grey with tiny fissures – scaled and leathery around the blackened wings. Another difference was in the eyes. They were open. This was not unusual in itself; the wizard had handled many mummified objects in the past, had in fact been engaged in the methods of mummification himself, though not this one. Yet, he had never seen a bat, living or dead, with eyes of white marble in its head. Against the grey and black skin those eyes formed an eerie contrast. They compelled a fascination in the onlooker, a compulsed repulsion. Conversevitae felt this, despite all the macabre sights he had witnessed in his life.

The servant looked towards the alchemist. "Sire, do you want to keep this for your experiments or shall I burn it?"

"Burn it," he said.

But it was not quite enough. Irritated with his own squeamishness, Conversevitae reached out and touched the wing.

Immediately, the creature began to flap its wings. Both master and servant recoiled in shock. The dead had suddenly come to life. What happened next was just as quick as the initial movement.

Rolling over the bench, the fleshy bat dropped onto the floor behind Conversevitae. As soon as it was on the ground, its body began to grow as if inflated. It stood up on its two lower legs like a man raising himself and in brief seconds there was a beast taller and immovably placed between the two men and the door.

The servant grabbed a knife from the bench but before he could use it to any effect, the creature had sunk its fangs into his swinging arm and the poison broke through his bodily defences. He collapsed.

Conversevitae was able to call out for the guards. He just had time to exercise the spell of camouflage. For any ordinary being this would have been a successful ploy. Effectively for human sight, the wizard had disappeared. What had once been a man visible to others became blended with the wall near to the bench.

The creature stilled itself and then slowly turned. At the same time, extending its wings to confine the space, a highly pitched sound reverberated from its mouth. Through its blind eyes the bat could sense, amongst the sound waves bouncing back, a lumpen mass crouched beside the wall. It leaped. In his final conscious act, Conversevitae felt a hot stinking weight drop on him and a flashing pain in his neck. Cocooned in the flesh of another animal, he punched out a final shriek before dying. His spell died with him and visibility returned.

By the time the guards had run into the room, it was all over. They found a strange scene. Both Conversevitae and his servant were lying flat on the floor, the servant with a bloodless knife in his hand. On the neck of the magician, worn like an oversized necklace, was the small corpse of a mummified bat, its eyes open and black.

48
Water City

Having reached the city of their origin, the Water Sidhe and her people were exhausted. It was the continual swimming through lakes and rivers that had drained their energy, with only sporadic halts for rest. Once they had got to the destination though, their spirits revived. Apart from her own son, Su-Lance-du-Lac, very few of those travelling amongst the refugees had ever seen Water-City. It was a magnificent spectacle to which Penlac, in its previously unburnt state, could bear no comparison.

Su-Lance-du-Lac had seen it previously, it was true, but he continued to be thrilled by the city's appearance. In no other part of Briton could there be found such structures which appeared to grow naturally out of the landscape and yet were a distinct element within it. The Celtic settlements were very much low-level in the type of buildings they contained. There were the megalithic monuments of course, but they were reserved for rituals to the gods such as at the Plain of Rebirth and very occasionally to mark the burial of kings or chiefs. They would be positioned away from places where people lived. The highest building structures in the settlements were the defensive walls and the palace or Great Hall where the governing officials lived and worked. Here, in the Water City there were defensive walls preceded by an outlying boundary of jagged rocks packed tightly together and partially buried into the ground to deter attacks by mounted riders.

Above the walls what made an immediate impression were the towers. Not great in size, being three or four storeys in height but they were numerous. Also, there was a curiosity about them. The walls of these buildings were cladded in green-leaved plants and as it was spring, many were in bloom. The effect was extraordinarily colourful. Reds, yellows, pinks, blues and russets shimmered as petals in the breeze. And design had been put into the growing. Some towers were covered in vertical bands, each band a specific colour. Others were striped in horizontal lines of colour. Only the windows in the buildings interrupted the pattern. Su-Lance-du-Lac guessed that beneath the plants the structures were stone-built and ingeniously the Orsook had trained these plants to grow as they did.

In these towers, the Orsook lived and through the middle of their city flowed a broad river that brought the clean, fresh water from the mountains essential to their lives. Arterial canals had been dug from this waterway which branched off between the towers and other buildings. They were in effect the streets and along these, boats carried goods that were sometimes sold direct by the basketful to those who lived in the towers. These baskets were winched up by hook and poles that had been built into the towers for that purpose. The rivers and canals were the features that had given the city its name. The canals were very deep and had been a massive undertaking at the time they were created under the rule of the second Water Sidhe centuries ago. Orsook swam in them for their pleasure and necessity; all goods came into and through the city by them. These artificial waterways were shaped like the slim wings of a gnat or hornet. Leaving the river, a typical canal would run up one street of buildings, loop around the end and come down the other side to rejoin it. Thus, each looped canal would contain within it a row of buildings and serve the need and aesthetic viewpoint for two others. Orsook cleverness in engineering was not only visible at street level in their city but also hidden below it. For one canal was dug lower than the rest and covered over in brick: it conducted Orsook bodily waste to the sea, a short distance away.

Food and other goods were not only sold from the canals but as well at certain points along the river. The two most significant points for this were the internal harbour created around the main city gate which was an initial trading market for some imported goods and then the chief gathering place for Orsook trading and information called *Poblach Cearnagach*, situated in the city centre.

It was to this place that the Orsook from Penlac were first shown. They were in a sorry state after their hard journey and the inhabitants made a great fuss over them, bringing them food and dry clothes. It was a welcome that certainly cheered them. *Yet strange*. That is what the Water Sidhe, Brun-du-Lac, thought as there appeared to be no one in authority there, to greet them. Spontaneous expressions from the crowd surrounding them were made – several individuals sprang onto the public pedestal placed there for giving speeches and did so, voicing their sympathy for those who had endured the destruction of Penlac. But there were no guards to escort them or smiling officials engaging in the usual courtesies. Brun looked for an explanation and spoke to her son, Su-Lance-du-Lac.

"Su, you have met the Water Lord – why is he not here? Or at least someone to show me to him."

"Mother – I have no idea," answered Su, "apart from perhaps that the news of our arrival has just reached him. There is someone coming this way now." Her son indicated and Brun saw that indeed there was an Orsook mounted on a horse, which was unusual in itself, making his way in a leisurely manner towards them. This Orsook was dressed in exceptionally fine clothing: a red, silk, loose-fitting shirt over wide black linen pantaloons. His feet were encased in wooden sandals and he wore a thin hoop of iron around his head while a gold chain decorated his neck. Brun was slightly disconcerted. An Orsook was not given to such luxury, no matter what position he occupied in the community. The Water Sidhe kept to this frugality in her own dress, as did her administrators in what was once Penlac. Her family kept to this principle with an occasional exception when Su-Lance had to be reminded of it.

The rider was old and that could be seen by his hair which fell in long yellow strands to his waist. Unlike human ageing, Orsook hair did not generally become white but changed from its original dark green or silvery grey to a straw colour and the curled ringlets became straightened. He may have been old, but he was still vigorous in his voice and dignified.

"Su-Lance-du-Lac! We meet once again and the City-Over-The-Water welcomes you."

"In very different circumstances, Duke Ote, as you can see," called out Su, "but we are glad to find that fellowship and solidarity amongst the Orsook remain strong and the citizens here are generous. We are grateful."

"This?" said the mounted official, taking note of the many gifts being offered and smiling, "This is the least we can do and much more shall be done," he said firmly.

Su was relieved. Seeing Duke Ote reminded of the time he had spent here – a very pleasant one and much was different to the life he knew in Penlac. There was the luxury for a start. At the assembly of the Water Lord munificence was displayed in the statuary and the furnishings of the Great Hall or in the jewellery on both male and female Orsook. He knew it could not compare to some human settlements he had heard about but for the Orsook to be interested in what was artificially created from the natural environment around them rather than in beauty grown naturally – that was a remarkable change. Su had assumed this had been brought about by the expansion and development of Water City itself. He felt an impatience at his side. "Duke, may I introduce to you my own mother, Brun-du-Lac, who is of course, the Water Sidhe of Penlac?"

"My dear Lady Brun," said the Duke. Hurriedly dismounting, he walked over to her, after tying his horse's rein to a stall. "I am so glad to meet you. It must have been a desperate journey, yet it seems that you have led a good number of your people to safety." He was assessing the crowded pavements around the *cearnagach* occupied by the Orsook from Penlac as they were sitting surrounded by an even greater crowd of citizens from Water City.

"Over one hundred and fifty," responded the Water Sidhe with some pride, "excluding those who went to fight with the Telemachons. We did not lose anyone in coming here."

"Such courage! But there is much to discuss with the Water Lord concerning the Telemachons and the Celt who pursues them. His real intention is to destroy the Orsook. I believe they call him Formus. All that can be dealt with later. The immediate urgency is to accommodate yourself and all of those who survived with you. I don't mean just on a temporary basis. The Water Lord has made provision for your permanent settlement within the City."

Now it was Brun's turn to be impressed. "Already? I did not think you would know about Penlac's destruction until we arrived."

"Oh, we heard much sooner than that," replied Ote. "Our water messengers are very quick. The arrangements for your new homes were completed yesterday. Do you want to hear about them?"

"Why yes, we would very much appreciate it."

The Duke went to a pedestal and climbed the short few steps up to the stone platform. As soon as he got there, a market stall holder, recognising him, took a long horn from behind his trade counter and blew a loud blast on it. The noisy chatter abated in the square. Duke Ote spoke out and his voice could be clearly heard. "My friends, this is such a pleasing sight! Orsook giving badly-needed help to Orsook! We prove today that the lives of our people matter to each and every one of us. The happiness of all is the concern of all." There was light applause. "If our homes were destroyed and our families left in a desperate state, we would want to believe that somewhere in another place we would be offered the chance to start again. Through your concern with the plight of these people from Penlac, you have begun to relieve their utter distress – your generosity is what marks us out as a civilised people attending to the greatest happiness for the many, not the few. We are a big city; our resources are great. Do you believe we should use them for the sake of the many that live here?" The direct question created loud applause amongst his listeners and cries of "Use them, use them!"

"I believe you do," said Duke Ote, smiling. "So do the council and so does the Water Lord who is advised by it. Therefore, we have allocated empty apartments in two home towers to the newcomers. They have now become permanent citizens of Water City!" There was louder applause and Ote stepped down from the podium.

"How can we thank you enough?" said Brun-du-Lac, making herself heard with difficulty, above the noise.

"By being happy here," Ote replied, "and helping us to defend the city in a time of peril and I, for one, believe that is very near. You must tell us all you know about this deplorable human being, Formus, when you and your son come to dine with the Water Lord, myself and a few others. Meanwhile, can you gather your people in readiness for taking up their new homes?"

The Water Sidhe said she could do that and the Duke walked to his horse, mounted it and rode away.

He had not been gone very long when a small group of young male and female Orsook appeared which set about organising the newcomers into their families and then into larger groups according to the tower and which section of that tower the Orsook from Penlac had been allocated. They then began to escort them there. The two towers were close to the Great Hall and palace occupied by the Water Lord and his council.

Brun-du-Lac and Su walked at the head of the refugees together. Their accommodation was not far from the *Poblach Cearnagach* either.

"You told me the rulers of this city were courteous in their manner and you were not wrong," said Brun to her son.

He realised that she was referring to the time when he had got back from his diplomatic mission to Water City, many months ago now. "They have undeniably given us everything we could wish for under the present circumstances."

"Don't think me ungrateful, my son, but under natural Orsook law they could hardly abandon us outside their gates. We are not human!"

Actually, he did think she was showing ingratitude but refrained from saying it. "Mother, we have been given accommodation that is at the same standard as those Orsook who have lived here for years and have been born in this city."

"Was Penlac not born of Water City? As the Duke implied in his speech, the Orsook have a responsibility for each other that is ingrained." It was a hurried interruption and she made it worse with another comment. "Anyway, we have not actually seen this accommodation yet. It could be worse than you think."

He could not believe it. They had just been given the kindest opportunity that could be given to help them to a better life and here she was, behaving as if it was a slap in the face. It was not a good foundation for their lives here.

"How do you expect to live, here in Water City? We cannot begin to make demands on the Water Lord and his council. What would you require them to do if you could? We have just lost a settlement and the circumstances in which it was lost do not cover us in honour. We allowed it to be abandoned without a struggle. If the Water Lord had been a human king faced with such a failure in responsibility, he might have closed the gates of his city to us forever."

"Does that still anger you – that I gave instructions not to fight? My son, our prime responsibility as community leaders is to our people, the Orsook of Penlac, not to the buildings or property or place called Penlac. Judge our actions by that one aim and you will know that they ended in success, not failure. Have the good sense to understand what is behind you."

"Meaning?"

The Water Sidhe pointed to their people from Penlac walking behind them, the adults and the young. "*Everybody* has been saved," she said. "Can you imagine how many we would have lost if we had opposed Formus and his army of five hundred, even with the help of the Telemachons?"

"We did not even try," said her son morosely.

"And if we had, what do you think might have happened? Let us imagine the Telemachons and ourselves had defeated Formus

– it probably would not have been an easy victory. Penlac was a small settlement. Who knows what kind of weapons Formus could have brought against it? In battles it is always the soldiers who win, never the citizens."

"If you felt like that, why did you allow Chanson and the others to leave?"

His mother began to lose her temper. "Su, what is this actually about? Let me remind you that it was you who represented my viewpoint to Tyracides and skilfully so. Why this sudden remorse when we have done exactly what we set out to do?"

It was true. He did feel guilt. There was some sense of resentment too. Resentment that his sister was in the place he should be: with other brave Orsook and the Telemachons to oppose Formus and his Orsook-hating army. At the time he had himself been divided in determining what to do. Duty prevailed. He understood the route to Water City and he had made the necessary contacts with the governing class there. He wanted to ensure the safety of those who intended to escape from the advancing army. That is why he went. Secretly, he had to admit to another motive and that was to return to the magnificence of the City-on-the-Water. If any place on land was his natural home, it was here. His mother's voice broke in again. "We both attempted to dissuade Chanson and the others from leaving us. They were adamant. It was their own free choice as Orsook. I could not order them in a matter such as this. So now, I suggest we consider our position carefully. My people continue to have trust in me."

"But for how long?"

"Exactly."

Su was caught out by the quick agreement and was startled into silence. His mother continued. "You are thinking as a leader should and we must predict what might come next. It is imperative if we are to do the best for our people that we gain some influence with this Water Lord and his council." Brun took a surreptitious glance behind her at those following and was satisfied by them being far enough away to say to her son in lowered tones, "which is why I will be passing my authority in leading the Orsook from Penlac over to you."

Again Su-du-Lac was stunned. This was the last thing he had expected. "But why? There has always been a Water – Mother guiding our people. Won't there be opposition? I thought Chanson would be the inheritor."

"No opposition," said Brun with conviction. "Don't you think that in recognising the way this city is led by a Water Lord, that they will be happier to accept a change in tradition with your appointment – particularly in their demoralised state and away from familiar surroundings?"

"I believe you are also considering how we may make ourselves acceptable to the ruling council."

"Especially that. By doing this, we may find ourselves gaining influence in the council rather than treated as some kind of divisive faction appealing to the past."

"That is if they are willing to grant us any political influence at all. It might be that we are to be ignored or an official is imposed upon us to represent our interests."

Their escorts stopped them in front of the two towers that had been their destination. The long line of Penlac refugees were broken up, as family groups left to be shown their future homes. The new accommodation was more than just adequate and Brun-du-Lac lavished praise where previously cynicism had dominated. Su guessed that this was because she had been given a complete apartment to herself as he had too. In a way it further reassured Su about their future treatment by the Water Lord and his council. But then, it was meant to.

49
Telemachus Leaves

Telemachus was making his way from the bed to his wash bowl when the arrow struck. He heard a whip-crack sound as the bolt buried itself into the wooden frame of his window. Immediately, although he had just awoken from sleep, he fell to a crouched position and rushed over to the opening. Princess Byncor had given him the top floor of a guard tower on a wall of Overblown in which to take up residence and for a few moments he wondered if the city had come under attack. Yet, remaining motionless there, he did not detect any more signs of it: no sudden hissing onslaught from either arrows or yelling men coming over ground to assault the walls. Very cautiously, he raised his head to get a better view. It could have been an assassination attempt. He did not want to give the murderer a second chance.

His position on the tower gave him a perfect view over the surrounding countryside which, this side of Overblown was fairly flat and grass covered, with a few wooded areas before it became green rolling hills. Beside one of these clumps of trees were two mounted riders. They were close enough to be recognisable. It was Eris and Faramund! Eris had the crossbow in her hand which Faramund had made for her and had just shot the arrow that had become an extension to his window jamb. Eris was waving and Faramund had another arrow in his hand, while pointing to it with the other.

Realising, Telemachus looked towards the arrow that had been fired. A piece of parchment was wrapped and tied to the shaft. Raising himself now, Telemachus reached out and retrieved the message. Written in Greek, it told him Conversevitae was dead and that Eris and Faramund were fleeing north to rejoin the Telemachons. They wanted to know if he was going with them.

Telemachus wondered how the old magician had died. The fact that both Faramund and Eris were outside the city walls, in a hurry to leave and had contacted him in this extraordinary way was suspicious. But he knew Faramund to be gentle in manner. Surely, Conversevitae had died a natural end to his many years. Whatever the cause, Queen Byncor would miss him. He had, after all, conquered the Windlander disease and rid its pestilence from her land. They were escaping her displeasure maybe.

He viewed their small figures in the landscape and understood that this was the moment he, too, had to leave. He had completed all he could here in the country of the Borrumani and Queen Byncor wanted to reward him handsomely. A rich estate and an influential position at her court could be his. He was supposed to be still considering it. Telemachus was not inclined to serve another, good or bad. His was not a duty owed simply to himself either. The intention that ran through him was as natural as the blood that circulated in his body. His life's purpose was owed to the Telemachons.

Eris continued to wave. He signalled back and made it clear that he would be riding with them, but they were to continue their journey until he caught up. They galloped off and he noted their direction.

Going to the table beside his bed, Telemachus lifted the simple cord and wooden pendant that he had placed there. The pendant was a piece of the timber from 'The Telemachon' which he had ordered to be dismantled in Europa. Each Telemachon had been given a tiny piece from the ship to be hung around his or her neck. His, he had carved into a likeness of the Greek trireme that had brought them all the way from Sicily and along the Danu. A simple flat image with potent memories. They had argued violently but Telemachus was sure that Tyracides still kept the precious remnant swinging close to his heart. It was a bond between them all, not to be broken.

He hung the cord around his neck, buckled on his sword and put his Corinthian helmet into a leather pouch. Taking some coin for his belt pouch, Telemachus made his way down the tower through each level to the stables below. There was a problem: he passed guards on the way down from the battlement walkway and they nodded to him respectfully but there was an urgency with their movements. They must have been too busy chattering with the new patrol who had come to relieve them, to notice Faramund and Eris in their activities on the other side of the wall.

The stable-boy offered to prepare his horse but Telemachus declined, wanting to get away as soon as possible. The boy shrugged his shoulders and left him to it. In minutes, Telemachus was mounted and on his way to the main gate into the city. If there was to be any trouble it would be there. And so it proved.

"Halt sire!" The voice called. It came from a guard who appeared to relish giving commands to a superior officer. The opportunity did not happen frequently.

There were four gatekeepers in all – two on the left and two on the right. It was a very large gateway and people were freely travelling through it into the city but the command had been delivered to him.

Telemachus leaned down to peer at his face. He recognised him.

"Cranogus! Good to see you again! And even better to see a man alert to his duty. How is the old war wound? Healing well, I hope?" The injury had been gained in the heat of battle with Noremac's supporters and if, while riding past, Telemachus had not delivered a fatal blow to his opponent, Cranogus would not, now, have been guarding the gate.

"Much better, my lord. Thanks to you."

"No – it's down to your courage and strength that you survived the battle." The man was flattered. "Is there any reason why you are stopping me?"

"We have orders to turn back anyone attempting to leave the city. Lord Conversevitae has been found dead in his chamber."

"So I heard earlier – very sad. But the physician was advanced in his years and beyond saving himself with his own medicines. I, on the other hand, am still fit and intend to take my own form of medication that will keep me like that in a village not far from here." He winked at the guard, then taking a silver coin from his belt gave it to the soldier saying, "When you are off-duty have a drink with your friend here and celebrate the fact that we are still standing to enjoy it." The two guards looked at the coin knowing full well that it would buy more than one drink and when they had spent it, they would not be standing. The grins split their faces.

"If we had recognised you straight away, sire, there would have been no calling out," said the other guard and he turned to his fellow. "Cranogus, what could you have been thinking?"

"That's alright, lads. I'll be back soon," said Telemachus. The two men drew back and with a wave, Telemachus back-heeled his horse which trotted quickly through the arch.

He turned right and started on the path that Faramund and Eris had taken a little earlier. After galloping for thirty minutes, he caught up with his two friends who had hidden behind trees until they were sure it was him. Jumping from his horse, he greeted them warmly.

Faramund told him what had occurred when he had come back early from the iron-master's forge. How he had discovered Conversevitae exercising his depraved influence over Eris through magic. Then the agreement to leave.

"You must have been greatly angered at what you saw. Tell me, how is it that you knew he was dead, after you had both left him alive and healthy? That is the impression your message gave me, anyway."

Faramund and Eris cast a look at each other. There was guilt. Perhaps hers for allowing herself to be experimented upon and his for losing control.

"Did you kill him, Faramund?" asked Telemachus directly.

The Celt was slow to respond. "I was not there when he died but it occurs to me that Conversevitae might have disturbed certain specimens I left behind. If he did not understand what he was handling, it could have been lethal for him."

"Not 'could' Faramund, 'was'." Telemachus saw in the Celt's face something different to the young inventor's face he remembered from the first meeting in Europa a long time ago. It had been thinner then, innocent. Today it was fuller, the eyes more hooded. He had learned much, perhaps too much, from his mentor, the wizard Conversevitae. A pupil's knowledge had destroyed his master.

"Shouldn't we be moving on, away from here?" Eris' anxious voice brought them to the immediate danger and the need for action. "It will not be long before the Queen sends after us and we are captured."

"You are right," agreed Telemachus. "We must decide which path to take and attempt to find the Telemachons. I suggest that the quickest way northwards is by the route that King Noremac took down here with his army not so long ago."

"Won't that lead us to the northern garrison?" asked Faramund.

"Only if we stay on the road all the way to the end. We shall divert at the best point for reaching Monithcound. Somehow, we have got to get hold of news concerning where Tyracides and the others have gone. It will not be easy, I am sure. I hope, Faramund, that your tracking skills have not been worsened by the time you spent in Conversevitae's laboratory."

"No, not at all. In fact, I have acquired new methods for detecting where travellers make their journeys."

"We will certainly need those," said Telemachus remounting his horse. "Now let's work our way through the trees out of sight of the city walls and make haste to get onto the road to the garrison."

"Won't that be one of the first places the Queen's guards will search?" suggested Eris.

"Possibly, but if we are to add speed to our travel, then we have no real choice. We must keep alert and try to get onto the road further up."

There was no more discussion and all three hurried off on their horses through the tree cover.

It was a long hard ride through the fading day and up the road to the fortress. Fortunately, it appeared that no one had been sent to pursue them from the capital and they covered a good distance. There were few people on the same route and those who did travel, travelled southwards to the city either to sell their farm wares or their own labour. When it got too dark to ride any further, the three left the road and tried to make themselves comfortable amongst the trees. They had brought blankets from tinkers along the way and these, together with the dry weather which had prevailed for several days meant that their sleep was relatively undisturbed. At sunrise Telemachus found himself roused by the smell of cooking meat. Faramund was turning a skinned rabbit on a spit as he sat before a small fire. Eris was still asleep.

Telemachus joined him.

"How did you manage to catch that, Faramund?"

The Celt fixed him with a contemplative stare. "Oh, I called it."

"Called it?"

"Yes, just as Conversevitae called my wife."

"I suppose," said Telemachus after a pause, "We must eat after all."

"Just as you have your sword and spear to hunt or protect so I have my own means," said Faramund. "You don't approve?"

"Like others, what I don't understand I am suspicious about."

Then there was another pause and Faramund said seriously, "Telemachus – do you trust me?"

The other looked surprised. "Why – yes – of course I do, Faramund. Why shouldn't I? You have done some good things and been a great support to the Borrumani people and to the Telemachons. This business with Conversevitae, well, we might all have reacted in the same way under similar conditions. He committed an offence and it should have been punished, quite rightly, as you did punish him.

Some of the concern lessened in Faramund's face, "Thank-you for that, Telemachus. I think you don't completely agree with the action I took but you have offered me comfort in what you just said."

Telemachus nodded and saw that Eris was beginning to stir. "We have a long way to go – have you any ideas about the best means for covering ground?"

"We have passed three *steles* already since leaving Overblown. When we get to the tenth marker we need to divert north-westwards through the trees. It will get us to Monithcound."

"Yes, it remains abandoned since Coryumberix and his villagers left, although Queen Byncor has plans to resettle people there. What we must discover is where the Telemachons have gone. The news from the northern garrison is that Tyracides led them north with the women and children from the village. They were followed by the High Druid Formus and his army. There was a battle at a settlement over the border in the territory of the Ordovices. It did not involve the Telemachons."

"As soon as we get there," said Faramund, "I will have a better idea of where Tyracides went."

"Let's not waste any more time, then."

The ride to Monithcound took them two days and as Faramund had promised, he found the track the Telemachons had made towards Penlac. Off they went again and a day and a half later came upon the shadowy remnants of Penlac.

Telemachus and Eris were truly surprised when Faramund told them it had been inhabited by the Orsook.

"Surely," said Telemachus, "Formus must have massacred them all. His hatred towards the Fish People is well known."

"No-one died here," came Faramund's equally surprising verdict." In fact, the Orsook used the lake to escape and both the Telemachons and Formus after them are journeying through that great forest there." He pointed. A mass of beech, elm and oak trees stretched out before them, huge in height and grand in appearance. "I have learned something about that woodland from Conversevitae's library. It contained several books about the northern territory adjoining Borrumani land. There was some reference to the Forest of the Bracken Ones, much in the form of a warning."

"A warning? About what?"

"Certainly not about the animals – wild hog, wolves and bears – you might come across there. More to do with the creatures that the forest is named after: the Bracken Ones. Their origin is lost in the roots of time. They were believed, once, to be people, but now have come to resemble the branches, twigs and leaves they live amongst. It used to be that they were numerous in the forest but great as the forest is now, at an earlier time it was even greater. Since then, men have cut down the trees to increase their grazing land for the cattle they hold. As the forest shrunk so the numbers of the Bracken People dwindled."

"That does not seem such a great danger to me," Telemachus commented.

"The destruction of their wooden territory has made them extremely possessive of what is left. Consequently, the few who remain living there are fierce and bear an instant detestation for any human. Believe me, when I tell you that their allies in the forest are many. The strongest friend to them is the river that winds through the very centre of the forest. It is the life-blood and is as important to them as any water-way is to the Orsook. In fact, that river is said to go beyond the forest and to be in some way important to the Fish People too, although the records in Conversevitae's library are hazy about the reason why."

"Does this river have a name?" asked Telemachus.

"Yes, the River Fusion."

His heart skipped a beat. He recalled the words Goreth had spoken to him before he stepped out on what appeared to be an ancient wooden causeway: *it is the River Fusion.*" Then what he had seen from that walkway was brought back to him in a sudden clarity. He gasped.

Eris looked on with concern. "Telemachus, are you alright?"

"Yes, I just remembered something Goreth once said to me. Faramund, do you know where this river has its source?"

It arises to the east from the mountains called the Dark Peak of the Atom. There is no other river like it in the whole of Briton."

"Perhaps we should travel by boat, rather than horse through this forest," suggested Eris.

"No, that would take too much time and we do not know if the water is consistently deep or wide enough at points along its route," said Telemachus.

"We may not be travelling on it but you can be certain that the Telemachons and anyone else trying to find a route through that forest will be following the line that the Fusion takes. I think it will not be long before we come across it. Do you agree that we should attempt to get to the river as soon as possible, Telemachus?"

For a moment, he could not stop the idea of dead, bloated animals being sluiced through his mind by a black, oily river current but he pushed his fear away. "That would be the best action to take," he said, "Let us go."

50

Formus and
the Bracken Ones

An army moving through a forest cannot keep quiet. It cuts and tears, pushes and forces an entrance and talks and shouts curses when sodden wet. At night it breaks down trees to kindle half a hundred campfires and must feed off the salted, dried meat carried by each man because the noise of its progress has scared the fresh meat off, running as fast as it can on four legs.

I should have sent half my men with the camp followers, thought Formus gloomily as he led his horse by its lead up a muddy incline and down again. *That way, we would be quicker and still have enough force to overcome the Telemachons.*

The Lady Andraste was with him. She was not in a talkative mood, just focused on keeping up with him. She wore trousers and long boots. Her dress was pulled up and tied at the waist, yet its muddy ends flapped around her thighs. That's what he liked about her. She was resilient, never complained, just got on with it.

Artemius was somewhat behind them, where he ought to be, with the main body of the men. In front were more of his soldiers, near a hundred. They went first to meet with any unpleasant dangers and deal with them. They were also clearing a path and most of the hacking and chopping sounds arose from their direction.

The sounds had been going on for more than several hours so when it came to a stop that was something noteworthy. Formus had been staring at the ground, trying to pick the driest way through. The quietness only came to his attention after a few minutes. He stopped his horse and lifted his head. "Andraste, do you hear that?" She was confused for a few moments but then she too stopped to listen and then realised what he meant. The silence was like a sound in itself.

Formus gave his reins to one of several soldiers who accompanied them. "Stay here," he ordered. "The rest of you come with me. But no noise!" His words were whispered and urgent. The men did as he said and followed him cautiously.

Andraste was beside Formus, who had drawn his sword as he walked forward.

Breaking tree cover, they came to a large, flat area and now the silence was broken because beyond that could be heard the swirling current of a river in full flow. The sun blazed down and full into their faces. Formus shaded his eyes with his hand for a better view. No sign of his men. What he did see was a very large area covered in tree remains; so thickly strewn and so decimated that it was as thick as turf. Here and there, tree branches stuck up. At the edge, just before the river, huge brown humps rose up but these were less solid. It occurred to Formus that they were rather like beaver dams. His eyes dropped to the ground again and he perceived something else that lay scattered across it. Swords and battle-axes by the score lay where they had been dropped. Of the soldiers themselves, other than this, there was no evidence. Nearly a hundred men, gone.

Formus told the others to fan out and to approach the nearest weapons. He himself moved out and so did Andraste but they let the guards go in front. The four guards reluctantly tested the ground with their feet. It seemed firm enough and they reached the weapons. They were just a few yards ahead of Formus and Andraste. One of the soldiers stooped to pick up a fallen sword. As he bent down there was a sudden eruption at his feet and the soldier's arm was caught by another that had come from the earth. Thick, twiggy fingers lashed around the man's forearm so that he was pulled off balance. Pitching forward, head first, the soldier dived into the woody ground which sucked him up and he vanished. Spontaneously, the other soldiers standing next to the dropped weapons felt the ground seemingly quake beneath them and their legs were grasped by other hands breaking from the surface – hands that looked more like tree roots than hands – and just as quickly they too sank down. Letting their own weapons fall, they clutched hopelessly at the roots and other vegetation either side. The last noise they made were their own screams as their bodies were pulled under.

Formus backed away. Andraste did the same, exclaiming, "What monstrous evil is this?"

"Keep quiet!" hissed the druid. "We may be safe as long as we avoid their attention and do not step onto that ground."

But already Artemius and the main body of the army had come up behind them, spurred on by the cries they had just heard. After hearing what Formus had said, the general passed the word on for silence to the rest of the men.

There was another hush and the Celts crouched down. From underground though, there started up muffled shouts and calls.

"What are they doing?" wondered Artemius aloud, "Applying torture before they kill our men?"

"Whatever it is," said Formus, "we must use the opportunity while these things, whatever they are, distract themselves. Artemius, keep your men close to the edge of this killing ground once we break cover. Those bulwarks over there may offer the solution to our entrapment."

"We are not yet caught," replied Artemius. "We can always withdraw into the forest."

"There is no time to argue and no place to hide once these creatures have finished with our men. Follow me."

His commander leaped up and Artemius had no choice. Running lightly along the perimeter of the flatland, Formus quickly led his men up to the brown slopes and onto them. They were made from mud and turf rather than tree waste and the soldiers found difficulty in manoeuvring themselves up to the top. At any minute Formus expected another attack but it didn't come.

Instead his army found itself on the brow of several hillocks, looking out across the river to the east. The hills themselves joined with the river and dammed it but in such a way that the water continued to flow on its natural course. The damming itself had caused scores of shiny small ponds along this river stretch.

But Formus was not concerned with the distant view. He was scrutinising what they stood on. "Get the men to search the other side of these inclines!" he yelled to Artemius. "Twenty silver pieces to the first man who discovers the entrances to the demon-ridden lair we have just walked around. When they are found, make sure no one enters or leaves!"

Soldiers scrambled down to the ground level and immediately began to hunt through the thick bushes covering it. A jubilant shout came up soon after and then others not so jubilant but excited. Ten entrances in all were uncovered: they followed the contour of the hills from which the soldiers had just descended.

Formus got to the first opening just as his men had finished clearing away the bush growth. This opening like the others was very large – as big as an oak tree and wide enough for three carts to pass through, side by side. Compacted mud shaped it and there was a suggestion of wooden beams but so hidden that the whole space seemed to have grown, rather than been built. Moisture oozed and dripped from the roof.

"My first thought was to either burn or smoke them out," mused Formus, "but seeing this renders that plan useless."

"Yes. Perhaps the smoke might have worked but for the size of this place. It would take days," said Artemius.

"Time we haven't got and anyway we don't know how far these tunnels extend or how many ventilation shafts there are," added Lady Andraste, coming up beside them.

"We cannot leave here – having lost a fifth of our force – without taking revenge," said Formus, his purpose fixed.

"You are right," said Artemius, "The men would expect it."

"Which is why you must go through that entrance with whoever you select, harry these creatures, kill some and return with their heads."

"Me?" replied Artemius, taken by surprise. "But why not a junior officer, my lord? There is a risk that any squad sent in there will be slaughtered. Am I not more valuable to you marshalling your army?"

"It is because I – and the men – regard you so highly that you are the best person to punish these creatures. All I want you to do is to engage with them and show that it would not be worthwhile to pursue us once we leave here. I will stay at these entrances with the army guarding, just in case these tunnellers try to exit. Remember, all you have to do is to engage with them briefly and bring back heads."

That's easy enough for you to say thought Artemius. It was not only that he was fearful to go into that dark place because he had always held a respectful dread for the chthonic gods and their suffocating embrace but he preferred to do his fighting above ground in daylight, when the risks could be more easily assessed. But his answer to Formus kept a head on his shoulders for the time being. "Very well, sire, I will choose the men at once."

"Good. We will give you two hours. Be back by then, Artemius, with plenty of trophies." Formus, as usual, was impatient to be moving on. He watched as his general selected fifty men and disappeared into the wide gash that marked the hillside.

Moving into the underground space with his men and their flaming torches, Artemius decided that the odds against this operation being successful were great. One of his men carried a glass shielded lamp with a marked candle. *Very well*, he thought, *as soon as that wax segment denoting two hours is burnt away, we will be leaving this place with or without heads on the end of our spears.* He was prepared to take any punishment that Formus' vindictiveness could deliver. Taking account that the High Druid's army had already been reduced by a hundred men, he supposed that the punishment would not be too great. Formus, despite himself, would not demoralise his military force any further by removing their most senior and respected officer.

The hint at the entrance that this whole hillside was an engineered superstructure became more evident as they progressed. Wooden beams interlaced with large stone blocks, smoothly cut and cemented with organic material, formed the walls and roof. Vegetal moss and lichens grew over the walls while it was surprising that at their feet sprouted large-leaved ferny plants. Another curiosity was that the further they went down the wide passageway, the *lighter* it got. It was never more than a shady light, of course, but it was good enough so Artemius could call for the torch flames to be extinguished in order that the brands could be used later. The light came from the roof but that was so far above their heads that they were unable to work out how it got to them. Sometimes there were smaller tunnels which deviated from their main route to the left or right. Artemius was not tempted to explore these. It was going to be difficult enough simply to walk this main route and retrace their footsteps alive.

He had men around him whom he could trust. They kept their mouths shut and their footsteps quiet. Men like Agolix. Agolix, like himself, had been a slave but whereas Artemius was from the Helvetii tribe, Agolix had been born into the Sequani. Getting into debt, his family had sold him to Corix's army. He had opted to come with Formus to Briton, like many others, to escape that slavery.

Suddenly, Artemius, hearing a sound, thrust his arm out to prevent Agolix going forward. His lieutenant understood and likewise gestured to the men behind to pause and then move forward more slowly.

There was a bend in the passage and the sound was coming from around that. Cautiously, they approached the corner. From their position it was observable that the passageway they had been walking ended abruptly in another large opening, as it had begun.

A massive chamber was before them and in it were contained what looked like numerous dwellings. They were circular and light poured down upon them from above.

Artemius was probably not the only soldier there who felt disorientated at the sight. After all, they could not have possibly walked that far – surely they could not have passed under the river. They had previously been standing on top of one of the brown hillsides along with Formus, next to the River Fusion. To get such light into this chamber would require a whole hill-top to be carved away. That was not what they witnessed when actually standing on one hill and viewing the others, assuming that the open arena before them was indeed placed at the bottom of one of those hills.

Something else that that disturbed them was the hundred men from their army who they thought had been lost - now some were apparent before them. Yet, what a sight it was. And what a sound. A sound like a creaking but multiplied.

"Are these strange creatures produced by the nightmares of Belinus?" whispered Agolix beside him.

Truly, thought Artemius, *Agolix is right – the beings he was staring at could only have been produced by the disturbed sleep of the earth god.* But to Agolix he said, "Take courage, brother, they have human shape and can therefore feel the cut an iron sword delivers."

That may well have been but nevertheless their attention and that of the men gathering near them as they came up, was fixed upon the moving figures a short distance away. It was fortunate that the tunnel they had travelled by seemed little used and there were many other tunnels connecting to this central chamber. It also helped that they were in the darkest part. Artemius wondered why no guards had been set at the tunnel mouths. He remembered the name that the Gorangun woman, who had attended the Lady Andraste, had used for these people. She called them 'The Bracken Ones'. It might be that these Bracken Ones had little to fear from intruders into their domain. Or that their actions were completely directed to the Celtic prisoners who they had earlier pulled from the surface. It seemed that they were engrossed in what they were doing and had no time for anything else.

"Our men over there have avoided death so far but it cannot be long for them now," whispered Agolix again. "What do you want us to do?"

Artemius had to agree with him. The creatures were preparing to sacrifice the men in some sort of victory celebration. He was glad to see that in counting the Bracken Ones, their numbers were few, far fewer than the number of dwellings would suggest and better still, less than the men he had around him, although not by much. He had not counted the females or children in their midst.

A timber construction had been made, a simple one where upright wooden poles, thick and sturdy, met horizontal beams across the top and from them hung long nooses. Between the ropes dangled ivy tresses touching the ground. It was a wall of green vegetation. The prisoners, tied and yet struggling if they were able, were having their naked bodies painted with a green dye.

"Seems a lot of trouble to go to for simply killing a man," muttered Agolix.

Artemius was trying to settle a course for action in his head, one that would work. The Bracken Ones were ungainly in their movements. They had long thin limbs that were slightly covered in roots rather than hair. This got denser over their necks and heads.

He made his decision. "Agolix, get the men ready to march out in formation. We will stop when I give the order but while on the move we are going to make a lot of noise. Each man is to beat his shield, all in unison and to sing the *Balgoch*." If properly chanted, the battle hymn to the war god was reckoned in Gaul to strike terror into the hearts of the enemy, causing them to drop their weapons and flee. He could not rely on that happening here but at the very least it would be a good introduction for the Bracken Ones to Celtic military discipline.

The men marched and swerved around the corner to come into full view. They stamped their feet on the chamber floor and shields were raised and beaten. Artemius and his lieutenant were at their head. Behind them was another man striding just before the organised ranks of the others. He started to call out the alternate lines of the sacred chant and the Celts answered with a booming refrain. When they finished each line, a rhythmic beating of sword against shield would mark it. They spread their lines out as the chamber opened up. The noise was impressive and echoed in that underground space.

But the Bracken Ones did not run.

The movements they made did not become urgent. There was no sudden rush to arm themselves.

They stopped what they were doing and waited – as if this invading military force had been expected.

The Celts reduced the distance between them and came right up to where the prisoners were being held. At their approach this near, a sudden action broke out amongst the Bracken Ones.

They were standing as a crowd but one that was thinly spread. When the Celtic force paused in front of them, these strange figures suddenly drew closer together so that they became densely packed. Artemius saw that in fact there were far more of them than he had originally estimated because additional figures joined on from somewhere behind the dwellings. As he watched, the crowd swelled and then a curious thing happened. A shape was passed above the heads; arms reached up to support its passing. He screwed his eyes to discern it. Incredibly, it looked like no more than a bundle of tied sticks – a faggot for a fire. Instantly on the alert – he had seen stranger objects become lethal weapons for war – Artemius shouted a command, "Shields forward!" The beating on them ceased, iron boss and wood rose up, interlinked, to defend the one military body from abrupt attack. As that sound finished, the other took over. The one they had heard at a distance. It was only at this point that Artemius and Agolix became aware of what it was. The squealing they had heard, as if coming from a great ship's wooden timbers rolling in a sea squall was actually caused by the movements these creatures made. It was not only squealing but also a sound like sticks hitting each other.

The bundle rolled towards them, borne by the fluttering hands but now it seemed to stretch out into a vague star shape. It rolled and spun as it came on. At last, it finally reached the outer edge of the crowd and tumbled down onto the mossy stone.

It could have been a fallen pile of sticks but there was a recognisable outline to it. A movement occurred within, one that could have been caused by a continual ground tremor only no one else felt it. The wooden sticks and bramble were more perceptibly a shape bent to the earth but now it rose up, stretching to its natural height. And in rising it was more like a natural growth, speeded up, than a movement by an animal. For it was creaturely, arthropoidal and no longer a bundle of twigs.

To the Celts it was a human skeleton but the bones were wood and the skull was a fleshy man's face with long hair and beard that was curled tree bark and dark moss. Its body was partly covered by a long open gown woven from ivy shoots and the eyes in its head were black jets of space. Opening its mouth, the words that came out were understandable but could have been made by a snake that might have squirmed its way through the wooden bone and moss from the stomach, all the way through the throat to appear as the tongue rattling at the lipless mouth.

"You have come in an attempt to kill us – the Bracken Ones?

Artemius stepped forward. "We come to recover our warriors," he said, pointing, "the ones that remain alive after they were pulled from the world above into this subterranean region."

There was a grinding creak as the head turned briefly to the prisoners and back again." They are the spoils of war and as such will be offered to our god."

Artemius was willing to strike a bargain, if he could, with this horror. Formus had told him to bring back heads. He could hardly argue if those heads were living ones and belonged to his own men. The army supporting Formus would not take kindly to a senior commander being punished for rescuing its own soldiers.

"If you give us our men, we will go in peace."

There was a short sound like the sudden fall of tree that could only be interpreted as laughter. "Do you really think you can overcome us when you see the numbers we have against your small band?"

"I see larger numbers, yes certainly," admitted Artemius, "but in any fight, there will be losses on both sides. Is it necessary to have any of your people die in this action?"

"In battle, death is natural. What is your alternative?"

"Many people dying on both sides is unnecessary. I suggest instead that we select two of each side to contest the battle. I choose my best warriors, you choose yours. If our men win, we withdraw taking the prisoners you release with us."

"And if ours is the victory?"

"Then we leave but without ten of our men. You will have more offerings for your god." *I will die before that happens*, thought Artemius.

The creature's head creaked, again musing. "How do we know that you will keep to this agreement?"

"We will exchange hostages for the duration of the contest. Those that are valuable to our people." Artemius went to the rank behind him, to a man standing next to Agolix and asked him to walk forward. He placed a hand on his shoulder. "This is Agolix," he continued, "my second – in – command. He will cross the space between us and become your hostage." The man chosen was not happy at the prospect but kept his face impassive and did his duty.

On seeing this, the creature called to someone from behind who likewise came forward. He spoke again directly to Artemius.

"I am Llyr and this is my son. Every one of the Bracken People you see before you is either my son or my daughter. They are the Children of Llyr. My son will cross over now and you should send your personal guarantee too."

The hostages were exchanged.

Artemius selected his two champions. They were seasoned fighters, Cosumbra and Gortoch, each having visible scars to show for their survival from previous lethal encounters in the field. Cosumbra, a small man, was speedy on his feet and as a skilled swordsman had tremendous stamina. He was seen to have fought much bigger opponents to a state of exhaustion and quickly finish them off. Artemius thought Gortoch would be a natural complement for him: a giant of a man, he could crush a man's fist in his own as easily as an overripe tomato. They were both well-armoured with iron breastplates, greaves and helmets. Cosumbra carried a sword in his left hand, shield in his right, while Gortoch bore a massive double-headed axe and a round shield that could have served as a table top.

Facing them were their two Bracken opponents. More wood than flesh, they did, at least, appear to be like two thin men. They were slightly taller than Cosumbra and surveying the ones collected behind Llyr, Artemius wondered why even bigger and more powerful figures had not been chosen as he could see that they might have been. Root-like hair covered their heads and was black on the one and red on the other. Both were bare-chested and wore trousers cut from a green leafy material. Pallid skin came from years lived underground.

The four stood opposed, waiting for the signal to begin. A Celt adjudicator looked from Llyr to Artemius and receiving a nod from both, he shouted an order to the contestants.

There was an abrupt movement as the two Celts struck first but as each swung out with sword and axe both were countered by shields blocking the lunges. In the case of the blow struck by Gortoch, it was so vicious and heavy that it split the Bracken One's shield straight down the middle. His opponent moved off quickly with the huge Gortoch coming after him. He swung the double-headed axe again in a sweeping downward curve but the

Bracken jumped aside and the metal head buried itself into the ground. The Bracken One leaped forward and thrust at Gortoch's chest. Gortoch moved, but not fast enough and the blade drove through the muscle in his arm. He gasped and blood flowed out. To have been caught so early and quickly in the fight was not a good sign. The Celts behind Artemius started to shout out encouragement to the giant. Fortunately, it was not his axe arm and the injury could have been much worse. Nevertheless, he was hurt. Gortoch, did not back away as the Bracken probably expected but pushed forward with his shield raised for maximum impact. It worked. The Bracken found himself knocked to the ground. Gortoch, having lost the axe, pulled a knife from his belt and slashed at the shape underneath him. His opponent moved far faster than he expected and rolled just in time. Jumping to his feet, he circled the giant.

Meanwhile, Cosumbra was doing rather better in his own combat. Parrying several flurried blows from his opponent he had returned the tumult and driven his enemy back. At this juncture it was all the Bracken One could do to stand upright. Cosumbra could see that the rocky floor behind him was slippery with wet moss and wanting to take advantage of this, he forced the creature back further. The Bracken took one more step back as Cosumbra's sword rushed down again. In trying to protect himself his opponent raised his shield arm, yet Cosumbra's strength, as small as he was, overwhelmed the creature who fell flat on his back. Its shield was sent spinning.

This was an extremely vulnerable moment and Cosumbra was not slow in using it. He threw away his own shield and with both hands held the sword hilt for a final downward stab into the neck of the body that lay transfixed beneath him.

Then what occurred was something that the watching Celts would never have witnessed in a duel between two ordinary human men.

A long root whipped up and wrapped itself around Cosumbra's two locked wrists, forcing them away slowly. The Celt's neck and forearm muscles bulged as he struggled against the power that was being exerted on him. Slowly, slowly, the sword moved away and pressure from the root tightened around Cosumbra's arms so that he cried out with the pain.

Artemius and his men looked on horrified as they saw that the root had been projected from the head of Cosumbra's assailant.

To be precise, it had shot from between the base of the skull and the top of the spine.

After the yell, Cosumbra dropped his sword with a clatter to the ground. The root unravelled quickly and instead transferred its attention to the Celt's ankles, tying them and then with a sudden jerk upending his whole body so that it could be pulled closer to the Bracken One. Cosumbra felt himself helpless around the legs. If it had not been for his helmet, he would have been knocked unconscious by the fall.

Gortoch, aware of Cosumbra's trouble, gave a huge kick to his opponent's shield which sent the creature flying and with his great battle-axe cut in two the root that had imprisoned Cosumbra. Not red but bright green blood spurted from the end which then retracted like a startled snake back into the Bracken's spine.

The creature himself was clearly in pain and for a few moments was groggy in his movements. Cosumbra loosened the root from around his ankles, sprang up and delivered two strong blows with his sword to either side of the Bracken One's neck. Wood-chip and dust flew up; the creature groaned and fell to his knees. Cosumbra brought his sword around in a swift swooping motion that sliced off the Bracken's head. The head bounced on the ground and rolled away while the remaining body slumped forward into its own pool of green blood.

For Cosumbra, there was no time to celebrate his victory as he rushed to help Gortoch. Both men were wary about the additional danger they faced after what Cosumbra's opponent had just done. On either side they attacked the Bracken One, who defended himself with raised shield and hacking sword. Yet outnumbered, he was not likely to last long.

Then there was another dreadful hiss and again the root, that may as well have been a rope, lassooed out and caught the necks of Cosumbra and Gortoch in two loops before pulling tight. The men gasped, instinctively letting their weapons go while their hands reached for the organic torcs stricturing their throats.

The onlookers assumed that the Bracken One could have used his own sword to finish them off but it became obvious that the effort to wield both the 'root' appendage from his own body and at the same time the sword in his hand, was too much. But it appeared that the sword would not be necessary for Cosumbra, whose face had become purple and was showing bloody track marks from his nostrils. At last he went limp and all life left him.

Gortoch, however, was still fighting strongly and was pushing the thick coil away from his throat with some success. Desperate, he saw an opportunity and opening his mouth bit into the root, tearing a chunk away with his teeth. The root quivered, snapping back into the Bracken One's back. This time and with this creature the retraction of the wounded limb did not have the same disorientating effect as with the Bracken One whose head had just been sliced off. No, this creature leaped on Gortoch's back and started to hammer at his face with the pommel of his sword.

Gortoch, blinded, whirled on the spot, reaching up to drag his assailant down. He caught him by his fists and yanked hard. The Bracken One rattled down, an avalanche of wood, onto the flat ground. Still temporarily blinded, Gortoch jumped on him with his whole weight and taking his head, twisted it to the right. There was a sickening crack and the Bracken's neck was broken.

The giant got up off the ground and the dead body to loud cheers from the Celts. He wiped the blood away and with the vision remaining in his left eye was able to make out the figure of Artemius saluting him with lifted sword.

The cheers died away as Artemius lowered it and then, addressing himself to Llyr, King and Father of the Bracken Ones, said, "Our champion, Gortoch, has prevailed. Now, it is your command to honour our agreement and release the captives you have taken.

There was the sound like a storm wind through trees and the creature, grinning, replied, "We are the strong, you are the weak. It is not here, in the home of the Bracken Ones, that you will take what we are unwilling to give."

"We made an agreement. I have your son to prove it," said Artemius, placing his hand on the Bracken hostage's shoulder. An arrow just missed his hand and thudded into the woody flesh below. The Bracken One keeled over, instantly dead.

"My sons live, only to die for me," hissed the Bracken King. Artemius saw that the man he had sent, the man he had called Agolix, was standing near to Llyr. He and the other Celts watched with foreboding as a tall Bracken One stepped behind him and then struck him to the ground with the club he was holding. "And your people must die for you," continued the Bracken King, "…... all of them." He turned to his children and raising his voice bellowed out a command which echoed off the rocky walls in the chamber." The Celts must die – every single one of them. Leave no one alive!"

From somewhere, horns blasted out and then the Bracken People rose like a swelling tide and swept towards the Celts.

"Back! Back! To where we came!" roared Artemius. If they could only make it to the tunnel passageway, then the narrower space would at least reduce the violent onslaught from superior numbers. "Front two ranks defend the entrance – kill your man, then fall back," commanded Artemius. He was hoping that the charge by their enemy would be impeded and simultaneously give some of his men time to escape. The front ranks would also be given the same chance once they had paused the speed of the attack, although not much of a one.

Artemius' detachment ran into the tunnel and most continued to hurry on but a score of men stayed to hinder the Brackens. They fought bravely, stubbornly, but in the end it was a hopeless effort. Those who were archers in the front ranks picked their targets easily and having obeyed Artemius' command, were able to retreat. Many stayed to kill one or two more Bracken before leaving. The sword fighters however, had a much more difficult task in fulfilling their duty. Even in the narrowed confines that the passageway offered there were at least three Bracken to each Celt and gradually the pressure from the growing Bracken numbers in the tunnel mounted against the shield wall put up by the front rank and broke it. Agolix, who had stayed behind, shouted out for a second shield wall to be raised but by then it was too late – the two ranks were overrun and he himself lay on the damp, mossy floor, stabbed through the neck.

Trampling over them, the Bracken Ones charged onwards. They caught the fleeing archers first and after making bloody work of them, pursued the remaining Celts.

Later, Formus waited impatiently outside the same entrance that he had commanded Artemius into, to rescue those captured by the Bracken Ones. He sat astride his horse alongside the rest of his army – all prepared to wait for a short time more and then to leave.

The Lady Andraste was with him. She had changed her mud bespattered clothing for fresh garments and was also mounted. Her horse was a white mare flecked with grey on its haunches. It had carried her all the way through Europa and the Britannic Isle.

"How much longer should we wait, my lord?" she asked Formus.

He didn't answer and seemed to be listening for something. Andraste noticed that her horse's ears had pricked and it began to whinny. The mood passed to Formus' mount as it started to shift its feet. Formus patted it, "Steady," he murmured and then looked intently at the cave mouth.

A sound was growing from it, getting nearer. And now it was unmistakeable. Clashing swords and screaming men. Some screams chopped short, silenced by Death's hand clamped over mouths.

Formus alerted his men, not that they needed it. "Unsheathe your swords, prepare for battle!" There was a grating sound as four hundred swords were unsheathed from their scabbards.

But then the loudest noises in the tunnel suddenly came to a stop. It was replaced by a panting as of someone running, breathing heavily.

Out of the cave gloom came a man's figure. He was running one moment and then became stock still. He was bloody, one arm hacked away, a face bruised, eyes closing and his head unhelmeted. There was an obvious reason to the watching army as to why he was motionless. What looked like three long tendrils had shot out from the depths and wrapped around his legs, torso and head. The root around his head covered his eyes and tied his neck. Only his mouth was free.

"Run!" shrieked Artemius and that was the last word the army heard from him, before the roots slid him back into the darkness.

51
Misgivings

The River Fusion was different to all other rivers in Briton. Some said it was unnatural. Created by the inhabitants of the Shadow World rather than the gods of earth and sky; whoever those inhabitants were. It was unnatural because unlike those other waterways, it did not flow directly from mountains to the sea. It did not travel from east to west or north to south. If it appeared to travel in any direction, it moved from south to north. There was no logic in it. No rationality. Just a water mass. Changing. Being its own energy. Reproducing.

Reproducing, in that very occasionally along its course, the mighty river became a trickle in its channel. And then further on there would be an unexpected expansion of its mass and the river's roar would tumble into a listener's ears. The River Fusion was a fascination to certain druids and passed over by others. The former wanted plot its course. They thought that if its power and flow and material presence could be captured in some way, there would be great benefits to the Celts. They wanted to *quantify* it. The latter said how can you measure something that is unquantifiable? They avoided any further analysis, preferring to spend their money, time and effort on more tangible advantages for their people.

In its course through the forest of the Bracken Ones, the Fusion never lost its power, maintaining its size and speed with consistency under the tree cover. Sometimes the rate of flow was slowed at a bend but there were not many corners to be turned in the forest. Beyond the trees, it was then that the river lost its strength more than once or twice and of course the Celts living near those stretches blamed the Bracken Ones in the woodland for its diminishment. The water soon recovered, nevertheless, it was this renewal that they found wonderful.

So, the River Fusion came to be regarded as particularly different and especially protected in comparison to other rivers. There were small shrines erected along its course, though not where it ran in the Bracken Forest which was a place no Celt would choose to go with just a few friends.

The Orsook, in travelling with Tyracides and the others, had taken to bathing in the river before they took their breakfast every day and Goreth led the way into the river.

Hebe watched him enter the Fusion along with the other naked Orsook and recalled the time she had seen him running into another river when the Telemachons had been journeying through Briton at what presently felt, to be a very long time ago. Then, as now, she was missing Telemachus. But Telemachus was becoming a distant memory. Goreth had also left the Telemachons but at least he had returned.

Agenor was beside Hebe, sitting and eating his breakfast. He noted her attention. The Orsook were wading into the river after Goreth and the respect they showed for him was obvious, even Ol-du-Brec's attitude had changed. To Agenor, the sight was a little disturbing. The Water People were gaining strength, he perceived, from the Fusion and from Goreth. Ordinarily, this would have pleased him. After all, the Orsook were their allies. Yet, ever since he had gone to them as they gathered closely around their fire with Goreth a few days ago and thought he had heard them speaking almost furtively together in another tongue, his suspicions had been provoked.

"Do you think he has changed?" He asked Hebe.

"Isn't that obvious?" said Hebe, regarding Goreth's more feminine figure. Agenor followed her eyes.

"No, I don't mean that: a change in his attitude to us. That is what I am asking."

Hebe brushed the hair away from her face. "Perhaps he has. But then again, we need to understand that he is back together with his people. And if most accepted him, there were one or two who didn't. Goreth might have thought that he should make an effort to get closer to them. What did Tyracides say when you spoke to him?" Hebe guessed, rightly, that Agenor must have relayed his concerns to Tyracides after visiting the Orsook at the campfire.

"Like you he thought that Goreth was wanting to renew friendship and respect amongst his kind but it would be only sensible for wariness about their future behaviour towards us. The history of the relationship between human beings and the Orsook has not been a happy one."

"No, but at this moment we have a common enemy: Formus."

"Enmity is not enough to bring people together. In fact, it is a shaky ground on which to establish friendship." Agenor leaned forward, confidentially. "Hebe, we must have someone from the Telemachons more familiar with what is happening amongst the Orsook, a person who can give us fair warning if they intend to break the alliance with us."

"Is this your idea or Tyracides?" Her tone was cold.

"Mine. But Tyracides welcomed it. We have noticed that you seem to be the one person amongst the Telemachons whom Goreth meets with on an occasional but regular basis."

Hebe blushed. It was true. Once she had been attracted to Goreth, when he had been male. On his transformation she hadn't quite known what to think. They had conversed together after that first time when she really noticed him and she understood that she was no longer physically attracted. Yet, she found him fascinating.

"You want me to spy on him." It was more a statement than a question.

"Yes." Agenor, as was his way, spoke plainly.

"Don't you think he will realise?"

"Again, yes. But if his attitude to us has changed, he will suspect any and all of us."

"Then what is the purpose?"

"Nothing," said Agenor, patiently, "will come from an absence in communication. Anyway, I believe his perception of us has always been the same, whereas his manner has been a friendly one. He views us as a destructive influence on his own people."

"It was the Celts who massacred the Orsook in Europa, not us," protested Hebe.

"We have Celts among us."

"Women and children from Monithcound and a dwarf from Europa."

"They are Celts still and you forgot to mention Berengar. The friendship between him and Goreth seems to be a strong one. Why don't you ask him to do your spying?"

"We have and he has agreed to keep us informed. Before you ask, more than one report on the same source is better than just one or none at all."

Hebe gave up an argument in which she had no serious interest. "Alright, Agenor, I will do as you ask. The fate of the Telemachons and those with us matters as much to me, of course, as it does to you. If anything worrying had been raised from my conversations with Goreth, don't you think I would have already brought it to you and the others?" She forestalled his response. "Naturally, I would have done that. It would be foolish to keep such things quiet."

He fell silent and they both watched the Orsook bathing and swimming in the river. It used to be the practice that some Celts and Telemachons would bathe with them before breakfast but fewer were doing that now. Hebe could see Berengar's wife and young son with them. Ula was swimming in the river. Herne, however, was sitting on the bank, staring morosely. Berengar was not there. She was not surprised at that. The Telemachon men usually took to the water much earlier to clean themselves at first light. They did it after their military exercise involving combative sword duels. Tyracides did not want them to get lazy. Hebe saw how miserable Herne appeared to be. She wondered what was wrong.

Further down, Goreth had finished his swim and was out of the water drying and dressing himself. He was unembarrassed by any attention it brought. Hebe saw that his breasts were rather small and it gave him the look of a rather flat-chested woman. In fact, she noticed that his body could not be described as fully feminine since he retained the male genitalia between his legs. He was both man and woman, rather than having been transformed wholly from man to woman. His choice in clothing remained masculine and today particularly military as he pulled on cotton trousers cut off at the knees and seamed with leather. The shirt was padded with extra layers of linen specially hardened after being treated with flax-seed glue and could withstand an arrow fired from just a hundred yards away. It was curious. She had always thought of Goreth as a peace-loving being and why would a god need material protection anyway? She supposed it might be his desire to form a closer bond with his people as had been spoken about earlier. In what she had been told about the Orsook, they avoided war and military activity yet that seemed to be denied by the Orsook who had joined them from the settlement of Penlac. From the very first, they had all been armoured with a short dagger and thin swords in bright scabbards at their waists.

When Goreth came up from the river, the other Orsook gradually followed behind to clothe themselves on the river bank. Hebe saw that Chanson-du-Lac was next to Goreth. With the Orsook there were no inhibitions about nakedness on display between the sexes. She slipped on a short cotton tunic that reached to her knees.

Agenor heard someone call his name and turning, discovered Tyracides walking up. Berengar was with him.

Tyracides stopped and stared at where Goreth and the other Orsook were preparing themselves. Without addressing Agenor directly, he said, "Berengar has come to me with information that he has just learned and which is very useful to us."

Berengar began, "It came from my son when I got up for military training this morning. He is always up at the same time asking me to take him to watch the duelling. Anyway, we got into a conversation about his young Orsook friend, O-ta-ke-re whom he is missing quite badly and it was then that he told me."

"How many days have we been travelling with them up to this point?" broke in Tyracides, addressing Agenor directly but not leaving him time to answer. "Three. In that time what has puzzled us all, is where the Water Sidhe and those from Penlac have actually gone. We have been met with vague references to 'the northern lands'. Well, Herne, in his childish way, has suggested that they might have had a clear destination for their journey. A place they could have already reached."

"It took me a little time to get it out of my son," said Berengar with something approaching grimness in his tone. "Children are better than adults in keeping secrets these days."

"You didn't use torture did you?" joked Agenor and then quickly regretted his words when Berengar fixed an ice-cool gaze on him.

Tyracides cut between the two. "The Orsook child was not so good at keeping secrets for his people. This destination for the Penlacians turns out to be a complete city that has existed for generations. They call it, 'Water City'. It lies beyond this Forest of the Bracken Ones, northwards, in a region dominated by mountains and lakes. Apparently, it is built over water and right at the heart of this city there is a statue. The statue is the image of the founder; the one who originally led them to that place and constructed its buildings, streets and waterways."

"You mean someone like Orsek, the High King, whose tomb we raided?" asked Agenor.

"No," said Tyracides, carefully, "I mean him." He turned, face towards Goreth, gesturing with his hand. "Or her."

Agenor's confusion was increasing. "But you said this city was generations old. I realise the Orsook live longer life spans than our own but even they, individually, cannot live for several generations at a time."

"Is this not further proof that Goreth or Danu or whatever he is, is more than man, more than Orsook? I, for one have believed it." Berengar occasionally recalled his conflict with Goreth, try as he might to repress the memory. "If he seriously decided, for whatever reason, to break his alliance with us, then we must make certain that Formus is the one he directs his power against and not us."

"Why should he abandon his friendship with us at all? He has supported us all the way from the time he joined the Telemachons in the lands divided by the Great River Danu. There would be no sense in it."

"You might want to put that idea to him. He is on his way over here," said Tyracides.

Goreth had said a few words to Chanson-du-Lac and Ol-du-Brec, his taller head bending near theirs and then all three moved towards the Telemachons.

"Tyracides!" greeted Goreth, "My friends," he added, with a nod to the others. Somehow, the expression rang hollow, even to Hebe.

"Goreth," returned Tyracides, "I am glad to see that you have been refreshed by your swim. We have had our early morning exercise too – in preparation for the day ahead. Another two days, so my scouts tell me, and we shall be well away from the confines of this forest."

"As for that," said Goreth, "I wish you luck and a good future but we cannot accompany you from this time on." There appeared a genuine tone of regret in his voice.

Tyracides kept his manner calm and without reproach. "I am sorry to hear that, Goreth, has the Water Sidhe sent a message for her warriors to return?"

"No – it is my decision and one supported by all the Orsook here."

"But I thought you were willing to come with us and fight against Formus – a man who hates and persecutes your people?"

"There are more ways than one to deal with men like Formus. Sometimes it is their own contempt and ignorance that can be used against them."

"Well, if there is a battle plan in that strategy, please inform me," said Tyracides.

"Actually," replied Goreth, smiling, "there is. But now is not the time and this Forest of the Bracken Ones not the place."

"So …. you cowards will run and hide instead!" shouted out Eucleides, who had been sitting apart but was now up on his feet.

Goreth looked at him coolly and then walked over to him. He smiled and said, "If you need to relieve your feelings about the matter, Eucleides, strike me."

Eucleides hesitated and then turned away disgustedly, "I would never hit a woman."

"Quite right," replied the Orsook, "And I would never hit a man." He laughed. "That is just as it should be. Otherwise, there would be chaos."

In his frustration, Eucleides threw one more taunt but this time directed it at another Orsook. "Ol-du-Brec! You were so keen on engaging Formus in battle. You would have saved the honour of your people. What has changed that you have decided to leave it to others to fight alone?"

"Let us just say that I have rediscovered my rationality," said Ol-du-Brec, carefully.

"We are only twenty in number," added Chanson-du-Lac, "And cannot seriously add much impact to your military force."

"Like the fish, you can breathe underwater. We could have done much with that kind of gift," said Agenor.

Chanson ignored the comment. "Far better for us to go northward and rejoin our people to persuade them to oppose Formus."

"I hope you have better luck with them, than we did with you," muttered Eucleides.

"Go north and organise your battle plan from Water-City, you mean?" suggested Tyracides.

It was obvious that the remark had stunned Chanson-du-Lac and Ol-du-Brec.

"How did you learn about that?" asked Chanson.

"You did not seriously believe that a city of such size could be hidden from us, like a mushroom in the undergrowth?" said Tyracides. Truthfully, he did not know to what scale the Orsook built their city but wanted to test to see if he would be corrected. He was answered by Goreth.

"Tyracides, when you meet Telemachus again, ask him about the Causeway – the one I guided him over. Then let him know that the same Orsook engineers who built that road were the ones who designed Water-City. He will then make you realise how difficult it will be to discover the location of that city. Not only is there an advantage in that but there is something in the very structure of the buildings, in their essential design, that not even the rulers of that place know about and which ultimately will protect the Orsook." He laughed. "In fact, the rulers understand least of all."

Chanson-du-Lac and Ol-du-Brec were staring at him wide-eyed.

Eucleides scoffed openly. "Who is this supposed to frighten? If the Orsook had such latent power, why is it that they were annihilated by Formus on the continent? They could not save themselves and you provided no defence for them. Tell these stories to children by the campfire that they may be easily entertained to make them sleep and dream when their parents tell them to go to bed. And if you intend to go, then go now and let those who are still awake, conflict with the real monsters that govern this world."

"Those that are awake are always directed by some idea or impulse and sometimes it masters them so that they lose their ability to think as a sensate being. You should know that more than most, Eucleides."

Eucleides just stared, unable to think of the words to answer.

"More than most but not better than I," continued the Orsook. "For though I have more power than most, yet sometimes I cannot use it when I choose to do so. I wanted to exercise my strength so many times in Europa. When you feel yourself powerful but being overpowered by something that is beyond your control, then you question your purpose. If it happens more than once, you begin to doubt existence itself. But here in Briton, away from Europa, my vitality restores itself. Every day that I swim in the River Fusion at the various points we travel along its connecting route to the north, I feel the flow of energy in my body become cogent. I am preparing. I am coming home."

Eucleides found his words. "How can we stop that?" he mocked with his hands raised briefly.

"You can't," replied the Orsook, "but we have and I hope we will remain, as friends. My people's only wish was to be left in peace. But they have only seen their own kind being exterminated.

When that happens, a people must choose either to die or defend themselves against the growing malevolence around them. We choose to live. If we lose our lives, they will be lost in a battle of our choosing, defending our own way of life, our own city - so not here, not in this way. Before we go, as we must, I will leave you with something to comfort your march north."

"What would make up for your absence?" asked Hebe.

"Perhaps not what I am about to tell you," said Goreth, "but only you will be the best judge of that." He paused. "It is not everything you would want but know this: Formus has lost his commanding officer, Artemius, together with one hundred and fifty men from his army. They were killed by the Bracken Ones."

The Telemachons looked at him, wanting the news to be true but were mystified.

"Who brought you this information?" said Tyracides.

"The fishes in the river, the birds in the sky. We are close to them than you can ever be."

Tyracides thought about the animal divination that had been practised in Heraclea Minoa where he had lived as a slave.

The priests who had predicted future events from bloodied entrails there were never as precise as this: they did not speak in numbers but in riddles. Tyracides suddenly realised that what Goreth meant as he kept those calm green eyes on him, was that he had got the news from the living animals, not dead ones.

While he was thinking about this, Goreth turned quickly on the spot and walked away, accompanied by Chanson and Ol-du-Brec. When they reached the others, there was some discussion and then all the Orsook moved off into the forest growth. Before they disappeared, Goreth raised one arm to them.

"Was that a wave of farewell or one of dismissal?" noted Agenor glumly.

"I would have liked for him to tell us a little more about the Bracken Ones," said Berengar, "they are a danger to us as well as Formus."

"I think that from now on," said Tyracides, "Goreth is much more likely to speak to the birds, than to us."

52

A Dead King, a Book
and a Seed

Brun-du-Lac, Water-Mother, slowly entered the splendid High Chamber that contained the Water Lord and his governing council. She did not want to show that she was easily impressed or overawed. This is what they would expect, judging her life in Penlac to be very different to the one she had led her in the city just in the last few days. And so it had been. Here, there was confidence in the air and the belief – although the Orsook knew Formus to be on his way – that the city was impregnable. Curious that, thought Brun. How could any settlement without walls to defend it, be defensible?

Her son, Su-Lance-du-Lac, was with her and they were escorted along the length of the hall up to the two high-backed chairs that had been placed for their benefit in front of the long table at which sat the Water Lord and his senior advisors. She had thought long about this meeting. Nothing must go wrong. It nearly did when she and her son reached the chairs and she first saw the Water Lord.

He could have been none other, since he wore the famous yellow crystal crown whose pearled points bent over like the spouts from an ornamental water fountain. It sat firmly on his head and the Water Lord himself sat next to the familiar figure of Duke Ote. On the ruler's left side was his wife, tall and elegant in her white silk dress cut like rippling waves. When she saw the Water Lord between these two, Brun-du-Lac found it difficult to repress a smile. Her son had prepared her for this but to see the squat, toad-like shape of this ruler placed neatly between the tall, dignified figures either side and be greeted by such an ugly face, was enough to tempt anyone's self-composure. A counsellor at one table-end spoke up when the two had got to the chairs.

"Please be seated, Brun-du-Lac, Water Sidhe of Penlac and her son, Su-Lance-du-Lac." To be addressed in such an indirect manner sounded like a discourtesy but nevertheless Brun ignored it and sat down, as did Su.

There were ten counsellors in all, spread along the table either side of the Water Lord and his lady. There were other attendants also in the hall. Good, thought Brun, what she was about to tell them would soon be out amongst the general population. It had not been easy to keep her own son and those she had brought from Penlac to keep silent. It was difficult and in the long term impossible so this meeting, arranged after three days in the city, would be the best opportunity to announce the news. She had no doubts that in receiving it, there would be utter amazement and immediate disbelief. It was her duty to deliver the message and with its effect buy an important place in the society of Water City for herself and her family.

"We are pleased to see you, Brun-du-Lac," said the Water Lord, "I have been waiting for a long time and of course, your son is always welcome at this council: he has been a tireless representative for the Orsook of Penlac." The Water Lord's voice was soft, melodic. It was a pleasant surprise.

"I thank-you, my lord, for myself, my son and all those from Penlac who in compensation for losing their homes, have been offered new ones and a chance to start afresh in Water City."

"Our great pleasure. All Orsook need to help each other against what is becoming obviously apparent as its common enemy. I mean humanity. We have tried to live by their side, at peace. But they, themselves, will not accept that. Our immediate problem is this Celtic druid called Formus, who leads an army of five hundred through Briton. It seems, going by the stories told of his actions in Europa, that he intends to rid the world of the Orsook. We have been debating how he may be stopped; it is that which has unfortunately taken up the last three days, otherwise I would have seen you sooner."

Despite all the courtesies, Brun felt sure that the reason why they had not been invited until now was because the Water Lord had not deemed it necessary. That would change.

"My lord, I can tell you that there is someone on their way to this city who can offer the people more than just hope."

"First, he must find it," answered the ruler. Brun wondered at his jocular comment and supposed that he might have taken offence at their being anyone who could offer his citizens protection other than himself. "That, after all, is our greatest defensive advantage, mathematically worked into the substructure of our buildings."

"The founder can always find his own city," said Brun, bluntly.

"Founder?" replied the Water Lord. "I don't understand."

"I mean the Orsook of Orsooks. She and he who swam the Great River in Europa, settling the Fish People on its banks and then leaped the encircling sea to course the River Fusion and create Water City, before returning to Europa."

A hush fell in which the realisation took hold. The look on the face of each counsellor was something neither Brun or Su-Lance would ever forget. Duke Ote was the first to prompt the answer to all their thoughts.

"Danu?"

"I mean," affirmed Brun, "Danu: the originator."

The Water Lord sat back on his seat suddenly.

For a few moments no one uttered a word. Then those around the table began to babble all at once – to each other and calling questions out to Brun. Quite unexpectedly a new voice rang out, strident, above the others.

"Stop the noise, let my lord speak!" Astonished, Brun saw that it was the elegant lady who had shouted, she who sat next to the Water Lord as his wife. The chatter finished on the instant.

Her husband, who appeared to have been physically pushed back in his chair by the news, leaned forward and scrutinised Brun. He did not look gladdened by what she had just told the assembly. In truth he was angry and directed his anger at her.

"All the Orsook of this city have done for you and those you brought from Penlac is to offer their help and generosity where it was needed. We gave you food and shelter. In return, what do you bring? Especially at this time, when the Orsook and their very existence are being threatened? You bring the loss of a settlement that was inhabited by the Orsook for generations – a place that now lies in smoking, burned-out ruins. You bring an unbelievable story about our own founder who, you claim, is on his way here right now and will save us all! It's as easy as that! What do you mean by this? I've been informed that you have a daughter, yet she is not with you. Has this Formus got her? Does he hold her hostage while you have been sent to undermine our resolve to protect ourselves – is that it?"

"No .... no!" replied Brun, shocked at the outburst, "that is not it at all…"

The Water Lord continued his vehemence. "Have you ever seen this Orsook who you claim to be Danu?"

Brun looked uncertain. At this moment her son took the initiative.

"A number of our people left Penlac to fight with the Telemachons against Formus. They say that Danu is with them. The features of this Orsook exactly resemble those that were seen on the wooden statue that once existed in our Hall of Reflection. Perhaps when he gets here, you may make a comparison yourself to the image at the Founder's Fountain here in the city."

The squat figure on the chair appeared to calm himself as he heard this from Su-Lance.

"There will be no 'perhaps' in it – I will certainly refer to the Fountain. But I and everyone in this city will not accept appearances alone to accept his identity. There will have to be a lot more before we can believe the impossible. One Orsook may look like another and claim to be that other, yet the substance behind his claim is as dust."

Su-Lance hesitated briefly and said, "Sire, when I mentioned that the resemblance was exact, I meant it."

"Well, of course you …." The Water Lord began to snap back and then realised what the other was actually alluding to. As did the others at the table.

Duke Ote placed his hands on the flat top and leaned over them towards Su-Lance. "A facial similarity between two Orsook, although not common, could still be coincidence. What you are pointing out is that this Orsook not only bears the same face as Danu but also the body? He is both male and female?"

"That is correct, Duke Ote."

"If this creature is a charlatan, he has taken great lengths to make his duplicity real," half-joked the Water Lord. At the same time, he thought that if there was trickery of some kind, it was a deceit that he could turn to his advantage. A returned god would do wonders for morale in the city and if he was not who he claimed to be, that would be an unarguable reason for putting him to death. It was prohibited for an Orsook to be executed by his or her fellow Orsook but in that instance the ruler was comfortably sure that his people would not withhold their permission.

"There is another matter, my lord, which will be of great interest to you and your council," said Su-du-Lance.

"One equally as important as this one?" replied the Water Lord, not wishing to be distracted.

"That is for you to decide but I feel it could be. These Telemachons that our Orsook travel with – they might have something which would be of great benefit to us."

"What is that?"

"They used to be led by a man called Telemachus, from whom they derived their name. But at this time they are led by a man called Tyracides. It is this one who carries with him the seed from the Plant of Infinite Want."

The crowned leader of Water-City fixed Su with a puzzled stare and repeated the last phrase, "Infinite Want?" He looked around to his counsellors and his gaze fell on an old Orsook with spiky white eyebrows who sat self-assured in his warm woollen gown dyed a rich green in colour.

"Myor, you might impress our guest with the great extent, indeed the almost infinite breadth of your knowledge, being the Keeper over the Orsook Mind and the initiator for public ritual – what does your *infinite* learning tell us about this Plant of *Infinite* Want?" It was a teasing tone, probably forced by his own embarrassment in being ignorant.

Su-du-Lance knew the gentle old counsellor from those previous visits he had made to the city, a fact which the Water Lord well understood.

"My lord," began Myor, "I know certainly that if this Tyracides has it, then he stole the seed or it was given to him by someone who did steal it."

"Theft?"

"A dead king can grant no further gifts. But he may be robbed." Aware that everybody's attention around the hall was upon him, extraordinarily, the old Orsook broke into song. Or at least, the tone he used was pitched mid-way between speech and song.

> "*The seed that settles*
> *Driven by the Wind of Change*
> *Under Danu's fertile force it wrestles,*
> *Overcomes the reluctant terrain.*
> *Sink into the dark matter of earth!*
> *Charm this High King's souterrain!*

Engage an age sped in light to the future,
Radiate an infinity in mechanical growth:
New promise to Orsook or human
- the Plant of Infinite Want."

Every Orsook sat in that hall realised the source for these lines but not the meaning of them.

Glad to recover something from his previous show of ignorance, the Water Lord asked, "That comes from the Orsook Book of the Water Current, doesn't it Myor?"

"Indeed, it does, sire. As everyone here is aware, that book consists of several thousand pages in content, which are contained within ten gloriously illustrated volumes. We have only five copies in the whole of Water-City; three of them have been created during my life-time by the ten scribes under my supervision and kindly paid by yourself, my lord." It did not do any harm to exercise a little flattery to maintain his position, thought the old keeper and besides, the Water Lord deserved it – the previous ruler, the Water Mother, had only given him three scribes.

"All very interesting to my lord and ourselves, I am sure," came a voice further down the table, "but what does it mean?"

Myor glanced at the young counsellor who had spoken, knowing that he cared little for the ancient text and whose place was assured at the table because he was the Water Lord's nephew. If it had been left to him, the keeper's scribes would be reduced to less than three. Myor cared about his position at the Water Lord's table but more, he loved the Book of the Water Current and it was his responsibility to make certain it survived even the death of the Orsook. That text contained not only the explanation for how all living things came to be on this world but also the possibility for future existence or existences. He could count on two fingers of his webbed hand the number of his scribes who were beginning to suspect what he had understood for many years: that the book contained a code within its volumes. Of the ten volumes there was one which held the interpretation. An index, if you like. However, unlike other indices, this was not placed at the end in the concluding book of the Book but somewhere between the first and last volume. Unfortunately, he did not know which one. So although he could not answer anything about that if asked, he could answer this ignorant fool of a nephew to the Water Lord, who was more like a human being in his greed for wealth and power at his uncle's table.

"It refers, Duke Baloose, to a seed that is able to produce huge plants from which you cannot only crop plentiful food but also medicinal drugs to cure all ills that you are likely to experience within one lifetime."

"I have heard about many wonderful things but that just seems an impossibility."

"Believe me," replied Myor slowly, with emphasis, "if human beings had anything further to do with it, those seeds would have been an impossibility."

"Why?"

"Many, many centuries ago, before the time in Europa when the Celts stole the body of the First Orsook and claimed him for their High King, there was an act they perpetrated which was as destructive and malign in its repercussions as the intermittent wars they pursued against us. In their raging desire for wood to forge weapons and boats that were required to transport goods and soldiers, they uprooted utterly an ancient woodland called the 'The Forest of Eternal Sunlight."

"Not so eternal, then," came the same voice, mocking.

Paying no attention, Myor continued, "There were many herbal plants in that forest, some of which could be found only in that place and nowhere else in this world. Our people at that time knew this forest down to the last twig and took the herbal plants and seeds for themselves that they required. But they only took what was sufficient, not wantonly as the humans do. This is how the seeds for the Plant of Infinite Want came to be in the High King's tomb. They were the last seeds of that plant in Europa and already a thousand years old by the time that the Telemachons broke into the tomb and stole them."

"Would the fertility in those seeds stale after such a long time and render them useless?" asked the Water Lord.

"Sire, the name is in the nature – this plant has an infinite want to survive. Those seeds are forever potent unless deliberately destroyed."

"It strikes me as strange that a growth with such marvellous produce should be hidden away in a mausoleum for all this time rather than be used for its benefits."

"As to that, I have no answer. Not presently," replied the old Orsook.

The elegant lady sitting beside her husband, the Water Lord, spoke up again. "It might be that the seeds were not farmed properly. The benefits may not have been as wonderful as predicted."

"In which case, why store it at all?" observed her husband.

"I, for one," said Duke Ote, "suggest that we should ask that question of Danu when he arrives here, for surely it would be a simple one for our Founder to answer?"

The Duke had neatly brought the conversation back to the more important topic of Danu's return. Sat deep in his wooden high-backed chair, carved intricately with images of river fish and water-weed, the ruler of the city pondered for a moment and then in a peremptory tone called out, "Myor, you seem to be the most suitable Orsook for this task: can you devise a means for finding out whether the Orsook who intends to visit us is indeed Danu or simply an impostor?"

The keeper over the Orsook Mind stroked his eyebrows with one webbed hand. Very few Orsook had eyebrows and with Myor this was a habit and there were some who believed that it was a deliberate and arrogant action to mark himself out as different to those around him. "I will refer to the Book of the Water Current, sire, I am sure that it will provide us with what we need."

"Good. Let the method be a civilised one, as befits the Orsook. If it turns out that he is an impostor, well …." The Water Lord waved an airy hand, "that means a different outcome. We can only take our politeness so far." He turned his attention back to Brun-du-Lac and her son. There was contrition in his face. "Water-Mother, I must apologise for my outburst earlier. It was rude of me and I can only put it down to the surprise at your news."

"Please don't worry," replied Brun, "you were right – much has been done for myself and others from Penlac. If there was any way we could be of service to you and the other Orsook in Water City, please make it known to us – we would gladly accept any duty."

"As to that – our thanks for your offer and we will let you know of our wishes very soon. But for now, I would be glad if you accepted a place on my council here to attend for its future meetings and ensure that the voice of those from Penlac is heard in our discussions and acted upon."

"Nothing would give me greater pleasure, sire."

"Good. Duke Ote will call on you to talk about the arrangement."

Taking his statement to be an indication that the meeting had ended, the Water-Sidhe and her son rose to their feet. After they had bowed, their disappearing figures were observed by those at the High Table.

"Sire," said Duke Ote turning his head to the small figure sitting beside him, "what if this Orsook they call Danu does turn out to be Danu himself?"

"What does the Book of the Water Current tell us about that, Myor?" asked the Water Lord, not wanting, or unable, to give an answer.

The official Initiator paused and thought for a moment, as was his custom. "The return of the gods is described there several times. Both to the Orsook and to humans. Their visit never turns out as expected."

The Water Lord did not want to hear any more. He determined to speak to Myor privately at another time and brought the council session to an end.

53

The Bracken Maze

Twenty shapes swam through the water of the River Fusion; bigger than the largest fish that inhabited the waterway – and some were human-sized in length – but the Orsook swam swifter, smoother than their human counterparts. The swimming stroke they used to slice through the water comprised a broad sweep around the head with the arms and the open webbed hands, accompanied by a pulsed, pushing movement from the legs. For a few moments their bodies would be perfectly straight and then the movement made again. Twenty Orsook could be counted together but further ahead there was another one. The rest took their lead from him. The current was strong as it flowed northwards, helping them to swim faster and the water here was deep.

Goreth checked that the others were still behind. The Fusion's water did not always run clear and could be murky at times. He had dealt with this by exuding a green light from his skin. The fluorescent glow made it easier for his companions to find their way. Disturbed mud in the water was a sign that not far ahead the river would be hitting some kind of obstruction, with a possible drop in the water level. He decided to slow his pace, swim with caution and just as he thought, a little further on the level did drop so that soon he was wading through it at waist height. Paradoxically, the Fusion's power increased in strength. It was a struggle for the others to follow Goreth out to the side and pull themselves onto the river bank.

Resting only until they had caught their breath, the Orsook pushed on – this time moving rapidly around the obstruction in the river which turned out to be a number of large rock boulders. A path beaten into the mud running alongside the river was a welcome route. It was difficult to understand where the rocks had come from since there were no rocky hills either side of the river, only dense forest. Perhaps they had been torn from the ground in the world's first making, before the forest had taken root. As if to confirm that suggestion, a little further on the river level was split. The water suddenly fell over a ledge; a noisy cascade blew up with a voluminous roar that belied its short stature. For though, indeed, it was not a long waterfall, as Chanson-du-Lac gazed at it she realised that despite the increased water depth in the river after it, not many of her companions would have survived the fall.

When they assessed the water depth to be safe again, the Orsook plunged back in. With renewed strength they coursed northwards to Water-City. It was an overwhelming desire that drove them on, an irresistible urge similar to the one that grips the new-born sea turtle scurrying across the sand towards the ocean. So they were impelled, to find their original home. This sense was stronger in Goreth than the others. Once again, he found himself questioning why it was that his body subjected itself to instinct, rather than rational control. Why was it that he who should be so powerful, sensed only an obligation to the unknown? To give in, afforded the only relief. It was the only way, at least, to satisfy curiosity.

But once more, there was another barrier. The current slowed and a dim impenetrable shape loomed ahead. When the Orsook came close, they discovered that a great iron grid stretched across their path. The lattice spaces were large enough to let some fishes through but not the Orsook.

As they came out of the water, it was not just boulders and a water torrent that confronted them this time.

The iron grid under the river now appeared as a tall spear-pointed fence on dry land. It curved when reaching the flatter earth beside the river as if designed purposely to protect what was on the other side. And there was a material shape on its other side. Something huge, rising up to the sky.

Goreth led his Orsook up to it. Ferny, dark hair dripping water, he raised his eyes and their stare took in the tall trunk travelling upward. Anyone would have expected brown, wrinkled bark on such a body but no, this trunk was more stem than trunk and uninterrupted sea-green in colour rather than brown.

To Chanson-du-Lac and Ol-du-Brec as they came up behind Goreth and saw his face, it seemed that Goreth was almost afraid. They were disturbed and when seeing what he was stood in front of, it added to their unease.

"The Plant of Infinite Want," murmured Goreth. He stopped for a moment and then spoke louder, his tone confessional. "I gave the seed of this plant away to a human being once. He is now dead. But I did it because I had to."

One of the other Orsook suddenly called out. "Over here! There is an opening into this place." Those who had just left the water joined him, as did Goreth, Chanson and Ol-du-Brec.

It was strange that such a protective fence should have a weak point but it was true. The barrier gave way to an arch that had no gate to it but was simply an open entrance.

They argued whether they should use the gateway but then saw there was little alternative. Either side the river stood a rocky wall which had to be climbed. The perimeter fence coming from the river on the side they were standing met with one of these rocky walls and where it joined rose up higher than the other sections of the iron grid. The only way forward was via that arch or they could go back. By someone else's design their choice was made for them so the risk was taken and they reluctantly passed through the open gateway.

Once the Orsook had gone under the arch and passed by the Plant of Infinite Want they found themselves walking down a path between two high hedges, deliberately cut and shaped. Small daggers and swords were already in their hands and no order had to be given by Goreth or Ol-du-Brec.

The path turned and turned again. There seemed to be no escape from those high hedges. At times gaps became visible and the Orsook took them, only to immediately arrive on a similar path to the one that had just been left and which twisted at right angles again to lead onto other gaps and so on.

Finally, losing patience, Ol-du-Brec exclaimed, "Wait! What are we doing?"

"Finding our way out?" replied Chanson-du-Lac, gentle mockery in her voice.

"Hardly," replied Ol-du-Brec. "Not like this and not here on the ground. We need to go up." He stepped away from the hedges, estimating their distance from the ground. "Why travel down here, getting lost when we can walk across the tops of them and see all around? Those hedges are dense enough to carry our weight."

But before they could put this idea into action, something disturbed them.

Way ahead, in one of the green corridors, a moan erupted. It was human in tone and contained a whisper of wind through tree-tops. The sound was not so weak that its source could not be located. Soon the Orsook were at the corridor from which the sound had come. It was louder now and what made it could be seen. An untidy wooden heap, sticks jutting out, lay against one green border. Suddenly the whole rose up and became a tottering figure clinging for support to the hedge.

Chanson-du-Lac moved forward in an effort to offer help but Ol-du-Brec stopped her. "We need to be careful," he warned. Gradually, the helpless figure, either injured or sick, pulled strength from somewhere and lurched along the greenery, away from them. As it did so, the Orsook slowly followed.

This creature was not one that Ol-du-Brec had ever seen before and he had seen many in his short life beside the lake at Penlac. The silver flitting patterns under the water, reflected from one fish or a shoal's, blank round face that burst the surface, gulping with pumped, open mouths at the swirled dance of insects just above their heads. The insects themselves: from tiny spectral flies to bluely blazed dragonflies, half the length of your arm, skimming from one place to the next. Then the otters, the wolves, the bears and the soaring eagles. This creature looked like none of them but did resemble what was told in the stories of the Bracken Ones, those strange beings who ruled the forest north-east of Penlac. He put the thought into words for those around him. "A Bracken One!" he exclaimed in a low whisper.

"Are you certain?" replied Ol-du-Brec.

"As sure as I could be on the first sight of one, yes," he answered.

They all, on hearing it, grew warier still. The told stories had been listened to by them all. How the first humans in the forest near Penlac had grown to love the trees so much that the god of the trees, Silvanus, had made the people into bracken. But bracken shaped like men and women. Those stories that spoke about the lives these Bracken lived in the tops of trees or in deep pools by the dams built along the River Fusion or in the dams themselves. How Orsook women and human women would be travelling through the forest – this was before the histories and song cycles were created – and they would peer into the liquid surfaces, having been attracted by a silver flitting pattern or to recall the memory of a lost relative. At that unguarded moment, the long tendril arms of the Bracken King's embrace would reach out from the water. There would be no time to scream. Just an instant exhale. A soft splash. To accept. Disappear.

The Bracken creature staggered on again and turned a corner After some hesitation, the Orsook with this time Goreth leading the way, followed him. This close, they could see that the figure was a man. A beard like wild Hawthorne scrub tufted with white blossom wrapped around his lower jaw and what seemed an armoured breastplate encased his torso but this was made from tree bark not metal and might just as well have been his bared chest. Below that, he wore a short tunic plaited from river reed.

They rounded the corner without a problem but found that the Bracken was further away than he was supposed to be. Furthermore, beyond him was a gap in the hedges but instead of yet another green border to limit the view, this gap was filled with light and space. Behind them came a rushing noise and already the Orsook knew that they had just walked into a trap that had been sprung.

The Bracken creature ahead lost his vulnerability and from a stooped position, he stood up straight and strong, a wry smile breaking above his thorny beard. In a clattering command, sticks falling on rocky ground, he called out, "Drop your weapons!"

Ol-du-Brec and the others looked behind them to another sudden disturbance. There, on the hedge-tops, arranged to block their retreat and with arrows already notched into bows, stood numerous Bracken.

Beside Ol-du-Brec a companion impulsively threw his dagger at a Bracken stood above. An arrow instantly buried itself into his skull and he fell flat on his back, stone-dead. Meanwhile, his knife flew harmlessly by the Bracken over him, who was fitting another arrow.

"Stop!" hissed the creature near the exit as he saw two Orsook moving towards their fallen comrade. They obeyed. "I said release your weapons." Then, after a pause, "The alternative, of course, is to be slaughtered like penned-up cattle if you don't wish to do that."

Swords and daggers dropped to the ground.

"That's sensible. Now, I want you to follow me out from this maze garden we specially designed for all our guests. There is someone you must meet."

"First," replied Goreth, "you must let us bring our fallen friend."

"Good idea -" said the other, "best not to leave a mess in the garden."

Goreth ignored the jibe and walked back to the dead Orsook. He lifted him up as easily as if he was taking up an armful of feathers and proceeded to carry him through the gap. The other Orsook followed.

Deliberately ignoring the sight that he knew would meet him – for the moment anyway – Goreth found a place to lay the dead Orsook gently on the ground. The body was at the foot of the last hedge in the maze. That arrow sticking out from his head was an indignity. Goreth reached down and broke it off.

As he stood up straight, a voice like a dry rustling wind through tree-tops rose up behind. Goreth could see the fear on the face of the other Orsook.

"So, the rumours are correct. Danu has crossed the sea to the land of the Britons to join up with his last remaining Orsook!"

Goreth turned to see, at a distance, the Bracken King standing with his 'children' either side and behind him. They did indeed look like children as the tallest of them only reached to the chest of his king.

"I am here, Llyr, the question is: what do you want?"

"Me? I want? You break into my kingdom without permission and ask me that?"

"The gate was open," said Goreth, waving back to the maze. We assumed it was an open, friendly invitation to guests and we came to find hospitality."

"That maze was created to discourage all those who might want to encroach on our land. If you like, it is a polite form for denying entry. Once you were confused, you should have retraced your steps. But now, it is too late.

Goreth took a step forward, his face set into an expression that was grim and his body began to glow with an incandescent gleam. He surveyed the hundreds of Bracken creatures massed around their monarch and said, "Careful, Llyr, you might consider yourself safe behind the shield provided by your numerous progeny but their strength is nothing compared to mine. It would be best for all of us if you exchanged hostility for friendship that we may all go in peace."

"Oh, believe me, when I say I do not underestimate the power of Danu, the force that brought life to Europa. But you are not in Europa, you are in the land of the Bracken. It is a curious thing but ignorance is not just the prerogative of human beings – gods too may be oblivious to what can cause their own destruction."

At that instant, lassoes whipped through the air, three in all. They dropped over Goreth's head and shoulders and he felt his arms caught, pinned to his torso. But the reaction from Goreth was completely unexpected. He shrieked and dropped to his knees. A sudden pain had shot into his whole body and the phosphorescent shine that had been increasing through his skin before the contact with the lassoes, vanished. Pain continued to flow throughout his limbs .... and weakness. He could barely hear what was being spoken to him by King Llyr, who continued to speak as if nothing had happened. The other Orsook watched Goreth in charged despair.

"Your people might have the ability to communicate with the birds and the fish but our knowledge is given to us through the very roots of trees and plants beneath the earth. We knew you were coming the moment you stepped onto our forest floor." A groan escaped from Goreth's lips but Llyr continued heedless. He was speaking to be heard by his own subjects and the Orsook, glad to show the latter how weak their god really was. He would also predict their future.

"The Plant of Infinite Want is a truly wondrous thing is it not?" Another moan slipped from Goreth. Our forests extend everywhere – here in Briton and over the sea in Europa, where they are even denser. The species of vegetation that grow in them is countless. Under the soil, their roots spread touch and communicate more than life itself. They communicate everything to us."

"Stop it! You are killing him!" burst out Chanson-du-Lac as she saw Goreth trying to rise again and collapsing. The ropes, tight around his chest, were held from a distance by three Bracken Ones.

A crack across the rough bark on Llyr's face indicated a cruel smile. "He is not dying. A god does not die. Not yet. If anything could kill a divine inspiration while satisfying all human desire, it would be the Plant of Infinite Want. That is what those ropes are made from." The Orsook stared at the organic shackles and in the mind of each one was the hope of a plan to release Goreth from them. "It surprises me that Danu did not realise the threat contained by this plant to both him and his people, once the sprig had grown to its full height and been nurtured for a year. Because as much as it answers every human need, it is lethal to the Orsook and their god. Danu should have realised that when he passed by the one we had located next to the gateway into our garden maze. But from what I hear, he actually carried the seed of the plant around with him. Carried the seed that had been kept for safety in the High King Orsek's tomb and then simply gave it away to human beings. How strange is that? That the great river god and protector of the Orsook world give away the code to his own immortality to the weakest creatures on this planet?"

Ol-du-Brec had a desperate urge to rush forward in an attempt to release Goreth from his bonds. He saw Chanson slowly shaking her head at him, realising what might happen. There seemed to be nothing he could do, no command he could give his Orsook warriors to relieve the situation, no escape route. King Llyr's army gathered, the skin and hair on each making them more like vegetation in their forest of origin, rather than humanoid. They took root around their ruler. Behind, were more Bracken warriors, itching to kill another Orsook.

It was disastrous. The final, ominous, notes rang out in what Llyr said next.

"We must send out a clear message to the Orsook, to the human beings, to any other tribe on two legs. This forest belongs to the Bracken and will always be ruled by the Bracken.

Take them!

54
Telemachus, Eris and Faramund

Eris and Faramund put out the morning's campfire on which the fish had been cooking. They had all eaten and were ready to move. Telemachus was pleased to see how well they worked together. If only he could have found such a peace in another's company. Instead, he had only guilt as the legacy of a dead wife, recovery from a malicious spell cast by a Witch Queen and long separation between himself and the woman with whom he was most likely to forge a genuine love.

The short, murmured talk between the Eris and Faramund was almost comforting. Birds sang from above; the river flowed, partly shaded, beneath the overhanging trees and warm sunshine broke through the green canopy in bright mote-speckled beams.

Eris must have caught something of Telemachus' mood. "If only it was like this all the time," she said, wistfully.

"Like this?" said Faramund, staring around. "Certainly, it's pleasant enough at the moment but it was colder and damper last night. Moreover, that bear's growl startled you out of my arms soon enough." He paused and added teasingly, "If it was a bear's growl, who knows?"

"The campfire kept it away," observed Telemachus. "The forest is probably teeming with food that would be easier to prey upon than us."

"I wasn't startled," said Eris almost angrily, "I was alert, which was more than could have been said for you two – both snoring away. And Telemachus, I'm surprised. It was your turn for guard duty. Have you spent too much time allocating watch duty to others? We could have all died in the night as a trophy to your diligence."

"Eris!" warned Faramund.

"No," cut in Telemachus. "What Eris says is right and I owe you both an apology."

"We have been riding hard for almost a week now and it is two days since we came across the River Fusion," said Faramund.

"Does it take a man to defend another man against a woman?" asked Eris, the scorn clear in her voice. But she too was tired, even after a partial night's rest, following her own watch. "Let's just get on!" She went to her brown filly and using the stirrup, jumped easily onto it's back. With a tap of her heels, the horse was off. Faramund shrugged his shoulders at Telemachus and then they both got onto their steeds and rode after her.

It was a track running alongside the river that they rode on. The path was beaten, wide and well-used. Telemachus wondered by what or whom. Because it was so wide, Faramund was able to ride beside him. Yet, they rode in silence, Telemachus staring into the brown water that rolled by, its surface bearing fallen leaves and moving quickly on. It reminded him of something. Then again there flowed into his mind the vision on the causeway. He thought about that for a few moments and then he thought about Goreth.

The Orsook god had cast a long shadow over his life, despite the short time he had known him. And here he was again, chasing that shadow. Or was it Formus he was pursuing. Or Tyracides? He felt angry with himself now. He should be leading, not following others. *In Europa I was in control. There was a purpose. I was with my people and achieving it. Here in Briton that integrity has been taken from me, first by the Witch Queen and even by Princess Byncor. They have all been distractions from what he should be doing: settling his people in a new land.*

In a curious way, his own situation ran parallel to Goreth's. They had both travelled through the same lands, both undergone physical transformation. But Telemachus thought, no, he *knew*, that Goreth was not happy living in the form he currently held. It was not something he desired. The androgynous shape had been thrust upon him. Sometimes, Telemachus had wondered if the alteration was complete or was it a stage Goreth was going through to reach completion? When it was complete, whole, what then?

"Are those thoughts worth discussion?" smiled Faramund, having observed Telemachus studious expression.

"It is just this, Faramund," said Telemachus hesitantly. "Does Goreth support us or is he opposed to us?"

Faramund considered. "Probably neither. His motivation, naturally, lies with his own people. He is too intelligent to blame all human tribes for what happened to his fellow Orsook in Europa, yet who could blame Goreth or his kinsfolk for being wary, if not downright suspicious towards us?"

"We too, should exercise that same caution about him. Sometimes, I have doubted the implication that he is some kind of god. He has never said so himself but perhaps it is a deceit that he has encouraged for those around him, practised for his own purposes."

Faramund laughed. "If that is the case, then ask Berengar about what happened when he argued with Goreth. Such power as was exercised then did not come from a mortal combatant. Recall how we found Goreth chained in the tunnel underneath Glauberg and that Tyracides was convinced it was the face of Danu that he was looking at? See Goreth now – how his body has changed. Is that normal – even for an Orsook?"

"No, but is it understandable that a god should allow himself to be chained, unless, following upon that, he is not a divine?"

"Oh, there are many examples in the stories from both your people and mine concerning the entrapment of immortals. What is reliable is that they never die, and always escape."

Telemachus was sceptical about that. The most wondrous things could happen to him – had happened to him – but in the end, he remained sceptical. It was his strength. To dream and build a better future is a sceptic's enterprise.

"Those are just stories, Faramund."

The Celt observed the Greek commander's face with complete astonishment on his own. Here was a man who had been given the shape of a beast not once but twice through the power of sorcery and yet was denying that such events could happen. He searched for a suggestion that the speaker meant humour in what he said. But none came. It was as if he had deliberately blinded himself to the wonders in this world and had chosen ignorance. Faramund gave an inner shrug. He was certainly not going to waste any time in discussing it but satisfied himself with a rejoinder. "The stories we live can be more shocking and stranger than those told by the bards at starlight."

Telemachus made a derisory *hurrumph* and rode on.

They maintained a distance within sight of each other, dismounting and leading their horses by the rein over steeper terrain next to the river. The land got hillier the further north they went and the forest receded a little from the river's edges. Eris had gone further ahead again and it was becoming difficult for Faramund to keep her in view as she led the way for all three of them.

But when Faramund had peered for the umpteenth time at her moving figure he found that she had halted and got down from her horse, looking at some feature on the ground. Telemachus had also noted it and turning around to Faramund beckoned to him to move faster and catch up with Eris.

By the time they had reached her she had tethered her horse to a tree, disappeared over a small hill and returned again.

"What have you found?" said Telemachus as both he and Faramund drew up to her. But the answer to that question was plainly at her feet. The tracks in the wet mud suggested a number of people travelling together. Over a dozen, he assessed. There was something unusual about the prints.

"Orsook," replied Eris, simply. "They all came straight from the river." She pointed at the crowd of marks leading down and vanishing under the water.

"You sure?" said Faramund. "Might they not be a flock of swans exiting the river?"

For answer, Eris stamped her foot down next to one of the prints and lifted it. The mark she left was smaller than the one that had been made earlier there, only beside the clear pattern her boot had made, there was a webbed outline. "Swans the size of men perhaps, but with bigger brains?" She paused, "Do you hear that noise?"

The sound was loud, continuous and completely normal.

"It's only the river, what of it?" replied Faramund.

He, along with Telemachus instinctively turned towards the source if the cascading noise but the hill Eris had climbed over earlier, obliterated their view.

"On the other side of that hill, as the river turns, it divides into two levels. Anyone swimming in the water would have been swept by the current and smashed to pieces on the rocks below. That is why the Orsook left the river at this point. I have something else to show you. Follow me."

Without waiting, Eris led her horse over the hill. The other two followed and just as she had said, discovered the rapids flowing furiously on the other side. They also found themselves in a valley and its rocky sides grew in height as they continued to walk its length. After ten minutes Eris stopped and let the eyes of Telemachus and Faramund dwell on the sight.

Faramund was staggered. Instantly, he recalled the sorcery he had practised with Conversevitae. A simple seed had been converted to a weapon of war and King Noremac's horse troop had been destroyed under a massive collapse of vegetation.

"The Plant of Infinite Want? But what is it doing here? I thought the seed was rare."

"Scarce, if not extinct in Europa, but judging from this, more common over here in Briton."

Telemachus was studying the perimeter fence in front of it, seeing how it went all the way down to the river and noting the arched, gateless opening, with the fence on its other side covering the ground all the way up to the valley wall. The valley walls for some reason did not appear natural; they had been artificially created.

"More tracks," he said, pointing to the river edge. Indeed, there they were, the same Orsook footprints, leaving the water's edge and heading towards the arched entrance. "Do you remember what you said to me about what you had learned from Conversevitae's library, Faramund? Concerning the Bracken Ones, the River Fusion and the Orsook? It seems that if this place was built by the Bracken Ones then we have all three here together. That could be more than coincidental."

"Those hedges on the other side of the fence, mused Faramund, "– they could be hiding something. Let's go through the archway."

"Careful!" hissed Eris.

His horse trotted through the archway with him on it and there was a very short gap between his head and the stone. Eris went after him and then Telemachus.

They began to move through the green lanes silently and as they did so, Telemachus recalled that he had seen puzzling layouts with hedges such as these before. Only once or twice, back in Sicily, at the home of a rich merchant or tyrant with daughters to amuse. They were gardens kept and maintained for entertainment. This one, however, was on a different scale. On the horse, his head was at a lower height than the nearest hedge – just. He reined it in and then raised himself in his stirrups. They gave him the leverage he required, to see over the hedge-tops.

The other two saw the expression on his face and immediately paused their own mounts. Becoming aware of them, Telemachus lowered himself and pressed a finger to his lips. It did not stop them from doing what he had just done. What they saw filled them with dread.

55
Fusion

Over the hedge-tops in the distance was a gathering of the Bracken. Neither Telemachus nor his companions had seen these creatures before and their strange appearance struck fear into them. But what made them even more afraid was the line of wooden posts along the edge of the River Fusion. Each column was fixed sturdily into the mud and roped to it was an Orsook. Taller than the others was a post with a cross-bar. It was placed in the middle of the line and the reason for the cross-bar was plain. Whereas all the others had shackled to them an Orsook who could stand upright, this one held up a creature whose head slumped forward, while his arms were raised and the rope tied to his wrists had been lashed around the wooden cross-piece.

The distance away was not so great that all three there could not recognise who it was.

"It's Goreth, isn't it?" asked Faramund, shocked, and the others nodded in answer. "What have they done to him? And how?"

Telemachus did not want to waste time in discussion. "Whatever it is, they have overcome him and the others. We cannot wait here and be captured in the same way."

Eris eyed him with reproach. "You cannot mean, Telemachus, that we must leave them to their fate, without offering some help?"

"There are just the three of us," said Telemachus, firmly. "We must be sensible. The Bracken, for that, I take it, is who they are, must outnumber us by over thirty to one. What, by the gods, would you have us do? The only possibility for us is that we slip by them and continue on our way to meet up with the other Telemachons."

"You mean use the suffering endured by Goreth and his friends as a distraction for our escape?" said Faramund.

"Have you a better idea?"

Wordlessly, Faramund reached into his tunic and pulled out a small leather pouch the size of one of his fingers. It was tied with a sewn-through leather drawstring. Telemachus had guessed at the content before Faramund had finished unknotting the leather and had turned it out into the palm of his hand to show them. Surely, he couldn't have one, could he?

Yes, there it was – a small round white bubble in the centre of his hand.

Faramund eyed Telemachus with a slight smile on his lips. "With this, I can create chaos."

Telemachus had heard from Eris how her partner had destroyed Mitshid through occultic practice with the Plant of Infinite Want. Of course, at that time he had been led by Conversevitae. "Chaos for all of us, perhaps."

It was as if Faramund was reading his mind. The slight smile had gone from the Celt's lips to be replaced by the shade of a frown. "I learned a lot from Conversevitae about these seeds and the plant but more on my own account. If you want to rescue Goreth and the others, there is little choice. We have to use the one seed we have got."

Telemachus stared doubtfully at the white sphere in Faramund's hand. "Faramund, I managed to glimpse what they had tied the Orsook with. Metal chains for all of them except Goreth: he had plant tendrils around his wrists. Ordinarily, he would be able to snap them like twigs but I'm guessing that those shackles have been made from the Plant. Do you think I am right?"

"Yes, you are. There are many plants poisonous to the human race – hemlock, deadly nightshade, foxglove, ragwort and this Plant of Infinite Want differs from the rest in that although it brings some cures and benefits to human beings, it is completely toxic to the Orsook. It is why Goreth is so weakened under that post. Wrapped around his wrists is the poison that invades his body."

"You intend to use that seed to rescue the Orsook?" exclaimed Telemachus, incredulously.

"Be optimistic, Telemachus," said Faramund, "a malign influence can be changed to benefit all."

Eris smiled and placed her hand on Faramund's shoulder. "Now that is how a true man speaks."

*　　　*　　　*　　　*

In this blackness I cannot see, I can only feel the surging pain from my wrists, along my arms. Pain that saps my energy, leaving me useless and unable to flee from the black hole of pain. Darkness cocoons me. Sometimes my eyes open; at least I can feel them opening but they see very little – dim shapes moving at the edge and flowing river water to the front. There is that. It's fresh muddy smell rises and watery waves sparkle beyond the darkness. Another searing pain shoots along my limb. Someone screams. Is it me? Blackness folds over. A single voice shouts, saying a name: "Goreth! Goreth!" My name is not Goreth. It is Danu.

*　　　　*　　　　*　　　　*

The Lord of the Bracken, Llyr, called to his children, "Bring the wood! Prepare to burn them!" From two stacked waggons, dozens of the Bracken Ones pulled away bundles of tied twigs, bringing them to the shackled Orsook along the River Fusion.

Chanson-du-Lac watched the bundles stacking around her with growing horror. Water had been her source of life and happiness for a long as she could remember and now to be destroyed by fire was an abomination. Escape? She strained uselessly at her straps, then called out to Ol-du-Brec, "Are you conscious, Ol-du-Brec? Can you see what is happening to us?"

The Orsook moaned but then mastered himself. He was positioned on the other side of Goreth facing the river, while Chanson stood fixed to her post on the left side. Congealed blood covered one eye but with the other Ol-du-Brec understood why Chanson had called to him, rather than Goreth. The Orsook god continued to hang without any sign of consciousness, his head slumped forward, saliva and blood dribbling onto the muddy ground.

But then, not waiting for an answer, Chanson did call to Goreth in her despair. "Goreth! Goreth! Please wake up! See what is being done to us and help us!"

There was no response from the hanging body but Ol-du-Brec tried to calm her. "My lady, peace, peace. Goreth cannot help." Which, as far as his people are concerned, has been the case forever, thought Ol-du-Brec bitterly. "The only recourse for us is to prepare ourselves in as dignified a way as possible for what is to come."

The piling up of the wood fuel had almost completed and each Orsook was surrounded by a ring of bundles waiting to be lit. When the waggons were emptied, they were hauled away.

In their ranks the Bracken Ones fell silent, behind them the tall hedges of the maze garden that marked out an entrance to their land; in front: their king, the captured Orsook and the River Fusion.

Llyr turned his huge craquelured face to his people and addressed them. "My children, we will reduce these Orsook to ashes and scatter them as an offering to the River. No-one can claim this river as their own but us, the Bracken. The Orsook came from water and to water they will be returned." A cheer broke out from his army and the others gathered by.

Llyr waited for the cheering to subside and then gave his command. "Burn them!"

But as the last word fell away, an odd disturbance occurred. From behind him and his army, somewhere in the dark green maze that marked the entrance to the Land of the Bracken, came a loud sound. It was distinctive: like the jarring *clack* that was produced when a Bracken suddenly moved a limb but this one could have been made by a thousand Bracken together.

The order Llyr had given was disregarded as everyone's attention was pulled towards the disturbance. Then they saw, like a column of hot air, gas and molten rock shot from the central chamber in a volcano, a huge green growth rising up. The ground shook so hard, that some Bracken fell to it and lay there, gasping. Thick, leafy foliage sprouted from the stem, blotting out the sun. Now it could be seen that what had erupted from the earth was a Plant of Infinite Want but none there had seen such a size before.

And it kept on growing.

Llyr's mouth fell open as he saw the many branches sprouting from the main trunk, the stems dividing again from the branches, the countless leaves then filling every available space between.

*　　　*　　　*　　　*

There is a respite. The pain diminishing as if retreating or being called back to somewhere else. Around my wrists the tightness loosens. It is just a glimmer, a hint of warmth but I can begin to exercise some strength again.

*   *   *   *

At the first quake from the ground, King Llyr had tumbled down along with some of his subjects. Furious, he raised his clacking body up and heard some officer from his army shouting to him. "Sire! Sire! Look to Danu. See what is happening!"

The Bracken leader heard and saw what was unfolding where his chief prisoner was held. The green tendrils which had been tied around Danu's wrists and looped over the cross-bar appeared to have come alive. They were moving as if one long limbless body of a snake. First, the cords around the cross-bar had whiplashed off and down to the earth in one swift movement. Then those around the Orsook's arms had unravelled themselves and followed downwards to land beside the other end. For a moment, the heap of snaky coils lay still, taut as a bow-string. In the next, the wiry loops buried themselves just below the earth's surface and shot off to join the Plant that was still growing in the green maze. Its forceful intent in that direction could be traced like a moving furrow through the confused ranks of the Bracken army.

Llyr's attention was divided between Danu and the shuddering, towering bulk that was the Plant of Infinite Want. For the latter seemed to have attained its optimum growth. But a fresh bursting change was taking place. Between the leaves, there poked out spiky blue flowers. They were different to what the Bracken were used to in this plant they had cultivated for many years. The blooms recognisable for them were blue but wide-petalled, not the pointed daggers that presented here. Also, from each pin-end there oozed bright red sap.

No further movement was detectable but now the colouring in the plant began to change. What once had been a verdant green suffusing the main stem became pallid as if the colour was being flushed downward back into the soil. The white sickly luminescence contrasted strongly with the leaves, which somehow kept their greenery. Then, yet another sound broke out. The fear that swiftly overtook the expressions on the faces of the Bracken and it must have been true fear to bring about a recognisable change on those faces, showed that they understood what it was. Any woodcutter in the forest, having sweated for a whole morning wielding a single axe around the girth of a particularly large tree, would have instantly known the sound.

Shouted warnings, cries, rose up from the Bracken as they desperately ran this way and that to escape the falling monster.

The Plant of Infinite Want came down with a whistling roar to crush the running Bracken. Yet many would have escaped, despite the tall mass falling on some Bracken but for the fact that as the vegetable body hit the ground those spiky blue blooms popped out, flying like arrows from the pressure of a loosened bow-string. Where they hit woody, softer flesh on any Bracken their blood-red sap soaked in. Screams vibrated from those Bracken mouths and their skin burnt. The deadly toxin left them squirming and dying on the ground.

King Llyr had avoided the fall. There were two or three of his subjects between himself and the tip of the Plant. All the poisonous darts had been thrown out to the sides and not to where he stood.

Fear and rage combined in the Bracken as he turned around to vent it on what he assumed to be the cause for his misfortunes. From the maze garden he noted three figures come running through the sprawled Bracken as they lay dying on the ground. Three *humans*. Where were they running to?

He gauged their direction and saw that its aim was for the Orsook chained to their posts at the riverside. Specifically, to Danu. But then Llyr realised that Danu had been freed from his restraints and was groggily moving away from his post to the River Fusion.

With a snarl, the king grabbed a javelin from one of his Bracken standing by and moved off. A thought suddenly occurred to him. He went to the fallen Plant and finding a blue bloom that had not detached itself from the main body, he stuck the sharp bronze point on his javelin into the sticky red ooze and made sure the tip was heavily smeared in the sap.

After it was done, he began to run. Not after the human creatures. His concern, in the first instance, was the Orsook river god.

*　　　*　　　*　　　*

I can walk but just. I sense the light but my vision is blurred. What little consciousness I have, tells me that the water of life lies in front. And to it, I must return. Eyeee! With each indrawn breath of oxygen, my life is beginning to restore but my true life lies in that water. Something else is happening within my body. That thing I cannot control, that impulse which has so often regenerated the change coming upon me: from female to male to the unity of the two; from Orsook to god to animal or tree to god. This is the build-up in power again. It begins to roll through my

existence, an enormous tidal pull towards the water. There is a difference this time.

*   *   *   *

Llyr's height gave him an advantage when he ran. Every single stride that he made was the equivalent of two for any one of the Bracken he ruled. He was able to get quite near to Danu without him knowing, before the shout rang out.

"Goreth!" It had come from Telemachus who was also close enough for his voice to be heard.

The Orsook god who was walking now, dazed and unsteady at first but becoming firmer in his movement towards the river, turned at the call. He saw, through his restored eyesight, the man Telemachus, pointing to the Bracken giant running towards him, javelin at hand.

"Beware Llyr!" shouted the Greek. He had stopped and Faramund and Eris had rejoined him.

They saw Goreth now, beginning to run himself. Swift and swifter, he flew towards the Fusion's edge. The Bracken King stopped and levelled the javelin to his shoulder.

"Quick, Eris!" commanded Telemachus, "Your bow!" She reacted immediately, unslinging her bow and notching an arrow.

But Llyr had already started the run-up to his javelin throw. Over his shoulder, Goreth saw what he was about to do but continued with his own purpose, which was to reach the Fusion.

At a certain point on the river bank, he lifted off into the air for a perfect dive.

The Bracken King hurled his spear.

Eris had already loosened her arrow and fired two more after that.

Speeding javelin and diving god met on a malicious trajectory. The iron tip buried itself in Goreth's back.

Llyr raised his arm in jubilation but as he did so an arrow hissed by, then with a sickening thud a second one went into his eye, a third, moments later, into his neck. He lurched forward, all life extinguished.

Telemachus, Faramund and Eris were paying no more attention to him. They watched something they could not understand.

The spear had caught Goreth in his back but the dive did not falter. His body hit the water but then like a skimming stone across a placid lake it *bounced* and not just once but two, three, four times. Then on the fourth ricochet, Goreth flew up vertically into the sky. His figure was held there, still, as if by invisible force. Stillness convulsed in the next passing of time: he changed into a massive fiery wheel of sparks revolving and spitting those sparks down to the river beneath. But those lights did not fall as a scatter and they did not fade as sparks would have done. They fell, or rather moved, into the form of a turning double helix that was constructed from interconnected spheres, now shining red, now blue, now white and the colours giving place one to the other and back again. The movement was serene, not violent but the helix wound slowly as it neared the surface of the River Fusion. Strange to say that the object did not appear to go *through* the water but just above it part of the double helix quaked and vanished and then became visible again under the surface. The remaining shape above began to spin quicker and gradually all of it was swallowed by the air and then the black hole that was the water. The water churned in a great engine at work.

To the watchers – Telemachus, Faramund, Eris, the Orsook remaining tied at their posts and the few surviving Bracken – the river water from that spot had become flushing molten gold. It lapped at the bank and travelled upstream, transforming the other brown water into its own clear brilliance as it went. The gold liquid became a tidal wave moving further and far upstream. Nothing diminished its energy. In fact, its impulse grew stronger, the further it went. Miles and miles, it journeyed. Time halted. The distance covered - light in comparison.

One instant later, the brilliant yellow tide hit the city of the Orsook, Water City. A female Orsook sensed it first as she took up her filled bucket from the riverside in the centre of the city. She held her pail and was distracted by the shining glare. Turning to face it, the bucket was dropped in horror at the sight of the enormous golden wave coming her way. A warning shout began from her mouth but by then it was too late.

The wave rushed through the river and the canals branching from it, like blood filling arterial veins in living tissue. Yet here was a strange thing. The massive wave did not break the river banks, not even flood the paths that lined the canals. It did not overwhelm the buildings with a huge energetic watery onslaught. For it was not water that was the driving force. But what it did was to separate. What appeared to be the wave came away from the main body of water in the river and canals. It drew the glow from moving fluid and that became a glittering golden fog, which suffused the breathed air of the city. The scream had not finished from the Orsook woman's throat before the shining mist had entered it. Around the streets and in the buildings, the Orsook at their tasks found themselves taking in the spangled air before they could clap hands to mouths, not that it would have helped. The child at his or her school-desk, the bread-maker at the oven, the law-giver presenting a case in court: they all and all the others breathed in a charged, scintillated aura. It reached into their lungs, their minds, their blood.

*   *   *   *

My final re-creation is complete. The growth to non-existence. As an individual mind. Instead, I become a thousand. And more. Each scintillation, a mind and multitudinous twinkled thoughts. My energy: my people. My energy becomes them. It is why I have lived. To die like this.

*The end of Book Two of
the Telemachon Myth.*

List of Characters
with Pronunciation Guide.

The guide in brackets is phonetic and stress is indicated with an apostrophe after the stressed syllable e.g. Quant'um. Characters are listed in order of appearance in the myth. Vowels are pronounced short unless indicated otherwise in brackets.

Telemachus (Telem'-er-kus): Leader of the Telemachons, searching out a new homeland for his people.

Eucleides (You-klay-eed'-ees): Greek mercenary officer who had fought with Telemachus in Sicily and is a loyal friend to him.

Pelisteus (Pell-i-stay'-us): Former Syracusan slave and one-time lover of Belisama.

Belisama (Bell-i-sarm'-a): Celt, originating from the mountain tribe of the Helvetii and the land where the Danu has its source. Trained charioteer.

Tyracides (Tir-a-seed'-ees): Once a slave; becomes a rival to Telemachus, temporarily taking over leadership of the Telemachons.

Melissa (Mell-iss'-a): A Greek slave owned by the banker Porcys and rescued by Tyracides.

Histarchus (Hiss-tark'-us): One of the personas Goreth takes on.

Thocero (Thock'-er-oh): An Aeolian pirate who throws in his lot with Telemachus.

Xura (Zu'-ra): Young sister of Chalestrus and daughter to King Istar.

Chalestrus (Kal-es'-truss): Young son of King Istar.

King Istar (Is-tar'-sis): King over the Greek city Istria where the River Istros (Danu or Danube) enters the Pontus Euxinus (Black Sea).

Rhodessa (Roh-dess'-a): A female member of the ruling 'Pelt' in the city of Galati, whose mother had been a Libyan slave.

Bhusa (Booss'-a): Another member of the Galati ruling class and Rhodessa's male partner.

Cordyr (Cord-eer'): Manwyr's female Pelt partner.

Suhdo (Soo-'doh): Wolf Master for Galatean ceremonies.

Manwyr: (Man'-veer) A Wolf Master Merchant.

Zalso (Zol'-soh): One of the Pelts. Responsible for the city's defence.

The Psychezoion (Sigh-key-zoy'-on): The supernatural, phoenix-like pet of Zalmoxis.

Zalmoxis (Zal-mocks'-is): A follower of Pythagoras who on returning home had become, through a process of quasi-resurrection, a god.

Doctor Eudeos (You-day'-os): Philosopher and physician to the Pelt.

Agenor (A-jee'-nor): Friend and officer to Telemachus.

Sostis (Soss'-tis): Danuviad athlete and Telemachon.

Zipleus (Zip-lay'-oos): A Telemachon, dies in trying to capture the Psychezoion.

Taranus (Ter-an'-us): Dies with Zipleus.

Goreth/ Danu (Gor'-eth/Dan-oo): God of the Orsook, the Fish People-first inhabitants along the Great River.

Croebos (Cree'-bos): One of the crew of the Telemachon. Rhodian wrestler in the Danuviad.

Pelos (Pell'-os): Danuviad athlete and Telemachon.

Eris (E'-ris): Freed from slavery in Athens. An expert archer and lover to Faramund.

Hebe (Hee'-be): Joined the Telemachon at Athens and later, a partner to Telemachus.

Selene (Sell-ee'-nee): One of the women who joined the Telemachons in Athens.

Adrasteia (A-dra-stee'-a): Joined the Telemachon expedition at Athens.

Chara (Car'-a): An ex-slave woman who had become a Telemachon at Athens – infected by the 'Wind Disease'.

Chryseis (Kry-sea'-is): Joins the Telemachon at Athens.

Andromeda (An-drom'-ed-a): Joins the ship with Chryseis and the others.

Faramund (Farr'-uh-mund): Celtic inventor and later magician, friend of Berengar.

Berengar (Ber'-en-gar): Celtic warrior and friend of Faramund.

Thoros (Thor'os): A chief Druid under King Garudian.

Garudian (Gar-uh'-de-un): Celtic King of Belgrade and the tribes along the Danu.

Toruc (Toor'-uk): Celtic village champion.

Other athletes in the Danuviad: Polydeuctes (Polly-day-uk'-tees), Demaraton (Day-ma'-rat-on), Lysimachus (Lie-sim'-ak-us), Artorius, Stellarstasis (Stellar-star'-sis), Bauxus (Bawk'-

sus), Akeron(Ak'-er-on), Phildoktopes (Fill-dok -ter-pees), Eris, Herophon, Antipater (An-tip'-uh-tuh).

Artorius (Art-or'-ee-us): Danuviad champion caught up in the fight with the water divinities.

Herophon (Heer'-o-fon): Champion lost to the river divinities.

Folson (Fol'-sun): Dwarf guard in the city of Fol.

Costus (Kost'-us): Elected Grand Vizier of Fol.

Bollarchus (Bol-lar'-kus): Chief administrator and personal attendant to the Grand Vizier.

Ula (Oo'-la): Berengar's wife and mother to Herne.

Herne (Hurn'): Young son to Berengar and friend to O-ta-ke-re.

O-ta-ke-re (O'-ta'-ke-re): Young Orsook friend to Herne.

Leonis (Lay-on'-iss): Thocero's younger brother.

The High King Orsek (Or'sek): claimed by the Celts to be their first king, he is, in fact, the first king of the indigenous people living around the River Danu – the Orsook.

Corix (Kor'-icks): King of the Sequani tribe with his capital at Dunsberg.

Formus (Foor'-muss): Chief Druid to the Sequani who is determined to destroy the Orsook and pursues Telemachus.

Artemius (Ar-tem-ee'-uss): Corix's army officer who becomes commander over Formus' military force in Briton.

Lady Andraste (An-drast'-ee): Noble of the Sequani tribe and Formus' lover.

Aristopolis (A-rist-o'-polis): Telemachon soldier.

Bordoric (Bord'-er-ik): Helladore's fourth husband. Dies at the end of a trial-by-combat.

Ortix (Oor'-tiks): Bordoric's opponent.

Queen Helladore (Hell'-a-door): Leader of the Belgae tribe in Briton.

Lady Bellosa (Bell-oh'-sa): Helladore's sister.

Dorstoric(Door'-ster-ik): Bellosa's husband.

Helda (Hell'-da): Belgae village girl who knows Helladore's secret.

Calevenorix (Calev'-en-oor-iks): A clan chief of the Belgae tribe ruled by Helladore.

Runegar (Roon'-gar): Chief Druid, ruler over the Plain of Rebirth, a sacred place for Celts in Briton and Europa.

Borrum: wind god worshipped by the Borrumani.

King Hors Noremac (Whores' Noore'-mak): Ruler of the Land of the Four Winds and its inhabitants the Borrumani.

Netmapliar (Net-map-liar): Counsellor and court historian to Noremac

Princess (later **Queen**) **Byncor** (Bin-coor'): Noremac's daughter, opposed to his rule.

Conversevitae (Con-verse'-viteye): Noremac's physician and magician.

Coryumberix (Coree-um'-ber-iks): Clan chief of the Borrumani living in Monithcound.

Torcus (Toor'-kus): Officer in Coryumberix's guard.

Kellis (Kell'-is): Leader of the Ghost Warriors.

Dacius (Day'-shus): Commander of the northern garrison in The Land of the Four Winds.

Mitshid (Mit'-shid): Noremac's cavalry officer.

Arrevoes (Arr-ev-oes'): Supporter of Princess Byncor who takes over the capital city, Overblown.

Deophobos (Day-oph'-a-bus): Noremac's army commander.

Su-Lance-du-Lac (Soo-lonce'-doo-lak): The Orsook Water-Sidhe's son.

Ol-du-Brec (Ol-doo-Brek): Young Orsook warrior.

Dega (Day'-gar): Another persona adopted temporarily by Goreth.

Chanson-du-Lac (Shan-son'-doo-lak): Daughter to the Water-Sidhe.

Brun-du-Lac (the Water Sidhe) (Broon'-doo-lak): Orsook leader of those living in Penlac.

Duke Ote (Oh'-tay): Advisor and counsellor to the Water Lord.

Cranogus (Cran-og'-us): Guard at Overblown's city gate.

Agolix (Ag'-oh-liks): Sequani, a slave sold into Corix's army who leaves with Formus to go to Briton.

King Llyr (Leer'): King of the Bracken Ones.

Gortoch (Goor'-tok): A champion selected to fight the Bracken Ones.

Cosumbra (Cos-um'-bruh): Another champion selected by Artemius to fight the Bracken Ones.

Myor (My-oor'): Keeper over the Orsook Mind at the Water Lord's court.

Duke Baloose (Ba-loose'): The Water Lord's nephew.

Printed in Great Britain
by Amazon